Insatiability

Insatiability

A NOVEL

Stanisław Ignacy Witkiewicz

Translated, in a newly revised version, by LOUIS IRIBARNE

hydra books

Northwestern University Press
Evanston, Illinois

Hydra Books
Northwestern University Press
Evanston, Illinois 60208-4210

First published in Polish under the title *Nienasycenie.*

Published 1996 by Northwestern University Press.

Printed in the United States of America

ISBN 0-8101-1134-9

The Library of Congress has cataloged the original, hardcover edition as follows:
Witkiewicz, Stanisław Ignacy, 1885–1939.
[Nienasycenie. English]
Insatiability : a novel / Stanisław Ignacy Witkiewicz ; translated, in a newly revised version, by Louis Iribarne.
p. cm.
"Hydra books."
ISBN 0-8101-1133-0 (cloth : alk. paper)
I. Iribarne, Louis. II. Title.
PG7158.W52N513 1996
891.8′537—DC20 96-4251
CIP

Contents

One

The Awakening

The Awakening

Genezip Kapen could not bear captivity of any kind — had abhorred it since earliest childhood. (Uncannily, he had endured eight tyrannical years at the hands of his despot-father. But this ordeal was like a spring: he knew that one day it would uncoil, and this made him tough.) At the ripe age of four he would implore his mother and his governesses on their summer strolls to let him pet a mongrel, usually as it lashed out from its chain, or some small melancholic pup whimpering softly from a cottage step — just to pet it and feed it a snack, if unleashing it was out of the question.

At first he was allowed to take food from the house on behalf of his friends in distress. But soon this feeding mania outgrew even his circumstances: he was denied this one genuine pleasure. This happened mainly in the country, in Ludzimierz, a town situated at the foot of the Beskids in the Tatra Mountains. But once, on a visit to the district capital of C., his father had taken him to the menagerie. After pleading unsuccessfully for the uncaging of some hamadryad monkeys (these having been the first animals to meet his gaze), he threw himself at the keeper and kept hammering his tiny fists against the man's stomach until he scraped his hand on his belt buckle. The azure of that August day, so aloof and cruelly indifferent to the suffering of poor animals, remained in Zip's memory forever. Such a luxurious sunshine while they (and he) had felt so blue . . . blue in a disgustingly pleasurable sort of way . . . The episode ended in a spasmodic fit and a severe attack of nerves. During the next three days and nights Zip hardly slept. Horrible nightmares afflicted him. He saw himself in the form of a grey-haired monkey rubbing against its cage, unable to reach another monkey of the same color. There was something odd about the other one: it was reddish-blue and unspeakably ugly. Genezip could not recall having seen a second monkey. A choking pain in the chest, the intuition of some forbidden, disgusting thrill . . . The other monkey was himself; he had been looking at himself sideways. *How* all this happened was a mystery. Next came giant elephants, huge, comatose cats, serpents, and melancholic condors: all him, or rather not him at all. (In reality he had only caught a glimpse of these creatures as, convulsing, he was taken out through another exit in a fit of dry sobs.) For three days he inhabited a strange world of forbidden torments, excruciating shame, nauseating sweetness, and mysterious excitement, even as he lay unmistakably in his own little bed. When he had recovered, he felt limp as a noodle, yet endowed with a justifiable self-loathing and a loathing for weakness in general. Something had sprung up inside him: the embryo of a conscious use of power in the abstract. A prodigal uncle on his father's side, the black sheep of the family and a resident of Ludzimierz, said: "People who are kind toward animals are usually monsters toward their fellow creatures. Zip must be brought up strictly, or he'll turn out a fiend." And thus did his father raise him, though the elder Kapen did not believe that anything good would come of such sternness; he was strict, especially at the beginning, to please himself. "I once knew two young ladies of so-called good family, who were both brought up in a convent," he was fond of saying. "One was a wh . . . , the other a nun. And the father of both was surely the same."

By the time Genezip was seven, such symptoms became ostensibly subdued. Everything receded into the background. He sulked a lot during this time and went in for, among other things, games of a special kind. He went for walks alone or in the company of his cousin Toldzio, who introduced him to a new world of autoerotic perversions. Hidden in the bushes, with a stirring music playing in a nearby park, the two youngsters would excite one another by mouthing dirty innuendos and exploring various odors. Until at last, nestled close, in a frenzy, with cheeks flushed and eyes rolling in their heads from some inarticulate desire, they summoned from their healthy, pathetic little bodies the diabolical thrill of some ineffable, eternally mysterious, unachievable lust. They went at it again and again, trying for more — but couldn't do it. And again they tried. Later they would come out of the bushes, pale, with red eyes and ears, and slip away like thieves, suffused with some strange malaise, an aching sensation located in regions . . . Girls merrily at play affected them in an irritating sort of way. There was both sadness and alarm in these amusements, a vague yearning, futile, cruel, but agreeable. A sense of lewd superiority over everything and everybody made them disgustingly arrogant. They looked on other boys with contempt and a secret remorse, whereas the spectacle of handsome young men flirting with women filled them with a hatred mixed with a melancholic, mortifying envy, one that held forth the bizarre appeal of transcending normal, everyday life. Toldzio was to blame (later on, of course) for everything. But for the moment he was just that closest, truest companion who became the first to possess the bizarre mystery of wicked self-indulgence and who then condescended to teach it to Zip. But why did Zip *later* turn against him? The affair lasted some two years, off and on. But by the end of the second year their friendship began to deteriorate. Perhaps because of that initiation. Meanwhile, new symptoms related to those mysterious pleasures made their appearance

. . . Zip became frightened. Was this some awful sickness? Was he being punished for his sin?

It was also around this time that his mother, contrary to his father's wishes, began teaching him religion, although no mention was ever made of *that other matter* as something sinful. Still, Zip sensed that by indulging in such practices he was doing something childishly "ungentlemanlike," something *evil*. But this evil was of a magnitude altogether different from skipping his homework, being nasty to his parents, or teasing his little sister, who, apart from this teasing, did not exist for him. Perplexed – he could not explain this evil and these fits of ruing – he resolved upon the following decisive step: with the boldness of a condemned man he went to his father and told him everything. After a thorough hiding and haunted less by the beating than by the prospect of idiocy, he summoned all his willpower and quit these shameful practices. For Zip prided himself on his intellect, which, in discussions of the natural sciences, stood him above his peers and even above the perverse Toldzio, who was a year older and a count, while he was merely a baron, and a "dubious" one at that, as he was apprised by none other than Toldzio himself.

Then came the period of healthy brutalization. The memories of past events, however interesting "from the point of view of the natural sciences"(?) – his father had failed to offer a theoretical explanation – were exorcised by fights, sprints, and sports. But Zip's mania for liberating dogs from captivity returned with redoubled force. It came to resemble a sport, a noble test of courage. He returned home bitten, splattered with mud, his clothes torn. Once he had to wear his arm in a sling for a couple of weeks, which had spoiled a series of amazingly lifelike battles with adversaries known as the "Young Turks." Still, the accident cooled Zip's ardor somewhat. He set out on fewer liberating expeditions now. It happened always when he was seized with a desire for something else . . . Ersatz activities.

Then came the "sublimation" phase. School ended it abruptly. The best time in a boy's life – that time when a prescience of the unknown joins with a nascent sentimentality where girls (or, rather, "the one and only") are concerned, causing a mist of metaphysical wonder (not yet to be construed as awe) to envelop commonplace, everyday reality – was cut short by work of an almost mechanical nature – a compulsory and, for some (although very few), deadly work. In spite of undisputed abilities, Zip had a tough time in school. Coercion destroyed whatever real enthusiasm he may have felt. He spent the entire winter mentally stooped under this forced labor, while his brief vacations were taken up with sports, by now de rigueur, and with local amusements. Except for those classmates chosen to act as his companions, he saw no one and never "ventured" into the surrounding area. Just when early autumn began to find him unbending a little, school would be upon him, and so it went until the time of his examinations.

He had promised his father he would return to the country right after graduation, and he kept his promise. Having thus been spared those beastly postgraduate solemnities, Zip pulled up, pure and innocent but also smelling of life's diabolical possibilities, at the manor house, the so-called house of his ancestors, lying at the foot of the mountains in the vicinity of Ludzimierz. That's when it all started.

....

INFORMATION: Naturally, Zip knew, even before entering school, that he was a baron and that his father, the owner of a gigantic brewery, was "below" his mother, a countess in whose veins there coursed a sprinkling of Hungarian blood. There had been a brief fit of snobbery, but not very rewarding: on his mother's side everything was okay (a few heroes whose names he had all but forgotten, some Mongols, not to mention a few savage bloodbaths during the reign of Ladislas IV, etc.), while papa's ancestors did nothing for his amour propre. Hence, as early as the fourth grade (he had entered school in the third), Zip, guided by a happy instinct, became a democrat and thus managed to overlook the somewhat less-than-perfect fact of his origin. This earned him no small stature and allowed him to convert a certain self-abasement into something of a positive value. He was pleased by this discovery.

He awoke from his afternoon nap. He awoke not only from his sleep but also from that other business which had gone on for some five years! A desert now separated him from those beastly childhood battles. How he regretted that it could not last forever! The feeling that nothing was without importance and the feeling, unique and absolute, that not all was meant in earnest on this plane of reality — with that ensuing sigh of levity even in the face of defeat. . . . Gone forever! But that which was coming seemed vastly — oh, infinitely — more interesting! Another world. For some reason the memory of those childish perversions now shifted under the sheer weight of remorse for those "crimes" as if they were indeed *weighing down* upon his entire future. Perhaps they did so in fact. Years later he went through a similar phase of temptation, but he controlled himself. Shame held him back in the presence of women, who were as yet strangers to him, strangers to the core, for indeed only the day before . . .

. . . .

INFORMATION: Discipline in the school dorm had been nettling, while during the holidays — ha! — his company was never what he would have liked it to be! Still, he managed to get it all secondhand from friends who had bitten off more reality than he had. But this was of minor importance.

The fact remained: *everything is.* This was not the banal truism it seemed. A subconscious, purely sensual ontology, animistic in the main, is nothing compared to that first glimmering of a conceptual ontology, to that first general existential perception. Until now, the mere fact of his own being had not impressed him. Now, for the first time, he could grasp its sheer impenetrability. His distant childhood loomed up in his innocent imagination like some golden and enchanted world — a world of blissful, irretrievable days, shimmering in a dust of unearthly longing: the chateau belonging to his mother's family in eastern Galicia, a cloud heated to a white-hot intensity and lurking with storm, frogs croaking in the clay pits near the brick kiln, and the screeching of a rusty well. He recalled, too, a rhyme composed by a certain friend with whom he had been forbidden to play.

O the mysterious pull of a hot spell
Fruit's juicy store for the taking
A cool shade beside an abandoned well
Then a night given to wild undertaking . . .

Here is what that trivial little rhyme conveyed to him: life's immensity, the inscrutability of its each and every moment, insufferable boredom, and a yearning for something immeasurably great. It made sense only now. When Ptaś first read these silly lines aloud to him in the school privy they had meant nothing to him. In the bolt unleashed by revelations of the present, the past became illumined as another, hitherto unknown world. This vision lasted for a fraction of a second before vanishing, along with the memory of it, into the darkest interior of his subconscious. He stood up, walked over to the window, and leaned his head against the pane.

The great, yellow, winter sun sank rapidly, barely brushing the twin peaks of Grand Mountain. In the blinding light everything merged in a quivering mass of blazing gold and copper. Violet shadows stretched into infinity; a forest lying adjacent to the sun ran with a black purple that turned by degrees into a brilliant, pale green. The earth was no longer a mundane place, a place known and intimate in relation to our own human world: it was now like a planet viewed from a telescopic distance. With the jagged, sculptured ridge of the mountains rising on the left, far beyond the precipitous slopes of Grand Mountain, the earth seemed to go to meet the strangely "funereal" night now approaching from interstellar spaces. The sun, which by now was visibly sinking, became at times a dark green disk surrounded by a crimson-gold border. Suddenly, with a timid, almost hesitating motion, it touched the line of the distant wood that stood against a sky as though hewn into bloody blades. The reddish-black velvet was transformed into a dark blue, as the last beam, fractured into iridescent sheaves, pierced the heavy clumps of spruce. The eye, attracted to the infinite by this blinding glare, collided with the stolid resistance of the murky and infinitely more real world. Genezip's breast ached. That eerie moment wherein a mystery had unfolded passed, and real-life banality revealed its drab, jaded face beneath its mask. What was one to do with such an evening? This question reminded him of others, and he fell into a deep muse, so deep that he lost track of the present. He did not realize what a supreme happiness such distraction can be.

The princess rose up (reared up) in his imagination as though alive. This image was not a reflection of yesterday's reality. Suddenly he recalled some indecent prints seen in a library belonging to a friend of his father's when, taking advantage of these gentlemen's distraction, he had peeked inside an insecurely shut drawer. He gazed, like a spectator to some lewd effigy, upon her naked figure bathed by a torrent of dark red hair. A group of maliciously grinning monkeys was strolling about her with unbridled grace (each was holding an elliptical hand mirror) – an obvious attempt to render a design of concentric circles, which in turn was meant to symbolize life's various spheres ranked in order of their importance. Was the middle circle really so central? Two irreconcilable points of view were shown, giving rise to an annoying ambivalence. Roughly construed, the figure might have signified his father's idealistic agenda and Zip's own wish to indulge illicit pleasures, which, in some unknown way, was associated with his mother. Zip could almost feel this ambivalence in his breast and in the pit of his stomach. A moment ago none of these sensations had been there, but now his entire past, the time spent in school as well as his childhood, melded indissolubly, irretrievably into one, marred only by the absence of any solution for this newly posed and thoroughly enigmatic problem. The secrecy surrounding such enigmas became, from the moment of his first encounter, something disturbing, ominous. A morbid (why "morbid," dammit?!) curiosity overran him like some warm and disgustingly pleasant grease. He shuddered, and only then did he recall the dream he had only just dreamed. Another person's voice had reached him from the abyss of some impersonal gaze, which seemed to fix him with a fatal, unanswerable question. He felt as if he had not crammed enough for an exam. And then briskly, stutteringly, the voice from his dream said: "The intralevelers feed at the sight of the black beatus, boovering moddlycoddlers." Iron arms embraced him, and he felt a ticklish pain below his ribs. It was the same awful feeling with which he had awakened but which had eluded definition. (Were such experiences really worth having, worth immersing oneself in, if later on . . . Ugh – more on that subject later.)

Only now, and with a feeling verging on joy, did Zip recognize in the *mental image* of that ugly hirsute face belonging to the composer Tenzer (introduced to Zip the night before) that same baffling ambivalence he had just experienced. The pent-up energy so discernible in that man's eyes had made for an unbearable tension. His utterances, which Zip had listened to (but not understood), suddenly became clear to him in their entirety as an unanalyzable mass – or, to be more precise, only their general tone had become clear. Meanwhile, the twofold meaning of life droned monotonously beneath the crust of conventional "schoolboy" secrets. Occasionally this crust was torn asunder by such inanities as:

"Let everything happen. I'll experience it all, master it, chew and digest it: every boredom, the worst calamity. Why do I think such thoughts? What I said just now was absolutely banal, and if anyone gave me such advice I'd laugh in his face. And now I recite this stuff as if it were the deepest truth, the most profound discovery." Yesterday such words would have had a more conventional meaning, but today they seemed symbolic of new horizons flung into a new dimension. The mystery of one's birth and the inconceivability of the world's existence without the positing of one's ego were the only luminous points in a series of otherwise obscure moments. Hence his life's mess. And why? If it was all going to end in . . . – more on that subject later. Only yesterday his recent boyhood had stood out pristinely, as something alive, forever in a state of becoming. Its division into infinitesimally small parts precluded epochs in spite of epoch-making events (like, ostensibly, those happening at present). But now, obscured and distanced by some secret decree, the whole "great" (?) span of his life had sunk into the realm of immutability and finality and, in doing so, acquired a fragile, elusive charm, that of the past's irretrievable capture, which Zip had tragically sensed for the first time. On this rough sea of changes, which were happening in a medium as trancelike as his former life – changes that left everything the same but that were incommensurate with yesterday's reality – the dream he had just recalled appeared like a cyclone, sharp and distinct in outline but inwardly tangled, on the indifferent, voidlike, water-transparent screen of the present. A lightning parting of perspectives, as when a tired gaze suddenly perceives things infinitely far away, minute and inaccessible, while at the same time a given object maintains its normal size – which fact, however, fails somehow to alter the real, readily ascertainable, objective proportions of the various elements making up the field of vision. (Perturbations in the estimation of distance, the seeing of objects in their actual dimensions, minus the factor of a consciously perceived distance, which, due to possible sensual impressions, modifies the immediate impression of spatial relations within a two-dimensional space. But enough of that.)

Genezip began recalling his dream in an order inversely related to its proper sequence. (Dreams are never experienced directly during the actual time of dreaming: *they exist solely and exclusively as memories*. Hence the singular, specific character of even the most ordinary dream. This is why memories which we are unable to locate exactly in the past assume precisely that special coloring of dreams.) From the furtive interior of some imaginary world there arose a chain of ostensibly trivial and insignificant events belonging to nobody's memory but his own, to Genezip's; and so special, so imbued with otherworldly power were they that, despite being petty, they seemed to cast a shadow, one full of foreboding and guilt for uncommitted sins, upon this time of postgraduate leisure and upon the amber glow of this winter sun expiring among the purple woods. "Blood," he whispered, and experienced, along with this vision of red, a violent constriction of the heart. He saw the last link in the crime and, pushing farther into the past, its mysterious origin, which gradually dimmed in the black irreality of dreamy nonexistence. "Why blood?" he half-murmured to himself. "There was nothing in the dream about blood." Just then the sun disappeared from sight. Only the forest gracing the slope of Grand Mountain, its border notched like a saw by the sun's fiery gold shafts, blazed against the pale orange sky. The world turned ashen in the bluish-violet dusk, while the sky brightened with the approach of a flaming, evanescent, winter twilight in which a fading

Venus flickered softly like a green spark. The dream grew more and more distinct in its anecdotal contents, while its real narrative, at once inarticulate and elusive, was submerged in the concreteness of the events provoked by memory, leaving scarcely any trace of that other, inaccessible life vanishing at the periphery of consciousness.

The dream: He was wandering down a street in some unknown place that reminded him both of the capital and of a small town in Italy he had once seen in passing. At one point he noticed that he was not alone and that along with his cousin Toldzio (whose presence in such dreams was compulsory) someone else was walking beside him – a tall, broad-shouldered galoot sporting a dark blonde beard. He tried to get a glimpse of the man's face, but in that peculiar and nonetheless perfectly natural manner of dreams it always disappeared the moment he looked at it. He only saw the beard, and it was this detail which all but formed the essence of this mysterious "character." They stepped into a small café located on the ground floor. The stranger stood in the doorway opposite Zip and began beckoning to him by means of imperceptible signs. Zip felt an irrepressible urge to follow him into the back rooms. Meanwhile, Toldzio was grinning ironically, omnisciently, as though he knew what was coming, which Zip likewise thought he knew but about which, in fact, he knew nothing. He got up from the table and walked out behind the stranger. They entered a room with a low ceiling billowing with a dense smoke. The space overhead seemed endless. The stranger then walked up to Zip and began squeezing him with a sickening cordiality. "I am your brother; my name is Jaguar," he whispered softly into his ear, and this whisper came as something fiendishly titillating. Zip nearly woke at this point, but he overcame the temptation. An insuperable disgust welled up inside him. He grabbed the stranger by the neck and began bending him over backward toward the ground, choking him with all his might. Something (it was no longer someone), some soft and inert mass, slumped to the floor, and Zip fell down on top of it. The crime had been committed. He sensed that Toldzio was perfectly aware of his total lack of contrition and of his one unambivalent urge: that of escaping his predicament. After uttering something unintelligible to Toldzio, Zip walked back to the place where the body lay. The face was visible now – only instead of a face Zip saw a huge, hideously shapeless bruise, and around the dead man's neck, underneath that *contemptible beard,* he clearly made out the reddish-blue streaks left by his own fingers. "If they sentence me to a year in prison, I'll survive; if they sentence me to five, it's all over," he thought, and he passed into a third room in hope of reaching the street from the other side of the house. But the room was full of police, and to his horror the murderer recognized in each of them his mother, disguised in a grey helmet and a gendarme's cape. "Request a hearing," she said quickly, "the chief will hear your case." And she handed him a large sheet of paper. In the middle of the paper was a sentence printed in italics, which in his dream had been full of sinister portent as well as hope, his last. But now, rescued from memories passing into dark oblivion, it merely had the character of misguided drool: "The intralevelers feed at the sight of the black beatus, boovering moddlycoddlers." End of dream.

The dusk thickened while the sky took on a deep violet tone, which affected him in precisely the same manner as the perfume (brand unknown) worn by Princess di Ticonderoga, his hostess at yesterday evening's soirée, had done. (The perfume, Zip later found out, was the renowned *Femelle enragée* by Fontassini.) Gazing up at the glittering stars, Zip formed the impression of an abominable void. His previous state – his dream and the feeling that some inexhaustible richness dwelt both within and beyond him – vanished without a trace. Something passed like a shadow, leaving behind boredom, unease, and a kind of sadness that was without charm and unworthy of sublime transformation. On the surface nothing had changed, though Zip was sure that something momentous had transpired, something decisive. This something was opaque, it defied comprehension – it was like a flawless block of granite. (Was such soul-searching really worth the effort if later on . . . Oh! But that, too, will have to keep.) An anonymous bookkeeper had multiplied everything by an unknown factor. Why was everything so strange? A metaphysical state without form. This much he knew: he could never believe in God (though his mother, it seemed, had lectured him a long, long time ago on this very subject – not about God Himself, but about the strangeness ["I believe in God, but in a God unlike the one found in the teachings of our Church. God is everything, and He reigns not over the world but only over Himself."]). In those days the world (as God) impressed Zip as the blue and concave bottom of a china cup, of the sort that stood in rows in their dining-room oak cupboard. It was an impression *intraductible, irreductible, intransmissible, et par excellence irrationnel.* Alas. For him, Christ had been nothing more than a magician. At the age of seven he told his nanny of his discovery, and it drove the old woman to despair. His mother's religious views acted on him more persuasively, and he was of the feeling that he would never have anyone, for as long as he lived, who was as close to him in his most intimate thoughts as his mother. Still, some insurmountable wall separated them, even during their best times together. His father, who was ferocious in anger and rigidly stubborn in peace, inspired him with absolute terror. Zip knew that he and his mother were battling life's evil power but that right invariably chose the side of evil. He wanted to go to her and to complain about how awful dreams were and about life's traps into which, resist though he might, he was bound to fall sooner or later. But with an abrupt reversal of pride, he overcame this weakness, and with a masculine toughness quickly reviewed all the pertinent facts: he had eighteen years behind him; he was old, very old – twenty, after all, was the epitome of old age. He was bound to solve the mystery, and solve it he would – a little at a time – alas. He would fear nothing, he would master everything, or else perish – with honor, of course. But why and for what aim this drive for the all? He suddenly lost heart. This noble proposition, absurd when it came to this world, acquired the force of a magical incantation, a cure-all for everything. Dusk crept up rapidly, and only a few scraps of light were now reflected in the pictures hanging on the wall. All at once the mystery of his dream and his erotic future became the mystery of *Everything:* it encompassed himself and the whole world. It embraced not just the inscrutability of life's each and every moment but the stunning mystery of the entire universe, of God and the blue concave bottom of the china cup. Nor was this the problem of belief or disbelief posed in the abstract: everything was and acted at the same time, yet was frozen in an absolute immobility and was dying in the expectation of some miracle beyond our imagination, some final revelation after which there would remain nothing but the most perfect, the most marvelous, the most inconceivable Nothingness. At such times Zip deserted the religious faith that had been forced on him and which, at his mother's behest, he artificially aroused in himself before his examinations (religion had not been a part of the curriculum). Anyway, his mother's faith, as symbolized by the blue china cup, stood far removed from the beliefs of the local vicar. Establish his own sect? Even that had lost its appeal. Revelation had proved a categorical flop. From then on Zip looked on all religious practices as a deliberate hoax; for this he was indebted to his mother (not even she, adored as she was, could inspire him with belief). It was this ambivalence toward his mother that one day would cause a small, seemingly minor scale to tip. For all his mother's notorious merits, Zip knew that she concealed an abyss, as yet unexplored but connected with the darker side of life into which, slowly and imperceptibly, he himself was slipping. Thus did he nurture a slight contempt for his mother, which he deliberately repressed. He knew that he would never be so close to another living creature as he was to her; he also knew that he was about to lose her. So why the contempt? Nothing in life was simple, dammit! Everything was a tangle, a muddle, a messy business, like some abominable salad of life deliberately dished up by an evil spirit. Now it only *seemed* that way to him — how much more complicated life would become in the future! Then again, from another point of view, certain things may have become simpler thanks to this little dose of life's meanness from which perhaps only saints are exempt. By what right was he contemptuous of his mother? The coexistence of two contradictory emotions — ferocious attachment and contempt — raised the whole scheme to the height of an inconceivable lunacy. Yet, everything remained exactly as before, nothing had changed. To make a breach in that internal dam separating him from himself; to open all the valves, knock down all the fences that artificially inhibited his schoolboy's field of vision! Oh, why had he been asleep for so long? Yet the thought, weird as the demonstration of it may have been (weird only to him), that only thus (i.e., by coming at all this with just such a past as his) he might get two, three, four times as much . . . But get what? Life as yet meant practically nothing to him as such. Not to speak of how guilty he felt for even thinking such thoughts – no, he would never mention it to his mother, never, for as long as he lived. Suddenly the old wooden floor in the next room creaked, and a faint childish quiver was blended with budding manly courage in a delicious mélange. For the first time Genezip was conscious of the fact that a full twenty-four hours had passed since the time of his arrival.

....

INFORMATION: Final exams were held in winter. Because of the war scare, the school year was terminated in February. The country was desperately in need of officers. Extraordinary events were expected to take place in March.

The advance guard of the Chinese Communists stood already at the Urals and was now only a step away from Moscow, which was drowning in counterrevolutionary bloodbaths. Brainwashed by the manifestos of Czar Cyril, the peasants avenged themselves horribly for the necessary evil inflicted on them (for the good of the cause), not realizing that they were cooking for themselves a fate a hundred times worse.

Kapen senior was having the ground cut out from under his former life. He could not even be as strict as before, although he was good at shamming strictness. He already had visions of his glorious Ludzimierz beer – whole streams, rivers, and oceans of it – being channeled off into different directions; of its being nationalized and socialized, of his plants being denied their little gimmicks, many of which he himself had introduced after inheriting the brewery from his father in such a primitive state that it sooner reminded one of a thing that had sprouted spontaneously out of the earth than of something built by human hands and brains. The future looked as dull as dishwater. He might rectify things with some "coup" (?), and by the capriciousness of his behavior head off any possible coercion by superior forces.

The thought of his father sent a small and unpleasant chill down

Zip's spine. When was this tyranny, which he had put up with for twelve years, ever going to end? (His tortures prior to that were drowning in the dimming phase of early childhood.) Would he be able to mount a permanent defense against the force that was stifling his every impulse for independence? Yesterday's experience in this regard had left him torn and undecided. Right away Genezip had announced that he would not make a career of beer; that he was not going to enter the institute of technology but that, instead, in September, provided that war had not broken out in the meantime, he was going to enroll at the university and study in the Department of Western Literature, for which he had already begun preparing during the last semester. Literature was to be the ideal substitute for life's nagging multiplicity: through literature you could devour everything without suffering food poisoning or becoming a cad. So thought the commander's future aide-de-camp, still naive and as yet ignorant of his life's fate. His father's reply, despite all his mistrust for what the future held, had been a mild apoplectic fit. The old man could not imagine what sort of future awaited his slouch of a son — that future borne out by recent events and by internal changes — but filial disobedience had nearly asphyxiated him. Genezip endured this scene with the stoicism worthy of a marabou. His father's life had suddenly ceased to interest him. He was just some character standing in his way, opposing his all-important vocation in life. Immediately after this scene Zip put on a dress coat for the first time in his life (his father's seizure had taken place at exactly seven in the evening; meanwhile, it had grown dark and a snowstorm was raging about the Ludzimierz manor), and at nine rode off in a sleigh to the ball being given that evening by the Princess di Ticonderoga. The princess's face suddenly loomed up before him in a swirling mass of beery boredom — a boredom Zip had rejected. "Whatever you do, don't act like a figure out of one of those man-of-his-time type of novels," he whispered sternly to himself along the way. This occurred in a little clearing destined to serve, on more than one occasion, as the site of monumental changes. He had whispered these words without fully comprehending — for lack of experience — their meaning. The unerring instinct of self-preservation (the voice of Daimon) functioned independently of, though somewhere in the region of, the intellect. The princess's face – or rather, the mask which was removed from that face at the peak of sexual frenzy – was a mysterious dial on which the hour of his test and the shape of his future destiny were to be revealed in signs known only to him. As a matter of fact, he already saw something there, vaguely outlined. How to decipher these symbols? How to avoid falling into error if one knew absolutely nothing to begin with?

....

INFORMATION: The anticommunist war created a curiously paradoxical situation in each of the nations taking part: they were beset by chronic bolshevik revolutions at home. Meanwhile, in Moscow "White Terror" was "all the rage," with the former grand duke, now known as "Czar" Cyril, at its head. Thanks to the seemingly furious efforts of a handful of people (one of whom was the present Minister of Internal Affairs, Diamond Quilty) (in fact, their famous mission owed its success to something else entirely), Poland managed to remain neutral and to abstain from taking part in the antibolshevik crusade. It had thus escaped any internal revolution. Miraculously things held together as if by a thread, though no one could explain why. A theoretical explanation was expected from the students of Professor Tarfinger, founder of the "binary system of social analysis." It was Professor Tarfinger who held that the sociologist of today who did not labor on behalf of a conscious dualism (as the prelude to an eventual, utterly swinish pluralism) could only be *une dupe des illusions* of objectivism, and at best could describe a theoretical magma representing the views of a given social stratum. The practical gist of this system, which those same students later bungled massively, was the scientific organization of labor – a boring thing in itself, like listening to some fogy ramble on about the good old times. Thanks to this system, everything held together like a suspicious-looking pile: people had become so stupefied through automation that in time they ceased to know why they did anything and began to blend into a homogenous and stuporous state of "poopefaction." Work somehow went on, but *au fond des fonds* no one knew how. The idea of the state *as such* (not to speak of other illusions flowing therefrom) had long since failed to power even the most modest sacrifices or the repudiation of individual swinishness. Still, things dragged on through a mysterious inertia, the source of which ideologists loyal to the *ostensibly* ruling party – the Syndicate for National Salvation – researched in vein. Everything took place *ostensibly:* this more than anything else summed up the epoch. In this rapidly Americanized, curiously atavistic age, women grew alarmingly more intelligent than men, now cretinized by automation. The *précieuse,* once considered a rarity, had declined in value due to an overabundance of the same – at least this was true for one *précieuse.* Yet their numbers set the intellectual tone for the entire country. Ostensible people, ostensible work, ostensible country – only the preponderance of women was not ostensible. There was one man, Kotzmolochowicz by name – but that, too, shall have to wait. Meanwhile, the communized Chinese were poised beyond powerless, disorganized, depopulated Russia. "We saw it coming," people kept repeating, shuddering with terror, outraged, yet still tantalized by the prospect of prosperity. At heart, they were immensely gratified, though perhaps not sincerely so. They had predicted all along that something like this would happen. "Maybe if we'd kept our mouths shut . . . " What then?

After his awakening, the previous evening towered above Zip like a dark and ominous mirage rising up from beyond his former sleepy life, spilling over into the present half in grotesque figures, into the part of himself that had begun in the shadow of the most awesome historical changes since the Russian Revolution. This last had been a *déclenchement;* this time, however, mankind was literally rolling over onto the other side of history. The decline of Rome, the French Revolution – mere child's play by comparison. *Now,* at that very moment, which was slipping away and would never come back and which, according Whitehead's method, was being asymptotically squeezed out by events completed in time. "The present is like an open wound – unless it's filled with pleasure, it may . . . ," the Princess di Ticonderoga had said with an ingenuous smile as she crunched on an almond cookie that was made of the same stuff as he: the sensation of the same taste, of the same idea of this taste divided into two animal faces (yesterday he was of the opinion that everyone was a beast in disguise, which was not far from the truth), condensed in him his sense of the present, of simultaneity, of identity, with which everything seemed to swell beyond its borders. Nothing could contain anything anymore. But why only now? Because – oh, how tedious! – for the "reason" that certain glands had just shot their stuff into the inner core of the organism instead of discharging them by the usual routes. "Do I have that frump's eyes to thank for all this?" Zip wondered, knowing that he was committing a *gross* injustice, that he would soon have to repent (yes, repent – how Zip couldn't bear that word!) because of his love for her, that he would have to confess all this to her – *this* to *her* (he shuddered at the thought of that sickening, animal, faintly malodorous intimacy that was bound to befall him) – with a ferocity of youth that can bring to a boil the last, dried-up juices of decomposing cunts and septuagenarian coots. Of course Zip was oblivious to his whole nauseating charm: he – a "*Valentino obraznoe sushchestvo,*" as the princess had called him yesterday, for which he had been severely indignant at her; with a nose so straight and short it might have been taken for a snub nose, a small and meaty nose with a slightly cleft but by no means flattened tip; with his crudely outlined, blood-red, arabesquely carved, but by no means negroid lips – was moderately tall (a little over six feet) but wonderfully proportioned and contained within himself a whole sea of womanly travail. Unconsciously all the cells in Zip's healthy, taurine body secretly rejoiced. His soul was lifted high above this "Olympiad of the cells" (there was no other way to put it) – slightly knock-kneed, anemic, a little freakish looking even, but above all undeveloped (what more can be said – except, perhaps, by some psychiatrist, but only a good one – Bekhmetev, maybe?). Fortunately such types were becoming less socially differentiated, and even their total integration in a given time and place would not have been enough to influence the capricious course of events. And so: yesterday he had still been asleep in that schoolboy past of his, yes, and even at the princess's soirée, where willy-nilly, in spite of himself, he was made to feel as if he represented the whole beery might of the Vahazes (Kapen de, lately of Ludzimierz). And today? He was not a beer drinker, and the image of himself as a parasite living off the lives of unhappy (yes!) workers – even as the latter were drowning in an artificial, Polish, American-style prosperity and had become so exquisitely automated it was laughable – was painfully embarrassing. Expiation could only come in a field of work having nothing to do with all this. His choice had already fallen on literature as something embracing the whole of life, when – kabloom! – his father had nearly dropped dead. Now the truth was known: he did not love this great and renowned brewer (or "king of the malt," as he was dubbed) – that is, not when measured by the dolorous, bloated, ultimately boring love he felt for his mother. No! He would not live off the suffering (be it even subconscious) of these pseudo-human, slaving-the-devil-only-knew-what-for semibrutes. (Oh, how easy to transform those toiling apes into enlightened souls! But for that one needs ideas – well, and also a snippet of those scraps left over from the old stock exchange, scraps that, still rank and filthy from market dealings, had been floating around in the slum districts of the Polish soul – soul, that is, with a capital S [yes, capital, even though lately the subject of such bombast]). At most, he stood to inherit a certain percentage of the estate (this being already a compromise) along with his mother and sister (the pretext for the compromise). "Avoid at all cost any self-contradictions on 'awakening.'"

Today, however, this decision took on new meaning; it encompassed his entire soporific past, arousing in it echoes of nonexistent reproaches; it shook the foundations of certain established facts such as his home, his mother, his family, and, standing quite apart domestically, his fifteen-year-old sister (whom he had barely noticed until now), the flaxen-haired Lilian. Now, among other things, his academic studies began to evanesce as though they had never been very academic or respectable or serious: just a lot of bunk, which may have been aimed at this or that or at nothing at all. But any moment now, with a little patience, life would begin: perversions, crises, interesting experiences, pornography . . . Oh, stop! What in blazes had come over him, anyway?! A worried feeling in the lower part of the stomach, provoking with the help of a glance from the princess's omniscient eyes, which stood out like turquoise balls in a pornographic frame (Genezip's eyes were nut-brown – a splendid contrast), a slight humiliation born of the following proposition: Was he to be the function of such absurdities? The memories of that evening, which only now were beginning to arrange themselves into some seemingly intelligible riddle, belonged to a strangeness of a lower order compared to the revelations of a moment ago. Images flashed before his eyes as in fast motion; conversations passed by in the form of huge, dark pills that whizzed overhead like missiles through a jungle of some highly meaningful sphere. Oh, how differently did he grasp their meaning now!

A Soirée at the Princess di Ticonderoga's

A blue-eyed vulture on an enormous settee and a limp little hand, almost indecent in its limpness. ("What if *it* did what Toldzio on those unforgettable days in the woods . . . " the thought vaguely arose. "Oh, so *that's* where it's all heading.") A painfully shy and obscene little hand, no less omniscient than the eyes. Was there anything in life it had not already touched – or was not about to touch – in that realm?

"I graduated from school early," Zip had just finished saying. "And now I'm waiting for the future like someone waiting for a train at a small out-of-the-way station. It may be a foreign express, or it may be the local boneshaker wending through suburbs of minor entanglements."

The princess's eyes were rolling around like the eyes of an owl, though her face remained perfectly immobile. Her bearing bespoke "grief for life's hopeless passage" – the title of a waltz performed only a few moments ago by the bearded, dress-coated, longhaired, slightly hunchbacked, long-fingered, lame (as a result of a partially withered leg) Putricides Tenzer, composer, forty-two, genius sans official recognition.

"Putrice, my pet, please go on playing. I feel like contemplating this boy's soul as it's being wrapped in music. He's so marvelous he's disgusting in his inner neglect," the princess said with such malice that Zip came close to slapping her. "Oh, if I could just do it – but I haven't the nerve," a child's voice whined inside him. The easy chairs swelled, consuming the other guests who kept melting and merging in the smoky haze. Among the guests was that worshiper of Onan, his cousin Toldzio, who had been wasting these past two years in a diplomatic school for young boobies. Ticonderoga, inwardly senile but outwardly a stout and hearty old man, was there, too, as were ladies from the neighboring estates accompanied by their precious sons and daughters, plus an assortment of that enigmatic and eternally suspicious tribe of businessmen and bankers – even a real-life stock market king of the old school, lately a rare specimen, who was taking the waters for a liver ailment. (He was stuck with the domestic spas because the "authentic" spas abroad were teeming with bolsheviks from all over the world. [No "majority" Pole had the right to enter the fashionable *cultural reality* outside: one might entertain illusions, so long as one did it at home.]) Also present was an orphan by the name of Eliza Frockette, a distant cousin of the lady of the house and rumored to have been a princess of sorts. At first sight, she was a nondescript creature – tiny blonde curls, eyes turned inward, and cheeks the color of an autumnal dawn. But the mouth, the mouth . . . With his life-detecting organs in their present phase of development, Genezip was utterly incapable of noticing her. All the same, something was quivering inside him, in that nub of forebodings where the future –

dark, possibly gruesome – was marshaling itself. "She's the wife for me," this prophetic voice, which he feared, almost despised, said. Meanwhile, in a circle of amused but somewhat terrified women, the young (twenty-seven-year-old) novelist Sturfan Abnol was almost shouting above the wild piano music of the now slightly drunk Tenzer:

". . . and you mean to say, with my grasp on life I'm to perform before this audience which I abhor, which is as sickening to me as a hunk of rotten, worm-infested cheese? Before this revolting mob mesmerized by movies, dancing, sports, the radio, and by train-station newsstands? That I'm supposed to entertain them with train-depot romances just so I can live? I've got news for those – " (he was obviously stifling the urge to swear – the phrase "fuckers" hung in the air) "for that tribe of prostitutes and platitudes!" He was choking with rage and indignation.

....

INFORMATION: Neglected artists were one of the princess's specialties, whom she often helped out financially – but rarely with more than was necessary to keep them from reaching the "shoving-off-due-to-starvation" point. Otherwise, they would have ceased to be neglected. The princess could not stand people who had achieved celebrity status in the artistic realm; somehow she regarded them as a living insult to her inherent sense of good breeding. She adored art but could not tolerate its having "got so fine" (as she put it). This was curious in view of the cessation of art generally. There may have been flickers on the domestic front, fanned by abnormal, artificial social relations, but all in all – good grief!

"No, I refuse to be their jester," the foaming Sturfan continued to crow. He *zakhlyobyvalsya* (as the Russians say), and spewed out his poison. "When there's nothing left in art, I mean *real* art, then I'll start writing novels – but me-ta-phys-i-cal novels, understand?! I'm sick of all this 'connoisseurship of life' stuff – I leave that for the second-rate hacks who crib off mediocrity and then knowingly reproduce it. And why do they plagiarize? Because they can't imagine anybody but themselves. They can't manage superior types who aspire to what our critical parasites refer to as 'the serene, pseudo-Grecian smile of indulgence,' from the heights of which they proclaim that all, including myself (for which I excuse both them and myself), are swine. To hell with Greece and all that rehashing of pseudoclassical puke! But no! They call it 'objectivism,' those critikons, those tapeworms and trichinae infesting the dying body of art – and they have the gall to invoke the name of Flaubert! No – I'll tell you what a *pseudo*-objective writer is: a grinning porker, shit-stained from the universal vulgarity, a man who hangs out with his 'literary creations.' And what do they mean by 'creativity'? Spying through keyholes on people who allow themselves to be spied on. Superior people, if such really do exist, are not so eager to be spied on by just anyone. So how do they create characters? Very simple. They hang out with the crowd, drink from the same trough, and then, pissed on a morbid and useless mania for self-humiliation, unburden their souls to people unworthy of becoming their heroes – there you have your 'objectivism'! And what do they call 'literature of great social significance'? Exposing the vices of various creeps; inventing positive, artificial, and paper-doll characters who can't even rescue a blind and shallow optimism from the jaws of defeat. These are the sort of hacks they glorify!" He coughed, maintained an attitude of despair for a moment, then resumed drinking.

After a frantic, thumping finale, his shirt front crumpled, his hair mussed but still matted down and covered with perspiration, Tenzer tore himself away from an exhausted Steinway. His eyes were burning *bleu électrique*. Visibly agitated, he advanced toward the princess with an unsteady step. Genezip was sitting beside her – he was already a changed person. He knew who was going to chart his future. "Although, who knows, maybe I should just run with the pack," he mused, conjuring up some vague image of official debauchery of the sort his father had outlawed and which he couldn't even entertain in the abstract. Something ripped inside him like a piece of linen – only the initial tear was painful (animal paws did the ripping, beginning in the pit of the stomach and gradually extending to the abdominal part where . . .), after which it progressed swiftly and with perilous ease. It was then that he lost his virginity and not, as he later imagined, the following day.

"Irina Vsevolodovna," said Tenzer, paying not the slightest attention to Zip. "I insist on addressing you not as the humble erotic surrogate of bygone days, but as your conqueror. Let me come into that locked chamber once – just once – and I shall conquer you forever. Irina Vsevolodovna, I promise – you won't regret it," he groaned.

"Trot on back to your plow girl," replied the princess. (Later Genezip learned that Tenzer's wife was a young and robust mountain lass whom he had married for her money and a chalet. In all fairness, however, it should be added that he had found her somewhat attractive in the beginning.) "You've had your share of good luck, so what more do you want?" the princess whispered with a benevolent smile. "Maybe it's better for your music if you suffer. An artist, a *true* artist, and not some overintellectualized blending machine for every variation and permutation, should not be afraid to suffer."

Genezip felt a hideous polyp fasten itself to the hot, viscous walls of his soul and start crawling higher (in the direction of his brain?), tickling as it went, mercilessly and with obvious relish, hitherto dormant regions. He was not about to suffer, not he. He felt at that moment like a bit of a rake, like Toldzio's father, for instance, his mother's brother, Count Prattle – still very much the "Galician," a curiosity that had withstood the test of time. He once dreamed of becoming just such a blasé bastard; now, though there was nothing to warrant it as yet, the prospect of such a future turned his stomach with dread. Time was moving at a frantic clip. Hundreds of years became squeezed into seconds – what De Quincey experienced while under the influence of opium – as if time had been compressed into pills of condensed duration. Everything had been irrevocably decided. He fancied he would summon the courage to overpower this she-monster who, with a magnificent gesture, had discreetly sprawled herself out before him on the settee. He knew that, girlish as she sometimes appeared, she was a little on the old side – somewhere between thirty-eight and forty – but at the moment it was precisely the staleness, the omniscience of this exquisite maid that drove him insane. No sooner had he exercised his vision than he was standing on the side of a life forbidden him by his father. Then came the sobering thought: I'm destined for evil.

Leaning over the princess's exposed arm, Tenzer was visibly sniffing with his broad, malformed nose. He was an exceedingly repugnant man, yet there was no mistaking the force of frustrated genius in him. Just now he reminded Zip of one of his chained dogs from out of the past. But this was one dog he had no intention of unleashing. No, let this one suffer; there was something rank about it, criminal, something so foully delectable it turned the stomach with a mysterious horror. (The presence of that woman was enough to bring out the worst, the most perverse in everyone. They came away swarming with evil thoughts like a worm-infested carcass.) And this under the guise of an artistic soirée, to which every species of buffoon had been invited as a diversion for the "best" society. Even Zip, until now little more than an innocent child, had become a candidate for a decomposing psychocorpse intended for the pleasure of an unsatiated female body. The former boy, the pure and good Zip, was pounding inside him the way a butterfly beats against a windowpane to avert disaster. Sexual pleasure! Oh, to be a beast, ignorant of that human dignity inculcated in him by (a) his father during the school holidays, (b) Madame Vigilia, an impoverished aristocrat with princely pretensions at whose house he had once boarded, (c) his professors, and (d) certain high-minded and lugubrious schoolmates hand-picked, at his father's request, by the school principal himself. Oh, how he detested it, that pale, insipid "humanity" dictated from above! He had his own sort of dignity, in no way inferior to theirs. If he had not repressed it, they would have trampled it, stifled it. And what was his version of dignity if not the incarnation of revolt: unleash every dog; disperse his father's workers after dividing up the beer among them; free all prisoners and lunatics; and, having done this, march through the world with his head raised up high. And then came the denial of it, this dignity, in the form of a shameless wench and the pleasure connected with that very denial. But why had she come to symbolize the inverse of those former, personal, dictated ideals? Could he really "come to know life" through her and still remain true to himself? Ghastly, but delectable. Oh, well.

Zip's noble-mindedness (the simple kind that eludes definition) – thoroughly stirred, hitherto artificially elevated under pressure –

and his idealism (i.e., the belief in some vague "higher aspirations" designated by the middle circle within his own self-styled diagram of the ego) had met a dam of personally refined and externally female animality bristling with sexual armor like a dreadnought or a fortress with cannon. But behind his life's every undertaking was his father, that corpulent brewer with his grey mustache *à la polonaise*. He could have stopped him from attending this *Kinderball*, as he called the princess's soirées. But no – it was he who had pushed him into this *gomon* of pleasures and dissipation, he who had coaxed him into it soon after recovering from his "attack." To divert him from his passion for literature? Perhaps. And what sort of model was he if he assigned his class a leading role in the march of civilization (on the condition that labor be streamlined, socialism repudiated, and religion restored – the Catholic religion, of course)? How could he cast himself as one of the elect in view of what was happening the world over – he, that old pseudopalatine bon vivant sprung up like a monstrous fungus from the muck of misery and injustice endured by his workers, whom, because of that very streamlining, he had sucked dry, meanwhile telling them that two hundred years hence they, too, could count on a Fordian prosperity (which over *there* had gone bust long ago). (It turned out that people were not such cattle after all; that it was no fun living without ideas. Fabulous America was rupturing like a gigantic ulcer. They might pay for it later on, but NOW, at least, they realized, if only for a short while, that they were not simply robots in the hands of similar but slightly cleverer robots. Anyway, the end result was bound to be the same: total automation – barring a miracle.) (Zip could not stand the sight of his father's workmen without shuddering and getting queasy in his lower gut. [And yet, wasn't there something erotic about it, too? Erotomania? No – but a person shouldn't stick his head under the pillow while thugs are carving up his next-door neighbor.] There they were now, a trailing column that stretched along the road that led from the factory compound to the manor in the pale azure dusk of a fading winter evening broken up by the violet sheaves of light given off by the arc lamps. An immense sadness brought on by two eternally irreconcilable contradictions – the life of the species versus the life of the individual –

took possession of him now as he sat there contemplating this picture [as though it were a postcard from a place not of this world], and once again he settled down to the words of that young man of letters, Sturfan Abnol.)

"No, I won't play jester," Abnol, by now thoroughly drunk, obstinately repeated. "What I do serves the mysterious aims of my own inner development. I'm poisoned by unspoken things that I can know only by writing novels. Chemically dissolved in my brain, life's mysteries produce ptomaines of sloth, confusion, inertia. I must go beyond appearances. What do I – *I, personally* – care if I'm read by a bunch of quasi-automated apes with pretensions to being demigods but who are unworthy of real art, and perhaps by a few from the vanishing breed of intelligent people (not that I know very many). I have no intention of manufacturing booster shots for flagging patriotic feelings or degenerating social instincts, for all those moribund worms infesting the rotten carcass of what was once a magnificent beast! Not for me to portray those people of the future exuding their void of animal health. Besides, what can a truly intelligent person say about those who fit into their fate as easily as a sword into its scabbard or a gem into its case? A function perfectly adapted is psychologically dull, whereas the epic is the pipedream of sterile scribblers. More interesting is man's *absolute (!)* alienation from existence. This only happens in decadent times. Only at such times are the metaphysical laws of existence made visible in all their naked horror. People can reproach me for inventing wimps, idlers, contemplative dreamers, men too paralyzed to act. Let people of lesser intelligence write of other characters, of tropical adventures and sports. It's not for me to describe what any halfwit can see and describe. I must delve into the unknown, enter the bedrock of what those other morons can only see on the surface and narrate so effortlessly. I wish to explore the laws of universal history, not just of things here, but wherever there are thinking creatures. I have no ambition to write vast panoramas of life – they are as tedious to read as listening to a lecture on the theories of Einstein – that last great innovator in physics – would be for my cook."

Tenzer stopped smelling the princess's arm and stretched himself out, thereby accentuating the grotesqueness of his dwarflike frame.

"All the same, Sturfan, you'll be a jester," said Tenzer, towering above the entire salon in a gigantic vision of his own future. (Even Princess Vsevolodovna surrendered to it, and, in doing so, suddenly saw him in a different light – in a superbrothel of some pan-metropolis, at the top of a pyramid of naked and beautifully costumed girls [not the same], honoring the inventor of some new narcotic just as the world's supply of cocaine, peyote, and apotransformine was drying up. She herself sat beside his legs [the palsied one (his enemies maintained this freak would have stunk less if that leg could have been amputated); he was also naked], those hairy, twisted legs with their hideous, froglike feet. The addict-adepts of his poison were rolling around before him on their knees and stomachs in the final throes of madness.)

....

INFORMATION: This was all a gross exaggeration. Art was bankrupt, though a handful of maniacs in certain limited circles clung to their snobbish pretensions with unprecedented fury.

Tenzer, that benevolent poisoner of vanishing ghosts, stood grinning like a fiend, saturated with a triumph and a glory that filled the ambient space to overflowing. Billowing ether cascaded into infinity, magnetic fields expanded perpendicularly (oh, who the hell cares except for a few moribund theoretical physicists!), transporting into barren interplanetary space the sound waves borne from the grimy, gloomy soul of this aging gentleman – this rusticated gent – who had got his fill of life too late. Tenzer continued to address the writer, who was collapsing in utter prostration:

"Nothing can save you from becoming a clown, no matter what you may think of yourself. Which is the real 'you': what you imagine yourself to be or what you are in fact in the coils of a society – of a clump of worms – by metaphysical, transcendental laws? Artists have always been jesters serving the mighty of this world and will remain so, as long as the leftovers of a magnificent order – like our Prince and Princess di Ticonderoga in their palace here – continue to strut about the world." (The princess was on the verge of fainting, so intensely gratifying was this to her vanity. She adored this display of social audacity on the part of guests belonging to a "lower caste" – impertinences were collected and entered in her "diarette," as she called that bunch of male incivilities.) "You can make believe you write out of your own metaphysical soul-searching, but socially you're a clown whose job is to amuse the jaded, cloying souls of yesterday's elite who are today's dregs – which, in our country, have stayed afloat, like a film of scum, on the violent rapids of a newly arisen humanity. I, at least, realize this and can't be other than what I am, while you . . . "

"I have no desire to know society. Live in this mire I must, but I can insulate myself from it," Abnol proclaimed with sudden emotion. "Unless it were a model society and not this hypocritical democracy of ours. In the West maybe, or in China . . . "

"All right, if you insist – not socially, but in reality, unclouded by any personal illusions, vis-à-vis the centuries to come. No need to wait for the Last Judgment. In a couple of hundred years each of us will be what he or she is – minus pretty dresses, minus all those little trinkets none of us can live without, minus our personal charms."

"Especially you, Putricides," interjected the princess sarcastically. Tenzer did not so much as throw her a glance.

"Then we'll see what personal charm can accomplish! This might not even be so bad for the art world, let alone for politicians, conquerors, and other revolutionaries of real values. Oh, if only I weren't a hunchback with a palsied leg . . . "

"We can all see how you're flaunting your mental powers and your musical dexterity. But it's precisely your mental stability that's a little suspect. If the emotional effect of those musical sounds wasn't so . . . "

"You're talking" – Tenzer made it a point never to address titled persons by their titles – "about all those teenagers I'm supposed to have seduced?" (Homosexuality had become quite respectable, thereby losing much of its attraction.) "About those ephebes compensating for a life of frustration?" Putricides spoke bluntly as if vomiting on a magnificent Russian carpet. "There's no reason for me to conceal it." His face was lost in a cloud of voluptuous power. "When a disgusting cripple like myself, without a shade of desire, can defile an innocent, beautiful . . . it's a triumph, is it not?!"

"That's enough, Tenzer!"

"And when they go back to their girlfriends – it doesn't matter anymore, because then I'm already beyond that, I can sink into my world of pure sound, calm as Walter Pater himself, away from all this sickening sexual longing, away from the random quality of such moments, in a nonqualitative realm of absolute necessity and freedom! Because nothing is more terrifying than that afternoon hour between two and three when you can't hide things, when the sheer metaphysical horror bores like a tusk through the ruins of those everyday illusions with which we try to kill the emptiness of a life without faith . . . Oh, God!" He buried his ugly face in his hands and turned perfectly still. The horrorstruck guests shook their heads. "What ever must be going on in that shaggy skull of his?" Yet there was hardly one who did not envy Tenzer that abstruse, wildly impractical world of his in which he was so at ease with himself, comfy as all who inhabited their island of belated, quasi-fascist-Fordian, enervating-because-economically-prosperous galimatias. The princess, absorbed now by the prospect of old age, stroked Tenzer's head. Suddenly something wrenched inside her. It was the thousandth time it had happened, and it terrified her out of her wits.

Genezip had comprehended nothing, which did not prevent his guts from being torn infinitely asunder. He was drinking now for the first time in his life, and strange things were taking place in his head and in the rest of his body. Yet everything stood out as clearly as in a photo slide – *interesslose Anschauung*. The present moment, detached from both the past and the future, removed from the stricture of his former tumor-ideals, and with its hackles slightly up, turned its back and receded into infinity where someone even more personal was standing now, some young god (that "moment" had been the princess): "The rainbow was his belt, the moon lay at his feet" (Miciński, "Isis"). The infernal thrill of license: suddenly he understood those last words spoken by Tenzer, "absolute necessity" – oh, what profundity lay in that phrase. "That's me, that's me," he whispered ecstatically. He saw himself as if situated beyond reality, beyond some river that reminded him of the Styx in one of Doré's drawings. He stood flawless in his consummate beauty, while all worldly desires, now drowned in the river, floated away like bloody intestines. (This wasn't the worst of it, not by half.) *It* had happened. He regretted his ignorance – now that it was too late. He longed insanely for that *genuinely* free period of childhood with its tranquillity and discipline. Yet, the last scale of deceit and hypocrisy had fallen from his father (who was probably near death from an apoplectic fit), and a single, naked shoot, indecent as an asparagus or a young bamboo, shot up from the moist, steaming dungheap. He was both – the god in the distance and this stupid shoot; he had taken on a split personality, "henceforth and forever more." Again the experience was all within him: the strangeness, the world – this salon, these young ladies, this lecherous old vixen (her vicious smile, provoked by wild regret for bygone female depravities, by her hold over the "dumb-but-clever long-tailed monkeys" [men never appeared in her thoughts but in this fashion]) – *all this existed inside him.* For a moment he doubted the reality of this fantastic landscape: he was alone and he felt marvelous. Little did he know that he was being scrutinized by a pair of girlish eyes, that nothing escaped those eyes, and that they were trying to rescue him: these were the eyes of Eliza. Compared to his massive internal realignment, their effect was like a mosquito bite on a mutilated thigh. If he had only pried himself from the gaze of that bawdy bitch and turned his attention to the corner where the piano stood, life might have looked different somehow. "How humiliating to have your fate sealed by a wench, by creatures of a lower order" – he might have thought five years ago while fleeing from the kisses of some wicked chambermaid (about whom, by the way, he had completely forgotten). Not anymore. (But what were all these petty drunken visions compared to his present "awakening"?! He knew everything now; but how many more initiations, each time to an increasingly higher degree [or lower, depending on the nature of the involvement, on its exponent in the ethical sphere], into the mysteries of the world did he have before him?)

The princess turned on Zip those eyes omniscient in pleasure and perversion and licked him up and down with her glance: he was hers. "It's she who's going to initiate me," he thought in panic, and suddenly felt his mother standing beside him as if to protect him from this depraved superbawd. But wasn't his mother cut from the same female monstrosity – if not actually, then potentially? Was she not such a profligate, too; if so, what then? "Nothing. I'd love her just the same," he went on thinking with a somewhat strained magnanimity. "Still, it's a good thing she isn't." He felt his mother's jealousy and the awesome mystery of motherhood (that she still had a claim to him, which aroused not the slightest gratitude in him). Despite all of these apparent earthly bonds, he had descended quite by accident (all the more terrifying for being inevitable – hence the mystery) into this world, and no one was the real cause of it – not even his mother, much less his father. The origin of his existence, that succession of complex tragedies involving so many bodies and souls at war with, and among, each other (and all this to engender a misfit like himself!) suddenly became intelligible. "I was meant to be this way, I guess, once and for all eternity – this way or not at all." He had strayed intuitively into the mystery of the causality of existence: a sense of the static equilibrium of all physics, of the derivative nature of a psychological causality issuing from two sources – from logical necessity and from physiology – the latter being ultimately reducible to physics. But he was not *conscious* of this; that would come later. And then the corollary to all this: death, the supreme sanction of personal existence. Oh, but at what a price . . . ! Again he thought of his mother: "She might protect me if she were dead – alive, she can't do a thing for me. She's too human, too ordinary, too imperfect, and too much of a sinner in the catechismic sense. Because she and father must have done it to each – Ugh . . . !" Having seen through to this terrible truth – somehow it struck him as unworthy of a child – he felt proud of himself. It was as "a man of the world" now that he surrendered to the princess's gaze, and with a look of bewilderment said (with eyes only): "Yes." And at once he was overcome with a disgraceful, "boyishly" disgusting embarrassment. As she turned to the others, the princess licked her lip triumphantly with her sharp, pink, catlike tongue. This lecherous, cunning old vamp knew now that the spoils belonged to her. The thought of depriving this magnificent young Valentino of his virginity made her clever body shudder. Even Sturfan Abnol, the ex-lover who had exorcised her presence (or, more precisely, her erotic dexterity), suddenly knew a twitching in the nether regions. Oh, why not take her on the spot while she lusted for that other boy, with that smirk on her face, so self-controlled – oh, how lovely! But the urge quickly deserted him. Tenzer, on the other hand, was wallowing in a state of sexual despair as in a pile of manure. "Forge for yourself such a power / And at your feet these carrion will cower," he muttered, quoting a rhyme from one of those young, totally talentless ultrarealists fond of pasting together words with the glue of a perverted semantics rather than with the force of inspiration. Prince Basil's house of retreat loomed up in his memory from a time when this most *svetleyshy* of men still recognized drugs, that is, before his having attained to the ultimate narcotic, that of mysticism. Mysticism, and not religion. "Religion is the profound truth. Its derivatives are not to be confused with faith; the former are the delusions of feeble souls who can't look their own metaphysical void in the face. That's not religion. Some of them know this, yet knowingly poison themselves on their own intellectual flabbiness, their queasiness before the truth, and their fear of the absurd, which sooner or later every definitive truth reveals if it's not hermetically sealed by all sorts of qualifications. But not everyone can afford the luxury of such qualifications." So Tenzer had said once to Prince Basil. And yet, what bliss to venture beyond, far, far beyond the aquamarine, to the boundless realm of the "Black Strudel" – the name they had given to that continent on which the essentially nondimensional ego seemed to land after traversing the perilous but finite ocean of absolute Nothingness: a miracle. Their last trip there, managed not without some strain, had been two years ago, after the three of them – the third was the logician Afanasol Benz, alias Bends – had downed a quart of ether. But the barrenness of those worlds at the outer limits of consciousness; those purely sensual trips into the realm of nothingness and of absolute, *pseudo*metaphysical solitude; the futility of using them on behalf of his private, esoteric realm of self-constructed sounds had turned Tenzer off the illegal stuff. And then there was his wife, who rapped his hairy face whenever he came home reeking of it. For these two not quite compatible reasons, Tenzer had sworn off the ultimate in high-grade narcotics and had stuck with good old alcohol – there the effect on one's work was immediate, even stimulating, not to mention technically advantageous in condensing his elusive musical vision. Not for nothing had a certain Moscow superconstructivist once said of Tenzer, *"Etot Tenzer pishet kak khochet,"* for there was virtually no visionary combination of sounds that this metaphysical volcano in tablet form could not reduce to a set of rhythmic and melodic symbols. But even this gift was predestined for the sphere of finite miracles: the plenitude of life had broken this glorious talent, which blossomed in proportion to the disproportion between desire and its fulfillment. The princess, like all the *précieuses* of her time, had been right.

Genezip was suddenly befuddled out of his wits. He was telling the princess something, something in the way of a promise . . . Things were taking place in some purely irrational realm, even assuming the existence of "Lebesgue's psychic dimension," that is to say, the possibility of differentiating the most minute aberrations of the human psyche. The world seemed to be exploding from extreme self-insatiation. Musical "soul phrases" were being torn to shreds and strewn into unknown regions by a flaming vortex of alcohol mixed with an adolescent brain. At a certain point he stood up, marched out of the room like a robot, got into his coat, and ran out of the Ticonderoga palace. And not a moment too soon. He puked out his guts. A moment later he was enveloped by a storm of ice pellets on the Plain of Grains. But he had not yet awakened that evening: the real horror of those irrecoverable moments had yet to sink in.

His father was fading fast. He had been given only two or three days to live. An awful thing had happened, though no one knew for whom it was "awful" (for some of Zip's aunts?): even before the old man died, Genezip had dismissed him utterly from his mind.

The wind howled and whistled, winding about the brewer's mansion the whipping braids of the "storm witch." Except for Miss Ela, the nurse, Zip was all alone in his father's dark green study. He bent down and without the slightest emotion kissed his father's swollen hand.

"I know you'll be her lover, Zip," his father gasped. "She'll teach you life. I can tell by your eyes; there's no need to lie. May God protect you, son, because there's not a person alive who knows that reptile's mind. I was one of her paramours some fifteen years ago when I shone at the court of our dearly departed king." (The kingdom that was Poland for years was largely fictitious. A kind of Bragançe. It was thrown out like so much garbage.)

"Rest, sir," Ela whispered succinctly.

"Hush, woman – you are the personification of death. This Ela is nothingness incarnate. I know I'm dying, but I cross this little bridge cheerfully because I know nothing new awaits me on the other side. I enjoyed my life; not everyone can say that. Expand, grow – in short, produce – there you have it. I was unlucky with this young shaver of mine, but I'll knock some sense into him after I die – so help me God, I will. I'll make mincemeat out of him."

Genezip froze. For the first time he saw his father not as that tyrannical, familiar, lovable (fiercely, with-clenched-teeth-lovable) old man but as someone else, a stranger, as some indifferent passerby. He seemed to Zip so much more likable at that moment. He could have become his father's friend, hated him forever, or strolled away with a shrug. For Zip he was just some nameless Mr. X, where the X might have stood for anything. He stared at his father from the incalculable distance created by imminent death, the first in Zip's life.

"Forgive me, Papa, and I can do whatever I set my mind to," Zip almost pleaded with emotion. The "knowledge" that his father had once been the princess's lover drew him closer to him, though in a tainted and not very palatable manner.

"You're forgiven," said Kapen senior, and, even though it was painful for him, he burst out in a sinister, beastly laugh, his tiny green eyes flashing in folds of fat with a ruthless intelligence and a ferocious, rhinoceroslike meanness. An abominable old man from a long-forgotten dream: in penumbra, while a stiff little wind whispered in the junipers, an old man was gathering brushwood; his face was lost from view and all one could see, or was permitted to see, was his beard – the rest was beyond description. By giving Zip a free hand, old man Kapen knew what he was doing, though even he had been guilty of one miscalculation. Zip promptly lost all interest in literature. He stood there psychically stripped, shivering from the cold, from a lack of sleep, from having drunk too much, and from a posterotic fever. A storm-tossed, labyrinthian future had blocked his view of the present, which was shrinking as if examined through the wrong end of a telescope and was nearly obscured by the vague terror implicit in coming events he had already devoured in the abstract.

"Good-bye, Father; I'm off to bed," Zip said brusquely, and he left the room.

"He's got my blood all right," Papa Kapen whispered to the nurse contentedly, almost in a voice of triumph, and he lapsed into a deathly slumber. A pastel-blue dawn, enveloped by galloping clouds of snow, was breaking beyond the tapering hillocks of the Ludzimierz landscape.

....

INFORMATION: The political background was for the moment quite remote. But something was sliding down like a glacier from the gloomy Mountains of the Unknown. Small and impetuous avalanches were forming at the sides, but no one took any notice. Statesmen of all parties, now almost indistinguishable in the general, artificial, pseudofascist, and *au fond* mindless prosperity, were positively drowning in ideas and in a cheerfulness bordering on blissful idiocy. The mobile Chinese Wall was looming larger and more awesome, casting an ominous yellow shadow over the rest of Asia and the West. Two shadows: there was no telling where the light came from. Even the English, their Empire having been broken up and bolshevized, finally saw that they were not a single, homogenous nation. Indeed, apart from the Poles no one spoke of "nations" anymore. Their disappearance accorded with the latest anthropological findings.

Kapen senior was ruminating: "An attack of sclerosis . . . hemorrhaging in one of the brain's lobes — oh, why try to diagnose it? I'm a changed person. If I somehow survive, I'll probably end up socializing the factory. What I mean is, I'll turn it into a collective and hire Zip as a common laborer. I might even stay on as a foreman. Who knows, I may do it anyway – the former, that is, not the latter. I'll take a nap now, then I'll make up a new will. I won't die in my sleep – not a chance!" (But soon he was visited by thoughts having to do with his son: about his strange friend Kotzmolochowicz, the quartermaster general of the army, who had fallen for his wife back in the days when she was unmarried [and who today was as feeling as a tree stump].) "I've gotten soft in my old age, dammit," he continued to muse. "It's good I'm going to die. To live and not be ashamed of going gaga – ugh! But on my deathbed I can permit myself a little 'mischief.'" He wrapped himself in his distant, faded life as in his blanket adorned with lilacs. And having simultaneously rolled himself up in these two existences, he went to sleep with courage, confident that he would live to see the world again. Whether he woke up tomorrow or the next day, what did he care? – he thought with satisfaction.

Genezip felt in possession of a malevolent authority. Even so, he had to live as prescribed by his father, who though a changed man went on functioning, like some defective machine, according to old, deeply ingrained habits. Went on despite the world's being "other" – it was strange beyond words, but nothing like the eeriness with which everything, absolutely everything, had become charged after today's awakening. An unnamed light was rapidly suffusing forever new, far-flung regions of his soul, like the sun's light when it chases the darting shadow of a wind-driven cloud. Then he recalled that just before his exit, at his intoxicated peak, he had agreed to a rendezvous with the princess at two o'clock in the morning. He was shocked that he had let matters go so far. "Theoretically," Zip knew everything – that sexual "everything" of an innocent eighth-grader – but he never dreamed that this theoretical knowledge could become so easily entangled with reality. Suddenly everything stood stock still as if fixed, anchored to the ground: the past stood before him whole, as though on a tray, devoid of time, cold and stiff. The present moment was also stuck in this wilderness without duration, like a knife planted in the belly of an enemy. He heard his life "babbling" amid the ruins like a tiny brook, but it only served to increase the uncanny quietness of everything. It was as if the entire world had halted in its orbit and was staring goggle-eyed at itself in dismay. "Nothing will ask for nothing in its own hollow grave," one of his "forbidden" playmates had written. Then "something" let up momentarily, only to resume its course at a still more furious pace, like a rampaging river demolishing the ice floes in its path. The passage of time, seemingly arrested a short time ago, now became an insufferable tedium.

"I'll never make it by myself," Genezip said under his breath. Again he conjured up Tenzer's hirsute phiz and eyes as the composer had talked yesterday of music. "He must know everything. Maybe he can explain to me why nothing is really itself and yet is precisely *what it is*." He made up his mind to go see Tenzer at once. He was seized with restlessness and felt like some exercise. He wolfed down his late-afternoon snack (the old sort, the kind he ate as a kid, when matters such as these . . .), and left the house, heading almost unconsciously toward Grand Mountain where Tenzer lived with his family in the woods. He hardly knew this man, had met him only yesterday, but for some reason he seemed closer to him than any of his other new acquaintances, this despite the absence of any special feeling toward him. He was guided by the certitude that the composer would grasp his present situation and perhaps offer him some advice.

A Visit with Tenzer

Zip stumbled along with his eyes fixed upon the heavens, where the daily (but certainly not everyday) mystery of a starry night was celebrated. The kind of astronomy he had been taught in school held no great magic for him. He had been bored silly by the horizon and the azimuth, by angles of declination, precessions and perturbations, by all the complicated computations . . . The only thing that had aroused in him a slight anxiety verging on a very primitive, metaphysical ferment had been a short survey, all but lost in the heap of other required subjects, of astrophysics and cosmogony. But "astronomical angst," once a cousin to loftier states leading to philosophical meditation, was rapidly being brushed aside as a luxury by an age of mundane pursuits. Now, as he sauntered along, Genezip felt as if he were looking up at the night sky for the first time in his life. Until tonight, despite what scientific knowledge he possessed, he had thought of the sky as a two-dimensional plane sprinkled with more or less luminous dots. Even though he was knowledgeable, emotionally he never got beyond this rather primitive notion. Now space suddenly acquired a third dimension, revealing differences in distance and boundless perspectives. The mind, catapulted into space by a furious force, was circling about worlds in an effort to penetrate their essential meaning. Zip's textbook knowledge, which lay at the bottom of his memory like an inert mass, began to surface and cluster around questions, now posed differently, not as intellectual problems but as a cry of terror before the omnimystery contained in the infinity of time and space, before the apparently simple fact that everything was so and not otherwise.

Above the three limestone stars of his Hunter's Belt, Orion soared like a gigantic kite, trailing the frantic Sirius on his heel. Orange-red Betelguese and silver-white Rigel stood guard on either side of the belt, while Bellatrix, slightly paler than the others, cleaved through interstellar space. Shining with a peaceful, steady light between the Pleiades and Aldebaran were the two star-planets: orange-red Mars and lead-blue Saturn. The dark ridge stretching from the Hunter's Belt to the northernmost star of Auriga stood out like the spine of some antediluvian lizard against the luminous dust of the Milky Way, which sank perpendicularly behind the horizon. Genezip became dizzy from stargazing. Above and below had lost all meaning for him: he was suspended in an abyss, terrifying, amorphous, undifferentiated. For a second he had comprehended the infinity of space: it had *been* and lasted during the very moment he experienced it. Eternity was as nothing compared to the monstrous infinitude of time within infinite space and the heavenly bodies inhabiting it. What to make of the thing? It was beyond imagining and yet impressed itself on the mind with absolute ontological necessity. The same mystery had shown him its unmasked face, but in a different way. The immense world, and himself, metaphysically alone (he would require companionship), without the possibility of cognition (what were ideas before the horror of the immediately given?!): still, there was something painfully sweet in this sensation of loneliness. At the moment he felt quite small in the infinite tangle of the universe – not small in relation to the vast expanses of this nocturnal sky, but in his deepest feelings toward his mother and the princess.

Genezip walked along now with his head bowed, listening in despair to the snow crunching beneath his feet. The past few idle moments were sinking, in a welter of frustration, into the past. He had already tired of the stars, of their mute contempt and meaningful winking. He felt an antipathy toward everything, even toward his prospective talk with Tenzer, but he pushed on through the inertia of his former determination. The road led uphill through a spruce forest. Decked with tufts of snow, the trees seemed to stretch forth gigantic white paws with enormous black claws, invoking a mysterious spell over him. Now and then starlight penetrated the dark growth, keen and disquieting like a danger signal. The moment he caught sight of the yellow lights of Tenzer's house blazing brightly on a hill beyond the forest's edge, Genezip knew that this was to be a turning point in his life, that an entire chain of events would be decided by this evening, whatever their external configuration. He felt possessed of a terrific power to manipulate reality however he chose; let a mountain collapse on him, he'd dig his way out – so long as he clung to this fugitive moment! Gossamery cobwebs moving blocks and bulwarks of steel; the capricious form of an evening cloud pronouncing a life or death sentence for nations (like rain on the eve of the Battle of Waterloo) . . . But everything was veering away from chance, from the Great Numbers, toward conscious manipulation, and he was going to be a part of that movement, not some disorganized piece of crap, not some pebble stuck in the gears. "The illusions of pseudoindividualism raging like a nasty little tumor on the comatosely swelling carcass of society moments before the final explosion of history," the logician Afanasol Benz would have said.

Genezip surveyed the glowing windows of the cottage as though they were something to be overcome, yet somehow intimate and familiar, and entered an enormous hallway lighted by a small and quaint lamp. The furs and overcoats hanging on the coatrack filled him with superstitious alarm. Somehow they struck him as incredibly powerful and portentous, more powerful in their bulk and immobility than the man to whom they belonged. The eerie inertia of those garments suggested the manifold possibilities of things waiting to be accomplished, even though Tenzer himself appeared as but the momentary phase of a fleeting personality, insignificant, devoid of substance and durability.

He could hear the sounds of a piano coming from the next room. Tenzer was not to be seen, while the music only augmented the impression of his mysterious power. With a twinge of dread, he rang a gong that hung on a door to the left of the entrance. (Oh, how differently it was to have transpired! – the good guardian angels in whom no one believed were sobbing in despair.) The piano music was lost in a prolonged and metallic crescendo, and a moment later Genezip saw before him in the doorway that hairy monstrosity of a face he felt he had known since time immemorial.

"Come in," said Tenzer sternly, imperiously. Zip stepped inside and was enveloped by the pungent smell of forest herbs. They moved deeper into the room. Very spacious; covered with a black shag carpet and lighted by a lamp with a mottled shade. To the right, in the corner, stood a gigantic sculpture of a giant's head from which hung a small, grotesque hobgoblin.

"I hope I'm not disturbing you," Genezip said timidly.

"As a matter of fact, you are – on second thought, maybe not. It's probably better I interrupted that improvisation when I did. No sense in overdoing it. To be quite frank with you, I'm not fond of men your age. I can't hold myself responsible for them when it comes to . . . – oh, skip it."

"I see. That's what you and the others were talking about the other evening. But I don't understand what . . . "

"Stop! I was drunk then. Anyway" – his tone suddenly mellowed and he shrank drastically in his psychic dimensions – "let's you and I be friends. But, remember, I take no responsibility for what happens," he solemnly repeated. "From now on I'll call you by your first name."

 Genezip squirmed with discomfort. Still, something lurked

beyond this moment for which he was willing to pay the price of a temporary self-disgust. "Then again, no one can say I invited you exactly; on the contrary, I was not in favor of this visit. You were drunk – you couldn't possibly remember." He turned silent, as though pondering something exceedingly bitter, all the while his gaze remained fixed on the intricate design of an oriental carpet hanging on the wall. Genezip's feelings were hurt.

"In that case . . . ," he began in a voice quivering with wounded pride.

"In that case, sit down! You're going to have some coffee." With a shove from some invisible force, Genezip plopped down on the sofa. "You must have had some urgent reason for coming here if you weren't put off by the tons of fluid surrounding my person." Tenzer went into the next room, where Zip could hear him fussing with the coffee grinder. A short while later they were seated at a small table on which two tea glasses of very strong and heavily sugared, if not particularly aromatic, coffee were steaming. "Well?" asked Tenzer against a backdrop of silence broken only by the distant, "wistful" sound of sleigh bells. Genezip moved closer to Tenzer and took him by the hand (the latter shuddered). Why had he done that? Why all this posing? Was it really he who was acting like this? Surely not. And yet . . . Oh, how complex were the psyches of certain people! No one, not even the offender, can claim to know all the layers of their alien personalities, of all those hidden compartments, those secret drawers the keys to which have been lost . . . Despite a genuine metaphysical curiosity and the hope that Tenzer would dispel all his doubts by a single utterance, something else had now arisen, something abominable, uncanny, hitherto unparalleled in his life. And yet, it all seemed so disgustingly familiar, as if it had already . . . *Yes, Toldzio was to blame for all this!* Wasn't it Toldzio who yesterday had briefed him in such lurid detail? Zip had been aroused to a morbid curiosity. But Toldzio was not to blame now, only for what happened much earlier. Meanwhile, Zip, naive kid that he was, decided to deceive Tenzer by pretending till the "very last" – i.e., till the moment of violation – to be his latest prey. He had to see for himself the power of this man, to take possession of it, to appropriate it for himself. And it was he, the once-proud lad, who was having such thoughts – it was not to be believed; he, who from the very beginning had wanted to discover everything on his own, who in school had been ashamed to hear of what others had done – now he was to live by sponging off others! "Wow, I'd be one hell of a mathematician if I could just rewrite the whole of mathematics," he blurted out in one sentence. He had said it flippantly, almost blithely, but for Tenzer it signaled in a big way the possibility of gloomily triumphing over his own ugliness. Who knew (well, who?) whether such moments weren't more essential for his music than all those really quite entertaining and humiliating-because-not-fully-it, normal sort of "involvements." (The word "involvement" makes one want to puke. Incidentally, there are many Polish words that are *gebrauchsfähig* only in quotation marks – e.g., such "shameful" words as "rakish," "perky," "frisky," "verve," "overtures," "penetrating," etc.)

"I'm not the least bit afraid of you. I have no feelings toward you one way or the other. So there's no need to stand on ceremony. I'm really quite innocent, a 'virgin' as they say, but I know the whole story and I have this fantastic knack of ruining everyone I get close to." (Tenzer was suddenly and disgustingly set aflame; measured by his previous display of emotion, it was almost genuine.) For Zip, what he was saying was too corny for words. But it gave the boy an immense satisfaction to think that a dumb, still-wet-behind-the-ears graduate could put on such a diabolical act and fool this supposedly omniscient hunchback. Here we see a possible aftereffect of having stared too long yesterday into those eyes of blue enamel. But Zip was ignorant of any such connection.

Tenzer, wishing to probe the coefficient of his new friend's "revoltingness" ("repulsiveness," "hideousness" – no phrase or proper suffix will do), or simply put, to see how easy it was to make himself and his ways revolting to Genezip, suddenly leaned over and, with his broad mouth that stank (or rather did *not* stink) of raw meat and an animal's drooling muzzle, kissed him.

Oh, it was revolting all right! So take off, stop pretending, forget you ever knew this man – or that vicious vamp, either – puke it all out and go find some poor, simple young girl to fall in love with. And then came a single thought, coolly formulated, and the revulsion was objectified, was rendered harmless as a defanged snake, as remote as the pain of a broken leg after an injection of morphine: "Being initiated into such mysteries is worth the hassle," some alien creature without any heart, without any conscience, without any sense of honor, thought inside him. He would go on nurturing this little freak and began keeping a diary (the same diary published by Dr. Wuchert in 1997 as *Notes of a Schizophrenic;* it made him famous and led many to suspect he was the real author) as a way of recording his (this little freak's) experiences. Genezip was petrified as he submitted passively to this first kiss on the lips. Tenzer went on slobbering him, but meeting with no resistance suddenly stopped: it did nothing to titillate his vanity.

"Listen, Kapen . . . What I mean is: forgive me, Zip. This outburst is not what you think it is. I had a brother of whom I was very fond. He died from the same disease" – why had he said that? It was obviously a lie – "which I was lucky enough to overcome. *Osteomyelitis scrofulosa.* But it left me a cripple. So I'm always dreaming about a glorious end where my life can be an eternal feast. But I'm a stranger to love and probably always shall be. I'm sure you don't understand that. But you get my drift."

Genezip was choking with disgust, as though some grimy, stinking, sweating hulk of a body the size of Tenzer's house was pressing on top of him. Tenzer's words were even more offensive than his repugnant kiss. Yet he felt an odd sympathy for him, greater than the sympathy he had felt for his dying father. He grabbed Tenzer's arm and squeezed it.

"Why don't you tell me the whole story, right from the beginning. For one thing, you're married. The princess told me your wife is an attractive woman."

"Ours is not a marriage. It's one enormous crime-cum-torture. I even have children. My illness isn't hereditary until the third generation. Adolf Tenzer will grow up to be a healthy, normal person and will enjoy a life his father and uncle never had. Ninon will be a good mother because my wife is a good woman. And that's why . . . " Tenzer suddenly began to sob. Genezip's eyes nearly popped out of his head for shame. A feeling of compassion, revolting as a crushed cockroach, was cruelly, pitilessly (just so), tearing his insides.

"Don't cry . . . You'll see, everything will be okay. I came here today to see if you could solve life's mysteries. You must know the answers because your music is omniscient. But I have to understand it with my brain, which is quite another thing. You'll figure out a way, though, because you said something last night that went beyond the fact that everything was so and not otherwise. I don't know how to express it." (Tenzer gradually stopped sniffling.) "Last night's soirée, my father's attack – this last is probably the least of my worries – then today I wake up from an afternoon nap and I'm completely mixed up. My mind's a total blank, because everything I took to be normal in the world is poised above a cliff and unable to go over the side. Down below is mystery incarnate. But I've never gotten far enough that I could plumb that mystery, so . . . "

"The moment of revelation or, as they say nowadays, the first signs of lunacy," said Tenzer, wiping his eyes. "I've had such moments myself, friend." (Oh, that word "friend"; it made Genezip squirm.) "But fewer and fewer in the course of time. Because before I know what's happening – pfft, the whole thing turns into sounds – not into the actual sounds themselves, but into an arrangement that gets beyond me – and a lot of others, too. It's what saves me from going insane. I have a fair idea of what I am, but if I'm never understood, not even after I'm dead, won't this prove that I'm a musical hack laboring under the illusion that I was somebody? Because, dammit, I'm too smart to entertain such illusions. And won't it also prove that music has come to an end, that just as Judas was singled out to be a traitor, so I was chosen to bring down the curtain?" (Genezip was of the distinct impression that life, hitherto so atrophied in its monotony that it had ceased to consume time, had swerved onto a new but equally precipitous course and that the acceleration he had been waiting for, even hungering for, was about to begin. Familiar states, bordering those of the present, zoomed by, remaining in the past like the scenes of one's native realm in the windows of a train hurtling faster and faster into distant and unexplored regions.) Tenzer went on: "And that's how it ought to be. I accept the transcendentality of that law, its absolute finality – that law," he repeated, "which says that art, on whatever planet, will follow the same evolution of forms as our own; that it must be related to religion and metaphysics, which, at least for thinking beings, are as basic a necessity as art. But only in its own time. After that it has to perish, consumed by the same force that created it, by the social mash that, after crystallizing into perfection, has to expel everything that dares to get in its way. But why should I be the unlucky one? Still, it's a great luxury: this sense of your own individuality, of its absolute necessity in the scheme of things, this one and no other. Ha! I'm better than others because I won't give in. Even if I wanted to, something would stop me, a force mightier than myself – my own pride. But pride not before the world, but before infinity . . . " His eyes burned with a power that looked, it seemed, into the navel of the universe, and suddenly this apparently feeble, hirsute freak stood before Genezip like some powerful idol (but not ideal) with a special function or mission; for the whole of existence there might have been forty to fifty such people, each corresponding to a primary phenomenon: music, the other arts, the winds, the elements, the weather, natural disasters . . .

At the same time Zip thought: "He sees himself as necessary because he's an artist. He'll never understand me or explain to me why I find it so incredibly strange: my *this*ness as opposed to *that*ness." Suddenly he was stricken with doubt: "But who cares? This piano thumping that's not worth a damn to anyone? What an exaggeration! Would-be profundity! No, I prefer thought – but *what* thought? I don't have a single one of my own, not even the start of one. Think one up! My God!! Instead of chasing illusions and kidding myself for the rest of my life. Revelation? But who can say that what descends on me is really the truth?" Something told him that only by a supreme exertion of will, self-sacrifice, ruthless asceticism; that only by avoiding what now looked so inevitable and which enticed with its powerfully alluring naughtiness (strangely, it struck him as the opposite of unleashing a dog) could he have that other world revealed to him. Ha, just try playing the ascetic! It was then that he forever renounced the possibility of self-knowledge. There are natures that cannot live in debauchery and blissfully know the highest truths: one has to choose. Oh, blessed are the select few who can discover themselves while destroying themselves and thus achieve perfection on earth. Never mind about the state of their souls; at least they've reached perfection down here, even if in evil. Today was a trial, a turning point. But *whose* day? Was it worth being an accidental speck in the abyss of the unknown, this and no other among the *alephs* on the periphery of other specks? (*Aleph* = Cantor's first transfinite number.) (In the whole of infinite being [and then *only on the periphery*] there can be only one *aleph*, and not – God forbid – a *continuum*. This is not the place to prove why this is so.) The existence of an individual speck cannot be expressed by a general law in which values of arbitrary magnitude can be posited as variables in the hierarchy of particular existences. How did Husserl put it? One of Zip's teachers had quoted the philosopher in a lecture on mathematics: "If there's a God, then His logic and mathematics cannot differ from our own." This was the point, not how some clown or pseudointellectual or even (o blasphemy!) some genius felt! It was a question of *laws*, not this or that case. Such was the whirl inside Genezip's wee brain. Imploringly he said to Tenzer (a whole lifetime can be decided by such moments, by one opportune word, but people are dumb and trample one another [often on behalf of ideals] into the muck of a reality botched and bowdlerized by ideas. Reality allows its most precious juices to escape under the pressure of ideas. But the quality of the latter determines whether the former will be a poison or the most nutritious vitamin):

"Putrice" (that's what Putricides Tenzer was called for short), "I don't know who I'll be tomorrow. Everything's all crooked inside me, not at an angle on one and the same plane but in some other space. These ideas are just too far beyond me" – (*with irony, sarcasm*) – "I'm not as convinced about art as you are. Your ideas are on a higher level than the things they refer to – higher, because born of the mind; you overestimate their basis in reality. I like literature because it holds more of life than my own. Life is concentrated there in a way I could never find in reality. The price you pay for that concentration is irreality." (Tenzer was grinning broadly. "Ha-ha, he can tell the difference between reality and illusion! He's an illusion himself. No need for me to have a guilty conscience.") "But it's *this* life I care about. That it be unique in its own way and at the same time necessarily *different*, a model, a perfect ideal, even in things that are, or could be, evil – perfect even in defeat. That's the ultimate in life . . . " He stared blankly, feverishly into space. "But now all is changing so powerfully, so fantastically that I'm no longer sure whether I'm me or someone else. This contradiction between change and continuity . . . "

"Always keep in mind that we can only doubt the continuity of our ego because it's continuous. Otherwise, your question does not even arise. The cohesion of the self is immediately given, due to its continuity; all our doubts have as their source the stunning multiplicity of fragmented complexes. Even for those afflicted with a dual personality, time must be continuous; there's no such thing as an infinitely short time span . . . "

"I understand intuitively what you're saying. But these are again vague concepts. I loved my father and was afraid of him. Now he's dying, and I couldn't care less." (Tenzer looked at him intently, but with the sort of expression one makes into a mirror.) "I've never felt so low, and for no real reason . . . I feel as if nothing in the world is as it should be; as if everything were covered with a wrapper – even astronomy. I keep wanting to touch everything naked, just as I touch my face with my own bare hand . . . I want to change everything so it'll turn out as it should. I want to have it *all*, to choke it, crush it, squeeze its guts out, torture it . . . !!!" Genezip cried out hysterically, on the verge of tears, not recognizing himself in what he was saying. Once formulated, an idea that was once trivial was becoming the only reality.

INFORMATION: Tenzer kept silent and grinned sarcastically: he faced these things nearly all the time. Except that he knew how to convert (he had no other choice, really) it (this metaphysical insatiability) into sounds, or rather, into sound patterns, which usually appeared to him initially in the form of vague *spatial* potentials and then fanned out into time sequences, weighed down like branches of berry clusters with preposterous dissonances which no one could fathom, much less cared to listen to. He had not yet rejected themes, in the old sense, but was teetering on the brink, about to plunge into a teeming morass of musical abstruseness – potentially understandable but instrumentally impossible – verging on complete chaos and a purely musical (but not *emotional*) nonsense. Neither ordinary feelings, as such, nor their musical expression meant anything to him. It had been a long while since this or that emotional state – still generically expressible in words – could be the soil on which his initial musical concepts might sprout like simple, modest little flowers. Yes, they had been simple compared to his latest work, but not to Stravinsky, Szymanowski, or to other celebrities of a bygone era. Latent in this simplicity was that potential whirlwind at the border of the expressible with which, having mastered the art of resolving immediately identifiable sound complexes in time, he was presently battling. For this he was detested and blacklisted everywhere. Contemporary music in his native land was bent on ruining him. He was barred from concerts; virtuosi were discouraged from performing his works through insinuations of "difficulties"; all communication between him and the outside bolshevik world, the only place where he might still have hoped for any recognition in his lifetime, was officially cut. Deprived of his only means of intervention, that is, of money, he became powerless, and after a brief struggle he stopped worrying about it. He was "holed up," as they used to say, in Ludzimierz, in a big chalet built on land belonging to his wife, and had just enough to be spared having to earn a living – his only consolation, too, since with his bad name (despite an enormous musical erudition, acknowledged even by his enemies) tutoring was out, and, because of the length of his fingers, he was little more than a mediocre pianist. Except when it came to playing in jazz bands, another casualty of the times. But he could not stoop to it, to jazz. He avoided it like the plague; besides, he was too old for such racket. And this made him especially furious, since he had a special little side talent for such compositions. Somewhere he had a portfolio full of the crap. But he was too much of a coward to use it commercially. Besides, jazz bands were dying out; people had forgotten how to have fun, leaving only a few surviving cretins to dance in the old style.

In "scientific" terms, Tenzer's fiercest problem was his "sexual life." A young autochthon of a girl, a wealthy mountain farmer's daughter – whom he had seduced with music made deliberately primitive for the occasion (Tenzer was also an extraordinary violinist, but here again he was stopped short of perfection by his crippled condition) and with his being a "flatlander" ("flatlander" = anyone from the low-lying regions, i.e., a "gentleman"; after all, he was the son of an organist from Brzozów!) – his wife had stuck by him through the blacklisting and, under different circumstances, might have helped to develop his seductive powers. But his experiences in this area were horrendously pathetic. Enticed and mildly enraged by his music, women surrendered to him more from perverse shame than sexual desire. Later, humiliated by his appearance (by his palsied leg, by his hunchback, not to mention by the mushroom smell he exuded when he was aroused), they ran from him in disgust, leaving him prey to his unsatiated passions. His "romance" with the princess had been one such fiasco, nearly causing him an acute seizure. He remained in an abnormal state and during this period indulged in some fairly unsavory practices: experiments with photographs, stolen nylon stockings, ladies' slippers, etc. – ugh . . . But he soon cured himself of that. In the end he always returned to his wife, who, having been tutored by him in wildly sophisticated acrobatics, was his best remedy against these abortive excursions into the inaccessible realm of genuinely "worldly" love affairs, doomed beforehand, of course, by his crippled condition. "To hell with it! If I was meant to be a loser, then let's *really* be a loser," he would say, and immediately plunge himself with redoubled fury into the world of his increasingly monstrous music. Piles of "posthumous works" (only some youthful preludes dedicated to the memory of Szymanowski had been published) began to accumulate – the nourishment for future pianists in an age when innovation would be considered passé; when music, inwardly consumed by its own insatiability and innate complexity, would, in Tenzer's words, "turn up its toes for good" – a churlish expression, that – alas, this was how he spoke, this citizen of Brzozów, this husband of the prosperous mountain lass Maryna from the neighboring village of Murzasichle. It was there that they had met; he had been wandering aimlessly through the local swamps covered with a thin autumnal ice (*sichle*, by the way, is dialect for "swampy"), having journeyed there in the hope of curing his hunchback in the Ludzimierz sulphur springs. He met her late one evening (wrapped in a cape so that his hump would not be noticeable) and seduced her on the spot while playing one of his youthful preludes on the violin. (Having just come from a wedding reception, he had been half-crocked since the morning.) Maryna was *fiendishly* musical. She forgot (as she often did later) about his hunchback and his withered leg, and she did not react at all to his funguslike odor, as she had known odors far worse in life: cows, goats, sheep, hides, cabbage, to say nothing of the stench of peasant life in general. The love of the local worthies she happily exchanged for Putrice's *fiendish* music and his "man-about-town" tricks, which for all the world she could not understand but craved more and more. What Dick or Harry would have dared such things with her? Humiliated her in such morbidly fetishistic fashion? She became swollen with pride, much like a head of cabbage or a pickled herring. She had become a "lady," and, true to the ways of other peasant women wedded to our country's artists, was "seen" wherever her husband's music was recognized.

The country itself was in the exact same state it had been in prior to the antibolshevik crusade. By now, political double-dealing had congealed into aspic; this aspic, covered with the sauce of "bolshevik" foreign money, had remained firm; and thus everything went on as though in a thoroughly fascist-Fordian fashion, but in reality exactly as before, because an unheard-of commotion was raging along the eastern border. The "yellow peril" (who knows, possibly the greatest danger to our dull planet today) had passed from the realm of contemptible myth into bloody, everyday, not-to-be-believed reality. Our country was absolutely unswerving in its heroic defense of the idea of the nation – in the old-fashioned, almost prehistoric style of the nineteenth century, before the invasion of the Fifth or Sixth (the older people had lost count) International. Syndicalism – whether of the workers', Sorelian, or the American-fascist-intellectual model – hadn't a chance. How much time has passed since then! As always, Poland was the "redeemer," the "bulwark," the "pillar": for centuries this had been its historical mission. By itself Poland was nothing; only in national self-sacrifice (this idea was too deeply entrenched) did it begin to acquire a life of its own. Even so, some people made out fairly well (sigh – can an absolute corpse sacrifice itself for someone else's sake?), while the lower classes, drugged *svoebraznym fashizmom na psevdosindikalistichnom fone* (as a certain bolshevik once wrote in the old manner), were unable to mobilize themselves. The reason? (a) Complete pulverization of any sort of ideology, (b) specialized automation, and (c) a suspicious little "boom" economy fostered by "bolshevik" money from the West. People were waiting for the occurrence of certain events, for a solution to come from without – in short, they were waiting for the Chinese. Even the Syndicate for National Salvation was subconsciously waiting for them: at all costs avoid any liability, even at the risk of a life sentence. Liable? Fine, but to *whom?* There was no "to whom": horrendous. And yet . . . Such was the unbelievable state of things that once prevailed. There was only one man preordained to respond, by some outrageous act, to the enigma surrounding a destiny terrified even of itself. This was the one known as the "quartergen," Kotzmolochowicz, that great organizer of the army (his guiding principle: "Have an army on standby – an enemy will always turn up – if not now, then later."), that brilliant strategist of the old school (that is to say, non-Chinese), that most unpredictable demon from among the intrepid souls still roaming about on the vanishing horizon of individualism. (The main quality here was courage in the face of internal dangers, not the ordinary, animal, physical sort of courage – though even among the toughest leaders this too was becoming rare.) All the other so-called "remarkable men" (except for a few *Überkerle* belonging to the general's staff, who, though similar types, were of a decidedly inferior quality) amounted to no more than a herd of cringing phantoms and castrated social pimps: they were not masculinely sexed. Given the general disappearance of human values, the stature of the quartermaster general was assuming gargantuan proportions. Mentally craning one's neck to see the most ordinary things had become commonplace. And this from Poland's not having taken part in the antibolshevik campaign! The forces that, contrary to their predestined mission (contrary even to one another), had been held in check were now fermenting various toxins, which, having worked their way through the system, were being used in turn by the architects of foreign policy in the bolshevik West to poison all sense of history in our country. Only the "quartergen" could not be poisoned: he was immune, and with his toughness he had immunized those closest to him for ventures utterly mysterious – mysterious, because unintelligible even to him. Oh, to be such a man! To be in his shoes for a split second, even at the price of a death most heinous, but *to be* him! But let's move on.

Tenzer stopped chuckling and studied Genezip as one does a prospective victim. A brilliant thought had lighted up the inside of his skull like a lantern: get this boob under his control, let papa kick the bucket, then the brewery, money, fame, triumph would be his; his enemies would be crushed; Maryna would be his queen; hordes of women at his disposal; and all on their bellies before him . . . SATIATION! "Subconsciously we're all bastards," he used to say, judging the behavior of others by his own. A rather banal truism, but, then, Tenzer was not much of an authority when it came to life's vicissitudes or to theorizing about life.

"Time will tell," he said. "Only art can do justice to the greatness of being. Art is the mystery of existence staring us in the face like a boar on a platter, as something tangible, see, and not as a system of ideas. The thing you're talking about I render in the form of sensuous material. But I don't hear it in the orchestra – and that's disastrous. Someone has said that music is a lower art because people use hammers to bang on sheep guts and wire, rub against gut-strings with horsehair, and blow away on slobbered-up horns. Noise – what a marvelous thing it is: it can deafen us, blind us, overpower the will, and produce a real Dionysian frenzy in an abstract dimension. And yet it *is;* it's not just some intellectual tease. Silence is death. Painting, sculpture – they stand still, they're static, while poetry and theater are too freighted with life: they'll never be able to give you *that* . . . " He went up to his treasured Steinway, the one luxury in which he had indulged himself after a long and protracted battle with his father-in-law, Johym Murzasichlański, and commenced playing (did he ever!!!). It was as if a peal of thunder from man's subterranean guts had banged against the sky – not an earthly sky, but the cosmic sky of nothingness, truly infinite and vacuous and from whence, blossoming from metaphysical storm clouds, it crashed, bottoming out in a creeping, fire-engulfed, flattened-out, *barren* mystery. The joists of the world trembled; in the distance glowed death's tranquillity, transformed into the peaceful sleep of a mysterious deity broken on the wheel of superdivine tortures: the unmediated perception of the real infinity. The eye of satanic knowledge of ubiquitous evil bulged over the desolate expanses of ultimate, seemingly benign concepts; a glare, insufferably hurtful, pierced the thick armor of primevally dark Being, and went painlessly berserk, in a sort of French *malaise* raised to the power of a *continuum*. Genezip froze like a hare in the field. He had never heard music so shamelessly, so *metaphysically indecent:* it reminded him of Toldzio, of their . . . with strains of a light park music in the background . . . But that had been childish make-believe while here it was actually happening. Metaphysical masturbation: there was no other way to express it. That was to say: supreme loneliness (is there any lonelier person than a masturbator?), lewdness, pleasure, pain, the superterrestrial oddity of pleasure and pain mixed indissolubly; and unattainable beauty, buried like a fang in some sublime and incalculable horror. Oh, it was wild!!! Zip turned into a tiny worm inhabiting the infinite wastes of a bottomless solitude; he was compressed into a pill with the density of iridium that kept trying to swallow itself, snakelike, but couldn't, his guts stretched endlessly across the geographical (and no longer astronomical) latitudes of the boundless globe of spatial Existence. He had effortlessly leapt some mountain pass in himself. He could never return there, to the normal, pregraduate vision of himself and the world. As recently as half an hour ago he might have become another person. *Zufall von Büchern und Menschen* . . . (always at the wrong time) – to quote Nietzsche, or words to that effect. Now Zip was cascading down a cliff like a boulder broken loose from the summit. Of course, in reality he was ignorant of the change. To be aware of that one must be old, with extrakeen skewers of self-analysis, a psyche rampant with rot, someone of sagging flesh and dwindling mind. (For some, of course, self-analysis amounts to licking oneself, like the self-stroking of an elegant cat.) "Still, this is something," he whispered calmly to himself, or rather to someone he had yet to recognize in himself, some menacing spirit. Now he shunned such "matters," knowing that one day he would have to look them squarely in the puss. Tenzer's playing grew more horrendous, more inaccessible; in this musically uncultured upstart he reckoned he had found a suitable audience. ("For my stuff you either have to be a savage or a hyperultrasophisticated expert – to hell with those in between," he used to say.) It was not an improvisation, either, but rather a transcription for piano of a symphonic poem called *Diar-*

rhea of the Gods, which he had composed over a year ago. In his portfolio of sketches lay works infinitely more outrageous, works almost not performable: not only were they too difficult for a pianist to execute, but they were by and large unplayable, indecipherable, and musically inexplicable – "inexecutabilia" as he called them, and quite aptly so. And yet one of these études had just begun to "tweet," as he liked to put it, and little by little the score had blossomed into whimsical patterns of ominous signs latent with the potentially metaphysical outcry of a solitary beast in the bottomless pit of the world. Suddenly he broke off, slammed down the lid of his one and only faithful animal, and went up to Genezip, who sat there shaken to his bestial-metaphysical depths, reduced to something akin to amorphous human dough. Tenzer said triumphantly, savagely:

"Noise – that infernal, mathematically organized noise! Let people exalt static, noiseless works, the fullness of the impure arts with their whole gooey concoction of contradictory elements: noise is still the most sublime of all the arts. Oh, how I'd like to moisten women's crotches, but they're not mature enough yet. Ha, somewhere in California little girls are growing up . . . just for me . . . still in diapers, probably, like my Ninon a few years back . . . " (He snapped out of it.) "*Musik ist höhere Offenbarung als jede Religion und Philosophie*. Ha-ha! Words spoken by that great child of the eighteenth century – Beethoven! But he would have vomited to hear the things I'm doing. The broken-down old cunt is on its last legs, but I'm the last of the last, because all those Pondillacs, Gerripenbergs, even Pujo de Torres y Ablazes – they're field larks compared to me. There have been thousands like them. Perversion is the path to greatness – but where are the ideal limits of that world, because in reality it ends *here*," he said, as though to himself, tapping his bushy skull with his monstrous, froglike finger. But all the while he kept an attentive eye on his new protégé: he knew him inside out. "Today it's your turn to be her lover, Zip." (Genezip's body was atremble with that sickening sexual panic typical of virgins.) "Don't be scared. I went through it too. It's better to lose your virginity with that aging bawd than risk getting the clap in some anonymous whore – "

"Oh, no!" (He was hearing echoes of his father's deathbed advice!) "No, I don't want to! I don't want to! First I want to fall in love. . . . " He jumped up, but then settled back helplessly into his chair.

"What?" Tenzer asked. "Don't pretend to be a prude with me. And not a word about love: either it's a shabby fantasy or else it makes for a life like mine. You're strong-willed like me. And you'll grow even stronger, provided you can find an outlet for your energy in this miserable world of ours. But it's getting harder for guys like you. You're not enough of a robot. Because whether our side wins or the other, whether it's our fascism or it's Chinese communism – I don't count Western-style accommodation – the result will be the same: a contented machine, which is about as banal as saying that the world is infinite. I'm just waiting for the Chinese. Barring a miracle, their power will be broken right here in this swamp of ours. Because they're bound to swallow Russia like a pill. And that's as far as they'll get. Because over there" (he pointed to a corner of his chalet standing to the left of Genezip) "they've burned themselves out in the West. Communism is the first layer of manure for what's coming next and for what will be sticking around for roughly an eternity. On that day, there will be no more music in the world. Maybe on the satellite of Jupiter or on the planets of Antares or Aldebaran – though maybe it won't be music anymore; maybe their means of perception, based on different sorts of vibrations, will be different; but something *must* be there and *is* there in that eerie and infinite existence atomized into nebulae of Living Entities – those stupid globes where colonies like our own are born: you and me and her and all the others . . . " He became paralyzed with prophetic inspiration, this last avenging deity of the future but for the present the husband of a prosperous peasant, a hunchback reeking of fungus, a bearded loon and a megalomaniac – or, as he described himself, a "relative" megalomaniac. Genezip snapped out of it, though he was now totally in the other's thrall. He thought, citing Miciński: "I am guided by an avenging hand, by some eternal misery . . . !"

Through Genezip's imagination flashed a vision of eternal things: the mute pain of moribund space; in the infinite distance a somnolent God the Father with a beard covered with a hoarfrost of helium; and on a balmy little planet, the cross on which His Son had been crucified in vain, His flaming heart rent asunder, the only veritable fire in the otherwise glacial desert of the universe. But what had come of it? Even today (through a tolerance truly greater than that of Torquemada) a gentleman decked out in title and frock coat and escorted by a guard armed with halberds (oh, those halberds guarding the Vicar of Christ were absolutely the last straw! though people were so used to it they no longer noticed) – and so this gentleman gives the wise ruler (a thoroughly "Taylorized" ruler!) of souls some red bonnet during a ceremony that would have made a Philip II, Xerxes, or Cambyse blush for shame! And this in the West, despite the worldwide trend toward "bolshevism"! If not for such spectacles (we had our share, too) and the Church's habit of compromising, that sacrifice on the cross might not have been in vain and there might not now be this "mobile Chinese Wall" tumbling down on Europe. Or would Buddha have been reason enough? Not likely. For without our social problems, nurtured by religion itself, would those petrified masses have set out from the East? "What makes me so convinced?" Genezip whispered to himself, and this vision was immediately followed by one of a village confessor wearing a biretta, of mortals at work in fallow fields, flickering candles, a mean-tempered baba (this time not a man) gathering kindling on a frosty autumnal evening, and, above all, the conversations with his mother. ("I haven't given her a single thought for several hours!") Yes, these had been the things of eternal life. Until now, anyway. Henceforth it was to be different; other things would acquire an eternal dimension. Meanwhile, Tenzer chatted on ("Oh, how much longer would this rigmarole last?"):

"But you have to promise me one thing, Zip – after all, I love you – why, I don't know . . . "

"Just don't ever kiss me again," whispered his prey. Here a press of that repulsive paw.

"Promise me you'll never become an artist. All right?"

"I promise," he said. "I was overwhelmed by the power of your music. But these are symbols, expressions with a conventional meaning, like those in Benz's formal logic. I want life. All that noise is a phony illusion."

"Right. And it's for the sake of that illusion that I live like *this*." (The word *this* summed up everything: all the misery and internal glory of a madman obsessed with an idea.) "But I wouldn't abandon it, not for all the triumphs of all the aviators, engineers, inventors, singers, rulers, and penitents in the world. But you'll not do that. You've got talent, I know, and maybe one day some devil in you will be roused to something creative. But I'll tell you something in all frankness: I'm the last of the line. It's frustrating enough as it is; I'm choking inside on my own forms, which are now beyond my control." ("Sooner or later insanity awaits me / It is I and not the world who am the enemy" – again Genezip recalled a line from the pen of a "evil" comrade.) "You'd be had from the very beginning, and since you seem strong in character this would be all the more dangerous in your case. The tougher a person's nature, the more violent the burnout. The only reason I'm able to hang on is because physically I'm as flimsy as a noodle. On the other hand, I have nerves like steel cables. But one day they're bound to snap. Do you understand?"

"I understand," Genezip replied, though in fact he had understood nothing. Yet he sensed that what Tenzer was saying was true, even if he himself had never been personally threatened by such dangers. (Tenzer tended to transpose everything into the artistic realm. He was a stranger to any other psychology: subconsciously he divided the world into artists and soulless robots – which may explain his streak of amorality. Other threatening gestures [in the form of a finger, or of something worse, belonging to a person pointing at him sternly from other worlds] glimmered beneath the murky ruins of vague premonitions and were immediately extinguished, like the sparks thrown by a locomotive zooming into *unknown* territory.) "I have no such ambition. I want life itself without any of the frills." (What had become of literature, for which he had once lusted?) "I'm content to occupy a tiny patch of existence as myself." There was little sincerity in this modesty. Quite simply, he had panicked, like a horse in front of an automobile.

"It's not as easy as you think. I'd like to give you some guidance, an anonymous force to be used as a sword in battle. You can kill anyone you like – yourself included. Killing yourself even has its advantages – it's carrying on afterward, that's the very trickiest part. You have to learn how."

"But what does it look like in practice?" (Genezip had never been told.)

"A routine sort of thing," Tenzer replied, now lost in his thoughts. "Is this my doing? I'm in the power of a strange and cosmic force . . . "

"Do you mean in the astronomical sense?" (At heart, everything reeked of insufferable banality, so badly that his skin ached from the indomitable boredom hovering above the entire world. And then there was this mighty contrast between the artist's life [though damned if he could sleuth out any details about its more practical dimensions] and his work – it had come as something of a revelation: it was as bad as trying to "rationalize an irrational number." Just when you thought you had it . . . pfft – gone. Ugh – enough of that! You've got to take life in bits and pieces, even if every little piece contains an infinity.)

"Don't be silly. When I said cosmic I had in mind the great laws of existence." Because of his present lassitude, even the moment of musical exhilaration that had just passed now impressed Genezip as a lousy comedy, a quite ordinary and irritating racket. (To himself: "It was like listening to a gigantic noise machine. Right, a machine – but a really gigantic one. Here, proportion takes the place of greatness. Well – and what of it?" This wasn't the prize he sought when he came here under the influence of that "revelation.")

"I never wanted to become an artist, anyway," he said adamantly. "Please don't get angry with me, but what does this or any other noise mean, even if it's tidied up a little, as in the case of music, or made artistic? Literature is far more meaningful, because there, at least, you have a narrative based on the experience that gives rise to it. To ruthlessly tamper with that material, which is dished up hot and juicy . . . " (He was astonished to find himself talking thus.)

"Form – don't you see?" said Tenzer, tightly clenching his hairy fists. He bore the look of a man who feels himself to be losing ground. "It's a question of form, which has to bend itself to satisfy itself. Worse, it has to bend reality." (Genezip's amazement grew. Needles of revelation were piercing his brain. But he was beginning to feel darkness converge on him. His cognitive apparatus was too small, not yet broken in. Tenzer had brutally but somehow unwillingly dampened his fire.)

"Form," he repeated, "form evoking the Mystery of Existence! The rest is darkness. Ideas won't do. Philosophy is dead, now that it has nothing better to do than piddle around with the finer points of causality. Philosophy departments are being phased out at the universities. That leaves form as the only medium . . . " (He had a vision of his own work, which was still in progress, which verged on the incomprehensible, and which was totally self-indulgent.) "This snotty little ninny's right," he almost groaned mentally. "Still, I have to make the most of things."

"So what? That's a convention – the importance of art. People have been kidding themselves, but now they've stopped. Artists are expendable. There you have the cause of that misunderstanding with the public, that lack of recognition, which you quite unnecessarily turn into a sort of heroism."

"Spoken like a true man of the future," Tenzer uttered contemptuously. "You're right, though, Zip. You're extremely blunt – count it as a blessing. You're tough, but watch that toughness doesn't poison you when you can't find an outlet for it."

"You still haven't explained why today has turned out so strange and all."

"Give up trying to understand that. Take it as it is, as a most precious treasure, and don't waste it, don't think about it – because you won't discover anything new, your sense of wonder will just crumble into bits of dead concepts. I'll show you a man who did just that. He lives not far from here. Above all, don't try to give it a form: don't breathe a word about it to anyone, otherwise you'll wind up as an artist, and you can see by my example where that leads – I need everything in greater and greater doses of weirdness, one improbability on top of another, just to cope. But this brute has an insatiable appetite – nothing will satisfy him. You can get used to intensity, just as you can to vodka and worse things. And then there's no stopping it; you have to keep going, farther and farther, deeper and deeper, until you're up to your neck in madness."

"How do you define madness?"

"Do you want a classical definition? The discrepancy between reality and a person's internal state, pushed to such an extreme that it violates the safety standards accepted by society."

"So then you're a lunatic, too? Your music's dangerous, and that's why you're ignored."

"To a certain extent, yes. You're pretty blunt for an upstart. You won't screw up in life; just be sure to guard against madness. Treasure that wonder you experienced today for the first time, cherish it without thinking about it or trying to verbalize it – which is hellishly difficult. It should shine like a lamp behind a shade of frosted glass, but never try to shatter that shade and stare into the light. Or you'll have to increase the brightness to the blinding point, which is the danger I now risk. If I could live the way I'd like to, I probably wouldn't be an artist. That I'm a cripple has a lot to do with it, I suppose. Anyhow, that's what our arty types are like nowadays. Surrogate activities . . . "

"But practically speaking . . . "

"Why this fixation with practicality? I can't advise you on how to be raped by your aging whore or what you're supposed to eat for breakfast tomorrow. My only advice to you is: keep in its original state that which you discovered in yourself today, and learn to be master of your own power. Believe me, that's a lot harder than trying to reform yourself."

"Am I really as tough as that freak thinks?" wondered Genezip. "Nobody really knows how strong he is until he's been tested." Then he recalled one of his father's maxims: "We're always stronger than we think." And another, taken from a third-grade handwriting manual, came to mind: "Fortitude is the overcoming of momentary weakness." But none of these homilies applied to the present. Why should he worry about fortitude?

Tenzer was satisfied. The drudgery of his material existence, despite his horrendous struggle with the unknown in the realm of pure sound, was relieved by what was popularly described as "sneaking up on people." (The expression had been coined by the princess.) He had to tell people about the dangers confronting them, to ferret out of others the subconscious motors of their behavior, to prophesy, to advise – in a word, to pervert the destinies of others to the maximum. He thrived on it, in a way surpassed only by music, though rarely was he able to find a suitable object for his experiments. He had latched onto Genezip like a tick. Quite apart from any financial prospects, he had found in Genezip a perfect subject for increasing his own self-importance by projecting quasi-imaginary concepts onto someone else's ego.

Then the woman of the house entered, a petite little blonde whose spiritual air, alas, was only skin deep. Narrow eyes with irises shaded a light nut-brown, prominent cheekbones, and a perfectly straight nose. Only her somewhat slender mouth betrayed signs of a perverse sensuality, while her broad cheeks lent her face (but only on closer examination) a wild, almost bestial-primordial look. She had a low voice, metallic sounding, guttural, faltering as though holding back tears and a secret passion. Tenzer introduced Genezip somewhat reluctantly.

"Will you do us the honor of staying for dinner, Baron?" asked Tenzer's wife in a somewhat humble tone.

"No titles, Maryna!" Putrice snapped angrily. "Of course Zip will be staying for dinner. Right, Zip?" he said, tastelessly calling attention to the fact that he was on intimate terms with the brewer's son. He was obviously trying to impress his wife.

They passed through an unheated hallway into another part of the house that was furnished in the rustic manner. Tenzer's two children smelled of whey. A nauseating psychic-malodorous atmosphere made Genezip gag. The discrepancy between that other room and the present one, between their conversation and reality, was woefully evident. But this, too, gave testimony to the wicked power wielded by the master of the house. "Strong ambition does have its ugly sides," Genezip reflected, observing that both husband and wife actually formed a couple. Despite his innocence in these matters, the mere thought of any physical contact between these two was painfully repugnant. Through an open door leading to another room the couple's nuptial bed could be seen, the visible symbol of that obscene combination. The sexual relations of such a couple must have been an insufferable ordeal, similar to the acute sensitivity of the skin that often accompanies the flu, to the tedium of a parlor filled with third-rate guests — but raised to an infinitesimal power, to a prisoner's abject despair, to the powerful longing of a dog on a leash watching other dogs gambol in freedom. Together they comprised such a dog. And yet it must have had its moments of perverse pleasure. (Genezip found Tenzer's wife somewhat appealing, though more explicit feelings in that direction were overshadowed by the image of that other hellcat.) At the moment he had but one wish: to unleash the two of them. It was with them as he surmised, though Tenzer had managed to automate his sufferings in such an ingeniously cunning way that even though theoretically he had visions of another, happier life, relieved of that underlying boredom swollen like the bladder of a uremic, still, practically speaking, another existence was no more possible for him than a prism casting a shadow onto a sphere located in the fourth dimension, while luxuries as banal as, for example, a private motor tour along the French Riviera, lobsters, champagne, and expensive women appeared as abstract as Afanasol Benz's symbolic logic. Life's imperfections first had to pass through the osmotic membrane of pure sound followed by a sublimated transference of blatant vulgarity into the realm of self-justification. How this actually worked was a mystery, even for Tenzer. The transition was so abrupt, like passing from a drinking habit to a cocaine addiction, without knowing how or when it took place: "Part of the mystery of genius," the founder of this method used to say while boozing.

All were internally oppressed by the heavy silence. Even the children, for whom Tenzer was endeavoring to show some affection, sensed the strange atmosphere, which had congealed, like acidified albumin, because of this mysterious guest and the powerful dose of conversation that had just taken place. (During the school vacations Zip had been forbidden to go anywhere, except on sporting trips with the gamekeeper Ziegfried, and so was a stranger even in the immediate vicinity. Nor was he allowed to join in the family receptions. Such was the boy's isolation imposed by the older Kapen. His son was to be allowed impressions only when he was worthy of receiving them. That was why, now that he had suddenly "matured" – not because of some diploma, but because he had been unleashed – the tiniest thing made the most fantastic impression on him. He could hardly believe in his new freedom: he was afraid he would wake from it as from a dream.)

While Genezip was saying good-bye after dinner, without having satisfied his desire, that of seeing the exasperating mysteries of his awakening unraveled, Tenzer quite unexpectedly said (he could not bear to part so abruptly at 9:30 in the evening. The projection on his psychic screen of his rotting away in boredom was too haunting. Besides, he needed a more tangible triumph over this delectable-but-disgusting kid – over his body as well as his soul – to feel again the power of his masculinity. Was this not the secret, unknown coefficient of his transformational models for transforming reality? If so much as a tiny wheel were missing, the whole machine might collapse. The inner tension was fierce. *Vy zhivyote na bolshoy schyot, gospodin Tenzer,* as Bekhmetev had once told him. But no one knew how subtle was his game. Besides, who cared? Maybe some biographer centuries from now, when none of the facts are available. His latest symphony, which loomed up in the field of his imagination as his crowning work, had yet to be teased out of its author's sanguinolent depths. Actually, it was a symphony in name only, being in fact a veritable Tower of Babel of uncoordinated themes, structurally questionable even for its would-be composer. Was this to be his last work? And then what? A noxious void spread beyond the nebulous contours of this momentous thought. That he couldn't hear his work performed was driving him to a wild despair verging on frenzy. Abstinence had refined his musical imagination to such a fantastic degree that he could catch sound associations, their coloration and rhythm, not imaginable for others. But for him this was nothing – nothing, dammit!):

"Come with me. We'll visit Prince Basil at his retreat. It will be a test of sorts."

"I'm unarmed." (The retreat was nestled deep in a forest stretching eastward all the way from Ludzimierz to the foothills of the mountains.)

"My automatic will do. It was a present from my father-in-law."

"I'm supposed to be at her place at two in the morning."

"Oh, so that's it! Well, all the more reason for you to go. Too much pep the first time around can only discredit you." Genezip quietly acquiesced. His sense of wonder was paralyzed. He was overcome by inertia; he was ready for anything; his fear of the princess was now a thing of the past. Over this day and over the future hung the tedium of things irrevocably settled in advance: thus did he imagine the final transformation. He calmly reminded himself that his father might have been dying on the other side of the forest, surrounded by a stupendous quantity of his own beer, and felt no remorse at having abandoned him. He even rejoiced from behind a little (psychic) screen that it was now he, the oppressed son, who was destined to become head of the family. The only discordant note in this idyllic prospect concerned the exploitation of those sullen figures from life's "other side." But he would somehow cope with it.

"But please don't ever kiss me again — remember that," he murmured softly to Tenzer. They were tramping through the crunching snow across a vast plain that stretched some four miles before reaching the Ludzimierz forest that now darkened the horizon. The stars sparkled overhead with a rainbow glitter. Orion was already sailing toward the west, parallel to the spectral summits of the mountains in the distance, while from behind the horizon in the east enormous, orange-red Arcturus uprose. Illuminated in the west by the moon's fading crescent, the amethyst sky arched like a canopy above the deserted earth with a sort of counterfeit majesty. "All of us are prisoners, in ourselves and on each of these globes," Genezip mused. The apparent aimlessness of his "postgraduate" vision of the future, a vestige of his undergraduate days, contracted now into the ineluctable oneness of everything. All the days never come to pass, all the impending evenings filled with longings and adventures — all expired in anticipation of the inevitable: of life, of character, of a premature death beyond reason — of a living death, even. Time had stopped again, though in a different way — oh, and how! It had stopped not as a compressor for the next phase, but simply out of boredom. An aimless terror (not the sort inspired by ghosts), one Genezip had never experienced, stirred among the uniformly shaped pine trunks and in the haze of the juniper brush.

He tried, but failed, to summon his enthusiasm from earlier that afternoon. He was dead. He was no longer in the mood for talking. "Where's this spastic dragging me to? What does he want from me?"

Tenzer observed a grave silence for the better part of an hour. Suddenly he stopped and pulled his automatic out of his holster.

"Wolves," he said tersely. Genezip stared into the wood scrub and caught sight of a single yellowish glare. Beside it flashed another, then all at once three pairs. "He was looking sideways," he thought in the fraction of a second.

Though not exactly the courageous type, Tenzer was obsessed with the idea of testing his nerve. Despite his many encounters with wolves, which seldom moved in packs but mostly roamed about the land in bunches of four or five, he had never "come to terms" with them. And even now he became needlessly excited, emptying his revolver in the direction of the mirrorlike flickers. The bullet thuds echoed from the middle of the snow-covered forest. The flickers disappeared. He reached for his holster belt: there were no more cartridges.

From his behavior Genezip guessed the truth. He took out a pocketknife – his one and only means of defense. As usual, he showed no traces of fear in times of danger (of which he had experienced not a few already), and sometimes it took several days before the fear actually caught up with him. But a terrible regret wrung his heart and his innards, all the way down to that bundle of his inscrutable guts whose general message had eluded him until now. "Uh-uh, never again," he rued in a surge of miserable self-pity – miserable in comparison to his former "boyish" courage. He beheld again the omniscient, enamel-like eyeballs of that old "ooze-bag" (an expression coined by Tenzer and now irrevocably associated in his mind with the image of that lady), who, at that very moment, was waiting for him in the safety of her strawberry-colored boudoir. Two A.M. became for him an ungraspable eternity, and in this short interval he came to despise the princess as his worst enemy, as the symbol of a frustrated life that was likely to escape him forever on this damned forest path. If he had known how, in nastier times, he would gaze upon this relatively quaint episode – namely, the possibility of being asininely devoured by wolves – with nostalgia, he might have abandoned the will to live, gone back to Tenzer, reloaded his automatic, and ended it right there – or maybe at Prince Basil's place, or after his two o'clock rendezvous . . . Who knew? He felt as if someone had just snatched from under his nose a wildly entertaining novel he had begun reading. And all the while he positively knew that he knew nothing: neither the person he would become nor who he was *in essence*. Before him yawned a hole, bottomless, narrow, inhospitable. The world, as though suddenly swept away, disappeared under his feet. He hung suspended over some abyss. But suspended over *what?* This abyss was not a measurable space . . . His ignorance as to his real identity was becoming the height of self-awareness, though it was quite unlike the state in which his awakening had left him. He knew for certain that he knew nothing, but absolutely nothing. The mere fact of existence was imponderable. So Zip plunged headlong into that hole; down and down he went until he suddenly found himself standing, his feet planted firmly in the snow, on that same Ludzimierz forest path. "Where was I? My God, where was I?!" Everything spun in a whirlwind of thoughts indecipherable, until suddenly they expired as if snuffed. All this affected him so strangely that he momentarily forgot about the wolves that might have sprung out from anywhere – from the sides or from behind.

Tenzer stood in silence, holding his automatic by the barrel. (With him, fear always appeared in a disguised form: as despair for his not being able to transcribe the stuff in his awesome, shaggy skull and to finish all the countless projects from the red morocco-leather briefcase, the only thing he owned by which to remember his deceased mother, the organist's wife from Brzozów. He was attached to that briefcase almost as much as to his own children; they, in turn, were the source of almost as much pride as his wildest works: that a mutant like him could "beget" such hearty, strapping, tough-fisted, sturdy little "zombies" [as he called them]. It was odd that these same children, with their presumed fate, never served as a pretext for a normal, purely animal fear.)

From deep inside the forest came a rustling sound, and the snow on the trees fell to the ground with a dull, weak clap, snapping the small, dry twigs in its path.

"Come on," said Tenzer, the first to break the silence. His voice, even though shots had been fired, resounded like a cannon salvo in Genezip's ears: it had interrupted one of the most bizarre, one of the most unique moments of his life, possibly one destined never to return in any remotely similar form. He tried in vain to break it down into fragments of memories: himself, the forest, the wolves, Tenzer, a nostalgic yearning for life, for his not having been in love (oh, my poor boy!) – all of which was still very much in the present. But the last interval, the one just transpired in the immediate past, stood out in the course of events like a point wrenched loose from a straight line in three-dimensional space. "O mystery: take up thine abode within me; abide for just one second in the poor little brain of an inexperienced jack-off, so that I might commit thine face to memory and recall thee during those most troublesome times and tribulations that are bound to come. Enlighten me that I might avoid those abominable things inside me, for those which are outside me do not make me afraid." Such things did Zip mutter to himself as he trudged along, head bowed, behind that apish monster in a mountaineer's four-cornered sheepskin cap. His pleas went unheeded. The forest murmured softly, motionlessly – as though it were the stillness itself that was murmuring.

Before long they were standing in the Bialozierska Clearing surrounding Prince Basil's retreat. It was eleven o'clock.

A Visit to Prince Basil's Retreat

Through the windows of a log cabin shone the orange, subdued light of kerosene lanterns. Smoke, redolent of resin, hung among a few scattered pine and beech trees. They went inside. Besides their host, who was dressed in a brown monk's habit, they were met by a middle-aged man with fishy eyes and a dun goatee: Afanasol Benz, alias Bends, a Jew. Benz was a famous logician and once upon a time a famously rich man whom Prince Basil had met while serving in the czar's imperial guard, the Pavlovsky Regiment. The prince had just been revisiting those glamorous days when he had marched as a young second lieutenant to the special "Pavlovsky" step, brandishing (o marvels!) his unsheathed sword while soldiers stood armed and ready for attack. They had been the envy of the guard, as had their grenadier caps — shakos dating back to the reign of Paul I. This was in the time of the brief second counterrevolution. Long afterward Benz, in despair, after having lost his estate, took up logic and in a short time obtained the most startling results: on the basis of a single axiom, which no one but he was able to grasp, he had constructed a new system of logic, in terms of which he proceeded to define all of mathematics by reducing its previous definitions to a combination of several rudimentary signs. He had, however, retained Russell's notion of class, and on this subject he was often heard to quip, paraphrasing Poincaré: *"Ce ne sont que les gens déclassés qui ne parlent que de classes et de classes de classes."* At the moment he was a mere schoolteacher in a Slovakian secondary school in the valley of the Polish Orawa: these were not the best of times for geniuses of Benz's stature. Inexplicably, in circles close to the Syndicate for National Salvation his ideas were viewed as a threat to the mechanicofascist — not to mention artificial — equilibrium. On the other hand, he was constantly refused a passport to go abroad.

Prince Basil Ostrogski, not surprisingly an ex-lover of Irina Vsevolodovna di Ticonderoga (and a recent convert to a degenerate Franco-Polish version of pseudo-Catholicism), was living as a forester on lands belonging to her husband, in what was supposed to be the final "incarnation" of his first phase. The guests were received rather coolly. The two men, obviously engrossed in recollections of the past, returned to the mundane world of the present reluctantly. (They were so much at home in Poland that, even though Russia had been in the grips of a "White Terror" for almost a year now, they were undesirous of returning. In this they may have been guided by the uncertainty surrounding the new system and by the alarm created by the "mobile Chinese Wall," which, to listen to our own politicians from over one-half year ago, was bound to be checked by the obstacle of Poland. Moreover, Basil, a man now in his fifty-sixth year, had unexpectedly discovered his Polish ancestry. Was it any wonder? The Ostrogskis, after all, were once Polish magnates and had embraced Catholicism. Basil himself had never belonged to the Orthodox Church and, in fact, was far from being a believer. Recently he had been visited by a revelation as a result of some literature – stuff written by Frenchmen frantically in search of salvation – sent to him in his "retreat" by Irina Vsevolodovna. It was this exposure that led to his becoming a hermit *en règle;* until then he had been an ordinary forester.)

A few hours ago these two had ended a discussion in which Afanasol had tried to persuade the prince of the spurious nature of his conversion. These ex-monarchists had also alluded to the new religion of Murti Bing, a Malayan as mystical as a De Quincey vision, which was spreading across Russia, was even catching on at home a little, and which, on the *surface,* was similar to theosophy. News of it was reaching them even in this secluded place. Both were agreed that the whole thing was a hoax, the success of which testified to the absolute decline of intellect among the Slavs. In the West people were unfazed by it. There, tolerance had bred indifference, and people still believed in the rebirth of mankind on the back of material prosperity. But unfortunately prosperity has its own untransgressable limits, and after that – ? How this "rebirth" would come to pass was altogether a mystery and would remain so until the day the sun's fire was extinguished. Unless by rebirth was meant: tranquillity, the end of creativity (except in the realm of technological advancement), and a bovine contentment produced by grinding out a fixed quota of mechanical labor.

After a meal of roasted wild pig washed down with an exquisite gin, the conversation returned to the previous topic. Afanasol, the founder of a new mathematics – or rather, of a mathematical system based on the analogy with geometry – was generally frustrated at his having been ignored by the community of established Polish scholars. Together with Tenzer they formed a trio of perfect malcontents. For even Basil, despite his neo-Catholicism, would not have been opposed to having the hundred thousand acres of his Ukrainian properties, especially the Ostrogski castle, restored to him. But even with the counterrevolution in full swing, there was no reversing the agrarian reform, especially not in the Ukraine. Nor was he really in any shape to resume his former way of life: in his retreat he had grown sour, cantankerous, and ankylotic while absolute sexual paresis had eliminated any thought of women. If Genezip had guessed in what reversal of fortune he would next meet these two gentlemen, he might have wished for death out of fear of the unspeakable anguish that awaited him. Tenzer was saying:

"There's only one thing I don't understand: if I'm to be good, why must I, in order to be good, swallow that incredible bull which even as a child I couldn't . . . ?"

Prince Basil: Because you can't really be good without it . . .

Tenzer: What do you mean by "really"? A spiritless insertion that's supposed to convey a purely "make-believe" difference. I've known perfectly good people who were inveterate materialists, a product of that neopositivist vogue born of the dancing-and-sports era. Besides, being good is not my life's dream. I've never thought of it as a subject in itself, at least not consciously. I leave that for the feebleminded.

Prince Basil: But thinking about it consciously *is* a source of goodness, not of feeblemindedness. Virtue can never come from weakness, only from power. And as for those others, remember that even today's materialists are the unwitting heirs of Christianity. Of course, exceptions may occur. But let's not talk about the exceptions, only of the general rule. Imagine what those people would be like if they were blessed with faith. Good works without faith somehow seem uncoupled, isolated, irrelevant; they lack that higher sanction transposing them to another hierarchy. An amorphous pile of something is always inferior to something having a certain structure – to the system of those same elements. Doing good for one's self-satisfaction and not for the glory of God and all creation or for the sake of eternal salvation – which is the only way the world will become perfect – is pure folly, even contrary to nature. Even people who are basically evil can act that way. Only within a hierarchy can good deeds acquire the true higher sense of something structured, as the function of a collective consciousness. (Genezip's boredom packed a wallop reaching hundreds of dogpower. He was sick of intellectual approaches. Oh, the boredom of imperfect things! Ha, if only he could have grasped this as it is philosophically construed by the most august minds! Not a chance.)

Tenzer: The same goes for bad deeds committed on the premise that the world is evil, that it pays to do evil, and that the world is governed by an evil power. And in view of what Leibniz, possibly the greatest Christian mind . . .

Benz: Assuming that he really was a Christian and not merely posing as one for the sake of appearance, for social reasons, and for the sake of his courtly career.

Tenzer: Hold on. Leibniz could never prove the necessity of the proposition that God is infinitely good in His perfection. It could as well be posited that He's infinitely wicked. There is much to be said for the proposition: the abundance of evil in the world, the fragile nature of good, the futility of Christ's redemption in combatting worldly evil.

Prince Basil (reluctantly): One shouldn't risk propositions that are offensive to God; rather believe in those things that are given to us to believe. That's the point.

Tenzer (exclaims, with irritation): Well, then, give us this faith, force it on us! Why does disbelief exist, why does evil exist? I know what you're going to say: that God is mysterious in His aims, that He's a mystery beyond human comprehension. And I say to you: I'm a moderately good man, to the extent that my Christianity is a subconscious one and that my illness has ripped my animal guts out – although that same illness is to blame for a certain percentage of amorality in me. I have a *right* to indulge, dammit, it's my reward for these twisted bones of mine! Maybe I *am* a trifle rotten – if so, then it's more from bitterness than evil or *Schadenfreude* – and I wouldn't want to be otherwise, not for what you take to be a superior idea. I might become a better person, that is, I might try to become one if I could be sure that by doing so I might become a better composer. But, then, I doubt whether any external force could ever change my internal dispositions. (Basil kept silent. "Yes, faith is not something that can be inspired by reason. How often have I felt as he does, but now that I understand his whole miserable dialectic, I can see that his case is different. Why can't I simply transfuse my feelings into his veins? Then he'd believe without that intellectual senility he's so afraid of.")

Benz: I must confess, Basil, I couldn't abandon my convictions for the sake of a better disposition – unless something awful happens to my brain and I grow softheaded without my realizing it. I once came within an inch of religion when I allowed ontology to sully my system. Now I believe only in signs and in the rules governing their behavior – everything else is a contingency, in other words, is unworthy of discussion.

Prince Basil: Yes, you've found your trump. *(Turning to the others.)* He thinks he's escaped life with all its moral laws. He's taken refuge in some meaningless signs and that gives him an air of absolute certainty. Never mind that he has yet to be recognized by a single one of our own logicians. If it wasn't for some foreign idiot . . .

Benz: Lightburgh – the world's greatest mind. Oh, Basil, how low you've sunk intellectually with that religion of yours . . .

Prince Basil: The greatest mind because he lends an ear to this devil who no longer believes in anything, not even in the fact of his own living personality, to say nothing of the immortality of the soul.

Benz: But aren't I happier, Basil, than you believers who are too intelligent not to see that spark of awareness at the bottom of your religion, which tells you that your only disciples are inferior beings who are terrified of the moral darkness of the universe and who are searching for a way out of that darkness, even at the expense of reason, so they can assent to the fact that morally the world is not an absurdity. But it's not an absurdity, all your doubts to the contrary – which tell me more about your ignorance than your religion does – and the reason why it isn't is because logic is possible. There's your proof. The sense of an ideal world whose pathetic function is nothing but a limited – not absolute – rationality means far more than whether some boob can endure life or not . . .

Prince Basil: How can you compare the living fruit of a faith that has allowed me, a man who had wasted away in the desert, a man bereft of all, to be reborn again, here in this retreat, and to live in complete abnegation of all that was once my life? How can you possibly compare this with the empty and godforsaken edifice of your signs?!

Benz: How much greater the feat if you had done it *without* all that!

Prince Basil: And yours, if you had not stooped to your formalistic logic. A person just has to be willing.

Benz: There you have your fallacy, in that "willingness" of yours. I'm sorry, Basil, but faith or no faith – whoever *wants* to believe is already strongly suspect.

Tenzer: You gentlemen remind me of a couple of down-and-outers who'll invent any sort of fiction to justify the end of a frustrated life.

Benz: My ideas are not a fiction; I can prove the necessity of my system. In time all truly intelligent people will come to accept it.

Prince Basil: Given certain premises – without premises there are no proofs – but not automatically. I, too, assuming my own premises, can prove the necessity of my religion. Ultimately, I declare there's no difference between religion and mathematics: they're merely different ways of praising God. Except that the latter can be contained in the former.

Benz: That's where you compromise, by trying to reconcile everything at any price. Lukewarm water, the smoothing over of irreconcilable differences. That's the compromise made by Catholicism in general, because Catholicism has to do with the scum of humanity. Until now, the Orthodox Church has not had to resort to compromises.

Prince Basil: You see, Benz, that's an argument in my favor, it wasn't a slip; only Catholicism has tried to educate the best part of humanity. It was the Protestant element among the Germans that wreaked mankind's greatest misfortune, The Great War. The Orthodox were the most unenlightened people under czardom, and who if not they have ushered in that ruin of civilization which will mean the end of all culture such as we now see in the West: bolshevism.

Benz (bursts out in a wild fit of laughter): Isn't that just the point? Mankind may well choke on its own chaotic culture. Religion won't stand a chance.

Prince Basil: Wait a moment. The English were once a model of imperialism for the entire world; it was they who taught other nations how to oppress the so-called "inferior races." Revenge is being visited on us by the Chinese, but the deeper explanation is that it was the English who paved the way for what the Germans later put into practice. It was they who established the greediest, most stultifying, most barbaric state that built on money – an older version of America which, by its example, has reduced us to a state of sluggish manatees through its perfidious organization of labor. Automata have no need of religion. Ultimately they wound up with a kind of pseudobolshevism, for no cars or radios, no mass prosperity, can ever take the place of ideas. Instead of religion they made revolution, even though the class struggle was long over.

Benz: So why has your God permitted it to happen? Can't you see that what for us is artificial – I'm talking about our pseudo-Fordian prosperity – was for them quite natural, because their society was young. And if a revolution ever takes place here, it'll be the Chinese who'll do it, not we. Because on our own we'll never accomplish anything.

Tenzer: Who's "we"? The Jews?

Benz: My dear Tenzer, the Jews have yet to show their stuff. No, I was speaking about the Poles as Poles. Hee-hee!

Tenzer: The Jews will beat the Chinese, I suppose? Ha, ha!

Benz (to Basil): Whenever I hear such monstrous bull I feel as if I'm not inhabiting the twentieth century. I shall not try to prove anything, since you will not admit to proofs of any kind. Besides, Basil, you're faking; you don't believe everything you say. If one were to stack your faith up against that of a true Catholic, yours would show its true colors. Neither your God nor your Christ nor your Virgin Mary mean to you what they mean to a true believer. You have no idea how greatly you differ from a genuine Catholic, not only in matters of dogma but in your behavioral mechanism.

Prince Basil: What you take to be a compromise is just an elaboration of an idea already existing in Catholicism. It's a living science, not a collection of moribund doctrines.

Benz: That's where you're grossly mistaken. When it comes to absolute truths, to rationalism in general, evolution is an absurdity. It ceases to be a defense of religion proper, only of the institution that gave rise to it. The institution tends to live by tradition and makes compromises with its own religion; it transforms it by adapting itself to it. Thanks to this flexibility, it's able to win over adherents like yourself. But that's poor material for a Church that wishes to fight and still aspires to world domination. It's not quantity that counts but quality. When the Church was still a living church, active in worldly affairs, it burned and executed heretics . . .

Prince Basil: Those were purely human errors. Only now is the moment of reparation at hand; neither a bolshevik paradise nor fascist prosperity can lead to anything. Internal evolution still awaits us: when all are good, all will be happy.

Benz: Your brain has grown moldy in this retreat. Such pet notions aren't worth discussing. Your "internal evolution" will last until the doctrinal basis for it is demolished, then *finis.* And what will you say about the East, which has adopted our civilization – though not our culture, which, as Spengler shrewdly observed, has expired – with all its social problems and which is pouring down on us and within a few months will probably be here, in this land of darkness surrounded by the ramparts of the unholy trinity: parochialism, ignorance, and cowardice . . . ?

Prince Basil: You're a self-cynic, Benz. That's a horrible vice of the Poles and even of certain Jews. It's worse than our self-flagellation, because it's only skin-deep. And Buddhism is the only religion whose only merit stems from the fact that it somehow resembles an abortive Christianity.

Benz: Isn't the opposite true? Buddhism never "evolved" in your sense of the word – I use that word ironically, in quotation marks – because from the beginning it was a profound philosophy based on concepts borrowed from Brahminist metaphysics, a religion for wise men. But your Christianity began with simpletons, which is why it must now seek loftier minds. But in the very process of seeking, it lost that which formed the essence of the idea, just as it forfeited its crude simplicity for the sake of its social survival. The Roman emperors made a fantastically wise move – and may also have given the patricians a motive for conversion – when they officially recognized Christianity. In doing so, they undermined its social prestige and enabled the rulers of the world to make it disappear by magic and to make of it a "Church," one that for a while enjoyed the status of an equal power. It was not until later, after it had assumed a more imperial form, that its successors began waging a struggle for world domination. When this became a lost cause, then fearful of the consequences of its social doctrines, which were based not on any metaphysic but solely on the idea of material well-being, it began looking for a way out, and that's how your compromise arose. The only way to revive the Church is to restore it to its original form, to what it was before it became a state. But no one will risk it, and those who might are the ones who refuse to join the Church out of conviction. So actually it's not your compromise, Brother Basil (Benz addressed the prince in this fashion only when supremely irritated), but that of the Church's leaders, who try to lure disciples of your caliber into the trap of their own little free thought.

Prince Basil said nothing. His noble, eaglelike face, saturated for centuries with physical refinement the way cloth is soaked with rubber to make it waterproof, reflected his every doubt like a shield. But what were its internal lineaments? It was a pretty sorry little morass of subcutaneous contradictions that sustained the magnificent profile of that former lord. It showed no signs of a vitality rooted in the depths of a robust organism. Such people lacked authority, not because they had been unlawfully deprived of it but because they had lost the knack of exercising it. They were hollow shells, all the meat was gone out of them. Prince Basil's god was not even the same (was not so surfeited with ontological divinity) as the one being propagated by quasi-religious optimists from the West, by those with so much extreme boredom on their hands they were becoming monsters in their antimetaphysical void: the French. Basil had just mumbled something apropos of these French "renaissances," to which Benz retorted:

"Why is a religious revival like that unthinkable in Germany? Because there theosophy would arise as an expression of insatiability brought on by the negative effects of progress and of a philosophy unable to fill the gaps it had helped to create. But don't assume that the Germans, with their intellectual training – I obviously don't mean Hegel and Schelling – quacks both – could ever return to their old costumes, shake off the dust, and stage a religious *Kinderball* where the role of God the Father would be played by old man Reason in his customary mask. No, only a facile, antimetaphysical French rationalism of the eighteenth century, the begetter of that monster positivism, which is today's popularized version of physics passing itself off as the only legitimate philosophy – only it could have sprung this thing called religious revivalism."

Prince Basil: I feel sorry for you, Benz. All your symbols notwithstanding, you still have the mind of an incorrigible materialist. You have no faith in the spirit. Your whole rigmarole about creation comes down to this: on the one hand, formal logic gets raised to some ideal level of existence, whether Platonic or Husserlian, to a fictitious world from whence you can look down upon any *non*-negative idea as an absurdity; on the other, you champion the utterly primitive position of a simp-pimp who for the sake of convenience refuses to believe in his own ego or human nature. You haven't the courage to hold a worldview for fear it might contradict your system. Maybe it's your system that needs changing – into something positive.

Benz: There you go, trying to apply your evolutionism to the immutable principles of the thought process! You completely miss the point, Brother Basil. The theory of types allows for every sort of absurdity, since everything is relative except for the theory of types itself. The absence of contradictions is the most sublime thing of all.

Prince Basil: A purely negative desiratum. Unduly modest. But how did you arrive at this theory of types?

Benz: From the unavoidability of paradoxes. Russell deserves credit for this, though in my opinion . . .

Prince Basil: Oh, enough! And you call that a proof?! I can't listen to any more of this. One day you and your kind will wake up in a horrible void. Maybe from all your mental somersaults will come a system that will satisfy you in the realm of pure signs, but it will be a system without any application: it will always be a vacant building without life or tenants, and that's where you'll die, in a sterile void.

Benz did not respond. Similar thoughts had occurred to him when his work with signs wasn't proceeding well. What would come of a system free of contradictions, a system derived from a single axiom and wallowing in the perfection of some ideal world? The boredom and emptiness of a spent, thoroughly mechanized mind. What marvelous machines there would be, but, alas, machines having nothing more to apply themselves to. (Just like our contemporary prose, which, fearing the problematical, has expired in the purely stylistic exercises of people who have nothing to say. This was Abnol's opinion.) Okay, this was a problem for the future; meanwhile, there were still signs, apart from them: nothing; they were *it*. Benz tried to be witty:

"One day I'll logicize Catholicism – then you'll see what's left of it, Father Basil: nothing but a bunch of signs." He laughed cynically, but the echo reverberated from his own depths with a hollow sound, the sound of a stone being thrown against the wall of a volcanic chamber.

"There you go: you crave total destruction, not creation. You are the living negation of life, of any intellectual thought or movement."

"Better a petrified truth than an 'upbeat trend,' the latter merely expressing a primary fallacy. The multiplicity of views is not a manifestation of life but proof of its imperfection. The law of mental entropy."

"Nonsense. You accuse me of evolutionism, but your ideas are evolving no less. You have said yourself that logic has been standing still ever since Aristotle, that only with Russell has it begun to move forward again."

"But it must come to an end – and it will with me. You understand nothing about logic, and you don't know how to take a joke. A certain gentleman not well disposed toward logic has remarked that all one had to do was posit a single sign, a point, for example, and adopt the following as a rule of procedure: 'Attempt nothing with this sign' – and perfection will result." Benz continued his "joke" (such jokes actually exist), hoping all the while and at all costs to become ultimately reconciled, for a conversation ending on a note of discord left him feeling perennially depressed. But suddenly he turned morose, introspective, brooding. Basil went on arguing, to the puking-from-sheer-boredom point, about the flexibility of religious notions, a flexibility that in no way impugned their validity.

What intuition could have guided Tenzer in bringing his protégé here? Zip was hardly a newcomer to such matters; he had been involved in *x* number of such hopelessly convoluted (in the geometrical sense) discussions (?). But in the case of Genezip, the present discussion could not have been more timely. Or more untimely – depending on your point of view. More likely it was the former. To be turned off, on the same day as his awakening from childish ignorance, first by art, then religion, science, and finally by philosophy – maybe it was indeed a blessing. It all depended on events to come. In proportion to the irreconcilable split between the two realms represented by these men, he was being more and more propelled into his own unambiguous world of ineffable, not-capable-of-being-analyzed, primal mystery. Benz and Basil were like two poles, with him suspended somewhere in the middle: the possibility of some unique truth. Neo-Catholicism + symbolic logic divided by two: one of the two halves represented that elusive principle he was seeking. "Such that being and thought might coalesce, and one's personal life, in all its unpredictability, might constitute its perfect function" – he reflected, unconsciously echoing Hegel's dream. What had become of his concentric circles, of those "most subtle impressions" that had stood centermost, of that whole blasted aestheticism which had been pushing him into literature? It had evanesced in the fume of their conversation, reduced to something hopelessly superfluous, sickly.

Genezip was maturing with ferocious speed. Something had broken loose, was cascading down with increasing momentum. Waiting at the bottom like a spider or a polyp was the princess and the problem of her orgasm, the final one. Was it for *that,* this whole transformation of his – was it just for "sweetening" (yes) the final moments of some sexually fading gluttoness? Again, at this moment of consciousness, he felt an evil power surge within him. No, it was he who was using her, for the ulterior aims of his own internal metamorphosis. At last he understood. The present (three older and wiser men; himself, alone in his ignorance, a mere greenhorn embarking on life; here in the Ludzimierz forest, on a frosty February night, with the purring of Prince Basil's sumptuous samovar [a present from the princess] and a whispering pine forest in the background) seemed, for all its apparent calm (at the moment all four were sitting in silence), to be charging in all directions with equal speed.

In despair Tenzer fixed his blue eyes on the red flame glowing through the frosted bell-glass of the kerosene lamp. It was that not-to-be-sublimated-in-anything sort of despair before the All, before the world's minutely apportioned multiplicity. To hug and to smother it all in one fatal embrace, like some female carcass . . . To experience it just once, the fiendish metaphysical orgasm as you rape the totality of being, even at the price of eternal nothingness! "Any cocaine addict can have that," he thought with disgust. No, narcotics were out of the question: he would not stoop to such tricks to attain to the unattainable. Forever the same balancing act between death, the ultimate satiety, and life, hopelessly diffuse in its contingency (that was the real fiend), in that ephemeralness seen even in his art – oh, how he despised such words at the moment! He visualized some unspeakably hideous music lover (a Jew most likely – Tenzer was an anti-Semite) listening intently to his works, devouring the sounds (not likely to be performed by any orchestra during the composer's lifetime) *begotten by himself* (thus adding to the many pleasures which he, Tenzer, had been denied)! He was a plaything in the hands of a ruthless power aimed at showering with perfection some musical "bigshot" – anyone, but in any case not some wretch like himself – posing as the mediator of public, even class, interests. (Even if he gained a mass audience through the radio, he would be *understood* only by "that one" – his present adversary – and by others like him, of whom there might number less than a dozen, while the rest would admire him out of snobbery . . . But if such a rascal were suddenly to appear now – ah, then he would not be your enemy; for him you would wag your tail and yelp for happiness.) Oh, miserable life! But forget it, the working class hasn't time to savor such fricassees; it is the soil on which such fungi who are its voice are to grow. As for our ex-*aristos*, why waste our breath, they've become so crass they no longer stand out in the drab offal of the mass. Though, who knew, perhaps they were preferable to those ________. Putricides Tenzer did not know how that brain of his, which artistic creativity and a frustrated life had helped to deform, could twist things around. Long and brooding tapeworms of the mind were crawling off into the distance, far beyond this hovel and the Ludzimierz woods. The sum of these "false notes," if randomly compressed, might have changed the course of history at any moment. "On the one hand, the fate of mankind is arbitrary, the future being contingent upon the sum of all these utterly superfluous minibrains; on the other, there was the fait accompli of society, massive and disturbing in its unambiguousness. It was inescapable in its universality. Minor aberrations might occur, but the end product had to be the same, here as on the planets of Altair and Canopus: fascism or bolshevism – *ganz gleich, égal, vsyo ravno!* – a machine or a beast. The law of great numbers: the chaos of particles in a gas mass produces though sheer quantity such exact laws as the interdependence of temperature and pressure – these and no others, not just laws that are logically indispensable – what the Germans call *denknotwendig*. On the other hand, there were also unlawful intellectual experiments, what the Germans again call *unerlaubte Gedankenexperimente*, staged by optimists who believe in the reversibility of social progress in the area of intellectual and artistic invention. This is tantamount to positing a multidimensional time to account for spiritualism and telepathy, or to believing in another system of logic. 'Perhaps 2 x 2 = 5 somewhere else,' they would say. But say to them, 'You might as well posit that A is not A,' they become indignant. The term *somewhere else* can hardly escape the identity of concepts, since it signifies not another world but an absurdity. In which case it's better to howl one's lungs out rather than dabble in such concepts – such was the conclusion reached by Bergson." Tenzer's thought lost itself in vast and nebulous expanses. He roused himself.

Prince Basil had the odd feeling that he had overstated his case today. Unhappily for him, the revival of Catholicism and of religion in general loomed larger when he preached it rather than practiced it. Yes, being a good man was greatly satisfying – indeed it was. Being good made everything simple, neat, pomade-slick, unctuously and spiritually lubricious – in a word, smeary. Ugh . . . Suddenly he was overcome by such a nasty "pricking" sensation: the palace in Oblivia; his deceased wife (of minor importance, to be sure, but *even so* . . .) in whose memory he had renounced women for a period of seventeen years; the murder of his son (a fifteen-year-old boy in command of a doomed antibolshevik party formed of a squadron of violet cuirassiers under the banner of *"Evo Velichestvo"*); then his escapades with that woman and with others; his waning looks and potency; life become "a downer"; and a horrible regret for the past tugging at his most sensitive gutstring, which lay hidden from view, deep in his hitherto wonderfully well-preserved body. But all was a "downer," a "downer"! And with only that lousy virtue to remedy it; not the bright and serene sort that lavishes everything on everybody (well, perhaps not on *everyone*) generously and unstintingly, but rather the kind that's wrested from a heart hardened by pain, from a worn-out sack knocked about for the sake of unworthy things – that sorry, insincere, awkward, *singular* sort of goodness, festively adorned with flowers like some miserable little wayside shrine bedecked by an idiot of a shepherd who not even on Sundays is granted a moment's fun. Something kept gnawing at his insides, mercilessly, every day, from the crack of dawn, while another life rolled by, inaccessible. His love affair with Princess di Ticonderoga had taught him that the time for such adventures was over. He had lost his former boldness – and not being the sort of paunchy, ruddy-cheeked, sprightly old fellow who coats his physical senility with a varnish of frivolity that too often gets turned into a second but nonetheless bogus adolescence, there was only one thing left for him to do: withdraw. Then followed five years of life in seclusion, and if it hadn't been for this hypocrisy, which could not escape even the dry and obnoxious symbolomaniac Benz, life in society might have looked altogether different. So many people had passed through this retreat! So many had been converted, so many duped, so many saved from death! No, it had doubtless performed a "social" function, thus atoning for misdemeanors going back to his guard days; yet something was nibbling away in the pit of his stomach, a vague but festering boredom, a yearning for another, more tangible end, something besides this slimy, salubrious virtue in which not even he believed. It was nice to be converted, but not to live like a convert. External expansion merely served to conceal the void – to which a priest might have replied: "God sends us doubts to make our faith all the more precious." But this didn't satisfy Prince Basil, who was a fearfully unhappy man. While Basil mused, Tenzer began to speak, which turned out to be an unspeakable agony for all – including the reader. (In general, each was engaging in a game of self-deception so as not to see life's abyss yawning at every step.)

"To believe in the meaning of life is a privilege of the simple-minded. To live as though existence were rational, being all the while conscious of its irrationality – that takes class, something between suicide and a mindless bestiality. Everything profound had its origin in doubt and despair. But the latter had at least one virtue: its effect, unlike its cause, made people conscious of their individual worth, which in turn made for society, which in turn precluded any further doubts. But doubters are a thing of the past. Today, it's 'act without thinking' (not in the technical sense, of course) and 'produce at all costs.' Everything we do, and that includes us, is an attempt to blind ourselves to the supreme absurdity of existence. Mankind is stampeding toward a state of blissful ignorance, silencing the visionaries – today mere midgets by comparison with their forebears – who are trying to halt the stampede without offering anything in return. In the past they were there to enlighten the herd, they allowed the mass to organize itself socially. Now they're superfluous – worthy of being liquidated, so vastly inferior are they to their predecessors. This much is certain: existence as such is monstrous; it presumes the suffering of others, starting with the millions of beings dying inside us every minute – and being born, it is true, but for the very same hell – just so we can endure this miserable scrap of time."

"There's nothing worse than the concept of timelessness," said Benz. "I wouldn't mind killing myself, but my bones freeze at the thought of my not existing." Suddenly he shouted hysterically: "The only certainty, I tell you, are my symbols and all that can be deduced from them – mathematics, mechanics, everything! All the rest is uncertainty. Symbols are pure while life is dirty and squalid by definition. Tenzer was right."

"It's a fad every bit as much as Prince Basil's neo-Catholicism," said Tenzer. "This cozying up in a corner and deluding yourself with tears in your eyes that some good still exists in places, that in essence the world is good, only it has been temporarily obscured by evil due to our own imperfection. That's wrong! Not to speak of the harm I do the cells laboring inside me or that which is dying because of me, in the realm of what is supposed to be inorganic matter but which is in fact a prescribed mass existing in every theoretically possible combination. For even though existence is infinite, in any given enclosed space the number of lesser beings must exceed that of greater ones. The fact that being is infinitely divisible is, after all, the basis of physics, which is based on an approximation, in a finite order, that's forever inaccessible in its extreme magnitude . . . " He got bogged down and was unable to complete his thought, of which he had an intuitive but clear grasp.

"Cut out the metaphysics – it's more than I can stand," Benz broke in. "How dare you preach that stuff in my presence?! Pay no attention to it. This drool is just theosophy by another name. I can explain it to you in much clearer terms; I'll even grant your idiotic assumption that only living creatures inhabit the infinity of space. Within each category there will be some so small they provide for its inorganic matter, which can be mathematically approximated. But what becomes of infinity in the ontological sense? What would infinitely minute beings look like? How could they be said to exist? And what about atoms, which are real and not merely hypothetical? Or electrons, which are as demonstrable as stellar systems? Do you postulate the continuity of such aggregates within each category, and do you assume that the formation of organic matter takes place independently and that it has its own structure? That's nonsense."

Tenzer smiled sarcastically while tears of humiliation, pumped up from the nethermost region of his viscera, clouded his eyes like a mixture of yogurt and water. He was gagging on his once-insatiable intellectual appetite. Too late now to bring it off in grand style. With insurmountable envy he stared at Benz, who swelled in his eyes like a sponge soaked with absolute knowledge – of a negative sort, to be sure, but absolute, drat! All the while he knew that the sum of it was as nothing beside the bottomless abyss of omnipresent absurdity and of the mystery that begets that absurdity.

"Even so, I'm right," he insisted. "My system may need perfecting, the expression of it may be inadequate, ambiguous. Yet it's the only valid one, for it allows for what is. If I could ever perfect it, the bolsheviks would have to grant a materialism superior to their own – a biological materialism, because there is only organic matter, individualized, sentient in the sense that even microbes have feelings and a rudimentary personality. For us, consciousness is associated with the intellect – that's a luxury, a superstructure. It's easier for us to imagine a gradation going upward rather that downward, whereas the direction depends on how close or loose the connections between the different parts of the organism are – cells are complex things, too. This composite nature can be approximated through complex chemical formulae." (Benz gestured contemptuously.) "But even if this were not so, neither of you could be for me a model of perfection. In you I sense none of that spiritual drive of the ancient sages or prophets, nor do I sense about you the element of intellectual risk. I detect only two cautious snails taking refuge in the sanctuary of their shells out of fear of being crushed in today's ruthless social struggle. How it must comfort you to know that nothing exists except your signs. How differently life's sorrow must look then, even a life like yours, Mr. Benz. Of course, it's more fun to be recognized. Yet when I think of the dangers to which a man of fame is prone, a man who wishes to uphold his own standards, then I think we're both better off as outcasts. We may be excluded from life's pleasures, but we'll create things all the more profound. I don't know how to be mean, but I know how to express nasty truths. As for you, Basil, if the whole world started falling for that neo-pseudo-Catholicism of yours, you'd lose all your personal charm, for who would be left to convert?" (The other two were writhing in discomfort.) "I realize my music is just a defense against the metaphysical – not to mention the everyday – horror of existence. But I also know this: it's grown out of me the way a snail's shell grows together with the snail; my music and I are the natural product of something that transcends me; while you people remind me of a caseworm that builds its cocoon out of anything that comes along – the kind whose color blends in with the general shade of its surroundings."

"How do we match our surroundings?" asked Prince Basil, cut to the quick by this last remark.

"That shows how little you understand about yourselves. I, at least, know who I am, in my time. Your religiosity and symbolic logic could be blazing a trail for some Murti Bing or other. You treat him with disdain, but any day now you could embrace his religion as the only narcotic capable of saving you from yourselves. Certain social changes in Asia are likely behind all this. Meanwhile, these masks of yours will allow you to worm your way through life and to salvage the little tail of your own psychic well-being." He was being flippant, not realizing how close he was to the truth of the not-too-distant future.

Genezip's internal vistas were expanding. He knew that it was happening, here, within the walls of this forest hut: the final convulsion of his hitherto innocent existence. Life, or rather not life itself but its armless and legless torso, was dragging itself aimlessly along. What was to be the shape of his own personal life – his *life* and not some taxonomical description minus entrails, balls, brains? He bolted. Time was racing by. These men were trapped in the contemplation of ultimate truths and fallacies. All three were looking at him: that for which he had a powerful yen had somehow eluded them, each in a different way. All were aware of it and felt obliged to bestow on this moppet the absolute wisdom that not one of them was capable of realizing himself or, on the contrary, to watch the ignorant little sap suffer as they themselves had suffered. The "ultimate truth" was that nothing was ever what it ought to have been . . . Why?

The forest sighed from the pressure of the wind blowing from the mountainous distance. A horrible yearning yanked at Tenzer's insides. He had run out of remedies. Every antidote had been exhausted, unless he wished to traipse back to the chalet and start arranging little signs on staffs – signs that were essentially no different from those used by that dried-up pork chop, Afanasol Benz. What the hell for? And yet he felt sure that, beneath the chaos produced by these would-be nonsensical sounds, some little surprise lay in store. Not an internal one, either: he was fully enlightened. What else was left him in life? A little nastiness. But was it worth it? He perceived more clearly than ever the awesome truth of the futility of transcending the bounds of one's own ego – odd that it should come now, so soon after his meeting Genezip. He stiffened with some obscure but acute pain. It was time to act, to aspire (who said?), to go after something – meanwhile, nothing – everything remained stuck in a "lamentable," nondescript, hard-set metaphysical humdrum. All four rose to their feet, hoisting as they did so their hopelessly forlorn lives onto their shoulders. The wind outside was gaining. Why were they all, "to a man," suddenly overcome by the same sensation? (The whelp was straining on his leash, but what did they care?) At the moment, despite all their differences in the past and in their bodily constitutions, they were nearly as one.

Sexphyxiation

As soon as Tenzer and Zip left the cabin (Afanasol stayed overnight at Basil's), something awful happened outside. "It can't go on like this," Tenzer said to himself, and he began talking to his protégé as follows (this monologue was equally painful for both of them – alas):

"Zip . . . " (a blast of hot air, the reflex of a gathering spring storm, passed through the forest; heaps of wet snow dropped from their branches). "Zip, I'll be frank with you. You have no idea how awful life is. Oh, not in the ordinary sense, not the way it is for some civil servant who's just been fired, say, or for the organist's son who has to marry a farm girl so he can get on with his posthumous masterpieces." Here Tenzer broke out laughing, even as a ferocious appetite filled him to the brim like a hungry pig salivating before a pile of slops the size of Kilimanjaro. A desire for purity and sublimity, of the sort that depended on some nastiness of the first order (what else, except for the odd pseudohomosexual encounter, was left him?), pricked him in the subcoronary region. His skin ached from frustrated desire, as it does when you spike a fever. He saw his reflection in the mirror while bathing: the withered leg, the left one, with all the grace of a kid goat's leg; the right one, as normal as a truck driver's; the protruding collarbones; the sunken clavicles, and the "Christlike" (to quote some sentimental scribbler) thorax, with the long monkey-like arms appended to the sides; and still other bodily parts as swollen as those of a rhinoceros afflicted with elephantiasis. If he, freak that he was, could get to this young virgin before he was seduced by that aging whore, that would make it all the sweeter: revenge for the fact that he still lusted after her – even though she was unworthy of him (she – at her age?!), a cripple. "Unworthy of a cripple, yet he lusted" – these were rough words, yet he had no choice but to digest them the way a starving person, belching and heaving out his guts, will wolf down a rotten sausage. Meanwhile, walking at his side was a fabulous, nineteen-year-old kid – a baron, too! ("God! How miserable I was at that age!" Living on beans, secretly composing utterly fantastic things on the harmonium, going around barefoot because there wasn't enough money for shoes, and loving – passionlessly, onanistically – the petite, red-haired Rosey Faierzaig, who had dropped him for some silk merchant in Brzozów.) He swallowed all this for a second time like some horribly bitter medicine. To say nothing of his present circumstances, of his wife and children, the lot of it dished up in a pile of disgust, guilt, and safety in the sauce of his truest, most worthwhile feelings. "Zip, life is awful – by that I don't mean those mundane little headaches that the Norwegians once used as an excuse for manufacturing a lovely little fruit juice in their literature. Making everyday life seem quintessentially magical; making believe that all are equal in their fundamental passions; positing the most banal similarities between a prince of the blood and a brutalized common laborer – why not between a man and a mollusk? – that's not 'the truth and the way.' Christian equality, or rather the illusion of it, and all that self-perfection à la Basil are the fabrications of the feebleminded. There will be equality when . . . when a model society has distributed all the roles according to human abilities. But a hierarchy will never disappear. I drive myself cruelly and I'm the end of the line, that's why I enjoy absolute license." Something wild was vibrating in his voice. He put his right arm around Zip and looked up into his evasive eyes. Wet snow was falling on them from the spruce and pine trees rocking overhead; the forest gave off a mysterious, damp, fungous, sensuous, almost putrid smell. Genezip did not dare push Tenzer away. Disgust or no disgust, he was curious to know the outcome of this encounter. He would go the limit, then resist with all his might. But he underestimated the softness of his heart, that heart which bade him unleash dogs as a child. Foul, foul. Tenzer went on: "I don't want to pose as some mangy, overaestheticized Greek, but think of it: Didn't they have the right idea?" Zip was completely in the dark. "Creating something hermetic, unisexual, immune to alien influences? Pure thought, coupled with an ecstasy no less pure because made up of compatibilities, that marvelous Hellenic levity free of the humiliation which every heterosexual relationship entails – that's something you have yet to discover . . . " (With these words Tenzer let go of Zip and swallowed a pill of some potent aphrodisiac recommended to him by the princess [he was incapable of physical desire; he cultivated only the aftereffects].) "I'm going over your head, I know, and hopefully Prince Basil's God will spare you from having to deal with this depression. The point is not that you're bored, bored in a purely negative way, but that this boredom creeps into your very last cell in the form of an unbearable ache, as something with an existence all its own, and it nibbles away at your most priceless treasure, the singularity of your ego, and turns it into an impersonal chunk of living flesh that wastes away in a waterless desert. Oh, I don't know . . . And then you feel that none of it makes any sense – or worse, that it's a crime, the fact of your being here, this very creature and no other, why you and not someone else . . . , and you're left with these horrifying words, horrifying because of their uniqueness . . . And it kills you, as if you were being roasted alive, that you can only be yourself and not everything, and so you soar to infinity. And then you're terrified that you're *it*, that beyond you there's nothing, because what could be more wonderful than two creatures of the same sex, in arbitrary space, coming together in time . . . ? But you don't believe that a second creature can exist, and yet you *must* . . . But with a woman, never . . . Oh, God! Words fail me, my dearest Zip . . . " (Suddenly he felt such an insane hatred for this beautiful young buck, which only fanned his excitement.) (Hearing this last ["dearest"], Genezip felt his insides being twisted into a knot of stuporous agony, cynical revulsion, and a shame without earthly limit . . . It was really obscene.) "I'm not up to it," stammered the composer, foaming with the most profound abomination.

Meanwhile, from out of the nocturnal distance, as though uprisen from the other side of this forest filled with a snow-driven, powdery fury, there came a wave of unfamiliar sounds that was lifted up into a diabolically horned edifice bristling with sinister-looking towers. Putricides Tenzer was seized with inspiration. Neither the wolves nor Beelzebub himself could arouse any fear in him. His spirit was sailing over worlds in a metaphysical storm. All the while his tongue went on blabbering incredibly ugly things in disguise: " . . . I run from such moments, I can't do it, see? I can't! Yet I'm consumed by such a burning desire for these things, because only at the border of the monstrous does real profundity exist. And there's nothing perverse about it – everyone knows that; only it's better to close one's eyes to it for social reasons. In the past it was different – gruesome atrocities, human sacrifices, religioerotic orgies – some people even got through it splendidly and nobly. And today? Some unacknowledged musician waltzing around in a snow-covered grove . . . " (Greater twisting of the entrails; even so, Genezip felt obliged to listen, because what Tenzer was saying, as he showered him with that noxious breath of his, was helping to illuminate his own muddled state. And that made it all the more repugnant. Tenzer rattled on.) "And then I'm afraid of myself, afraid that I might commit something so hideous that afterward life would no longer be livable! I'll tell you something in confidence: sometimes I feel like murdering my whole family." ("But that's madness," thought Zip with alarm. "Is he planning to murder me, I wonder . . . ?") Tenzer spoke more calmly now: "But they say neurotics never go crazy. I know I could never bring myself to do *that,* but I must have its equivalent. Bekhmetev has analyzed me but could find nothing wrong with me. And then suddenly," said Tenzer, dropping back into the same tone as before, "such a calm sets in amid the storm, and everything freezes in awe at the senselessness of every gesture, and I feel as if I'm standing between two walls of wonder in me, as normal as the walls of my chalet, and I can't understand why only a moment ago I felt like howling from terror and bewilderment. Oh, if I could only be sure that this was the truth and not a hallucination, not the effect of cocaine, ether, or hashish – I'm off all of them, by the way – then I swear to you, for one such moment I'd endure not decades but a millennium of suffering; I'd pray to anything for a mere second of that revelation so I could die *there* and not here in this gruesome world of cruel chance. But I am not *certain* of anything."

"Oh, if that were really so," said some fairly unfamiliar "adult" in Genezip, the one that had appeared a week ago as the graduation list was being read aloud and when the "poor kid" (as the newcomer called him) must have known the truth. Which truth? Well, the one which b-b-b . . . To quote Wittgenstein: "*Wovon man nicht sprechen kann, darüber muss man schweigen.*" All that about which volumes have been written in vain for a couple of thousand years and which has been banned at last from the universities. Genezip did not know what narcotics were yet. (And he never found out, either.) But Tenzer knew, and he dreaded like fire any faking of reality because he knew how thin was the partition dividing these two worlds, which were as similar as twins (two still-lifes by the deceased Fujita, the princess would have said) and which were distinguishable on the basis of details that were at first glance imperceptible. *Identité des indiscernables.* And were it not for the aftereffects, invariably negative, who could have differentiated between them in a moment of duration: between a moment of metaphysical inspiration and the thrill of some thoroughly depraved act.

"So you don't pretend to know, either. That's awful. That means you're as much in the dark as I am," Genezip said bluntly and without the slightest sincerity, while squeezing in his pocket the revolver lent him by Prince Basil. The only certain thing now was this cold, inanimate, metal object. "In such matters there can be no shades: it's either black or white – every halftone is equal to darkness. Either I'll be made wise or I'll smoke my brains," Genezip yelled hysterically, and with a theatrical gesture he pulled the revolver out of his pocket. He might really have shot himself at that moment, if not for Tenzer's interceding.

"Give me that thing, you dirty snot!" Tenzer roared in a cloud of raging snow. He squeezed Zip's wrist and pried the "instrument of death" out of his hand. Genezip broke out in an artificial laugh: such pranks were blatantly inappropriate. "That's why I brought you to see them," Tenzer said calmly. "What you have here are really two pinnacles of consciousness – not the highest, but good enough to serve as an example. Their 'truth' is a nice little trampoline for jumping into a comfortable bed of feathers plucked long ago from the meaning of ideas. What was once great has been reduced to a trained guinea pig. Truth – absolute or not, it doesn't matter – and faith were once founded on necessity." Reluctantly, Tenzer rambled on, knowing that with a masquerade of feelings alone, without a higher dialectic, he would never seduce this – possibly unique in his way – upstart; unique only by comparison with the present generation being fashioned into apes through a fitness campaign that was absolutely anathema to Tenzer; a generation being artificially manufactured in degrees and dosages suitable for partial solutions: social, political, existential; a youth minus any country and minus any commitment; in short, a filtered, popularized, vulgarized, homogenized, decadent youth. And this process was not about to be reversed for anything in the world.

"What about those other two? If there were some way their thoughts could be combined . . . ?" Genezip began, freeing himself by force from the other's unholy grip. Not that he regarded himself as something sacrosanct; still, there were certain things . . . certain childish playhoops . . . Oh, why had he lacked the courage to plug away at that pathetic skull of his? The stranger in him was taking pity on the kaput kid. There was no denying the multifaceted greatness of this hairy pile of deformed flesh and bones trudging beside him through the melting snow in his short sheepskin coat. He realized he was consorting with an "archetype" – and yet, strange to say, he felt no snobbish satisfaction. Greatness – no longer limited to the musical-artistic kind – emanated from this freak, suffocatingly so, but Zip was revulsed by his corporeal person: as the spouse of that countrywoman whom he even professed to like; as that psychological whore who was unburdening all his excrementally insipid thoughts in the presence of him who was little more than a child.

"That would be like trying to mix melted iron and oil in a single emulsion. They're polar opposites. Between them lies that whole forsaken land, that deserted valley wherein I dwell. The one, having read up on the history of religion, fashions for himself a God analogous to every other deity. Such tolerance exposes the nullity of his faith. His Mother of God is no different from Astarte, Pallas Athena, or Cybele; his God differs in name only from the Brahmin's world; and his saints are Chinese idols acting as patrons for you name it. How difficult today to distinguish between a real idea and its counterfeit. How is one to tell, for instance, whether it's not a tidy bunch of fading clichés about something that once breathed, or a beam of light transpiercing the darkness of eternal mystery?" Genezip thought he detected a note of falsity in these last words.

"All right, but what about the other one?" he asked in order to postpone for as long as possible the event that was advancing rapidly from out of the future.

"It's the same. Only the other extreme. It's a horrible machine, maybe even flawless, though some may not believe that and may see in it a basically flawed premise. This only satisfies the intellectual desires of its author, the appetite of a sick stomach that can no longer digest anything. A soulless machine from the heights of which – yes, from the heights of a machine, why not?" – Genezip liked this self-admission of error, and owing to such a trifle surrendered 80 percent of his resistance – "one sees only the uniform poverty of the world's ideas – the quality of which may vary, but poverty nonetheless." ("He runs them down the same way they run down others, though his vision lacks substance" thought Genezip.)

"No – out of the question," said Tenzer with distaste. "I won't let you – " Once again he brought his stinking, shaggy mug up close to Zip's cold, peachlike cheeks redolent of downy youth. " – get involved in a sterile metaphysics. You have to feel it, not think about it. That gut-feeling – my thought is deliberately obscure – is the engine of my art, and I couldn't care less whether or not those ignoramuses get it. If I were to analyze it, it would instantly vanish, like burning a hundred thousand tons of pyroxylin out in the open. This way, it sets up a positively fiendish tension inside me. I'm like a missile that inches forward through sheer willpower – think of what that means! It's like prolonging erotic pleasure through artificial means. But that's something you wouldn't understand. When did you last give yourself that kind of pleasure?"

"A year and half ago," Genezip lashed out at Tenzer. At the same time, there was this fierce temptation to relieve his overburdened glands on the pretext of something extraordinary. He feared disgracing himself before the princess and had decided not to admit that this was his first affair. (Little did he suspect that he had already been unmasked.) Then, too, it *had* been a long time. His previous disgust melted, took on a more positive meaning. Everything was driving him inexorably toward the act of submitting to this improbable pyramid of contradictions – which is what this miserable mutant walking at his side was, not only for Zip, but objectively speaking. And then there was the analogy with the dog . . . Once the notion of submission had gotten into an arbitrary stratum of his emotions, he had become a slave of this man. Until now only in a minor way, of course. He had witnessed this kind of progression before: the situation was becoming dangerous. Time was moving quickly; as it sped by, it seemed to whisper warnings in his ear.

"So you see for yourself, you must let me try. All I want is for you to enjoy it. One day you'll come back to me – later – when you discover that the alternative is just as repugnant." A fierce compassion for this man paralyzed all the centers of Zip's defense. Naked and defenseless, he offered himself in sacrifice, aware at the same time that to do so, on this day in particular, was positively a sin. He found the air titillating now, hot, as though everything, both inside and outside him, was dissolving in some sweet abomination, some unbearably pleasurable agitation: it was enough to revive his onanistic past. Tenzer fell to his knees, and Genezip surrendered to the humiliating triumph of diabolical lust. He was not alone in surrendering – how strange it was. Strange. STRANGE . . . "Ooooooo . . . !" he suddenly howled, and as the violent spasm ripped through his body with both pain and a gut-rending hyperpleasure, some internal mask was shed – and he could see. Oh, how often was he to be awakened on that beastly day! Never had he experienced anything like this. It was all over, of course: no trace of homosexuality had been aroused in him, not in the most secret recesses of his being. But it had been worth it, nonetheless, like one of those high-school lab experiments with hydrogen or rhodium oxide. But that which loomed before him seemed an endless, even more haunting dream.

Tenzer was also affected, even though he was not wildly thrilled with the outcome. In the snow like that, without the boy's body in full view, without that contrast with his own crippled condition, he had failed to "bottom out," as he liked to put it; still it was a double triumph: over the young upstart and the vicious vixen. The inspiration mounted as the sounds began to cluster, to pattern themselves diabolically, to marshal themselves on the soul's dark side. Their cohesion grew stronger: an authentic creation in the grand style was emerging. Tenzer breathed a sigh of relief; the dirty deed had been exonerated, the last resonance of that erstwhile ethic of exploiting evil for the sake of art.

Genezip was also raunchily contented. He had received a thrill greater than any he had ever known in this domain, and he was without remorse. The world was somnolently drawing itself up into a symmetrical coil like some loathsome snake preparing for sleep. To doze off together with the world – what a fitting conclusion! Yet this day, or rather these past twenty-four hours, which had seemed so infinitely long, crept mercilessly on. There was so much yet to be accomplished! But Zip no longer felt intimidated by the princess: he would show her what it meant to be a man. (Alas, the poor lad overestimated his powers.) The term "awakening" now connoted something else. Having listened to the two extremes represented by Basil and Benz, he was fairly turned off by metaphysics. If these were to be the consequences, then better to give it a wide berth: let life itself be the bearer of marvels. Ha! Such as that marvel in the snow, perhaps? (So there *was* a pang of conscience festering somewhere in the background – not to worry.) Thought alone could only kill those nebulous monsters spying with curiosity through this bloody hole of the present that saw the world teasing the unknown. Genezip felt no urge to believe in anything definite or to take up symbols. Thus was he saved from the greatest danger facing modern man: metaphysics. (Somewhere the devil of automated ennui was chortling and piping gleefully as he turned wild somersaults in the air.) For all this he was indebted to that enigmatic, repulsive, flabby, hirsute semibrute whom he loathed as a living creature and yet admired as a mysterious instrument capable of fusing every awe-inspiring-to-the-point-of-choking wonder into an ordered and readily decipherable sound montage. Zip was very musical; hence, he had no trouble integrating Tenzer's horrific musical gallimaufry, with greater skill, perhaps, than professional critics swollen with erudition were able to muster.

They walked far apart from one another, as though each were inhabiting a different world. The church tower in the distance struck one as they emerged from the darkness of the Ludzimierz forest. Their inscrutable destinies were interlaced. Suddenly a terrible ache shot up from Genezip's bowels. How he longed to be something! Oh, God! For somebody, at least, not for everybody, not even for the vast majority. He was envious of Tenzer (with whom he had just parted coolly) because, although not even a dog would dare to recognize him now, one day he would be celebrated. What a joy to make something perfect, distinct, something with a life of its own. For its sake one would happily renounce the All. And yet, when you stopped to consider that the sun would one day expire and that nothing would remain of all this, was it so crucial to be something "in the hearts of millions"? What was going through Tenzer's mind at that moment? Oh, for just a fraction of a second of those thoughts! Then he would have known such cleverness as to be invincible. But why this urge to defeat people? He would never manage this chaos. He lacked the proper device for it. Tenzer's confession, although messy and embarrassing, detracted neither from his greatness nor from his enigmatic character. Was it art that lent him this psychic armor? "Unconsciously we live as though we were meant to remain on earth forever, or if not we, then at least our works. But let's imagine that astronomers are computing the end of the world. Some obscure heavenly body joins our own system and together with our sun circles around a common center of gravity, whereby the earth slowly, in two weeks' time, let's say, withdraws as far as Neptune's orbit. Next let's suppose that the realignment will come to pass in three hundred years, this being determined beforehand on the basis of perturbations in the movements of the planets. All right, so what happens now to the generation that makes the discovery? Will it change its way of raising children? How will the next generation be raised, and the one after that which lives to see the catastrophe? Will childbearing be outlawed and, if so, what will become of posterity? Oh, what a marvelous idea for a novel! I must tell Sturfan Abnol! But God forbid any formula writing! Let writers first enter into the psychology of these people and *then* see what happens, what the natural 'outcome' is. A few – like Conrad – may have let their works write themselves, but they pretended otherwise so as not to have their grades lowered by those addlepated, would-be literary critics."

It was a quiet but restless night. Dogs were howling in the wind, a wind turning increasingly more humid, more sensual. Indecent things lay in ambush, inviting the sleaziest, seediest acts. Awful (everything was awful!) desires slunk stealthily along the surface and began tugging convulsively at Zip's body, the body of Baron Kapen, nineteen, probably the last of that tribe: the line of Kapens had to be preserved. Genezip invoked the decisiveness of the moment. It didn't work. Someone – some instinctive passenger inside him – immediately dismissed everything the way Afanasol Benz had done with his symbols. But how was *he* doing it – he, that instinctive gent who could not bear higher tensions that were not justified in practice? Maybe it was actually better this way.

At the foot of the limestone quarries, beyond which the limekiln was located, in an old and slightly overgrown garden, stood the newly built palace of the Ticonderogas. It dawned on Zip that he had forgotten to bring the gate key the princess had given him. With effort he managed to scale the high outer wall, the ridge of which was covered with glass fragments. Just as he was about to jump he suffered a severe gash on the wrist. The blood spurted out in a hot stream. "My first sacrifice for her," he thought almost with love's fervor. And for a second, lust became wedded to feeling, thus approximating true love. He bound his wrist with a handkerchief but was unable to stanch the flow. Bleeding profusely, he cut diagonally across the park through a clump of giant ash and linden trees whose leafless branches howled in the wind. Presently a façade in the Renaissance style (is there anything more abominable than the Renaissance? For Genezip, architecture began with the gopuras of the Brahmins) emerged at the end of a lane that ran downhill and was lined with spruce trees trimmed in the Versailles fashion. Not a sign of any dogs. Along the right wing on the ground floor two windows showed a subdued, blood-red light. This was the bedroom, the room that had been foreordained two centuries ago (and the wench who had been foreordained some decades ago) where (and upon whom) Baron Kapen de Vahaz – "the last of that house," as Claude Farrère would have written – was to lose his virginity, to be "sexphyxiated." Genezip felt his aristocratic origin, felt himself the son of a countess, and that warmed his insides a little. "Well, that's something in my favor," he thought, and was immediately overcome with shame. His aristocratic pride persisted. His father (dead or alive) continued not to exist. He had been callous enough to think that his father's death might arouse some emotion in him, an emotion he had long been repressing, and that then he would begin to suffer pain. He dreaded the prospect; on the other hand, to go on feeling nothing was not very pleasant, either: one pang of conscience might one day rise to the pitch of real pain.

He rapped on the window. The *dark-red* silhouette of the princess appeared behind the curtain. She made a circular gesture with her hand from left to right, from which Zip gathered that he was supposed to enter through the main entrance of the palace. The sight of this ferocious bawd (who had been waiting for this and only this) made a perverse impression on him: a tail had curled up to his stomach from a strange bouquet of lust, terror, courage, and revulsion. He felt like some store salesman transacting a petty sale of perversities. He passed between the columns of the palace esplanade like an animal being led to a ceremonial slaughter in the temple.

....

INFORMATION: The princess was sitting in her bedroom with her husband, the most addlebrained politician of his time, one of the founders of the country's program of domestic stability (in a sea of chronic revolution, this program was an island from a bygone dream of a nice, pat, democratic life) and of a foreign policy based on noninterference in the Russian counterrevolution. In return for granting armies free passage, otherwise known as "military transit," Poland had avoided active participation. This ideal arrangement, with all its mutually sustaining contradictions, was now being shaken by the avalanche of Chinese communism rolling down from the Altai and Ural mountains onto the Moscow plain. Huge sums of capital, the source of which was kept secret and which had been expended on improving the workers' standard of living, had ceased to pay any dividends in the form of submission to the new methods of organizing labor. All efforts to the contrary, something was beginning to ferment at the very foundations. Despite an unprecedented passport control and a campaign of disinformation in the mass media (which had become a gigantic, quasi-sexual organ of the Syndicate for National Salvation), Poland was finding it harder and harder to maintain its absolute isolation. There came a time, however, when the isle of bliss began to shrink, if not physically, then morally. The country had yet to lose an inch of its territory, but it seemed, increasingly, a small patch encircled by glowing magma. The ground under the syndicate was getting hotter by the moment, but it stood firm. For the sake of what? No one knew; nor was there any place to escape to. People had even become disenchanted with life in the old style: clearly such a life could not last . . . Officers had quit feathering their own nests (Kotzmolochowicz was summarily executing those who were caught); businessmen had stopped handing out bribes in "appropriate places" and making "blockbuster deals"; supper clubs were going bankrupt; and except for utter whores and bona fide cads — a vanishing breed — the dance halls stood empty. The sport craze was being transformed among white-collar workers into a daily fitness hour; thus was this mania becoming thoroughly democratized. Not only that, but movie theaters, that nemesis in all that concerned the loftier aspects of human activity, were slowly but systematically disappearing. Only in some cheap arcades in the suburbs could one still find a few inveterate star-crazed cretins who idolized eclipsed film stars and some megapills of masculine ugliness and vulgarity in a state of utter decay. Even the radio was falling into disfavor, but not before it managed to reduce 50 percent of the musically mediocre among the semi-intelligentsia to a state of absolute moronism. The press, standardized by the syndicate, could not "outdo" itself in trying, through a proliferation of dailies, to fashion public opinion based on the reigning party doctrine (parties as such had all but disappeared), with the result that universal accord now prevailed. Some drab, colorless mass of languishing phantoms was heaving aimlessly about and no one knew why. Quite spontaneously, however, without any help from the paralyzed centers of propaganda, the Bottom was beginning to protrude slightly and ascend upward. Some people, being more accustomed to the level foundations of society, had the impression they were treading on some slightly tilted, swamplike plane or on one with extremely broad amplitudes. But mostly this feeling was dismissed as a hallucination. People talked about, and even hinted quite explicitly at, the potential of the yellow mass beyond the Urals to alter the ambient space, the psychosocial environment, in a non-Euclidean fashion like some gravitational potential – but no respectable person took it seriously. Isolationism, or rather the momentary illusion of it, could endure because none of the bolshevized states in the West relished the thought of becoming fully bolshevized in a pungent Chinese sauce. Despite the bolshevik doctrine of worldwide revolution, the respective governments of the world kept an artificial conservatism alive in Poland, using vast monetary sums diverted from communist propaganda (there was no one left to convert, simply); in return, Poland was to be a bastion, a role which in her torpor she gladly assumed. A certain breed had begun to flourish, previously rather rare, and this mainly in the realm of art and literary criticism: namely, those we now call "simplifiers" as opposed to ordinary "simpletons." The first referred to individuals who were capable of simplifying, at will, any complex problem, in contradistinction to Whitehead and Russell, for example, who, in a manner befitting philosophers (mathematical ones, at that), could create a complex problem out of any trifle whatever. ("We can define this kind of people as those who, by means of introducing suitable notions, can give to any problem, as plain as it may be, any degree of difficulty that may be required" – taken from a speech by Sir Oscar Wyndham of the MCGO = the Mathematical Central and General Office.) The Spirit (with a capital S), "milked" categorically by the neopseudoromantics, teetotalers, and malcontents, now reigned supreme. It had triumphed suddenly, entering into every aspect of life, but it was as if some unspeakably hideous beast had put on the mask of an exalted angel, a mask perfectly suited to its slobbery muzzle. Those who promoted this trend – or whatever you wish to call it – were plainly unhappy: there was nothing left for them to promote; even the most obdurate materialists were in agreement, though their convictions rang hollow and were devoid of passion. Prince Ticonderoga was the prototype of a "simplifier," a ninny without peer – Michelangelo or Leonardo da Vinci could not have added another stroke. Precisely for this reason he was regarded as one of the pillars of that peculiar greyness – a greyness that had none of the tranquillity of our Tatras mist or the haze of an October dawn, but that had the more sinister and forbidding aspect of a coppery and in places lead-grey sky just before a tremendous electrical storm – not the "scattered" variety, but the sort our mind's eye can transform into a storm-sow that nurses the smaller emissary-clouds the way a bitch nurses her litter. Enough – down with literature! That universal harmony; that indecent spirit of "love one another" and "shoulder to shoulder," beneath whose skin one caught the subdued grating of a dormant hatred; that orgy of praise that masked a mean-spirited jealousy; that lewd hypocrisy which saw people rolling around tearfully like dogs wallowing in their own excrement: it was sheer horror. But few took any notice – at any rate not Genezip and not the prince. And those who did had taken cover in the recesses of the four capitals, or in the ostensibly close-knit battalions, squadrons, and batteries of the quartermaster general. Rurally, of course, no one suspected a thing, our farmer being a hopelessly inanimate object, material for anesthetizing the ideas of mealy-mouthed democrats, those social parasites who, high on universal nostrums, endeavored to build a jolly little world in which workers, already bamboozled by spiritual sublimities and pseudo-benefits, could be ruthlessly gouged and exploited; to stuff their guts so full those toiling apes would forget that they were or ever *could* be men; to deaden with material prosperity any higher spiritual aspirations and weave into these tethered bolts of lightning a cozy little nest for their own personal consumption, which was on a level only slightly higher than that of our slaving brutes. Such was how some of them thought, while others, pointing to the steady decline of production and the increasing rate of poverty among workers in the bolshevik countries – and this under the guise of noble ideas (noble, indeed) – argued for fascism as the only solution. Who was right, or could one even speak of right and wrong? Were such terms relevant here?

Everything exuded a horrible stench. As if from spite, legions of pseudomen claimed they detected an odor in the air and that it was even sweet smelling. Under the uniforms of some (mainly members of the syndicate) there quivered wormlike intestines instead of muscles – but no one noticed. Due to some strange inertia, these contradictions held together like an emulsion of pulverized lice in a solution of slightly sugared, lukewarm water. Its cohesion was supplied by the Spirit, with a capital S, and by communist money. There was something really terrifying about this lofty but insidious mood that, except for a few haute-aristocratic boobs, now pervaded nearly every layer of society. Meanwhile, the good guys were saying, "Aha, you see? You didn't believe everything would turn out okay" – thus to our lachrymose pessimists who, all mushy and teary-eyed – eyes more accustomed to sardonic winking – were asking themselves: "Could we have been wrong in deliberately tormenting ourselves, in dashing every hope for the sake of those future martyrs (one day they would have to open their eyes) who chose to ignore the evil surrounding them and the impotence threatening every sphere of creativity?" – as if it had been such a breeze half-deluding themselves with such pipedreams as reviving religion, reversing the process of deindividualization, combatting automation through milk-drinking and Bible-reading, promoting art among the proletariat, processing food into pills, etc.).

Shyly, with a suddenly scabby heart, Zip passed through the lighted rooms. The Princes Zavratynski winked at him from their frames. Once, while traveling on a diplomatic mission to the Pope, one of the Zavratynskis had eloped with the Italian Princess di

Ticonderoga. In time, the Russian name was dropped in favor of the Italian. The youngest son took the quaint title of Marquis di Scampi. The marquis had just arrived from the border by a Hungarian night express with some important news. For the past two days, the Chinese communists had been attacking Moscow. An airplane pilot who arrived in Budapest the following morning confirmed the news, which was not divulged for fear of aggravating the Bottom. Besides, no one believed seriously in the Bottom: the situation appeared bottomless in the strictly spiritual sense. People felt removed from the effects of their actions; only the accompanying psychic states seemed to matter. It was impossible to live like this for long; sooner or later it would have to end in bankruptcy. "Bottomlessness of the spiritual deep" – like the "ding-dong" of a monstrous bell, this sonorous chant had lulled the world into an eternal sleep, from juvenile illiterates to senile literates with trim, grey beards and duplicitous eyes long since gone blind. Everything had become self-contradictory; nothing had any self-consistency. What to do, though? Facts were facts. Most curious of all, the new faith (which those two in the retreat had mentioned), this so-called Murtibingism, had begun to spread not from the heights of society, as theosophy and other semireligious confessions had done in the past, but precisely from that undulating Bottom.

The twenty-year-old marquis was not worried about the fate of his country. He knew that, even if all hell broke loose, with his good looks he would always amuse himself. Women flocked after him, for the marquis suffered from what was known in the Russian guard as a "*sukhostoy*" (a dry wick). The family's cynicism infinitely surpassed Genezip's naive vision of life. A year older than Genezip, the marquis was – and had been ever since the age of twelve – the perfect specimen of a bon vivant who suffered no illusions. It was even rumored that his mother and his . . . But surely it wasn't true. "A dark and handsome man, in a custom-tailored suit of Airedale, lay sprawled in an armchair munching canapés, and standing over him, imposing as a thoroughbred boar in a den of density, was the Papa Prince."

"Mr. Kapen de Vahaz," the princess announced, pressing the hand of her future lover promisingly. The others, who were engaged in political discussion, barely said hello. What did they care if their housemother (their mother and wife) had a new lover? "Please sit down and have something to eat. You look tired. Tell me, what has happened to you since yesterday?" inquired this dazzling-in-her-decay, maternally affecting beast. "Have the evil spirits of these parts – Putricides and his friends – been molesting you?" Stunned by this obvious clairvoyance and generally panicked, Genezip stared trancelike at his executioness; for a fleeting moment he had caught a glimpse of himself devouring an elusive, remote life – life with a capital L – in bloody chunks freshly carved from the interior which pulsated with mystery. But it was clear the princess was speaking flippantly, to fill the awkward void. A horrible *gomon* of feelings was seething inside her withering body. (The worst was when she managed to forget, and then, suddenly, the sharp pain of recollection, like being slapped in the face with a dirty washcloth . . .) Her head, wise as an owl, towered above that whole monstrous show, while her thoughts, these cold automaton butterflies, appeared to flutter freely and lightheartedly over it; but, in fact, each of them was dripping with blood, coagulating, odorless, as though mixed with pus – the blood that oozes from the pain of approaching old age . . . Oh, to cross the line and really become a matron! But as the optimists say, the Chinese Wall would sooner stand at Ludzimierz before that beautiful, pathetic body would roll over onto the other side of life and let itself be crushed by the spirit, which was, and still is, powerful, only it has never had time for itself, having always had to serve some *précieuse*ly organized lust such as that heap of unbridled organs. For some time now, the princess had been reading the biographies of the world's most wicked sovereigns and depraved courtesans; they consoled her, just as Napoleon was cheered by his readings of Plutarch. But the horror marched on; now it was not enough to deceive others: she had to deceive herself. Something was spoiling it for her, meaning she went less often into that realm of cruel triumph over the male, spent-from-its-crass-exertions body; to that jellied sphere of perfect contentment where the juices ejaculated from the genital depths overflowed the world's banks with only one possible meaning: the maximum of bestial, in its essence so mysterious, delight.

Oh, those were the days when these apes, so untouchable in the testicles of their essence, so strong and cocksure, so *interchangeable* – did not simply dismount her but found themselves trapped, marmaladed in that region from which everything flowed, heaving their spirit into the abyss of universal nonsense. And now this one, with her, in wild despair, decay, and yet with power . . . She shuddered. Before her stood just such a dish possessed of the very thing that was driving her insane, that was getting away from her: youth, dammit! But – if she now had both the right fella and the pills of Dr. Lancioni . . . Ha! Something positively f-i-e-n-dish might happen . . . Such was the terrifying thrill which the suicidal pall over the universe now pushed past all endurance: perhaps this was it, the last time, before she became a reject, a useless old *bas-bleu* for the rest of her days. This thought, forefelt not even in the bloom of her youth, created an abyss of wildly – unbelievably – exquisitely – fine oblivion, or rather torture . . . But no! Why go on . . . Surely there was no describing it in these terms! Let it really begin to happen (that, that, that inconceivable thing) and then, in that fiery place, the source of all earthly powers, words might be found to capture the elusive moment of incarnated wonder . . .

Despair. Genezip, a handsome young man, ferocious in his naïveté, stuffed his exquisite mouth with canapés and kept on chewing for so long that the tasteless pap refused to go down his dry and constricted throat. The princess, who seemed to inhabit his body, its most secret fibers, and even the center of its separate cells, said (no, her spirit was transported into intercellular spaces, not unlike some organic matter belonging to the highest magnitude among the stars, for whose structure our stellar systems are but mere reference points, similar to what electrons are in relation to our own living substance) – and so that metaphysical bawd said – her voice, clear as a silver bell, fell from above, somewhere from the crystalline chill of the interplanetary heights (or depths): "Drink something – otherwise you'll choke." And she broke out laughing, childishly, healthily, agreeably, like a sweet little girl. Oh, what a wicked fiend she was! And dull-witted Zip could not begin to appreciate that wickedness. Why was it so asininely fixed that no one could appreciate anybody in time = the proposition that the total number of years for a sexual pair should be more or less equal to sixty: he fifty – she ten, she forty – he twenty, etc. (The theory of that same Ruthenian who devised the Taylorization of erotic relationships.) If only such a fading flower, such a weird piece of tail, could have been appraised by a genuine connoisseur! (What could possibly be more repugnant than sexual "connoisseurship"?) But no, if there were such a gentleman, he would surely be a physical wreck, an ascetic, or the sort who tracks down foolish adolescents to instruct them in the follies of his youth. Ah, but even that has changed now. A certain confusion, a general devaluation, now reigned over that entire hierarchy. It was being invaded by a triumphant spirit, perhaps for the last time before the final collapse into nothingness. It was only logical, of course, that the battle should have been decided in Poland, that "bastion" defending against the most critical destinies. Nations, like people, have their destinies (not in the sense of necessity, however) and missions. Provided one is able to live long enough, then eventually (so long as one is not obstructed by powers and events such as imprisonment, madness, the loss of certain limbs, etc.) one achieves one's destiny, perhaps in a modified form, in caricature, but one achieves it. The East, checked in its expansion by that "cursed Poland," had, in its curious ultra-Western transposition, in its raw and undigested form, begun at last to move on the West. Communism had blazed a trail for it. For the fact is the Buddhists have always been more consistent than the Christians, and from Taoism to socialism the journey is a short one. Aristocratic Confucianism was easily adapted to the norms of European utopianism. Above all, owing to the deeply metaphysical foundation of their conscious existence, these yellow devils were not so worried about their stomachs and the boorish pleasures of life: social transformation went hand in hand with the pursuit of inner perfection. Their spiritual slogans were not simply "cosmetic": these people really had a vision of another world of the spirit, unattainable perhaps, incomprehensible for us perhaps, but they had a vision. And yet: infected by the problems of the West, imperceptibly, themselves unaware of it, they were beginning to lose more and more of the original character of their superhuman drive: any moment now the belly might overtake the soul. Rarely was it the case, however, that as the masses were literally being infused with spirit, their leaders were becoming surfeited. The Chinese were not interested in satisfying material wants so much as in creating new possibilities for internal development, which for the past twenty years had become a complete fiction in Europe. At long last, the white man had ceased to believe in the myth of infinite progress and now saw the wall of obstruction in himself and not in nature. Was the Chinese faith a hoax, or was it based on other psychic data? The most ardent pessimists claimed that it was merely a stage, limited with respect to time and space, in the general leveling of all values that was to be followed by an even gloomier period of social tedium and metaphysical humdrum. Meanwhile, from underneath, from the bones, from that primordial layer, from the quarter of the "most destitute," something was beginning to "putrefy" ("rot" doesn't convey the proper shade required here, while the aforementioned synonym appalls). This was demonstrable proof that on a *sufficiently low* level of the *outer, hereditary* culture, the ideocreative elements in human nature could not be stifled either by stuffing the stomach or ear (i.e., by means of the radio) or by applying certain means of locomotion (i.e., the automobile). Demonstrable proof lay also in the Western bolshevik countries. But some "deep-thinkers" claimed this was merely a "short-term" experiment. Despite a profound drugging by the "Spirit," all were exasperated by the slowness of social transformations. That brute of a higher order (society) had time – society as a whole, naturally. What did it care if the refuse ejected by a centrifugal force, indeed, the remnants of the innermost, essential core, perished in agony? Does a cocaine addict care how the separate cells of his brain feel?

Marquis di Scampi sipped his liqueur through his teeth while listening to the lamentations of his father:

" . . . if there really were a force, I mean in real, honest-to-goodness reality, it would be dis-or-gan-i-za-tion. Anarchy has always been, and still is, Poland's greatest strength. But since the automagnetism of the masses is expanding in geometric proportion to the internal tension of the syndicate, we will cave in – not absolutely, Matthew, but in time. Because a reaction is bound to follow. I'm a firm believer in the reversibility of society, but only over the colossally long haul. God exists, and He alone rules – that's so. And you will see again a world ruled by pharaohs, only these will be more sophisticated ones, uncorrupted by totemistic superstitions, rational like true sons of the Sun of supreme knowledge." ("Oh, what the blazes is the old jackass blabbering about," thought the marquis with a feeling of lassitude.) "But we neglected to keep pace with the corresponding changes taking place in other countries. If, I repeat, if we already had bolshevism behind us, and by that I don't mean this communism of ours but rather the Russian brand – ha, we might have immunized ourselves against its belated phase; we might have put up with a hundred Genghis Khans from some International or other. For years I have said, even when I was an inexperienced colonel in the artillery and politically underage: let them into the country – in the long run it's bound to pay off. They'll last just long enough to immunize us for another two hundred years . . . "

"Oh, no, Daddy," interrupted Scampi. "You overlook one thing: our compatriots' lack of panache. I have in mind such risky political notions as courage and the capacity for self-sacrifice. National slavery, romanticism, and political traditions have reduced all our best people to a state of potentiality. The 'kineticists' are either a bunch of sluggards with no great ambitions – at most with petty ambitions – or do-gooders like our dear Uncle Basil. Time has passed them by – they're not inventive anymore – they belong to the eighteenth century. Today's benefactor of humanity can be a first-rate heel, so long as he's clever and has some knowledge of economics – which is becoming harder all the time. Nothing has changed in our country since Targowica. We have had some exceptional people, I won't deny it, but whatever they accomplished owed more to purely fortuitous events. If we had let in the Russians when they were still bolsheviks, our country today would be nothing more than a province of that Russian monarchy which is crumbling under the Chinese avalanche. Today at least we're still free to act; we're in a position *vykinut takuyu shtuku, chto ne raskhlebat ey vsey Evrope.* Right now Kotzmolochowicz is the most enigmatic person in either hemisphere, including communist Africa and the countries of North America, which are moving in the same direction. We in the Foreign Office are pursuing a slightly more independent policy than you people at Interior. We even have our own Secret Service."

"Matthew, for God's sake, is your father about to start experimenting at this late stage?"

"Why not? He's gone completely stale. Oh, when it comes to our own personal lives we have imagination to spare, but in politics we're stale, banal, and spineless. That's been our Achilles' heel throughout our entire history – that and letting ourselves be mesmerized by phony traditions. Kotzmolochowicz is the only man in the country who can measure up to a Batory or a Piłsudski – and what's more, he's an enigma. The ability to be enigmatic in our day and age I regard as a supreme art, as a basis for unrivaled possibilities. It's one thing if some effete and prematurely degenerate artist is enigmatic, we find nothing unusual about that. But when someone stands in the limelight, at the very center of historical forces, and as a matter of fact is the only secret ray of light in this whole murky affair – I'm speaking of our country's history during the past several years – and then in the seemingly modest role of a quartermaster general; when you can be illuminated by the most powerful searchlights both at home and abroad and still remain a mystery – then I say, that is class. The contrast is made even greater by his manners: he's positively sweet."

"You people in the F.O. treat everything as a sport; you trivialize life's seriousness. We want to go on living our lives to the fullest, as before."

"Of course life must be treated as a jolly sport today. Be happy, Papa, that you have such a son. If I were a man with your principles I would now be one miserable, disillusioned ass. The state can be defended the way you defend a goal in a football game. But even if the antifascist syndicalists were to score, I doubt that anything dreadful would happen. And the state socialists, in whatever form, with the exception for the time being of the communists – for the time being, I stress – are doomed anyway. I admit that there are very few among us – I mean among our own kind, of course – who will go along with this view. I suggest that we disband the Syndicate for

National Salvation and that we willingly resign ourselves to a revolution. And judging from the latest reports out of Russia, it looks as if we're next. But if we refuse to confront these events, but *really* confront them and not merely settle for some immunization shot, then we may have to pay for it with a slaughter the likes of which the world has never seen. Kotzmolochowicz couldn't care less how many people die; all he cares about is his greatness, even if it's the posthumous kind. He's really a Caesar-figure. But what about us?"

"Not a Caesar-figure at all, just a miserable condottiere. If push comes to shove, he'll become a lackey of the most radical group."

"I'd advise you not to speak so rashly, Papa – one day you may have to swallow those words. If Kotzmolochowicz had wanted to pave the way for the Chinese, he could have done it long ago. I suspect he has no positive plan at all. For myself, I wouldn't think of dying for the sake of an idea. Life is a goal in itself."

"Your generation is truly inventive, that's because you're nothing but trash. Oh, if I could pull off a reversal like that! But I don't know how to spit in my own navel."

"Papa, your ideology, your Syndicate for National Salvation – haha, national, in our day and age! – is nothing but a sham. What it really means is the exploitation of life by a class which forfeited that right a long time ago. No, I'm not laboring under any illusions. Not until your ears have been sliced off, your genitals shoved between your teeth, and your belly pumped full of oil will you ever learn, Papa . . . "

They began talking in a whisper now. Genezip listened to their conversation with growing apprehension. Two distinct fears – his fear of the princess and his fear of political profundities – were hoisting the sense of his own ego to dizzying heights. He felt like a nit in the company of this underage cynic who was barely a year or two his senior. Suddenly he despised his father for having raised such a clumsy ass. How could SHE possibly take him for anything when she had *such* a son! He did not see that it was quite the opposite, that his whole charm lay in his abysmal ignorance and naïveté, not to mention his fairly impressive physical endowments.

The princess was studying him closely. By a sexual intuition she was able to divine the scene in the woods, not the actual place (the woods), of course, or even the exact manner (with Tenzer), but in a general way. Something "of that sort" had transpired in this precious boy whom she longed to devour, raw and fresh as some tender shoot bursting obscenely forth, as some gullible, frightened, inexperienced kid, as some poor darling to be caressed and then, if it showed its horns and claws, "tor-choord" (as she used to say) a little. But would she have the nerve to inflict such tortures? She was far from being an outright sadist, and besides she had even taken a liking to the boy. Perhaps this was really to be that "last time" she was so loath to contemplate. "As we age our demands increase while our possibilities decrease," her husband had once said to her, endeavoring for the first time to explain to this unsatiated *mégère* in an ever-so-delicate manner that he had tired of her physically. This conversation marked the beginning of a series of official love affairs.

" . . . worst of all," said the prince, "is this fad of psychoanalysis and its intrusion into areas where it simply doesn't belong. Psychosociology, for instance, is a farce. If all were to tow the line in this respect and were really consistent, human nature would soon be extinct: nothing sacred or specific would be left of it."

"Why, even the syndicate might turn out to be the hallucination of a collective psychic state of a certain group of social malcontents," Scampi sneered. "But if someone had the courage to be a consistent psychologist, someone like Kotzmolochowicz – and to be a consistent psychologist, Papa, you have to be a *solipsist* – then even as a quartermaster general one might accomplish things marvelous in their monstrosity."

"To listen to you prate, Matthew, is more than any man can bear."

"Oh, Father, you're such a hopeless old dinosaur! Don't you see the time has come for a bit of political extravagance and that it's precisely up to us? What we're seeing are the death pangs before we're all tranquilized – and that in yellow, *à la chinois*. Those bastards only indulge their imagination in an abstract way; in reality they're flawless, fearless machines. On the other hand, we who are nothing but loathsome canaille have become so inwardly vulgar that, unlike our dull intestines, that which is most sacred, politics, has turned into the sort of freak show found in the paintings of cubists, hyperrealists, and Polish anythingists. I plan to stay here for three days, and if in that time I'm unable to make of you a statesman in the new style, then I predict that you will die a painful death. And who knows whether it won't be I who'll supervise it – for the sake of my principles. But it's already 2:30. It's time to go to bed."

The marquis rose and kissed his mother goodnight with a feline tenderness that Genezip found odious. For the first time he had to admit that the princess was an aging hag: it was a fair while ago, after all, that this polished young man had crawled out of his mother's belly. But a second later he found his curiosity aroused, his previous fear somewhat ameliorated: he had found an advantage over his lover-to-be.

After sprawling out on the sofa a little, Scampi resumed speaking (are there any more ill-mannered people in the world than Polish aristocrats and pseudoaristocrats?): "But I completely forgot about our young man. What's he doing in the bosom of our family at such a late hour? But why stand on ceremony . . . Is this Mama's new lover?" Genezip jumped up, suddenly speechless with rage. "They have the gall to treat me like a child?" His temples felt stuck with thorns, a violent flame seemed to shoot from his burning nose . . . There sounded a howl of wounded pride: they would *now*, of all the times . . . ! He was now staring at existence from outside its absolute forms of time and space; or rather, from two sides of a duality belonging to one and the same form. A life hitherto barred to him, a life so foreign he could have wailed from envy and yet was insufferably beautiful, was whirling about on the periphery of unexplored destinies. And then, like that "brilliant bird of comfort" from childhood dreams, honor was hatched from the egg, the egg of humanity and manliness. He took a step, intent on retaliating, but the princess grabbed him by the arm and sat him back down in his chair. A strange current rippled through him: it was as if they had physically coalesced. And there was something lusciously obscene about it . . . All his nerve vanished. He could no longer view things objectively, the way life really was. Marquis di Scampi was gazing at him with an indulgent, omniscient smile: he knew such moments of revelation, but he had little time for them; they were not very profitable in his world of catlike, almost childlike intrigues and aimless diplomatic subtleties; besides, they indisposed one toward life. No, moderate bestiality was better. Meanwhile, the old prince was hundreds of miles away in his thoughts, in the capital. He envisioned Kotzmolochowicz, the solipsist (elliptical, like a snake sucking on a tapeworm in the stuffing of a sofa full of soot), sitting in his green-and-black study which he knew so well . . . What a ghastly spectacle, like sleepwalking with a lighted match through subterranean crypts filled with pyroxylin. How unpredictable life was! "In the worst case, I'll become a solipsist too," he thought, and felt somewhat relieved.

"You're a stranger to our little nest," the marquis said to Zip. "Under the guise of cynicism we are the most perfect family in the world. We love and respect each another and we are free of that petty-bourgeois filth powdered over by superficial prejudices. We are truly pure in spite of our outward appearance, which some naive souls may find abhorrent. We do not disguise our betrayals, nor do we dissemble – we are ourselves because we can afford not to be evasive and abjectly hypocritical. You are not the only one with principles."

"And yet," interjected the princess in a light and casual tone, "people must respect us for other reasons." (She seemed to derive a wild, sadistic pleasure from this obligatory respect on the part of people who despised her.) "There's our money, my husband's position in the syndicate, and son Matthew's personal charm. To be sure, Matthew is a dangerous man, as dangerous as a tame lynx. Adam, my other son, is no match for him, even though he's serving as our ambassador to China. No one actually knows what's happened to him, that moron of a diplomat – the last I heard he was on his way home. Matthew, on the other hand, is like one of those Chinese boxes you keep opening without end – until you come to the last, which is empty. And it's this emptiness that makes him dangerous – a psychological sportsman. But don't be afraid of Matthew. He loves me dearly and for that reason wouldn't do you any harm. If you like, we can wangle you a position in the Foreign Office."

"I don't need any favors! To hell with your stupid Foreign Office!

I plan a career in literature, the best thing going today – unless, of course, I'm drafted into the army." Again he rose to his feet, again the princess sat him down with force, this time with a certain impatience. "How strong she is. I'm not worth a damn. Why did that hirsute brute rob me of my nerve and self-confidence? I'll bet I have a masturbator's rings under my eyes." He nearly spilled his wimpy insides in a mixture of impotent rage and suicidal despair.

"A very likable fellow," said Scampi without a trace of affectation. "Please don't judge us prematurely. One day we may turn out to be the best of friends." And with these words he extended his hand to Genezip and looked searchingly into his eyes. His eye sockets resembled those of the princess, while their charcoal-grey color recalled instead the old man's eyes. Genezip winced. It seemed to him that there, in the depths of those mendacious eyeballs, which inexplicably pass for "the soul's mirror," he caught a glimpse of his most opaque destiny: not the events themselves, but rather their most profound essence, their most ineluctable truth. His body trembled in wild dismay. Oh, what he would have given, if not to avoid it altogether, which now was unthinkable under the circumstances, then at least to defer that rapidly approaching moment in which he was to lose his virginity! Young people once used this as an occasion to join the priesthood or enter a monastery. For the first time in his life he summoned up the image of his ailing father (like God), who was either dying or was already dead, "for deliverance." And immediately he felt guilty for having waited this long. But what else was he to do? A person, even in his most uncontrollable thoughts, is what he is in reality. Should he begrudge the tiny bit of freedom that is his in this abominable prison which is both the world and man for himself? Outside, an Oravian wind was blowing, setting the palace chimneys and recesses to howling. Everything seemed to strain and bulge from some terrific tension, the furniture swelled, any moment the windows might explode under the pressure of some massive, mysterious force. Impatience, mingled with fear, expanded in his intestines the way a ball of cotton compressed with fat expands in a rat's intestines (such a barbaric method of extermination actually exists – the poor creatures! has no one any pity for them?). An intolerable state; yet he felt positively powerless to make the slightest move, not to mention that *mouvement ridicule* (which he had heard about), and then under *such* conditions! Nothing seemed more monstrous than the sexual act. And precisely that he would be *obliged* to do: insert this into that, etc. Inconceivable! With her!! *Ah non, pas si bête que ça!* The very existence of female sexual organs was becoming problematic, if not inconceivable. He was being compressed into a mass without a will and was frantic that unless she said something or touched him at once, then he, Genezip Kapen, would immediately explode on the princess's pastel blue settee and be dispersed into the infinite. All grossly exaggerated, of course, but still . . . Simultaneously, he had a boundless (theoretically, that is) craving for what was about to transpire, even as his eyelashes were quivering in a weird apprehension: What did it look like in reality, and what was he supposed to do with it (with *it*, O ye powers of darkness, O Isis, O Ashtoreth!)? – that was his worst fear. This was a test to beat all school exams. It was as tough as one of those diagrams in descriptive geometry in which the rotating shadow of an ellipsoid is projected onto a prism intersected by an oblique pyramid. He groaned, or rather mooed, like a cow in unspeakable travail, and this saved him from exploding. He managed to shoot a furtive glance at the princess. There she sat, with her vulturelike profile turned toward him, mysterious, like a sacred bird from some exotic religion. Immersed in her thoughts, she seemed so far removed from reality that Genezip again began to shudder and stare bug-eyed. He was sure he had passed imperceptibly into some utterly different world, a world separated from the previous one (which continued alongside the other) by the immeasurable abyss of the "psyche." The transformational equations of this passage were never revealed to him. Altogether, the entire day (these past twenty-four hours), and in particular the evening, were to remain a mystery for all time. What a shame that such things cannot be integrated later on in life. While the moments may stand out clearly enough, the totality of these profound transformations, the underground current of these mental permutations, remains unintelligible like a weird dream that cannot be recalled. From that point on everything became "cockroached" – of that he was sure;

he had once seen two cockroaches joined together so bizarrely . . . Ordinary fear, combined with lust, erupted from his intestinal centrum (from the corporeal center of his personality) and flooded his being to the farthest extremities of memory. So strong was this sense of duality that at times he truly expected his soul to exit his body, a phenomenon being reported by the disciples of Murti Bing for popular consumption. Imagine it! The soul escapes the horrendous business of sex for a world of absolute harmony, pure thought, a genuine but by no means frivolous freedom, leaving behind this sickening corpse as food for demons and fiendish monsters. But no such land of liberation existed. This would have to be accomplished here while hauling about some insatiable sack of organs with their demented cravings; some infernal case of raw flesh set with precious, iridescent stones. No, this was no ordinary fear: it was the last defense of masculine dignity (not the repugnant sort) against the greatest humiliation of them all: surrender to the power of unchaste female dreams. Only love could have justified it – and then not very convincingly. Something was smoldering there, but it was not love. How to live, how to live? Was he always to walk a tightrope over some abyss, fated to fall despite all his (basically futile) efforts? What a Catholic he was now, the type known as a "negative Catholic." His hands were sweating, his ears were burning, and his mouth was so dry it could not pronounce a single one of the words with which his stricken tongue was laboring. Meanwhile, the adversary was so intensely fixed on something that she lost sight of Zip's presence. With a costly effort, Genezip got up from the sofa. He was a small, pathetic child; there was not an ounce of manhood in him, and even if there were, the effect would have been obnoxious, since his physical appeal was deadly.

The princess started as if she had just awakened from a dream and directed her absent gaze at that woeful but lovely caricature of sexual panic. Seconds ago the princess had been reviewing her life in drastically condensed form. She realized this was a terminus of sorts: this boy, followed either by absolute resignation and a prolongation of life with its horrid, unrelenting pseudopain in the skin; with its enervating torpor in the loins arising from insatiability; with its mute affliction somewhere deep inside the belly – that, or several more years of compromise, for which she would surely have to pay – if not directly, then indirectly, in a backhanded way – with a self-loathing and a hatred for the lot of male "rotters." Neither "*précieuse*ness" nor her quasi-intellectual life would help her then. (They had served her well in diverting male attention from those organs manifestly dilating with lust.) But such a life in itself? "That, madam, would be positively boring," Parblichenko had advised her, the same blasted Ruthenian who was going around Taylorizing everything. Oh, how repulsive men were to her! Not this poor babe sitting next to her petrified with fear (she could sense it), but *he*, that member of a plurality in the abstract, that abominable, hairy, always elusive, mendacious Male. "Oh, they're much more deceitful than we are," she mused. "While the whole world knows we do everything for the sake of *that*, they pretend to have other passions in life." She looked at him, or rather at that "something" out of which (with the help of her diabolical erotic technique) she was determined to make a man, one of those males the very thought of whom made her wince in disgust. Genezip sat down again, reduced to impotence by a contradiction that shot past him into that unverifiable realm where fancy became wedded to reality. "Ha, our will be done," thought the princess.

She raised herself up nimbly, gracefully, and with a girlish, sisterly gesture took Genezip by the hand. He stood up obediently and trailed after her. He behaved as if he were keeping a dental appointment to have a tooth pulled, but by no means "repairing" to one of the country's foremost demons for his first night of pleasure. Compared to what lay in store for him, however, a tooth extraction was a mere trifle. "It's what I get for putting it off, for procrastinating," he fumed. "My father, everywhere my father. If it hadn't been for him and his 'morals,' I'd have acted differently." He felt only hatred for his father now, and that strengthened him. The whole charm of the situation, of course, lay precisely in that procrastination which annoyed him. Oh, to *be* two contradictory things at the same time, not merely to *contemplate* them! What a joy! We may strive after it, but the results are invariably partial and incomplete. Except for madness . . . But that's too dangerous. Besides, then one is not wholly conscious . . .

He found himself in the princess's bedroom, which smelled of wild thyme and something he was at a loss to define. The general impression made by the room was that of one colossal sex organ. There was even something vaguely obscene in the arrangement of the furniture, to say nothing of the colors (lobster red, carnation pink, blue, greyish violet) and the smaller accessories: engravings, assorted knickknacks, and albums filled with the most crude pornography, ranging from ordinary photographs to the subtle drawings of Chinese and Japanese woodcuts – an abnormal symptom even for such a *bas-bleu* as Irina Vsevolodovna, since the collection of such sleaze is treated as an exclusively male preserve. A warm half-light suffused with a slightly offensive odor penetrated him to the bone, now softening and relaxing his body, now making him tense, savage, bestial. Once again Genezip felt a masculine urging, the body's deep intestinal bidding. His glands were beginning to mobilize, independently of the soul. But what did he care about the soul: we glands are going to live it up, to hell with everything else!

The princess quickly got undressed before the mirror. In the oppressive silence that ensued, the rustle of fabrics seemed like a tremendous noise capable of rousing the entire household. It was the first time Zip had beheld anything so magnificent. How could the most spectacular mountain vistas compare? The hazy dusk all but obliterated the tiny (minuscule) blemishes of that exquisite animal face (grinning at him in the mirror with that tear-out-your-guts sort of smile), around which blew a mighty spirit like a hurricane around some unassailable summit. He could feel her swimming about inside him, acquiring an indomitable power and a kind of diabolic, supermundane charm that ripped through his adolescent soul with the pain of a life somehow imperfect. With all this witchcraft, how utterly unimportant were her wrinkles (which he had previously noticed) and that slightly porous but otherwise gorgeous nose! Dreams, statues, the paradise of Mohammed, and having the good fortune to be born an insect (formerly one of his ambitions) – what were all these beside this pageantry of flesh that immediately grabbed hold of the throat; that was as gigantic as something that can shrink on occasion to the size of a slit, a pitiful turd before the world's greatest conceptual hoaxes. Only in this world was this an impracticable mixture of random fragments, of scraps left over from the practical instinct of the human herd – "Sir, she's standing before your very nose" – an insurmountable pyramid of apparent nonsense whose texture was not some axiom floating about in an "ideal existence," but something real (a scandalously misused word!), consistent, flawless, without a blemish, something as smooth as glass that cannot be penetrated or analyzed except possibly by a stiletto or an artistic lunacy that has been held in contempt for some six thousand years. (In contempt because at one time other tools were used: gruesome religions rank with eroticism, great art, great renunciations, the grim prophecies of narcotics, and, above all, a sense of terrifying mystery: "Our last resort," Sturfan Abnol once remarked, "is nonsense – otherwise, forget it.") It was as elementary as any quality of the senses (color, sound, smell, etc.), or as any concept for ("hee-hee") Husserl. "And now, that same mankind which for so many centuries [from the point of view of rationalism, of course (which, as we know, is by no manner of means always and for everybody [*y compris* the most august minds] valid)] has been floundering around in the most gorgeous religious rubbish is upset about the death of art because it is unable to reproduce its moribund world of forms without a slight distortion of 'sacrosanct reality,' which is to say, that vision of the world entertained by the most banal, average, common man of our time," the obnoxious Marquis di Scampi had remarked half an hour ago *en passant,* the devil only knows apropos of what. But this body, this body . . . Now, before the astonished eyes of this sexual upstart (or nonstart), the fearful mystery of another personality was unveiled; now, as he beheld her wrapped in this voluptuous body, which beauty and material resistance rendered inaccessible (unless it was butchered, ripped to shreds – in a word, annihilated). She was all that, this hellcat. And he was like an archpriest standing before the statue of Isis. All the hideous oriental myths and lewd sexual rites that this creature personified, a creature cursed by its very perfection, passed through the polluted imagination of this ex-masturbator as a sensuous vapor given off by that indescribable something sprawled out before him with such gloomy impudence. With a sullen grace – the princess was indeed sad – she exposed her body's deadly curves – *"des rondeurs assomantes,"* as a French admirer had once described them to her. Zip's bewilderment (she was watching behind her as well in the mirror) scorched her skin like the burning plates of a diathermic apparatus. "It's worth suffering for such bliss," the poor thing sighed.

For Genezip the world had become unbearably huge. In it, as in a feverish nightmare, the princess appeared small as a tiny stone inside some colossal fruit; gradually she receded until at last she vanished altogether in the limbo of destinies towering over him. Once again, fear. "Am I a coward?" Zip wondered, stretched out on his portable cross. This little cross was to grow into a mammoth cross that would never forsake him; on the contrary, it would grow into his body and even into the lower extremities of his soul. No, he was not a coward, he, Zip Kapen, a graduate deflowered a trifle late for his age. By now his fear had become metaphysical in essence: it brought no discredit to the man nascent inside the boy. Genezip was actually conscious of the fact that he had a body. Sports and gymnastic exercises were never like this! The muscles of that "system" (as the English call it) were twitching madly. He walked up to within two feet of that ominous deity standing before him – a deity from which a pair of very lovely panties had just fallen onto the luxurious carpet. But what did he know of such matters? This body and that red-haired fire down there . . . ? He could not bear the sight of it. He lowered his gaze and examined attentively the multicolored design of the carpet as if impressing these Persian zigzags on his memory were now a matter of extreme importance. Only by a lateral adjustment was he able to take in the lower part of that truly diabolical picture. The princess turned around, jumped nimbly out of her panties, which still lay on the floor, and, not looking at him, removed her shiny stockings with the graceful motion of a little girl. The sheen given off by her stockings had a touch of cruelty, like the polished steel of some high-powered machine. The dimensions were being altered from second to second: the world kept oscillating between Brobdingnagism and Lilliputism as in a peyote vision. (Note: Irina Vsevolodovna always wore a pair of garters above the knees.) Genezip gazed at her legs, which were so beautifully formed that no Grecian statue – but why waste our breath: they were like two distinct deities, each having a life of its own, barefoot, naked, indecent . . . In fact, one leg by itself ceases to be so extraordinarily beautiful; on the contrary, it is something infernal, perhaps the most obscene thing of all. But here, meanwhile – oh, hell! – it was indeed a marvel! And that it should have been ordained so and not otherwise, at this juncture of time which was desperately retreating, sinking into the abyss of the past . . . Genezip looked into her face and was petrified. She was "an angel of lewdness." Yes, there were no other words for it: AN ANGEL OF LEWDNESS. AAA, aaa . . . This beauty run wild, this beauty bathed in an otherworldly, not-to-be-touched holiness – it was un-bear-able. And then in combination with those legs and that crinkly, red-haired tuft holding the awesome mystery of our origin. Would this beautiful, sorry galoot depart from *that* into the world he had just discovered? Zip was plunged into wild dismay that had as its counterpart such a damnably *unpleasant* pain in his sexual-vital parts that he simply burst from within like a puffball, like a bedbug bloated with blood. He would never muster the courage to go up to her, there would never by anything between them, and he would never recover from this insufferable dolor. Instead of genitals he felt only an inert, mushy wound, painful for being so numb. He was a castrate, a milksop, and a bumbler.

"Are you afraid?" asked the princess with a bewitching smile on her finely arched lips, lusciously tossing her mane of copper-red hair. So what if he had behaved suspiciously today; those misgivings were behind her now. A powerful affection had entered her indomitable thighs and in a paroxysm of other misgivings had shoveled her intestines into a greedy pit. A thick sweetness, so pleasing to the senses it pricked her, had crept into her aching, throbbing heart that was bleeding for some sublime fulfillment – she could have consumed the world and not just this babe, this cuddly kid, this simp, this runt, this snotty little jack-off, this splendid little cherub who was already being transformed by manhood into a powerful stud and who had something for her there in his drawers – something soft, shy, limp, which in a few moments would rise up menacingly like a finger of providence in a black summer sky and, saturated with itself (even with his soul), maul her (both he and it together – O the ineffable wonder of carnal delight), ball her, and wreak its throbbing lust until both were mangled in a degrading, base, and triumphant (for it, the author of this fiendish orgy) orgasmic spasm. Oh, what do men know about the joy of sex? They run the show, but what they miss is that it is the woman, some she who through her passivity raises the frisson to a frenzy by her being built so and not otherwise (we leave aside a few minor emotions). The poor things, do they know what it is to feel inside oneself, inside one's own intestines the deflated, humbled, and yet great and almighty instigator of that pleasure? And it is *that* which does all this to me, that thing down there! The helpless surrender to a foreign power – that alone is the climax! And it is *you* who brings about the downfall of that beastly thing. "Oh no, I won't make it . . . I'll go mad," she whispered, torn apart by the lust that had gripped her whole body, a body that this numskull was too timorous to look upon as a conqueror. Such was what Irina Vsevolodovna imagined. But what happened in reality? Perhaps we should not discuss it. And we most certainly would not discuss it were it not for certain details which argue that it would indeed be better that we did.

Only now did Genezip discover the truth of his afternoon awakening from childhood dreams. (How many times did that make?) Infinite are the tiers of the human soul: one merely has to know how to push on intrepidly – either one conquers one's summit or one perishes, but in any case, it wouldn't be the sort of dog's life led by mediocrities only dimly aware of their existence, such as it may be. Ha, give it a whirl! Suddenly the discourse between Prince Basil and Benz became illumined as when the sun, forging its way westward, flings its dying, raspberry rays from behind the horizon upon clouds bunched in the east. Where he was at that moment he did not know. He had transgressed the boundaries of his former "I" and had forever renounced the use of his intellect. It was his first self-inflicted crime. The collision of the worlds personified by those two in the retreat had yielded a net result of zero. "Life for life's sake" (the most chimerical notion of the most crass human offal) had led to his downfall. In renouncing what he had supposed to be boredom, the proper conceptual realm for novices, he had, in effect, renounced the life for which he had sacrificed this realm. (This law is by no means valid for everyone, but how many people today conduct themselves according to this fallacy?) A terrifying deity minus panties and stockings, with *chut-chut* drooping but nonetheless (the menacingly raised finger, alone in the air) beautiful breasts (Genezip had a vision of some strange fruit from another planet) was standing there before him, silent, affectionate, meek. And therein lay the terror. But the poor kid was too dumb to see it. Nor did Zip know what a powerful attraction he possessed for her because of his confused and discombobulated state, what a profound emotion (it, that emotion, unstitched her insides with tears frozen into crystal spikes) he aroused in this ex-mother who was almost beyond the pale of lust because he was such a puerile erotic boob, a positively priceless specimen during those horrific times. And then came the kicker, that self-disgust . . . How can such self-contempt on the one hand be the equivalent of self-exultation on the other? A mystery. Inscrutable are the decrees contained in the scheming concoctions of glandular secretions! Such a cocktail can always surprise one by its taste. But, hell, everything has it end, and the sequel is not of our doing, and meanwhile the moment passes us by, that unique moment which ought to be savored, *saavored* – ahhh . . .

"Come," whispered this mysterious goddess through a throat choked with desire. (Where to, O God, where to?) He made no reply: his stiffened tongue belonged to someone else. The princess drew so close to him he could smell her arms. It was a subtle, fragile odor, infinitely more poisonous than all of the world's alkaloids combined. Mandjune, Davamesque, peyote, and "lukutate" – none could compare to that poison. It was his undoing. He almost puked. Everything was going haywire, as if some vicious outsider had put the whole machine into reverse. "Don't be afraid," Irina Vsevolodovna continued in a deep, slightly tremulous voice, not daring to touch him. "There's nothing evil about it; it doesn't hurt. You'll see how sweet it is to do such a lovely, indecent thing together, a thing no one shall ever see or be ashamed of. For what could be lovelier than for two bodies that burn for each other. . . " (Oh no, not again, dammit!) ". . . to penetrate in the pleasure they give each other . . . " (That demonic woman morosely affected by her body's decline did not know how to tame, lull, and seduce this poor intimidated stud-boy. Her soul took wing, splitting its sides with laughter at the expense of her poor, defiled, senescent body quivering with "abysmal" desires; a body that in the twilight, in the eyes of this obnoxious teenager, was blossoming in unprecedented glory, perhaps for the last time. Her morose condition enhanced the charm of that moment in a singular way. Everything was covered with the grey sauce of a woman's torment in which a few tiny raisins of a would-be genuine and virginal but in reality almost senile shame were floating about. But the grandeur of the gesture gained the upper hand, and only then came the delayed corresponding feeling: a mysterious amalgam of maternal tenderness and outrageous animal lust – a woman's rare good fortune provided, of course, a scapegoat can be found for such a mélange.) (So thought Sturfan Abnol – but the point is, no one knows what a woman is really like.) She took him by the hand. "Don't be embarrassed; get undressed. You'll feel more comfortable that way. Don't try to resist, just give yourself to me. You're so lovely – you have no idea how lovely you are – you can't see it. I shall give you all the nerve you need. Through me you'll come to know yourself; you'll become tight as a bowstring for that flight into the distance which is life itself – from where I have returned in order to lead you there. And to think this may be the last time I shall ever love . . . love . . . ," she whispered on the verge of tears. (He looked at her hot, flushed face close to his, and the world, slowly but systematically, revolted. *There,* in his genitals, an ominous calm persisted.) And she? Wrapped in its silken scarf of pride, locked in its metal mask of cynicism, and cowed by a cunning (for a wench, at least) spirit and by a body with secret defects (very negligible, by the way), her heart, that ball of immature and overmature, conflicting, and hopelessly complex emotions (she was a mother, after all), flung itself open, savagely and impudently, before this young, ferocious, and, judged by the cruelty with which he was innocently torturing her, disgusting adolescent. Strictly speaking, adolescence is a rather dull and tiresome affair, unless it's illumined by an intellect of fairly high caliber. This light had yet to appear in Zip, but all the same something was beginning to rumble. Today marked the end. He would never be found on the other side again. An evil, vicious life was rolling over him like some beast from an atlas of monsters – a catoblepas, perhaps, or something worse (for example, a docile sheep). Carnal desires, like long, crushing elasmosaurs, had coiled themselves around him and were preparing to drag him into the darkness of the future, where some people could find no relief except in narcotics or death or madness. *It* had begun. Again the words of the princess:

" . . . get undressed. You have such a cute little body." (She was slowly undressing him.) "How strong it is, too. What muscles – enough to drive a person insane. Here's a cuff link; I'll put it over here. Oh, my poor, beloved, impotent one. I know, that's because you were waiting all this time, weren't you? And what is that stain, may I ask?" (Her voice was trembling.) "Oh, my little pet has been masturbating. But that's not nice. You should have saved that for me. And now it's like a noodle. But you were thinking of me when you did it, weren't you? I shall break you of that nasty little habit. Don't be embarrassed. You're so marvelous. Don't be afraid of me. Please don't get the idea that I'm so terribly wise. Why, I'm just a little girl like you – what I mean is, you're not a girl, no, of course not. You're a big boy, a regular he-man. Let's you and me play marriage like a couple of seven-year-old Papuans in a jungle hut." Indeed, while saying this she had really looked like a little girl, the kind Zip had previously despised. "I'm really not that awful, you know. That's just what people say about me. But don't you listen to them. Don't you believe a word they say. You'll get to know me yourself and fall in love with me. It's inconceivable for you not to love me, especially when I kiss you like this . . . " – and the first kiss of this omniscient female fell on his innocent mouth while her wildly sensuous eyes ate their way into his eyes like sulfuric acid into iron. At last he discovered what a dreadful thing the mouth is – especially such a mouth, belonging to such eyes. Suddenly he burst into a cool flame and embraced her on the spot, briefly, violently. He stopped at once. Mouth or no mouth, he was put off by the wet mollusk working his face over, by the frenetic "slurps" of her convulsed tongue. His body split in two all the way down to the floor. But what did she care?! Showering him with kisses, she dragged him over to the sofa and, though he tried to resist, stripped him naked. Next she took off his shoes, all the while covering his smooth, beautifully tapered calves with kisses. Nothing. So she resorted to another method: taking his head in her hands, she forced him to kneel down on the floor, whereupon she spread her legs fiendishly like some abominable succubus. Then, mercilessly and pitilessly, she began shoving his head and the desirable face up there. And even though he was already on the brink of disaster, defending himself against a lifelong curse (except for infinitesimally brief moments of self-delusion, it doesn't matter whether it's a curse or a blessing), even though he was potentially doomed and already sliding downhill, Zip fought back with the sheer instinct of personality against the herd and against the multiplicity of existence that personality engenders out of metaphysical necessity. It split him apart. He gagged, vomited internally, grunted, and snorted seeing before him the one thing he dreaded most. He felt not the slightest urge to gratify this woman's lust, not to speak of how little he appreciated that which he had been given to inspect: that monster shaded by a patch of red hair (the princess had a positive disdain for artificiality), preposterous, nauseating, salmon-colored, redolent of Hell (you bet) and the freshness of the sea, the finest of Rothman's tobaccos, and a life forever wasted; that belly, a seemingly ordinary belly, but one which was domed in a sacrilegiously delicate manner like the cupola of some forbidden Eastern temple; those breasts which were like white pagodas with tips illumined by the rising sun; and, finally, those hips, somehow familiar (from subconscious dreams, perhaps?), both alien and intimate, untouchable, unbeatable, and unapproachable in their splendor, dammit, thus remaining a perpetual tease, a testimonial to male shame. Not to mention that face, that infernal puss . . . ! And love. (Now we all know what it takes to master all this with one heroic thrust, to realize something beyond oneself: the past and, however briefly, something "other," impersonal. But an ill-omened calm prevailed there like the calm at sea an hour before a cyclone.) Again a welter of unidentifiable feelings that conflicted with his "previously reported state"; and a burning shame for being so silly and inept (physically speaking). A wasteland of senseless, merciless experiences totally obliterating eight carefully wrought years of his life. This was how the ineluctable future was molded during that interval of anguish and pudency . . . (Eh? A hateful word, to be sure, but you try to find a more revolting synonym for "shame.") And there she was, a woman as savory in her licentiousness as milk chocolate, as a licentious cow, female roe, crocodile, capybara. She had become so large and ponderous and uncomfortable – in a word, superfluous – but as for Zip, nothing, not a twitch. And instead of doing what she demanded of him, he snuggled up to her breasts, those slightly but ever so slightly drooping breasts, which were nonetheless such perfect specimens of "pure form" that they might have eclipsed the roundness of not a few sixteen-year-old virgins. At last that whole scheming contraption known as the Princess di Ticonderoga ran out of patience. Tossing back her mane of hair, she again offered him her mouth, a mouth so uniquely obscene, so repugnant in its slushy sensuality that Genezip's whole being recoiled in abhorrence of the one thing he coveted most – an abhorrence that managed to have its pleasurable side, its profoundly flattering side: he returned her kisses. But still he would not take that magnificent mouth, the moron. Then she took him herself, and he was again subjected to the humiliation of those kisses from which there was no more escape – except by offending this pernicious creature crawling all over him. But that was the last thing Zip wished to do, however great his terror and nausea. He could have gone on admiring her naked like this for ten hours without interruption. An almost sincere but somehow weird affection, not exactly the filial kind but in some ways similar (brrr), had suddenly sprung up in him for that basically benign creature who was simply playing unbelievable tricks down there, shamelessly going into ecstasies over the object of his hitherto neglect. Still nothing. Limp as a noodle. And yet he had such an insane urge for something that he nearly exploded – though for *what* he longed, he could not say. That is, he knew abstractly: what he lacked were the right internal connections.

At length, bored, exasperated, disappointed, and furious, the princess (she knew that within half an hour she would forgive him everything and that – someday – she would give him a second lesson, this time applying a different method) cried out at him in a shrill voice and shoved him away in disgust – just as he was beginning to warm up to her with a thoroughly genuine passion.

"Get dressed. It's late and I'm tired." She knew what she was doing: he looked as if someone had just whipped him across the face – that innocent "babyface" – with a birch switch.

"I'd like to wash," he literally rattled out, his feelings now in utter shambles. He felt extremely foolish, inwardly humiliated, and sexually disgraced.

"What for, I wonder. Oh well, use the bathroom if you must. You don't suppose that I am going to wash you." And saying this, she pushed him gently, scornfully out into the corridor where he stood barefoot, naked, dripping with loneliness and awkwardness. Even if he had been a man of titanic will, he would have been outclassed. "I wonder how Napoleon, Lenin, or Piłsudski would have handled it," he mused, doing his best to smile. Oh, if he had known the night was going to end like this he would have gone all the way with Tenzer in that primeval, wolf-infested Ludzimierz forest. A monumental resentment was welling up inside him.

It was daybreak now. It was still blowing outside and had grown visibly warmer. The trees looked black and damp, while from the neighboring rooftops water was pouring down and being carried away by the wind. After what had just transpired, this ordinary, commonplace morning, begun in such a farcical manner, now offended by its triteness, by its hypernormality. Zip gave a snort and felt a new surge of masculine dignity. And yet this day which was dawning without compassion – oh, what a drag it would be! What was he going to do? Had everything come to an end? Was he to remain like this, an open, bleeding wound, till the day he died? How would he ever get through the day, or life, for that matter? Alight on that other shore where the blasé, thoroughbred pusses of all-knowing antediluvians skulked in the distance? Or rather: fling open some hitherto invisible gate leading from this dirty courtyard of the present, let the true Sun of knowledge break through, and then, bidding the place farewell, set off for that other place, out there, there – but where was *there?* Recollections of long-ago dreams, of aimless, childhood aspirations for something great: timely recollections, to say the least. But seeing his present state, he broke out in a bitter laugh. This in turn acted as a provocation: you must force such moments to happen. But how? Where would he find the will? He clenched his fists with a ferocity that seemed capable of transforming the world into his own creation, into a docile beast akin to his dog Nirvana. But reality was not the least bit fazed. Muscles alone were of no use here: there was also the matter of a tiny mainspring. Suffice it to say that Zip lacked such a spring. He had dismissed his intellect, having renounced it forever. How could he transform this palace, where he was nothing but a nasty interloper, and that alien bitch (he was now thoroughly disenthralled with her) into his own domain and his own woman (but without all that "eternal love" stuff, and minus marriage, the possibility of which had never occurred to him, to say nothing of children), into objects meant for his own private use, objects belonging to the rite of those symbolic hoops comprising the sort of puerile metaphysics over which he had ruled until now. The world weighed on him like an insufferable burden: only this last hoop had any zip left in it (Genezip Kapen: *"je ne 'zipe' qu'à peine"* – "zipless" – as he was known in school). This last hoop was himself, or rather his nondimensional ego, which now seemed to exist outside his body. Although he could flex his muscles, not even his body belonged to him anymore. He had been reduced to various disparate elements devoid of any chemical bonding. He was standing there naked, slightly chilled, in a hostile place, in a labyrinth of rooms inhabited by that equally naked ogress, who was presently waiting for proof of his manhood while all maternal feeling for him escaped like water from a leaky pot (like milk from a cancerous breast).

It was a nice change, an amusing twist, even if it was only for a few hours in her twilight period. (She had been through such an ordeal once before, not with an innocent boy but with some pious celibate of long duration.) But if this was his idea of foreplay (maybe he was sexually abnormal – oh God!), then flatly no, out of the question. If this youngster couldn't do it to her, one way or another, and then under *such* conditions, that would be a tragedy squared; then for the umpteenth time (only for different reasons) she would have to make the procedure a little more demonic, raise the diabolical element with that phony act she had been perfecting . . . But now she just wanted to relax, indulge in some simple love-making, stretch out and calmly, sensuously slide her lithesome body onto the guileless heart and tight little bundle – *sur ce paquet des muscles* – that was this lovely boy. And then how wonderful if this "laddie," on his own, in the absence of any artificial stimulation, should go wild, work himself into a rage, and all in a soft and gentle but nonetheless interesting manner. . . Such were the musings (the idle dreams!) of the princess as she lay there drowsing, her entrails in pieces, her body sheathed in an aquamarine dressing gown embossed with gold flowers (how luxurious!), or: a lounge-gown, a sprawler, an idler, a loller, a snuggler, etc. She was sure this whimsical package would not try to flee directly from the bathroom. Although, after that scene in the bedroom . . . He was capable, for instance, of grabbing a fur coat out of the hallway and making his getaway in a pair of her husband's galoshes. The princess was beginning to wonder about the future of this romance. But her most troubling doubt was whether he was in fact normal. The time was past when she could indulge her wildest fantasies, however much she may have so desired in recent times. Once again some vigilant animal (an adorable little creature like a marmot, that guardian of the herd) stirred inside her, pricked up its ears to hear what the little bare-assed beauty (ugh . . .) was doing down there, that "wonderful, smooth-to-the-touch, hearty young thing, but yet so packed with muscle and brawn, so whimsical, so unwillfully sarcastic and difficult to please (by such a pageantry! – honestly, what a scandal!), and so sensitive, too!" She started. For the first time in her life she found herself contemplating what was taking place in HIM, in *this* particular man (a total license in the case of this "kid"), in this, her very own male (as yet unmaterialized). A dangerous novelty. Never had she tried to investigate their male thoughts, unless it was before her marriage when, as a young girl, she had wondered about some prehistoric fops, dozens of whom she was to know as serious lovers. Or were they really so serious? She had gone without love for such a long time, a lifetime it seemed: it was all so evident to her now. And now this one (she realized now that it was love, her first and last) would have to be poisoned, defiled by the more or less demonic *trucs* of old, by her truly terrible but much-regretted past, which she could not throw off all at once. A powerful grief took possession of her heart as well as that thing below.

Meanwhile, that moron of a kid, totally ignorant of the verdict passed down on him by her body's dark and secret powers, stretched his muscles in the hope of rousing some puissant spirit in himself. In vain. Reality was unyielding, which is to say: this palace, these bathroom walls, the oncoming day, and the surrounding woods being swept by a warm, Oravian, February wind. Spring's terrible nostalgia hung in the air; it was intruding itself into this palace so burdened by the past, into its innermost recesses. Life was to have been so different, not at all "lousy and ridiculous"; somewhere there were to have been decent worlds in which every object was assigned its proper place and slipped as snugly into its appropriate destiny as into a jewel case; a "happy ending" for everything. But what were the conditions? Tremendous self-mastery, renunciation of a whole lot of things (that was the first condition), unbounded sacrifice, goodness, but the unpretentious sort that flows straight from the heart and which is free of any pragmatic or theosophic baloney (hence unattainable nowadays without acting like an idiot and without all that disgusting self-denial and continence that sooner reminds one of constipation), and, finally, the killing of your own personality, ripping it out of the world by the roots so that all that was left in the earth was a tuber for sustaining other people and beasts, plus a few leaves and flowers necessary for nourishing and propagating this tuber – nothing else. Okay, okay! Genezip did not actually *think* this way, he was still no match for such notions (despite their simplicity). These notions were merely the qualitatively inarticulate stuff out of which, under certain conditions, such words could "effloresce." And then, as if by a lightning bolt, he was struck by the following ingenious thought: she, that wench, was the one and only *soft* object (alive, too) within reach (in the distance, far beyond the horizon of destiny, the image of his house, and in it his dying father and his somehow distant mother – all, indeed, of what was about to become the past – passed before him), and he perceived at once that she was just as soft in spirit, whereas his own was a blunt hammer made of a different substance, a mallet for pulverizing that female stuff of hers, for turning it into a mighty compound, if only as a foundation for life's future construction projects. It was a shabby idea, of course, but could he see that? Suddenly the instinctive ferocity of youth flared up in him and, standing there as he was (he had no choice), barefoot and naked, he "set out" for the bedroom on a new expedition.

The light was still on and the shutters were closed: the princess preferred not to be seen by the servants in her present state of defeat and was mortally fatigued. She was in no mood to greet this day on which she was to have celebrated a new happiness. The bedroom was still under the spell of the previous night. Zip entered with a confident step, ignoring his continued state of impotence. (A strange figure wrapped in aquamarine on the sofa glanced up at him with an apprehensive look, rolled herself up into a ball, and buried her head in the pillow.) After the relative cold of the bathroom between six and seven on a February morning (that whole messy business had consumed a total of four hours!), the atmosphere of fragrant, opalescent, and nearly palpable sensuality affected our obnoxious pubescent as a conquered city might affect its battle-weary plunderers. This, above all: to erase through some perfectly mad and "supernatural" deed that compromising fuck in the woods with Tenzer and all this puerile fumbling on the very threshold of paradise. He had ceased to be aware of this hag's age: she was a female simply, a protofemale à la Przybyszewski, "stinking with lust" (a very unappetizing expression, that) to the very heavens. Soon savage desire, primal, instinctive, unadulterated desire, erupted from the centers of his brain and completely inundated his glands and muscles, including his sphincters. Without turning around, the princess sensed that something was mounting behind her. She waited in a state of insufferable numbness that spread slowly from the nape of her neck all the way down to her hips and thighs where, with a tingling sensation of boiling water, it bubbled over into that eternally greedy furnace of bestiality, the source of an eerie, inexplicable, preposterous, forever new, somber, suicidal joy. Her instinct told her that *it* was about to happen. How? Should she help him, or should she leave him alone? Lust, like a meaty, bloody ball with fiery tongues, rose up in her throat and engulfed her mouth, nose, eyes, and brain. She felt now the same guilty-luscious wave that coursed through her as she dwelt on descriptions of tragic accidents, sadism, suicides . . . mounting in stages to an ever higher lust . . . an egoistic, nauseating, sordid, intensive, sleek, slimy, clammy, suspiciously *tainted* lust . . . the greater, oh, yes, the greater for being a little . . . and then the climax, engorgement by the Infinite, in the hurting capitulation to an alien nihilism . . . They were that nihilism, the bastards! Oh, off with their hides! But this one she loved as her own child, almost as much as that monstrous brood that had crawled out of her belly into the world, prying open her thighs with an unbearable but blissful-fertile pain. For the princess was a good mother: she adored her sons and had given birth to them with a wild satisfaction. (The oldest, a manic-depressive, had recently committed suicide; the second oldest [whose whereabouts had been a mystery for over a year now] was at twenty-one the syndicate's ambassador to China; the third was Scampi – the aforementioned.) The princess was confronted now by a vision of all three as one spirit conceived by her; this spirit had become incarnated in Genezip, Zip, the last of her darlings, her "lambkin," her private little "fuckee," so innocent and so callous, brutish, alien, hairy, hateful in his maleness. How could she repress this motherly love if she had failed to get a rise with the other kind?! Wrapping the anticipation in grief like this only made the thing spicier, fiendishly so, as when a piquant English sauce is added to a piece of beefsteak. These "weir-r-rd thoughts" – to quote an old Jew who used to deliver various wares to the palace, the only "peon creature" with whom the princess would speak regarding matters of a more serious nature – were interrupted by the very thing she had been dreaming about.

He grabbed her viciously by the shoulder and with his naked, impudent kisser glared brutally into her face, rendered positively pretty by the preceding thoughts. Carnal desires were already copulating madly in the space between their bodies. The princess glanced down below and saw everything exactly as she had fantasized it, and this time she did not let him out of her famished, frantic arms, but without any perverse preliminaries guided him by the sheer force of passion into her all-knowing body's most secret seat of pleasure. Their bodies meshed, interlocked, and Zip perceived that life was really *something*. She had the same sensation, only on the brink of death, or worse: of a living death. And that young stud truly went berserk, gorging himself on the fatal passions, both his and hers ("the old bag with one foot in the grave," as, struggling with his feelings, he later told himself), now melted into one floorless ocean of insanity. She became for him the embodiment of life's essence: insolent, naked to the point of excoriated. And lo, the inarticulate became articulate in this amalgam of piggish delights bordering on the metaphysical. Later they moved over to the bed, where she commenced to teach him. The tutorial left him inwardly exalted, then collapsed him till he no longer knew whether he naturally inhabited that Hell of desires – private but divined – which she was dragging out of him like guts from a carcass; at home in that diabolic proliferation of inadmissible spider-thoughts or hydra-thoughts. Until he was cast into the pit, and this time for good. Meanwhile, the "demoniacal" Irina Vsevolodovna, the subject of so many monstrous rumors, rumors easily surpassing every previous (and potential?) subject of human gossip, was kissing the filthy – filthy only in a certain sense, of course – hand of this lug who, immersed in the mute recollection of freshly consummated lust, no longer knew for certain whether he was sane. He had been annihilated, so to speak, but his fatigue was delectable, sweet as some rare narcotic. Showing pride and affection for her lover, the princess stroked his soft, silken hair and, closing her eyes like a cat drowsing off to sleep, inhaled its honeylike fragrance.

The time was eight o'clock. While they were still lying in bed, not having the strength to part company, the maid, a voluptuous, red-haired thing, brought in a breakfast of French lamb chops, ham and eggs, smoked fish, porridge, café au lait, and a superb cognac. (The princess prided herself on her female servants, boldly risking comparison, whereas when it came to entertaining "ladies," a strict etiquette was observed at the Ticonderogas'.) Zip hid beneath the cover. Titters and whispers were heard overhead.

Despite his having to endure this minor humiliation, he had finally sunk his teeth into the horns of life. He could feel it in his bones, an asinine, adolescent triumph: at last he was a man, and he knew wherein his future lay. Oh, how grievously mistaken he was!

A short while later the old prince came in wearing a green dressing gown of felt (?), followed a moment later by Scampi in cream and gold (how marvelous!) pajamas, who barged into the room without knocking. Genezip nearly died from shame when the prince, as was the custom on such occasions, began interrogating his wife. They held themselves in such high regard that nothing, but literally nothing, could shock their sensibilities. From underneath the cover Zip heard the princess's subdued voice:

" . . . a bit strange at the beginning, but extremely nice later on – exceptional, I should say. In some ways he's just a kid. Show us that baby face of yours, dearie," she said sweetly, pulling back the cover and lifting up his face by the chin. "You know, Diapanasius," she said, turning to her husband with that so-called effusion of heart, "for years, almost since the first time I betrayed you, I haven't felt so metaphysically exhilarated as I do today. Oh, I know you bridle at that word; you and your cronies say I abuse it. But how else is one to express such marvelous things in such a succinct manner? You – and not just you but all men of action who want to be stricken from the living – you don't see that life may possess another dimension. It was Chwistek, I believe, who proposed something similar when he wrote about the 'plurality of reality,' but he failed, of course, to carry his ideas to their logical conclusion, and predictably the public treated them as so much humbug. Not even Afanasol Benz, who they tell me – I have no way of telling whether it's true – has deduced his first axiom from nothing, not even he acknowledges the theory of this man. But I'm convinced there must be something to it and that his followers are to blame for making a mess of it . . . "

"The news from Moscow is going from bad to worse . . . Those yellow devils have some general who's come up with a new offensive strategy. At last our people have cracked it. I just had a call from Kotzmolochowicz's adjutant – you know, this chap who's supposed to be on our side? But this will enlighten us as little as

Napoleon did the coalition. Only one way we'll ever find out: from the Chinese themselves."

"What do I care – I have him." The princess was holding Zip's head under her arm. It was here that Scampi made his entrance.

"You may not even have that for long, Mama. Rumor has it they're going to announce a general call-up tomorrow. The armies of General Cuxhaven are pulling back to our lines in panic. Moscow is officially a bloodbath. The Chinese are imposing a brand-new social plan. Something about swallowing the white race. Nor do they respect our military – they look upon us as mush. And all this on behalf of the most exalted ideas, namely, raising us up to their own level. Given their work ethic and the disproportions that exist between them and ourselves in this respect, well, the prospect is not very pretty. Even if we manage to survive, we'll have to work ourselves to death. I should like to know whether an ideology, for whose sake people are willing to die – not all of a sudden, but gradually – is not in fact something incidental. The bolsheviks, by contrast, have kept Russia well in hand. That may suit the workers who have nothing to look forward to. But what about us? How are *we* going to justify our existence in the new order? That's the question."

"Didn't I say so! Now where is that syndicalism of yours? That product of a bourgeois clique pretending to resolve the class struggle? Now where is that pseudoworker's socialism of yours? It's a lot of rubbish, I tell you. We should have set up an independent monarchy and then perished with honor, without disgrace, like my Czar Cyril . . . "

"His fate is uncertain," Scampi interrupted. "I see him regularly at headquarters in Kotzmolochowicz's company . . . "

" . . . or swam with the tide. In the end, it will be we, the last remnants of humanity, the only ones capable of life, who will surely be victorious, and *après nous pust vsyo propadaet.* Yes, we've been duped in a most vulgar fashion by that pseudobolshevik but *au fond* fascist West. I mean it. With us everything's a fraud . . . "

"Shh! One doesn't say such things out loud. Well now, with all her talents Mama will surely survive, even as the mistress of some Chinese chief of staff. But not we men. There you have the fallacy of today's aristocracy and even of a fraction of our crass bourgeoisie: aprenooledelugism. The present system has hung on for four thousand years because the great of the past were people of vision and, theoretically at least, stood before an eternity. Not until this faith was lost did all the trouble begin and the mob start to rear its head. Its *head*, that's the point, and not the rump, with which it once kicked over the traces. But as soon as it raised its head, the game was up – there I'm in agreement. Mama, you were right: we should have resisted, but for that you need . . . honor – hee-hee . . . But Kotzmolochowicz will take care of that for us, and we'll all be left stranded."

"So that's how politics get made – by people like *these!* But where's reality?" thought Zip, who had quite suddenly matured beneath the cover. (The famous and infamous bosom of Irina Vsevolodovna was an excellent incubator for such timid little souls.) And strange to say, *simultaneously*, against the "generally confused background," (naturally, he realized it sequentially) he felt alternately oppressed, smeared, puny – to the point of altogether blowing his sexual self-confidence, despite his having just made up for his boyhood bouts of guiltless expiation, so acute was this self-belittlement in relation to the immense chasms of the unattainable: knowledge, position, influence, power, the gratification of appetite. And, quite astonishingly, he had forgotten about his father, also a bigshot, also a dabbler from time to time in the political cesspool. But this feeling had nothing to do with "domestic pride"; no, other values were at work here. And yet he knew that Matthew Scampi was nothing but a common pleasure-seeker and a shitass, a revolting tapeworm inside the disintegrating body of what was once Poland (which was in the process of surviving its own death) (how many are there of these living cadavers today?!), *un simple 'gouveniage' polonais,* as General Lebac used to say, the head of the French military mission who, immediately after the bolshevik coup, remained on duty in our country in the service of "true democracy," as it was ostentatiously couched. "Oh, you poor naive soul, you're a self-deluded lackey of our fat bourgeois belly, and all under the pretext of pseudosolidarity and scientific planning." *(Oh, vous autres, Polonais, n'est-ce pas – mais tout de même la démocratie, la vraie démocratie, est une et indivisible et elle vaincra.)* Such were the grudgingly sincere thoughts of Erasmus Kotzmolochowicz, with whom Lebac was "collaborating" (?) (although the latter couldn't hold a candle to the ingenious Kotzmolochowicz!) in the task of "saving mankind" from the "cultural catastrophe" of the Chinese invasion. Kotzmolochowicz was positively spewing such ideas. For he was a man hungering for the truth, that bloody, steamy, quivering truth, not the sort dished up to him in public by the Syndicate for National Salvation and until recently in private by his wife, a wasted but, for that swarthy, sinewy bull of a quartermaster general, fiendishly seductive little blonde, née Dziedzierska and supposedly a Galician countess. Ah, that truth of hers! It was the nadir of irrealism: a "panthosophia," a synthesis of all the sciences (duly distorted of course; purely abstract structures of the various disciplines, dreamed up for pure convenience, became in her version the wildest ontology imaginable) and systems, from totemism to the logic of Russell and Whitehead (no one in those days knew Benz from a hole in the ground). Until at last a miracle transpired on earth: Djevani, the great emissary of Murti Bing appeared . . . The quartermaster had other antidotes for this trend – but more on that later. Marquis di Scampi was fleetingly acquainted with it as well, though oddity belonging to a higher realm refused to stick to his slickly polished pinhead – "a typically Polish and polished excremental fellow," as Lebac's colleague, Lord Eaglehawk, used to call him. Kotzmolochowicz was sick of this international clique. But with the patience of a truly great man he was biding his time for the right moment, not knowing himself what would follow. In those days knowing how to wait was a supreme art. And yet these thoughts, these "weir-r-rd" thoughts . . . He was powerless to expel them; often he felt that someone else was thinking for him (not in the form of concepts, but of images) and arriving at absolutely inescapable conclusions. At times he detected another presence in a room of which he was visibly the sole occupant. He would utter a word or two to confirm this presence, only to confirm that he was alone and that, in truth, he did not know himself what he had said. Images merged and vanished without leaving so much as a trace, a scent, or a sediment as to the contents of those mysterious complexes making up the subliminal sphere of consciousness. Bekhmetev had prescribed a short rest at Zegiestów, at the sanitorium run by the descendants of the celebrated Doctor Ludwig Kotulski, but Kotzmolochowicz could not spare the time. Oh, if only his enemies and detractors had known! Enough – let's return to the princess's bed. Genezip continued to meditate in secret beneath the cover. (A warm animal stench, at once eerie and acrid smelling, filled his nostrils but no longer aroused his senses: he was savoring what it was like to be a man, a bona fide stud, a gentleman, a *mister*, failing to see how disagreeably, how obnoxiously this new role suited him.) Still, he was mortally ashamed that Scampi, an intellectual zero and cynical careerist, that "cold-blooded lugworm infesting the dissolute belly of a Poland in decline ever since the Saxon period" – had managed to impress him. Where did such an arcane politics come from? Wasn't it all a gigantic and *au fond* ridiculous fraud, a third-rate hoax based on a crass understanding of human nature, a proficiency in the shabbiest possible dealings verging on the criminal? All right, he was impressed, but the very thing that Zip had esteemed as noble, nay, as sacrosanct, now appeared drastically diminished. And because of this reduction in size the world was covered by a prosaic, uncouth, proletarian veneer of boredom and misery. Zip was wrong, of course, but the question of who was right would only be resolved, in another millennium or so, by generations scientifically bred for the new utopia – provided anyone would be around to recall so remote a past. No, in those days politics truly did not belong to the noblest of endeavors. Perhaps in the Far East, where new ideas were gushing forth (a number of "simplifiers" contended these ideas had been around for some time, even in China itself; but, what the hell, is there nothing new on this earth? Does that mean we should all lie down and give up the ghost?); perhaps there, in that boiler room of creativity, something had a right to exist, even as a necessary evil, a by-product of the gigantic transformation begun by those yellow noggins: a new domestic policy (their foreign policy was already in high gear, its mode of operation being unprecedented by Western standards: Murti Bing's followers [along with their bizarre narcotic Davamesque B_2] were slowly but surely going about their business). But more about that later. For you see, the whole of European "bolshevism" (Lenin would have died a second time had he been there to see it) was merely the final burning and smoking of rubble left over from a previous fire. But about new people, in the traditional sense, barely a word. Renewal could have come only from the relatively new societies of Australia and New Zealand. But it was getting late, besides which those confounded Mongols, who never hurry and who always seem to have time to spare, were going about it their way (which was different, oh, radically different from how we would have done it). Patience was by far the most prudent course. But how to be patient when the proletariat of Europe had *no time* at all?! Just try (if you're not a Chinese) to live with dirt, lice, bedbugs, roaches, in hunger, cold, and in a state of abject despair for the duration of a generation, and take comfort in the thought that one day, within three generations, say, a cabal of immaculate and wonderfully nourished (and, alas, hopelessly specialized) experts and capitalists would finally see the light and put up cozy little bungalows replete with gardens, radios, and home libraries. But how will *we* benefit, we who are, and always will be, nothing but manure? Now, would it not be better to resist with our intellect rather than settle for such a dog's life? Intellectual resistance, however mad, is better than rotting in despair without a glimmer of hope. Try to understand, dammit! Might it not be better to live, *from this moment on,* in the same style as before, but guided by some idea and always with imagination, even the frenzied, wild sort but *imagination* all the same, and not with the feeling of being harnessed to the infernal treadmill of production? So what if this idea leads to the same thing; that is, to *a certain limited prosperity, beyond which the human race will never advance* – to ennui and greyness ("The fly cannot sit down," as the zoologist Janusz Domaniewski once quipped), but at least it will happen *at once,* without all this infernal waiting. Eh, it's all well and good for you to talk, you gentlemen of the "elite." All we want is what you have had for centuries, and we want it now! "A policy of internal consumption?" Just try to "consume" as much as we have! Anyway, it's no use. America and the Old World (which had been given up for "fascist") had gone bolshevik, which is nearly the same as going fascist, but gone bolshevik it had. To repeat, ideas . . . Such were the quaint notions held by Kotzmolochowicz the trooper as well as by a few other high-caliber misfits. But not consciously: they took it as given in the form of a mentally inarticulate mush. "How can one make crystal out of shit?" the quartermaster would ponder to himself, then lose himself in deep and aimless reverie. Once upon a time, a politics based on individual will had been something respectable; a knowledge of human nature was not regarded as a dirty word. Today, except for a fanatic, purely theoretical extremism on behalf of a gut-basis for the imaginary advancement of the spirit, party politics means a mass hypnosis using notions like democracy and national sovereignty. This might have worked when people took such things as the gospel truth; today they ring false. Hence that mindless struggle at the pinnacle of the collective mob, that struggle against the hegemony of the coin, is something real, and all the rest is just a tug-of-war between that same coin and democracy, between *trucs* and tricks, plots and chicaneries, a poker game based on a universal bluff – a boring subject in itself, except perhaps from the historical point of view. But by what miracle that colloidal island, i.e., Poland, was able to hold its own in the trend toward greater crystallization of the mass, no one knew. People made much ado about "Poland's inertia," "Poland's indolence," "Poland's lack of redeeming virtues," etc., but such explanations were inadequate despite the modicum of truth they contained. It was indeed a historical miracle, but didn't history testify to several such miracles? To wit: the violent spread of Christianity, the perseverance of bolshevism in Russia, the very fact that an independent France untouched by revolution still existed, or, for that matter, Poland's unswerving faith in its own messianic mission. No, historical materialism could not explain everything; the laws of physics are nothing more than the sum total of a vast number of arbitrary incidents, and such approximations, such *pseudo*necessity breaks down when its laws are applied in an absolute manner to the immense social complexities that, in our range of magnitude, are arbitrary par excellence. The property of arbitrariness is immediately posited for every animate creature: it is an elementary fact of existence; under certain circumstances resistance engenders a feeling of limitation and relative necessity, whereas absolute necessity, because of the abstract elimination that occurs at the periphery of Particular Being or of living creatures in general, is *necessarily* a fiction. Enough. The causal relation between events has nothing to do with the absolute causality of the physicist. Whenever a sufficiently large number of uniform, unidirectional tendencies happens to coincide (which, because of the immense quantity and minuteness of elements, is impossible for us in chemical or astronomical terms), a historical miracle takes place, similar, in fact, to the one that obtains when an individual performs a feat involving a phenomenal exertion of will.

The family discussion was drawing to a close.

"Come out, sonny," the old prince said to Genezip through the golden damask bedcover. "Think of it – what a range of experience! The death pangs of the old world, and that includes us, you know . . . it's unspeakable . . . she was right . . . metaphysical . . . it makes the mind reel . . . that great word . . . she's always right. Mark my word, sonny, you listen more closely to her than to your own mother and you'll escape this devil's trap called life. I know what's ahead of you, lad, and I'll be frank: I don't envy you. Still, no one can say we didn't enjoy our last tidbit of reality in this seclusion of ours. As for what's coming, it's an illusion."

Genezip, morally warmed by the old man's soothing tone, stuck his embarrassed little head out from under the covers. The princess smoothed his hair, and said:

"We'll make something of him yet. At home he had no one to show him the way. That will be my last great mission in life – I'm through with politics anyway."

Zip was horribly set on defying this bunch of shadows "dancing their macabre dance on the carcass of comatose Poland." But his future was still hazy, even if last night had shed a lot of light on the subject. Despite the pretty landscape and fuzzy emotions, despite the childish guilt, the sense of a newly flexed manhood, and, above all, despite the sensation of having gone *from here to there* and that even if he busted a gut he would never get beyond a certain point – none of this encouraged more decisive action. He felt strangely bewildered (it was a bewilderment of a different order) (someone had refurbished his brain without consulting his will); nothing was as it *"should have been"* (not like before, however; this time the world seemed full of hidden menace; as though by shedding reality it could turn into a monster from some insufferable nightmare; only on the other side could one awaken, while here was the *whole world,* and maybe all that remained was death, or rather, that something about which Zip had heard and failed to comprehend but which *he feared precisely because he did not know what it was:* madness. Once, seeing an epileptic in the street, he was reminded of his terror in connection with the Zoological Garden and the onanistic practices of his boyhood – a sexually tinged terror, as though his testicles were being tickled from *within* and were raising up his body suddenly deprived of its sense of balance [he was similarly overcome in high towers and balconies, though oddly enough mountains didn't bother him at all].). He felt separated from the world by the transparent but invincible barrier of that minatory strangeness through which all came at him slightly distorted, though how the distortion came about or where it lay he knew not. How to break through those layers of resistance that were thick as tar and yet untrappable? How to grab hold of that tangible something (something like this must exist somewhere, otherwise the world would be a dirty joke and should be tossed back to God like a filthy rag nobody will touch – which would mean the death penalty, of course) beyond this trio of phantoms – or rather, quartet, since he was now one of them. Life was breathing a deadly anxiety down his neck; not he but his future fled in panic. Again he hankered for some deed. But above all to catch those fugitive devils' tails, reins, or plain old strings and tackle everything anew. And naked as he was, he sprang across the room, snatched up his crumpled clothes lying on the couch, and dashed into the bathroom. The old man blinked in bewilderment and chomped his toothless gums in dismay. The marquis snickered his perverse but subtle giggle.

"Well," he said, rising to his feet, "I see you have a hard nut to crack, Mama. But you'll crack it, you'll crack it." (To his father:) "Well, old man, let's go attend to business. Papa and I," he continued, again turning to the princess, who, without so much as flinching a muscle, was gazing wistfully into space, "have founded a *kruzhok samoopredeleniya,* like those crazy Russians who don't know who they are. The times are such that even we who are such knowledgeable reptiles, such hyperintelligent beetle shells, have to define ourselves. It's like intellectual masturbation. If some really smart fellow loses a portion of his God-given wits, then even if he bestows the rest on ten men of action he still won't get his machine to run: the engine must be proportional to the whole. And the reverse situation is no better, since in that case the motor could smash its own flimsy chassis to smithereens. That is the *cas,* I suspect, with your latest pet, Mama. But I must say I prefer his kind to cousin Toldzio. On the whole, the aristocrats of Galicia are an obnoxious bunch, and no one should know this better than we who come from the borderland. But how much younger you look after last night, Mama! It's better than a massage, no?" Irina Vsevolodovna did indeed look marvelous; her eyes of blue enamel scintillated. She could have summoned a crowd at the drop of a hat if she had so willed: she was a female "standard-bearer" par excellence. And perhaps, at times, she had even entertained such dreams, now that there was nothing else . . .

"Get out, you facetious little snot!" she shrieked, and she flung her pillow straight into her son's grinning puss. Tickled, the marquis trotted quickly out of the bedroom behind his panic-stricken pappy. It was unwise to expose oneself too long to the wrath of this miserable *mégère.* "Will he come back, or won't he? Anyhow, sooner or later he has to come back from the bathroom," she mused, wrapping herself in a blanket. "No, he won't come back now – this evening . . . " And she began devising a series of devilish ploys (variants of those perfected from past experience) with which she meant to overwhelm him in the event he resisted. This had always been her method. All trace of motherly affection had been blown to hell. If an incurable impotent had seen her now and read her lurid thoughts, he would have been instantly cured, so fiendishly depraved were those expedients of hers. What a shame such pearls vanish without a trace, much like the drunken improvisations of a Tenzer, Smorski, Szymanowski, and so many others. A dull bang of the heavy house door removed any further doubt concerning this defeat, her first. Ten years ago he would not have dared to pull a stunt like that. But now? Old age. And the princess began to weep softly, despondently, as never before.

The Return, or Life and Death

Enveloped by a snowstorm growing more violent by the moment, Genezip made straight through the woods for home. He was quite content with his performance – with his "manly feat." In retrospect this feat assumed gigantic proportions and took on the meaning of a sublime symbol of power, will, and courage. It was 9:30. At last he emerged from the woods and began plowing his way across the hills through the snowdrifts. The blizzard made it impossible to distinguish the various buildings of the manor "already partially obscured by the park trees screeching in the wind." He trudged past the dreary-looking brewery, whose towering, pylonlike stacks (symbolically denoting his father's omnipotence) were spewing a black smoke; now and then the smoke merged with the falling snow to form imaginary mourning veils. "Mourning," whispered Zip, and an evil foreboding gripped him in the pit of his stomach like some malicious midget dwelling inside him. Neither the night, nor the princess, nor the future occupied his thoughts now. At length he gained the manor house.

"His Grace gave up the ghost at six this morning," the footman whispered in Zip's ear while removing his snow-covered fur coat. (This last was "Joe," an old codger known for his eccentricity of speech.) (This time, however, he had gone too far.)

"Shut up, Joe!" the young heir cried, and brutally shoved aside the "quailing, wrinkled paws of the faithful servant." Zip momentarily failed to grasp the import of what he had heard, this despite his premonitions and his general clearheadedness. Small wonder: this was the first dose of bad news he had ever received in his life. Even so, it was as if some heavy ball had wrenched itself loose from his young and unruly guts. "What was I doing at six this morning? Oh, yes, that's when she was showing me that number between her legs! Oh, how perverse! While simultaneously he . . . *Simultaneously*" – he reveled at the thought, gloated over the words. The "communication" of his father's death intensified (retrospectively) the already catastrophic pleasure of some four hours ago when he had touched those insanely and inexorably beautiful and obscene legs – and all because of the element of simultaneity, not in the present but in retrospect, mentally or abstractly speaking. Oh, if only Zip could have read an article by a certain Sicilian prince and member of the neo-Mafia, a pamphlet entitled *Gli piccoli sadismi,* he would have been greatly enlightened, although, strictly speaking, no mechanopsychological theory can divest these realities of their specific character of inscrutability. Not because they have to do with the preservation of the species, but because they touch on a far more basic issue: the divisibility of Existence among a plurality of individuals, each of which conceives of itself as a unique self, defined once and for all as this one and no other, despite the theoretical arbitrariness of being anybody at all. From this combination of what is given semiarbitrarily and the random nature of its development arises a situation in which these particular beings must address themselves as "I" (though, in the case of an infusorian, only potentially so). And even if a thousand William Jameses were to hang themselves on their own brains, the problem would remain unresolved, and a denial of the immediately given cohesion of the personality invariably results in a very ingenious, but for all that superficial and artificial, conceptual construct that does nothing to elucidate the heart of the matter. Enough.

Genezip moved mechanically through the empty rooms until at last he encountered his mother. She looked composed. Fifteen years ago she would have privately rejoiced at her husband's death. For she had been a woman locked up, immured in his principles and his brutality like a living person in a tomb. Despite these conjugal horrors, she pitied him now; having overcome life's centrifugal drive, she had resigned herself to her fate long ago and, for a second time (though differently), fallen for that jovial brewer many years her senior. But death had come prematurely, leaving her defenseless in the face of life and loneliness. It lay upon her fragile, quasi-mystical little head the awesome burden of responsibility for this adorable strapper who (it was plain to see) was fairly bursting with an insatiable appetite for a life not, in her present condition, within her ken. Zip was all she had; her duty to protect, combined with a certain maternal attachment, engendered in her a force that elevated the object of that attachment far above herself, to the point of fashioning a protective power out of him. She folded him in her arms, and for the first time since the calamity wept, unrestrainedly, from the bottom of her intestines, hitherto a rock of frozen tears. Until now (since six o'clock) she had shed only dry tears, with short, intermittent sobs. Genezip also felt the urge to cry, but the tears would not come; he was as dry as sawdust, cold, indifferent. The bottom of his soul felt chapped; he had been in a mood for relaxation when, hello, along had come a new mess, a new batch of problems. He was still impervious to his misfortune, or perhaps in his case it was no misfortune at all. Besides the obligatory "painful anticipation," a tiny, mischievous flame of wild satisfaction was prancing about in the most extreme layers of his still-inviolable ego. Something had been liberated down there, something had finally *happened*. From the moment he learned of his father's death, life had suddenly embraced wholly new and fantastic surprises. Already he was feeling jaded (and in his jadedness missed out on the real action), this despite his erotic screwups and his newly acquired, but somewhat blasé, syndrome: "Did he love the princess, or was it merely lust?" The problem was modeled on a subconscious *Mutterproblem:* Did he love his mother for her own sake, or was he just egoistically attached to her? He awoke for the umpteenth time. But now life was really stampeding into the stagnant mire of his soul like a herd of horses into a pond. The last mask was shed: he would have to deal with it. But on the surface, behind a façade of obligatory distress, he was truly delighted that his father had "given up the ghost." (In one of those youthful transpositions he recalled how much he had envied, as a child, classmates in mourning for their parents, as well as the special, almost painful subsexual urge aroused by their sisters in black – a kind of morbid perversion combined with a subconscious desire for emancipation, manhood, the mastering of one's destiny.) The future was acquiring a mysterious charm. The taste of life, sharp and heady like that of some narcotic herb, coursed through his veins like some tingling, titillating wave. He delighted in the fact that he was a man, that he was having an affair with a "real woman" – to hell with the bogus ones: his mother, his sister, Miss Ela, etc. . . . He was the head of the family now, he, that same Zip who was once bullied by everyone. Toward his mother he felt something special, now that he had reached the other side of sonship: from milksop to family sovereign and protector. Swelling with a superiority that even he found comical, he embraced his mother, and, locked in each other's arms (with a peculiarly sweet pride he noted that his mother nestled against him differently), they moved toward the bedroom where the corpse of their father-in-common (this, indeed, was how Mrs. Kapen had come of late to regard her husband) was lying in state. His mother was now like an older sister and as such he loved her all the more poignantly. What happiness! He was brimming over with himself; it was by far the happiest moment of his life, something he had never dreamed possible before. He dissolved completely in a spiritual opulence such as he had never known and sprawled himself out in the world as if it were an armchair. At last he felt like somebody.

Coming to greet them was the fifteen-year-old Lilian, a lovely little blonde with the slightly upturned nose of the Kapens and her mother's enormous, dark-set eyes – which, at the moment, appeared small, red, and puffed from weeping. She alone had sincerely loved the old patriarch. In her eyes he had always been a good man, a kind of Saint Nicholas. Zip put his free arm around her, and thus did the three of them approach the body. The two women immediately began sobbing, while Zip radiated a morbid outer confidence stemming not from real power or solidity of the ego but from the accidental collision of two mutually antagonistic forces of weakness; it was the net result of contradictions, even though it gave the appearance of being a genuine fortitude enabling his body to move forward obediently like a broken-in horse. The entire scene was a farce from beginning to end, not worth noting, though neither Zip nor the two women saw anything farcical in it. For all three this interval of time possessed an almost otherworldly significance. Abruptly, and for some unknown reason horror-stricken, with a certain false solemnity in their movements, they entered the room where, on a makeshift arrangement serving as a household catafalque, Mr. Kapen's freshly washed and fully dressed remains were lying. Genezip was never so acutely aware of his father's omnipotence as now. The hands of the corpse had been bound together with strips of cloth, while a kerchief kept the lower jaw from drooping. He looked the part of some monstrous titan, bound up by those who feared him posthumously. A hidden power seemed to lurk in those chops clamped shut by the kerchief, a power capable of grinding chunks of granite or porphyry into powder with its soft teeth. Suddenly an awful, violent grief wrenched Genezip's insides. As if telepathically divining his state, Zip's mother and sister fell to their knees with a groan beside the kneeling Ela. Genezip was paralyzed by some incomprehensible and un-en-dur-able pain. His friend had taken leave of him; now when he might have gotten to know and respect him. Why had he ignored his father's friendship? He realized now the high degree of discretion and wisdom his father had exercised in not imposing his friendship on him. Mutual distance was preferable to a father-son relationship distorted by false perspectives. It was up to the son to take the initiative. Why had he not done so? A relationship with a friend, if it becomes skewed for whatever reason, can always be broken off; with one's father, it's harder. Hence his father's discretion in revealing anything about himself. Hints to this effect had been given on that grim morning, but Genezip had not been attuned, thus squandering the final moment before his death. Too late. And now his father would get even for having had his friendship spurned and become a tyrant beyond the grave – of that he was certain, this profligate of a son. Why was it so that no pleasure lasted longer than five to ten minutes?! Suddenly he was reminded of his bout with the princess. That had lasted longer, of course. But how it pained him to recall it now! He wagered he would never know such pleasure again; he was even ready to make such a vow to atone for the wrongs he had inflicted on his father. But he was prevented from doing so by a parade of other "psychic states."

He felt disgustingly alone now, as if he were wandering aimlessly about on a cold and rainy night in a suspicious suburban district, with no place to "lay his head," among a crowd of foul, aloof, and hostile strangers. Thus did he view the world and, except for his immediate family (though not excluding the princess, Prince Basil, or Tenzer), all its inhabitants. (His schoolmates = a pulpy mass showing not a single face, except perhaps for those "forbidden ones" whom he had never really gotten to know.) Suddenly he fell to his knees and broke out in a spasmodic, visceral, childish weeping; he was embarrassed but went on howling anyway, which was also a form of penance. His mother gazed at him in astonishment (what self-control he had shown until then!), and even Lilian sensed that inside this uncomplicated giant of a brother, the brother she knew so well and soon to be a brewer like daddy (oh, how she adored that mustached old walrus whose nature had always bordered on the mysterious where she was concerned), there lurked a complete and enigmatic stranger. And for a brief moment, in the still inarticulate, grimy, slushy, sordid, female recesses of her subconscious innards (located somewhere between her heart and her pudendum), the thought flashed through her mind that perhaps she, too, was harboring someone inside her, an absolute stranger. Someone else *must* have been instrumental in liberating in her that other, more primal "she": on her own she was incapable of it. But how had it been accomplished? She was ignorant about sexual relations. A pyramid of marvels as hard as reinforced concrete shot up into another dimension and then immediately crashed down to the floor of this gloomy room like a broken paper toy. Lilian now began to love her brother, though in a different, somehow funny way, from a distance, from beyond the impassable border of gigantic, unassailable mountains. It was all so incredibly sad that she broke into tears again (these tears were *different*, too, not the "postpaternal" variety; by and large, they were more agreeable) like an engine shifting into high gear. In Madame Kapen, meanwhile, under the sway of Zip's protective embrace, curious changes were taking place at an alarming rate – though *whom* they alarmed was not quite clear. She wept now – three minutes after that hug – in the serene contentment of having been liberated, profoundly grateful to him, her husband, for having departed when he did. So grateful was she that she almost wished he were still alive, though, alas, this wish contained an in-sur-mount-able contradiction. A new life was unfolding, a really new life, not the sort she had perpetually begun inside the old. Each of them had somehow profited from the death of that wise old patriarch, to say nothing of how they would profit from his estate. And they loved him more than ever now, each in proportion to his or her previous coefficient.

....

INFORMATION: Then they suffered a frightful blow . . . though for Zip perhaps it was really for the better, since it may have hastened his . . . But more about that later. After the burial, which went off in a decidedly routine way ("Conventional things should be left to that special breed of writers known as 'kitsch artists,' for how else can the poor bastards earn a living? Some even say it's not the theme but its execution that counts – which is hardly true for the novel. That's why today we have such an army of brilliant stylists with nothing to say, because ignorance and stupidity breeds that sort . . . ," to quote Sturfan Abnol) – and so after the burial, when the will was "unexpectedly" opened, it turned out that Kapen senior had converted his factory into a workers' co-op and had left all his capital to the moribund Polish Socialist Party (to be spent on propaganda) and not a dime to the Syndicate for National Salvation, of which he was a member. The family received a modest annuity, enough to prevent death from starvation. All attempts to contest the will were nipped in the bud by the unerring and irrevocable decision of Professor Bekhmetev, to the effect that the old man had been sane and in full possession of his faculties at the time of death and that only his motor centers had been affected by sclerosis. Wild days followed. Zip's mother went crazy with despair: her new life had been dealt a powerful blow from beyond the grave. Lilian, that comely, sweet-natured, Pre-Raphaelite Lilian, her father's pet, began to despise the "dad" she had once worshipped, so much so that even Genezip, now elevated to the "someone" special in her life, could not convince her that it was unbecoming, even *indecent*, to reproach the dead in this way. She matured so rapidly that they found themselves addressing her as an adult and soliciting her views. Genezip spent those extraordinary days and nights in the most daring excursions into the realm of life's forbidden knowledge. Despite a growing sense of life's external consistency, he was becoming more visibly split from the bottom up. He had mastered his ambivalent feelings toward his mother, his sister, the princess, and The Greatly Departed, who was assuming in his mind the stature of a ubiquitous, supermundane power: he, the father, became identified with that "not-quite-digested" God of childhood. Genezip did his best not to repress such thoughts, which kept circling around "the night of his life's turning point" until, subsiding by themselves, they lighted on those familiar and boring hills of reality like a flock of ravens during a spring sunset. Little by little this man, hitherto essentially more child than man, was turning into a pure spectator: his "Genezip" was as an actor on the stage – a sweet feeling, if not for the certainty of the play's finale. And yet the need for a decision pressed itself on him with growing urgency. Wasn't he the head of the family, responsible for its welfare? But responsible to whom? To his deceased father? Wherever he turned, everywhere his father's ghost . . . secretly commanding . . . Which of the two persons wrestling inside Zip would decide the outcome? That was the question. One of these was the *tout court* metaphysical, life-thirsty brute that, having tasted from the first waterhole, wanted to go on guzzling (there was something bottomless about everything in those days); the other was that well-behaved youngster eager to consciously, painstakingly fashion, forge, and build a life for himself, but who was not quite sure how or where to begin. Those horrible nights with the princess, devoted to exploring the infinite shades of carnal pleasure and the metaphysical monstrosity of sex – and those solitary walks that left him feeling alienated from reality and unfailingly (though to no effect) brought him back to that crucial day (Oh, if only he could have turned back the wheels of time, only once . . . and spliced his previous state of hyper-awareness to what he knew now! But alas, nothing in life is free, because the price of such knowledge is the debasement of childhood fancy.) – they were like two poles. He kept his internal state scrupulously concealed. People admired his maturity, the cool and evenhanded judgment he displayed in the matter of his father's will. (His papa had known all along that Zip would never make it as a brewer, but that he could not dispose of the brewery on his own; sensing a foul compromise in the making, he had decided that *this much* he could do for his beloved son.) The plant was snatched up before his very eyes by some suspicious-looking gents arrived from the capital. The family of the deceased, having no further business there, was forced to vacate its melancholic perch, where it might have maintained its power surrounded by wealth, but in poverty, never. There were no alternatives.

Tenzer stayed clear of Genezip altogether. On several occasions he closed his door to him, and once, having bumped into him, he declared himself to be in "a state of inspiration" and bade him a brusque, almost curt farewell. It had taken place on a cloudy, windy, springlike afternoon. The image of that omniscient, musically surfeited hunchback receding into the distance, against the backdrop of a windswept landscape, made a somber impression on Zip: it was as though some better part of himself (something indivisible, despite all his dabbling in perversity) were taking leave of him forever in the form of that hairy, creatively robust, otherworldly little freak. The last "refuge" left this sorry dualist was the princess, to whom, regardless of his tremendous progress in the realm of pure erotology, he had become attached as to a second mother. Meanwhile, however, the first symptoms – negligible, to be sure, and fleeting – of a certain erotic, almost subconscious contempt had become apparent. Of course Irina Vsevolodovna spotted these symptoms at once, and they pained her, sent her into a fury of insurmountable contradictions: genuine affection struggling with the demon of spent youth on the ruins of that precious little body. Zip's deepening involvement with the princess was helped along by the revelation within his own family of certain character traits – traits personally repugnant to him – arising from the loss of the estate and the death of his father. She at least was free of any materialistic *mesquinerie* – there was even a touch of grandeur about her, like the breath of the Mongolian steppe, whence her ancestors, the descendants of Genghis Khan, had come.

All seemed to be taking place not on this earth but far away, beyond some mysterious partition that existed not in external reality but in himself. It was not he who was involved in all this. Bewildered, he would ask himself: "Can *this* be me, is this *my* life unfolding? Oh, why out of a billion possibilities *this* way and not some other way? Oh, God!" He was thrown into a bottomless cavern, a subterranean prison presided over by the desiccating, eternal, and suffocating pain of "so-ness" (and not "other-ness"). And there was no exit. "Life's an open wound that can be filled only with sex" was the message he kept hearing from that witch who, with words lethal as caresses and with caresses more lethal than the most sinful words, was amassing in him a punishing carnal knowledge of the world's monstrosity through a lust ever hungering and never satisfied. He had only one favor to ask: let him find out what a beast he was, then let him die like one. A jolly ideal! So much for the usefulness of mind and guts. But for some it is precisely the simple route by which they try to escape their own complexity that in the end turns out to be a sealed labyrinth in the alien desert of life. The world was reduced to a tiny prison-scrap that might as easily have been infinity (space as a form of limitation! wasn't this squirt hankering for too much freedom?), while internally something was distending – something nameless, momentous, *immutable* (the stony visage of a "livid corpse," the kind from dreams), as fatal as the trajectory of a bullet, as systematic in its unswerving functions as a rotary machine. Zip sensed that he was being shaped, crystallized in some fixed order, that henceforth everything (even his wildest behavior) would turn out to be a function of his present attitude, not exactly willed by him, toward life. It was not an attitude he could have defined rationally, though he could sense it in his response to passing clouds, in the taste of certain fruits – in those terrifying spells of heart-rending ambivalence when the princess became split into a wild voluptuary and a pseudomother.

The princess was also struggling, and this in a way that corresponded exactly to the mental states of her lover (or, "lover-boy," "stinker," etc.). At first she had let herself be guided by her "maternal instincts" (ugh!). She taught him how to enjoy himself, how to elevate a trivial, titillating, and rudimentary thrill to the level of a metaphysical ache and an otherworldly gloom of final appearances beyond which there was nothing but death, the redemptrix from things too profound in essence. But Zip was charging too quickly into the future, and even though he could not see it – the precipitousness – the princess sensed it for him, in certain of his gestures and glances and in those thoughtlessly cruel asides that betrayed a jadedness and satiated lust. Scampi and the prince had warned her repeatedly of the dangers involved in this final love affair, urging her, for her own sake (as well as for his), to practice a modified demonism instead. They had grown quite fond of the little bugger, that "brewer manqué," as Genezip was called around the palace of the Ticonderogas. The princess spent many hours in thoughtful meditation before deciding on a compromise on behalf of loftier aims: she would keep Zip's feelings in their original state of strained desire and make of him a "man" (?) based on the notions prevailing in their house; i.e., a brainless cad, a social parasite equipped with a maximum number of sucking organs, an ametaphysical hedonist – in a word, a prick. She admitted to having been made miserable by an overdose of latent mysticism, and vowed to mercilessly repress such tendencies in her sons. As a pseudomammy, on the other hand, she would end up no better: an abandoned woman condemned to rot away in despair, in the purulent secretions of wounded vanity. With this marvelous little snot, her former world had come to an end – of that she was certain.

Genezip had no idea what jealousy or betrayal meant. These words were practically meaningless to him. But when he suddenly panicked at the power wielded by this shrew over his internal matter, at her emotional superiority, her experience, he would find consolation and support in the realization of the following truth: "Still, she is an old woman." (This was hitting below the belt, and not even the princess would have expected *that* from him. Generally speaking, women [even the shrewdest and most depraved among them] cannot possibly know all the intricacies of male self-defense, and certainly no upstanding member of the tribe will ever disclose them.) Genezip could rationalize her age variously, depending on whether, at any given moment, he was in a position of power or one of weakness. Or else he would tell himself: "She's really not that old, and besides she's kept herself marvelously fit" – when, after having shot his lust, he would feel a nagging discomfort (this mostly occurred in the morning while the two took their coffee in a sumptuous bed that had once served as the bridal bed of the Ticonderogas). These were not very noble thoughts, and he would rather not have had them. Unfortunately, they belonged to "the intrinsic and inescapable order of things." (Only, for God's sake, please don't go around advertising this notion, otherwise *nobody* will resist anymore.) And now, in a manner altogether clumsy and ridiculous (how odd that "*it*" had made him no bolder vis-à-vis the opposite sex – alas, he had become overspecialized), he was already making eyes at Zuzi, the princess's fetching little chambermaid. This was clearly a portent of the future, in relation to which the present events were a mere phase. He had time, but did the princess . . . ? This is how far he had come in his thinking. Oh, how can anyone not versed in such matters appreciate the horror of watching that "sexual time" slip idly away – when nothing else was worth living for! The princess perceived this more acutely than he, with all the clarity of a peyote vision, hence the fits of moaning and "mooing" to which she now became prone. She had no choice (as little as those recruits during the Russian Revolution:

either be killed at the front or fight for freedom – *tryn-trava, vsyo ravno*): she would have to go the heroic route – either keep him captive for a year or two, or lose him forever. She would have to gamble. She had no great desire to dabble in the muck of a third-rate demonism; she hated the thought of him being dragged through the mud of sexual humiliation. "So you don't want to shove your business up there, is that it? Well, you'll be sorry that you don't. It'll be always on your mind, you'll wind up polluting not only your body but your mind as well. You'll be totally obsessed with it, you and that proud little masculine mind of yours. See how much fun that will be!" Thus did poor Irina Vsevolodovna muse at times, squeezing her luscious thighs with a morbid excitement bordering on delirium. Antidotes were few and far between – it was a bad time of year in the countryside. Tenzer? He might turn him off her for good. Toldzio? Toldzio could always be counted on because of his morbid taste for older women. Oh, how tacky . . . So this was . . . Such was the outer scaffolding of vulgarity that surrounded the whole nasty affair. How shocking to peep into the behind-the-scenes technique of what's commonly known as the theater of love. Behind all the ideal marriages, lovebirds at the altar or sarcophagus, behind all the oaths of fidelity there hide dirty "rear kitchens," where saucy little devils concoct their magic against the abject poverty of existence, or whip up high-grade narcotics even more life-distorting: counterfeit virtue. Brrr . . . And hung on this scaffolding were the emotional subtleties, seemingly fragile, that in the future would weigh heavily on everything, dragging down these frazzled, poisoned-from-the-bottom-up minds into the abyss of subconscious crimes. How hideous is the dialectic of emotions, and how putrid the practices implied by it! But without it? A short circuit of sheer lunacy and death. Possible in the diluvian caves of the past, but not today. Then it might have panicked a few of the "elite," excited, stirred hideous visions of future epochs looming up from beyond the horizon of human destiny! Yet they ate, drank, pawed one another, and had fun in the meantime. Among them the most celebrated men of action, or perhaps they most of all, necessitous of a "wee" rest after the extreme tensions of daily work. But the rabble get upset if they learn some revolutionary hero has taken a mistress (although if he bullies his wife, that's okay). The fools! Don't they see that he must be allowed his fun so that he can later rollick ecstatically on the carcass of history, burrow into the future with his proboscislike brain. "Oh – *qu'est-ce qu'on ne fait pas pour une dupe polonaise!*" as old man Lebac used to say. Or, as the late Jan Lechoń once asked in private with feigned naïveté: "But what other life is there besides the sexual?"

While Zip could not decide whether to move to the city, the day "drew" closer when the future was again to be focused in its entirety – but with what a "reversal of fortune"! Like an iridescent fly buzzing about a sticky spiderweb, Zip behaved as if he hadn't a care in the world, reckless of any danger, proud of having conquered *such* (!) a man-eater. He was like a commander who, heady with the success of an easily won victory, neglects to set up night watch. More and more, himself unaware of it, the meek little kid of the past was disappearing along with the dwindling snows atop the sunny Beskid range above Ludzimierz. Then one afternoon (on one of those ghastly afternoons when the oncoming evening can only be drowned in alcohol, after which it's curtains), Genezip (despite his aversion for living off the labor of his dearly lamented workers) began, now that he was busted, to resent his father for having shafted him like this before his death (this resentment had been festering in the deep for some time). But old Kapen had loved his son deeply and knew what he was doing; acutely aware of the global instability, he had wanted to spare Zip the loss of the estate in the event of a revolution. Thus did he remove from his son's path a slew of dangers most foul and save him from a paralyzing social embitterment. Besides, there were no more banks (anywhere in the world? amazing!) for depositing reserve capital. Except in Russia perhaps. But deep down Kapen senior had believed in the indestructible might of the Chinese Wall; and while he may have miscalculated as to the time (despite the latest news reports), his intuition had proved basically sound. Although ignorant – like everyone else – of Kotzmolochowicz's precise plan, he alone sensed that inside the swarthy skull of that crazy man lay the whole crux of the present situation, both for us and for the world. Just before he died (at precisely the moment his stud of a son was trying desperately to lose his virginity) he had composed, with his paralyzed paw, a letter to the quartermaster commending his son to him.

> . . . an adjutant's post in your regiment. When the pot boils over I would like Zip to be in the thick of things. Death is really not that bad. Being far away from great events is worse, especially if they happen to be the end. Zip's a brave boy. I made him sit up, for that I run the risk of being despised later on. He's the only "thing" (I don't believe in the personality as preached by the Americans – and what good are these new religions, except for keeping the numskulls in harness), the only thing, I repeat, I have ever loved – except for beer, of course. Alas, your former flame, my wife, could never satisfy me spiritually, despite the difference in our ages. Don't feel bad about it and don't hold it against me. Zip might well be your son.

(The old man knew that only Kotzmolochowicz could have been at the center of that pot [if he wasn't, nobody was] and that a blind rapprochement with the Chinese would have been a disgrace.)

> If no one can be found to represent us, even in this loused-up affair, we'll wind up as cattle unworthy even of communist aparatchniks. You're the only one – I tell it to you straight, because I'm a goner, if not today, then tomorrow. You sure knew how to keep yourself a mystery, even for me.

(Kotzmolochowicz burst out in a wild fit of laughter. Old Kapen was a rotten gunnysack, and the sooner he was dumped overboard the better. Still, he was quite fond of him, and while reading this garbled mess he tied a mental bow in his brain not to forget Zip.)

> You know how to bear the horrible strain of loneliness. Praise and glory be to you for that, Erasmus, but triple woe to your country, because there's never any telling what you'll do next – you and that gang of the most contemptible bastards that ever walked the face of the earth. You damned next-moment man. Farewell. Your old pal, Zip.

 Thus did Kapen write to his friend "Rasmus Moloch," ex-stableboy of the Counts Chraposkrzecki, whose coat of arms bore a frog's spawn (skrzek) and a horse's nostrils (chrap). This coat of arms was emblematic of the quartermaster's whole career, for, having been hatched from the anonymous spawn of society's "bafonites," he had gone on to become a somebody – certainly not your run-of-the-mill! – thanks to horses (and their nostrils, of course). And yet it terrified "old Zip" to see his country reach a state when it might have to depend on a single man as on a slab of mediocrity. What if the leader came down with scarlet fever or an attack of appendicitis? What then? Before Kotzmolochowicz there had been Piłsudski, and then it was precisely this ballast of mediocrity that had saved the day. And now they were counting on it happening again. People have never learned how to draw lessons from history, preferring to play the game of analogy instead, just like those Russian patriots who, equating the revolution of 1917 with the Great French Revolution, pinned all their hopes on the warlike instincts of the masses. A woeful lack of leadership and not knowing how to use those who were only "tenuously" well placed – this was Poland's great forte in those days. The country's fury of organization was a farce; things held together because "we were a nobody," as a certain gentleman was heard to quip afterward (after what, though, what?). Instead of "in anarchy lies Poland's strength," people now said it lay in its "lack of leadership," while others claimed Poland had been laid to rest, that it was laying it on a bit thick, and that it couldn't have laid a soul (!) (obvious borrowings from the Russian). Still others argued that under different conditions even Kotzmolochowicz would have turned out to be a nobody, a zero. But compared to that grey mass of cocktail-lounge, coffee-house, boudoir, Pullman, cabinet-level, cathouse, automobile and airplane men of action, Kotzmolochowicz had assumed the proportions of a star of the first magnitude, a mammoth diamond on the putrid trash heap of the personality. And perhaps he actually was a great man, not so much in comparison to his own social peers, but great in relation to that whole fuck-up of a world that was so bent on impressing us – us Poles! What nerve! And even though Kapen had hinted at some ideas of his own (the idea of introducing a genuinely fascist regime, among others), the quartermaster kept silent as a dead mackerel and went on biding his time. He knew how to wait, dammit! Therein lay much of his strength. For he had perfected the knack of withholding his opinion in what seemed like the most candid conversations. At the proper time he intended to use, for himself and for his own aims (which were as much a mystery to him as to anyone else), that whole pseudo-organization set up by the Syndicate for National Salvation. He was already dreaming of some fantastic sortie against those yellow conquerors, using for this the drab, crystallized mass of his mechanized army – he, K., the only great military strategist around (he used to laugh up his sleeve at the Chinese and their new techniques, all the while publicly acknowledging them as a threat in order not to tarnish his own prestige), a clod-becomegent, without parallel since the Egyptians (for when in the history of the world has there ever been an event like this or a man like him: "a mysterious man in a mysterious place"), a lowly quartermaster general. But deep in his soul (a dog let off his leash), there always drowsed The Unexpected, something so infernal that he was wary of contemplating it even in those moments of tortuous and sweeping clairvoyance when he felt as if he were shitting into the very navel of the cosmos. He was riddling the future with his lurid and sinister thoughts the way a shore battery might pepper a battleship with high-caliber shells. But the depths of his own fate he never plumbed. Fascism or bolshevism, and "Was he a phony or a crank?" were the quartermaster's most pressing dilemmas. The "quartergen" was confronted by the immediately given and it greatly surpassed his ability to analyze it, though no one but he was aware of this: he had, in addition, the reputation of being an avatar of self-awareness. If the country as a whole – suddenly, as a collectivity – could have seen him now, it might have shivered in horror and cast him off like a hideous polyp into the bowels of Hell, where most likely other captains of humanity were roasting. If he could have seen his own reputation integrated into some infernal, infinitesimal calculus – ha, then he might have come tumbling down from his somewhat lathered-up "steed" of unpredictability into the most prosaic rut of a lackluster noncom. Fortunately, darkness reigned, and this darkness only served to nourish an unconscious, internal monster, one that lay in ambush until . . . until . . .

zap! curtains, because life would definitely pale after it, The Feat. Occasionally he dreamt of some superbattle and about something the likes of which the world has never seen. He never bothered with the social details – unlike military details, of which his head was crammed like a can of sardines – and looked after his personal charm vo chtoby ni stalo. Meanwhile, his legend grew, though he knew how to keep it in hand (and in obscurity as well). A legend brought to a head too early, or one that is overly explicit, is a real ball and chain for a statesman with a future. He will be plagued by that which plagues the successful artist: how to keep from straying from the line by which that success was achieved? And he will begin to reproduce himself in ever paler copies, stop being a trailblazer, surrender freedom and inspiration, and generally peter out – unless he's a real titan. Oh, then it's a completely different story. Everybody knew that in the worst case Kotzmolochowicz would "show his stuff," but except for reorganizing the army and staging some minor strategic maneuvers, no one knew what. His only reaction to the letter from Kapen was to have an induction notice sent to Genezip ordering him to enroll in the officer's academy in the district capital of C. – otherwise, he put it out of his mind.

The draft notice arrived on the very same day the princess had set aside for a rehearsal – but after Zip had already vacated the main house (his father's will had left them three rooms in the annex). The baroness and her first lover (yes, indeed – installed not five days after the funeral), one of two state-appointed plant supervisors, Michalski (Joseph), were sitting in her (the baroness's) comfy, immaculately clean, whitewashed little room, snuggled up like a "couple of lovebirds," when the mailman, grey, "covered with snow from head to toe," respectfully laid before them the important document whose envelope was stamped: "Executive Office of the Quartermaster General." That seal was enough to strike fear in the hearts of the greatest dignitaries – how much greater then was Michalski's fear! He came down with the shakes and had to excuse himself momentarily. The baroness sobbed freely, generously. Fate's paw had touched her: Zip, an officer at the side of her former admirer (she had turned him down when he was still a young cornet in the dragoons; she was barely fifteen at the time), Kotzmoloukhowitch le Grand, as Lebac used to say while privately grinning to himself. The document "provided" that on graduating from the cadets Zip would train as an adjutant, after which he would be assigned to the quartermaster's personal staff as an aide-de-camp à la suite. He was to report to the capital of C. in three days. Military induction also brought with it a family allowance, and Madame Kapen, who did not fret when it came to the physical dangers facing her son (if not those dangers bred by the war, then those in the form of a knee in the groin from the commander in chief, which, if rumors circulated by the syndicate were to be believed, was how one of Kotzmolochowicz's former adjutants, the young Count Koniecpolski, was said to have died), was inordinately pleased. With redoubled fury she surrendered on the spot to Michalski, who, as a widower of many years and as a stranger to the world of grandes dames, went wild in Ludzimierz. His masculine powers, enhanced by the sudden gratification of long-repressed snobbish impulses, reached alarming proportions. She, on the other hand, enjoyed a second adolescence, and gradually forgot her material misfortune and the problem of her children. She fantasized at times about creeping into some corner, about burrowing under the bedcovers, even with him and even if it wasn't "quite," well, you know . . . Only now did she realize the full horror of her marital ordeal. How lucky not to have realized it earlier – lucky, indeed! It was as if she had just left some cold, unfurnished room she had occupied for the past fifteen years (ever since Lilian's birth) for a warm eiderdown bed teeming with still warmer, virile embraces. For Michalski, despite his forty-three years and his somewhat bug-eyed look, was built like a bull, au moral et au physique, as he liked to characterize himself – a fair-haired, slightly megalosplanchnic bull. They went about it in such secrecy that nobody (not even Lilian) suspected anything. And theirs was a relationship in the fullest sense of the word, the sort found in tiresomely "risqué" French books. The similarity of their situations created, over and above their liberated senses, something on the order of real mutual understanding. Michalski was physically chaste (he even had a tub), and apart from a few imperfections in his social behavior (a trifle too jovial and exuberant), in his table manners (he had a habit of laying down his cutlery incorrectly after every meal), in his manner of dress (yellow shoes in combination with a black suit), which Madam Kapen would correct with her innate sense of tact, he was beyond reproach, except for the fact that he was . . . Michalski. But even this annoying dissonance was being rapidly effaced in the baroness's life-hungry soul, which made her ancestors turn over in their graves somewhere in eastern Galicia. But what did she care? She had LIFE, and "they were living together": how comforted she was by this thought! These were the times.

Demonism

It was March. Alarmed by the approaching storm of events, the February guests had scattered in all directions. Only Toldzio, that brooding demon of poor Genezip's sexual transformations, chose to remain. And now he had been appointed by fate to act as that chemical reagent "by which ye shall know all things," or something like that. At the moment he was on sick leave after suffering a severe attack of neurasthenia (psychasthenia?) from working in the Foreign Office, which had sucked his brain like an invisible cuttlefish. Unsuccessful in getting the princess to resume a life of sporadic pleasures, he was staying in a *Kurhaus* and was a frequent guest at the palace of the Ticonderogas. The fact that Zip was seriously in love with her excited him in a very special way – a regular little rotter, Toldzio was (he had plenty of company). Let's face it: those "subconscious layers," those cute little engines generating multiple unpleasantries, the sum of which form the backdrop of a given person's behavior, are a shitty business. Fortunately, ignorance reigned supreme here, despite all the fuss over Freudianism; otherwise, the result would have been a mass puking in general self-disgust. That's how Sturfan Abnol thought at times, though he made a point never to write about such matters.

Having been invited to the princess's for supper, Genezip cut through the woods in his large hobnailed boots, carrying under his arm a pair of patent leather shoes and tuxedo pants that were to be pressed at the princess's. That morning he had received a letter from Irina Vsevolodovna which had briefly thrown him off balance; he had almost had time to recover by now. The poor fellow had no idea what awaited him. The letter "ran" as follows:

Dearest Zip,
For some reason I feel so depressed today. Right now I would like you completely inside me. But *completely*, do you understand . . . ? If only you were small enough to fit inside me and could swell until I popped my innards. Ridiculous, isn't it? Please don't make fun of me. You'll never understand (neither you nor anyone else) what awful things women feel, and especially a woman like me, and especially when – [the next word had been crossed out]. Even if I'm a bad woman you should love me anyway, because I have a better idea what life's all about. [Genezip was somewhat moved by these last words, and vowed never to hurt her feelings, no matter what.] And that's not all. *Then* I would like for you to become as big and strong as you know what when I appeal to you, as the he-man you'll turn out to be someday, though maybe not for me – and for you to stuff me, asphyxiate me with yourself. [Reading these words, Zip experienced an odd internal illumination; again he beheld in himself some vast and limitless horizon, its throat full of insatiableness, gagging on a panorama of the-devil-only-knew-what, anonymous crime-things psychophysical-

ly inscrutable in essence, whose *optical* equivalent might have been weird and imponderable monster-things of the sort that appear in peyote visions. As in that *criminal* afternoon dream of his, a metaphysically far-off world flashed by against a still more far-off and spaceless expanse, then all sank headlong into the mysterious depths where huge, grotesque motors or turbines were ceaselessly at work, propelling the real future into channels never before seen by ordinary reason.] Be *good* for me today [she added, choosing precisely these words and no others, the miserable swine, having already planned her next move down to the smallest detail], and forgive me if I seem a little on edge. My whole past is bothering me today. "Sins are a drag," as Basil once said. I leave you with a kiss, you know how . . . I would like so much for you to be really *mine.*

Your ever-faithful I.

P.S. I'll have some of your favorite cheese dumplings waiting for you.

This postscript had moved him most of all. Then came the usual division into pure feelings and sensual feelings, though "the latter" paled beside the former. The poor beggar simply had no idea what lay in store for him. He fancied himself, in this his jaded phase, a superblasé rake, even caught himself contemplating the red hair and the tiny, rodentlike, obscenely blue eyes of the princess's chambermaid Zuzi without ceasing for a moment to feel for Irina Vsevolodovna. A delightful, late March afternoon lingered over the Tatra Highlands as though trying to prolong itself, to feast on itself, to slake the longing of all creatures on earth for another, immutable, unheard-of life. And it was precisely this passing quality that lent it such priceless value. The snowcapped mountains, visible through the reddish trunks of the pine trees in the clearings, bathing in warm meltwater, cast a rose glow over the cobalt-blue banks of the spruce stands in the distance. In the foothills, the land was laced with snow patches that lay in the hollows, beside the balks, and along the timberlines. Spring was everywhere. One could feel its breath gaining by the moment: in the indescribable fragrance of scorching hot soil; in the hot, musty effluvium of last year's dry rot coming off the bogs; in the fungous odor of the damp forest floors; in the hot blasts pouring down from the conifers that were shot with a pungent, ether smell. It was as if some material force was grabbing hold of its muscles, tendons, innards, and nerves, and relaxing its bodily ligaments grown stiff in the winter paralysis. To say nothing of how "relaxed" Zip had become during the winter! Suddenly, while walking across a sunlit clearing, he was thrust into a very specific springtime despair, the sort once known as "*Weltschmerz*" and which the French, being strangers to the word "longing," have diluted into some kind of *mal de je ne sais quoi*. This sense of despair was actually a baser, more animal, and vulgar form of what was essentially a metaphysical terror, one of those moments when we confront ourselves and the world without the intrusion of mundane habits involving things and appearances appropriately labeled and packaged in the banality of mundane associations. His earlier awakening did not recur with the same intensity: only the memory of it glowed still, slightly altering the contours of the normal process of duration and softening the sharp outlines of known complexes. Its derivative was that brutelike "veltshmertz," a subconscious, sexual, ludicrous, and quasi-profound sadness, a state the Russians render in a way that is absolutely unrepeatable: *vsekh ne pro* . . . "Oh, if only one could rise above that *fond de feminité, impersonelle et permanente* . . . the breakdown into *this and no other* woman or girl – into that *other*, which also had a claim to humanity; above the necessity of having to shit all over another ego by fucking the body appended to it – altogether one hell of a fix, eh?" Such were his thoughts, this lad precociously come of age but still ignorant of the meaning of love, having come to know its surrogate form in the worst, almost posthumous version deformed by a disproportion in age and an incongruity of epochs. ("A slightly aged demoniacal woman is fine for a young chap, so long as he's already made love to young virgins and has a certain, even rudimentary, erotic experience – otherwise he can go crackers," to quote Sturfan Abnol.) A morbid, protracted, sapping desire took possession of him now, not so much for the princess as for that whole contraption of stupefying lust that she alone knew how to set in motion, innocently somehow, imperceptibly, and yet prescient of the most secret, most abominable, soi-disant "mental" states of men, of that which "one does not talk about" (one doesn't talk about women either, though with them the drive is a lot more simple). What a shame that this will all be gone in two or three hundred years. Matters like these belong to those shocking phenomena – "epiphenomena" – the description of which is thought to be more scandalous than the thing itself, more scandalous even than the most graphic accounts of genital contact. Exposing those states is more wicked than exposing the body in the lewdest poses. Not even Sturfan Abnol, our boldest contemporary novelist, disdainful of the literary public and of political factions eager to enlist the services of certain stylistic geniuses for promoting certain ideas – not even he was willing to broach the subject. That beast the princess had a gift for sexual banter; it could eviscerate the most potent male, to say nothing of a Zip Kapen. The knowledge that she was fully conscious of her conduct down to the last detail augmented the charm of these things incalculably. The pleasure increased in proportion to the perversity. Without the certainty that the torture was being inflicted by a henchman well disposed to such work and who understood perfectly the ties linking the patient's psyche to his behavior, the pain would have been nil. Compared to a single twitch of deliberate cruelty, when it comes to the dose of suffering that can be endured, the cruelest instrument of torture is the epitome of mildness. Then, like the fusion that occurs at the farthest reaches of a spherical infinity (as represented in the popular version of Einstein's theory), sexual depravity merges with the cruel instincts of preservation to form a hideously perverse rationale for the existence of the personality. Discouraged by the conversation in Prince Basil's "retreat," Genezip had yet to arrive at the first tier "in the commonplace lesson of Kantian pseudocomplications." "For those dopes stuffed full of a cheap materialism, metaphysics is something dry and boring, even *arbitrary!* The numskulls! This isn't theosophy, it can't be acquired *ready-made,* without any brainwork. As for the 'behaviorists' and those American pseudoprudes: metaphysics and the positing of a self as something immediately given make them so nervous they demur something awful. Shouldn't we just ban metaphysics outright when a guy like Russell, despite a promising start, can write a book like *The Analysis of Mind?*" – to quote Sturfan Abnol. Before these vastly more sophisticated desires, the aplomb of the seasoned, all-knowing gentleman vanished, and an insufferable, springo-sexo-quasi-metaphysical unease began to quicken the muscles, sinews, ganglia, and ligaments of that "self" wandering through a forest permeated by the breath of reawakened life (*"dieser praktischen Einheit"* à la Mach, as if the notion of a "practical unity" could be arbitrarily introduced along with the concept of the herd, and then *from a composite of elements!!!* – someone had once ranted, though it was more than Zip could comprehend). There were times, especially at such melancholic moments, when his present state of penury began to pall him. There were even times, short in duration, when he hated his father. But he took comfort in the thought that "the gig was very nearly up" (to quote the doomsayers), and the future presented itself to him as a woman-sphinx luring him on with a farrago of unknown adventures. Subconsciously, in the form of images, he foresaw what his father had foreseen while composing that last letter to Kotzmolochowicz shortly before his death. With "daddy" around, he might have enjoyed his inherited wealth without compunction (whether he would have enjoyed it in fact is another question), but never on his own. The ambivalence of this brewer manqué grew more distinct with every problem. For now, however, it was no cause for alarm. It expressed itself in a boundless curiosity; it lent a certain charm to moments of further "awakening," but, alas, on increasingly lower levels of the hazy outline of the person-to-be. This future Zip, already subject to so many sublime transmutations, seemed to be converging more and more with the notion of a perfectly functioning machine. All the internal peripeteia of the adolescent were pointing in that direction. But it was *precisely this* that he took to be true, a priceless treasure, the very one he was wasting in a manner befitting adolescence. Every step had been a mistake. On the other hand, what is perfection (even in art) if not something machinelike? Today, at any rate, it is – "now and forever more," which is to say, so long as the sun's little fire continues to blaze in the galactic void. The age of individual "extravagances" is over; authentic being is achieved through madness; only through perversity whose boundaries are a primordial chaos can art in the truest sense be realized. Philosophy has surrendered; it can never return to the creeds of the past, a fact determined by its own internal law. This is obvious to all but to old-fashioned dunces . . . and to future generations who, cut off from the past, will never understand it.

The borders of existence had not yet closed on the projectile of Zip's youth that was being released in a gradual explosion. Beyond every hill, beyond every clump of trees from which escaped huge, billowy, summerlike clouds hounded by a spring wind, there seemed to lie a totally new and uncharted land where The Unnamed was about to be realized: to be realized and trapped in a motionless perfection. The fact that life itself was un-real-i-zable; that the time would come (but would it come before his death?) when beyond those hills he would distinguish only more hills and plains and, farther on, the spherical shape of a lifelong prison situated on a tiny globe in the boundless wilderness of a *spatial* and metaphysical nonsense; when those hills (oh, to hell with those hills! But is there anything quite so lovely as a hill?) would dim on the screen of infinity to become mere symbols of limitation and finality – all this the skunk did not understand. A multitude of experiences and phenomena had not yet jelled into solid, immutable, specific, well-defined, self-perpetuating, ontologically depressing complexes. "So that's how bad things are! Damn! How can I construct my life in such circumstances?" Genezip wondered, not sensing that the project must be made independent of *any* circumstances, that it must be an "invariable." But tell that to someone who thinks the world should oblige *him!* If only he could have seen the benefits of that "skunk doctrine," pluralism; if only for a second he could have settled for being a *conscious* pragmatist (everyone, starting with infusoria, is an unconscious pragmatist), he might have been the cheeriest of men. Not a chance: *mais ou là-bas!* But a person of his temperament is either pragmatic at the price of being stupid (what's the value of anything if it's unconscious?) or is conscious of everything at the expense of Love, Happiness, The Great Unknown, even (!) the Orgasm of Supreme Lust – of that which must turn to the rot and ash of boredom, while from the ashes parasite-notions ascend like a specter into the realm of metaphysics and start to feed on the Eternal Mystery, which, because of the mind's knowing, can no longer muster the energy to incarnate itself in the tiny tidbits of reality making up daily life . . . Only pure thought . . . But for that one must be ready to sacrifice the juiciness and bloodiness of life, the manifold creature comforts that numb and immobilize one, that glue to the face a mask-persona at times bearing little resemblance to that other, true, repressed self. "Only rationally and over longer periods of time can we, the average people, see (and then only seldom) the sense of existence, regardless of our life's success or failure, regardless of whether our ambition, in no matter which domain, has been satisfied or not. Only the greatest minds can grasp the necessity of their destiny and the necessity of overcoming (in life, not art) the seemingly accidental quality inherent in the course of events." But how did Zip stack up to such giants?

All the more baffling, given his present train of thought, did his fundamentally inscrutable father seem to him. For his father had possessed this sense of absolute finality. How had he come by it? Surely not from beer. He had carried the secret with him to the grave; too late now to ask, as one friend to another. Quite simply, his father belonged to the megalosplanchnic type; he had no need of any external sanction beyond himself for the robustness of his mind and body. He *was,* simply. Not treatable in fiction; at best one can characterize them *externally,* as is the current practice. For the first time in his life Zip was aware of his father's presence, not as the possible would-be companion of recent days but as one closely related in body and in spirit and yet strange and unfamiliar as only someone quite ordinary can be for someone who feels extraordinary. His father appeared before him as though alive, but soon his mother shunted into view with a look of mute supplication, her weary-from-a-life-of-frustrated-appetite face upstaging the mustached, patriarchal phiz of that cunning, self-made man, that gentleman-rube of the old school. His mother's image brought home the extent of her present transformation. He had been aware of it — and unaware of it — all along. Quickly he tried to analyze the change vis-à-vis the mother just recalled, and the thought vaguely crossed his mind: Michalski . . .

But this unformulated thought gave way to a more immediate problem: how to exploit a duality for the sake of healing the division, a problem put to him by Scampi in a conversation. On this subject his mind was a blank. At the moment the only certainty seemed to be this vast, sun-drenched Ludzimierz wilderness; these snow fields shimmering with a matte, gunmetal glare; and these pine trees describing shadowy patterns of indigo on the white land. Compared to this flawless, immaculate, perfect, self-contained beauty, the ferocious and forever insoluble maze of human contradictions was an obscene heap of litter strewn on a mountain peak, a pile of excrement on the carpet of a modest little parlor. Beyond the forest, in the spiritually dark but materially resplendent abyss of reality; beyond these mountains vibrating milky-red through the coppery pine trunks; and farther, farther even than the unexplored south and the poor earth's outer rim, lay the future, condensed in a pill of timelessness. Only in this flight into the temporal-spatial distance did the sense of everything seem to be contained – in the flight itself, not in the things encountered along the way. Oh, if only one could keep such thoughts always before one! Thinking – that's a trifle. To *feel!* But to feel one must be tough, knowingly tough, or a robust brute like Zip's father, wanting life for its own sake, not being pressured into it by doubts, vacillations, anxieties . . . "Give me a goal and I shall rise to greatness." Ha, there was a vicious circle if ever there was one! "Worse to be weak than wicked," murmured Genezip, suddenly exulting in the world. All of his present emotion was contained in that one awful word: "longing." This state was the central hoop in his former conceptual model: the ego, wrapped in a mist of metaphysical longing. ("When a woman longs for something, it's beautiful; whereas a man in such a state is ridiculous and worthy of contempt.") But how to achieve greatness when already at the trailhead he was blocked by a vamp like Princess Irina (her name alone was suggestive of urine, irrigation, a retching of the gut caused by something incredibly spicy, a wretched internal howling . . . etc. [every name lends itself to this or that interpretation, depending on the person involved]) and by such disgraceful, bestial, rotten-to-one's-psychic-marrow pleasures? Tenzer's music was there: beyond the mountains, beyond everything, beyond time itself. But even though that music was rooted in the wasted little leg and the fungus odor of its creator, it lacked reality. Genezip was starting to sense (quite erroneously, like so many other boobs) the "illusion of art" and at the same time (this time correctly) its absolute, timeless value despite the transient quality of the work itself, which is subject to *le principe de la contingence*. With its limp and listless fingers, music lusciously caressed and fondled that primordial something, the big homogeneous slop of panexistence, which lost its essential flavor when it was scavenged down to blood and bone by tooth and claw, leaving behind, in those insatiable talons, not pulsating life but the rotten, moldy, fetid refuse of ideas. Zip's love for the princess involved a similar devouring. So what if he was choking that luscious, all-wise quasi-corpse in his youthful mitts? So what if he sometimes loved her as a pseudomommy not of our galaxy? Would everything he touched elude finality, like the sexual insatiety of his onanistic past? The princess had become for him the living symbol of imponderable life; and so it was with mute despair in his heart that he went to today's rendezvous.

Still immersed in such thoughts, Zip changed clothes in the presence of the princess's footman Jegor (who, ever since the promulgation of Kapen's will, had treated Zip with a scornful sympathy, this despite generous tips from him) and entered the Ticonderogas' drawing room looking every inch the jaded, blasé "man-about-town." He behaved flippantly toward the princess and ignored the ironic gibes of Scampi, who, aware of his mother's intentions, was studying Zip as though he were an insect being skewered alive on a pin. Naturally, Tenzer was there, too, this time accompanied by his wife and children – along with Prince Basil in tails and Benz in a dinner jacket. While being sweet and gracious toward all, the princess paid no more attention to Zip than to a "hole in ether": he did not exist, however hard he tried to catch her distant and coldly indifferent glance. As if from spite she looked incredibly beautiful. Beelzebub himself, assisted by Zuzi, had lavished on her the most extravagant jewel-charms in return for a truly diabolical pledge. It was a quite a display, rare in that period. She drove the men to despair, and not only Zip. She was like a spectacular day in late autumn when the world seems to expire from a wild autoerotic love. She was having one of those days when, as she put it, "my legs and face and all the rest of me coalesce into one inscrutable synthesis of erotic attraction, a battering ram pulverizing the brains of strong and arrogant males into a gangrenous and slimy jelly of wounded sexuality." The futility of life, even a rich life, and not-to-be-vanquished female beauty were thus made manifest in a most indecent and humiliating manner. Shortly Toldzio arrived, and for some reason became the main attraction as soon as he set foot inside the door.

Afanasol, who at Basil's urging was making his first appearance at the princess's, was desperately trying with his symbols (what else did he have going for him?) to become master of a situation that was rapidly gaining mastery over him. "Symbols are one thing, the aristocracy another, by Jove!" some ironic voice said inside Benz. The fact of his Jewish origin (he was the great-great-grandson of a Jewish leaseholder or something) loomed vaguely – vague even by comparison with the mystery surrounding Kotzmolochowicz (an enigmatic man in power is always the unwitting comforter of every malcontent) and that mobile yellow wall rumbling across Russia – in the background. (Benz was impatient for the arrival of communism and with it the professorship he had been denied for engaging in some agitprop on behalf of the social dregs, quite needlessly, too: the dregs had never had it so good. He had been recruited by various unscrupulous individuals hoping to exploit his symbolmania for the purpose of "logicizing" Marxism. The experiment proved a fiasco. [Apropos, what is a fiasco, anyway?]) He was flustered because the princess, having interrupted him in the middle of a passionate and devilishly interesting critique of Wittgenstein's theory, had launched into a political tirade, trying in this manner to lay the groundwork for her pubescent lover's final undoing. Her voice resounded with triumph as though from heights unassailable, evoking ominous echoes of sexual irritation in the guts of these exasperated males. Genezip felt like an intellectual sluggard, while Toldzio's intimate manner with his, Genezip's, mistress, whose harangue he had interrupted with that typical Foreign Office arrogance of his, began to arouse in him something new: a sexual animosity. He felt an attack of sexual frenzy coming on; he was on the verge of committing an outrage. But like a hypnotic he remained stuck in his disgrace and, rocked by internal, snakelike spasms, expanded in the coils of a fury like a balloon being filled with helium. Every word she uttered stung him in a gross and indelicate manner, while his sex organs felt like a *sluggish* wound in a flaccid body gone completely limp. But he was tongue-tied: he had nothing to say. He did not recognize himself . . . And he felt strangely light. His body seemed weightless; he was sure that in another second some unknown force would dispose of him; that his mind and will would be loosed from his motor centers, continuing to function somewhere in the vicinity (in the realm of Pure Spirit, perhaps?) as if in derision of what was taking place in this carnal jungle. He was horror-struck: "No matter what I do, it won't be me who's doing it, but I'll have to answer for it all the same. Oh, life is awful, awful!" This last insight and the terror of his own unpredictability momentarily calmed his nerves. But his meditations in the forest now belonged to someone else. He could not believe the princess had once been his sexual property. She was immured by a cold wall of invincible charm. He was a mere nothing and had strayed into captivity. He was a dog on a chain, a solitary monkey in a cage, a prisoner in the hands of a sadist.

" . . . and I understand that Kotzmolochowicz," the princess said casually, criticizing with that peculiarly awesome levity of hers the most enigmatic figure in the country, possibly in the whole world, "having turned the army into slavish robots, has been trying to force the issue of whether we should join forces with our own White Guard. Or, failing that, whether we should rationalize trade with the West. Our industry is dying from a shortage of exports or something – I'm no expert in such matters, though I suspect it is as I describe. The complexities of economics are now so far beyond the power of a single brain that even the most experienced businessmen are speechless. And our economic councils by which that sphinx lets himself be guided are driving me to despair. Our country cannot boast of a single expert in anything – " (here she glanced at Zip, but with such contempt that the latter turned slightly pale) "not even in lovemaking," she added insolently, after a pause. Here and there laughter rang out. "Please don't laugh; I'm being quite serious. This drive toward isolationism is madness. Unless, of course, it's all a hoax to save an economic situation that not even a genius of compromise like Tarfinger can figure out. That's what my son Matthew believes. Literally nobody can explain our country's present prosperity. We hear of secret funds being funneled by the no less secretive syndicate, of the latter being in the service of the communist countries of the West. But not even in our age are such fantasies credible. But when someone has power," the princess said, raising her voice to a truly prophetic pitch, "and refuses to exercise it openly, then that *is* a crime! But what in blazes can you do with cryptonoodles like our statesmen? You have to be either a cryptotyrant yourself or go raving mad. That makes him tragic, I suppose," she added in a more subdued voice. "I never knew him personally; he was afraid of me and always avoided me. He was afraid I might give him more than he could handle." Her male guests sensed she may well have been speaking the truth, and they suddenly felt giddy in their sexual centers.

INFORMATION: Kotzmolochowicz would have died laughing if he had heard this last comment. But then, who knew, maybe he really was trying to fend off such an exalted destiny. No one can know without having tried it. Certain fateful encounters can yield fantastic, hitherto unknown, high explosives. The princess had once been so given to democratic impulses that she had actually dreamed of becoming this ex-stableboy's Egeria. But that numskull had refused, although he might have proclaimed himself king with her beside him – or "under him" (like a horse), as he used to say of his women. (There were two of them, but more about that later.) But nothing doing. So, failing to become a light in his nimbus after bringing it to a dazzling intensity, the princess had chosen political abstinence rather than prostrate herself before one belonging to the "lowest sort."

She went on: "I'm reminded of our Social Revolutionaries during the revolution of 1917. We Russians will never learn. Nor will you Poles. Our émigrés were so lacking in self-confidence that after their compatriots from the lower classes finally took power in Russia, there was hardly a man among them willing to rush to their aid and accept an important post. Our intellectuals lack the courage even to revive themselves; we only show courage in renouncing life and parading our wounds before the world." (Prince Basil stirred as though about to object.) "Don't bother, BASIL, I know what you're going to say. But is your neo-pseudo-Catholicism, your treacly, do-nothing virtuousness not a cowardice in disguise? A *shkurny vopros.* You'd rather be my forester than risk your flabby hide. *Des hommes d'État, des hommes d'État, voulez-vous que j'en fasse?* as General Trepanov said at the last session of the War Council, parodying Napoleon's famous statement about his reserves at Borodino . . . "

"*Des balivernes, ma chérie,*" Prince Basil interposed. "The time for social experiments is over. Only by radically changing men's souls can new values be born in a new spirit of . . . "

"Mere cant. None of you can say what the values of the future will be. It's all wishful thinking. The first Christians were as optimistic, and look at the result: crusades, the Inquisition, the Borgias, and now this Catholic revivalism of yours. The hypocritical death pangs of your decadent selves you take to be the labor pains of a magnificent – ha, ha! – future! Oh, at last I've hit on the vicious blackmail being practiced by the optimists of today. The beginning and the end can easily be confused; you need a different kind of brain to see the difference. We women know, because its all the same to us. We shall remain constant, unchangeable in our nature, long after you've been turned into drones. But how boring it will be on earth: there will be nobody left to dupe. You can't fool a machine. Unless we take power, in which case we, or approximately 20 percent of us, will keep a few pseudoartists and Don Juans around for our own amusement. The time has passed, Saint Basil said, the autocoprophagist. If all thought as he, there would be no more human culture. Epochs are measured by the work of individual genius. When this one is over, we'll take mankind in hand and . . . "

"No, Princess," Afanasol interrupted in an exceedingly loud voice, having finally rallied the courage to speak. "What you just said can be applied to your own theory as well. Women have always been domineering when great ideas were in decline. Beginnings are the work of men. You thrive on a rotting corpse, which enables you to overcome your own slavish instincts . . . "

"*Tiens, tiens,*" mumbled the princess, looking at the exalted logician through her *face-à-main* (once the custom of every female aristocrat).

"Yes, yes," Benz blurted out, frantic with envy, humiliation, and sexual frustration. (Why did the poor fellow let himself get flustered and thus risk "losing altitude" in such important spheres?) "In today's general equation we have to replace the word 'individual' with the concept of 'the mass' and then multiply it by an unknown coefficient." (As he spoke he was conscious of both his superiority and his inferiority, an insufferable contradiction.) "By the law of great numbers we can expect new values to come from the masses. They alone can defeat that 'ruthless,' disorganized, rampant capitalism eating away at mankind like a tumor twice its size, and in fact have already done so. They'll produce their own economic planners, not a pseudofascist gang of sexless, classless specialists. Besides, does it really matter how it's done? The result will be the same: spiritual death in the absolute void of the soul . . . "

The princess: Nonsense. You're just sore because you can't be on top of the masses. You'd feel princely up there. That's the reason for your whining. Mr. Lenin was no worse than his predecessor – hypothetically, of course. He was a gifted though deluded man who deluded others . . .

Benz: He was an exponent of the masses; he dealt in ideas that shape reality and not with fictions long out of fashion – except here, in this fetid hole, in this nursery of mediocrity . . .

The princess: Right now that fiction of his is going out of style in the West, too. Only the Chinese, who still lag behind in the evolutionary process, have fallen for it – to our own undoing. Anyway, I'm not in the mood for a *printsipialny razgovor.* I care only about the present. This pseudoglobal bolshevism is a toy balloon that would pop in the hands of the right people. But it might last for centuries through sheer inertia . . .

Benz: They aren't being born anymore, *chère princesse.* Not the best of climates . . .

The princess: Please, keep your distance, Mr. Benz. If a Kotzmolochowicz can turn our army into an obedient tool in the syndicate's hands, if we've demonstrated that prosperity and economic planning can easily take the place of revolutionary ideas – something not even the Italians have managed to do – and all with the help of misfits like my husband, Zifferblatowicz, and Jacek Boroedder (nearly everyone blanched; the princess's temerity in pronouncing the most horrific names in the land was well known, yet she never failed to shock her listeners), it goes to show what trash, what a lot of living fossils exist in other countries. The Australians I can understand; they were thieves to begin with, the descendants of criminals. But that's not a proof. What we need are people with courage – there are enough brains to go around.

Benz: But how do you come by such people?

The princess: You cultivate them. The future is here among us tonight. Consider poor Zip, a boy stripped of life's possibilities even before he's out of the "gate." I've taken him under my wing, but that's not enough. (Genezip blushed horribly, briefly; much as he was offended for his father's sake, he kept quiet. A humiliating paralysis had come over him, affecting even his centers of honor and masculine vanity. Meanwhile, the scrofulous Toldzio was pie-eyed with joy at the way the princess had squelched the "logical Jew." It infuriated Zip to think that it was precisely this dandy of a cousin who had initiated him in onanistic practice and practically emasculated him – infuriated him so intensely he could have butchered the bugger with glee. He was truly frothing, but, alas, only inwardly. He visualized himself as one huge mass of an almost fluid ineptitude, his hopelessly sad and beautiful eyes made bleary by his own impotence. He was inhabiting a novel world of ordinary failure, a living offense to his recent dreams. Where's your "strangeness" now? Oh, to hell with "the strange"! The banal triumph of third-rate evil powers. Only one thing left to do: spit on everything and leave. Maybe it wasn't necessary to spit; while the latter [i.e., leaving] was, well, out of the question. He had wandered imperceptibly into a trap, swordless and destitute of armor: his childhood toys were rusting away in the attic. In his present mood, overwhelmed by the princess's erudition [she was not much more knowledgeable than he in such matters – and who is, pray tell? Who?], the precious little that remained of those meditations in the forest now vanished like a gossamer spirit, and a diabolical [but truly diabolical], petulant, adolescent, and hitherto unimpeded lust snatched him up like a rag with its red-hot pincers. He had to get away, immediately, or who knew what might happen. But no. The conversation dragged on like a nightmare devised by the devil during a moment of extraordinary inspiration.)

"And who will do the cultivating?" Benz once again butted in with all the obstinacy of a true logician.

The princess: Who? We women! There's still time. My whole life has been wasted on love affairs; I'm so sick of it.

Benz: Yes, I can well imagine you are . . .

The princess: Don't interrupt! There's still time, I say. I neglected my sons for the sake of those idiots Fate sent me as lovers. I didn't raise *them* in time. But I'll show the world. I'm fed up, I tell you! I plan to set up a gigantic institution run exclusively by females. And there we'll nurture the new – even if I have to become the mistress of Kotzmolochowicz, whose manners I abhor as much as cockroaches. You don't know me yet, you swine! (She didn't realize, the poor thing, that the sinister wave of Murti Bing's irrefutable teachings was heading her way from out of the depths of the Malayan jungles; she still believed in the invincible charm of her physical paraphernalia.)

Genezip was petrified. Was this an omen of parting? Was the monster planning to *educate* him rather than sleep with him (with him!)? Oh, that would be a catastrophe! The poor sap felt his impotence so acutely that he actually believed it possible. Under her wing, eh? There followed what might be described as a "spiritual wrenching of the genitals." The wound had opened, a wound of titillating gauze, through which, riding the juices filtered through his stupefied brain, the spirit flowed down into corporeal prisons, into those torture chambers of the interior. The "blasé gentleman" suddenly deserted him, having been brought to a white-hot blaze and converted into a fetid gas by the phenomenal temperatures of sexual despair, leaving behind only a poor frazzled *blanc-bec* in a colloidal state. He turned stiff in his lounge chair, utterly transformed into an enormous, panting, but nonetheless naive lingam, and waited, waited, waited . . . Something would have to give, because what was happening now could not possibly be real. Her head seemed no larger than a pinhead, while the rest of her body – we can skip all that, because there was only *it*. (One of the compartments of Hell is surely a dismal waiting room where people are condemned to wait in the continual expectation of something they know will never come to pass.) What good here were courage, those recent illuminations in the forest, life's distant horizon in relation to this pernicious female carrion whose every word was a lie and who was wise to every bodily twitch made by her enemy the Male? He continued to stew, utterly stranded. So much for her "motherly" affections! Was this her way of making a "somebody" of him – by punishing him the way King Spirit treated his own hellish subjects? He had not the knack of redeeming his punishment, of forging from it a new kind of force: he lacked the proper machinery for that. Some obscene misfortune had taken him "unawares." He surrendered himself to annihilating thoughts, and from this self-scourging and self-profanation, from this sense of his own nullity, of his own paralysis, derived a perverse kind of pleasure – as with Toldzio in the garden of the Ludzimierz *Kurhaus*.

"Our instinct for life, our *female* instinct," the princess went on declaiming, "is still sound. Because without men around to admire, life would be a sorrow and a pity. For what could be worse than for a woman to despise the man she loves, or merely desires, without sensing his superiority over her?" (These words fell upon the gathering like a rock in a swamp. Something splashed in the private little quagmire of each. Still, the following truth emerged from all this: men had gone to the dogs, women had not. Of course, one could have pointed to various extenuating circumstances. But what was the use, it was all the same to these broads. The causes paled by comparison with the irreversible fact. Silence. Prince Basil remained absolutely motionless in his seat, his gaze turned inward. His artificially constructed faith was teetering on the brink of the most awful doubt. The "poor misguided soul," as he *endeavored* to call her, always knew how to plant her fangs in the most sensitive spot. But life still stirred, and so absolute was his faith – despite its artificiality; what was missing was a live-wire connection – that the rusty all-purpose sustaining hook in need of daily maintenance held. For some reason Benz felt his symbols and his heart "in his breeches" [as the English say]: he was beginning to develop a mad, futile, desperate, altogether rational liking for the princess. Oh, to be *a member of that class* for a mere second! What fantastic things he might have achieved, even in logic, and all so effortlessly, so casually, like Cantor on the margin of some book. To become a "brilliant" *[blestyashchy]* dilettante and not *this*, a specialist in crummy suits and run-down shoes! Toldzio was squirming in what was obviously a powerful sexual agitation. Tenzer, his whole body convulsed by an aimless and ineffectual rage, was eyeing his wife in despair: at the moment he despised her with a vengeance. He despised that "gunch," too, but in a different way. She represented for him something unattainable and at the same time something "grossly" beneath his erotic "standards." He recalled the inspired lines of Słonimski:

> What, O nature, is a litany of your charms
> Compared to the passion your dark realm arouses!

A hopeless predicament. Only one solution: to improvise some satanical piece by which to transcend the feculent swamp both in and around himself. He was waiting for his chance. But the discussion dragged on, a frustrating, boring, fruitless discussion.)

Benz: Pardon me, "*Your Highness,*" but in my opinion our country should be deprived of its own domestic policy. Geography and national temperament demand that it should be made a function of external agreements. Self-negation has fed our country's decline and lowered our culture, which no amount of prosperity can ever replace. A full stomach will never fashion those possibilities, those unprecedented possibilities so dear to our pious optimists, who, at heart, are do-nothings willing to let things happen from sheer inertia. The radioactive minerals of the human soul have to be ripped out with teeth and claws. Ideas still command a price.

The princess: Wait! That's more or less what I just got through saying. You're repeating my words in your own jargon. Though, for my taste, you have too much of the sophisticated Jew in you. It irritates me to think that, although we're both saying the same thing, our points of view are so diametrically opposed. Unconsciously, or perhaps even consciously – damned if I know; inscrutable are the secrets of the Jewish soul – your axiological vision is shot through with Jewish nationalism. I'm a rationalist in all things, you see. Individual progress I view as a function of belonging to this or that nation, itself a member of a larger family. On the other hand, because of your leveling, antinationalistic ideology, you're *au fond* a *selective* nationalist. (Benz definitely felt intellectually superior to this woman, despite her arch, patronizing manner. He decided to poke a little fun at her on the sly.)

Benz: Alas, *chère princesse*, there courses the blood of Jewish priests in my veins and I'm proud of it. Except in biblical times, the Jews have always given the world individuals; someday we'll show you what we can do as a people, and when we do, it will be on behalf of a sublime socialism, not of pseudoideas like *your* nationalism, which is to say, the instinct for self-preservation and the crass consumption of life's leftovers by social classes historically defunct and mentally bankrupt. We shall act as the universal oil in the gears and transmission of that great machine that's bound to transform mankind, elevate it to a higher level, a superior species, a superorganism. We managed it once before – the last world revolution was our doing. It's our mission; it's why we're called the chosen people. But the goyim won't praise our work for another thousand years. In the meantime: Cantor, Einstein, Minkowski, Bergson, Husserl, Trotsky, Zinoviev – that should do. And of course Marx, who started us down the true path of the elect . . .

The princess: And you, above all. Ha, ha! Oh, do be serious, Mr. Benz. In one breath you mention Bergson, the biggest *blagueur* in the history of philosophy, and Husserl, a truly inspired madman whose mistakes are worth a hundred times more than all the correct assertions of academic pseudoprudes too squeamish for introspection in psychology, even for conceding they *exist* as far as logical symbols are concerned. ("That cow isn't as stupid as I thought," Benz thought gloomily. "Ah, to construct a perfect mind-boggler of a system with her as a mistress!" Against the shimmering, iridescent backdrop of his intellectually charged love affair with the princess, his wasted life flitted by like a dirty rag buffeted by a bleak autumn wind of prosaic, ordinary doubt.) But it's not for you that I worry and weep, Mr. Benz. (Her prophetic gaze seemed to penetrate to the heart of each and every national destiny slowly fading away in the twilight of history.) When I consider our Catholic Gothic – now, an *Orthodox* Gothic, wouldn't that be marvelous! – then I'm numb with shame. This country should abound in Byzantine temples, golden, dome-shaped temples brooding in their own otherworldliness and profane splendor. Ah, now, a Poland allied with the East, not a Poland in Western frippery that ten centuries later still looks like a pair of third-rate pajamas worn as a coronation robe by the chieftain of some tribe of savages. What a people you would be! Not a trace of your obnoxious frivolity, none of that falsity, that ostensible civility masking a self-loathing and shame. Historically your biggest blunder was accepting Christianity from the West rather than from us. And how much this mistake has cost us, because instead of treating them as allies and leaders we look on the Poles as enemies – and not the noblest ones, either. When I think what a splendid type a Byzantine Pole would make, I could cry. Because I know it will never come to pass. In 1920 you could have let our bolsheviks into the country: either assimilated us or been assimilated by us – painlessly, too, not like by the Germans – and in that way redeemed yourselves historically. Now it's too late to join forces with our White Guard – such as it is. Some mysterious force always manages to drive us apart at the last moment.

Prince Basil: That force is none other than the instinct of self-preservation on the part of a nation to which I now have the honor of belonging. As the commander in chief, Trepanov, said recently: *"V kazhdom russkom samom blagorodnom cheloveke jest v glubine nemnozhko grazi i svinstva."*

The princess: Oh, you demi-Polish neo-Catholic! Not only we Russians but everyone is a swine. Once upon a time there were magnificent swine; now it's a distinction of the small and petty. I'm talking about fading, crumbling individuality, for which there's no more room even in literature. But in this swinishness there is still some gold to be extracted, smelted, and purified. Of course, the supply of gold ore is down by at least 80 percent, and another method of extraction has to be used – of the chemical variety. And there are still women around who understand that science – psychochemistry, I mean. First you break down the elements, then you resynthesize . . .

Scampi: A pity you didn't master the science earlier, Mama, because it's nothing new: it's a symptom of old age. It was also practiced in Roman times . . .

Benz: Anyway, it's too late for that – not only in Russia but globally. The Chinese will smelt that ore, but for other purposes. Too late for the Russian people, too late for the rest of the world, at least in the traditional sense of that word. Only in the West have the remnants of radical social ideas survived – but not here.

The princess: With the exception of yourselves, O oil of that universal social machine! But it's also too late for your utopia: the power of elements is finite. It wouldn't last anyway, no more than you can build a five hundred-story skyscraper out of bricks. And a social foundation of reinforced concrete seems unlikely – the bodies may hold out for a while longer, but not the brains. You can lump their bodies together into a kind of megaheap, but not even you, Mr. Benz, can create a megabrain, and especially not in an age of increasing specialization. No sooner does mankind become aware of itself as an integer than it's choked by the complex existential base out of which that self-awareness came.

Benz: I fully agree with you. But do you suppose that your pseudofascism can halt the trend toward increasing complexity? No; everything's bound to move faster – it *must,* don't you see? – because production must expand. Not every race can stand the pace. Only we, the Jews, who are oppressed but at the same time poised and tensed like a coil, are predestined to serve as the future brain and nervous system of that superorganism which is now in the making. Vested in us is the knowledge and the authority; others will be as comatose intestines laboring in the dark . . .

The princess: All the more power to you, you nationalist in disguise! The only hope is that you'll burn out – or that we'll use you for our own project. (There was a touch of insincerity, apathy in what she said.)

Benz: The sun will burn out one day, too . . . (The thought was never completed.)

The princess: You logicians are a funny people. Whenever you stray beyond your symbols you're as correct or incorrect as anyone else. But you can risk such sloppiness, because you always have in reserve that realm of absolute logic where your prudishness can be downright laughable. As soon as your backs are to the wall, you play prissies and even boast of it. That way you don't risk a thing. All the same, you're sterile.

Benz broke out in a broad and triumphant laugh. He had succeeded in making the great lady (she was that) angry. He was pleased with himself for having subdued this eighteenth-century salon. *Faute de mieux.* Genezip felt pulverized, a zero. In a last-ditch effort he tried to reorganize his ego, or rather its final soupçon, rapidly dissolving into a greasy substance. He watched as it oozed away and crept under the (still quite magnificent) feet of his lover who was bound to betray him. That much he knew, however stupid he may have been. How could she have taken him seriously? A "genuine" sophisticate like her, one who spoke so intelligently about whatever came into her head, and in the company of such brainy people. "Such a dilapidated piece, such a raunchy old macaque," his mind kept on repeating without sincerity and to no avail. The princess rose to her feet and, with a magnificent gesture, tossed back her mane of copper-red hair, as if to say, "All right, enough of this chit-chat – let's get down to business." With a young and indomitable step that could drive her sacrificial victims to despair, a step monkeylike in its agility and tigerlike in its ferocity, which was accompanied by a slight swaying of the hips and invited the most perverse and perfidious acts, the princess strode across the room and stood before a thoroughly demolished Tenzer like a statue of some omnipotent goddess from a sexual Hell. She brushed his arm lightly, absently. Putricides winced as if he had been pricked with a needle in the most sensitive spot. Straightening up, he shot a furtive glance at his wife. The bulge on his leg (the withered one), the basis of his barely tolerable existence, grew taut with a steadily mounting desire for revenge. "The fur is going to fly," he thought to himself on the sly. (Outside, a March day was expiring. The lily-white clouds that had crept out from behind the mountains in the west were now stampeding boldly over the linden and maple trees in the park. Spring's ferment, infinitely more triste in this region than the gloomiest valley autumn, was storming the windows, which seemed to buckle from the strain, and was settling on the guests in the parlor, who rose up like a wave of exotic vermin summoned by a fateful, blind decree whose fulfillment was contained in the rumbling Chinese thunder.) In the glare of the electric chandelier, the faces of the men appeared crumpled, emaciated, sepulchral. The princess alone was radiant with the nauseating power of sex, which she now flaunted in all its autumnal splendor, outdazzling with the diabolical glare of her charm the youthful, rustic beauty of Tenzer's wife. This was the crowning moment of her twilight period; the risk she was running in today's test was immensely – "down-to-the-gullet" – gratifying. She reverted to her female self – feminized herself – as the irretrievable past came back in all its sweet delectability. "All right, maestro, to your instrument," she whispered to Tenzer, who stood there teetering. His mortified wife, the country lass, mired in her hatred, quickened the princess's appetite to a frenzy. Tenzer's children were wide-eyed with fear and clutched each other by the hand.

Grudgingly Tenzer found himself sympathizing with Genezip, now suddenly grown hateful in his eyes. He had failed to humble him, and now "that woman" had humiliated *him* by wresting Zip away – because of his sorry circumstances, obviously. If only he'd had money – oh, his time would come . . . The princess's dubious superiority, the flippant way she spoke of the most intricate social questions, struck him as a cheap vaudeville. True, all this had a history, long festering and as yet vague in form; he had only to formulate it in words, to express it. The improvisations would come later; no way was he going to play on command. He poured some green liquor made from Indian hemp into a wineglass and raised it to his ugly, hirsute mug-face bursting from the pressure of his spirit, a face lost in tufts of sweat-soaked hair.

"Not now – later."

"Now!" the princess hissed in her old imperious tone. It might well have been her "lucky day," but her tone failed to produce any effect. Tenzer brutally shoved her aside, spilling some of the sticky liquid on his dress coat and on the carpet.

"You could at least pay attention, Putrice, and stop swilling like a fish," Maryna from the backwoods suddenly cried – her voice sounded strange, as though she were speaking through a thin metal tube.

"Now it's my turn to speak." He filled his glass again, emptied it in one gulp, then launched into a tirade, as long-winded as it was pointed: "Your political philosophy is a joke. Kotzmolochowicz is the only real mensch – if he ever gets a chance to show his stuff," he said, tossing in this cliché then making the rounds of the country, from slummy apartments to swanky mansions. "A joke, I say, ever since the time of the French Revolution, which unfortunately never made it this far eastward. Oh, we tried, but – nothing doing. We might have led the world, and would have if we'd been willing to slaughter one another, if there'd been a man courageous enough to get things started – in a big way, I mean. From unrealized dreams came all that messianic drivel, though it would have taken a greater messiah than France. But it didn't happen, dammit, and all because of our flunky nobility. Is there anything shittier than our Polish nobility? And there are so many of the buggers! Myself, I prefer the Jews any day; I'd rather see Poland Jewish than aristocratic."

"Bravo, Tenzer!" exclaimed Benz.

"And the Congress of Vienna was the posthumous product of the grand aristos and their screwed-up politics. The vicious democratic lie born of the French Revolution has endured to our own day. This hoax was the womb that begot wild, unbridled, cancerous capitalism, that cuttlefish which came dangerously close to devouring mankind. And now, as thanks for our not having marched against those butchers from the north, our land has become a capitalist haven. They say Kotzmolochowicz deserves credit for this, even though he was only a captain and *fought* the bolsheviks. But he'll pay for it, don't worry; I clearly foresee it. He'll have to lick the heels of those yellow monkeys and submit to a bamboo caning. If only there were still time. Meanwhile, what have we in our snack bars, restaurants, nightclubs, couloirs, and other pissoirs? The petty diversionary tactics of chess pros, having as much bearing on the future as the princess's lamentations over a Poland that's not Russian enough and a Russia that's not Polish enough. Meanwhile, the 'gangs' jockey, the 'parties' parlay, and the simpleheaded and the simplifiers feast merrily on to the end, knowing their final hour is at hand. And I ask myself: what for? But no one will give me an honest answer, because no one knows. The old argument of the 'state,' even the egalitarian/elitist/corporative kind, won't wash anymore: it's a ruse for grabbing what cannot even be *imagined* anymore. Impotence. How asinine, how egotistical, how sickening to tie oneself to the apron strings of the past."

"Wait until we're all butchered, Tenzio, then you can have your success," said Irina Vsevolodovna sarcastically.

"Well, well, look who's being familiar now! If my symphonies were being performed in some lousy salons before ignorant howling dogs, you wouldn't be talking to me that way. You, you're nothing but a cackling bitch, a Phimosa Syphillisova, a bassarid, a coelenterate freak, a priestess of the mournful fartophone," he cursed, having run out of material.

"And that's how it should be. A failed artist today is an unbearable anachronism," the princess, delighted with Tenzer's invectives, responded with unruffled calm.

"They exist so you can be a patroness of what's known as a 'neglected artist,'" Prince Basil interjected with a shade of malice that could not by any means be described as neo-Catholic.

"What's this? A concerted attack against me?" asked the princess, and she scanned the guests menacingly until her gaze lighted on her minion's head looking almost livid in the glaring light. She felt besieged, pity was beginning to tug gently at her weary heart. Oh, if the brutes only knew how much her every triumph cost her! How they would commiserate with her, coddle her, drop this bullying of a poor defenseless creature. There appeared before her (in her imagination, of course) her vanity containing all the cosmetics she had acquired but had never dared to use. Just a little while longer . . . , and then: the horrible, hollow, empty days of the future (what she had said on the subject of cultivating future generations was pure bombast) when she would be anybody's lay —

dolled up by some Evarist, Ananill, or Asphodel, the one friend and confidant to whom she would pour out the details of her life every morning, the grisly life of a dried-up nymphomaniac. Then she recalled her diabolical scheme, and she again wrapped herself in an infuriating mask of arrogance and lewd indifference. (The men, for all their spiritual airs, were again all muzzles and snouts.) In this last twitch of repressed despair, the princess discovered (a precious gem beaming in a grey rock fissure) a sentimental gratitude to History (imagine!) for having sent her at her life's end a cosmic calamity in the form of a Chinese invasion. Better to perish in a universal storm than die in bed with bloated legs and a body oozing with purulent sores. Suddenly the beauty of existence, the perfection of harmonious composition, and the splendor of ineluctable death flashed before her with a dazzling inner brilliance that illuminated like a nocturnal bolt of lightning the brooding landscape of life's autumn littered with scattered ruins and abandoned tombs. Her unbridled charm, radiant with metaphysical voodoo, cast a refulgent glow over the world. The men were helpless. She was about to say something when she was interrupted by Tenzer. (It was better so; words would have detracted from the wondrousness of the moment; what was needed was a grand gesture, not some dialectical, drawing-room conquest. It'll come, dammit, it'll come – there was still time.)

"No attack at all. *Vouz avez exagéré votre importance, princesse,"* Putricides suddenly exclaimed in a shrill voice, pronouncing these words with an outrageous French accent. "Listen to me, please!!!" The combination of alcohol and hashish had slammed into the back of his head like a torpedo into the hull of a battleship. He was not himself; he literally had no idea who he was; he was incarnated in each of the guests, even in inanimate objects; and all multiplied to infinity. It was not enough that the infinite number of all things persisted bull-like, even concepts began to proliferate – that of a piano, say: *an infinite number of piano-concepts!* "A logical vision in hashish – wouldn't that be grist for a sterile logician's mill?" He scornfully dismissed the idea. Internally he sounded like some improbable instrument being hammered by God or Satan (he could not tell which) in a moment of fantastic inspiration born of painful dwelling in loneliness and desire, beside which Infinity was a prison and a perimeter. What could possibly beat this?! A satanically new, but still *musically anonymous*, creation filled his being like a raging linga engorging a female, illuminating him from within until, perfected at last, he stood out in the cosmos like a flawless crystal embedded in the grey mass of a crag whence he had come. He flared up out of his own nonentity like some monstrous meteor in the interstellar void rubbing against the atmosphere's outer edge. This atmosphere was for him the transcendent (but not transcendental) unity of Being – what else, pray? His material was, at the same time, his catalyst: a little slip of a bawd, sir, a domestic spat, a shot of vodka with hashish, sir, some mucking around with the teenaged crowd – in short, a bouquet of life's tidy little proclivities belonging to *this particular freak* and to him alone, a cripple charged with a billion-volt current of metaphysical wonder, foaming with insatiable desire, sprung from the gut-engines of protoexistence and only by accident differentiated in life's anarchic mess into this particular individual. "Centrojob" – this curious word (an advertisement for a French brand of cigarette paper called "Job"?) seemed to be the cohering substance of that whirling magma, the guiding compass in the chaos of spiraling equivalent possibilities. Exploding now in the purest artistic, compositional frenzy was that oblation of higher forces, Putricides Tenzer, a man pulling back on his inspiration like a runaway horse perched on the brink of an abyss: let it condense itself, purify itself, for he, the great supermundane master, would wait till the gods granted him the poison prepared for him and for the whole miserable staff of his ego. For such were the *produits secondaires* of that whole farce known as Art. He knew that he would play something (a mere drop of what had been fashioned in the musical crucible of his being) and demolish this gang of psychic mutants not reaching up to his belly button, grown moldy in a comatose pseudonormality, and sunk to an intellectual mud puddle, a shithole, through a glib pseudoknowledge scavenged from the garbage heap of the mind. Benz was different; Benz understood something there, despite his symbolmania – but those "paragons" of a drawing-room pseudointellectualdom can never be made to understand their own fatuity . . . Ugh

. . . The "howling dog" crouched at his feet strained its ears and muscles in expectation of a musical earthquake. Contempt filled him to the brim – but would not *out*. Why? They would discover why after his death – discover not from his music but from the papers, that truly abominable "press" of minds that was grinding millions of people into a brainless jelly compatible with the prevailing political fiction. The proliferation of newspapers and of cheap-pulp literary tripe: it fucked the mind. Sturfan Abnol was right.

He, miserable cr*eee*pple that he was, was the sanest of them all, perhaps the sanest in the land. Despite all his artistic perversion, he was the *truth* – he and perhaps Kotzmolochowicz (he seriously believed it – he was that far gone), two poles qualitatively measuring life in society, two sources of an untapped energy charged with fantastic potentiality. How and when, if not now (the ulcer, already lanced, was beginning to back up and to infect the deepest crannies of the body politic), would that deliverance from the mobile Chinese Wall come, poised as it was above the "putrefying" West (never mind the appearance of a revolution there) the way he, Tenzer, was poised above the black hole of his inspiration, where, wide-eyed and teeth bared, the ugly embryo of his work-to-be seethed, writhed, rumbled. Oh, if every birth could be as unequivocal, pristine, immutable, and necessary as that gradual bodying forth from the occult wilderness wherein art is born, why, life among one's fellow creatures might become a joy! On the other hand, the poverty of the métier, however sublime the art; the artist as prestidigitating clown, as metaphysical juggler; that whole sleight of hand, *lovkost ruk* stuff, which sooner or later gets into the mental act . . . : the model was unworthy of the unfulfilled ideal. It was not "art's subterfuge" that irritated him – this was a polemic fit for morons and aesthetic prigs. Art is truth, but one conjured up in the accident of *this particular* work. And him? He was an accident, too . . . Okay, so long as the thing was inspired. He was entitled to use that word without irony = he was neither an overintellectualized musical hack nor a slave of fame and glory. Not that he was averse to the very success he scorned, but – what the hell – if it couldn't be had, then better to ridicule it. Such transference may be immoral when it comes to people, but not with things of a more abstract nature. A life as screwed up as his own body frightened him not nearly so much as the prospect of a creative vacuum rearing its head as he wrestled with overwhelming banality, psychophysical want, and boredom. It was boredom that he feared most. He had not yet attained to the summit, but he was already acquainted with its sinister, desperate, vicious roadside ditches where a hideous, preposterous death crouched in ambush: a dried-up, festering, hunchbacked old harpy, the death of a man killed by boredom, by a frustrated life, by stunted genius. For even when he occasionally made the summit, his private ambition urged him higher into that region where, cleansed of body, he might have thrived as pure spirit. This was the third epoch about which he had dreamed; *there* (in the throes of guiltless expiation), where his buggered life found its fulfillment and vindication. Just make a leap for it, either kill yourself or soar to that hitherto untrappable realm of moral and artistic purity. But even a smattering of success could ruin things. And this Tenzer feared even more than boredom. Meanwhile, the sweet aftertaste of another life, put there by his quick (twenty-three days, to be exact) infatuation with the princess, was frantically tickling the spiritual palates of his life's various doppelgängers, who were sponging off the body of a refuse artist actively disintegrating alive. He went on:

"What inspires your hush-hush, hurrah, peek-a-boo politics that you talk about as if it were one of the sacred mysteries, the experiment of scientific wise men? Not any grand or universal vision, but a slug of fairy-tale ideas hatched, like worms in a cadaver, from the moribund state as such. The state is a malignant tumor; it has ceased to serve society and has begun to devour it — much to the delight of all who live off the scraps and illusions of the old regime. Your would-be political party is a mask hiding a screwed-up, cartoonlike ideomummy from the seventeenth century. The only truly great idea today — that of equality and of an economy planned down to the last pariah — is being parodied everywhere in quasi-bolshevik Europe — except here, of course — parodied in Africa and America, and is, in fact, being realized by four hundred million marvelous yellow devils who are about to show the world, and show us not in the style of Kotzmolochowicz, our only actor on behalf of a universal destiny. *His* great feat may lie in his not showing us anything – except a finger to the world, his way of demonstrating genius."

"Oh, for heaven's sake, you poor rube," interrupted the princess. "Bolshevism was obsolete even before it was born. In theory an attractive idea, like Christianity, but impracticable. It owed its existence to the ignorance of the preceding period. Recklessly – it had no precedent – it made too bold a leap into the future. The West took note and went fascist in the name of a pseudobolshevism masking various sinophobic and domestic tendencies. But it turned out that Lenin's dream of equality and communism had its price: economic recession, poverty, misery on all fronts. And not only in agricultural countries but even in the highly industrialized ones. So you can dispense with the state-as-anachronism argument."

"You talk," interjected the musician, impassioned, "as if you'd already seen the next millennium. Your ideas are not credible in the short run, whereas mine go for every historical contingency, even for irreversible progress, which only a moron would try to refute today. But our country has only megalomaniacs dealing in 'expedient ideas,' by definition petty and stopgap. A friendly chat appealing to the shabbiest instincts of somebody's soul; cozy midnight suppers at which, over liqueurs and cocaine, people unburden their raunchy reptile-guts of revolting and equally rotten secrets; greasing the palm of worthless social pimps . . . And all without any real motive, just to slow down the forward motion of that glorious machine on this incidental earthly patch that is our miserable country . . . "

"Until now self-flagellation has been regarded as an exclusively Muscovite specialty." (The princess was a trifle perplexed; this was the first time Tenzer had ever preached *undisguised communism* in her salon. Unheard-of! Even though passionate speeches of this sort [including those contrary to her own convictions and instincts] made a perverso-sexual impression on her, the princess was delighted that such outrageous things were being uttered in her salon. It represented a clear case of disguised snobbery.) "Instead of doing something about it, all you do is sit and bitch – there's nothing cheaper."

“Action has its place, but sometimes all you can do is puke. You can’t make meringue out of cow shit and saccharine . . . ”

“Sir,” Benz began sputtering, “I quite agree with your ideas; only, your methodology strikes me as a bit queer. Ultimately everything can be dismissed the way you dismiss politics. What is logic? Setting down signs on paper. And your music? The same; except that the signs are arranged on staffs. And that gives some cretin the right to blow on a brass tube and saw on sheep guts with horsetails . . . ”

“That’s enough!” Tenzer suddenly bellowed like a castrated steer. “Screw that logic of yours, which is useless deadwood, the measly flimflam of a fucked-up mind, a mere plaything for jaded intellectual appetites, mental impotents, and not for potentates of the mind such as you imagine yourself to be. But keep away from my work! ‘Let neither you nor God approach the threshold of my abyss,’” he said, citing the poet Miciński. “Now for some real music! Some fragments only – enough to fragment your heads,” he sneered, at the same time noisily throwing back the lid of the marvelous four-legged oval-shaped clavichord, custom-made by Gutstein of Adrianopolis. The princess was altogether thrilled. An intellectual tiff, combined with one of Tenzer’s wild hashish improvisations, formed a rather congenial backdrop for the act of pure demonism – that *cochonnerie féminine pure,* as Prince Basil liked to put it – stirring in her brain. The beatitude of perfection (the sense that all was as it ought to have been and could not have been better, the basis of Leibniz’s theory of the world’s perfection), increasingly harder for her to obtain, suffused her body, which grew younger, more taut, killer-tense as it gloated on the past, on those criminal and triumphant deeds that composed themselves at such times into pure works of art. She had enjoyed her life, she had not wasted it – only don’t spoil the finale, step back from the trough before you’re shoved aside!

Tenzer pounded on the keys as though he meant to tear them from the keyboard. All had a vision of him flinging, as he played, parts of the instrument into the four corners of the room, and this impression lasted even during the pianissimos. He played fiendishly, brutally, savagely, inhumanly, sadistically, extracting his listeners' entrails and wallowing in them the way Gilles de Rais was said to have done with his victims, gorging on the metaphysical pain of these human wrecks, rescuing them from the quotidian and catapulting them into a boundless eschatological awe and wonder. This *was* art, not the sort of piano-thumping performed by blasé virtuosi or intellectual designers of new sensual thrills for hysterical females. And so *full* was this music that, although it still appealed to the emotions, one had only to breach "life's barricade" to enter that secret underground where life existed really, inaccessible to cheap and sentimental breast-beaters. All but Benz made it. The world of sound, into which Zip was driven like a stray ram by a gale wind, joined with this all-too-real soirée at the palace of the Ticonderogas, with people as contingent in their existence as everything else, to make of him a spiritual spastic *beyond description*. The undraped windows were flooded with ultramarine as the expiring March evening looked in on these rapt martyrs of existence. Everything retreated into the impenetrable deep. Alien and fundamentally opposed souls were coalescing in a column of smoke, a burning sacrifice to a vanishing deity. (Somewhere in the capital of C., a weird theatrical spectacle was unfolding under the direction of Quintofron Crepuscolo, while here, at their very feet, music itself was being put to death, music with an enormous capital M.) Fused by the sounds flooding the threshold of being, the listeners lost all sense of their own personal existence. Something brutish, almost sexless, was faintly musing in one of the side chambers of Irina Vsevolodovna's soul: "Oh, if he'd been different! Young and handsome and pure, this miserable darling, this musical butcher of insatiable cruelty, this half-rusticated wretch! If in making love to him I could feel I was being engorged by him who makes such wonderful things possible . . . " (The princess was no "howling dog"; she knew how to respond to music musically through her almost palpably shaken body – only not now, for God's sake, not now . . .) Then, as if from spite, she recalled Tenzer's clumsy embraces, those feeble, spastic embraces that were as maladroit in their wild endeavor as the rest of him . . . She was mortally offended that fate could have permitted such an injustice. "If he would handle me the way he handles that Gutstein . . . If he'd take me with his music and not with that godawful body puked up from some unimaginable place." He was possessing her in reality now. She experienced a moment of metaphysical frisson. The ferocity of clanging and clanking was grinding her down, dissolving her into a sensual morass teeming with leeches and polyps and wicked enough to swallow Lucifer horns and all. The devil of sexuality astride the swollen carcass of pure art was regaling himself in her belly, lapping up art's decline, gagging on the impure juices of its "spiritual" expiry. The sounds' mental filters had ceased to function. Evil, suddenly incarnated in this essentially harmless banging away, had entered her body, dismembered and consumed it in a ravenous blaze, leaving behind her raw and aching entrails. Meanwhile, a demoniacal plan was beginning to ripen, a plan of the most ordinary, infallible, forever new female depravity, the base weapon of a declining cunt that, having failed to sack love outright, now sought to trick fate by purchasing it from the commonest of devils with a criminal act – on a small scale, but criminal nonetheless. For, once injected, the poison of sex can last a lifetime, kill love – this one and those to follow – and can even prove fatal to the killer herself.

Not for a moment did Genezip experience any metaphysical thrill; he was too immersed in life itself. On that evening in particular, music was for him a bodily torture – terrible, not to be endured. He understood now how one could be affected, depending on the appropriateness of the moment, by a set of intrinsically harmless sounds. Tenzer had assumed the proportions of a symbol of evil, a heartless god, a consummate shit. Zip writhed in his seat, as though being ground in the mortar of his own baseness by the awful pestle of the metallic, masticatory, insatiable chords collapsing on him, reduced to a tiny piece of excrement in the wilderness of evil created by these zigzag, angular, stabbing, piercing passages. The music had a recurrent theme, a theme worse than the desecration of the host during a Black Mass and so powerfully resonant it overflowed the universe into Nothingness. Here were peace and consolation – the music deliberately fell short of both, except on its completion, perhaps. It was not a creation so much as a miscreation: a horny, fanged, prickly affair, being a cross between a dinosaur and an Arizona cactus. Stop! The music became in his eyes the symbol of a cosmic sexual act in which some exotic being was violating existence in a manner most foul and perverse. When would it ever end? (Tenzer, bathed in sweat and reeking of fungus for a radius of five feet, was in a frenzy.) Then Zip recalled what the princess had said once of Putricides. She had mentioned it several times, each time arousing in him the gloomiest, most crimson, most morbid lust positively dripping with malice. Just before, and even during, orgasm, as the two hung above the gloom of near-satiety, fagged from indulging their whipped-up passions, the princess would turn to him and say, pert as a mischievous little tease: "Imagine if he could see us now!" That was all. But it was like the sting of a blazing-hot whip. And then the pleasure would "overflow its banks," as the princess used to put it, plunging his body's senses into a diabolical anarchy culminating in complete annihilation. He recalled those moments now, and was visited by a Hell of temptation, surrounded by a sticky, prickly, humid flame of a materialized lust. He rose to his feet and staggered about the room. His muscles and tendons all felt torn, his rubberlike bones were being twisted. And who should have been the one playing there, but *he;* yes, it was he who was putting on this shitty show full of tragedy, the same Tenzer who had got him to . . . Oh, no! To take her now – what a way to climax life! But just then Toldzio was whispering something in Irina Vsevolodovna's ear, sticking his sophisticated, fatuous, "effo," toady's puss into the unruly mass of her copper-red curls. The humiliation seemed to last an eternity. The world ballooned painfully in its time-space dimension as in the opium nightmares of De Quincey, even as it contracted into some skinny, basically obscene object, shrank to that site of maximal male humiliation, a place joined to this and no other female. The princess perceived everything, and a wild triumph (the typically female sort of triumph that comes from having reduced some "character" to one enormous phallus, devoid of any thought or feeling) twisted her S-shaped lips into a grin that might have driven a hollow stump insane. At last, with the passage of time – dense, unfathomably rich – *("einer lockeren Masse zusammenhangloser Empfindungen ohne 'Gestaltqualität'")* – the outsiders left the room, leaving only the three of them: herself, Zip, and cousin Toldzio. (*Il fornicatore* [D'Annunzio] was furious at the princess for having invited that hateful auntie's-boy to supper.) He remained sulkily and deliberately silent, gnawed by degrading carnal desires now divested of all metaphysical charm. The charming kid with interesting problems was gone, sucked up, resorbed, and ingested by *that* and by the fearful gent he was lugging around inside him – an impotent gent, no less. A common "excremental fellow" with only fornication on his mind sat at the table now. He drank heavily, but the alcohol ran off his brain like water from a raincoat. But then he thought: Soon this piece would be his for the feasting (he lived a hundred times more intensely in his imagination than corporeally), afterward all would be forgotten, then back to "dear" old world, which was now looking a bit crazy and weird for the moment. All trace of his flickering "childish" affection for her had vanished. He despised that witch as he had never despised anyone. Unuttered words, stuck somewhere in his gullet or possibly in his heart, were choking him, spreading their poison, shooting through his insides: he was speechless with rage, a rage condensed into a toxic pill along with an animal desire for things indescribable. But two things: his anticipation of the possible (the impossible!) pleasure and now this sexual jealousy, which was so new to him, gave him the strength to endure. "This is going to be wild," he thought, not conceptually, but in terms of images suffused with blood and all sorts of juices. This time, by God – this time he'd show her what he was made of. But in his own eyes he was a nobody; the "Sperm Princess" (as she was dubbed) had transformed him into one huge, thumping, stupendous, horribly exasperated obscenity, an inert mass of a thousand high-strung, nameless, solitary, suffering monsters.

Contrary to his expectations, his tormentrix did not see that contemptible fop to the door (o woe, triple woe!). Instead, all three moved into the princess's bedroom, that torture chamber, after passing through three sedately furnished bedchambers presenting themselves to Genezip as small and tranquil ports at which he would have been delighted to "call." All the while, he carried on with the princess as intimately as if she were his own mother or aunt, thus playing his part to the end. The poor wretch was acutely aware of his abject role in the situation. He despised himself, but could not shake the feeling. He commiserated with all men humiliated (even in triumph – that was the dirty part) by these she-brutes who are always correct even in the wildest configuration of events: *they were innocent of deception.*

INFORMATION: Located directly behind the bedroom was the princess's private bathroom, which had a second door leading out into the corridor. The bathroom's only window, made of thick, multicolored glass that strongly refracted the light, faced the bedroom. This may seem odd, but such is how it was – as if from spite.

(The light from the bathroom filtered iridescently through the crystal glass fragments. How many glorious memories did Zip associate with this rainbow of mysterious colors. He observed now firsthand how the same phenomenon may assume different aspects depending on the ambient shading. He gazed at the miniature panes in astonishment: their otherwise sumptuous hues were unrecognizable – so utterly perfidious were they.) Before both rivals the princess took off her evening dress, and with the grace of a little girl slipped into a purple dressing gown. Genezip vaguely detected an odor that twisted his brain into a unicorn's horn. "Ten more minutes of this and I'll cave that idiot's face in," he thought. He sat down at a safe distance and averted his gaze – alas, a moment too late. Two minutes later he caught himself devouring a demoniacal scene with burning, bloodshot eyes that expressed, alternately, indignation (almost holy), malice, and desires sorely exceeding the capacities of a nineteen-year-old. Sprawled out on the couch, that wicked teaser had begun stroking her precious Chinese bulldog Chi, which Zip despised with a passion. In this house it was the lone emissary of that mobile wall beyond.

INFORMATION: The country was apparently swarming with the disciples of Djevani, the "footstool" of the renowned Murti Bing, that great heresiarch of bygone Oriental religions in their generic form, a form allegedly devised by Lord Berquith for a declining England. (People were grasping at everything possible, and even at things impossible.) Djevani's teachings were replacing traditional theosophy, which was thought to be too mild a "preparation" for socialism in the Chinese version. But at home such drivel was known only from hearsay. And how else was one to know about it? That was precisely the point. But more on that subject later.

The princess's petting of the dog grew more and more passionate. At one point, she turned toward her man-sufferer. She looked extraordinarily young, twenty-five at the most; it was un-bear-able. Toldzio began squirming. "Why so isolated, Genezip Genezipovich? Don't tell me you took all that talk about isolationism to heart? Why not play with Chi for a while? Look how triste he is." She brought her flushed face up close to the chocolate-colored fur of that contemptible animal. Everything was contemptible. Oh, for just one of those smooching kisses! Surely, beyond all doubt, he might have settled for this supreme pleasure and, momentarily at least, walked away a free man. "I don't exist," he thought in an extreme dither that bordered on a childlike contentment.

"Princess, you know I can't stand to touch animals unless afterward I can . . . "

"Don't worry; you can wash up. What a purgatomaniac your cousin is," she added, turning to Toldzio, who snickered triumphantly. "At heart, he's a little bugger like all you men." Toldzio was bubbling over with laughter. Genezip groped his way over to the couch as though hypnotized. With the look of a condemned man he began playing awkwardly with the little Chinaman he hated so much. But he was resolutely afraid of appearing even more childish, and so, setting his teeth, he played. The princess played, too, but with the expression of a willful little girl. Suddenly their hands touched . . . The process of self-indulgence had now become ir-re-vers-ible. It was the skids now; he knew what lay ahead, knew he'd never make it, that he'd snap. She knew it too, and she laughed. "What's happening to her? Good Lord, what's going on here?" Once, while both momentarily had their backs to Toldzio, Irina Vsevolodovna quite deliberately brushed his cheek with her lips — those hot, moist lips, loose and relaxed. Her tongue grazed the corner of his mouth, triggering a pingle-tingle in his back and thighs. "Okay, you can go and wash yourself now. Chi would like to go beddie-bye." (Her every word, even the intonation, had been coolly calculated beforehand.) "Isn't that right, Chi, my one and only friend?" She folded the dog in her arms, completely smothering him. A leg as though *plated* in sheer silk suddenly flashed before Zip's eyes — cruel, indifferent, completely ignorant of its beauty. Genezip took a few steps as though drunk. (He was indeed a little drunk, but it was not quite the same thing.) "Not that way," she said. "Use mine, if you like." He turned around like a robot, and the next thing he knew he was standing in a carnal sanctuary: it was here this living statue of Isis got herself ready for the worship of idolatrous males. He belonged also to their company, if not spatially, then temporally. This last thought robbed him of whatever was left of his sense of uniqueness: he was a particle in some nondescript mass, a zero. The whiff of fragrances revived him somewhat. "I'll never indulge such a luxury again," he thought glumly, by means of some tiny lateral brain functioning like a tumor on a debauched, already-doomed body. Because of the noise caused by the running water, and because he was standing with his back to the door, he failed to hear or to notice that the door had been opened and its key removed by a delicate (delicately cruel) white hand, or that a pair of enamel blue eyes had run furtively over his bent, muscular figure, or that wistfully, fearfully, even despondently they had lingered on his brawny, bull-like neck. "It can't be avoided," sighed Irina Vsevolodovna. The door closed quietly, and the key turned noiselessly in the keyhole on the other side. Zip washed his hands and face, and immediately recovered some of his cool. He grabbed the doorknob: locked. "What the hell?" He cringed from head to toe. Misfortune was staring him in the face, though he still could not see in this banal happening the beginning of an even more calamitous series. So this was to be his first test. So *that* is what his father had . . . Oh, that father of his! He was manipulating him from beyond the grave. Some friend!!

"Hey!" he cried, his voice a bit shaky. "Open the door. None of your stupid pranks, Toldzio!" He distinctly heard laughter coming from the other side of the oak door. They were l*aaa*ughing. It didn't occur to him to go out into the corridor through the other door. (It was locked, too, by the way.) He climbed up onto a chair and peered into the bedroom. (His movements were as predictable as those of Fabre's lab insects.) He had already noticed the other room's intense glare: an enormous chandelier was blazing away in the ceiling, bathing the entire room (= a temple erected in honor of this female fleshpot) in a garish light. He saw everything, now strangely blurred and polychromatic, through the stained-glass window, the color shifting from violet to red, from red to emerald green and sapphire blue, and he saw, quite distinctly, something so improbable that he proceeded to *rise* (not fall – there's quite a difference) in a decidedly negative manner (with a minus sign) into a world of mortifying shame and rank sorrow. And all because of her, who had begun to slip in proportion to his treating their "romance" as something below his "standard," or "norm," to use the fashionable term. He looked, he saw, he tried not to look but was unable to tear himself away. At last he understood – not with his brain but with his whole body – the meaning of demonism. Zuzi the chambermaid ceased to exist, much as if she had been sucked up into a tornado of fire, as did all the women and affairs of the heart he had evoked in his booziest fantasies. Only that fiendish Irina Vsevolodovna existed, and *how* she did! Oh, babes be damn . . . She had planted herself – with her unyielding beauty and dirty mind – like a bulldog in every cell of his body, in every atom of his soul . . . Out from there! Meanwhile, that abominable cousin of his, that onanistic professor of his boyhood, was taking her (himself being overtaken with joy) on the couch. Genezip was a spectator to that whole comedy, to that whole scene of masculine debacle: a live peep show in some thrice-forbidden penny arcade. And who had sentenced him to this? She whom he loved (i.e., the wench who was insulting him with her intellect). Was there no justice in the world?! But the worst was yet to come, because soon all this male indignation, humiliation, wounded pride, and outrage subsided, that is, it was transformed into a lust approaching something absolutely irrational in the sexual sense. An absolute of obscenity produced by an internal transformer capable of converting any

Inhalt into a unique category: the "sexshual," or "seksooal," as others pronounced it. Where was he in reality, most damnable Hell, this detestable Zip (detested by whom?)? He had been turned into some lewdly suffering *thing*, flattened by that bitch of a *person* into a hideous pancake. But what about his personality? It had vanished into the wild and magical March night lingering over Ludzimierz. All – this palace, himself, his tragic situation – was like a tiny stone expectorated (by whom?) in a general panic before Nature and the march of events. If only they had known! But the universe was brimming over with *their* personal problems and tribulations. The most notorious fictions could not diminish their own self-importance: *they* were healthy brutes. And, and, and – and, meanwhile, that "other guy" (who had no right to exist, a guy irreparably damned) was going hog-wild, while she (the horror of it!) shared with him the pleasure unfathomable, inexhaustible, which, at the same time, she was cruelly denying Zip for Toldzio's sake: a vicious circle. Monstrosity not-to-be-believed. Toldzio's movements grew faster, more ridiculous; hopelessly silly. How embarrassed Zip was. The whole being of this scatological runt, this Zip who had surpassed himself on so many occasions, expanded into a sticky, odorless, astructural "sexual mass" that had glued itself to the window like an octopus in an aquarium tank. In terms of primitive intelligence, he was inferior to nothing, not even an amoeba. The princess wrapped her legs around Toldzio (how beautiful they looked at the moment), and for the longest while they lay still, rigid, as though dead. (The fact that he was watching [she was certain he was] excited Princess Irina to a frenzy rare even by her standards. She had pulled such a stunt before, but it had backfired when the poor beggar ran off into the woods and shot himself in the stomach; this time she felt secure; she was not in the least afraid for Zip's life.) Stuck to the windowpane, Zip also did not move. He was viewing everything in gold now, a color that permitted maximum visibility. He wanted the best possible view; he insisted on it, because if he was going to watch *at all*, then under the best conditions. Meanwhile, Toldzio and the princess stood up and started getting undressed – quickly, frantically. With his eyes (and, along with his eyes, his whole body) Genezip devoured this scene not, it seemed, of this world. He had discovered something in himself (and indirectly in the world) so ghastly that he turned mentally speechless. The one called Zip was no more. The fetters of his ego had burst asunder; his personality had fled. (Oh, to profit from this flight of ego! But he was too dumb for that.) Blood clots had clogged his brain, external forces had a stranglehold on him. It was worse, perhaps (of course "perhaps": *perhapsness*), than death by torture. In his head he felt a live, exceedingly restless octopus consuming him alive with its tentacles, clucking its broad, titillating lips lecherously. He momentarily lost consciousness. Even so, the outrageous image persisted – real, incomprehensible, bizarre. Why? He understood now: existence was a perfidy; nobody except his mother really cared what happened to him; to the world it was *ganz Pomade* that he was suffering to the point of insanity. He caught a glimpse of her naked legs and the indecent, ephebic form of the other. Stark naked, they flung themselves onto the couch. The perversity of it all became limpid, stark: it passed through him like an irresistible wave and entered outer space to apprise other planets of the injustice. But they, they went at it like a couple of spiders gone berserk . . . The sight of it was more than Genezip could bear, and so, reaching through his fly, he fixed things with a few quick strokes. He popped. At once everything dropped from him: some live, gigantic mask with an existence all its own dropped onto the blue tiles of the bathroom floor, quietly chuckling to itself, while the raunchy octopus stopped sucking and like a tiny worm began invading the coils of his brain – the leftovers that had survived the catastrophe, that is. But the dirty deed failed to restore his peace of mind. Doubly despairing, he realized the truth: the monstrous bitch had crept into his blood and meant to fight him to the death. His first dose of demonism had been too strong. Something had snapped forever in the realm of eternal wonder aroused by his afternoon awakening. How serious his debacle he could not know, though it would continue to fester out of sight of his consciousness. He got down clumsily from the chair (the clumsiness was proportionate to his self-disgust) and gazed into the mirror. (All was calm down there in that most infernal of infernos.) He examined his face, which looked so hideous and repulsive he hardly recognized it. Eyes, raked by an insipid madness, fixed him mockingly through the rubble of irreversible decay. This mockery bothered him most of all. Somebody was looking out at him from the inside, alien, loathsome, erratic (the worst), sinister, lowdown, feckless (no, no, this was the worst!). "Okay, now I'm going to kill you," he thought, referring to the intruder. In the mirror he tried to mimic the once-ambitious boy. No luck. Some mysterious force hoisted him back onto the chair and made him look in *there* – this time in green. He was mortified by what he saw; he was sincerely outraged. What were they up to, those beggars – who were now beyond beggarliness and into buggery – wrestling like a couple of demoniacs?! A feeble rage nearly triggered a new eruption of dark desires, and he was, just briefly, haunted by the morbid thought that he had a right (because of what he had just witnessed), an absolute right to indulge himself this minor pleasure again: *morbid* compared to such (such!) a spectacle?! Fat chance (or so he had heard it rumored at school). He shuddered and, feeling totally wrecked, crawled down cataclysmically from the chair. (The door was, after all, really locked!) Toldzio and the princess lay dead still, spent from their frenzied bout. It was a premeditated *demonicheskaya shtuchka;* and yet Irina Vsevolodovna felt a wild exhilaration, a gut-rending joy at the thought of what she had inflicted on Genezip. Even "my-loat*hhh*esome-as-a-dog" Toldzio seemed changed because of the blithe cruelty of it all: more aroused, more piggish, and more conscious of his every move. No, in this respect the Foreign Office had been an excellent laboratory – "*a molodets,* Toldzio." And yet all was overshadowed by a powerful nostalgia for the "life-that-should-have-been," marring this brief interlude with a bitter aftertaste. Would he return to her now, the scrumptious bugger, the poor dear? Oh, how he must have suffered on that chair. . . ! That he had actually stood on the chair and watched she took for granted. There was not the shadow of a doubt in her mind.

Genezip began rapping like a madman on the door leading into the corridor. It was opened a moment later by an ironic and contemptuous-looking Jegor. Genezip was led into a small room adjacent to the prince's dressing room and there given another pair of trousers.

"Is Zuzi here, Jegor? I have something important to tell her." (He had in mind seducing the princess's chambermaid on the spot – as an antidote. Everything was drifting into drab banality. Jegor grasped his intention at once.)

"No, sir. Zuzi has gone to a worker's ball organized by your late father's brewery," he said glumly. (Why? Oh, that would take pages to explain. Besides, who wants to dwell on the psychology of a *butlehhh?* Not even they care; they would much rather read about arrogant princes and counts.) (Today they had solemnly observed the handing over of the factory to the workers; Kapen senior had been praised to the skies.)

Internally demolished and physically wrecked by an onanisto-alcoholic *Katzenjammer*, Genezip again headed through the forest for home. It had been love all along – he was only now, oddly enough, convinced – and not lust which he had felt for the princess. But love's analysis, so foreign to his generation, was of little help to him in this his hour of peril. Besides, was this emotion really worth all the broken teeth and words expended on it over the ages in trying to dissect it in what have always been the most vulgar terms? Frankly, it is *unanalyzable.* Zip was pained by the damage done to this love – keenly, bitingly, scaldingly so. Only secondarily did those wounded, humiliated, excoriated, agitated, and hateful symbols of mortal corruption – those devil's ganglia known as genitalia – suffer. Oh, why not slice them off with his pocketknife and be done with the humiliation. Damned appendages! How much safer and more aesthetic if they had been appended *inside.* Yes, he was furious with the author of such an idiotic contraption – how fast he was progressing – ho, ho! In that one asinine night he had discovered realms of experience it sometimes takes others years and even decades to discover. But he still could not figure out why (oh, why?) she had done it. Had he been anything but kind and affectionate toward her? And if he had blundered, say, through youth's folly, then it was her place to forgive and to reform rather than to punish him so. A knot of contradictory feelings writhed on the purulent, *reddish-pink* floor of his being like a clump of nauseating worms . . . The world now seemed to him so unlike the commonplace world to which he was accustomed that he refused to believe these were the same pine trees from his childhood, the same junipers, the same clusters of huckleberry, and, above all, the same sky, now so hostile, so disdainful in its sulking, melancholic, spring-dawn gloom. All joined the clouds in a frantic race into the yonder (a vile, ugly word, that), leaving him like a fish on the sand in a world without value. He walked up to one of the pines and ran his hand along its rough and scaly bark. The tactile impression was foreign in its ordinariness, in the oddity of its visual dimension. These two worlds, so qualitatively different, coincided without producing a single, unified vision. Genezip suspected something was wrong inside his head. The soul's elements were improperly aligned; there was only dislocation, disorder, upheaval, like the belongings of fire victims found strewn in neighbors' yards — in the uncharted regions of his ego enlarged by an event forcibly undergone. Above all, he saw that there existed within him, in the realm of life-as-it-is-really-lived, such an abyss of the unknown that in essence he did not know, nor would he ever know, anything about himself: absolute unknowability. (There was only one way out: renounce life forever. But Zip had yet to reach this extreme.) To say nothing of this alien world through which he was passing like a tramp or a rover (the one in the childhood picture — a forest, a figure wading through the snow, and, at the top, a tiny vignette of happy souls gathered around the dinner table, possibly on Christmas Eve: steaming plates, a hanging lamp . . . — such worlds existed, after all). For the first time since his homecoming he missed his mother. What vast expanses of feeling had been occupied by that other female! — who knew, maybe forever. Even *after* her "retreat from the field": he pictured her now in the form of tin soldiers on the pages of an anatomical atlas, in hopelessly desolate and arid regions.

It was turning brighter now. The torture session had lasted that long. One way or another, he would have to decide. The urge was bound to flare up later, in the afternoon hours, with a hellish intensity and with uncertain consequences. The provocative image lay dormant now, but at any moment it might be aroused. Very well: he would stop seeing her. Simultaneously came the thought: Why take it so seriously; pretend you love her and imagine you're visiting a high-class whorehouse, and let it go at that . . . ? But immediately he saw the fallacy of the idea, of this quagmire that was avoidable only by avoiding life itself. No, there were some kinds of humiliation a man could not tolerate. Though he was thoroughly demoralized, something "human" still stirred inside him, something had managed to survive that shipwreck amid calm seas. He had no idea, the poor sap, what it had cost the princess to raise up that reef on which he had been dashed; so fixed was he on the screaming injustice inflicted on him that he overlooked the meanness of his own thoughts. How "keenly" he regretted having performed that antiseptic, annular (a snake biting its own tail) rescue operation. True, he had recovered his presence of mind (for the time being, anyway), but at the perilous price of resignation. Hence his unease. And if the urge came on as suddenly as it had while he was a spectator to that obscene romp staged before his very eyes? And to think it was Toldzio, his tutor in evil, and that it was he, Genezip, who had profited from those lessons . . . How low! He must have known beforehand. The whole story. How that bitch must have excited him with the details! "Oooo . . . !" he groaned "internally," excruciatingly. His embarrassment peeled him like a potato, leaving only the thinnest mental peel so that he might not lose all sense of his identity: the rest was one irritating, tingling Nothingness.

Oddly, he was reminded of Eliza, the girl he had met at the princess's party but had completely neglected, which is to say: he had briefly considered her as a possible wife, but then dismissed the thought as a mere fantasy. And yet, strange to say, her image persisted and began to acquire various colors against the backdrop of this weirdly altered forest softly murmuring in the breeze of a dropping Oravian wind. A small crescent moon had risen against a turquoise sky and joined the greyish-red clouds scudding in an easterly direction. Some august and unknown agent had arisen in the distance with the windswept morning (there was no telling the source) and was inscribing his destiny with invisible signs in a world grown brighter and more wondrous. But the meaning of these signs — portentous, mute, and yet seductive — lay within himself, and he grasped their eternal sense from present horrors pervading the farthest reaches of time unto eternity itself. "Stop searching for salvation; start by saving yourself." The grandeur of the moment was slowly being drowned in the sauce of this Ludzimierz landscape. It was as if some huge, mortally exhausted brute had slumped down on the horizon, which, for lack of anything better, was represented by the sad, distant horizon of the Ludzimierz countryside framed by this sprawling, gloomy forest. Far beyond the mountains lying passively in the distance, a grudging charm (but a charm nonetheless) was being squirted out of the floppy, dried-up tits of existence. And then despair, mighty despair at the thought of the irrevocable, irreparable, and thoroughly ir-re-deemable fact: he would never come to know the meaning of love – never . . . For the first time in his life, he fathomed that abysmal word "never"; for the first time, death came flying up to him from its own private and obscure world to formally introduce itself – not as a goddess radiating a rather dubious celebrity, but as some pedantic individual, a little on the masculine side, with an insuperable passion for order, meticulous, deadly boring, authoritative in a purely schoolmasterish way, in short, death as a duration in absolute Nothingness. Life had died, expiring like a small and unwanted lamp – a life without much grandeur to it. A black plate in Zip's skull dropped down like a damper in an oven or a shutter in a camera: located on one side were his immature feelings of the past; on the other, a black thought sprouting up in a fallow field of doubt. The end – poof! – and a new Zip was born. This disastrous, nightless evening-morn – whether or not he returned to that *mégère*, whether or not he managed to beat her at her own game (he realized now that the bathroom routine was a trick, that in fact he was free to return – which was an even greater disaster!) – this Hell-bent, astronomically predetermined interval in time had fixed things once and for all: he would never know real emotion. A web of lies, as though the windowpanes of his interior compartments had become fogged, and, beneath the mist, a film of dirt, then a psychic stench and mitts so steeped in filth they would never again hold anything pure or beautiful but would leave their disgusting prints everywhere, to be used at the Last Judgment (at some point everyone is forced into the docket, even if at times we affect ignorance) as evidence of his spiritual crimes. Although . . . perhaps . . . after some fantastically "fervent" penance . . . like swearing to himself he would never reenter *there* (by "there" he meant not her but *it*) – then, with more sweat and tears, grunt, grunt . . . oof! ugh! ahhhh! . . . (a woodcutter in the forest) – but this vow would not come, try as he might to wring it out of all the pores of his soul with his vanishing will. There was no one to comfort him, certainly not the surrounding landscape: the sky was skipping off with the wind, indifferent, not so much higher as unfamiliar, a stranger to such matters (if it had been a sunny morning, would things have turned out differently?); the earth now seemed unapproachable, hostile, prickly. He awoke, finally, like a drunk in a ditch, stark naked, one who's lost everything the night before in the fog of a drunken stupor. He would have to start afresh.

Domestic Affairs and Destiny

It was daylight now, and a pale, yellowish, cadaverous sun shone through the faint clouds as Genezip passed through the side gate and entered the annex in the palace's left wing, where the family occupied three rather small, sparsely furnished rooms. With a tenderness impossible for Zip, his thoughts now turned to Lilian and eventually to his mother. What if he broke down in a sweet, maudlin, do-goody sort of way, made a clean breast of things to his "mum," and behaved oh so nicely (toward Lilian, too) – perhaps he could still turn things around and whip that monster, a part of whom had remained in the Ticonderoga palace and another part (inseparable from the first) of whom had embedded itself in the bedrock of evil infesting his animal personality. Never was the split so powerfully manifest. And this in a purely physical sort of way: the right half of his head and body belonged to one person (contrary to all physiological theory, of course), who was surely himself, since a split personality presumes the immediately given unity of the personality; that is, it implies an asymmetrical relationship between the various complexes integral to that unity. The right side was the steel fist of a lowdown gent whose blow was aimed at the darker power of life; the left represented the corpse of the former pubescent now reduced to a sensual clump of worms. A lethargic, inert *Oberkontroler*, ignorant of what the two halves could do, hovered above them like "a soul above the abyss": *au commencement BYTHOS était*. To whom should he turn but to his mother (in her was the unity of origin; his father, on the other hand, towered like a sinister shadow [he saw him outlined against the clouds] on the border of these spheres which had swelled to become the cosmos, and *threatened him with life* – the kind of life he presently craved)? – yes, to his mother, as in the old days; to that all-purpose glue capable of cementing every conceivable crack (even those hiding hellholes not-to-be-consumed). Zip could not take comfort in *the charm of his own self-importance* (the charm of a lowly speck) – or he would have leapt for joy; he was just a milksop maturing in the artificial incubators constructed by his father. This was the secret of his weakness – quite nasty, judging by recent experiences. Mothers should be exempt from the practices of panfemale skulduggery, especially in their demoniacal version. But, alas, in this case it could hardly have been avoided.

But even here Zip took a hit. "God gave him a new shot," Tenzer would have said. He peeked into Lilian's room (as usual, the door was open). She was sleeping in a curled-up position, her exquisitely formed mouth slightly parted and her golden hair spilled over the pillow. Something vaguely erotic tugged at him: the world would have been a much cleaner place if only she, his sister, out of all these broads (the princess had already proliferated into a plurality, into a bawdpack [wolfpack], into a bawdnest [snakenest], into a *vseobshchee babyo*), had existed. Lilian suddenly made him recall Eliza, and (lo!) he identified with both: he so, so envied their virginal purity, their expectations of being loved, truly and in grand style, by some horrible jerk, possibly one little better than himself. About Eliza he did not even *dare* to think; then again, maybe she had slipped in status to a mere symbol. "Female psychology is such a bore – why bother," he recalled Sturfan Abnol having said, and felt infinitely relieved. A banal stone had fallen from his cankerous heart. (Thank God, too, because he was in for a ghastly surprise.) He insanely regretted having lost his virginity. He had a vision of that she-brute, who possibly even now was spreading her thighs for a hyped-on-hyperyohimbine Toldzio . . . Oh, not-to-be-borne misery!! And then to entertain *that* with Lilian's "angel-face" before him . . . It stabbed him like a burning rod, from his prostate to his brain. "Mommy, mommy," a whining, sniveling pip-squeak of a voice whimpered inside him, a voice Zip took to be the voice of conscience at the very nadir of his being.

He pushed open the door to his mother's room (it was slightly ajar), and found her sleeping almost stark naked in the arms of the reddish-blonde Michalski, who was also sound asleep. *Ah, nom d'un chien!* This was too much – or, if you prefer, the last straw – so gauche was the sight of it.

An amber light "trickled" from a tacky white shade, gently modulating the couple lying in bed. They looked like a pair of statues that had faced each other from their respective pedestals, coolly and impassively, until they could take it no longer and suddenly coupled – something so improbable was there in that embrace of theirs (for Zip, at any rate). He took in this scene with the bemused detachment of one who, being the recipient of bad news, cannot grasp its significance while still in a state of shock. His brain was boring into the roof of his skull like a corkscrew. In a second it would squirt up to the ceiling and spatter the ridiculous stucco ornaments. And to think his dearly departed father had this addition built for his clerical staff so that, one day, his disinherited son might catch a glimpse of his own mother sleeping off "love's euphoria" beside the liquidator of his business . . . It was plain, all too plain, they had drunk themselves silly and passed out, oblivious of where they were and who they were, after wildly indulging their long-repressed desires. Lying on the nightstand, on a gaudy-looking tablecloth (Mrs. Kapen, who hated inconsistency, had sold everything that was even faintly suggestive of their former luxury), were some pieces of fruit, party snacks, a jar of some pathetic-looking mayonnaise, an empty demijohn of Dzikowski vodka with a large coat-of-arms and a count's coronet on the label, and two *half-empty* bottles of wine. Out of a strange sense of tact they had refrained from beer: the Kapen insignia (to drink another label in Ludzimierz would have been unthinkable) would have represented the height of dissonance in such a composition – the labels on the bottles had not yet been changed. A regular orgy – and just when he had needed his mother as an antidote to life's beastliness! He winced with a shame that seared his insides like a ten thousand-volt current. He turned white instead of red. He could see his mother's "still warm" shining beige panties lying on a green settee in one corner of the room. And this now, now . . . ! Implacable hatred swelled his entire being, driving shame and all other noble sentiments out through his cheeks into the air with its mixture of various odors – among others, that of cigar smoke. He had detected the same stale odor in Lilian's room, not realizing . . . His shame, now thoroughly objectivized, was already riffling the crisp morning air and being spread in what was certain to be the usual manner: gossip. Is there anything lower than backbiting – after literary criticism, of course, the kind that made Sturfan Abnol foam at the mouth and that consisted of reading the author into his work, imputing to him every foul deed committed by his "heroes." But it was very well for Abnol to scorn those dummies passing themselves off as critics, not so for Genezip when it came to gossip about his mother. Besides, it would be *true.* He fell headlong into the abyss he had been courting since yesterday. And those metaphysical flights of the recent past? Even his "love" for the princess seemed sublime in comparison to his present low. Some monstrous parasite had attacked life's fundament, hitherto neglected – and now the whole thing was collapsing.

Michalski was snoring lightly in his sleep, while Zip's mother puffed her lips like a pipe smoker. A small spark of sympathy suddenly broke through the dark ruins of contempt like a lantern signaling hope for those stranded on the side of some unassailable mountain on a dark and stormy night — and then went out. If not for that spectacle of several hours ago, etc. . . . But to have these two images superimposed *(hyperposés)*, juxtaposed as in some pictorial illustrating life's sure disappointments — it was too much to bear. All the same, it would have to be borne. But his internal ligaments held some abominable bomb that was exploding through its inability to explode. And how could it explode, after all? The detonator used in Princess Irina's bathroom was not usable here. Because here it was his beautiful mummy, who had always demonstrated one unmistakable quality: no matter what she did, one need never be ashamed of her. And now this! Not only was it without style, but it was stinky low-class groveling to do it with Michalski: "jumpin' Jehoshaphat!" "thunder and tarnation!" etc. A cheap, barroom fantasy! Some other time, perhaps, a year from now (little did he know that like Irina Vsevolodovna his mother had no time to spare, nor would she have in the future), and then not on *such* a morning (how selfish can you get!), it might have impressed Genezip as being the quintessence of style, as something grand in its own way, a glorious affirmation of individual caprice. But today it loomed as an excremental fact in the extreme, a powerful toxic dose of unknown etiology, a below-the-belt fact polluting the last and indissoluble crystals of nobility that lay buried at the core of his ego (in its middle ring); that broke down a person's resistance to life's abomination on all fronts. Now he understood his mother's role: although barely a part of his consciousness, she was the fundament on which, unconsciously, he had based his entire life. She loomed larger now, more immense, only in a downward direction, as a reproach, as a regret for what she could no longer be in the loftier realms of the spirit. Too late. But a loophole had to be found, if one had no desire to explode or go insane, if one wished to go on living. One loophole was *compassion* (ugh . . .), followed by (a) mawkish charity, (b) self-sacrifice, (c) "heroic" renunciation of the unattainable, and (d) self-deception, endless self-deception, a thoroughly disguised, sublimated, and sublime self-deception that consumed everything like a bottomless swamp. But charity can also make corpses of the living, both actively and passively: "Indiscriminate charity is often a worse crime than crime itself," Tenzer once remarked. But this danger posed no immediate threat to Zip, who had unconsciously resorted to sympathy as a temporary nostrum, as if swallowing an aspirin.

How could his luckless mother have guessed that she was annihilating her darling son (as if, while strolling leisurely along with his gaze fixed on the stars, he had been dealt a treacherous blow from behind the corner of a seedy barrack full of dirty bunks and hoarse, obscene voices streaming out of the darkness – a fantasy, but would that it were true! He, on the other hand, went along with his gaze fixed on his "metaphysical navel," which was rotting away before his very eyes.). Although he was not yet skilled in the art of "making every moment magical" – it takes a seasoned veteran to do that – he saw the princess as a diabolical red star setting on an impassable bog, be the bog in himself, of horror (a horror not without interest). He saw her and smelled her as though she were a putrescent (a vile word, that one, implying a dry stink) sack of guts swinging before his face, getting in the way of life, a sack into which, even as he affected to repel it, he longed to plant his teeth like a bulldog. If he had run into his mother hustling on some street corner, it would not have shocked him as much as this outrage with its perverse allure. Two images of carnality, overlapping: it was like a knockout punch to the jaw, an insult that could never be redressed. A punk's fist was motioning from the bottom of a quagmire its willingness to help – if properly paid. With what, though? He was stripped "clean," he had no cash "on hand." What was more, he didn't have enough psychic cash to cover the costs of being pulled out of his present slump. An interminable ordeal lay ahead of him. But boredom is death for young people; it's strictly for wimpy artists, for a veritable titan of musical staffs like Tenzer, who was immune to life's griminess because he knew how to work it up into "artistic structures," into something necessary, absolute, sanctioned in a realm qualitatively different from, and essentially incompatible with, life. Zip had no such backup, he was not your pseudoartist type; he lived for the sake of living, like a regular animal – if not an irregular one. One had to seek support in real emotions.

Suddenly he was positively glowing with a sincere, poignant, lovable, lachrymose, and downright obscene pity; one so fulgently and fulsomely bright it took in his mother, his dead father, the sleeping Lilian, and even the obnoxious, snoring Michalski (Joseph). For as Tenzer used to say, travestying Słowacki, "And then there are those glorious mornings when you wake up brimming with love for all the creatures of this world – including man." His old aristocratic prejudices had been revived, but only briefly. (Possibly if his mother had been raped before his eyes by one of "their own," the comedown would have been less dramatic. He was appalled at the thought.) His sympathy for these creatures, having caught on the last rock sliver of sentiment located on the brink of despair's one-way chasm, engulfed with its indecent flames the warehouses of hitherto-dormant feelings accumulated since his school days. They now formed his emergency backup, for which he could again thank his father and his tyrannical rule, under the pressure of which those sensibilities had been preserved in their original state. Little did he know that lying on his nightstand was his future in the form of a summons, the source of new tribulations but also of power, and again all by the will of that slyboots, that artful dodger, his pappy. His present travail, his body's very real pain became now a measure of what his mother had endured all these years. What a hell she must have suffered to go on such a spree *á la russe* with this blondie (rumored to have been a mental whiz) less than two weeks after the death of her tormentor and next door to her own daughter. (It looked as if the party had started right after the workers' ball – the one attended by Zuzi – at the brewery.) Or was her behavior really so shocking? He forgave her – and himself (thereby abruptly rescuing himself from his own little jam) – and was even grateful – not expressly so, but in a decidedly backhanded way – to Michalski for having ended the drought suffered by this almost sacrosanct body, so fiercely adored "*for* him" (but not *by* him – there was the difference). Such magnanimity, such generosity of spirit – did he not owe these to Princess Irina and . . . to his father? A curious coupling. For a second he fell in love again with that jade.

But he was obliged to save his mother from an even worse fiasco. He tiptoed up to the bed and, stretching his arm over Michalski's rippling, auburn-brushed muscles, gently nudged his mother's shoulder. The black Hungarian eyes slowly drew back their livid blue lids, and a shriek-glance pierced the thick air pervading this new type of torture chamber. He had no time to analyze all the various odors. (When it comes to sexual misconduct, who the hell knows what is idiotic prejudice, spuriously and accidentally come by, and what is genuine, unadulterated morality, that is, a morality free of any metaphysical sanctions. Today we make do without sanctions: society itself has replaced all considerations of the beyond. You can be an inveterate materialist and yet live as virtuously as a nun.) Michalski, though he had stopped snoring, was still asleep. Genezip spoke straight into his mother's precious eyes, as though examining them through a microscope from a telescopic distance.

"Don't say anything. In a second I'll be on my way. I simply had to see you. I even had in mind some soul-searching, but it can wait. You mustn't think I'm put off by all this. No way. I understand everything. I'm not angry about a thing. But I'd get rid of him as soon as possible. I think it's better that way."

Shame, animal fright, a sexual afterglow notwithstanding the debacle (this last, a deep-seated cynicism, he felt he might have inherited from her), and unbounded gratitude to Michalski for services rendered . . . not to mention being head of the family, paterfamilias . . . In this effusion of fine sentiments, all three were immersed in a common swamp, even if all had temporarily risen a few inches above themselves. Not a bad arrangement. Michalski, who even now managed to look beautiful; Michalski, veteran socialist and master organizer of workers' co-ops, lay there peacefully, fast asleep like a baby, like a harmless little house pet. He looked curiously vulnerable in his present state and came close to arousing a certain pity. But in his arms he was holding a born baroness. It was quite unthinkable that he should wake up, too beastly for words. Neither Zip nor his mother seriously construed this as a possibility. All the same, Michalski showed a certain tact (despite his flagrant lack of social graces) even in his sleep.

"Don't be angry; you have no idea. On your nightstand you'll find your induction notice," his mother whispered, buried under her lover's powerful, inert, oblivious paw. "Now leave." With just these two words she managed to convey everything – a difficult feat even for an actress, but at times reality can lend a voice incredibly subtle intonations, even in the case of two lousy syllables. Genezip stroked his mother's head, then left the room with a smirk. He had no idea how beautiful he was at that moment. Through the *deliberately benevolent* expression of his nut-brown eyes there glimmered a *murky reflection* of concentrated pain; his internal breakdown lent his artificially clamped mouth the shape of a fruit brimming with sweetness, mysteriously toxic. His face had the look of an obliging waiter (from another world) crossed with that of a demigod hurled down from some (does it matter which?) holy mountain: the combined look of an inspired lunatic and a vicious kid. He looked positively out of character. An obscure madness preparing to flee the caverns of his spirit threw an ominous shadow over his features. Confused as he was, he was pleased with himself. His voice was not his own, and his mother's words had not yet sunk in.

"For a minute there I felt old, going on ninety. I'm not really here – I'm all over the place. It's only by accident that I'm . . . I feel happy." Impatience was reflected in his mother's face. "Go get dressed now, both of you. Quickly – before Lilian wakes up."

He passed by his sleeping sister, who had not changed her position by so much as a hair. He was exceedingly struck by this fact; it seemed as if centuries had passed since his arrival, and yet she slept exactly as before. He went into his room and found lying on the white enamel nightstand, beside a glass of buttermilk and cookies (how glad he was that he had forgiven his mother, and this magnanimity of heart – oh, beneficent joy! – braced him for the evil lurking in the grimy recesses of sex [no offense, eh?; he was a stranger to love, after all]), the official document, its seal still unbroken. The moment of wonder had passed: madness withdrew beyond the barricades of sex into his most intimate being, where it proceeded to wait for *its* time. He began reading, while the imperious figure of his father, his future's spoiler, loomed beyond the horizon exactly as he had last seen him: a kerchief-bound titan in a medal-bedecked dress coat – such was how he had instructed that he be buried.

The document read as follows:

Pursuant to ordinances L. 148526/IV A and L. 148527/IV A issued by the Ministry of Military Affairs, Genezip Kapen de Vahaz is hereby ordered to voluntarily enroll in the intensive officers' course at the Military Training Academy, commencing 12 April of the present year.

(Signed [typewritten])

Erasmus Kotzmolochowicz, Q.G.
As witnessed by:
Captain . . . (signature illegible)
Adjutant General of the Q.G.

The name hit Zip like a blow on the head. He had finally caught up with him. Was it possible that HE knew of his existence?! Like God in the highlanders' fairy tale who knew about the little worm locked inside the pebble on the ocean floor? He recalled the picture that went with the fairy tale: death searching for the pebble among towering waves. Again his father's swollen but powerful fist, reaching up to him from the grave during this momentous period of collapse. Genezip clasped it between his teeth, mentally sinking into it with his whole body. Like a powerful crane, it hoisted him out of the mire by his ears. But this new attitude toward his father (only his father could have brought his influence to bear on Kotzmolochowicz) implied no condemnation of his mother (who just then was waking her still half-stinko "fornication appliance"). For his mother, Michalski was as much a compromise as his surrender to the princess, though perhaps not quite as sweeping; while hers no doubt violated certain of her basic prejudices (religious, social), it did not mean poisoning love's emotion. But his mother's life was winding down, while his own . . . His new role fortified him in his battle with the perversity incarnated in that hulk, that torso, that trunk, that carrion – it was no longer a body. He was forgetting that the thing he feared and craved most also had a soul, a poor, fragile soul hounded by the prospect of old age. With a ferocity of will haphazardly acquired, he was exterminating the "*grande dame*" in himself, defiling her, desecrating her. By so doing, he undermined himself, forcing himself to let go of that fugitive tail of self-confidence on which he barely had a hold. He vowed never to stick his nose out beyond the safety of his own immediate family: his mother – along with Michalski, if necessary (oh, yes – the door was just then closing quietly behind the unwashed, unshaved, hastily dressed, hungover, reeking of liquor but still beautiful lover-boy) – and his sister, suddenly grown quite precious (increasingly so as she came to act as a mediatrix in love's eventual conquest [Toldzio had once betrayed a slight jealousy where Lilian was concerned, but it was tainted with a large dose of perversity – Genezip saw that now]). His mother and sister, and that was all. Let no one interfere with this deprived woman (necessarily deprived) – with the exception of Michalski. The latter would be his, Genezip's, penance for having indulged his mother this luxury and perhaps even greater ones. Let the old woman have her fling, enjoy life – why should she be deprived of what the princess had enjoyed? He suddenly winced in recollection: the monster was reminding him of its presence, telling him that it was on the alert, that it was biding its time before attacking his inexperienced glands and brain cells. Meanwhile, Genezip suffered the illusion that he would win this battle that had only just begun. He was ignorant of what lay in store for him – not on this but on more distant fronts.

He began packing at once. As head of the family he had decided they should all leave on the afternoon express. While he was fussing with the clasps on one of his suitcases, his mother came into the room dressed in her customary pink (!) wrap. She approached him hesitantly. Only now did Zip notice how much younger and more attractive she had become.

"Forgive me, Zip – you have no idea how awful my life has been." He was standing erect before her now, a noble and handsome specimen of a man.

"I forgive you everything, even though I'm the last to be forgiving anybody anything, least of all you."

"Then you don't mind if Mr. Michalski joins us? He was planning to leave today, anyway. He'll look after us. I feel so helpless, you know . . . " This last confession detracted somewhat from the glamour of his being the head of the household.

"You have me to look after you." (Mrs. Kapen smiled through her tears: "What a blessing in disguise!") "I've nothing against Mr. Michalski, or anybody else who is and will be necessary for your happiness. I've come to understand so much today . . . "

"And that other business?" his mother interrupted.

"Over and done with," he snarled. But a noisome echo from the depths of his being brought him an entirely different reply. The wench was repeating on him like onions. They stood in a long embrace.

That afternoon they sped across the surrounding (necessarily surrounding) hills on the "Hungarian Express" in the direction of C. Traveling with them (by a strange coincidence – Lilian was not at all stupid) was Sturfan Abnol, who had just been named the dramaturge in a bizarre little theater run by Quintofron Crepuscolo. The star of this *zavadenie* was the hitherto-unknown Persy Bestialskaya, the half-Polish, half-Russian great-great-granddaughter of that Bestialsky of Samo Sierra fame. She had yet another function, but it was a secret one. But this, naturally, will have to wait.

. . . .

INFORMATION: With intense vigor Sturfan Abnol had begun courting Zip's sister Lilian, who, on the surface, was as innocent as a rosebud. Despite the air of imminent catastrophe, everyone was in fabulous spirits. Even Genezip, ignorant of the calamities that awaited him, was frothing like a glass of wine made from young grapes fertilized with lava. There were times when having a mobilization order in one's pocket was a fine thing. In fact, that glorious afternoon spent in the second-class wagon of an express train careening wildly through the Beskid Mountains was possibly one of the most beautiful moments in his life. In the course of their journey he even became friendly with Michalski, who ever since yesterday had begun treating him in an oddly diffident way.

Two

Insanity

School

Horrible times befell Genezip Kapen. He could take comfort from the fact that the times were so for nearly everyone. So they were, yet some individuals still made the most of this, perhaps the final fling; in Zip's case, everything seemed stacked against him, externally as well as internally. The fool was blind to the fact that he was stranded within the "golden" kernel of happiness (golden in the sense of an autumnal sunrise, of an aspen leaf yellowing in the sun, the luster of a perfectly formed beetle) (for, as Marquis di Scampi used to croon while bathing: "If nothing bothers you and your pain isn't great / Don't be resentful of the grimmest fate"), in the stone of some luscious berry bursting with a perfection of color against the blue limpidity of space. It was a berry that others may have licked a little but that he was devouring from within like a chubby worm, or like a caterpillar destined to become a butterfly of iridescent color. But *would* it become a butterfly? That was the question. "When choosing my destiny / I chose insanity," he might have said along with Miciński. Indeed, all was conspiring to form one huge, flawless, perfectly efficient machine that was propelling him systematically and irrevocably in the direction of that insanity. When such a *psychopatisch angehauchtes Individuum tombera dans un pareil engrenage,* then *vsyo propalo.* But try explaining that to such a boob. Youth – oh, who can render the charm of that thing which only in retrospect is as wonderful as it could ever hope to be in actuality, were it not for the element of stupidity with which it is connected in an almost Husserlian *Wesenzusammenhang?*

....

INFORMATION: The country was being turned into a gigantic waiting room, gripped by a wild anticipation the likes of which have not been recorded in human history. Not even the Jews waited for the Messiah the way our people awaited the unknown. The chief pastime – aside from the automated-to-the-point-of-idiocy shift put in by every citizen in his or her own little sphere – had become "waiting for the sake of waiting" *("die Ewartung an und für sich").* Even the Syndicate for National Salvation (= once and for all SNS) ("The Society for Nervous Sissies," as the shades of ex-communists had it) was in a strangely lethargic mood, having deferred in panic to the unknown deeds of Kotzmolochowicz. The general, as mysterious as ever (nobody was sure which political side he was on, and nobody ventured to inquire), was madly organizing the army, preparing it for feats unknown. Whom he intended to slaughter no one could say, not even he: he was as much an enigma to himself as to others, perhaps even more so – therein lay his strength. In those days of omniscience and unbridled introspection, not knowing what one wanted was more difficult than knowing.

Moscow had been taken. Separating Poland from the Chinese avalanche was a belt of "buffer" (or "puffed-up") grand duchies: Lithuania, White Russia, and the Ukraine, where an indescribable and utterly ordinary chaos reigned. We all know what *that* is like (chaos matters only to those who are caught up in it; viewed from the outside, it is of little interest except for the "outcome," which can never be foretold), hence: (a) a contest between rival gangs bent on mutual throat-slitting, (b) the problem of knowing which convictions to hold at a given moment, and (c) the question of grub. The rest – sexual intercourse, metaphysics, the climate – remains unchanged. The reporting of this mess, by pen or by yap, had become pukingly boring. All of the grand dukes (even Nikifor Bialosielski of Kiev) had landed in Poland, where from morning till night they licked the boots of the SNS, which was shitting its drawers. Dissension had arisen within the rather obscure realm of "*Ewartungspolitik.*" Efforts were made to create a party of "Pure Anticipators," though Kotzmolochowicz quickly put an end to this enterprise, as the general was not very partial to vague causes: they gave him competition. From Romania, which had already been overrun by the Chinese, there was no news as yet. No cause for alarm; those "yellow monkeys" (resentment was growing) would not advance any farther. No one dreamed this state of affairs would last a lot longer than had been anticipated. In fact, only Kotzmolochowicz – and perhaps those of his immediate circle, though certainly not to the same degree – was relaxed (that was unquestionably his *perihelium*). No one who knew his fearless valor would have accused him of personal cowardice; yet among the "sabre rattlers" some panicky souls were shyly hinting that he should attack first before the Chinese had a chance to organize Russia in their own fashion. Meanwhile, strange things were going on in the only land where surprises were still possible. With the "worldwide" ban on the use of chemical gases and airplanes for warfare (the former were deployed in the realm of internal warfare as "psychic gases"; the latter as transportation) proclaimed by the all-powerful League in Defense of a More Humane War (headquartered in Caracas, Venezuela), which everyone, including the Chinese (thanks to Confucius, the only true gentlemen on our globe), observed with the utmost rigor, the chemical and aeronautic industries had ground to a halt. Military training at home was limited to the infantry and cavalry – the general's very own baby – and even these were neglected. The army was being increasingly mechanized at every rank. Parade marches now took up roughly half of the time once devoted to tactical drills. It was the Russian guard of czarist times all over again. The number of officers grew exponentially: there was now one officer for every five soldiers, hence the number of officers' schools was also rising. The pacifists computed that the amount of energy expended in saluting ran into the millions of ergs per day, especially because the two-fingered salute had been abolished in favor of the whole hand. The defeatists were crawling around on their bellies and exchanging hushed messages of gloom. The parliament no longer functioned; no one knew precisely what the budget was. There were even rumors of a "secret Chinese loan," but the editor of the newspaper who had insinuated something to this effect was executed following a very short trial (as an example to others) (from the point of view of the person being executed, is there anything more pernicious than having to serve as an example?). The insinuators had stopped insinuating: there was dead silence. The situation had turned so bizarre that the old-timers began clutching their heads, though they soon stopped: it was pointless. Universal love and harmony had suddenly, in mid-April to be exact, reverted to the universal mistrust of bygone days. The mighty catalyst to the East was dissociating and ionizing the unstable and explosive internal bonds with its colossal voltage field, the repercussions of which could already be felt in Germany. The suspicion arose that outside forces were at work, though no one could explain how, since certain individuals remained tight-lipped as fish, leaving those who were eager to know completely frustrated: they lacked the power to torture. That such conditions, attitudes, opinions, and institutions could persist within the ring of Soviet republics girding our poor country, with its escape route to what until then had been a Russia in the hands of the White Guard, was beyond comprehension. And those who were inclined to solve the riddle were dealt with in such a way that even the boldest among them were known to have lost composure. One thing was common knowledge: since April 1 physical torture had become routine. But to breathe a word of this was to risk being tortured oneself. Under such circumstances even the grubbiest, raunchiest blabbermouths and gossipmongering gasbags learned to keep silent — and that included the press.

Genezip was barely affected by the loss of his would-be wealth: he had never known how to enjoy it anyway. His mother consoled herself with her freedom and with the downright fiendish love she aroused in the middle-aged Michalski, a man as yet unspoiled by women. That she could wrest from this brute activist, human dynamo, and widower whole boxcars of childish emotions and that she herself now beamed with the sort of fully blossomed femininity she had abandoned all hope of achieving had opened her eyes to a world that, in her imagination, was transformed from a dried-up fleck into a gushing fountain of unknown colors, impressions, odors, titillations, sperm, and ebullient joy: it warmed the blood of her ancestors, the Counts de Kisfaludy-Szaràs (on the distaff side). She was developing as in some diabolical hatchery and was gradually being shed of those dusty old notions fed her by her dead husband (who was now fashioning her ecstatic lover from beyond the grave). Michalski had proposed marriage, though she had yet to make up her mind. The family relatives helped out financially, but it was done grudgingly, for they had always been opposed to this marriage between a well-born orphan and "that brewer." "If you're on the skids, why not go all the way," Madame Kapen told herself, and she grew more and more accustomed to the thought of linking her destiny to that of this energetic stud, this "King of the Pee-ess-pee Cooperatives," as her darling Joe was called. Only Lilian rebelled against her bitter fate. The loss of her aristocratic title, which meant no more snubbing of the lower classes – until now one of life's unceasing pleasures – was hard to bear. But it wasn't long before even she discovered her own sloping plane of comfortable descent, one more interesting than her mother's dramatic "nosedive"; that is, she had begun performing silly little roles in Quintofron's theater (otherwise known as the "Quintofronium"), where, after winning over the baroness, she had been installed by the exuberant and ebullient, in-love-to-the-point-of-*ostervenenie*, and absolutely unmanageable Sturfan Abnol. Sturfan wished to make of the Kapens' daughter a wife – as he used to say privately – of the "new type." The family lived together in four small rooms in the abandoned palace of the Gandorowskis on Holy Bombast Street – a street well known to all.

Three days after their arrival in the regional capital of C. (= R.C.C.), Zip was caught in the vice of a type-C officers' school known for its phenomenal discipline: two days' imprisonment for a wrinkle in one's bedsheet, regardless of the circumstances. They were called the general's Provincial Guard, but went under the popular name of "Cuepeegees." HE HIMSELF had acquired an almost-mythical stature in these circles, despite his all-too-real existence (in itself a miracle), which was apt to manifest itself at periodic inspections, after which an aura of panic lingered in the school like an almost-material fluid. His spirit was literally present at every lecture and military drill; only the latrines, where the rendering of honors was prohibited, were off limits to it. Once, however, the following – and, from the military point of view, amusing – incident took place: One day, curious to see whether the order in question was being observed, the general unexpectedly entered one of these charming little rooms where the receptacles cordially inviting evacuation were arrayed in a circular fashion. The place was packed. His entrance proved too much for the terrified and as yet untrained civilians, who in a body jumped to attention without regard for the stage of their present activity. They were thrown in the clink for five days. "I like it when they shit their drawers out of respect for me – they won't do that at the front," the commander would say as he twirled his big, black, thumping, Cossack mustache. But the young "junker" (as the cadets were called in the Russian fashion), having endured his father's reign of terror, was unfazed by military discipline. He quickly grew accustomed to all the senseless maneuvers (whose deeper sense he was even beginning to fathom), while that whole juggernaut aimed at transmogrifying the sort of normal personality alien to the army became for him a perfect antidote against his recent experiences – in effect, a workshop for Tenzer's "anonymous force." With distaste, almost with contempt, Genezip's thoughts now turned to that shaggy freak. They could stuff art – and there he had a point: what good was art in those days? To say nothing of metaphysics: time had been crammed to the bursting point, life marched mechanically on. Not once during the first two weeks of training did this embryo of an officer leave the somber-looking building that stood upright with its mass of red brick on the slopes of the limestone hills outside the city: he had flunked the prescribed method for rendering honors. In the evening, during the brief half-hour rest period before dinner, he daydreamed about the city and his family as he contemplated the dusky red horizon lit by the green flashes of streetcars. "Serves you right – now you're in for it," he told himself. A force was gathering in him, not an obedient instrument but something like an anarchic explosive, not containable and therefore spilling over into those secret and – for this primitive introspectionist – hitherto-unknown alleys of the soul, solidifying into something evil, self-threatening, life-threatening. He sensed, increasingly, layers of alienness in himself, but he had little time to fuss over them. And so that force kept on building until – "kabloom!" . . . and then . . . but more on that subject later. But there was one symptom, the worst: the force that had arisen was now turning against its creator. Off to the side, in the soul's margin, another hand was inscribing runic signs to be deciphered only at a later date. These symbols were a function of the memories smoldering in the underground of his ego – memories of a nascent weirdness and of freedom's first cursed days. (Or were they to be his last?) It was as though a cave full of treasures, marvels, and monstrosities had suddenly opened and was blazing in the refulgent glow of an otherworldly lightning – and then the crossbeams (necessarily crossbeams) snapped, and it was no longer altogether clear whether this was just a dream. And how ghastly it was: this first glimpse into the abyss of the unknown, beckoning with its bizarre charm, with the richness of experience, the possibility of satisfying unconscious appetites – from the lowest to the highest. His intellectual appetite, already dulled that evening at Tenzer's place and later at Basil's retreat, gave no sign of life. "Literature," which once had embraced the whole of life's fugitive allure, that *ultimate* which was unattainable in life, no longer tempted him. Life had become fractioned, scattered into thousands of uncoordinated riddles from the mystery of being to the opaque realm of feeling – which was beginning to intrude on reality, alarmingly and ominously so. A duality: the former boy and the nascent officer so foreign to him. These two selves jostled one but would not merge into a single personality. So *that's* how it was to be? What fiendish disappointment in that *that!* But he blamed himself, too. His future had depended on that one day and night. And what had he done?

He had probed the pit of mystery with his grubby adolescent mitt and pulled up a pile of bloody intestines. Or maybe it had been a treasure in disguise; perhaps by grabbing he had squandered everything and would never be allowed to make amends.

Genezip began venturing into the neglected realm of friendship. Toldzio had been completely discredited. The pseudofriendships of his school days sank into the amorphous past along with his changed circumstances. The period that once seemed so charged with meaning and colorful experiences was turning paler by the moment, disappearing behind a grey curtain, due to events that were puncturing his consciousness like steel blades, drilling artesian wells in the previously unexplored wilderness of the spirit, and, like fishing rods, wresting from mysterious depths forever new deep-sea monster-thoughts and a keener awareness of the real world. But none of this was IT . . . "So this is the big world?" he sighed, and in this one sentence were contained levels of untranslatable meanings whose general formula might have been any postulate expressing the randomness within necessity — the arbitrariness of our each and every act that nonetheless *had to be* at this very juncture of time and space, acts that supposedly are governed by the laws of physics but in fact are open to an infinite number of theoretical possibilities — a postulate expressing the contingency within causality and embracing the whole of Existence along with the impossibility of conceiving not only of Absolute Nothingness, that absolute absurdity, but also of such follies as the following proposition: "What if I don't exist at all?" which, from the logical point of view, cannot be challenged any more than the assumption of Nothingness. Laws and the absence of laws, along with the relativism this entails, racked the brain of this protoplasm of an officer during his leisure hours. (For a Kotzmolochowicz, such notions equaled a silliness not-to-be-stomached. Not on his deathbed would he have taken such high-class garbage seriously. Nor were young people [despite some endowment of intelligence] any better at detecting these subconscious states in themselves, at distinguishing them from the quotidian world of animal humdrum.) Every passing moment seemed rich with a supreme understanding of that everywhere sought, but eternally elusive, life; each succeeding moment seemed to deny the element of finality by exposing new levels of the interior and new domains in the existential realm – in other words, everything was screwed up. Genezip was blind to the blessings of his present phase, was annoyed by the mutability of things, by the diminution of what had appeared to be unlimited possibilities. Already he had a premonition of the wedge that was going to jam him into place: such was his destiny (generally speaking). What destiny? He didn't know. So *that's* what this life was like – elusive, shifting, slipping away just when one thought one had gotten hold of its most inscrutable navel, from which everything could be squeezed, pressed, eviscerated. What was needed was, to use the vernacular, a principle from which to deduce the proper response to any given experience. Aim as he might for a higher perspective, life's trifling, everyday decisions invariably backfired, while surprise occurrences in the outer world (i.e., officers at the academy, classmates, the military mentality, and the tons of responsibility being heaped on him) along with his own internal reactions – unpredictable and ungovernable – filled him with self-disgust. He had resigned from mastering this chaos. But *they*, those inscrutable (that was the really sinister thing) classmates of his: they were so hopelessly different that any rapport with them was unthinkable, even if one used the same signs and references. Zip was awed by the multiplicity of human types. His late father and the equally "late" princess now seemed mere figments of his imagination: he had never known them. Nor would he in the future, for he had sworn never to lay eyes on the princess again, and his father, as a matter of fact, was dead. And that was the point: it was a fact, but his was not the death others suffer or even the same as his own eventual death – no, it was different: an imperfect death. The old man was living inside him, unrecognizably paternal, having assumed the appearance of a new personality, pupated, manufactured, and of course falsified through an extrapolation beyond the field of perception: he had grown to the size of an omnipotent titan. If Zip still believed in an afterlife and in ghosts, then it was because of his father. His own hypothetical death, a "fact" quite unlike the death of other people, could be differentiated: one was that distant, all-inclusive death, the symbol of life's termination, of which he was mortally afraid at times; the other was that perilous, cheerful, "glorious death of the valiant" followed by a new kind of life. Despite his disaffection with art, despite his own feelings of revulsion, he began pining after the omniscient Tenzer – if only he weren't a cripple, one who kissed – ugh . . .

His persistent solitude – even when he was among people, even in the raucous din of his off-duty hours – produced a frenzy of mental self-indulgence, involving not specific concepts but formless images, sketches, and fragments of future concepts still in a germinal state. These germs were creeping in a concentric way toward some imaginary (for the time being, anyway) center that promised to provide a structure for the whole. But the incompleteness of it hurt – hurt awfully. He had wanted everything to become effortlessly perfect, ordered, irreproachable, flawless – but instead, chaos, disorder, bedlam, internal dissension, quarreling among the various parts: a riot. He hadn't a moment to lose. Oh, if only a person could live to be five hundred, could live thirty times over! *Then* one could have done something, achieved something. (The sluggish tempo – what the Russians call *bezalabernost* – and the gooey *milieu ambiant* meant that life was proceeding as in a tar barrel; a great many of our compatriots [including Kotzmolochowicz] felt the same way.) Alas! "*Il faut prendre la vie gaiement ou se brûler la cervelle*," as Lieutenant Wołodyjowicz, director of the school's riding academy and one of the meanest characters in the cavalry, the type known as an "ornery cuss," used to say, quoting Maupassant. (The words were meant to inspire the cadets.) Genezip had premonitions of a short life; not even he knew on what these premonitions were based, at any rate not on impending events. Twenty-one seemed like an eternity – but more on that subject later.

His classmates were of a decidedly jejune sort. One of them, a rosy-cheeked, "intuitive" chap a year younger than Zip, was fairly sensitive but daft. Another, a thirty-year-old former bank teller of primitive intelligence, was actually possessed of higher intellectual aspirations but was so obnoxious in his social manners that this redeeming feature vanished like a tiny diamond in some mammoth junk pile. He was surrounded by semiautomated mental flyweights only dimly aware of their own existence. Malice, envy, mutual contempt, and arrogance made of private conversation an excuse for subtle allusions and vicious innuendos, to which there was no responding. Since Zip was anything but malicious, he suffered from an acute case of *esprit d'escalier.* He would not respond the first time, not the second, third, or even the fourth time – but then suddenly threw a tantrum over some snide little remark and part company, which eventually earned him the reputation of a "high-strung wacko," which in fact he was. "Too much sensitivity," he would reflect bitterly. "All right, but isn't that a sign of a refined nature? Why does no one report me? Should crudity and vulgarity be our ideal?" But why this soul-searching? Best to keep one's distance, because "let a *lumpen* into your confidence and soon his tongue will be in your face." Besides, Zip was not a troublemaker by nature; he was far too kind for that – yes, *kind* – what more can be said?

Oh, the average white-collar worker of those days was so revolting! Big-time crooks were better, or even the masses (from afar, of course) in whose coils and tendrils lay the ominous, pitiless future of mankind's surviving elements. Society, corrupted by a bogus American prosperity financed by the bordering and nonbordering semibolshevized states, those protectors of the "bulwark" – society, I say, was behaving like a spoiled only child before he loses his parents and estate and then discovers, much to his astonishment, that no one cares a damn whether he has had his supper today and cannot get into his head that nobody gives a shit one way or the other. So it was later on.

Having raided the white-collar class in his craze for producing officers, Kotzmolochowicz had begun recruiting from among the semi-intelligentsia and was even scrounging among the "intellectual dregs," from whose ranks he selected the psychologically toughest the way Frederick II recruited his grenadiers. Genezip, unaccustomed to the way of life of this breed, naturally recoiled before the more than three hundred companions who had the *right* to treat him with unrestrained familiarity. On the other hand, this snobbery of his deeply mortified him. After all, he was a nobody; worse, he would remain one. He had against him: (a) the times, (b) people, and (c) a lack of time. He had a yearning for other historical epochs, forgetting that they had known worse (although, who knows?) screwups than in this period of monumental transition, a revolution whose goal was revolutionary in the deepest sense: the leveling of mankind in ways not foreseen by any previous theoretical doctrine, for who could have foreseen that the monster of civilization would grow to such proportions and that no counterinsurgency would be mounted in time? Fascism claimed to have found a way, yet fascism was still too tainted by nationalism and individualism. Zip resorted therefore to a few naive masks in the presence of his immediate superiors, who, fortunately for him, were not men of great perspicacity; otherwise, he encysted himself. He was being molded, slowly but systematically, by military discipline, but only on the surface. At times he was content to be a would-be member of that social machine spinning around in an ever greater vacuity. In the center of his guts, which, clawed by the princess, were still trying to heal, a subconscious desire for erotic adventures was beginning to swell. But until genuine love came along, Genezip swore a "life of purity" – a pious wish, to be sure, but the noblest thought this forlorn kid could muster. (As a "line of conduct" it was a pure abstraction, having nothing to do with the main drift of his life, and was therefore worthless.) He foreswore the usual remedies, and his vow was made easier because after his two weeks of mandatory confinement were up he was again placed under a week's arrest for suddenly having forgotten how to make his bed and for having switched on the enormous furnace in the squadron dorm. (The old post-Hieronymian [or postpneumatic] building and former palace of the Herberts had inhaled this more worldly, nay, military effluvium with rare delight.) The vague shapes of past metaphysical experiences – of the "on awakening," oval-shaped, omnio-insatiable kind, slipperier than a fruit stone and yet so meatily, pulsatingly firm – defied all analysis. However rare and fleeting those moments of clairvoyance (as evanescent as a distant flash of lightning on a summer evening), Genezip sensed that his destiny, the mystery of his inscrutable character, lay *there*. Some may wonder why we bother with such a cocky sucker (with such a c . . . r) – the matter is not so simple. He awaited the decree of some foreign power in himself, of his "prisoner," as he had lately begun to call that passenger (but not doppelgänger) in himself, that stranger whom he knew only by sight, who was more mature than he, and who was running the whole show unconsciously. But he was not afraid of him, not yet, not altogether; that would come later. Meanwhile, this momentary passenger, this internal prisoner, kept to his own compartment, only vaguely graspable conceptually. His barely pronounced thoughts and presentiments were not yet hooked up to Genezip's motors: a transmission was missing. Military drills were turning that boy's body into something truly marvelous – no exaggeration. (To hell with all these cavalier niceties – let's leave the cavalry to the cavalrymen!) He was not a troglodyte of the square-in-the-shoulders, lean-in-the-hips-and-trim-in-the-gut jock type. This mass of organs formed a hermaphroditic synthesis of masculinity and femininity bordering on maximal harmony, not devoid of animal power. Despondent and disgusted, he would sometimes contemplate his magnificent members (onyswahkeemalipawnse) and wonder to himself: Why doesn't somebody make use of these masculine splendors? Why is such a first-class hulk wasting away in these barracks? Maybe the body's tougher members will survive this meat grinder, maybe even the bulk of it, but only if bullied by a soul deadened by a mindless discipline totally indifferent to individual destiny – in other words, materials useless for erecting a solid personality. The distant and glorious idea of Kotzmolochowicz, unknown even to him at the moment of its conception, weighed upon each and every *internal* fate (the notion of fate must be differentiated), modeling individual lives according to its own ticks and quirks. Strange, wasn't it? Somewhere in the capital a human *Hochexplosivum* was sitting beside a green lamp and blindly ordering some adolescent, his admirer in advance (on credit) and one on whom the "eye of Providence" was now turned (be it only in a novel), upon some unexpected course and elevating him to a social symbol. Indeed, outside of a few friends and his immediate family, no sap was any the wiser. The day society finally comes to power (whether through some Sovnarkom or elitist economic council – it makes no difference), such communion between disparate souls will no longer be possible: only boredom shall reign.

After serving out his sentence he was grounded for the three days leading up to the holidays. And he began to show signs of the strain: an aching sensation in the skin, mild fever, a continual ache in the genitals and guts, which were returning to the depths – blind monsters desiccated by an internal heat. Life had suddenly flared up – remote, inaccessible, "alluring," as only some mysterious woman can be.

....

INFORMATION: Classes lasted a total of six months. During the first three months spent in the junior division, the cadets were granted one day's furlough a week, on Sundays, but were not allowed to spend the night away from the dormitory.

A Meeting and Its Consequences

A solitary mind, momentarily exiled from life, was boiling away in some kettle. Petty spirits, those shy emissaries of The Great Evil, without which there would be no such thing as Existence, were secretly preparing a fiendish brew with which it had been decreed, in subconscious realms and in the ancestral past, to poison that young "organism" ideally fashioned for other spheres. Alas.

One evening, at the end of a *metaphysically routine* day, at that hour when the most sublime wonders can become manifest in the most prosaic surroundings, Zip, his mind now thoroughly emptied by the military, was summoned to the reception room. The moment he was approached by the officer on duty, he knew why he had been summoned. The secret dam that had been separating his heart from his lower belly, a dam he himself had privately (unknown even to himself) erected in order to minimize the significance of this reunion, suddenly burst. He had worried over its ability to hold. And now it had cracked because that moron of an officer, Kwapek, had "endeavored" to approach him in such a solemn and official manner. An evil foreboding gripped his heart; a procession of preordained events paraded before him: the poison he would consume down to the last droplet; a black storm cloud stealthily descending upon his bloodstained brain, which was protruding on life's aching plain like some uninhabited South Sea island. The fiery tongue of higher consciousness was teasing the exposed cortex of his brain throbbing with suppressed thoughts. Just so, just so: his thoughts were being flushed from their sanctuary before they had time to arm themselves.

The prolonged execution began on May 13 at 6:45 P.M. The smell of damp lilacs drifted through the corridor's open windows. An odor redolent of sexual affliction merged with the sultry humidity of a drizzly, springo-melancholic evening. He was flooded with despair – stranded. Never again, never: an internal life sentence. This school, these walls, they had already *been*, in some other life, oppressing him since time immemorial through memory (down with memory!) to the point of amnesia, of an infinitely slow dissolving of the self in Nothingness. But along the way a mini-Hell awaited him. "Why do you wish me to go crazy?" he whispered as he tearfully descended the familiar, unyielding, manly "Stairs of the Knights" or "Stairs of the Spur," now made, it seemed, of warm gutta-percha. He realized what it meant: fate, that henchman from a German fairy tale, had picked out some figurines from a child's toy box and was stationing them in his path. They were not alive; no, they were exquisitely made robots posing as his "relatives." (Fate was a seedy gent wearing a jockey's cap and a crimson scarf barely covering a bland and sinewy Adam's apple with huge welts along the throat glands.) And this he was supposed to kiss while turning the other *cheek* (the other one had already received a good wallop)? Not in a million years! He loved no one at the moment; he was becoming a solipsist. The duty officer and the world at large were merely synthesized elements à la Mach. He entered the waiting room reserved for guests, consciously thinking that his mother, his sister Lilian, and Michalski (the threesome had already paid him one visit) were waiting for him – though he *knew*, with the lower part of his gut, that it could only be his destiny most foul that awaited him. For, say what you will, "eroticism *is* a diabolical thing and cannot be treated lightly," as a certain composer once remarked (only, alas, one cannot capture his tone of voice, that luscious sense of terror, nor that expression of the eyes made moist by a stinking, morbid fascination). The last time around, he had escaped the devil's slide; rescued by his father's hand, he had escaped the dark trap into which all his muscles, ligaments, and the nerves of his body were pulling him. Then his father had reached out to him from beyond the grave. From this moment on, Zip knew he would be acting alone, and he also knew that, even if he were a superman, he would never elevate his fate to the higher plane ascended from the middle circle of that childish metaphysical diagram of the past.

An ominous calm full of mortal terror prevailed in the sexual depths of his soul. Not with his own eyes (they belonged to someone else now) but rather in some compartment of the mind did he see HER. How fantastically seductive she looked. "So like a young girl . . . the beast! She will never give up . . . Oh, God (that dead God), save me from this monster!" he whispered as he walked up to the princess, who, dressed in a dark blue (i.e., *bleu Kotzmoloukhowitch*, nowadays quite the rage; so called after the uniforms introduced by the general) velvet "frock" and a marine blue hat, was leaning up against one of the pillars in the hall. The place was empty. A loud and terrifying silence descended upon the building. From a tower in the distance, in the world of life, freedom, and happiness, a clock struck seven. A despair of metaphysical proportions began sneaking down to earth, where it was transformed into a dull sexual ache – thus will the devil tempt a person with incalculable heights, only to hurl him back into the muck. The medicine bottle was within reach; all he had to do was to reach out for it with his male fist gloved in "boyish" sensitivity and shyness. (Somewhere in the nation's capital, the "Great Kotz-Moloch," steeped to the elbows in a genuinely Augean mess of which he meant to cleanse his country at the price of God-only-knew-what, was at that very moment reading a report by a Chinese doubled up before him like a man about to be beheaded. Kotzmolochowicz asked: "Does anyone know his thoughts?" The Chinese, a second-class mandarin of unknown age, replied: "His Onlyness is absolutely inscrutable. We know only that he is the most sublime, the most universal spirit. He can solve that which cannot be solved by you, not if you summoned a council of the world's greatest wise men. Your knowledge has outstripped your souls. You are in the power of a machine over which you have lost all control, which is growing like a living creature with a life of its own, and which is sure to devour you. The priests of various dying cults have tried to decipher His thoughts by means of serums and hypnosis. But He divined them telepathically and they perished; their heads were cut off, though under a different pretext." The general shuddered and reached for a whip hanging on the wall. Miraculously, the Chinese made his escape through two rooms crowded with aides. Kotzmolochowicz remained fixed in the center of the room, whip in hand, and became lost in thought up to his navel. His ego had collided with the totality of existence in an unutterable spasm, then with that miserable worm known as humanity. Sobbing inwardly, he staggered over to a green table littered with papers and pressed a buzzer. An aide entered . . .)

Genezip witnessed this scene as he stared into the face of his fate incarnate – it truly might have been mental telepathy, since it had transpired at 7:13 P.M. in the office of the omnipotent "Quarter*meister*."

....

INFORMATION: What is simultaneity and what is reality? Neither physics nor philosophy can (according to some) resolve this question, any more than they can answer so many others. Telepathy offers a plausible explanation, although such an explanation (that is, a mechanistic one) is based on the fact that we *shall never transcend the physical point of view* and will seek methods for transferring the energy produced in our brains through certain processes, an energy capable of affecting other brains by evoking analogous processes in them. But here we enter psychology, which allows us to posit connections between incompatible phenomena. The same applies not only to mind reading but also to the power to see and hear at abnormal distances and through obstacles, insofar as such a thing is possible. But such bunk as the "materialization of the mind" (?!) is as asinine as, say, the calorification of locomotives, but even more so. The same can be said of the stuff that passes for "supernatural phenomena." All these arbitrary solutions making the rounds of the public stem from an ignorance of psychologism (the philosophical trend, not the science) and its relation to the physical mode of perception, which is statistical and approximate and can be expressed in terms of psychologism.

"I've missed you" (with a capital M) "so much, please don't be upset that I came." Her whisper coursed through the upper half of his body along the most sexual route until it came to rest there. "I made up some excuse to come, but the real reason was to see you. You're so grown up now; surely you must realize why, oh why I had to behave the way I did. You can't appreciate me now. Only when I'm not around will you understand what I've given you; only when, thanks to me, you won't want to hurt your second or third, she whom you'll really love or *think* you love. Because I'm the only one you have ever loved – or ever will – maybe forever, I don't know. You're not angry, are you?" She crouched down like a submissive bitch, while her glance, a cobalt-blue, "celestial," bleary-eyed, wide-eyed, gut-rending gutter-glance, affectionate to the very core of existence (all the way down to the kidneys, and even lower), ripped into his stern eyes like a razor-sharp claw. The shot landed, exploded, killed (thoughts only), and annihilated like a papier-mâché toy his artificially and childishly improvised barricade (or bridgehead). Through the breach poured legions of long-imprisoned passions, sweaty, grimy, stinking, exasperated – and with the chains of many still clanging they marched off like some steel-clad vermin to conquer the soul. Above them was unfurled a tiny blue parasol pretending to be the real sky: a pure and noble love. He loved her immensely now, this pathetic, somewhat matronly girl, as he had never loved before. Suddenly the universe was lit from below by a rising happiness while the far-flung and mutually unrequited spaces (regions? territories?) of his soul joined in a wild and delirious embrace. Never had Zip experienced anything so fiendishly, so sublimely sensuous – not even (!) when, with his eyeballs glued to the pane of the bathroom window, he had pulled that clumsy, sluggish stunt on himself (or rather, on that gent he had discovered in himself, at present a quite *lewd* gent). A blood-red, clammy fog had engulfed and invaded his body wasted by a lust not-of-this-world. And yet the great adversary of the spirit, that solitary, stupid HE, who was all-powerful in struggles of the flesh, had not as much as twitched or budged. So where was it, then, that desire, or rather lust, that was a foregone conclusion? Having demolished the body, it had folded the entire world in a fatal and everlasting embrace. He loved this bitch unconditionally, as much as during their finest moments together, as he had never loved his mother, his sister, or even his father. So pure was the feeling . . . It was comical. At last, through a throat blocked with some sensuous pap, *il fornicatore* said:

"Upset isn't the word. I hate you and I never want to . . . " She silenced him with her naked, omniscient hand (fifteen seconds ago she had quickly removed her glove, knowing that she would perform just this gesture). Genezip pushed it away roughly, but the memory of its warmth and fragrance persisted: the world had flipped, but the scent of Fontassini's gentian lingered on. "I'm quits, see? What's the point of it? Something so monstrous! And I loved you so much!" For some reason he was lying through his teeth, that is to say, he was deliberately lying; in reality it was true; it had become true at that moment – besides, what the hell, nobody knows what it's like, much less how it was, not even those who . . . and so on. "I loathe you like a toad; I get sick to my stomach every time I think about you . . . " The princess squeezed his hands firmly so that it hurt; the wench was strong.

"No, Zip, not until now have you loved me. But it's too late to bring back the past." The princess looked him straight in the face with those ardently amorous eyes of hers. There was madness there, in that look of hers; for added courage and charm she had taken a drop of "empedekoko," as she called it. She resorted to such devices seldom, only at life's most critical moments. "We can go on seeing each other," she continued in a voice infinitely more indecent than a pair of spread thighs, than bare feet, than a mouth kissing the-devil-only-knew-what, "but never again will I be yours, beg though you might." This last was the height of artifice: Zip had a vision of himself kneeling before her as she sat, with her bare legs crossed, and gently brushed his nose with those wonderfully pedicured toes and pink toenails of hers. A claw of *dun-red* grief sank into his intestines, while a lust as somber as an execution on a spring afternoon, a diabolical, tawny, brown-gold yearning for a happiness that would never be, spread itself like a funeral pall or casket lid over the *golden-red* future flowering in the hothouse of his body. Despair had coated his sexual organs – once symbols of power but now vile-looking squids visibly contorted by the contempt shown them by THAT THING – with a sensuous film. The nerve! He was thoroughly dazed – he was, after all, a man. And just because he didn't understand, he behaved exactly as he should have. Ha, he owed it to himself to conquer, distasteful as it seemed, that swamp of a woman steaming with a multitude of spiritual crimes and to risk falling in love again, a risk worth taking, it seemed to him (but not to her). He swung his arm and struck her pale neck with his naive and inexperienced fist. Then he evened the score on the other side, instinctively grabbing with his left hand the princess's hat, an exquisite creation from Herse Ltd. (which had survived every calamity to date). The princess was gasping with delight . . . (He was tearing her hair now, and swinging, swinging – how marvelous! [He really loved her!]) But just as he was getting warmed up and could feel the first wave of desire traveling from the small of his back down to his loins and buttocks, the princess tore herself free. On the landing (in his confusion, he had neglected to close the door), steps were "making themselves heard." He quickly picked up the hat that had been thrown to the floor and brutally slapped it on her head. Such a lovely opportunity and . . . spoiled, dammit! By whom? Not by that man who was coming down the stairs, but by someone else, in the distance: his father, the one who had put him here, the one-time lover of this female carcass, of his "ideal," at a time when it, this carcass (which was not the least bit fat), had radiated youth (around twenty-eight), leaving him, Zip, a few scraps, scraps he had yet to even *conquer!* Oh, how disgraceful! How hopeless! He wished fervently for some pure, virginal sort of love. Then he remembered Eliza, that sweet, somewhat flustered creature he had met that evening at the princess's. His strained soul revolted, it bitterly lamented the sluggish body assigned to it. He was crucifying himself in an agony that was worthier of a better cause. But how could he have known better? What should have been his standard of comparison? He had neither Basil's serenity of faith nor Benz's precious signs nor was he born a freak like the composer Tenzer! No, nothing: life for life's sake. "Never surrender, not even to yourself," he thought, recalling a remark made by Putricides, who, despite life's mediocrity, was struggling, grappling with something, if not with something sublime, then awesome. And he? She, that contemptible she-monkey, for a touch of whose body he would have willingly sold the lot of those ideals (honor, fortitude, honesty, and other such malarkey [or rather, palarkey]) pumped into him by his father – this Beelzebub in skirts was for him the only symbol of forces if not sublime than at least powerful. He sensed the terrifying emptiness of that which sustained him. He would have to lay a new foundation out of psychic concrete, or be a pushover for anything and anybody. But the material for such a project was missing; he would have to quarry the distant, forgotten lands of metaphysical wonder. When? He had not a moment to spare. Life was pressing like gas in the stomach, forcing him to engage in obscenities. A few more jolts and he would wind up at the bottom of existence: a filthy, malleable mass minus any ambitions, backbone, and balls, that is, sexless and disgraced – ugh . . . Fear and self-loathing saved him. He collected himself – that he might realize his destiny in a more roundabout way. What if he really loved her? The truth was, he despised her (all four levels of her – which was the real one in this layer cake? oh, you lucky vagotonics who are not troubled by such things!); such lies were a sign of pettiness. One more about-face and then: a life of virtue, the scurrilous kind, motivated by cowardice and a fear of punishment. Just then the duty officer, an "enemy" of his – Wołodyjowicz, a young and nasty lout of a lieutenant from the previous graduating class – came down the stairs.

"Visiting hours are over," he declared in an artificially dignified manner. "Junker Kapen, to your squadron at once. Allow me, madam, to escort you to the front gate. I once had the pleasure of being introduced to you at the theater – at a gala in honor of our commander . . . "

"A mere trifle," the princess replied haughtily, nonsensically. But the lieutenant began fawning upon her with the sort of masculine attention women adore, and whisked her away. Over her shoulder the princess threw Zip one of those wistful, searing, prickly glances that seem to convey everything and nothing and that made him feel as if he were stranded on some uninhabited island. Only she existed (the princess, that is, not the island); she had succeeded, the beast. If she had imposed herself on him, hounded him, *groveled* before him – ah, hitting her would have been such a breeze! But this way? He realized how deeply the hook had embedded itself in his thickening blood. His whole being, his innermost circle, was inclining toward those evil powers reigning in the subconscious part of his personality that he had always feared, almost superstitiously so. He had leaned out over the abyss a little too far: Would he pull himself back in time? Annihilated, Zip ascended the marble stairs. A quarter of an hour ago he had walked down those stairs a completely different man. He failed to recognize himself in the black mirror of the Unknown, a mirror in which our passing doubles can catch a glimpse of themselves. The tumult of the city pouring through the open window of the corridor, the black heat of a May night, and the scent of wet lilacs affected him like an embarrassing pain in his swollen, beaten, and horribly agitated genitalia. Now, at that awkward hour, he would have to mount the final battle. He covered himself with willpower as with a coffin lid. Every second he was dying and being born again to endure some new punishment, some new disgrace. Meanwhile, those ganglia continued to lead their private, personal, autonomous life; to swell, disagreeably so, even when, with the grimmest of determination, he would manage to repress those scenes of past and potential license.

There, beneath his grey blanket, in the fetid atmosphere of the school dormitory (few in those days knew how to wash properly), his body bathed with perspiration, alone, with itchy skin and other appalling symptoms, he, the junker Kapen, bristling with guts spewing their noxious gases, was conquering at last the barbican of the spirit.

She had no sooner turned the corner of the building (she had come on foot) than the princess howled in a fit of awful, female sobs (a sobbing fit of female howls) into the scorching density of a black May night capable of hatching every imaginable sexual depravity. (That punk greenhorn of a lieutenant was doing his best to comfort her.) The little stud – Kapen, of course, not that comforter – was all that was left her on this earth, and he was not to be had. She had become boringly transparent, single-minded, one-dimensional. She was not worth writing about. Her whole demoniacal method had been blown. But there were still three days between now and Sunday. In the meantime he would toughen, grow in manhood, in horniness (to the core; she could feel her venom circulating with an accelerated pulse through his clotting blood), so wonderfully horny that "I'll go crazy if he . . . oh, no . . . it's too good to be true . . . can't be! And how cute he looked in that uniform! A little in need of a wash, perhaps . . . Oh, he can be as dirty as he likes and can even *stink* for all I care" – (she deliberately repeated this awful word under her breath) – "I even love those nasty odors of his," she ended shamelessly, defiantly. Women are impossible at times. The danger of her surrender was not lost on her, still she could not resist: just one more time, then a life of total despair: the autumn of drab and hopeless old age, covered with the hoarfrost of a lifetime of depravity.

....

INFORMATION: In Ludzimierz, meanwhile, Putricides Tenzer had also given in and compromised (until then he had scrupulously avoided any compromises, e.g., by playing in beer joints, giving singing lessons to schoolkids, proofreading the works of *reine Fingermusikanten*, etc.): he had accepted the post of musical director – which is to say, that of pianist and composer – which Sturfan Abnol had wangled for him in the quaint little theater run by Quintofron Crepuscolo. Tenzer's music was to "season," much like salt pork in meatballs, those hair-raising "improvs," "comewhatmayoramas," "shockeroos" (for God's sake, no "surprises"; the word, become as trite as a washcloth, was prohibited in Quintofron's presence) that had already given rise to a peculiar ebullience among the intelligentsia and semi-intelligentsia, whose ranks were being decimated by "military" service. The latter, by now nearly extinct in the West and in the East, flourished in our country in those days. The scholarly societies were swarming with characters attempting to solve the most intricate problems by the Finksteinian or Kotzmolian method, whereas the truly wise, not wishing to associate with this outfit, observed a glum silence: the former were beyond reason. Threepenny explanations had taken the place of intellectual rigor, lately driven beyond the pale of society. In making his compromise, Tenzer had been influenced by the lust-for-life argument, that is, by a desire to vary his female "menu" at whatever cost. The insatiability motif had begun to dominate his latest hypermusicalia. Out of the blue he threw off the mask of the semirural freak and in his new role as malformed degenerate, as genius-become-ape, fled with his entire family to the capital (C.) on a Hungarian express. In going along with this, Mrs. Tenzer was not without an ulterior motive of her own, but it was carefully masked by her concern for raising the children in the best circumstances. Everything was turning out for the best, only in a small way. A maximalist program was no longer possible.

A Repeat Performance

At last the day of Genezip's first school furlough arrived. It seemed as though the wave of terror and discipline – what Zip called "the punitive thing" (not in the disciplinary but judicial sense, i.e., "to institute various punitive measures" – ugh . . .) – was mounting by the hour. A perfectly innocent man could land in Hell's kitchen for the slightest folly, then be court-martialed for showing any sign of weakness. Torture: here was a concept the scarcely delineated shadow of which was enough to turn even the most adventurous daredevils a bedsheet-handkerchief-wall-plaster white. Authority, structured after the Chinese model, ascended through the ranks to the door of the black-and-green study occupied by the Great Master of the Future's Uncertainty, where it ended. Above him stood God, now pale with age (livid with fear, others would have said), or Murti Bing, whose name no one even dared to breathe.

Furious with all the waiting and what for him was unusual idleness (he was working an average of eighteen hours a day, but even so the waiting was too much), not knowing what to do with himself and his army, the general began extending his personality (which saw itself being frustrated by events – or rather, by a lack of same) into the realm of military education. There he was forging a power with which to overcome a purely negative situation: that of isolationism and preservation of the *status excrementalis*, as the contemporary state of affairs was being dubbed – i.e., the government of the Syndicate party and a reigning, hypocritical pseudofascism. Already strained to the limit, the country's internal, spiritual structure was trembling from the field of tension, ominously so, but it remained standing. Exactly what the source of that tension was no one knew, since the inertia of the population was enough to arouse even the admiration of foreign visitors – especially the regular ones, those of the old school. "*Das ist nur in Polen möglich*," old Field Marshal Count Buxenhein (the last of Hindenburg's younger colleagues), who of course had already found a haven in the traditionally hospitable "bulwark," used to say.

A measly speck, an amoeba like Genezip could hardly have braved the most profound states and feelings, those things that from a certain point of view make life ultimately worth living – a view obviously foreign to the notion of reality entertained by the majority of gown-and-tuxedo-clad cattle (that's putting it mildly, being in fact a compliment). Even in the most subtle palpitations of his being – there where the hunger for free existence abides – he had to be a measly function of some grand (Lord have mercy! grand for whom?) (and possibly even nonexistent?) scheme devised by some Kotzmolochowicz, who, in exchange for his power and influence, stood to lose a portion of his soul, the latter being the privilege of only pure contemplatives. But this "scheme" (about which no one, not even its future author, had a clue) had its own secret origin: certain hormonal imbalances in the general's hairy, well-proportioned, swarthy *(in spite of its whiteness)*, and flexible-as-a-whip (as-his-own-will) body. That hulk of a body was determined to survive, along with its raptorial, insatiable, and (to be frank) sordid (because power-hungry) soul, with which it was fused in an indissoluble lump. In this simple, servile, sloppy manner, out of such random combinations of personal screwups was the stuff of history made. "Backward or forward, rise or fall / History is the grandest hoax of all," as the poet has said. A few hundred years from now the human brain will be not be capable of integrating life's mounting complexities. A thousand projections will not shed light on a single moment of this most bizarre of epochs. Bizarre, yes, but only for someone from another planet – not for us, alas. Otherwise, there was only the law of Great Numbers, the last instance of universal necessity, in physics as in (though in a slightly different way) the history of living creatures: an office of statistics as the final arbiter of Truth – rock bottom, in other words. And no one saw (or ever would see) the mass stupefaction of the times, of existence itself, which was then in the making; for as private life lost its strangeness, history was becoming the epitome of banality. The point was not that reality had actually become banal: facts that in themselves might have struck a Louis XIV or a Caesar as weird or odd were sprouting like astral mushrooms after a metaphysical rainstorm, and no one cared. And what is the value of something that exists but which everyone ignores? None at all. Unless Particular Existence, the mere positing of a unique and solitary "I," is something intrinsically interesting. But then the *world* would cease to be interesting, even in the eyes of a superobserver – if such a one really existed. The whole thing was amusing, a fraud, unfathomable. Abysses yawned in places where they were not expected; social perfection became a carrier of a poison intrinsic to itself – an ultracomplexity vastly exceeding the capacity of the individual. The faint voice of the simplifier was dying in the maze of impersonal complexity; affluence (ostensible affluence) and the mass had produced a void. It was like someone wishing to draw all the pores, blackheads, and pimples in a miniature portrait two inches in diameter: the facial features and any physical resemblance must necessarily get lost. Mankind had lost its face because too much attention had been paid to the most minute elements. A faceless and indistinct blur had arisen on the periphery of history like a somber, crimson, autumnal moon lighting up a battlefield after a senseless slaughter. Beyond the seemingly endless horizon, the terrifying metaphysical law of limitation had thrown up insurmountable barriers and tollgates. A mounting wave of "progress" and "evolution" was surging at the foot of some obstacle un-assail-able: the futility (relative to Being in its eternal aspect, not only to Poland or even globally) of escaping a certain degree of complexity without becoming mired in a hopeless chaos; the irreconcilable division between the individual and the whole which is engendered through its plurality. Unless one withdrew. But how?

Zip knew even as he was getting dressed that he would not be at home long before "dashing off" to the "Palazzo Ticonderoga" on Border Street. Naturally, not with any erotic intentions (honestly, shame on us!), but to clarify their spiritual relations, which clarification would have come if they had not been interrupted by that duty officer. The combination of the military and the erotic; of a military ruthlessness and uniform-and-belt-buckle strictness applied to psychologically subtle things, to physically soft and slimy things, possessed a special charm for Zip. The sharpness and the clang of his spurs seemed to cut (the first with youth's callousness, the second with a casualness arousing despair) straight into the hot and panting guts of all the world's females. What was a dumb princess to him?! Women were so many exhausted nags, cringing bitches, fawning kittens, and he had them "between the legs." Women's "inhumanity" had become manifest. (Mothers might have rated an exception, although the matter was by no means clear – unless one waived the period since childbirth.) Life was unfolding like a teasing fan, tempting impetuous, eager youth; it teased with its myriad unknown colors and devilish surprises the cold-hearted accountants lurking in the still-dormant coils of his brain: insanity and death. Zip unleashed himself and plunged into the boundless distance of the inscrutable night. How could he break off a relationship with someone who had allowed him to experience the horror of things sexual and who was, after all, "somebody" and not your average street girl, about whom he knew nothing. Thus did he delude himself, nearly denying the reality of the object of his meditations. Even so, he was so run-down, so macerated from military discipline, so glandularly emaciated that at the sight of the first woman on the street he was amazed. "What is *that?!*" the frustrated animal in him thought with lightning speed. A split second later he was convinced of the existence of women as such. "It's okay; not all is lost." Still, without IT the world would have been an un-trav-ers-able desert. And then came the shallowness of the "concept," the ersatz quality of all "abstract" (abstracted from what?) male affairs. In his muscular rather than visual imagination he caught a glimpse of his mother and the princess locked together on some sacrilegious merry-go-round of animal indecencies. Now, for the first time, and only through such a juxtaposition, did he despise his mother as a woman. Still, he resented this shabby business with Michalski and, oh, how "fervently" he wished his mother had been not a female but a pure spirit bewitched into becoming a child-bearing machine. Immaculate conception *was* a marvelous thing, after all! That which is aptly called "maculation," on the other hand, is a sinister invention. One would have to be an unconscionable fiend to make it the motor for the preservation of the species *and* the most sublime of creations. Alas: all had its justification in the fact that the old world was coming to an end — here, in this pissant country stewing in its own juice — and that there was no foretelling what form existence might take after the secretly awaited debacle — the hope of all those disenchanted, underdeveloped, half-baked, undercooked psychological *semi-mesyachniki,* of which there were legions. Even the conservatives (moderately religious and moderately democratic) were waiting for the end, if only to be able to say: "Well? Didn't we tell you . . . ??"

Zip found nobody at home. He was furious. He had been so eager to pose before Lilian and his mother in his new dress uniform of the last Polish junkers. Worse, he found a card notifying him that they had been invited to the princess's for tea and would be expecting him there. Oh, no! On the other hand, maybe it was better if he went there, as if duty-bound, so that his mother would be none the wiser. What messy, infantile problems — a pile of dirty, smelly diapers woven into a "garland" embellished by this, the most extraordinary moment of his life: his debut as "someone," now symbolized by a marine-blue uniform with gold trim. He was awed by the splendor of the "Palazzo Ticonderoga": a fortress (he could still recall it from childhood) outwardly transformed into an "eiderdown, obscene, mandrill-like dithyramb" in praise of debilitated bodies and purulent souls – no other words would do. Already on the palace steps the juxtaposition of hard parapets and the interior's lewd softness produced a soothing, sexual effect on him. His former "palace" in the capital, which he had visited only once in recent months, now seemed a miserable shack beside this nest of delectably decadent depravity and of centuries-old bullying at the expense of human cattle. This last thought made him furious. The young and parvenu blood of the Kapens was beginning to stir, having suddenly become *bolshevized* by the collision of his own impoverished state with the symbol of those ancient, immemorial, and now vanishing protopotentates. So what if his mother was born a countess – to hell with her, that shameless frump-bag brimming with the proletarian secretions of her "Mister Michalski": may they "pour his body into the coffin through a funnel!" He was not in the least revolted by such snobistico-blasphemous turd-thoughts; it would take a while before he would swing back to the other side.

The surroundings made it all the harder to bear the obligatory rhapsodies over his handsome appearance and uniform: the shameless pride beaming in his mother's eyes; Lilian's astonished look ("What a prince that Zip is!"); and the doleful, benevolent, somewhat ironic smirk on those omnipotent lips. At home, this inspection would have had a different impact; here he was just a pathetic squirt. His composure was blown. For some reason he felt grimy, even though he had scrubbed himself (with a brush [brand: Sennebalt (Bielsko)]) as spick-and-span as a saucepan in some swanky hotel kitchen. He saw as clear as crystal the folly of resisting something as powerful, as erratic, as possessed of such infinite resources as the princess. One sensual slurp of her all-powerful tongue, and he saw himself transformed into a raging animal writhing in a revolting, humiliating, oscillatory, comatose motion; one contemptuously wry grin from those sinister mandibles, and he would be plunged into the melancholy pout of a whimpering cry-baby, a trashy "troubadour" (what could be more obnoxious than a troubadour?), an onanistic monkey on a chain! Now, in this "uniformed" state (what had seemed such a blessing only moments ago now struck him as ordinary), the princess impressed him as truly great, like . . . who the hell knows what . . . a phenomenon, perhaps: a war, a storm, a volcanic eruption, a waterspout, an earthquake, and she was even sexless in her grandeur! (A repressed sexual eruption slammed into his brain: Genezip was investing the princess with the negative equivalent of his *Minderwertigkeitsgefühl.*) Un-be-liev-able! Nothing like this had ever happened to him before, nor was it likely to do so again. Try as he might, he couldn't quite grasp the cause of this sudden exaltation, this sudden bestowal of dignity, this compulsion to "crown the old cunt in another realm of greatness." It was not her pedigree, nor even her beauty (objectively speaking), nor the influence she had in the Syndicate for National Salvation, which was being threatened to its very foundations. Then what was it, dammit?

There was something so inexpressibly terrifying about this *Ur*-wench that in the eyes of this would-be metaphysician she became the incarnation of life's mystery, all but dead in the realm of practical experience. It was in her and not in him that the personality emerged as a mystery from out of life's dark tangle and rose up like an invincible citadel in the boundless expanses of nonsense. Why? *To be,* dammit! Full stop. All other questions were for cowards and fakes, for those who, by elevating social fictions to the rank of supernatural powers, were trying to cover up the depressing, irreducible monstrosity of Existence. For such a thing as joyful monstrosity may also exist – but, alas, only for pure cyclothymes.

Having endured two weeks of bone-crushing punishment, Zip bathed in this "opening-of-the-wounds" atmosphere with a feeling of unspeakable anguish. (It was the background, oh the background that was wanting; with a *podkhodyashchy fon* one can tolerate anything.) He looked upon these inscrutable persons as exotic animals in a menagerie, as monstrous fish in an aquarium – through a barred window three inches thick. He would never set foot inside those cages; he would never make their – these beasts' – way of life his own; never swim in the medium of these monsters as naturally as if it were his own. The only way to break through to reality (as boring a task as the hopeless waiting of an autumnal spider in an empty, disinfected room) was by performing the sexual act with that witch. But he was stopped by his pride, which he never would overcome. What a terrible thing not to be master of one's pride, to see with absolute clarity how such a powerful force can ruin one's whole life (that supreme one, the one visited on us in moments of clairvoyance) for the sake of fictions totally out of fashion today. And even if he had, so what? Even, I say, if he had overcome his revulsion, what then? How to make use of it, how to exploit it, how to achieve something durable with it (that was the whole point)? You may ask: "To achieve what?" "Well, life's essence, its fugitive charm, so perishable it knows no duration; that something which is becoming increasingly rare in the world (and about which only lunatics have any true knowledge), which is not pleasure or success or devotion to a cause, but which bestows on all these a higher value: a reflection of the inscrutable mysteriousness of everything." (These were Benz's words, spoken while drunk.) All such sensation escaped the tightly clenched claws, fled the transfixed mugs of these brutes in frock coats and uniforms, and left them feeling utterly stuck in the quotidian. Even the toughest schizothymes have known the feeling. Thus far no fixative for it has been found, nor are we likely to see one. Of course, one could ignore it altogether and thus be spared all the hassle. But then what is there to differentiate the human beast from his animal counterpart?

The world was beset by mounting anxieties requiring a millennium of soul-searching. But no one was pursuing life's trillion- or quintillion-fold possibilities. Life had become such a horridly one-dimensional affair, *beside* which a man merrily bumbled along as though on a track (from the metaphysical point of view, quite apart from any physical discomfort – if left up to him, he would probably have settled for being a hundred-brained monster equipped with a million feelers) *at the very same time* as he tightroped across the abyss: maximal slavery and, hence (precisely hence), maximal danger, the sort posed not only by an aerial bombardment but by a hushed drawing room or bedroom surrounded by luxury, calm, comfort, and the pretense of a happiness not to be had – at least not by schizoids. With these, or perhaps similar, thoughts in his duffel bag (or knapsack), Zip entered the parlor where he was awaited by "the family," which he presently despised to the point of wanting to commit murder. And all because of the contrast he made with this female slug, this medusa, this crampfish, with this dehydrated semicorpse from the metaphysical whorehouses of Astarte. Sprawled in the muck of her sensual ambience, the princess sat in a frail little armchair, at the same time rising up in the expanses of Zip's soul like a gigantic boulder blocking the last possible exit from the gullies of eternal degradation and "pudency" (ugh – what an awful word!), herself outlined against an otherworldly sky of the eternal mysteries (the personality, sex, death, and, of course, infinity), basking in the glow of her truly unfeminine, waning, but *tout de même* extraordinary intelligence. Rejuvenated (by the miracle-working "Andrea" establishment), insufferably beautiful, *foully* beautiful, titillatingly seductive, and lovelier than ever, she was an inexhaustible symbol (inexhaustible even in the wildest pleasure) of "life's longing," of Zip's guilt-ridden childhood (despite his uniform's insignias, jocosely referred to as those of a *portupeyny* junker [Kotzmolochowicz had a positively perverse obsession where things Russian were concerned]), and of his boundless, indelible shame. He realized now that he had wound up on the tracks: all his postgraduate freedom had vanished.

His mother embraced him tenderly, yet because she was *his* mother here (how dare she!) (had she no respect for his manhood?) and because of Michalski – something not-to-be-overcome – he hated her: fluctuations of this sort were bound to occur. If she had been free of guilt, had greeted him naturally, he might have found in her an ally – as head of the family. But even this had been defiled, made ridiculous. He could see it in the smirk of the monstrous lady of his idiotic heart, now as distant as the constellation of Andromeda. Everything had been staged by a diabolical hand: he was being set up for some cruel humiliation. He had barely greeted his sister, who came bounding up to him like a sparrow, when she, too, was snatched away from him by that lucky dog Sturfan Abnol, who had the whole world by the ass, by some metaphysical hyperderriere. Except for his uniform, which was choking him, Zip had nothing to call his own. A pauper, dammit! And all because of that slyboots of a father and his sudden, deathbed conversion! He, Zip, the head of the family, might have done the same; it might have lent him a certain grandeur. But the last internal springboard for such a gesture had been snatched away from him. He was a marionette (or rather, an "irinonette"), and he was moving through the air as through a thick tar.

After he had made his excuses to the ladies in a voice choked with rage, the conversation took a new and perverse turn. Everything had been so meticulously planned! Quite simply, he was being pushed by his mother into the open arms of that frump whose sexual allure was growing more fatal by the moment. Surrender was inevitable, and the thought of his hopeless struggle quickened his desire to a wicked frenzy. He vehemently detested everything and everyone, but without a trace of contempt. No other woman but she existed – ho-ho! – and in a moment he was going to squirt all over these carpets, paintings, knickknacks, gewgaws, over the whole shebang with the concentrated juice – the hate-spiked juice – of his most profound essence. What annoyed him most was a grotesque bust of the princess, sculpted in nephrite by Kocio Zamoyski, grandson of the world-famous August Zamoyski, in which the SOB had somehow captured precisely that air of invincibility which was driving him insane. Valiantly he kept within a hairbreadth of falling into a most routine rage. "A hairbreadth," he muttered to himself. Needless to say, a reddish-gold hair that had stuck to his palate during hell-only-knew-what – mum is the word! Blood-lust and *Lustmord* engulfed the crumbling ruins of his brain, leaving only the tips of his most supreme control centers exposed. He wanted to wrestle with her as if she were some neighborhood tough spoiling for a fight – a duel to the death . . . She read his thoughts, and in a slow voice said:

"As soon as the ladies have left – oh, it's not I who am chasing them away – why, it was your own mother who said . . . " – ("So they're planning to leave me behind . . . yes, that's right . . . I have to, I have to . . . ") – "we'll go over to the gymnasium for a little *escrime*. It will do you good . . . "

His mother was prattling away. With a hiss in his voice he interrupted their insinuating chatter that reeked of their intent to launch him on a career of depravity.

"So, Mother, you'd like me to become this woman's secret adjutant, is that it?" he said, crudely nodding toward the princess. "Surely you know how deeply split the syndicate and the war party loyal to our commander are. The syndicate would defeat the Chinese diplomatically and save . . . "

"Keep quiet, Zip . . . "

"No, I will not keep quiet. I'm going to expose all of you . . . "

"You don't understand, my child. You mustn't spoil your relations with people who are as well-disposed toward you as Irina Vsevolodovna. She told me that she went to see you at the school and that you were rude to her. Why? You shouldn't discourage people who desire . . . " (He knew perfectly well what that woman's desires were. Had Michalski really made his mother so soft-headed and depraved!?)

"Mama, don't you know . . . ," he began, but glancing over at the princess and paralyzed by the ferocious, greenish-yellow glare in her eye, he broke off. "Can you be so naive . . . ?" Again he stopped.

"Why can't you appreciate the good will of Irina Vsevolodovna, who has promised to introduce you to politics? After all, you're about to become the quartermaster general's aide." (Only in certain circles was the general referred to in this manner.) "You can't remain a silly little officer forever; you must seek out people of distinction, learn how to handle yourself in extremely complex situations. You must acquire some of that finesse which your late father was always so dead set against."

"Leave Father out of this. I shall do as I please. If I can't acquire a political head on my own, I'll serve as a combat officer, which would suit me fine. I can sacrifice my life without all those scurrilous intellectual graces that are required in scurrilous political parlor rooms to justify a policy of appeasement . . . "

The princess (with delight): Another cup of tea, Zip? What a pity that someone of your ability should do what any fool can do. Think of the perspective you'll have. Anyone in literature should be the last to turn his back on life, especially not when it tries to show him its profile from the most interesting angle.

Genezip: My views on that are quite different. (The princess smiled ironically: "He has views!") Life has nothing to do with literature, except for writers who have no business being in literature – literal-minded photographers of life's musty little corners. Literature proper – not the theater and not poetry, but fiction – invents new realities, in the sense of Chwistek's theory. His theory is useless when it comes to pure art, of course, but luckily that thing which I don't even understand is disappearing before our very eyes. I look at art neither as the manufacturing of the asinine and utterly useless stuff known as "pure form" nor as the plagiarizing of reality, but as the fashioning of a new reality to which we can escape when we have a bellyful . . .

"Is your belly really so full, my dear Zip?" said Irina Vsevolodovna, now laughing openly.

Mother: Zip! What a vulgar way you have of talking! It's time you associated with . . . (The princess suddenly turned serious.)

The princess (to Zip): Sturfan Abnol, that schizophrenic, that brilliant dreamer of emptiness incarnate, has been fuddling your brain with his theories. That's all right in Quintofron Crepuscolo's theater (she added, noting the look of indignation on Lilian's "fair visage"), a theater quite extraordinary in its way. That's really the place for an artist like him – and he is one, despite his avowed hatred of art – there in the theater where an absolute void, in the sense of a lack of any substance, is realized as a collaborative piece. The individual is dead in art. Nor do I believe you can invent a new fictional world to take the place of yesterday's formalism. I attended a performance, and it was *nothing – but nothing.* We must go together some time. Lilian will be making her debut next week in a marvelous little bordellesque written by her Sturcio or Fanio. But a literature (she continued in that most erudite manner of hers) that is not socially based, that ducks controversy and distant horizons for the sake of some didactic fantasies, with no desire to uplift the masses – then I say, such a literature must be a fraud, a narcotic *tretevo razryada* for cowards who can't take the simplest reality by the scruff of the neck. Even Abnol has shifted all that hyperrealism of his into the theater . . . (Our teenage fornicator was thoroughly mollified. The princess's drawling Russian accent had the same effect on him as yohimbine.)

"What a mishmash of ideas in that red head of yours!" Genezip started out in a deliberately condescending tone, but, running out of material and mettle, he suddenly stalled. "Why don't you ask my mother point blank why you're so nice to me? Do you need some specimen to observe? Some fiendish experiment to work on because you're bored? Oh, Mother, if you only knew!"

"She does know – I've kept nothing from her. Your mother understands me as a woman. Isn't that right, baroness?"

"Oh, how well I know *you!*" He buried his head in his hands, livid with rage and shame. How cute he looked! Tsk-tsk!! Lilian was absorbing the inscrutable and not-yet-dismembered "essence of life" with the suction discs of her subconscious. Something inside her was getting poised for the kill; in another second she would know everything. Then she would go to work on Sturfan, straddle life like a panther astride an antelope, rest a bit, then suck out his blood . . . She strained her pink little ears that lay beneath innocent golden locks.

"You don't know me yet; and you never will. 'Befriend me well, lest you lose me like dreams painted by benevolent spirits' – now who wrote that: Słonimski or Słowacki? Oh, *vyso ravno! Glupie poetniki.* You're a child, a brutal, pathetic child. One day you'll come to understand a lot of things, but then it'll be too late . . . " Something was groaning in her voice, in her poor heart, and it was getting louder and more protracted. At the moment she was a big, overintelligent, extremely pathetic little girl. Genezip was being asphyxiated by a wretched compassion. "You judge me wrongly. You're one of those people who can never be intimate with anyone except themselves; it's your luck and your curse. You'll approach life with thick, warm gloves – not with the latex variety. Nothing will ever wound you, but neither will you ever be perfectly happy emotionally." ("She could be talking about herself," Genezip thought dimly.) "How do you know what I've been through, or what anguish I'm suffering right now?! Pain can make a person bite the hand that caresses him. You're replacing the sons who have been lost to me – Matt has become a stranger and Adam is never coming back from there . . . " (The princess let out a dry sob but immediately regained her composure.) "And instead of thanking your mother for being so tolerant, you spurn her precisely on account of it."

"Mothers shouldn't pry into their sons' dirty little masculine affairs as long as they don't break the law . . . The affairs, that is, not the mothers. Ha, ha!" He laughed insanely, like one of Przybyszewski's heroes. (The baroness, who was obviously braced for anything, did not so much as flinch.)

"The princess is very upset and feels abandoned. The prince and Marquis di Scampi had to leave for the capital, and Prince Adam has been arrested. Just think, she's all alone – she ought to have a young companion. Youth is such a precious thing. Much of it is squandered, but for others a mere drop may be enough to restore their full powers . . . " ("The language of Michalski," Zip mentally groused. "So that's it – I'm to be this babe's portable battery.")

"My side mission in this miserable little world" (in her imagination she suddenly saw herself presiding over a magnificent court, the mistress of some young king: all-powerful in love and politics . . .) "is to introduce you to the world at large. In return I shall enjoy a second adolescence."

"What's the real reason you didn't go to the capital?" Genezip asked abruptly, suddenly transformed into a grown-up, thoroughly evil-minded male. For the three women it was as if he had suddenly acquired a hide of hair, had reverted to an ape.

There was an awkward silence. Worlds were collapsing, worlds bearing no resemblance to the one in which this chat was taking place. And even if by coordinating their respective points one could have deduced one from the other in a collinear fashion, not one of these four individuals, each of them obsessed with life, was privy to those transcendental realms where they lived like phantoms endowed with a superior sense – all four, at the exact same moment, even as they sat sipping their tea, there in that very drawing room.

"Yes, why, why?" the princess frantically repeated, and she plummeted from that other dimension like a wounded bird. "It's my duty to look after my husband's friends, and besides, I have a personal reason . . . If I had gone with them, I would have had to plead for Adam's release. And since my personal charm is well known there, they would be tougher with me than with others – to show their impartiality, to prove I had no effect on them they would go out of their way to be strict."

Genezip heard not a word of this explanation.

"That personal reason you mentioned is me, or rather my 'mortal coil.' Yes, that's right – my *obolochka*." (He was so overcome with self-disgust that he "could not help but wonder" why they didn't simply bounce him out.) "For you I'm just an appetizer, nothing else. The truth is you don't even like me. You treat me like a stupid little pet – to be used and then discarded. I only marvel at my mother, that she could conspire against me and try to undermine me, my sense of responsibility."

This last drivel severely taxed Zip's mother and the princess. Things were beginning to come apart. The absurd social standoff between the syndicate and that OTHER thing about which not even the bravest souls dared to talk or think; a country adrift in a strange and faceless complacency – all had become incarnated in this drawing room, had found in it the most perfect symbol: the utter superfluousness of these people. Superfluous for whom? Among themselves, or in the eyes of those thoroughly stupefied and complacent workers out there? At times both sides appeared superfluous. Even the world was superfluous, there being no one left to do it justice. All that remained was the landscape and a few scattered beasts – which wasn't much. There was a cure: the mobile Chinese Wall, but this was a little like an avalanche: an unknown element. Better yet would have been a *Weltkatastrophe* like a planetary collision or entering some unknown galactic nebula.

The princess: You are impossibly rude. We had been having such a nice chat before you came, things were under control, everything settled . . .

Genezip: Under your *female* control, you mean! Mother has *Mister* Michalski, and you would like to have me. Mother doesn't need me anymore; I'm a nuisance to her in this *(with irony)* "new life" of hers. She'd be glad to get rid of me, both as her son and her protector. An Anadyomene out of beer foam (he foamed) – a cheap female cook with hygienic love-cakes. No, I don't want to be anybody's *Selbstbefriedigungsmaschine*. . . .

Mother: Zip! Your sister is here. Think of what you're saying. It's sheer lunacy. I don't know who I am anymore! Oh, God! . . .

Genezip: Please don't invoke the name of God; for you He died ages ago, just like Father, His spitting image. (All right, but how did *he* know that, the rascal?) And in a few weeks my sister will know more about life than I do – if she doesn't already. I've got nothing against Abnol, but only when he's not around Lilian.

"A brother's subconscious jealousy," the princess pronounced with a scientific authority.

Mother: Sturfan is descended from Romanian boyars. They can be married within the year; Lilian will turn sixteen in September.

Genezip: Oh, do as you please! Such a lovely reception on my first day away from school! Everybody wants to do me a favor, but no one knows quite what. And what for? None of you knows the answer to that, which makes it even worse.

The princess: How lacking in imagination your generation is. It's what we mean to combat, beginning with you.

Genezip: Show me an idea, and I'll fall flat on my stomach before you. The applying-the-brakes idea – that's *your* pinnacle of thought!

The princess: Oh, we have some positive ideas, too – the syndicate, for example. Our car will descend the steep grade of modern times with the brakes on. The brake is the most positive thing of our day, it gives us an alternative to the bolshevik impasse. The idea of the nation is a necessary . . .

Genezip: The idea of the nation *was* a positive idea, but only briefly; a sort of pack-horse idea transporting other ideas on its back. An auxiliary line in a complicated geometric diagram. Camels are giving way to locomotives; when the diagram is done, the auxiliary line can be erased. Any compromise between the nation and society is impossible. And you *will* perish on the new ramparts of the Holy Trinity – only without God, that's the trick. And what is your trinity of ideas if not a frantic consumption, the pretense of power (even if you have to lick what you consider to be the grubby paws of the proletariat), and the willingness to cheat in art.

Lilian: The future sage of Ludzimierz, like the future saint of Lumbres in the first part of Bernanos's novel.

Genezip: Right you are! Just you wait . . .

The princess: Don't tell lies, my dear. I once entertained such thoughts, too. But compromise is the way of the future, at least for the duration of *our* lives. Why have the Chinese stalled? Because they're afraid of Poland. They're afraid that here, in this land of compromise, their momentum will be broken, that their army will fall apart when they see a contented land free of any pseudobolshevik ideas.

Genezip (gloomily): You mean a mire. Is our country really so contented? The deeper one delves into this cesspool . . . ("Why does he drift off into this *printsipialny razgovor* when there are so many more immediate things to attend to?!")

The princess: No need to delve into anything. To *live* – that's the real trick! (Her affectation at that moment struck him as frail, pathetic.) Oh, something momentous is heading my way from out of faraway spaces, something to prove me right! Zip, as a covert member of the syndicate you could do us an immense service by penetrating the general's most intimate circle – lately he has been surrounding himself with politically sexless people.

Genezip: In other words, you want me to spy on that man you call a "general." He's no more a general than I am. No, never in a million years. I'll be what I want to be, and that's final. I shall persevere on my own. From now on, hands off my affairs, or I'll handle you in a way you'll remember – or won't remember, which is worse. Don't provoke the secret powers in me or I'll demolish you.

Zip swelled like a balloon giant inflated with an imaginary power – he could sense it but was powerless against it. Something, some foreign presence, was beginning to occupy his brain; someone was fumbling around in that complicated machinery with a clumsy hand; some unknown, terrifying customer who, without stopping to introduce himself, was taking over for him – insolently, hastily, impulsively, confidently, commandingly. It was just the beginning, but it was enough. "Was this that gent he had detected earlier (if superficially) but who was only now coming out of hiding? Oh God, what next?? No one can guess that, not even God, although some people claim that it is HE who deprives creatures of their reason, who takes and gives – just as He does everything else, after all. Either He partially nullifies (or 'switches off' – yes, why not? He's all-powerful, isn't He?) His omniscience on purpose (for His own amusement or for 'the good of the faithful'), or He's cruel beyond all reason. And is there a crueler beast than man?" Thus, more or less, did Zip muse, in bits and pieces and against the backdrop of that cerebromaterial manifestation of the unknown. He was wresting himself *from* himself for some dreadful, mysterious world governed by its own laws. But where was this other world? He was in both places at once. "Where am I?" someone cried out mutely in formless, bottomless, vaultless caves, in those "grottoes fashioned by dreams and madness" (Miciński). Oh, so this is what is meant by madness. It's really not so awful: a slight "non-Euclideanness" of the psyche. Still, this "bum start" was bad enough to last him a lifetime. Not the thing itself, really, but its possible side effects. What would his motor centers say to that? His muscles, sinews, bones? Or would they all be reduced to dust and ashes? And then he would have to face the consequences – and *that* would be ghastly. Simultaneously, he saw with alarming clarity how ordinary and utterly stupid the situation was. His gaze fell on Lilian, who was like a level permanently suspended in this whirling vortex of triviality. He loved her, could not live without her; but this was behind a plate of glass, the same one that always managed to separate him from the world. The dagger of perfidious pride was stabbing his intestines from below, a furtive thrust from his deceased father. She was to blame for all this, his mother; she was a madwoman. It was from her that he had inherited this ugly mess in his head. Even so, he would not have exchanged places with anyone in the world. He would rise above himself, above his own madness. Because madness it was – that much he knew, as yet without panic. This thought was dazzlingly clear amid the surrounding darkness. Still, he was sufficiently alarmed as to come to his senses. The moment of lucidity lasted no more than a fleeting fraction of a second. How might it have looked in the case of simultaneity? It was as though time had split in two, and the two halves were racing each other on separate tracks.

Genezip leaned with his fist against the table. He was pale and swayed from exhaustion, but he spoke coolly and calmly. He could feel Kotzmolochowicz's polyp-spirit inside him: how nice to have a commander one could believe in! (The princess was inwardly squealing with delight. How she adored her little "troublemaker"! Now, just bend him a little, humiliate him somehow, and all that quaint, pent-up, misguided, frustrated rage would unload itself on her – violently, in those lovely little juices [a young birch bleeding in the sun]: "The canalization of abstract masculine rage and general frustration," as Marquis di Scampi used to put it.) Horror-struck, Zip's mother fell silent, as though internally numbed, and made herself scarce. Lilian, on the other hand, gazed at him admiringly: he was her cherished idol, Zip, the brother she had always wanted him to be: a virtual lunatic. Abnormality was for her a necessary spice in any brother-sister relationship, verging on psychosexual impulses (for him as well). How different he was from other men – "a phantom on another plane," Sturfan might have said. These three women, each in her own way, were humbling themselves before the imaginary power of the moment, without seeing (as usual) the long-range implications. It started up again:

Genezip: I'm going to be what I choose to be even if I have to go insane. So, Mother, you know that I was her lover and that she betrayed me with Toldzio before my very eyes. That's right; I watched the whole thing from her bathroom, which she deliberately locked. (He had hoped that by openly declaring it he might rise above all this female intriguing. Both women responded with absolute calm. Here was a new method for educating females: imbue them from the start, in the ovum of their emotions, with a thorough knowledge of evil. And these were to be the strong women of the future! Lilian knew all there was to know: first of all, rationally, and secondly, directly, with the lower part of her belly, where life-hungry monsters were poised.) And you would like me to . . . Where are you people, anyway?! – in any case, not in any world that I know. What a twist! The son is more conservative than the mother. I'll bet Michalski is to blame for all this – I mean, *Mister* Michalski – ha-ha!

Mother: There's meanness in your laugh. I remember how on that morning . . . Oh, how differently you acted then . . .

Genezip: Even now it turns my stomach to think about it, coming as it did right after that . . . (He motioned toward the princess.) I'd like to it shake off, be naked as an embryo, and start over. (A howl of laughter from the women, then immediate recovery. Incensed, Zip went dead inside, was transformed into a huge gaping wound. He was thrust into a mushy shame, a gooey ridiculousness, a bitter despair. A seesaw.) And Lilian – now I see that Lilian has been initiated, too! (He was trying to pull it out with a hysterical defense of his sister; in reality he wasn't the least concerned.)

Mother: You understand nothing about women. You see in them only a threat to your as-yet-unformed personality, you don't see how fragile their power is, how much ostensible evil they have to amass in themselves to put up with you. You have no idea how the princess has agonized over you. (She stood up and embraced the princess.) We both suffer so much for your sake. Understand her with your heart, understand your poor mother whose life has been only a chain of sorrows. You have no idea what its like to fall in love after thirty! (Zip was beginning to show signs of melting; he was positively oozing with a greasy, slimy compassion, but he stopped himself – rather, that "gent" stopped him – at the border of an absolute fixation. "There's strength in madness, too" – the thought occurred to him in the empty space between his doppelgängers.)

Genezip: And I don't want to know! It's sickening, all this emotional slobbering. Human emotions – yes, human – are an abomination, deceitful stuff packed in the refuse of social transformations. Oh, animals are much happier, at least they don't lie!

Mother: You're behaving almost like an animal yourself, my child. By playing a he-man you've gone beyond being crass and brutal. And as for Lilian, she is indeed one of the newly educated women. We didn't want you to lose heart prematurely. There's no harm in being initiated early in life – that prejudice has cost many generations their sanity. Anyhow, Lilian is about to become Sturfan's wife. Isn't it true, my pet – you feel a lot better now that you know everything?

Lilian: I sure do! Zip's just a kid, though wonderful in his own way. He'll get used to everything in time. After all, whoever heard of Freudian complexes in New Guinea? There, children start playing marriage at the age of six. Later, of course, everything is "taboo" within the village. And sisters are the biggest "taboo" of all, one touch and it's death (she added in an embarrassingly coquettish manner). We'll manage, though; we – not our children, but we ourselves – will produce a new, normal generation within life's mechanistic scheme. Imperceptibly, from the inside, we will change everything (she added again, this time with a scientific gravity).

"Those new generations will serve the Chinese as manure, as a foundation for what they mean to build in our country," interrupted a furious and humiliated Zip, whose head now swam. "Cant, idle promises, the self-delusions of incurable optimists – I know it all too well." At bottom, however, the situation appealed to him, despite everything he had ever cherished in himself; it was the beginning of perversion, the work of that internal cad. But what exactly was this "bottom"? (What was this to a Kotzmolochowicz?! A fart bubble! Yet it was precisely such minor distinctions [those "cerebropsychic molecules," to quote some effeminate Bergsonian count] that formed the raw stuff wherein all such statesmen operated, etc. . . . Little did Zip realize how similar they were, he and that *Ober*hypergeneral, whom he revered and who might have learned much by examining his microdoppelgänger through a magnifying glass. They had crossed paths too late, to the detriment of them both.)

Something was beginning to surface again. He was illuminated from within by a sudden bolt of lightning, by a revelation. He felt so airy and spacious (and even brighter) inside, like a plugged-up nose after two decigrams of cocaine. That nameless one whom he dreaded and against whom he was resisting; that other, more essential "he" whom he had flushed out of the underground and into the light – let him rise, expand, have a ball! ("A wacko can realize his potential only in madness," that man of genius, Bekhmetev, would have said.) A person will sacrifice anything to know his double, to subdue him or be subdued by him. But how is it to be done? By what crimes or renunciations? How long life seemed! That other fellow, though, he could show him how to get the most out it, how to get through it. Only *he* could swing it, while Genezip would always remain "behind glass," like a fish in an aquarium.

....

INFORMATION: Lilian felt nothing even remotely similar. She had everything to recommend her: she was perfect, psychologically rounded, flawless – like her cyclothyme of a father. The whole thing (oh, what marvels were implied by that "thing"!) amused her in a purely rational, abstract way. She had succeeded so wonderfully in adapting the mask of a mature adult to her inner frigidity. It was precisely her frigidity that drove Sturfan Abnol wildly insane. So far nothing had passed between them (God forbid!). A few kisses, during which she had asked him rather icily: "Why are you licking me like that, Mister Abnol?" – pronounced not so much with an air of disgust as of curious detachment, emanating not from where she lived consciously, since the dynamite below had not yet joined the fuse leading up to the detonators in her small, "well-balanced *servelka*" (as Princess Irina used to call her brain). But something else had also emerged: the fruit of life, formless as yet but in no way (for the time being) suggestive of Phallus. It seemed as revelatory as an aquamarine light parting the murky haze of an autumnal dawn, but in fact was a snakenest of drives and appetites stretched to infinity. For just as these two incompatible worlds of her personality were about to come into contact (like a pair of mouths, but perfectly formed, not like Sturfan's fleshy lips and Lilian's strawberry gob of jelly) and form a new chemical compound (deliberate female bestiality and power), Lilian had experienced something verging on religious ecstasy: her pure, timid little soul was bathing in the ethereal, unfulfilled beauty of an imaginary Existence.

The cell door closed again: the time was not yet ripe. Genezip had collapsed inwardly. His muscles had parted from his bones, his guts were in shambles. He may have been a little titan at the officers' school, he may have lorded over his enemies – the divisional and platoon commanders; but here, caked with the meanness and allure of a life impossibly magnified in the form of these wenches (the two who were related to him only increased the allure of that bitch-princess instead of diminishing it, as they were supposed to), he was surrendering unconditionally. Unless he were to chuck all three, dammit (but right then and there; otherwise, forget it), and swear, oh swear never to see them again. If only he could have done just it; there are people, incidentally, who actually can pull off such things. True, they are becoming rarer, but they do exist, dammit. But Zip lacked the necessary courage. His repressed madness had him by the scruff of the neck and was forcing him to guzzle from the trough of misery. Ugly compromise had insinuated itself from the side, like a muddy little creek polluting a clear stream. The accusation of being unimaginative had stung him. What sort of ideas *did* he entertain, anyway? How to justify his existence, naked, stripped of all those petty, everyday proofs of necessity, precariously alone in the bog – without any of the props of childhood notions in the form of small concentric circles? How?! Never mind that the harpy had a few political opinions of her own, not to mention a damned good head on her shoulders, and in that head a brain of fairly high caliber – a little on the masculine side and well-versed in dialectics. It was not so easy to dismiss this woman out of hand. Infuriating, no?

Things dragged hopelessly on. No one tried to argue with him anymore. The three women knew (like the witches in *Macbeth*) that he had surrendered. A female triumph reigned supreme in the drawing room, coating all the furniture, carpets, and knickknacks with an obscene slime. Lilian and his mother rose from the sofa with that characteristic forward lean suggestive of rarefied flight over a squalid, thoroughly demolished reality. The gesture also bespoke gratitude to the princess. Mrs. Kapen kissed her son's forehead without even asking whether he intended to stay behind. Her kiss made the commander's future aide shudder: he was without a mother, sister, or lover now, as alone in the boundless universe as after his prophetic awakening. His excremental friends? They did not so much as enter his head. So be it! He would depart from there and never come back – only not now, not right then. "*Der Mann ist selbst,*" as the school principal, General Mildew, was fond of saying.

He accompanied the ladies into the hallway. But as he was kissing her *fiendishly soft* hand in farewell, the princess managed to whisper, aiming her hot breath directly into his ear: "Please stay. Extremely important things. Your whole future. I love you so very differently now." He dissolved in her whisper like a teaspoon of sugar in boiling hot water. And suddenly, changed beyond all recognition, illumined by this comedown and no longer feeling alone or desperate (complacency has something smelly about it, but never mind), contented, moved, and almost orgastic in a soothing sexual relaxation (a soothing laxation) – he stayed. But just as soon as the other two had left, the princess turned cold, standoffish. Again Genezip was gripped by icy despair – roughly, by the snout. Was it for this he had betrayed himself?! In exchange for his internal ruin he was to receive not a scrap, not even the meanest scrap, of that body which he was actually loath to possess? The inspiration to commit some decisive act never materialized. No banging of fists, no murder, no booting her around . . . instead, he stood in his own private little corner, a well-mannered boy with a heart *en compôte*.

"This time not a word about ourselves – " (He was sitting stiff and erect, military fashion. That "pile of elements" before him seemed so far removed [it occupied that "other dimension" looming in the very same space] he wondered how he could have stooped to even the most casual, "sisterly" kiss. He was haunted by the thought of disintegrating alive. "Oh, to escape on some stupendous wave, without all these tests, ambuscades, these pits full of spikes!" He had the sensation of being tripped up always by a stick. Let him graduate – he was in his final semester – then he would show them . . . Only he must avoid a repeat performance of what happened after his last graduation: just when all the world had seemed fixed and ready – pow, a massive identity crisis.) "That (by which she meant "we") is the least of our concerns. More important is what you are going to become. You especially, Zip, with your nature, so full of a mysterious and unruly passion – you can't afford to live without an idea. At best, it would be courting madness, a crackup. All of mankind is reflected in you like a fleeting cloud in a mirror. I've discovered a great deal just by watching you wrestle with yourself. (She spoke like an old aunt and was *so* beautiful in the role! It was diabolical . . .) Ideas such as labor management won't lead to any grand and heroic deeds. Those are concepts meant for the drab future. But we have to bear witness to their presence in the passé social forms with which we are still somehow connected, and that's why we feel anxiety and boredom. We're becoming more and more ingrown in ways that are alien to us. ("'The bitch has something up her sleeve!'" thought Zip.) These are technical ideas to be *temporarily* exploited by every party for its own interests – as much by the syndicate as by some bolshevized Mongolian warlords. One day these ideas will rule the universe – by then, fortunately, none of us will be alive. But these are not ideas to live by or to devote one's life to – unless you happen to be a technocrat."

Genezip: Yes, but the idea of an increasing prosperity, of wiping out the class struggle in classic American style – a product of that very labor management! – this idea may work for advanced societies, may allow them to endure existence, to say nothing of reinventing it, of fashioning new values to which only opportunists, careerists, and common ordinary fools will give lip service. To endure – that's a lot these days, given the spiritual desert engulfing us; to accept the hopelessness of everything rather than be duped by utopian fictions that are supposed to come true any day now; to not confuse the death pangs of something with the birth of something new . . . (Hadn't she once made this very point herself?!) How easy to promise a bright and rosy future, to proclaim in teary-eyed fashion all sorts of trite platitudes for those who are incapable of grim reflection. There have always been periods of crisis and self-doubt, and somehow mankind has always found a consolation . . . (He was losing sight of the object of this sermon, whether it was himself or her he was trying to convince. He was simply parroting ideas palmed off on him by one of his colleagues, the ex-amateur economist Voydeck-Wojdakiewicz).

The princess: You're blathering like someone on the rack. Prosperity can't expand indefinitely, but collectivization as such – *als solche*, I repeat – can, with or without prosperity, whose progress it can halt and which no power on earth can then revive. Europe aside, this is most visible in America: for all its frenzy over labor management, maximum income, full prosperity among the workers, profit-sharing schemes . . . , nothing could save that continent from communism. Human appetite knows no limit.

Genezip: It's being dulled, mark my word. It was only a matter of time: the transition was very smooth. Maybe in the new societies . . .

The princess: We shall never know how they might have developed. Etcetera, etcetera. Anyhow, the facts bear me out. The American model teaches that an idea – and what idea is superior to the national? – is still, I repeat, *still* necessary . . .

Genezip: Now *you* are talking nonsense! (He had opted for the blunt approach.) Even without communism, the global economy left by the last great war proves that nationalism is a scam, a fiction invented by the knights of yore, secret diplomats, narrow-minded industrialists, and plain old dealers in lucre. The world has become too entangled to speak of sovereign and independent nations. (Again he was foundering, not knowing whether he was voicing his own beliefs or unconsciously aping Wojdakiewicz.)

The princess: What arose after the last great war was bolshevism disguised as supranational bodies granting countries a semblance of sovereignty. And that's why all those leagues and international labor congresses collapsed; that's why things are as they are today. (The princess deliberately chose the most common Polish words, unaware of their special flavor.) Either you have a nation or an anthill – there's no third alternative. And you too must live by this idea, because you belong to that vanishing part of mankind. It's no use pretending; you can't be other than your born self. Better to die young and be true to yourself than to live as a liar. Deliver yourself to my care if you don't want to become your alter ego, which is quite likely in your case. If you want to occupy the heights and not the garbage heap, become a secret member of the syndicate. (Genezip buried his face in his hands. This time she had him! How could she have intuited the words in the inarticulate forest of his being, have pulled from there the live and meaty chunks of his deepest existence, skewered on symbols as though on hors d'oeuvre sticks?! She had managed it with the help of her sexual organs, as naturally and "intuitively" ["hee-hee, Mister Bergson!"] as a tediously conventional gallfly depositing her eggs in some wretched caterpillar. Zip burned with shame, even though he had been fed the whole of biological literature starting with Loeb and Bohn, those two great men of science who reduced to dust and ashes the concept of instinct and in so doing indirectly demolished one of the most monstrous hoaxes ever perpetrated: Bergsonism.) There's something strange in the air . . . The final convulsions, I agree, but it smacks of greatness, the absence of which we all feel so keenly and rottenly: *"Die Freude zu stinken,"* as that poor sap Nietzsche has written. (And then:) So far, however obstinately we tried, we haven't penetrated the general's most intimate circle. Because you were handpicked by him – they say your father was privy to his plans – you could furnish us with extremely valuable information, if only about his personal habits: what he eats for breakfast, how he takes off his historic boots at night. Because, you see, none of us has the faintest idea how that monster spends a normal, routine day. Later, of course, you might gain access to other, more important matters . . .

From the lowest lowlands, from the swamps, from behind the most squalid shacks and muckheaps (his own), Zip replied (a reality, splendid but sickening, and a bed of corruption like a pallet of dirty straw in a dungeon: these two images danced about in his weary brain, neither one able to overpower the other. His tongue was working independently of his personality. It was surely that third party, that lunatic, who was speaking on behalf of the noble lad, *his* ultimate aim being far from noble: *der Wille Zum Wahnsinn*):

"There won't be enough time. Do you suppose the Chinese will wait out these nasty little vendettas carried out for the good of your plump but barren tummies? Silly illusions!"

"Ugh! What a bolshevik you are! Be sensible. And stop acting like some vulgar street agitator."

"I told you I wouldn't spy," he snarled, "not for the most sublime idea."

"But spying on behalf of a higher goal is noble. And this is certainly . . . Not even for the sake of my friendship?"

"I spit on your friendship! Was your love, all those demoniacal tricks, also a part of the scheme? Oh, how low I've sunk . . . " Again he buried his head in his hands. The princess gazed at him with a mother's sympathy and with all the rapacity of a cat about to pounce. Visibly swollen, her body strained toward him, though she still lacked the courage to touch him. It was possibly too early, though if she did not do it now she might never do it. Genezip was a fly trapped in glue; his legs were paralyzed, his wings were buzzing desperately in the air, supplying him with the illusion of freedom. He shrank infinitesimally from shame, from his own and that of the situation. Then he heard the front doorbell ring from out of the remote depths of that exotic palace.

"You don't want to understand, do you? It's you I care about, your ability to experience life in the only way possible. And, of course, your career in case the syndicate wins. Remember, it matters whether you view life from a box in the orchestra or from the rarefied atmosphere of the balcony. '*Die Leute sind dieselben, aber der Geruch ist anders,*' as a Viennese cabby once told Peter Altenberg. So far, choosing to become a social outcast hasn't helped anyone, and climbing back up the social ladder is harder than you think." (Oh, to stop this landslide of words heavier than the most stupendous steamtrunks [precisely – steamtrunks]!)

"Do you really believe we can stop the Chinese and hold out in this third-rate democracy surrounded by a sea of bolshevism?"

"And that spoken by the general's admirer and future aide! My child, you are contradicting your idol's fundamental premise."

"No one knows his thoughts – that's what makes him great . . . "

"A dubious greatness, to say the least. He's a force, I won't deny it, but a warped one. Force for the sake of force – that's his idea, force in its purest form. We, the syndicate, must use him for our own ends."

"What?! That jellyfish pretending to be a party is going to exploit him, HIM?! Ha, ha, ha!"

"Don't laugh. I'm all adrift in a sea of contradictions. And who isn't these days? You see, Zip, we're getting secret help from the West. Never mind that White Russia has fallen; it was lost without a man of Kotzmolochowicz's stature. Why from the West? Because the new bolshevik governments there, still suffering from a nationalist hangover, cryptically fascist on the pretext that the time isn't ripe for communism – what a contradiction! – are trembling in the presence of the Chinese steamroller. Not only must they help us by maintaining the status quo – that is to say, this swamp – but for purely technical reasons they have to move us in a way that violates their own ideology. Life's complexity staggers the mind! Funds imported from the West – there you have that 'Polish miracle' which these yellow monkeys with their sense of honesty and fair play can't understand. Ho*rrr*endous secrets, Zip, for which I could be put on the rack. If our plan fails, then the gates will be opened, followed by the yellow flood and the end of the white race. Alas, even the racial issue has lost its significance in the mass society: skin colors no longer matter, simply. Oh look, here comes Sir Cylindrion Piętalski, baron and chamberlain of the Holy See and former commander of His Holiness's own machine-gunners."

Genezip felt himself an insect in this house, a cockroach, a bedbug, a termite. Oh, if now and then we could retch our souls into the void without departing this life! Wouldn't that be fun!

They were joined by a hideous-looking gent (why hideous when we could have made him attractive? a fluke), a sallow, droopy, thin-faced but big-bellied, blonde galoot with whiskers brushed "à la lord" and a monocle on a black ribbon. He wasted no time in speaking (the man was obviously primed). (His sexless character was all too apparent – here at least was one who was not the princess's lover!) He spoke, and the cadaverous quality of his concepts made his listeners shudder. Nationalism in general, and the Polish variety in particular, had been so macerated in literature from the romantics to the most recent Neo-Saviours, had been so prostituted at every celebration, festivity, meeting, session, and anniversary in the form of empty clichés and idle promises, that it was now dead, expired, and so removed from reality that it would never move anyone again. The vicious lie had congealed life's living albumin as far as the orbit of Neptune. Whole planets and their satellites were dying from the boredom and futility of resolving "the national question." If on the satellite of Uranus or Jupiter something on the order of a new nation was being born, then Piętalski's breath, reeking of pious platitudes, would have parboiled and reconstituted that living germ for billions of miles. And everybody knows what *that* sauce looks and smells like, especially when it's used to baste a rancid reality. It was very dispiriting, this willful self-deception on the part of a "man of prestige," this conscientious humbug on the part of a high-ranking demon. Okay, okay – but what was his program? No, it was so politically absurd that . . . – more absurd than in the land of Hyrcania, where alongside a bolshevik regime you had a buffoon of a king, apparently left on the throne as a source of ridicule but who in fact involved himself not a little in the affairs of state and amused himself handsomely. Piętalski talked aimlessly. Phrases like "the fatherland," "love for one's country," "sacrifice for the nation's well-being," etc. (such phrases were in decline – many had even been forgotten – and only the less hackneyed still circulated, those in which the vestiges of meaning still thronged, like moths around some arc lamp, about the mysterious, dark fire of the Ultimate Sense of Existence), were dropping from the greasy, bluish lips of this greying blonde, one of the "pillars" of the syndicate. He existed only through these phrases; otherwise, he was a phantom, a minute speck on the retina of God.

Genezip was ashamed for that nation (for himself as one of its component elements). Wouldn't you know it? This pint-sized differential-Messiah even suffered for others in a collective shame! He had arrived just in time! A shabby thought: was it worth being somebody in such a flop of a country? Suddenly he was reminded of something Tenzer had said: "To be born a hunchback in Poland is bad luck; to be born an artist in addition is the worst luck of all." Lucky for us ("*Bonne la nôtre*," to quote Lebac) we are not artists. No, that blasphemer Tenzer was wrong. Such maxims were to blame for the present foul atmosphere. "*Die Kerle haben keine Ahnung was arbeiten heisst und dazu haben sie kein Zeitgefühl*," as Buxenhein used to say. And so: every man for himself, no consideration for others . . . But that still left the Chinese flood and the general lateness of the hour. They sensed, the beasts, that time was running out. Poised above their heads (in no way superior to those "shaved heads" of our heroic past) was a yellow wave bearing a fate without precedent. Too late. Better to wrap yourself in a dirty blanket and mind your own business; keep to yourself, think about nothing, read a silly novel, go dancing, climb into bed with someone, then sleep it off. But it was too early for such a routine; now and then people still had to think. Europe, consumed by a "wild and rampant capitalism," was unable to lend a hand to the East, which was rising up. "You have to blow everything to gain everything," as Tadeusz Szymberski once wrote. Such ideas still pulsated in some semi- and quarter-intellects, crawling out only after they had been sufficiently reviled. So what was this hateful thing that went by the name of patriotism: a wishy-washy pride in the country, and then such a maligned one; a purely sensual attachment to certain sounds (in the West, Esperanto was gradually replacing the native languages); an animal attachment to one's "native tongue." But in essence it was a mask for concealing appetites. And that, dammit, was the terrifying part of it!

And for such corpse-ideas hatched like mushrooms on the cadaver of old feelings like – oh, who cares what they were, anyway? – he was to stab him in the back? The only man with any balls, the ill-starred Kotzmolochowicz, who, considering the odds, was clearly doomed? No. Meanwhile, from the miasmic swamp of his ego that mystery guest rose up again out of the land of madness where everything was the way it was supposed to be – for a select few, anyway. And Genezip rammed his fist into Piętalski's face and shoved him into the hallway. He could hear him spitting and coughing outside; he felt bad about it, but at the same time pleased to have vindicated the patriotic idea. Unsavory characters like that did not deserve to be emissaries! He sincerely wondered what his own percentage (%) of nationalism was at the moment. He saw only the yellow cuffs of his uniform, however, and sensed that he, miserable pissant that he was, had pulled off a crackerjack thing. His intuition had been sound – the word *intuition* was quite apt in this case – though it might have turned out to be unsound as well. (As Husserl has correctly observed, those so-called intuitive [currently the pet expression of female prigs and effeminate males with an aversion to thinking] discoveries are always the work of specialists trained in the analogical method, in the use of the researcher's tools, the skipping of procedural steps, self-suggestion – that's *intuition*, my dear ladies. "You will prevail, but only because the mind is held in such contempt today; even so, you're wrong," as Sturfan Abnol used to say on this subject.) Little did Zip understand the consequences of his "feat": the face-bashing incident hastened by two whole weeks the outbreak of certain events. A minor "intelligence riot," as it was termed, was even staged at the syndicate's party headquarters. The patriots were as mystified by the country as they were by Kotzmolochowicz. Confusion reigned; people were gasping in the fumes of universal "obfuscation" (a term used by Karol Irzykowski; may he be damned for invoking this word, which now affords every moron the right to divest the most precious things of their value). A few drops of blood were needed to assess the actual state of things: "The tetht of litmuth paper dipped in freth blood," Piętalski used to lisp. (It never occurred to anyone that lives might be lost in the process.) With an early victory the attack might be broadened and could even lead to the downfall of Kotzmolochowicz himself, who, to the syndicate's great distress, had begun flirting (for the time being openly) with the army's radical wing, then under the influence of Colonel Monkempt-Unster. (Needless to say, this "radicalism" was kept vigorously concealed.) The leading members of the syndicate took no part in the "experiment," so that in case of defeat their subordinates could always be denounced as lunatics.

Piętalski continued to spit and cough in the vestibule. A pale, trembling, and breathless Genezip, his clenched fists braced against the armrest, was staring fixedly at the princess's indecent legs, which seemed imbued with a satanic, but incredibly focused, sensuality. How could a leg sheathed in silk and shoes of stiff shiny leather be so expressive? Why couldn't one rape a woman's leg, as one would a body, and feast on its (or their, as the case may be) morbid allure . . . A sudden bang put an abrupt end to these meditations as the front door was slammed shut, causing the door fasteners to rattle furiously. The condemned exchanged glances and embraced with their duplicitous eyes, with their mysterious fluid (= a routine compact between two similar natures), like two bubbles in a murky puddle of reality. The clash with Cylindrion had unleashed that something sprung from Genezip's depths, a hunger for infinity enticing him to the extraordinary, even abominable in life – so long as it was not that which *is* or eventually might *be*. But, alas, only madness or crime can break through the wall of banality

– occasionally art, sometimes not even that. Let's drop the subject. How Zip dreaded this risk, though it was precisely what made life beautiful. He was not himself; it was a brief respite, a momentary transcendence. A psychic hemlock of his own creation, conjuring up an alien, elusive (in the sense of "pure being") world of absolute universal harmony. No, he was not himself (o bliss!): that internal bully was peering through his eyes as through windowpanes, like an animal lurking in the dark.

And then *it* took over . . . They hurled themselves at each other as if from out of infinite, aimless, indifferent space. It had begun, that ripping apart of the pleasure embedded in soft meaty folds; that lewd parting of the flesh burning with wild lust; that ruthless engorgement of an almost metaphysical *pain* wrested from the guts . . . Engorgement of pain? Yes, why not? This was indeed *something;* he had reaffirmed it; and having resolved the problem of his immediate derangement, he plummeted deeper into the overpowering embraces of his own demons inhabiting the Land of the Deep. Howling like a wild boar caught in life's lowest abomination, he hung suspended above the world, boring with the glance of a rabid hawk into *those other eyes* slowly drowning in a bottomless evil. In the obliquity of those eyes, whose slanted expression lust only *magnified,* there glittered the Mystery of Being. But it was all a hoax – a passionate, idiotic, savage hoax. Genezip had reached the summit, but instead of beatification caused by the joining of two bodies, only the sensation of loneliness. The psyche had reached its limits. He felt lonelier now than he had ever felt with Toldzio, lonelier even than that time in the princess's bathroom.

The princess, sensing her failure to punish the brat as planned, gave herself to him in silent gloom. Oh, what an uncanny taste he possessed for her, now that she had inherited him by the grace of wicked chance! What their lovemaking had lost in mathematical precision, it now gained in a new and perilous charm. Say what you will, the twilight period has a magic of its own. "By the grace, by the grace," she whispered, exhilarated by the awareness of her fall, exulting in the tragedy, the somberness, the futility of the pleasure aglow with all the autumnal hues of youth. Meanwhile, the kid was also "banging" evil. And one evil was found to be so satisfying to the other that they conspired to form a single evil – pure, self-sustaining, asexual Evil. Love (whole and inviolate, i.e., not split in two), now banished from their "dizzying" clasps, was smiling glumly off to the side; it knew that what they were doing would have to be revenged, and it was peacefully biding its time.

....

INFORMATION: After his humiliation, Cylindrion set about his little coup d'état with redoubled energy. "*So*," he said to himself, "that's what you want, eh? We'll see about that! The truth is at hand." This seemingly minor incident at the palace so consumed the energy of the syndicate's "pillar" that his "experiment," though still in a green state at the time, began in the days that followed to swell into a gold and succulent fruit ripe for the picking. The whole thing proceeded so quietly that some suspected it was being directed by Kotzmolochowicz's agents. "Even he needs to know what's going on down below," they whispered. Events were bolting from their masters and racing off on their own – for the time being within a restricted field. The most powerful personalities were little more than the simulacra of various parties: prescribed in their behavior, deprived of any initiative. The only exception was Kotzmolochowicz, who continued to hold his own inside his own internal fortress.

The method by which all this was achieved was as tedious as the exercises of an insincere priest: someone whispered a word here, handed a note there, gossiped with a third, slipped something to another, did a little cajoling here, wormed his way into there, and then that person would engage others in a similar – but why waste words? Psychologically it was a real bust, with the exception of the commander's inner structure: a mélange holding varying proportions of ambition, impressive words with unimpressive meanings, dirty cunning, and at times just plain, ordinary, brute power. As a result, everyone thought everyone else a rogue, including themselves at times.

The "affair of honor" initiated by Cylindrion and conducted with the knowledge of the school administration led to honorably satisfying but bloodless results. For political reasons it was deemed appropriate that Zip should apologize to Piętalski. Included in the files was a medical document, blindly "endorsed" by Bekhmetev himself, testifying to the mildly abnormal state of the assailant due to a family ordeal.

Genezip left the palace of the Ticonderogas, otherwise known as the "fornication point," "foaming at the mouth with life." Asceticism was good, but good fornication was better. Unconditional surrender. He was amassing an arsenal in the secret enclaves of his psyche, and he intended to use it against the princess at the appropriate time. Meanwhile, he wallowed in his debasement, exulted in the consciousness of his comedown. Having sunk to depravity, he came up wheezing and snorting. To evade the syndicate's spies, this *podozritelnaya parochka,* as the princess called this pair, began meeting in a foul little place rented and sumptuously furnished by the princess, the instigatrix of this messy affair, and which was located in the suburb of Jada. The question of treason was never broached again. For a number of weeks this *geroj nashego vremeni* was rendered harmless.

A Commander's Thoughts and the Little Theater of Quintofron Crepuscolo

Three days after this depressing incident Zip moved back in with his family. His nights were free now – one of the privileges of being a "Senior Cadet." He spent those nights with the princess in a positively fiendish affair that, in anticipation of an early end, was multiplied threefold, even tenfold, in the eyes and hands of that little upstart now thoroughly unleashed by his voluntary collapse. Genezip learned at last the meaning of the word *surfeiture*. How bizarre! Those creatures which only yesterday had seemed flawless mysteries, making him bug-eyed and turning his hands to insatiable polyps, were today mundane objects intended for daily use. His complacency was short-lived. That ogress was infinitely resourceful in devising new thrills, in conjuring up new tricks from her inexhaustible store of experience, and this without resorting to any cheap demonism. Yet that moment in the bathroom still affected him from out of the past, beaming forth indefatigably like a chunk of radium: it sheltered him from love but served as a backup for purely sexual stimulation. Herein lay a peril and an evil of a most abject kind. Something had begun to rot, and for no apparent reason.

It was at this time that Genezip paid a visit to the theater of Quintofron Crepuscolo. He was practically dragged there by Sturfan Abnol. The author's second semi-improvisational piece was being performed there, and Lilian was scheduled to make her debut as understudy in the role of a horribly strung-out teenager. Genezip had refused until now to see his sister onstage, whether from subconscious jealousy or a hidden fear of the social stigma – an actress from the house of the Vahazes! – was unclear.

Life was moving at a snail's pace, not only for Genezip but for the country as well, most of all for Kotzmolochowicz. The general had a scheme that was not translatable into words, that was as elusive as a cobweb and as strong as the strands of a steel cable. He felt it in his muscles, in the lightninglike flashes of his will, in his special talent for self-transgression: he longed for a nation welded into a single personality as fierce as himself – a machine, precision-made down to the last nut and bolt, yet as ostensibly free as a cloud drifting blithely in the sapphire blue of space. That monolith was himself, and he wanted this solid block of raw material to be a sculpture of his own creation, with his own muscle-emotions magically transformed into an inert material bursting with the flawless perfection of a pristine unity. But so far all he had to show for his trouble were a few klutzy bricks. But even from these the general was determined to sculpt a pseudoconstructivist, improvisational mass – as from elements of a perversity. A peerless rider, he was mounted on a sluggish, sagging mare with sunken flanks. On the other hand, he was so *unconsciously* in love with himself that he cherished his own mistakes, this hypernarcissistic bull of a trooper. He was only one little mental platform away from true awareness, though had he ever reached that platform he would have lost the ability to act and exposed himself to the paralyzing metaphysical nonsense of the universe. He was a bullet; he could feel the country behind him the way a bullet feels (if it could feel) the pyroxylin packed in its own cartridge. And he was compressing the explosive mass below, the force that would one day skyrocket him out of the Quartermaster Building on Bulloid Street into the higher realms of his destiny. He read only at bedtime, and then only *Barcz* and Stevenson's *Treasure Island,* slept soundly till five, on his right side, and woke up with a mouth redolent of freshly mown hay. The women found him simply *adorable.*

The day of Lilian's premiere was doubly memorable (in retrospect, obviously), because that same morning the commander had made a personal inspection of the school. Out of boredom (the general's boredom would have easily entertained the world's more than fifty commanders in chief), Kotzmolochowicz had begun a tour of the provincial "war" colleges. The result was a colossal orgy of fetishism. But the general possessed one extremely rare quality: the veneration of others ran off him like rain from an oilskin, in no way inducing him to play the role of a venerated person. He knew how to prevent any idolatry, even that rendered by his most intimate circle, from entering his voluptuous inner organ (what he liked to call the "clitoris of vanity"), whose secondary effects could beget a second personality (not the one that one was meant to be) nourished on the flattery of admirers, a tumor known at times to devour the most robust characters.

There was no negotiating with the Chinese. Only recently, in fact, the princess's eldest son, the ambassador in Hankow, had returned to the capital in a sealed railway car. Literally nothing was leaked. After delivering his report, the young prince was *officially* imprisoned in a cell located in the general's headquarters, and that was the last anyone heard of him. The mystery was all the more exasperating in its courtesanlike coyness. Just as it was about to expose itself, it would do a little pirouette, wrap itself in a veil of preposterous rumors, and retire. All the princess's efforts to see her son met with failure. She grew irritable and tried to drown her despair in ever wilder orgies with Zip, who sooner resembled a zombie from a dream of squandered youth than the general's adjutant-to-be. Moreover, he had grown handsome as the devil. Manhood was invading that adolescent dimple-puss, lending it a stern expression of brute force and severity that, in combination with the commanding sensuality of his *himmelblau* eyes, affected women like a dilating-debilitating pressure in the lower regions. In public, unknown women groveled at his feet like dogs. Oh, if only he had looked . . . But he was satisfied for the moment – the princess was high-class stuff – minor flaws being obliterated by the proverbial "crimson lamp." (He, that fop turned brute, that ephebe turned killer, that livid mixture of blood and milk caused by the swelling of powerful meaty stems: the princess went stark-raving mad, covering her body's monstrous gash with a steady discharge of ecstasy.) Zip's schedule was as follows: tiring exercises and classes by day, homework and wild dissipation by night. He learned how to get along on two to three hours of sleep – valuable training. He began to drink a little (a "l*ee*tle") and during his beerier moments found himself transposed into a delectably, frustratingly detached state, a state he compared (for the time being) to "going quietly insane," an almost-catatonic stupor in which his intellect functioned with all the precision of a computer. That gloomy spirit-beast-man was looming more distinctly now, but still only faintly so: he was lying in ambush. At times he took to *thinking*, and soon Genezip began jotting down these thoughts in his diary, which he later read in the company of that . . . But more about that later. He was haunted by his recent, postgraduate past, to say nothing of his more distant childhood, now as remote as a mountain skyline behind a vanishing horizon. It left him feeling old. He inhaled being a stranger to himself like a rare narcotic. The initial stages are always rather amusing, though later . . .

> How strange to see the world with a madman's vision
> In his eye, sane one, you'll see it for what it is, a prison!

as his "evil" school companion had once written. (Genezip regretted having lost touch with him. With him around, how many things would have been made clear!) He had preserved his sense of danger without knowing what form that danger might take. From which quarter would it come? From that gangster residing in the underworld of his own psychic guts with which he, that stranger, seemed to be merging, assuming their shape and absorbing their very substance (pseudomorphosis)? Or from the outside, from the realm of this prolonged fuck in which he and the princess were both mired? Despite the deep disgust he nurtured for both of them, he gradually conceded that no woman would ever be so appealing as the princess, that is to say, so inventive in acrobatics and in reading his most shameful thoughts. Thus did he cope with demonism, naturally one rather modest in scale. Nothing to match the demonic intensity of that time in Ludzimierz. But *still!* Sudden refusals (even if based on feigned attacks of piety) ended in wild outrages. An artificially aroused jealousy served as an erotic auxiliary engine, starting up whenever their exhausted glands were tired and their souls craved that which gave the illusion of esoteric knowledge and joined them in a kind of hyperbeing: delirious sex.

....

INFORMATION: It was about this time, strangely, that things began to acquire a different aspect, even an introspective character. A wave of self-awareness was sweeping across the ankylotic body of society. Through all the dreadfully boring cant about labor management (even the worst pedants and time fetishists had had a bellyful), and through the old trash heap of patriotic flimflam, there peered something unknown. People were grinning at each other idiotically, incredulous that they could feel anything. Like a rock rising up in the receding waters of an ebb tide, one truth, one value, was emerging: society as a fact in itself. That's a silly thing to say, but to really experience it and conform to it in your daily habits – ho, ho! – is to know one of the most profound transformations ever undergone by mankind. Boneless jaws continued to jabber in the service of brains long ago dissolved in the rotten, tainted sauce of the past, while Foreign Office nits were, as usual, studying how to jam the flywheels of gigantic machines with slivers and shavings. Most intriguing of all, the new trend cut across every layer of society, not excluding some prominent members of the syndicate. But not everyone, not even in a moment of revelation, can part with himself when practicality demands it. How often do people plod along, keeping to ways they have secretly renounced long ago. Old and venerable sages, subject to some adolescent twinges of their own, put forward the theory that this was merely a long-range catalytic effect, produced by that prodigious yellow mass under great ideological pressure. They may have been right. (Admittedly, wars had not been abolished [not even in an age of "leagues and *blagues* / of freaks and fl*ah*gs"], despite the ban on air power and chemical gases – except in their psychological version, that is, in the realm of public and private relations, literary and scholarly debates, social and political matters, etc. – alas. By what miracle everyone [including the Chinese] observed the ban was impossible to say, though surely it was due to man's overwhelming martial instinct inherited from the past. Because war under such [the preceding] circumstances was unthinkable, and the urge to make war was visibly stronger than the urge to destroy one's enemy and neighbor.) The real causes for this state of affairs were more complex, although no one (with the possible exception of Kotzmolochowicz) had a clue at the time. Thus did this socially harmless (ostensibly so, in the overt sense) religion of the prophet Djevani, with which his emissaries were drugging society with their narcotic, starting with the lower classes, gradually and imperceptibly begin to alter the emotional climate among the educated elite. The worst dregs worked on those on the fringes; the workers did likewise with their foremen; these, in turn, with their supervisors, and the latter with the Central Economic Council. Maids were trying to influence their "mistresses"; ditto the scummiest bureaucrats with their superiors . . . And yet, the wave (despite a series of perfectly frank conversations with Djevani and his agents) had failed so far to reach Kotzmolochowicz and his immediate circle; but important events were expected to occur that would reveal beyond all doubt the position held by that locus of contradictory (national and purely social) forces, urges, and hopes that was the Headquarters of the Quartermaster General of the Army.

That moment in which Genezip saw the general enter the school dining room was a *real moment*, not to be compared with those droll orgasms got, often by cheating, from a rank, aristocratico-Mongolian carcass. His legs were buckling but his eyes sank into the eyes of that man with a hawklike ferocity. Black plums submerged in a glassy-spermatic medium, miniature rotary engines in a supermotor grotesquely transformed by indecent thoughts of a humanity beyond redemption . . . And it moved, it lived: that mustache was made of real, live bristles like a seal's or like Michalski's! Another moment's infatuation with that man's puss and he would behold his own destiny and that of a nation displayed like the innards of a dead animal. Such a destiny, too! The general had a clear enough vision of it, though words could not communicate it – not for a Cylindrion and not for himself in his deepest, most private meditations. Something positively great lurked in that demigod of the old school (not to be confused with our nobility riffraff), something larger than himself both in power and style. It was greatness as a phenomenon (defined as follows: immense willpower; a certain quantity and quality of followers implicated in a given venture; the ability to disregard individuals [not excluding human emotions]; a general lack of consciousness in the execution of a given aim once undertaken; a sense of one's insignificance as a focal point of historical forces; the recognition of a superior force, ranging from God all the way down to society, and including science, art, philosophy, etc.; metaphysical isolation; all the petty venalities of an ordinary crook, though distinct in their special function – enough said) rather than a "psychic state," and it resulted from a foundation too small in proportion to the towering, ever-expanding upper levels . . . But it's impossible to generalize on the subject. So let's drop the subject.

Zip, however, was a combustible element in close proximity to the detonator; without him, nothing happened. What, though? Some intuitive rubbish of which 5 percent comes true by accident (and which third-rate mystifiers never stop ranting about) while the other 95 percent is forgotten – which is probably just as well. Genezip was again plunged into darkness: his father, like a winged bull in the white vortex of the stars; Kotzmolochowicz, the blackness of panexistence, enveloping both his mother's God and Michalski; the breath of the world's endless, scorching night; the princess, like a golden needle (fake) piercing "through and through" the whole brothel of life's metaphysical dimension; and himself, a gleefully wagging tail behind some fagged mongrel . . .

And then came that whole ritual: shouts of "Attention!"; the cadets jumping up from their tables (with feigned surprise); shouts of "At ease!"; the general sitting down to a vile meal of fish and vegetables (after a superb breakfast in the "Astoria," it made him want to vomit); the obligatory "lip-smacking" scene (the general knew how to smack his lips when he had a yen to win over an audience; such petty faux pas on the part of eminence tend to create a rather favorable impression). Genezip experienced it not as Genezip but as some catatonic beast, insensibly, inertly. He revived as he and his fellow officers were crossing in "free formation" over to the squadron canteen. Suddenly he passed by HIM and his heart constricted. Everything felt loose on him, too slack – his garters, drawers, trousers; something itched; he felt as if he were physically decaying, as though he had no right to love the general. He was the epitome of a manifold and thoroughly shattered imperfection, he who had aspired to be a crystal – even one in a triclinic system.

"Fall in behind, you ass," Kotzmolochowicz snapped at his present aide, the pubescent Prince Zbigniew Oleśnicki, a fop of high breed and charm, a true aristocrat from the Almanach de Gotha and not one of those cocky, simpering little farts from the petty landed gentry devoid of manners and inner polish. The chief could not tolerate the latter and kicked them every chance he got. Cringing like a dun-grey bitch, the young "ed-de-kan" hurriedly fell in behind the general until he was practically trailing between his legs. How Genezip treasured that moment! Oh, if only it, that moment, could have been a person! What a joy to possess it! If only time could have been prolonged, stretched like a piece of skin over swollen reality! And then . . . Well – nothing. The orchestra had just struck up some furious cavalry march, a composition by the old and still respectable and classical Karol Szymanowski (whose monument from the chisel [or heels] of August Zamoyski had been defamed not long ago by a group of musical invertebrates descended from Schönberg and who, following his most recent religious phase, had worked himself into a military rage [blame it on the war hysteria (again!) of the "antibolshevik crusade" era] and in this state had ended his career); and Genezip's soul, swept up in a whirlwind of purely military, condottiere exaltation, soared off into a fantasy world of the so-called death-on-the-field-of-battle type. Oh, to die thus, with just such music in the background, in the presence of a supercommander! All the rest would be a *fartbubble* – yes, fartbubble, that gross and unsavory word of the clodhopping crowd.

"Baron Kapen de Vahaz, Genezip," Oleśnicki whispered between the downy hairs lining the general's meaty and *chut-chut* Semitic ear.

Genezip did not hear the commander question his aide, but he saw that ear . . . Ah, to be a *woman* even, so that he, he, heee . . .

"Halt!" It was *he* who had shouted! A left face, a clicking of the heels, a jangling of the spurs, and the incarnation of military fitness sprang up before Kotzmolochowicz's plumlike, currantlike eyes. Between the two men a steady and infinitely quick lightning flashed in both directions at once. Their cement-fluid congealed into an invincible, otherworldly wall. Here was the future. And what a future it was! "You there, don't get lost in the empyreans!" In-cred-ible! It was he who was talking to him. His words, like nonexistent birds of paradise hatched in otherworldly spheres, alighted upon Zip's head, adorning it with the plumage of a glory not of this world. It was inside his head that they became what in fact they were. And to think that both had a pair of buttocks; that both had taken a shit today; that both had just polished off a plate of fish. How odd. Even Kotzmolochowicz was having a slight hemorrhoidal attack à la Rostopchin. How diabolically uncanny.

Over Genezip hung a drooping Cossack mustache and the mocking grin of a wild boar, an eagle, a bull, a Hungarian, a horse breaker and a horse thief – and higher up, the grubby, fugitive, elusive, and most elemental, molocho-gossamer, tiger-grip of the eyes. (Photographs of the general were unknown, a capital offence; if a myth, then a powerful one, i.e., no facsimiles were allowed. Under no circumstances was that glance to become fixed, captured, preserved, reified.) In the commander's ale-brown, or rather, malt-colored, pitch-black gaze, which was nonetheless as alive as boiling water or fire itself, the mask of erotic mischief fell from his future but still peripheral adjutant-to-be. Everything was raised to the sublime in this ebullience erupting from the very testicles of the psyche. Even the princess was floating about like an angel in some unknown medium, like a spritely little infusorian in a glass of stale water – ho, ho! – sublimelike, cloudlike, incenselike, saintlike. Even his mother became singularly necessary, this one and no other – his mother and Michalski and her new mania for co-ops. This man's gaze was organizing the arbitrarily arranged mass of his intestines by means of its specific, marshaling, concentrating power. It was as if all he had to do was direct his gaze at the messiest junkpile and things would begin to stir, to compose themselves into a magnificent star beaming symmetry and harmony. Thus did it restore the disintegrating Zip and instill order into his doubting insides and mental *raspolozheniya*. The world turned painfully glorious, brimming (but not *overflowing*, since that would have been impossible) with the froth from his ebullient spiritual yap. Surfeited with himself, he reclined on the edge of omnibeing and *was*. And all because of him, this fabulous, brooding prick parading in the medal-bedecked uniform of a general. The music was ripping his guts into celestial flags, pennants, and banners in honor of the Unnameable One; "Kotzmolochowicz" was merely a sobriquet for the benefit of the masses; not even he knew how to label himself, so unique was he. His Onlyness did not need a name: he *was*, that sufficed. Or did he merely exist? Oh God, take away this cross from me . . . Or did the man not exist at all? But he is, he is! Oh! Just see how those pitch-black eyes are laughing; see how those medals and ribbons are glittering; how his legs (and what legs they must have been!) fill those magnificent patent leather spur boots! (What was it like for women?! One shudders to think. After seeing His Onlyness in a motorcade they were surely driven, to a woman, to change panties. Crotches surely awash in houndlike adoration. More arousing than the infernal racket produced by Tenzer's morbid musical bang-bang. Right.) A moment of *that* and a person would have died willingly – so long as death came quickly, without delay.

"Your father" were the first words of a more personal nature to fall from the general's lips, and they coursed through his arteries like a sweet poison bestowing strength, valor, unlimited courage, and a genuine desire for death. (His father! How could Zip have forgotten him! It was he, after all, who had made this unique moment possible! "Yes, yes, your father . . . ," he thought, tearfully repeating in his mind the beginning of the sentence just addressed to him.) "Your father commended you to me, Zip. In three months you are to report to me in the capital, you good-for-nothing little bum. And remember, the main thing in life is *not to wait too long! A beau se raider le cadavre.*" (The latter was the general's only, if somewhat lame, French proverb, for which he was famous.) "Gentlemen," he said, now addressing the hall as he stood beside the First Squadron's right flank. (Zip was the second man in the Second Squadron; the First had not yet risen from the table.) It was one of those extravagant hysterical-historical performance-productions of his, the one thing he was continually afraid of overdoing. Hysterical fits of thoroughly convincing and spontaneous sincerity which, while shedding light on certain details, made him *generally* more mysterious before crowds and even some brainy types. Thus did he evoke a mystery more awesome than his own personality: the actual state of society. And immediately he turned to Zip and, in a soft, metallic whisper, said (Zip reeled with joy, shit his drawers, and became pregnant with an unknown fetus in his head – which is to say, with the general's idea, not graspable conceptually: his dream of universal power): "You have no idea, you little kiss-ass, what a fantastic stroke of luck it was that you pasted Piętalski in the mouth." (Good God! How did he know about that, this god of a trooper? He had appeared as something so abstract as to be beyond knowing such banalities.) "All I need," thought Kotzmolochowicz, "is a pretext for a little show of strength." (Aloud.) "Gentlemen, we have to make a test. I know what I'm saying and to whom I'm saying it. My agents have been challenging the syndicate for the past two weeks. But they diddled us around – me, too. Enough of this blindman's buff. I can't go riding around on a centaur; I need a regular mount beneath me. The whole country can be a regular moron as long as it's strong. Instead of our *Wille zur Ohnmacht* I propose the following: 'Bend till you bust,' because 'better to bust than to rot,' even if that busting would have as much meaning on a cosmic scale as laying a fart. Gentlemen, the fate of every living creature is so shitty that it's not good enough even for itself. But I suspect that my notoriously mysterious personality – at least I have the courage to talk about it – there I differ from all other earthly redeemers" (everyone thrilled to this tone of confidentiality, being transported to God knew where by this inner "glow") "because of the proximity of the army of the Celestial Empire, the anxiety of that quarter which is hostile toward me and toward my army is great, and I believe that our challenge will have the desired effect. We shall then determine the exact rate of decomposition in this country. Of course, a few corpses here and there are unavoidable. But for every one of you guys who goes down, there'll be a number in my secret notebook – provided I have one. Ha, ha, ha!" At this point he "guffawed" with the sort of side-splitting, pig-squealing laughter heard at village weddings. "I have no use for any paper except toilet paper – *post factum*, so to speak: let history wipe my ass and find out *qu'est-ce que j'avais dans le cul ou dans le ventre même*. That notebook of mine, gentlemen, is a myth. Many Chinese stoolies have been hunting for it, but so far not one has got within smelling distance of it. Each of you represents another parameter in the marvelous equation that's being concocted here." He rapped his skull with his knuckles and the noise reverberated throughout the hall. A roar of unbridled enthusiasm and a mute but powerful urge to die for that horse-thieving broncobuster-become-general who represented a curious admixture of 80 percent Alexander the Great and 10 percent Prince de Lauzun filled the place. Down at the other end of the hall, meanwhile, some pieces of moldy, postpneumatic stucco suddenly came loose and began raining on the inflamed cadets. Twenty men were injured, though they were howling more from excitement (even enthusiasm) than pain, and were immediately bandaged up on the spot, right there in the hall. Kotzmolochowicz shook the yellowish-white dust from his uniform aglitter with decorations and said:

"And remember, boys, I love you, you alone, because they can stick the rest of my family, my wife and daughter, up the ass of my Grey." This was one of those uncouth sayings of his that earned him the wildest affection, even among the most exquisite fops. Oleśnicki was moved to tears, while the head of the school, General Mildew, broke down and grabbed a bottle of Dzikowski vodka and polished it off in full view of everyone, whereupon he inhaled, likewise publicly, a gram of the finest Merck cocaine into his blood-red nose. "Why should I punish myself to live another five years? The angels can wait! It's all that abstinence which zaps a man," the ninety-five-year-old used to say. Meanwhile, Kotzmolochowicz was squeezing him in a soldierly, pincerlike embrace. The whole school was drinking now – tomorrow was a holiday. On the eve of great events, of which this mustached stableboy, the dark and still-youthful "Kotz," was the living incarnation, all were seized with a fatal urge to capture life's supreme magic while sudden death breathed down hard. (A gram of coke is often quite harmless. One merely has to choose the right moment, to not mistake a bad one for a good. Moreover, this rule applies only to the strong: *Meine Wahrheiten sind nicht für die Anderen.*) The dial of destinies was being furiously wound; two discs – the one black, the other gold – were merging into a grey ball. What would life be like without death? A dirty joke, that's what: perfection made the world torpid. The sweet delectability of living in the shadow of death, in concert with the alcohol, droned in Genezip's blood like a high-voltage current. Oh, to wed life's contradictions for a hundredth of a second and then hold out for a split second longer! But, alas, all the joy lies in the overextension; don't count on any orgasm *there;* climax is nothingness incarnate. Woe to the one who holds out for too long; he or she will return to a boredom the likes of which the planet has not seen yet. And only by that boredom shall he or she know what death is actually like: nothing so terribly ghastly, really, just insufferable boredom on a grander scale, compared to which excruciating pain, despair itself, are trifles. But right now Genezip was "partaking" full-mouthed of the twofold, bittersweet fruit of death-during-life or posthumous existence.

Outside, a glorious spring sun was declining, casting a brilliant orange glow on the house windows and on the wet trunks of trees whose feathery branches, still redolent of the last rain, were tense with yearning. Just as night fell and the sky was fading out in the most luscious aquamarine quilted with the brass sparks of the first stars, the cadets launched into their drunken orgies in which the foremost rider in the country and former "god" of the Saumurian academy also took part. On such occasions he and he alone wore the black and black-festooned uniform (the bastard changed right after supper) and golden spurs of the "Saumarian god." Genezip, who in his drunken confusion had accidently grabbed someone else's horse (was the "long arm" of Piętalski somehow at work here?), suffered a severe blow on the head next to his temple. He lay in the fresh grass, half-unconscious from the shock of the blow and the vodka. The general stood close by, only a few steps away. He saw Zip, but neither went up to him nor asked how he felt. Instead, he carried on a lively conversation with several officers from the school, one of whom had just sprained his hand and with his other hand was nonchalantly (while he waited for the doctor) smoking a "Mr. Rothman's Own Special," which the general had offered him.

" . . . grand things on a minor scale. Oh, I know, they're important as a source of psychic tension, possibly the last of their kind. But if you consider the consequences, they're minor by comparison with the explosion of the masses. The world, roughly speaking, is a sphere, dammit! A finite carcass! Odd the way it hides behind its mask . . . " (And this coming from him, he who was the perfect embodiment of mystery and possibly a master of disguise! What a joy, what unspeakable joy to eavesdrop on this man, even as he lay there with a cracked skull, deliberately ignored [which he also knew was a good omen] by that supersexual, superhuman, antimetaphysical brute!) " . . . and the mask has to be ripped off, even if it means ripping off the face and head. This time it's curtains for us as well. But what's a life not lived on the tip of a blade stuck into the unknown, at the height of madness or wisdom? *Vsyo ravno! Trebiono nat*" (a euphemism, like *parbleu;* the general was especially fond of Russian *rugatelstva* – alas, he would have to break himself of the habit). "Oh, if only people would understand that! If all, even the lowest shit, would measure up to themselves in a dimension of greatness! But . . ." (Here he uttered his famous dictum concerning crystal, and Zip heard with his own ears what had been parroted so naively in the princess's drawing room. The glaring disproportion between these words and reality was now evident, thus further elevating this man in his imagination to a giant: he flooded the world with his presence, sat astride in it with his magnificent cavalryman's haunches, and ground it to powder. Zip's head ached horribly, and he identified this pain with that of his idol: the pain of disproportion and inevitable calamity: a furious eagle at the head of an army composed of grasshoppers and dead fish.) Meanwhile, that voice which was being poured into his junker's guts like molten ore went on:

"Isn't it time to commit the ultimate folly – the supreme one – because those for which they *otpravlyayut v zholty dom*, they can stuff up my Grey, begging your pardon, captain. Say, what's your name? Count Ostromecki? *Bon* – I'll keep it in mind." The word *count* was pronounced with a slight shade of contempt – but mild contempt. He knew how to appeal in this fashion to that lost sense of grandeur on the part of our better *aristos* – a breed bordering on extinction. And that titan never failed to address such comments to this or that staff officer at any of the one or two hundred military academies. "*Il a de la poigne, ce bougre-là,*" as Lebac once quipped.

Through sheer willpower Genezip forgot the injury to his head (he had collided with a tree stump almost completely covered by grass) and licked his wounds with a psychic tongue invigorated by his encounter with the general. At eight that same evening, his battery now recharged (Kotzmolochowicz, that solitary psychodynamo powering the land, was at that hour dashing off to the mounted artillery school in Kotzmolia to recharge others) and inwardly aglow with a beauty that brightened every cell of his body, he dined at home with "Mister" Michalski. After Kotzmolochowicz's inspection of the school, this tireless "king of the co-ops" appeared dwarfed in size, almost a homunculus. He was certainly no "man of the people" to inspire life "on the mountain peak" *à la Kotzmoloukh le Grand*. To whip up the mass of pigheaded, collectivized mediocrity into a sublime and majestic diapason. Because what for Kotzmolochowicz amounted to a perennial holiday ("*immer Sonntag,*" in the words of Buxenhein) became for that "backbone of a sentimental socialism" vulgarity personified – and for the grey magma? A disaster. Qualitatively different kinds of forces. First it had to be trampled underfoot, ground up, flattened like a piece of dough before the last dance of madness and drunken grandeur could be danced on it. Zip clearly perceived Kotzmolochowicz's faults, the terrible anachronism of his person, and loved him all the more for it. How much more difficult was his mission compared to that of some "cheap" Napoleon, to say nothing of earlier heroes? And *he* had to curb his greatness in an age of an ever-thickening mass: whereas the great of yesterday had moved in a vacuum, he was moving in a tarry grease.

In a moment Zip would see Lilian onstage for the first time – and on *this* day in particular! He felt as if life had something up its sleeve for him, that nothing was "without reason" (an ugly expression) here. May he always feel the hand of destiny, for better or for worse! Sturfan Abnol arrived and greeted him like the most brotherly of brothers. They immediately toasted one another. The afternoon's carousal at the school had not yet worn off, and already his brain was being swamped by new waves of liquor. Alas, the day had to be pushed to the limit, at the risk of snapping everything, including the ligaments of his brain. The vision of the general was a steel band around his skull, a vision grotesquely disproportionate to its extraordinary scale, to its unspeakable power. He could feel him, replete with boots and spurs, in the region below his heart as a big, black, indigestible metal pill. But whatever its positive effects, it only served to intensify, fix, frame, and confirm the existence of that gent from below. The latter had become a permanent fixture, a screen on which the eerie shadows of the present were being adumbrated, turning gradually three-dimensional, and taking on a sort of muscular reality. That was just it: certain muscles had been nearly appropriated, he was losing more and more control over them. This was dangerous as hell.

No: such a day should not be allowed to escape before being sucked dry of the sort of pleasure normal people cannot even imagine. There are flower days and days of spit and sweat. But how often do the former blossom from the wreckage of the latter? Sometimes it takes months of seemingly idle spadework before a person can "snip a quick fix," he thought, recalling one of Tenzer's rather infelicitous sayings. Another doubt of Sturfan's: "What if women are just disgusting little chapels where onanistic idolaters pay reverence to themselves on the pretext of love?" The princess was diminished by their ordeal, yet she was, faute de mieux, good to have around. His "tamed demon," whose presence could be interpreted in two ways and with whom (internally, at least) one could do as one pleased, was feeling no pain. The sex was positively lethal. Zip felt sure he would never meet another woman endowed with such a proportion of physical and psychic elements, and this excited him: that sense of the ultimate, of finality. But not today. Today everything was devoted to the surrender of young manhood faced with that most beautiful of deaths, the one personified by his magnificent chief – a death in which the world looms enormous, magical in its most minute aspects, an infinity that can be polished off in one bite, a world in which the personality explodes under its own pressure and is strewn to the farthest extremities of the All. Such a death does not tolerate mangy nostalgia, it converts it into its opposite: a *joyful* affirmation of nonbeing; a lust for life but satiated with a fury not attainable *in* life. The notions of "fear" and "courage" become absurdities, pale ghosts of creatures from another, inferior dimension.

"To reinvent language: to do that is to risk speaking at the border of absurdity, for what are so-called intuitive formulations? A repudiation of logic in favor of immediacy, of the *artistic* statement = a statement that produces an effect through its form and striking diction. Intuition (about which so many ladies and intellectual sluggards have been driveling ad nauseam) always involves a crisis of meaning. But, except for contradictions (quite limited in number), meaning in the positive sense is impotent; one has to maunder a bit in order to communicate the purely metaphysical wonder of existence and its derivatives. Except for this sense of wonder and for emotionally contradictory states, the intuitive mode (as defined above) cannot be justified. And then the fools accuse us of 'esoterica'!" It was the immortal Sturfan Abnol who was speaking. Then came the usual rant about that "gang of parasites infesting a moribund art" (as he liked to call critics the world over): " . . . that herd of spineless impotents too cowardly to come out and fight in the open, afraid that I might disgrace them publicly; who operate with a tortured logic, with mendacity, and who at times affect ignorance to banish me from the minds of a cretinized public . . . " etc., etc.

Genezip found such confessions tedious. In the past he might have been moved, even inspired to become a "serious critic" in the same way one aspires to become a chauffeur or mechanic. Now they could stick literature up the rump of his "Euphanasius," just as Kotzmolochowicz had relegated to the rump of his Grey everything but . . . More about that later (naive curiosity). Who cares about literature in an age of chaos, of collapse *de fond en comble?* Oh, once upon a time it may have mattered when somehow it had seemed to bear on life. But culture today, insofar as it exists at all, is mass-produced on the assembly line of purely socioeconomic values. Perhaps it is not to be treated as culture at all, in the traditional, Spenglerian sense, that is, a culture based on certain myths – not even if a hundred George Sorels were to pontificate themselves to death. This mania for overlooking the characteristics of the age was yet another attribute of the "simplifier." "Everything is the same; the human soul is immutable; everything was and will be; there are only oscillations," they spouted, the SOBS, as they went around blurring the essential differences, tracking down crises and eradicating them wherever possible. Conceptually they belonged to what were called psychologists, empiricists, and relativists. Exterminate the lot! But let's change the subject. Alas, the word has ceased to be creative; it trails social life like a supply column behind a victorious army. It regurgitates the same material, never inventing anything new. Not because the number of words is limited, not because we have run out of radically new concepts, but because the deeper wells of creativity have been exhausted; because the human personality has faded, withered on the vine. Once upon a time the word was stationed at the front. But today? What could a semiartistic (he was not a complete artist in the traditional sense – i.e., in the sense of extinct) moron such as Sturfan Abnol know about a man like Kotzmolochowicz? He wasn't even equipped to pick up that man's wavelength on his raunchy transformer. Life had outstripped art; not even the great "schlock artists" with their *dévergond*ified psyches could cope with it – except perhaps in music, because there emotions, and not the world, counted, whereas the visual arts, the moment they overtook life some decades ago, had already run the gamut of forms. Zip, standing as he was on the very point, or, if you wish, on the bursting point, where past and future intersected – only Zip and a few other schizoids had any clue of the impasse. Society at large, if analyzed correctly, was – except for those who were conscious of the split in their brains – as revoltingly petty as that "courtly" literary-cultural world reeking with the mindless beggary of measly personal conflicts and impotent personal ambitions. Such was Sturfan's assessment, the same Sturfan who insisted that literature was life condensed – which it most certainly was not, at least not during those awful times.

Kotzmolochowicz was the last defense against the ultimate, universally depressed state of things, which not even the noblest minds of the past had dared to confront. And what was this state if not intellectual paralysis; sloppy thinking; the lack of any sense of time (the sort measured by a clock); a certain historical backwardness; the lack of any discipline nurtured over centuries; the *inability to adapt?* "There you have it": what among individuals gives rise to new values becomes in the case of nations a farce and a scourge: national courage for a while, cowardice for ages. But in that case (which?), what demon had allowed that titan of a quartermaster ("He's quartering in masterly fashion the entire country in a sort of Chinese *cherezvychayka*," the skeptics were saying) to act as a general screen – an internal mask – for the country as a whole? How was the horror of the situation reflected in him? How did all this look *inside him?* No one knew, and – what was even scarier – neither did he: ignorance had made him what he was – a huge stomach in which the whole country was being only partially digested (the heartburn caused by this indigestion was the general's private awareness). His enemies were sure they existed only because they were his enemies and thus gadded about in a purely negative fashion. It was this which, along with the Mystery, had made him so Untouchable. And it was precisely on that mystery – and on those funds from the West – that everything depended. Oh, thin was that membrane, thin indeed! Though it would occasionally give in places, it had not yet burst. Creeping slowly out onto that membrane, however, was the new faith of Djevani, beyond whom, on a distant Malayan islet, the *anonymous* Murti Bing was looming like a ferrovapor tower, infinitely enigmatic. Meanwhile, under our noses naught but horror, horror, horror . . . Oh, let Armageddon come, as long as it was beautiful! Even hearts of pure gold and intellects of steel were beginning to exude a rotten, metallic stench in the perfectly organized society. Yes, yes, Kotzmolochowicz, the last refuge, containing just enough impetuosity and rude strength – not your dance-hall-locker-room kind of stuff, not the balls and brash of your prehistoric types, of paleontological beasts long ago become extinct (your modern mousy type has defiled the wild beast with his pitiful knowledge of same), but that *perverse* kind of toughness sprung from a softness and senility turned inside out – for spite – like a pocket. ("Man has fucked up the world. First he made a pile of shit and now he's sitting in it. Grab the little punk by the scruff, shove in his mug, then toss him into the cosmic void" – such was the general's "astronomical philosophy," as he liked to call it; as far as he was concerned, such problems ended at the Milky Way [though the only book he had ever read on the subject was Fournier d'Albe's *Zwei neue Welten* – a supreme intellectual luxury in itself – and he had nearly bust a gut while reading it]. Hypostatic space was his fetish – but not his deity. The element of Time he could stick up the rear of his Grey. The rump of that poor Grey [who later met with a tragic end] was a truly prodigious storage room, containing the image of a second Kotzmolochowicz engraved on an electrum made of an inferior substance – in other words, the one on the planet [located, of course, in his own belly] – while all the rest, including the Milky Way, was contained in the belly of a third Kotzmolochowicz of higher quality. Only one Kotzmolochowicz in the entire world: no one dared to call him the Polish Gutierez de Estrada anymore; he had become truly one of a kind.)

All the time Zip was getting sloshed with Sturfan, he was thinking: "How fantastic to have a commander, to trust someone absolutely, even more than yourself! Those poor, pitiable people, days, countries who had no such man! If you can't believe in yourself or your country or in some utopian ideal, then have faith in a madman who *does* believe in all that." To be other than oneself; to reside in someone else, in HIM; an atom of his power, a fiber of his muscles – and deep down the shabby thought: from now on, whew, no more personal responsibility . . . Even the general's enemies justified themselves in this way: being his enemies, they had no choice but to act as they did; thus did they absolve themselves from the burden of their own deeds as far as history was concerned.

Meanwhile in the club car of the Kotzmolian Express, Kotzmolochowicz was meditating in the solitude of his compartment. ("What do you think of all this?" his wife used to ask him. He would reply with one of his beastly grins, stroke with his awesome, sinister paw his silky black mustache, and then . . . On such occasions she overflowed with admiration for her husband. Odd: the more frequent these moments were becoming, the briefer in duration. If he still desired her, it was at times like these: he could afford to be himself in her presence, which is to say, a masochist . . .) "Here's how I visualize the national boundaries: landmarks in Zdolbunów, Żmerynka, Rohatyńce, Psiory, and Kropiwnica . . . Right – now all we need are some Kashubian words in our language. How awful." (The real, ethnographic Poland seemed to him something tiny, a child's fist, like that of his daughter, his precious Ileanka, one he could hold in his palm. He looked down at his beautifully shaped, masculine, hairy, criminal [as it was described by the fortune-tellers] hand and shuddered. He was staring *at someone else's hand that had no idea what he was thinking.*) He imagined the Chinese; he was well acquainted with those skulls fashioned from bone, with those shifty, slanted eyes – he knew them from his Russian days. Slanting back his eyes in the mirror, he felt positively villainous; he could feel an alien psyche inside him, someone completely different, someone he did not know personally, only by *sight.* Or perhaps it was the one soon to be revealed to him? But he had no time for such thoughts: they did not fit in with the sort of schoolboy's game he was conducting with his unknown adversary. And how could he have known who his opponent was if he didn't know who he himself was? What *would* he be, anyway? Ha! Let them figure it out afterward! After *what,* though? A cold sweat on his lower eyelids. A man had only one life to live. He was the one and only true "Polack" on the entire globe. Poland: an inferior nation, but unique . . . And he was in a way like the king of Hyrcania, Oedipus IV, only infinitely higher (even without a crown), since the latter was *au fond des fonds* a clown. And yet . . . A horrible doubt protruded from *invisible reefs* overgrown with the marine algae of known words. New words failed him, and it was perhaps better so. If he had discovered the words for certain things, they might have come to life, pounced on him, and consumed him on the spot. He swam along like a shark in a fishless ocean, condemned to die of starvation. Nonsense: the visions evaporated; he was himself again. Compressed into a dot. If anyone had read his mind at the moment . . . Supreme terror, as during his highs with HER . . . Not with his wife. And, wonderfully, one could feel it, the terror, coming from *inside* rather than *outside*. Such panic brought no discredit to anyone. Oh, stop being so hysterical; forget all that stuff . . . Just squeeze your muscles and brain into a ball of iron: it is no more. A leap into another dimension. On the whole, that "poor" Kotzmolochowicz, who for all his crusader-heroics in the land of Bolshevia had been only recently accepted by the more aristocratic members of the syndicate – the same Kotzmolochowicz who had eloped with a countess (whom he had loved, incidentally; lately his wife's family had been trying to make up with him, though he had declined, with an ironic smile and sincere contempt) – all in all, was a pretty rare bloke. And yet he would have traded everything for a measly count's title. For a moment he conjured up the beautiful and inspired face of the young Oleśnicki, that Roman prince from out of the sixteenth century, and he trembled with a curious hatred and mortifying envy. Was this the insatiability-engine of many of his actions? Yes, of course it was; better to be a measly count, but measly *qua* count. But his *real* self he would not have exchanged for a kingship or a crown. Would he have done so five thousand years ago? Oh, yes, with pleasure even. But at present he had no choice but to be Kotzmolochowicz. And suddenly he apprehended the metaphysical absurdity arising from life's multiple transformations – be it that of an NCO into a general – and the stunning arbitrariness of one person's being this and another that. Being this and no other, once and for all eternity, is a property of Particular Existence; only *it* can refer to itself as "I" – not "I" as an abstraction flitting from one body to another like a butterfly from flower to flower, but something unique, joined to the body indissolubly. The poor devil had just experienced his own "supra-astronomical" necessity. The moment of metaphysical bewilderment, both with regard to his own being and that of the world, came and went. Again he was Kotzmolochowicz, from top to bottom – small in his greatness, just as a moment ago he had appeared great in his smallness. He had no time to spare for such trifles. His self-loathing was as fierce as the loathing he might have had for any stranger, and this revived him, this saved him from himself. If he had ever really attacked himself, nothing could have pried him loose from his own claws. (Bekhmetev would have diagnosed it differently.) He might have squashed himself like a centipede and risen above himself as above a feculent swamp. The doubt he had long repressed suddenly overflowed his soul's banks, completely inundating its surface. "The country is a map, yet there's this horrible, infuriating, *absolute* uncertainty as to its destination. It's all so small, so small . . . How I could squeeze the old girl to death, recreate her, procreate her, then toss her out while she's drifting in an orgastic swoon (because *he* did it to her!) like THAT girl . . . " Stop. Oh, if only people knew what a mystery he was for himself, how amused they would have been. Although – if they had probed a little, say, on the subconscious level . . . He was circling now above his own "bottomless private hole" (his own "privy hole," as some fairly intelligent yokel once quipped). Don't stare into that abyss ("a real abyss, dammit, not one of those silly poetic abysses invented by some sophisticated Jew or coffeehouse mystic," to quote His Onlyness), because down there was madness, or suicide committed in a state of absolute awareness – from insatiability. What *else* did that pure potential of individuality want? A taste of infinity on earth – which was not likely to occur. The only salvation was work, work, work. Avoid poisoning yourself through an accumulation of unused forces. But Bekhmetev had recommended rest and relaxation. "There's so much of life, and all a man does is slave his guts out," cheerfully replied this man who was as tough as Napoleon on the executors of his will. And Bekhmetev, that celebrated custodian of souls on the brink of doom – and the protector of those already doomed – would say of his patient: "*Erasm Woj-*

ciechowicz ne imeet dazhe vremeni chtob s uma soyti. No eto dolzhno byt konchitsya kakimnibud vzryvom."

This much was certain: the general cared little for the nation or society as such, which he regarded merely as a collection of *sentient beings*. Nor was he fazed by the psychological mood of the masses. "Internally" he recognized : (1) his daughter, (2) his wife, (3) "that female monkey" (as the general's wife used to call HER), and (4) his bitch Babs. The others were numbers. He saw them with unmatchable clarity, brutally exposed as in an autopsy – from his closest admirers down to the lowest-ranking soldier, whom he knew where to knee in the most sensitive spot. But he would sooner have been blown to bits than try to analyze whether he was guilty of any national sentiments or social instincts. Destiny had hurled him down onto the peak of a pyramid, and there he would stick it out. But he was helping that destiny along. He was stirring the pot in order to later emerge as a celebrity, as a man recognized by the world at last – though not as the person he was now. He was not content that he was being written up from time to time in the muckraking press abroad. (Little was said in public about Poland, which was being exploited as a buffer state – that "bluffing, bungling, puffed-up buffer of a buffaloed buffoon," to use his own words. There was also talk that Poland and Russia were just a buffet snack – the "Great Kotz" went in for wordplay in his spare time – for the Mongols before they gobbled up the world.) Yes, this was the last refuge of creativity: stirring up the human anthill (if only in Poland) but good and proper, with style and panache; attacking the mass society and the external pressures being tightened around the country's neck like an iron noose. But his consciousness was like an intellectual tumor; in his blood the general was devoid of leadership in the primitive, instinctive sense. The latter was embedded in some overly developed gland of his brain; it was lodged there separately but firmly. Another plan, this one truly his: a decisive battle with the Chinese, staged along a front designed to force the enemy into a certain *peregrupirovka* (another pet expression), from which the Chinese command would see definitively the writing on the wall. The general was a born condottiere – herein lay the secret of his success – in addition to being an artist-strategist. This was the sort of ingenuity he despised as a "statesman." Politics served as a background from which to launch his grandiose military strategies. In his own mind, however, he regarded himself as a universal prophet, a prophet minus any ideas. *Something* may have been stirring in his "private abyss" – but more about that later. If so, then he didn't know about it, nor did he care to know. The plan was ripening in the diabolical brain of the Great Kotz without the aid of written records: a blank map, minus any freehand drawings, was all that he needed: his memory was one colossal war room furnished with a million pigeonholes and an electric circuit board linking an entire system of signal lights. The main button of that monstrous machine had been privately located by Kotzmolochowicz between his eyebrows, a little to the left where he had an irregular bump – his "Macedonian bump," as he called it when he was with HER. This button seemed to stick out (subjectively speaking) on its own, a safe distance from the coarser layers of his soul (from his strapping shoulders and thighs as well), which at times served as a wicked backup, hence were not to be taken lightly. "Ha – those mounted riflemen in Grudziądz – damned shaky. Inspection might backfire because of that damned Wolfram, and there's no getting rid of him. He sees through everything, or thinks he does, which is bad enough. The worst thing is, he's one of those 'cavalry gods.' Just lay low; he'll either resorb himself or pop, and then . . . Snip! We'll clip his wings. Swędziagolski will know what to do if things explode. More 'appropriate' measures will have to wait . . . Right – K., I., and W. – that makes three. Zifferblatowicz is convinced about some sort of secret deal with the syndicate. He underestimates the syndicate's strength. Never mind; the easier for him to be neutralized. Let him fight his own battle." He despised his enemies for making him stoop to such treachery. "Give him enough rope, he's sure to hang himself. Then there's Boroeder with his inscrutable Oriental face, which is his only drawback. He's nearly as mysterious as I am, though not nearly as interesting. And that shiny black beard where he keeps all his riddles hidden . . . The fucker uses it as a disguise. What if I tied him up and shaved it off? A brilliant idea: it would zap him completely. And that yellow hand with all those rings and fake rubies" – (spinels?) (the dresser!) – "he fondles that beard like a faithful hound. And his name – Jacek – a real bundle of contradictions . . ." Then: "I'll shave the son of a bitch!" the general shouted. "Civilians are the worst. He's got someone tailing me. Who, though?" He stared so intensely at the red velvet of his cushion that everything darkened before his eyes. And through his smarting eyes he saw Uhrynowicz's stoic stone-face.

....

INFORMATION: Three and a half days later Uhrynowicz died of a sudden attack of brain fever.

The general was a *dan-ger-ous* man. He knew how to fix his sights on a goal – however obscure – without looking to the right or left. The precipices whipped by as he sped along his glittering track. The awesome battle and ensuing victory rose up like a golden disc in the East . . . Then: "Ha – Quilty = a pillow. If I flatten him, he'll puff himself back up. Not worth the effort. Better to let the air out of him slowly by giving him impossible jobs to do. That way he'll collapse from lack of sleep." Again an abyss. Its concave horizon darkened, and among the "Pythian" columns of the Unknown there arose his future house in Żoliborz (then under construction) and the vision of serene old age, stuffed to the gullet with heroism. With his spiritual fist the general shattered the idyll tempting him with its serene banality, and just to be on the safe side split it in two with an enormous and halfway-real saber, the prototype of which had been borne by his page ancestors for the grand and mighty. He was mentally rubbing his hands at having remained financially pure; it had nothing to do with ethics; more in the way of a sport, one even more agreeable than horseback riding. Ah, that horse of his, Hindoo, otherwise known as the Grey, an Arabian from somewhere along the Persian Gulf. Together they should have been called a "Bucentaur" if the latter had not connoted something else. For a second he could feel his horse beneath him, then his wife, and finally – oh, *she* was by far the most wicked (more about that later) = *le problème de la détente, das Entspannungsproblem.* And again he beheld the numbers and colors of regiments, the faces of various officers, the doubters, those who would have to be provoked into a pseudoconservative, preventative, preservative, privylike pseudorevolution. Actually, it was being staged for his own benefit: among the "lower ranks" he was being accused of flirting with the "counts," a rumor that would have to be quashed before Monkempt-Unster began drawing his slimy conclusions. The embarrassing name of Kotzmolochowicz would soon be on everyone's lips, evoking something different for each, and out of this collective version would emerge a new truth, now known only to him but one day to all. "I may not be consciously aware of it, but I am an emanation of the masses, while they, the numskulls, can see in me only a dangerous 'individualist.'" (Those "numskulls" were Zifferblatowicz, Quilty, and Boroeder – hence Interior, Foreign Affairs, and Finance – the most powerful brains in the country, men more intelligent than he, but numskulls nonetheless. But here intruded a minor mystery: his positively fiendish intuition [the usual variety, not the Bergsonian sort] confounding the most artful dodger. Only one man caused him any unease: Djevani. There would have to be a showdown after his present tour of inspection.)

Oleśnicki came in with a trivial message and was invited to remain in the general's compartment. Totally exhausted, the young officer fell asleep at once. The general scrutinized his ephebic face with its slightly parted, girlish mouth; and before the exquisite mask of this "sleeping hermaphrodite" there arose a carousel of faces and conjectured "psyches" – or rather, psychoses. And himself? Better not to think about it . . .

In that eerie and enchanted land, madness stuck out from nearly every prominent face like the bone of some fractured limb. The masks affixed to these faces seemed to form or to symbolize a new, heretofore unknown, unforeseeable, and unforeseen collective soul – an immense *bestia*. Everywhere the same brutish faces; his was the only one without a *fellow* face on the same level (below him were stacks, pyramids of them, but not a single one on his own level). Except possibly one, the off-duty mask of the "family man" (it tore his insides with nostalgia, unbridled affection, and the fiendish *stench* of a life dissipated in myriad possibilities [such emotions still existed, and how! – along with their pseudoemotions. But both were beyond him, in the sense of being beyond his capacity, though he was as honest as Robespierre . . . (how painful was this debility)]): his wife, his little daughter, and even HER – her, despite all the terrible *things* they did . . . And Babs. But that, too, shall have to wait. And in this intimate circle stood another, and this other was himself, that formidable loner acting on behalf of an exceptional idea, exulting in his isolation, in the subconscious yet profound mockery and derision being showered on him in his own country; discoverer of his life's supreme moment, the wild and artistic magic of each and every moment, even the adverse kind – of which there were very few: the attack on Bezobrazov's cavalry at Konotop; the assassination attempt by that maniac Scrofuloso, who had tried to "Taylorize" him; and this somewhat drawn-out period of waiting – perhaps the greatest adversity of all. He shuddered and gazed down at Oleśnicki, who was sleeping like an angel, though snoring lightly. "A prince, and yet he snores," thought the general. Such thoughts were a form of relaxation. "Maybe I'm just an ordinary anarchist laying the groundwork for a fuckup on a grand scale? I suppose I'll have to overcome my aversion for organizations if I ever want to organize this bunch of cattle. And what about my scale? China – well, that's something. It does me credit that I can measure up to it. But in some ways a bedbug crushed by a cuirassier's (necessarily a cuirassier's) boot is 'measuring up,' too. Because even if we win the battle, we'll have to surrender. What then?" The fatal sense of his own insignificance returned – a self-doubt leading to a total paralysis of will. Suddenly he was alarmed that Oleśnicki might have overheard this last thought while pretending to be snoring in his sleep. Hadn't he lately begun to think out loud? The little milksop was sound asleep. The general felt in Oleśnicki's presence what Judy felt when she was around Korbowski in Żeromski's *The Homeless.* Oh, when would this damned, seemingly immortal aristocracy ever disappear from the face of the earth? And it was *he* before whom that young fop cowered like his bitch Babs. This was the last of his degenerate thoughts. Their vicious circle was closed. No, there was something else, the most terrifying thing of all: someone was barking and baying inside him like a stray dog, rapping out the following sentence as if on a typewriter: "Am I an independent variable (in the mathematical sense), or am I merely a relatively simple function of (a) that vicious Chinese scheme to absorb the white race, or (b) that communist-fascist conflict in the West?" Ugh! Looks bad, all right. Enough. Back to maps, regiments, some "serious work," unwinding. He rarely indulged in such leisure. At two, that latest of hours, in the morning, SHE would be in Kotzmolia; then all would be put right. A chill of abominable pleasure pierced him like a sword, from his cerebellum to his tailbone, and the general slept like a rock for ten minutes, in the manner of Napoleon – a rock that for all its colorfulness was still a drab, dust-covered, roadside rock lying at the end of a path down which a moribund mankind was headed.

If Genezip had "read" the general's thoughts, it would have been a catastrophe, a moral disaster. The boy needed a stronger chassis than his own. He himself was too weak to support his own complexity; his undercarriage could not withstand the irregular jolts of an overly powerful and poorly tuned engine. Without a shot of Kotzmolochowicz's "life-poison," how to face such mighty forces as the princess, the syndicate, his mother, or even Michalski? That had already been demonstrated. He was greatly indebted to the general. "What did my father ever give me? He accidentally gave me life, while you restored my faith in sublime undertakings," he thought, recalling the words spoken by Jan Tsimisches to Nikifor in Miciński's *Basilissa Teophanu.* The comparison was unfair, since it was his father who had been guiding him – even from beyond the grave. Had not his father placed him in the custody of his distant friend? Nor could Zip foresee the future, these final glimmerings of a normal life: his mother with her eyes fixed on Michalski, a meal of veal fricassee in a béchamel sauce, a taxicab ride on a rainy night (huge, bulky rainclouds were already settling in from the west as he made his way back from school). Never again would he savor the things of this world in their customary contexts and relations, and, worse, he would lose the power to distinguish between his present surroundings and the world of the past. If he could have afforded the time, he would have worried himself to a premature death over such a fate.

The first spring storm rumbled over the city as the three rode out in a taxi to the suburb of Chaizów, to the place where Quintofron's

"Temple of Satan" held court. Such, at least, was how this place was described by members of the syndicate. (At that very same moment, with strains of Szymanowski's "God Save Our Fatherland" in the background, Kotzmolochowicz, content as a dog let off its leash, was pulling into the Kotzmolian station.) From fields beyond the city a warm spring breeze brought the scent of that much maligned "native soil," the smell of fresh grass soaking up the carbon dioxide with its thirsty blades. A delicious inner slovenliness overran the banks of Genezip's soul. He was wallowing in a mire of sham self-assurance. He kissed his mother's exquisite hand, which she had just bared from its glove, and (inexplicably) kissed the forehead of a thoroughly bewildered Michalski, now rendered speechless by his general good fortune. (Actually, he lived in constant fear of blurting something inappropriate in the presence of his "countess," as he called her – to her great sorrow. It was another story in bed, of course; there he held all the trump cards.)

NOTE: "What can be said about a happy, carefree soul successful in everything in life? Such people are awful, in life as well as art. Why not pick on the 'losers' and *pust plachut* – now there's a swell ideal for a literatnik. If you're stuck with a he-man, then model him on one of Jack London's heroes: make him crawl around naked for thirty-six hours in 105-degree weather, scale a rocky mountain one-quarter of a mile high in three days with his bare hands, then stop a three-screw ocean liner by jamming his foot under its prow, and afterward – 'keep on smiling,' as the English say. Inventing such uncomplicated heroes is a snap." Thus the opinions of Sturfan Abnol, who at that very moment was kissing Lilian to death in another cab.

The last occasion . . . Oh, if only one knew it at the time . . . Zip's intestines were unwinding from a scurrilous contentment. This miserable parasite living off the general's "psychic supply depot" was drunk on life's supreme novelty: the sense of Existence. The universal oneness of Being could no longer contain itself; the world was bursting with perfection. On such splendid occasions, or during other similarly intense moments of despair, ordinary people incline toward sublimity as an outlet for the unendurable pressure of perfection – be it a positive or a negative one.

At the entrance they were greeted by a vulgarly mechanical, photomontagelike, puristico-infantilistico-Sovietico-late-Picassoesque, pure-blaguesque *bezobrazie* vomited up from a thoroughly acidic creative void, and by Chinese lanterns shaped like sprawling skyscrapers and weirdly deformed body parts adorned with masks (black). The latter were a novelty. It was the first time Zip had ever been a spectator to such raunchiness, and he was fairly horror-struck. Such monstrosities filled the art history books, but he never dreamed they could be so revolting in their irredeemable depravity. And yet it did have *something* = a desperate hoax driven to the point of exhibitionist obscenity. "Oh, Lilian, you poor, dear, unhappy little tart! What awful lives we must lead: I, a pseudo-officer (it's not in my blood, you know), and you, a spiritual, pseudoartistic little whore." His jubilant mood evaporated: he was standing stark naked, in a cold and muddy rain, behind some run-down shacks reeking of laundry and cabbage, within whose walls he was to consummate his life. He was reminded of a Russian song from his schooldays whose refrain ended with the words *ofitserov i bladey*.

And then the world literally exploded. Genezip had already heard something about the celebrated Persy Bestialskaya from Lilian and Sturfan. But what he saw in Persy passed all comprehension, went beyond his wildest, most fanciful, most extravagant imagination: *and she's got him in his negative phase*.

....

NOTE: The long-term effect of such a phenomenon can be gauged by whether it has caught us in a positive or negative phase, a phase characterized by seemingly banal and irrelevant internal fluctuations.

She had struck upon a little "mine"; it was all over. Even Kotzmolochowicz had momentarily blanched all along the line of his hastily formed inner front. But for Zip the effect of this encounter was a function of the day's events in which the principal role had been played by that dream, that cream of a commander.

Before the curtain, an utter monstrosity crying out to Witkiewicz's

Pure Form for revenge, stepped a modest-looking creature dressed all in grey and coquettishly *girlish* in appearance, between twenty-five and twenty-six; and with a voice that was suffused through the body's muscles and recesses like some warm and sensually, titillatingly weird *balm of insatiability*, like some diabolical salve of sensuality that softened the bodily ligaments the way paraffin wax is softened by heat, and that caused the maleness of males to rise upward in an assault on wild insatiability – she said a few words about the performance and announced that Dzibdzia would be played that evening by Baroness Lilian Kapen de Vahaz, who was making her stage debut. At this, a howl of disapproval and a stamping of feet rose up from the disappointed audience.

....

INFORMATION: As a rule, Persy performed in rather minor roles, mainly serving as a stage manager for women wishing to delve deeper into Mr. Quintofron's mysterious world of metaphysical frustration. (Quintofron, this sterile castrate [fertile castrates also exist, at least in the spiritual domain] driven by a creative frenzy, by the terror of wasting away in a frustrated creative urge, sought, by organizing others into an elaborate symphony of serene madness, to fashion his own world of illusion in which to stomach his own existence. During the day he napped and read; in the evening, high on colossal doses of cocaine, he would emerge from his darkened room and begin "organizing" that infernal theater of unutterable horror ["the last refuge of Satan in a world drifting toward perfection"], aimed at imposing incurable dementia born of insatiability. Horrible things went on backstage. It was here that Putricides Tenzer's unquenchable appetite was finally sated – to the ruin of his art. More about that presently.) At the moment, Persy was coaching Lilian on how to realize Quintofron's secret aims, the most apparent one being the one they called the "flight-from-reality jag." And Lilian, whose "soul opened itself to Persy's words the way a white nocturnal flower opens to admit a brutal, buzzing moth, the procuress of stamens and pistils," had begun unwittingly, as early as in their first conversations together, to generate what's popularly known as a "mysterious fluid" between her initiatrix and her brother. Her love for her brother (that "kid brother," known to

Persy only from some old photographs and bearing no resemblance to the real Genezip) – desperate, unconscious, untouchable – she had passed on to that creature whom no one, least of all herself, could fathom. Zip was totally ignorant of Persy's existence. Lilian had jealously concealed from her brother the real agent of her wild emotional transformation, though deep in her soul she must have sensed the possible repercussions. Whether it would be good for the two of them, it remained to be seen. "Live your life to the fullest (no matter how awful it may seem – if fate has decreed it). Spare nothing; exploit everything in yourself – and in others – if it'll help them to lead richer lives," that cyclothymic blockhead Sturfan Abnol used to advise her. It was all very well for such a brute to talk.

Above a skimpy grey costume and a pair (thank goodness there were no more than that!) of outrageously lissome legs, Genezip saw a childish, almost ovine (even bovine) face which at the same time was so beautiful and refulgent with a gentleness of spirit (not the treacly sort) and of such genuine class that his viscera fluttered and his heart swallowed itself in a sudden convulsion. His eyes, grown huge as mill wheels and thirsty as gigantic sponges, were transfixed by this extraordinary sight, captivated to the point of self-annihilation, and after devouring that lamblike face with one glance, claimed it, without consulting his brain, for their own eternal property (this was all a very one-sided and superficial impression), until his eyes were shattered like two golden (necessarily golden) shields protecting his brain from a direct assault by this visual image on its sensitive, fleshy coils, transforming this (potentially) neutral picture in the subtle palpitations of space into an arabesque of eerie, profoundly weird colors. His gaze met hers, and Genezip was sure that she (success at last! he was shivering from sexual malaise, a morbid satisfaction, and a triumph so somber it was exhilarating – or something like that) saw him. For some reason he was reminded of Jerzy of Podjebrad. He collapsed in the void of his being – he voided his whole being, wailing with contradictory emotions. His gut and other organs were ripped apart in a prolonged spasm of futile longing for all of existence, the one never incarnated, never materialized, the one denounced on all sides by infinity as being altogether a gullible, wartlike, navel-like, disoriented, individual pissant existence.

Zip realized that *he had to have her,* otherwise life would have become so ugly, so criminal, so tense that . . . that . . . I don't know what . . . that the fatal torture of his mother, Princess Irina, Lilian, and all the others (he purposefully omitted Kotzmolochowicz – which was a shame) would have been a joke compared to the ferocious abyss-void left by such an irreparable loss – forget "reparation" in the case of such a tragedy, of such an animalistic, onanistic, *livid* grief and outrage (at the thought of her being wrested away from him – never mind that she was not yet his for the taking) that made one want to chew one's plushy loge seat. She was no longer just a woman; she was life itself that, at the very moment his gaze met hers, dilated to the very edge of cosmic infinity, to the ultimate, hitherto unrevealed sense of everything ("Where are the soul's limits, anyway?" Zip whispered, suddenly awed by the gutta-perchalike quality of his own essence.). It kept expanding, yet refused to burst. Inevitably, all would sink into the slimy alluvium of triteness and banality – from one moment to the next, from hour to hour (oh, horrors!), from day to day (I'll never make it!), perhaps even year to year (out of the question!). "She must be goodness incarnate." (Another flicker of those eyes, another volley of utterly obscure but jejune phrases, and he was seized with a terrible doubt: maybe this was that evil incarnate of which he was so ignorant until now [just as he was ignorant of a great many other things in all their pulsating reality], the kind one only reads about in newspapers but never quite understands, that sordid, aching, coolly malevolent and usually fatal stuff which "decent folks" drowning in a dubious respectability never experience.) Her face was so elevated that neither of these concepts, that is, good and evil, could stick to its surface. And he sensed that all – his boyhood, high school, his childish affair with the princess – had been dumped into the – still bottomless, but no longer merely poetic – pit of the past. (It was Kotzmolochowicz, of course, who had been the real instrument of this abrupt transition between epochs, though he himself did not constitute an epoch, as he did not penetrate as deeply as sexual depravity.) Like an avalanche, life was beginning to stir at the summit. Internally

Genezip could almost hear the whistle of time as it zoomed by. Everything was taking place in slow motion, which is to say, at the moment there were only these late arrivals who were being seated, and she, that creature, whose exit from the stage was more painful than any previous partings, ruptures, or even death itself.

Persy had stopped speaking long ago – though about what, Zip had not the remotest idea. He had caught only the final spasmodic twitches of her mouth, which was only a light shade of red but chiseled in such an outrageously obscene and yet devilishly innocent manner. Every word she uttered was a kiss, criminally indecent and sensual yet holy as the touch of the most sacred relic. How she managed such an effect was a mystery, not only for Zip. Supposedly two rather sleazy painters had tried to "render" or "immortalize" that mouth on canvas, but were said to have masturbated to death in the process. Only Abnol could not abide her. He, too, had flirted on the brink of that abyss (it started soon after his arrival in the city), but finding a powerful antidote in his attraction to Lilian, he had turned arousal into emotional antipathy and contempt. There was something so sheeplike about both of their faces that people began hinting at the possibility of a brother-sister relationship. The rumors may have contained a grain of truth, but Abnol was quick to squelch such rumors with one swift and perfectly timed right to the chops, then began opening fire on the hall (the whole episode had taken place in the "Euphorial"), firing a total of forty rounds before finally being subdued. He was released from custody after demonstrating that he was an infallible marksman even while drunk. (Such zany exhibitions were an everyday occurrence in prison and were often attended by the best sharpshooters in the army, by officers of the artillery corps, representatives of the clergy, and members of the press.) Abnol was a trifle jealous that Lilian had to welter in this theatrical sauce, a psychophysical mélange of sentimental and naughty old whores of both sexes; in the secretions emitted by some malodorous sexual glands, by greasepaint, powder, Vaseline, and the daily frequenting of restaurants – yet thought so highly of the fact that she was pursuing a career in art (was it really art that Quintofron was fabricating on this "last barricade of the Evil Spirit"?) not to have overcome what in fact were superstitious phobias.

The show had begun – or rather, a grotesque, greyish-green (the color of a consumptive's phlegm) Mass in honor of some ineffable deity, which was neither good nor evil but infinitely raunchy in its apparent and fraudulent antithesis to prosaic reality. Genezip, numbed to the depths of his human dignity, rammed to the very keel of despair, watched this nightmare and listened to the "text," which deserved to be instantly covered with turf. In fact, everything escaped him, including the last supply of those human *couches d'émergence* he had been saving for a rainy day: the alarm system had malfunctioned. His breast was in a shambles, his head in a fog of blood-red boredom, while his lower parts swam in a brew of tickling sexual dolor. Ten tablets of aloin would not have brought relief. He itched frantically, morally and physically, though to scratch that amalgam – ouch! – a roar to be heard from the animal depths. (Apparently such rashes do exist, and if they are not yet common, they soon will be.) At last his soul deserted his mutilated body: it had no desire to suffer. But his body clung with its abominably (because sexual) supple claws and tentacles and refused to let it pass freely into the world of perfection: the world of concepts and death. (Death was, in fact, the only alternative.) But a curiosity (a gaping maw ten feet wide emitting a whisper that seemed to travel for miles: "What next? What next?") as prickly as the most pent-up lust, overshadowed every other consideration. Deep in the subterranean regions of existence, he felt his fate being sealed. "Silly, isn't it, to make such a fuss over the erotic aspect of life?" some make-believe old gent said inside him. "Why should the reproduction of cells be so earthshaking – not only as it serves the preservation of the species, but as an end in itself? A problem for the personality: how to conceal the individual's absolute isolation in the universe so that individuals can be fused into a society." Thoughts – naked, swollen, gross – strove upward and were engulfed in a vast ignorance, a boring, dried-out, humiliating ignorance, but soon grew cold and went into hiding. Then Zip remembered that the princess would be sitting in box no. 4 (necessarily no. 4). Before the performance had begun, he had asked Sturfan Abnol for its location, and with an uncanny sense of pride had gazed in the direction pointed out to him (he began searching for her the moment he had been turned to sexual jelly by that other woman). What he saw was a mass of feathers (arranged bouquet-style; it was back in vogue) partly obscured by the brick- and raspberry-red dress coats (a new fad) worn by a group of "gentlemen," which is to say, by a group of incurably anile, pompous, undomesticated, dress-coated swine. Cylindrion Piętalski was among them, clean-shaven and wearing a pair of huge, dark-rimmed glasses. His face had crept into Genezip's field of vision as a symbol (why precisely then?) of the most horrifying horror. A shudder of alarm and repulsion, combined with the thrill of being an *osoby obrazets*, passed through him when that birdlike profile, violated by his glance, turned around, and when those all-knowing, turquoise eyeballs bathed him with their obscene fluid. The "fraternal" poison injected into him began to "fraternize" with her "fraternal" glance in lewd fashion. Oh, gross was this rendezvous of poisons! And yet how fortunate that he had been lessoned in the art of love by that frump. Now he, too, was a seedy, all-knowing "man of the world." (He might not give proof of this expertise "right off the bat," but neither would he be embarrassed if and when the occasion arose.) Suddenly he was braced by the nerve of a conquistador; he was on the lookout for that other apparition hiding in the mysterious milieu of "stage and sex" (he had thoroughly dismissed the princess – well, that may be overstating it somewhat – let's say: almost . . .). He forgot, the lummox, just how much he was indebted to her; nor did he appreciate, the louse, these last, great, truly unselfish feelings of hers – as he charged, nose first, for that ovine profile behind the curtain where his destiny awaited him. "So she's really backstage? That marvel was not an illusion?" He had not actually believed in her existence until now. *Now* he believed, and because of this belief experienced a *starry*, subsexual illumination. Much of his previous burden (oh, you know: his "internal bully," the sexual, demoniacal toxin, his self-cynicism, and other such trifles) was shed. He could disguise his mouth, but his eyes were now ogling "new girls, new horizons," as some swell named Emil was reported to have said one Sunday afternoon as he passed beneath the window of a lovesick cook. He had fallen in love "at first sight" – *coup de foudre*, or *kudrefudrennoe raspolozhenie dukha,* as our own literary "simplifiers" might have phrased it, and they would have been right. At times even the "simplifiers" were right, the bastards. On the other hand, they say that schizophrenics achieve their finest, most insane moments during their wedding engagement. "No telling about anything anymore – *polnejshy bardak i Untergang,*" to quote a certain general with the look of a seal. But then a new source of worry ascended from the rank depths (outwardly he was as clean and immaculate as a cherub) of that burning boob of a body. Devils were furiously stoking the sexual furnaces; the poison factories were going full blast. Even Beelzebub, a fellow of Herculean strength, mean-tempered as a hornet and sporting a black beard that stretched down to his navel – in short, a hypermuscular athlete – was observing, with an icy stare of pristine, greenish, spiteful malice, the pressure gauge of that most filthy of human hoaxes. He did it with disgust, he, that great artist and rebel, after being harnessed to such lousy work as a punishment – ugh! *"Kein Posten für mich hier,"* he complained bitterly whenever his thoughts turned to that collectivized earth petrifying into drab perfection. "Fascism or bolshevism – *vsyo ravno* – either way it'll be the ruin of me." Yes, *the performance had begun:* never, never, never . . . "Words will fail you and all you can do is to scream inwardly for mercy." But they'll begrudge you even the screaming, those fine, sophisticated, elated henchmen delirious with sex . . . Who will? A species of seductive hermaphrodites, naked and smooth as hyperalabaster or onyx; a race of colossal, oversexed, and indifferent demigods of the sort known as "universal myths," capable of being incarnated at a moment's notice, *à la fourchette* (to the ridicule of all [of whom, dammit?!]), in flat little *bonbonnières,* sleek sauceboats, whatnots, whirling gallopades, and wobbly puddings topped with a meringue of toothless geezers and infants, and on top of all this: he, the KING, the Great Vermino Gutsie, an actor, holding in his foul and deceitful mouth the hot and evil-smelling guts of the entire hall, which was packed with the most sumptuously dressed but *au fond* nonsmelling (powerfully so; in the moral sense, of course) human worms. On with it! No, anything but that! Let's try to describe it: for one thing, there was not a trace of art in it, Art with a capital A (there was no other way to put it, except by consecrating whole volumes to the subject). No, Pure Form in the theater was dead, trampled by the dirty feet of smugglers bringing in their Western merchandise and by ordinary idiots like Master Roderico and his helper from the opposing camp, Desiderius Sluttery. Both lay six feet under. And good riddance! Perhaps it was really for the best, you honorable goonfriggers! And so this play was the very antithesis of art; reality, that fat old whore, reigned supreme in it, her legs spread out disgustingly, unwashed, stinking of raw meat and sardines, of Roquefort and our own psychic ewe's cheese, bonbons, and that cheap perfume known as *Kokettenduft. The bonbonification of monstrosity*. And yet, and yet? . . . There was no escaping it. "On the surface not a ripple / But underneath drooped her nipple," some foulmouthed pigs were crooning in the gardens of the goddess Astarte, which were as yet unknown to Zip. The maximal, *almost*-metaphysical licentiousness of a reality turned inside out like a glove, but by no means in the service of an artistic aim: no, it existed for its own sake.

A few people were already gathered onstage, and it seemed that nothing could have been more appalling; that, dammit to hell, there were limits to everything; but here, just to spite the impossible, each new stage entrance unleashed a vortex of the Unknown into infinity, each one qualitatively different from the one before. Humbug? Try it yourselves. You can't? God be with you. Our hearts bleed for you.

Genezip stared straight ahead like someone lying on a slab tilted over a steep cliff, clinging to the red plush of his seat as if it were his last grip on a rock that was steadily slipping away. Any moment he might plunge down *there*, onto that stage — or rather, into another, collinearly distinct existence where the vital temperature, even in life's most trivial aspects, was a hundred, a thousand times in excess of the temperature produced by the wildest acts: sexual acts, hypersexual (= megalosplanchnic, cyclothymic) acts, purely "intentional" acts, by the freakiest drug hallucinations, the reckless self-annihilation provoked by HER and her sadistic doings, by some imaginary female hyper-Beelzebub. On the whole, the tangible elements in this spectacle were rather few.

That was reality, what was happening down *there*. All the rest (this world, as it were) had become a cheap imitation, not of the reality onstage but of what ought not to have been in the first place, something not-to-be-endured in its awesome banality and not-to-be-sated-by-anything boredom. Existence, unillumined by a profound metaphysic, is essentially banal, even when filled with sensations worthy of a Jack London or even (even!) a Conan Doyle. How to go on living in this world having once tasted of that other? The insatiable Quintofron (not in the metaphysical sense, but in his cultivation of the *absurd*) aroused through his *thèâtre infernal* the same insatiability in others. Seats were outlandishly priced, and this brothel was officially tolerated (*which* officials no one could say *au fond*) only because someone in the Ministry of Internal Affairs (Picton-Grzymalowicz?) had concluded in his report that for the financially privileged this type of theater, by arousing a "cavalryman's whimsy" (his words), could actually help to militarize the country: *tryn trava, more po kolena.* This martial-mania was shared by both the general and members of the syndicate. That some animals can get along without metaphysics does not invalidate it. It all depends on the scale of values. But of all standards, why choose that of bestiality? Even worse was the quasi-absurdity of individual and collective life – universal "quasi-ness" was the hallmark of the age. Either absolutism or the anthill society, either fascism or bolshevism – *vsyo ravno:* either religious fanaticism or a thoroughly enlightened intellect; either Great Art or nothing at all; but in any case not a phony, pseudoartistic "product"; not that grey sauce on everything seasoned with the rotten extract of a mealy-mouthed democracy. Ugh . . . Quintofron's theater was something quintessentially rotten unto itself, something grand in the prevailing tide of greyish-yellow offal. Kotzmolochowicz had never been to a performance; he had his own criteria of greatness and so was not in need of any seasoning; he was self-sufficient like the God of the past. (Ideas trumpeted as great in the first or eighteenth century may turn out to be minor in the twenty-first. The priests never understood this, thus were doomed to extinction.) The black curtain came down. Everything turned pale, acquiring a greyish, louse-colored hue like a landscape at dusk, like a fireplace that suddenly goes out on a rainy evening in late autumn. It was hard to believe one's eyes. The brain of a consummate maniac examined through some hyperultramicroscope; the brain of God (if He had one and had gone crazy) examined through an ordinary cardboard tube without any lenses; the devil's brain, at the moment of reconciliation with God, viewed with the *naked* eye; the brain of a cocainized rat if the latter had suddenly penetrated Husserl's system of conceptual idealism: *bezobrazie*. This explained why the critics were so bad at describing it. There are dreams whose exact contents can be recalled but that exceed the recapturing power of words and images; one can feel it in the belly, in the heart, in certain glands, and damned if I know where else. This thing was totally mystifying as to its methods, yet it was *bezobraz*ing itself publicly: before a cross section of all the political parties, moguls of the police, etc. There was nothing to grab hold of, yet there was no denying the horror evoked by it. (Rumors circulated that the theater was being subsidized by Djevani, on behalf of Murti Bing, for softening up the souls of intellectuals prior to their conversion.) It featured the same sort of clowning seen in the futurists and dadaists, in Spanish and African psychovomito-jugglers, in spiritual autocoprophagists of one kind or another – but what a strange variant! For what in the latter was mischief, posturing, and plain fooling around was here turned into genuine, got-you-by-your-throat tragedy. The credit for this clearly went to the stage direction and acting, which reached the height of subtlety in the most trivial and disgusting details. We shall pass over in silence the backstage consequences of such artistic license. One huge mass of degeneracy bordering on the criminal. There was a time when such a crew would have been thrown in prison; in the present age, they constituted an island or submarine boat resisting the pressure of muddy waters exerted by a thoroughly nauseating society. It was here that the frustrated Putricides found his ultimate gratification. A few words on that subject later. Alas, the "naturalistic theater" was dead, done in by the first men of the feather in their craving for reality. Of course, the spectacle bore traces of those unforgettable, but in fact quite easily forgotten, "experiments" of Teofil Trzciński and Leon Schiller – but how diabolical was the reworking! The remnants of the "director's art" were being used here to mount the most furiously *naturalistic* staging of the *improbable;* instead of transposing the spectators into another – more metaphysical – realm through an execution in Pure Form, they strove to heighten insufferably implausible Reality. The illegitimate great-grandson of Trzciński and another extremely shady character posing as the legal grandson of "Witkacy," that shit-ass from Zakopane, had both been cast in the rather minor roles of "The Obscurantists." The story was, for reasons already given, not to be paraphrased. A summary with quotations would not elucidate anything. *"Quelque chose vraiment ineffable,"* as Lebac said, and his words were immediately repeated by his aide, Duke de Troufières. Whoever missed it can howl with regret. The skits might have been bearable if they had formed a pretext for purely artistic designs. But it was not for artistic purposes (oh no!) that they had brought together the latest techniques in psychoacrobatics. In their surrealism (not the one made famous by that rotten bunch of Parisian *blagueurs* on whom our pure-blaguists got the jump in 1921 with their publishing venture "The Litmus Paper") (the sets were the work of the grandson of Rafał Malczewski and the son of Krzysztof Malczewski – Rajmund Malczewski, the devil incarnate of hyperrealism in painting), even the most banal details assumed the dimensions of awkward disasters and the most sickening, festering, pus-oozing sores. The spectator experienced these "capers and caprioles" as his or her own, in his or her own thoroughly *sexualized* but still fairly trustworthy innards (such as the heart, stomach, duodenum, etc., not to mention other intestinalia; what was going on in *those* organs cannot be described in polite language – you can sulk, because *that* would have been extraordinary!) as their own intimacies, which were being shamefully dragged out into the open, to the ridicule of similarly dressed (or exposed, as the case may have been) patrons of both sexes now merging into a single mass of rotten, purulent putrefaction. Putressina and Cadaverina, those stunning daughters of Lord Ptomaine, of a mankind decomposing alive (before the last resurrection), reigned boldly supreme in that auditorium. Raw chunks of a butchered hyperreality were squirming in the dust and powder of what were once noble stage boards, all that was left of the old theater. After the first act, the gut-wrenched audience sank back into their seats like one limp intestine. Each pictured himself or herself as a preposterous toilet into which that gang below had been shitting, then frantically and mercilessly tugging on the chain handle – the last safety valve. "Society was stricken with acute malodoration," wrote some old fogies of formalism. Meanwhile, the refuse traveled through a common sewer far beyond the city, over quiet and innocent meadows, until coming to rest in the thatched cottages of flabbergasted peasants. "None of my stuff will finish in some thatched hut, because luckily by then the peasant will be history. The earth will be cleansed of all fun and joy, too, leaving only a bunch of evenly apportioned shit," the immortal Sturfan Abnol had once written in Lilian's album, though he was mistaken. People were only astonished that the government . . . but they should not have been surprised. Quintofron's theater was the last escape valve for intolerable psychic pressures (later referred to as a "spiritual fartometer, sir"), for mastodons too old to be "Taylorized" and who continued, like parasites, to thrive on the scraps of nationalism and religion, those indispensable little twin engines for propelling fascism – blame it on society's economic ignorance, of course. There they could indulge themselves; one evening in that theater was enough to render them harmless for weeks on end. Depravities blazed in them like ore in a foundry, with not so much as a trace left behind. Indeed, their own depravities paled in comparison with what those miserable folks saw onstage – paled like a bedbug that hasn't seen human blood in two years.

Genezip was there incognito and in civilian clothes – for which he risked a two-year sentence in the brig, which only made his being there that much sweeter. He realized now with all the clarity of a knife incision in living flesh that *she was.* Implicit in this seemingly banal phrase was the whole mystery of existence; its meaning went far beyond the words themselves; it overflowed the banks; it bore traces of primeval man's bestial metaphysics, of that almost religious ecstasy experienced by the first totemist. Never had Genezip experienced such terror before the naked fact of another person's existence, of another ego distinct from his own. The others – his mother, the princess, Lilian, even his father – were pale, nondescript phantoms beside the sheer "is"-ness of that incomprehensible presence. "She exists," he repeated in a whisper through parched lips, and in his gullet he felt something on the order of a wooden peg. His genitalia had collapsed to a mere kink, were reduced to a mathematical point by the pressure of billions of sexual atmospheres. At last the rascal felt truly alive. In this storm of realignments only the image of Kotzmolochowicz stood firm, like a chunk of infusible rock swamped by a river of lava – but far away, like a pure abstraction beyond the outer boundaries of experience. It was his first genuine emotion, still tainted by the manifold cancers produced by Irina Vsevolodovna's "princess-virus." His entire past had been obliterated, deprived of its mystery, its virulence, its pungent palpability – as happens; otherwise, life would hardly be worth living. Lucky are those who after their first or *n*th clobbering in life can still respond to the primal fact of *being*, and who can do so without stooping to the vulgar, all-leveling conventions arising from the mundane. What incredible harm is done to our most primary insights by ideas that are themselves partially derived from those same insights, only applied in a somewhat different fashion – that is, artistically rather than logically. (Ideas are very much an artistic element of poetry and the theater – something our numskull artists have never understood and which bothered that poor sap Sturfan Abnol above all, despite the fact that it no longer really mattered.)

With the disappearance of that nubile creature, or rather her semireal image (despite evidence to the contrary, Zip still could not believe in the existence of this female *as such:* she conformed to no existing categories, was asexual and impersonal, and was the first and only ego to transcend his own), every trace of reality also disappeared from the stage (which, for all its realism, was a hallucination from another world subjected to an orgy of realistic distortion), while her *backstage reality* (for Genezip these words possessed the sharp aftertaste of betrayal, wicked perversion, mystery, corruption, and a purely human [without any animal ingredient] evil sublimated and bawdtaminated [men did not count at all backstage]); this reality, I say, acquired such terrific force that no sooner did he fantasize what was happening than the mental image of the monstrosities just performed were effaced, corroded, and bedbuggered, leaving a purely *imaginary reality of the highest order* to collapse with all its unbearable weight on that pissant's collective "psychic furniture," flattening it the way an express train squashes a poor dung beetle (a cantharis, etc.) sitting peacefully on the track on a gorgeous autumnal day. And that imaginary reality consisted of (1) a moist, strawberry mouth, (2) a pair of sleek, bare legs, and (3) smoothly combed, ash-blonde hair. But enough said; what mattered was the ambience created by these banal elements of sexual attraction. *It was all her,* that creature who had glanced at him and spoken (he had devoured the words pouring from her mouth the way an anaconda swallows a rabbit), there, in that building, in the mysterious recesses of its interior: how in-cred-ible!! And to think that between those legs, hidden by some hair (oh, not just any, but a very *special* kind of hair!), she had what every other female had . . . smelling of her body's secret chasms . . . Eeek! No, no – enough – not now – un-be-liev-able! Here at last was The Great Passion he had been waiting for, the love "of his dreams" (of his cream, as it were), the first and the last. At any rate, such were the symptoms – a few, at least – by which that passion can be identified. But only in its unrequited, unconsummated form does it become really beautiful. In any case, *she was:* the awareness of her presence was like a blade in the belly, like a black bolt of lightning in a skull illuminated by a metaphysical ghost and seasoned with the tangiest sexual sauce. Once and for all: something is metaphysical when it expresses a sense of the absolute wonder of Existence, when it arises from a primitive grasp of its mind-boggling mystery. And just so people don't start bothering me with all sorts of little dichotomies – *Von,* away with you, back into your musty little holes!

An ungodly scream onstage. Two half-naked females are engaged in a fight, around them a group of indifferent men in dress coats and uniforms. A third, an old biddy, fully naked and the mother of one of the two girls, rushes in and kills her daughter (chokes her with her bare hands) to make sure the other girl wins. A man clouts the hag on the head, ditto to him, the rest pounce on the girl. A priest enters, and it turns out that the foregoing was a carefully rehearsed Mass in honor of the Absolute Poverty of Existence and the absolute futility of dispelling Monumental Boredom.

The words? Who can say? Flagrant nonsense, probably; in those days of conceptual salmagundi (of intellectual coleslaw), the average critic, or even the average "citizen" (how ludicrous the word "citizen" sounds today – a relic of wonderful bygone days, a vestige of the *honorable* democratic lie – for us who now stand in the sinister yellow shadow of the mobile Chinese Wall), had a hard time distinguishing between true wisdom and preposterous bunk. Occasionally some *prècieuse* would tease some sense out of it, but as for men – heaven help them! But the *way* it was performed, the way!! Too incredible for words. Dirty-toe-licking good. Had to be seen to be appreciated. Let's just say there was a lot of raving as people were ground into one huge, bloody, metaphysico-bestial pulp (if only the stuff could have been immediately canned and distributed to the appropriate, or even inappropriate, places – the world would have instantly become happier). When the curtain finally came down on this hellishness (no one could have endured another second of it), the auditorium stretched out as one (till it ached) and was suddenly thrust into another psychic space, into a world of non-Euclidean, waking dream states (and, yes, hallucinations, but of that other world – oh, my! . . .). And all this while in a conscious state, without the help of narcotics. Generally, it might be described as: a kind of amnesia of one's existence and the real-life circumstances that accompany it (home, job, tastes, people – mundane things that through the imagination were turned into exquisite monsters, the sort that made life altogether worth a shit. The regret that it could not be so was too great for words – a magnificent hound chained up for life, but condensed into a second.). Only there, onstage, did one truly exist. For the actors this translated into an atmosphere of self-immolation: they were utterly consumed by this supra-existential, elevated, really high-class clowning – which had nothing to do with art, except in the minds of the usual critical "heavyweights," who, for all their efforts, still could not tell the difference between a rhino and a locomotive.

Dragging Sturfan behind him, Genezip rushed backstage in search of Lilian's dressing room. She was not due onstage until the third act, in the role of an innocent little pixie in a number called "A Sexual All Souls' Day" – whatever *that* was we shall let pass.

(Her sexual immaturity and her mad affection for Abnol kept her reasonably in line.) A frantic Zip entered a narrow, garishly lighted "cubicle." Lilian was perched on a tall stool where two elderly seamstresses were busy fitting her with a bright orange knit top with black and white veils draped over a pair of bat wings. His sister suddenly struck him as being so pitiable that he could have fallen madly in love with her (with his spare heart, that is) if he hadn't been so pressed for time. His whopper of a main heart, meanwhile, was busy with something as incomprehensible, contradictory, and ominous as a thunderstorm or a violent quarrel with his mother.

"Lilian, I beg of you . . . "

"I know the whole story. It's all so weird. Actually, it's she who knows. She told me she spotted you. She should be here any minute now. She wanted to be here between the first and second acts. Only for a second, though, because we were planning to rehearse my part during the second act," she said. "Oh, I'm so scared," she added, her tiny "sisterly" teeth chattering away. Sturfan's heart, homogeneous as a block of stone, was swelling with love and pity (the worst possible spice) to the point of bursting, while the following thought flashed through his mind: "She's so young, so sweet, and already she's playing the pimp. My God, what will she be like when she really unwinds?!" He was in a daze. She reminded him of a small and unknown (astral?) rodent in a cage.

"How do you feel being a part of this?" her brother asked tenderly. The sight of his sister in such a setting, coupled with the expectation of that other woman, especially after what he had just heard, surpassed every batch of contradictory emotions he had ever known – and craved (even as he feared).

"Well, a little better than in real life." Sturfan was squirming in pain, but her naïveté only made life's charm rise a few degrees higher to that little red line on his own private pressure gauge. "Something strange is beginning to happen. It's as if I were liberating myself – you know, *surfacing*. Sturfan no longer strikes me as a quaint little beetle on a blade of grass as seen from a moving train; I see him now as the perfect male we often used to talk about as kids. Do you remember? The fox family in Domaniewski's zoological album? . . . " Genezip suddenly switched off. His brewery childhood, surrounded by an auburn glow of things irreversible, rose up in his memory: the tart, acrid taste of pears; the evening scuffles; and his mother, that *other* woman in his life, the saintly martyr with her mute faith in a God unknown to any prelates of the Church. (The look on Christ's face on visiting a mint where coins of the Papal State are minted; Christ with his gaze fixed on the blade of a soldier's halberd [!] guarding the throne of His Vicar . . . Why had this grossly banal image occurred to him now? Of course: that afternoon the newspapers had carried a story of how the Pope, after quitting an impoverished Vatican, had gone out into the street barefoot. But no one was fazed by such news anymore. It received as much attention as the news that Snootie Zweinos had savagely bitten her fiancé for stealing a safety pin. Alas, the Pope was a late arrival.) Oh, how recklessly, irretrievably, do we squander such moments, as though they were meant to last forever; how casually we bathe in that animal glow around us, subhuman yet rich and almost painful in the fugitive charm it bestows . . . Where had it all gone? Suddenly a new flash of illumination, hard and sharp, with a touch of something disagreeably masculine and crude: Kotzmolochowicz and his historic mission (which, if ever realized, would have made life impossible for Zip and for other, perhaps worse miscreants), an obscure apparition beyond the stifling horizon of upcoming events. Muffled thunder rumbled in the distance – not in him but in that other, anonymous, now remote, non-Ludzimierzian nature. Here he was surrounded by people caked with, oozing with the grime of human affairs. He felt such an aversion toward all, including himself, even toward that Unknown Woman about to enter Lilian's dressing room any moment now. She, too, like everything human, was "impure" when compared to the untrappable beauty of a spring thunderstorm.

A bell sounded in the corridors. The second act was about to begin, one of those self-fucking, self-sodomizing "acts" performed by the rotting elite of a mankind sinking into the putrid morass of social perfection. SHE entered. Again the sensation of falling into a void (of voiding himself). A touch of his hand convinced him that this was really *it*. Oh, to touch for the better part of an eternity, even if her face were a festering wound, just one square centimeter of that skin – and to hell with everything else. He would have kissed her tumor, the tumor protruding from her body in an anarchic desire to escape the laws of a normally functioning organism. An organism-cum-orgasm ejaculated from the abyss of nonbeing for the purpose of destroying him: an orgiastic organization of organs and cells – hers and hers alone. And why, dammit, why? He could have survived without it, but now it was too late: the point of no return. He was sinking (by degrees) ever deeper under the debris, while up there, high above the rubble, in the murky darkness of a *psychic twister*, a new edifice arose and took form, one built of tortures in the shape of children's toy blocks: four-cornered, angular, bristling with tetrahedrons of unknown tortures. Suddenly he was reminded of a "ditty" sung by one of the officers at school, Wojdałowicz, in the morning, with his boots on, while washing with ice-cold water (as did the majority of officers, alas) the upper half of his rosy pink body (to the tune of Allaverda):

Oh, the countless joys that make up this life
And the countless times you're put to the knife;
No sooner have you bit off some fun,
Than another round of torture has begun.

Another round had begun. All hope was abandoned. Something incredibly tense was going slack, though he was sure he appealed to her, very much so. Maybe the slackening was for that very reason. But he had no way of knowing. What could he know about the terrific psychoerotic perverseness of denial, the sort one gladly endures a thousand times over for the sake of a single, measly *frisson* of pure sex. "Kill, kill," something inside him hissed and then slithered away, having been suddenly startled, like a deadly poisonous snake, back into its place in the brushwood of the spirit, into the spiritual *bush*. In his overcrowded memory there flashed the grinning but nonetheless power-crazed face of Kotzmolochowicz. Say, what was going on?! Oh God, oh God! Whatever it was, corner it, grab it, and in a moment it'll be sitting in your lap: a clairvoyance. A terrific pressure in the brain, greater than ever before (or after). It was like the children's guessing game: "Warm, warmer, hot, very hot, burning hot, steaming hot, warm, cooler, cold."

Gone, never to return. A unique moment irretrievably passed. The intuition of a fu*rrr*ious (with three *r*'s) passion should have penetrated to the little metal (iridium) truth-pit inside the fruit he was trying to devour with the toothless jaws of his brain, the fruit of his *whole* life – but it had vanished. Not in this piece of fruit, honey (in *which* then, for God's sake?! Who was that speaking? It seemed as if *everything* was shouting, that everybody was in the know, was pointing fingers, busting a gut. What a lot of vermin, even worse than Vermino Gutsie), was the evil to be found (about that evil – what a chain of horrors! – more later): *it resided in herself.* Not as a plurality, not as a pyramid of ill-conceived demonic schemes, but as that consummate union, that metallic and indigestible pit, evil indissoluble, a unique chemical element: *malum purum elementarium* – even if she *was* a nurse dedicated to the licking of other people's wounds. It was an evil to poison the noblest deeds, to pervert them, turn them into crimes: this woman might have been the spiritual mistress of Beelzebub himself. She was so unlike the princess; the latter was a stray lamb by comparison, never mind that her life was littered with hopelessly scarred corpses. Those, my good sir, were qualitative differences. How he scolded himself for thinking that what had already happened was evil. Those, sir, were the silly escapades of a tapeworm, the petty flirtations of a monastic friar. Evil should not be insulted that way. Here he was on the path to liberation, when – whoa! an infinitely greater horror was coming to meet him with face beaming. But maybe it wasn't all that bad? Maybe by other criteria . . . ? Ugh, enough! Nonetheless, an irrevocable sentence had been passed down on him by the accidental collusion of hostile forces. What sort of forces? This time he was denied any clairvoyance. He was jinxed from the start by something "exactly" a head taller than he. But what, dammit to hell, was it?! Surely not that woman's intelligence. Even such a hypothesis – no, no, it was ridiculous. After the cunning shown by the princess, few could have impressed him in this regard. No, it was something absolute and universal: a fundamental opposition, moreover one that was (he knew, but still refused to acknowledge it) in-sur-mountable. What sort of opposition? He could tell that he appealed to her, as a down payment on the man-to-be. Exit this place and never set eyes on her again – the demon in him was saying in no uncertain terms. How many calamities could be avoided if people would only heed those mysterious voices that never lie? The Catholic doctrine of grace: a self-knowledge permitting abstention from certain things – things in which our wills have at least some say. But he stayed put, to his own detriment, and perhaps to hers as well. (A portion of her bestial power was consequently blown – but more on that subject later.) "Maybe it will have a happy ending," he said, naively and unashamedly lying to himself like a rascal. This honest and benevolent lie filled his throat with tears. "That's right – everything's going to end happily." Gloom filled the valley of his life, which only a moment ago had beamed. The faceless forms of forbidding, stillborn thoughts lurked in every corner. He knew for certain that he would never beat back the darkness, and yet he stayed put, amply fortified in this knowledge.

"Zip was quite taken with you," Lilian said in a voice choked with stage fright.

Genezip could have sworn otherwise, but the fact was that he had spoken, for later he was quoted as saying: " . . . there's such a 'suicidal happiness' about her that life would immediately cease for her lover." (Oh, how true: Persy was performing under the pseudonym of Molly Humper.) "He'd burn up in a second, burst to smithereens on the spot, in the would-be eternity of that moment and renounce everything in exchange. Everything except life. That would just make her more awesome . . . " (her = Bestialskaya).

"I didn't say a word. That's silly gossip. I can't stand the theater. The whole thing's a big fraud." His words fell like grenades into a swamp, producing a languid, obscene thud instead of an explosion. Persy smiled absently, obliquely, toward worlds located – ha! – somewhere between her legs where she harbored what might be termed a "between-the-legs obstacle" (so named by way of analogy with Mariusz Zaruski's skiing jargon). Just then his mother and Michalski came into the dressing room – they had box seats, while Zip and Sturfan sat in the orchestra. "May I pay you a visit sometime?"

(These words sounded so comically indecent, as if he had really meant to say: Would you mind if I officially stuck this thing of mine into that thing of yours?) "I'd like to talk to you about Lilian."

"But mostly about yourself, right? And about me, much too much about me." (She was dragging him, grinning all the while, into the deep.) "Don't bother. Some other people have already done it for you. It's all such a drag. But you'd better watch out: I'm a bad cookie, the kind you don't forget." (If Genezip had seen through her self-confidence, had known how little experienced she was in this area, he would have snapped right then and there in that cubicle, thoroughly demolishing the theater. Instead, he turned livid with a gorgeous, glossy purple, glaring, glassy, glans-penisy, and gloriously sexual anger. Then somberly, as though his sexual appetite was "on the move" without recourse to any onanistic prodding, he surrendered himself to the violet-blue mist of those virginal-Beelzebubian eyes. He was "ready.") "Although I am very innocent – too much so perhaps . . . " (This last was full of an insufferable, leg-spreading sort of coquetry. She had said it quite openly in the presence of the others. But on Sturfan she had no *Griff* whatever.) Madame Kapen was staring wide-eyed in astonishment. "What's the meaning of this intimacy?" Zip turned green with rage, shame, disgust. Little did he suspect that she was trying to do him a favor = that she was trying to discourage him by wounding his feelings. And his feelings really were hurt; his insides rose up in arms; at last he had found someone worthy of himself. He instantly overcame his wounded vanity. His laugh was lustful, almost triumphant. Persy frowned and looked a little peeved. But down below, Genezip felt nothing – a cold, empty, exiled sort of feeling: the sensation of a pile of useless guts withered into a timid, painful, and truly superfluous little sack. "What the hell – there'll be a war, I'll die, and that'll be that." From the auditorium came a wave of obscene, repulsive (coprophagous?) music (it was Tenzer who, now unleashed, was instrumentally banging away in his lowered psychic drawers), immediately followed by thunderous applause. Out of some odd perversion and in mockery of a declining Church, these musical interlubricants were listed in the program under religious, even Latin titles. But what does the title of a musical composition have to do with its intrinsically *musical* contents? Either it is a disemboweling of the composer's private experience, which is of no interest to anyone, or it serves an ulterior aim. Then they began playing another work by the same author, a piece called "Salivation" (a kind of overture-chorale sung by lewd flappers and primped galoots), dating from his latest period of debasement. Modest success had wreaked incredible havoc on this recluse from the world of pure sound. Not to mention his recent success with women, who were not always of the highest quality. He was in demand as erotic prey among freaks-*assortis* belonging to the theater's special choir and ballet section, both directed by the despotic and matronly bawd Mania Kozdroniowa. Grown jaded with the usual swells, diverse "poontang" (as he liked to call them) fought tooth and nail over the insatiable carcass of that abominable, by now berserk "creeple" – that vehicle for the most awful musical fusions, that guru for turning gyro-agitating bodies into the incredible dance figurations choreographed by a seedy and foppish dance master named Anestes Knocker, himself steeped to the elbows in the filth of the world. Under the influence of this music arousing a *boundless* desire for *indefinite* things (not in the metaphysical or even artistic sense, but from the guts), Genezip's innards unwound and his muscles contracted into a deliciously nostalgic, aching-for-a-fugitive-life knot. There was no telling whether he pined for the past or the future. Or was it simply a nostalgia for all existing things, riddled by the intolerable pain of futility? Unspecific and unfocused yearning. In this context Persy became a microscopic speck. And so on: the curse of schizothymes (read Kretschmer, dammit: *Körperbau und Charakter* – it's time someone translated this work, which should be read by all [except musicians]). Forward or backward, the past or the present? It was no longer possible to tell who was commiserating with whom. Meanwhile, the eternally elusive persisted somewhere like a rainbow in the clouds, while God continued to smile benignly on the devout being reduced to dust by a sunbeam parting the storm clouds. It was not Genezip but someone else who spoke, whose strange and unfamiliar voice could be heard in the hollowed-out, gourdlike void:

"I'll drop by tomorrow after twelve. We'll talk about Lilian. Not a word about myself – only under that condition. I'm just a miserable candidate for the post of general's adjutant." (How had *he* turned up again? For a split second, the general ceased to be the public statue of himself, as Zip had viewed him in the past, and became a live human being with a belly, intestines, and genitals, a man packed with petty and disgusting desires, materialized in purely prosaico-lifelike dimensions.) A *blood-red shadow crossed Persy's face* – not a blush, but precisely a *blood-red shadow*. Neither in his head nor in his testicles did it occur to Zip that he might have been a rival of that man. For she, Persy, was the general's only real secret, apart from his "idea" (his *idée fixe*, or in this case *"Fide X"*), a secret known only to a handful of people who were as dependable as the principle of contradiction. But as for her, nobody, not even her master, knew anything: she was just "SHE," the commander's woman, the only woman who . . . , etc.

....

INFORMATION: It was Kotzmolochowicz himself who was against her living in the capital. As a rule they met once a month for erotic purposes whenever she had her . . . etc. – and was given a four-day sick leave from the theater. The general's diet of morbid, leisurely, diabolical, and perverted fun consisted of eating (coprophagia); being horsewhipped in the nude (flagellation); and the supreme pleasure of submitting to the power of a woman, especially one so innocent (self-prostration). The raging of a furious beast in the lily-white claws of a delicate, gossamery, sexual cruelty: it was the equivalent of consuming a glass of molten lava in sips . . . Thus did the accursed "Kotz," that awesome spring in the hand of God, unwind. Thanks to this diet, he was able to maintain his ferocious, essentially Russian *bezzabotnost* so admired by the military representatives of fallen regeemes and captive nations. Unfortunately, opening a branch of Quintofron's theater in the capital was out of the question: the pressure exerted by a communist nebula in the embryonic stage was growing more extreme. (It was interesting to watch as communists the world over tried to combat this nebulous ovoweb [a cobweb of eggs]. All the same, something was beginning to take shape in the capital, at times noticeably so.) Maybe the separation was even for the better – for personal reasons ("The application of spermatic forces for more noble aims," as de Mangro says in Miciński's novel *Nietota*. "Rarely but in fine style" was another of the general's favorite maxims): in the capital there were fewer outlets for individual license. Actually, there was more extravagance to be found in The Most Sacred Rite of Politics. (Quintofron's theater was already very suspect, especially in Lieutenant Monkempt-Unster's circle, that bearded avenger of the perennially greedy lower classes.) Besides, if SHE had been at HIS side *always*, then, gentlemen, life would have become a nightmare, and all, including his wife Ann and his little daughter Ileanka, would have suffered. He loved all three; all were needed for his ferocious munitions factory, for wrestling with his own enigmatic fate and with the country's destiny incarnated in him. "Oh, I know all three like the back of my hand, / And that goes for you, *ma belle* Fanfan," the general used to croon in a beautiful baritone during his lighter moments. The fourth was that imaginary unknown woman, the Princess von Thurn und Taxis, as he sometimes called her: *"Gefährlich ist's zu trennen die Theorie und Praxis, doch schwer ist auch zu finden Prinzessin von Thurn und auch zu Taxis,"* Buxenhein used to sing in the presence of the general staff, whinnying gleefully. Still, the general must have had something up his sleeve, must have, gentlemen, otherwise – what was it I wanted to say? – nothing, just a double take, the kind people do as they sit sipping their tea at a railway station when they hear their train is about to leave without them. But they were wrong. And if the news had suddenly leaked out, the country would have been immediately transformed into an enormous mass of liquified rot, like Valdemar in the story by Poe.

After two more acts of even worse *bezobrazie*, Genezip, demoralized to the aching depths of his aroused spiritual viscera, trailed along with his family to the restaurant Ripaille for supper. As they were leaving the theater, Persy mentioned that she might come. Implicit in this "might" was a down payment of a manifold perversion. Why "might"? Why not "certainly"?! Oh, why was nothing the way it ought to have been?! The world had become vulgar in Zip's eyes, too painful to look at: waiters, aperitifs, hors d'oeuvres, Lilian's gaiety, his mother's half-pained, half-buoyant smile, and

Michalski's all-round cheerfulness. To make matters worse, the princess had dragged along her minions from the highest circles, who treated Genezip like a hole in a wheel of cheese and then proceeded to lay into the champagne. A tremendous "longing for the elusive," similar to that evoked by Tenzer's waltz, flipped Genezip (morally speaking) face down onto the ground in a fit of rank, brutal sobbing. He began to drink, and for a moment his regret seemed beautiful, and all was as it should have been – like the pigments in a perfect pictorial composition. But a second later the brutish fist of alcohol clasped this harmony by the throat. Drenched with liquor, that gent from below woke from his sleep, stood up, and gazed about the hall with his bloodshot eyes. Life, gone loco, was drowning in a brooding, vegetal stupor. Give it another second, then – zap! – fifteen years of hard labor. The reptilian eye of shady financial deals winked through *the entire hall* like the firmament on a starry night after a thunderstorm. The collective pig of Big Business, that new parasocial superpersonality, was cannibalizing new victims in its dirty embraces, indifferent to the sufferings of its individual components. It was in great spirits, feasting in the cyclone of crap, brashly devouring fancy dishes mixed with luxurious fabrics, precious stones, sex. The soft strains of the violins, seizing hold of that undifferentiated mass of the most sublimely dumb metaphysics and the most animal craving, dragged this mob's aching, sordid guts across the polished parquet floor awhirl with the stunning arabesques of lewdly shining calves, pumps, the most repulsively elegant shoes and breeches. The pig was having a field day. Thus did people party in the "bulwark" – though only in the choicer restaurants and clubs, of course. Such decadence was no longer fashionable in the West. Whereas there religion and nationalism had functioned as temporary motors for powering the fascist machine, in full awareness of the heuristics of such moribund concepts, here, in the "bulwark," they served as an excuse for the last great feast of the Great Swine; under their auspices people went to their lewd deaths feasting and reveling with a string of undigested offal sticking out of their sow-mouths. Joie de vivre is a wonderful thing; it all depends on who is doing it and how it is being done. There were still a few around (exceptional individuals, of course) who had not lost the knack; but gathered at the Ripaille were the leftovers. Ugh, ugh . . . enough, enough! Was there no force strong enough to pull *this* life from the cesspool? You would have thought these few waiters and devotees of life for life's sake were enough to bring down the Chinese Wall.

Genezip had completely forgotten about Tenzer's existence – it was Tenzer, after all, who so "lavishly orchestrated" (to quote the posters) Quintofron's stagings (Quintofron, that beanpole sporting a blonde mustache and wonderfully soft blue eyes, was busy drinking champagne with Madame Kapen and Michalski, explaining to them the meaning of realistic distortion in the theater) and whose music had lent his first meeting with Persy such a terrifically elegiac charm, otherwise known as "shooting for the infinite." It was the complete polar opposite of that music played in school (God, how long ago that all seemed now!), when he first latched onto the general's spirit. A tardy Putricides (by now a perfect specimen of depravity) entered the hall. At that moment the past erupted like an opaque ball of smoke, traveling upward from the cellar of Genezip's being to merge with the hideousness of the dance hall's coffered ceiling. Beyond this smoke there appeared, with all the terrifying clarity of a landscape of war, the customarily serene but now strangely altered backdrop of past events, and against this backdrop SHE, almost as forbidding as the reality of war, but now projected on the ordinary planetary level of mundane human affairs. With a concentration capable of drilling a hole in a cement wall, Genezip looked to see whether among the horde of theater freaks in Tenzer's tow there was not, by chance, she in whose existence he could hardly believe anymore. No such luck: she had been detained by duties affecting the country at large, perhaps even humanity itself, duties of an almost cosmic significance. Tenzer announced that Persy would not be coming due to a migraine headache. "Couldn't she have come for my sake, headache or no?" the half-crazed Zip complained in silence. If he had known what was going on at that very moment (the magic of simultaneity); the means by which *der geniale Kotzmolokowitsch* was preserving his cool and his life-fury, he would have gone up in smoke in a furious, devastating, onanistic orgasm. He began eavesdropping on the conversations through the transparent walls of unrequited longing and unmitigated despair.

....

INFORMATION: Terrible rumors were making the rounds. Rank gossip, hatched from the darkest, mustiest skulls and the most putrescent guts (in place of withered-up "hearts"), had materialized, ripened, and oozed into hard reality: in the flurry of aperitifs and hors d'oeuvres; in this atmosphere of desperate and suicidal gluttony, dipsomania, and debauchery; in step with the mesmerizing sounds produced by a fatally cloacal (and no longer simply honky-tonk) music capable of grinding everything and everyone into mindless crap. "Grand Ole Cunt" and "Peewee Prick" were wailing away on their hypersaxophones, tremolos, plectrums, gargantuafarts, and cymbaltingles, accompanied by a triple organo-piano, otherwise known as a Williams Excitator. (Imperceptibly, insidiously, certain dark powers, certain rotting social bacteria, had managed to corrupt life under the guise of physical fitness, joie de vivre, and a shallow, wholesome, Chestertonian sense of humor.) The rumor was that Adam Ticonderoga, Scampi's older brother, had died in prison. Supposedly the body had been released by three bearded gentlemen in top hats with the help of a forged document. The release order was believed to have come from none other than the offices of the Q.G. It was at this point, if one was to believe the palaverers of unclean mouth, that the investigation had backed off like a whining wolf from a dog's spiked collar. There were reports of a beating in a privy behind a residence known for throwing sadistic orgies with the help of a special machine – imported, no doubt, from Berlin. There was also talk of a secret duel (among the most lionhearted it was hinted that one of the duelists was Kotzmolochowicz himself), and that because of this duel Lieutenant Habdank Abdykiewicz-Abdykowski had swallowed phymbine in the presence of his mistress Nymfa Bitchgunt from the cabaret Euphornikon. It was a much agitated and grief-stricken princess who had just reported this last bit of news. Only one cure: drink, get high, then make love to that kid who sat there – aloof, drunk, brooding, plunged in a mysterious reverie, with her so close, so friendly, so affectionate, and so miserable. Poor Adam, her precious "little Chink," as he was called at home. He had not been allowed to see her before the briefing – before his having been executed (which was almost everywhere taken for granted) by those "cro*oo*ks." But who were they? No one knew. "Ho, ho, ho – dangerous times, these: clandestine politics, *lettres de cachet,* incognitos, kangaroo courts, disappearing acts . . . ," the naturally suspicious were saying. The prince must have delivered an overflattering report where the Chinese were concerned. Given the prevailing mood, it was a wonder that Djevani – after Kotzmolochowicz the next most enigmatic man in the world – was allowed to travel about the land so freely – true, on a litter and escorted by fifty of his most loyal (to whom, though?) lancers. Some incurable optimists rejoiced and began prophesying wonders: "You'll see, we're in for a moral revival; *les moeurs, vous savez,* are bound to change radically. In times of crisis people always step back for a better jump," spouted the fools. Meanwhile – claimed the more venomous wags and wits – one could never be sure of the day or the hour. Your best friend might have be spiking your roll with cyanide while your soup was being served – and so many courses yet to come, so many ways of being transported to "Abey's hairy bosom"! Dinner invitations were often a moral torture, like dining at the Borgias', and several political deaths were in fact reported following these official blowouts. More than likely they were the result of normal gluttony and, even more certainly, of an overdose of high-grade narcotics that were being imported from Germany by the carload; but in an era of complete ignorance they were explained in the most lurid fashion, thereby increasing the panic to *pale green proportions.* Panic over what? The government's embrace of the UNKNOWN – a historical "first," not counting that *official* show of secrecy mounted by the tyrants of old, those direct descendants of antique deities. Hardly a day went by when members of the cabinet were not observed in the most ordinary situations – at "work," or as they dined, dressed in their customary jackets and dress coats, on shrimps, artichokes, or on ordinary carrots; hardly a day passed when you couldn't engage them on this or that subject, on "the fillies," say, or on how fond Stefan Kiedrzyński was of writing; carouse with them, drink toasts to their health, kiss their asses, swear a blue streak at them, and meanwhile – nothing, nothing, NOTHING. Who these people were – *au fond* – no one had a clue. "Not even they know," people sang as their faces paled, "who they are *au fond*" (hold the last *o*). The general's mysterious shadow fell on them as well. And it was this aura of mystery that lent them a phosphorescent, spectral glow, which was mistakenly attributed to the Syndicate for National Salvation. They were essentially "pawns of the state," a race of precision-made machines. But that demon (for the masses, at any rate), Kotzmolochowicz, had filled them with the leftovers of his own stuffing – stuffed them like ravioli – then choreographed their *danse macabre* before a thoroughly confused mob. *"Who is the government?"* The question was being asked – ungrammatically, but not illogically – everywhere. Kotzmolochowicz and Djevani were alleged to have held secret talks at four in the morning in the former's black-and-green office. It was also rumored (but only under the couch, under the influence of cocaine, or through the ear) that Djevani was actually a secret emissary from a United East; that young Ticonderoga had spoken of the organizational wonders being achieved in the Land of the "Chinks," had strongly advised against imitating the Chinese model as being inappropriate for the white race, and had most emphatically implored the government not to take into its confidence any unofficial emissaries (or rather tentacles) from the East, i.e., those purveyors of the mind-drugging religion of Murti Bing. Instead, he had urged heroism in defense of the "bulwark" (a policy known as "bulwarkism") and had vanished like a bullet in the bog. But were not all, including the regime, in favor of such a policy? And who *were* these Zifferblatowiczes, Boroeders, and Quiltys? Mythic figures – but backed by a wall. "But to what end, to what end?" the republic was whispering in terror. (The end lay in itself: the historical consequences of that eternal opposition to whatever seemed like the best idea at the time, focused in a man choking with an excess of energy that would not be harnessed to drab, everyday work; all the rest was coincidental: the triumph of communism, the Chinese invasion, mankind's disillusionment with the democratic lie, etc., etc.) It was as if the degree of one's spectral glow was directly proportional to the stature one held. But even the opposition understood that this "bulwarkism," however ghostlike its sponsors, was the only thing that made life on this planet worth living during its final social phase. Nominally the government was run by the syndicate, though many believed that the psychiatrist Bekhmetev was right when he said, *"Proiskhodil protses psevdomorfozy,"* and that, in reality, it was being run by their surrogates. No matter on which vile street in the capital, no matter at what hour of the night or day, it was like inhabiting a weird dream. The confused sense of time and the state of rampant ambiguity may explain why so many rational people had begun to doubt their own existence, as people deprived of a sense of life's permanence do when faced with a calamity. Here, however, the spirit's essential ingredients were escaping through the valves of fear; the very navel of the once-magnificent personality had "split" like an almond from its shell. And yet, man's inner life had become more diversified, even by comparison with the first half of the twentieth century. The process had only just begun, but it was proceeding furiously. The agent of this transformation was unknown. The general was much too busy with his army to indulge in such trifles as the creation of a mood – *something* was expected there, but no one actually believed it was under way; in fact, a different sort of surprise was in store. A new secret government was being formed under cover of the existing one, while the official organ (the only real newspaper in circulation) of the syndicate was assuring the public that there would be no change of government and that, on the contrary, it was business as usual. Never had the parliament and the government worked so closely together: thanks to the financing of elections from abroad, the parliament was "stacked" with members of the syndicate and (for safety's sake, just to be on the safe side) found itself in nearly perpetual adjournment. The general's battle with the syndicate took place entirely in his mind and in the minds of the syndicate's most prominent fanatics. As far as the public was concerned, it was all a big mystery. Forces were being mobilized on both sides, but those at the junior level were kept in ignorance as to the real aims and long-range objectives. People were later amazed that something of this sort could have been executed in such secrecy. But given the generally stupefied state of society, it was indeed possible, as the facts show. A fact is a powerful master. Even so, a few distinguished scholars abroad (sociologists with no political axe to grind), in footnotes and references to other works, shyly alluded to the fact that not since the spread of early Christianity had there reigned such an air of mystery as then existed in Poland. The fact, for example, that representatives of foreign governments were barred from entering the country had turned diplomacy – that whole diplomatic *kanitel* (as the Russians say) – into a cloak-and-dagger affair. With Ticonderoga, the last remaining link with communism, and the yellow variety at that, had been lost. And six months had already passed since the Chinese ambassador had left the country as mysteriously as the forty thousand gods in the temple of Canton.

In the doldrums over the recent news, the princess arrived at the restaurant for supper, but not before having dumped Piętalski somewhere along the way. Her presence was a torture for Genezip. Nothing – he knew – could save him from a *"notte di voluttà"* à la d'Annunzio, for which he felt no inclination and which, after his most recent *coup de foudre*, he was even beginning to dread. To think that on this very day he would have to hug, rumple this poor, dissolute piece of – how strange – yet stranger still was the fact that he craved it: not so much her as the fact of possessing her. There was a difference – an enormous, fiendish difference: the poison of habit was taking its toll. And the effect was indeed poisonous. For such things can never be healthy for a budding crackpot.

Tenzer, strangely and disagreeably agitated, greeted Zip with an air of distraction. Employed for the first time in his life, tasting of "status" (oh, how pathetic!), he was savoring in little gulps the miserable swill of success. Not counting a few childish experiments at the conservatory (from which he had graduated as the future organist of Brzozów), experiments sabotaged by jealous rivals who were themselves mediocrities, it was also the first time he had heard his stuff performed by an orchestra – a miserable one, but an orchestra nonetheless. It was not a premiere of his more serious work, but rather the castoffs from that other, more essential realm which were now being turned out for the amusement of that "musical scum" whom he despised. The latter was his old nemesis, "the howling dog." But while in the past "the dog" might howl at a sentimental moon, today to make it howl one had to blow straight into its nose, tread on its tail, unstitch its insides. Compromising and degrading as his present position was (though it still left him room to lace his music with a wild originality), Tenzer prided himself on his recent success – and privately rued it. So far he had resisted surrendering to the demands of the moment and to the fickle tastes of the "howling dog," even when it came to the titles of his compositions. (The herd's comprehension of a given piece is almost totally dependent on what appears in the program and on the opinions expressed by the know-nothing authorities.) In the thickening rubble of life's high-grade shittiness (thanks to the conflict between the artist and society), Tenzer bore his artistic independence triumphantly before him. It gave him that self-esteem from which he was continually guzzling as from a rotgut whiskey. It was not a noble narcotic, though had he not been a cripple, all would have seemed somehow pure, idealistic, selfless. But in fact it was merely a disguise for his own internal ugliness, boil-infested buttocks covered with Brussels (necessarily Brussels) lace. This was one of those private little psychic privies which only he was aware of. (Even if they suspect others of shamming, normal people are not apt to reveal it for fear of being accused of the same thing.) For how if not from his own psyche could Tenzer have known of such secret and shameful complexes? These things belong to the most secretive of life's secrets; very often they are what motivate the great deeds of great people. At least he owned a piece of land and a shack to go with it. But what if he had been altogether destitute? He made it a point never to delve further. What depravity he might have accomplished in the realm of pure art! And now, from out of the smelly precincts of "mercenary musiciandom," these thoughts crawled forth like hungry reptiles or worms, and an ominous retrospective shadow fell across his previous work. He stiffened in sudden revolt against such thoughts, in defense of the last possible form of existence: there was no returning to the Ludzimierzian "hearth," no renouncing this riot of self-degradation among the fay, psychophysical freaks of Quintofron's choir. On the other hand, now he could create what he had neither the strength nor the courage to do before: he would turn that surrender into a springboard for the final leap into the heights (or depths?) of Pure Form, and thereby justify the filth in which his life had become steeped. This dangerous concept of using art to justify life's comedown had fastened itself to his brain like a polyp. He was reminded of a sentence from Schumann: *"Ein Künstler, der Wahnsinnig wird, ist immer im Kampfe mit seiner eigenen Natur . . . ,"* something about *"niederge . . . "* – oh, who cares. But it was not madness that threatened him. How he despised those prigs who dared to speak of *rançon de génie!* What if he wasn't a genius? Although such inane and sophomoric labels had never troubled him, he could sense his own cosmic significance (and what else mattered, dammit?!) while reading over his scores at night; he realized it abstractly, impersonally, as though it concerned someone else, a rival of his. He envied himself and felt sorry knowing that he would be an impossible act to follow; he experienced that characteristic and infallible sting near the heart from which not even the least envious natures are exempt. "Wow!" (Here one simply cannot avoid using such hateful expressions.) Now imagine he was being performed by some big-band orchestra at the Music Palace in New York! Imagine the following headlines printed in black and white in Havemeyer's Cosmic Edition (and not in some "posthumous" rant of his): "Let the 'genteel' crowd go wild – not me. I could, but I won't – only if necessary." Although his mother was a noblewoman (but such a "petty" one that she was not much better off than a peasant), he always alluded to it with genuine humor. For Tenzer possessed one extremely rare virtue: he was untarnished by any aristocratic snobbery. Now, after the few minor successes he had scored, he saw himself on the ascending part of life's sine curve.

"How did you like my music?" he asked the princess as he attacked a mountain of nearly priceless blue flounder smothered in mayonnaise, a recent favorite of his.

At the sight of her brooding and hitherto infallible medium, Zip, Irina Vsevolodovna inhaled a few decigrams of coke and regained some of her former levity: *tryn trava, more po kolena.* The princess, convinced that she was a doomed woman, had become oblivious to life's worries. Moreover, after a chat with one of Djevani's adepts, who had promised her a dose of Davamesque and further consultations, she had discovered something new in herself: a tiny, luminous dot illuminating with its glow the somber clouds of approaching old age. This little dot shone when life was at its bleakest, and (lo!) immediately things began to brighten – in another realm perhaps, but brighten they did. Her throat would fill with tears, things would take on a meaning not easily explained in rational terms . . . Thus did her grand affliction became alleviated.

"Marvelous!" the princess replied, nervously blinking her turquoise-colored eyes that began to fill more and more the black abysses of her expanding pupils. "I must confess, Putrice, it was the first time I found myself captivated by it. Only your presence was a bit overwhelming. You should try to illustrate more what is going on. Your music overpowers the action on stage."

"It was my first time out. I've never done such cruddy things before. But I wanted to show those ignoramuses. Did you notice how the critics and my worthy peers were out in full force tonight? I wanted to show them my stuff, and to do that I had to intrude a little, because I could never flaunt my knowledge in a void. They're not very *keen*" (a Brzozów expression) "on hearing my music, but just when they can't take it anymore and yet *must,* out of curiosity – that's when they get a taste of some real music, the suckers. Six months from now you won't find a scrap of officially recognized music that hasn't been influenced by my work. Even today there were a few from the capital: Powderpoop, Jr., and the director of the Music Academy in person, Arthur Demonstein, the most harmless of them all, I suppose – and, of course, Zombiosa and Bombossa. I have to admit I was tickled. And the whole crew, with the exception of Artie, made it look as if they were busting a gut, but deep down they were sweating it and diligently recording things only I know anything about. Supposedly these were just details – flourishes, as they say. But that's just to deprecate the weirdness of the formal *Gestalt,* which is the molecular soul of the thing and totally incomprehensible to them. Ha-ha! During the intermission I caught Bombossa in the john with a notation book in his hand. He got pretty flustered and muttered something about parallel fifths. I let the bastard have it with my fartophone . . . "

"You shouldn't drink so much, Putrice. You're trying to swallow life in one great gulp, horns and all. You'll either asphyxiate yourself or puke – to use your manner of speaking – like Alfred de Musset or Fyodor Jevlapin. You have to be more discriminating, even someone as starved as you are. You should be given a good psychic enema with psychic sunflower oil like those explorers who starved at the North Pole. You're constipated with life's coprolites, ha, ha, ha!" She burst out laughing in one of those affected cocaine fits of hers. The brakes had ceased to function.

"And you're one of them – relax, Irina, and lay off the coke. Above all, don't overdose – or no 'bangee' even if they drive a coach with a team of six horses up there." (Genezip felt like an appliance; he tried to get up, but was stopped by a woman's paw awesome in its limpness: "Oh-oh, it's a tumble in the sack for sure," some not-too-mysterious voice said inside him. "Love won't help you now. The whole thing's hopeless anyway." He surrendered.)

"I've got a regular doll picked out. Practically ready-made ('He traveled to C. to pick up a *lee*tle tail,' as you used to say) – and even an admirer of mine. Seduced, like all the others, by my sounds; what excites her is that a freak like me can be the medium; it gives them a new dimension of erotic mystery. Oh, if you could read my head *then*, see the fusions of my mind: *exkrementale Inhalte mit Edelsteinen zu neuen Elementen verbunden.* I positively screw my way up the genitalia of mystery. My wife formally allows it, as I her, and so you see ours is a marriage in the most modern sense."

"You're as naive as ever, Putrice. Half the country, if not three-fourths, is carrying on that way. A hundred years later, French literature has finally caught on here. But I'm curious to know if your wife really enjoys the same freedom as you. Because not everyone can do that. In this respect my Diapanasius is a true exception." A blood-red shadow passed over Tenzer's face before being absorbed, like a sponge, by a face suddenly become fiercely insolent.

"Of course," he blurted out with a forced levity. "I'm consistent. I pass my wife's lovers in the hallway without batting an eyelash. Freedom's a great thing, so great that you don't even mind paying for it with one's stupid, fictitious husband's honor. It only gets comical when you're deceived. But this way I know, and for all I care they can stick it up my fartophone," he concluded with one of his pet sayings.

"You won't be sticking things up there for long if you can never be sure whose mistress your wife's going to be next, you brilliant little puppet, nor she you," said the princess with sudden earnestness.

"*Knyaginya,* I'm a provincial. For the first time in twenty years I'm living in the city and not just passing through. But I have enough brains to know when it's beginning."

"When *does* it begin – that's the most interesting thing. With flowers, candy, stockings, shoes . . . ?"

Tenzer slammed his fist on the table; he was being carried away by the knowledge of his own genius, by an exquisite Dzikowski vodka, and by that male honor which had just been salvaged.

"Hush, you aristocratic whoranalia." (The princess's aides shook with laughter. Be offended by an artist? Nonsense.) "You bagiarchal, female *elementhaler* – shut up or I'll make elemental cheese of your milk and wash it down with the famous suds of the Kapens. And you – " he went on with a sudden clairvoyant gleam in his eye, "you picked a winner, didn't you? Watch that your Zip doesn't leave you in the lurch. Especially now that he's found a tidy morsel in that petite little stage manager who's trying to make a monster out of his kid sister. She's a little out of my class, but Zip can handle it. You see, we're all turning monstrous," he added, noticing that his remarks had provoked a fairly revealing reaction in Genezip, namely, he had just grabbed a heavy bottle of communist-imported burgundy and was swinging it in the air, splashing himself on the neck and all over the princess's pearl-white evening gown.

"Cut it out, Zip – you know I wish you well. But didn't I hit the nail on the head?"

The princess disarmed her lover by means of a trick borrowed from jujitsu.

"You forget that three months from now I'll be an officer and that you're just a cripple. One can forgive a crippled genius a lot of things, but now it's time to stop, okay?" Anger had sobered Zip completely; he was soaring above the table piled high with expensive food, above the world itself. In his hand he held the very nucleus of contradictory forces; he had the illusion that by sheer willpower he could reverse the course of the planets and transform every living creature into his own image and likeness. Reality was straining toward him, cringing before him; he could smell her hot and (faintly) rancid breath, hear the smacking sounds made by her inscrutable organs. "Feasting on reality is like trying to satisfy a woman: impossible to stand pat. When that happens – bang! – it's over. The super orgasm – psychic as well as physical – can't be had. Once the spring has been overwound, got to start over again, and on it goes till one day you no longer care. It's called the law of metaphysics."

The princess gazed at her lover admiringly. Never had he seemed so mature. (She was drinking heavily, now and then switching to colossal doses of coke.) He tore her apart with his manliness, with the terrible futility of possessing the All. The combination made him even more lethal in her eyes; with every passing moment he grew more inscrutably, more uniquely male. Sprawled out, flattened before him, she was oozing like a huge wound, enveloping him with her swollen and painfully outstretched teletentacles. Tenzer and Zip were swearing eternal friendship to each other; the atmosphere in the dining room was turning positively orgiastic. The hot breath of infinity had engulfed even the most vulgar human cattle. They were a social organism permeated with a subconscious awareness of the absolute wonder of everything existing. Individual orgiasts slithered between tables: an osmosis of frenzied entrails filtering through membranes of social prejudice and class barriers. (Dance halls were notorious for such moments of predawn intimacy.) Sturfan, heady with the triumph of his play (officially commissioned by that swine Quintofron), had just whisked Lilian off to the dance floor.

"Shall we dance, Zip?" the princess asked in a voice as powerful as a suction pump on a transoceanic liner. The old girl was overcome when a Malayan band (some of Murti Bing's most faithful disciples) began hammering out an ungodly "wooden stomach." Nor was Zip able to resist. He danced, gritting his teeth, and lusted for her, for that frump, for the high-grade sexual poison embedded in her, that stupefying narcotic into which this erotic ogress could transform the most innocent caress. If he had known that in that very same building, in a special office located at the rear – had known that SHE and the quartermaster . . . (Kotzmolochowicz was indeed a master in this quarter, a master of a masochism most perverse, lending him a true grandeur during this, the second and more historical part of his life. [After a special "menu" and a serving of jalaps, she was being treated to a dish of monkeys' testicles in a macaroni of capybara oviducts, sprinkled with the ground coprolites of marabous force-fed with Turkistan almonds. Who paid for all this? SHE HERSELF did – out of her salary from Quintofron's theater: it was the height of humiliation. But what are the most fiendish designs of the flesh without that diabolical spiritual mix which only certain persons know how to arouse? Any old whore can perform the wildest tricks – but not this sort.]) Oh, had Zip known, he might have actually barged in on them, smashed with his bottle of burgundy the euphoric skull of his supreme idol, then killed himself and her in some superviolent act the likes of which has never been seen. ("What a pity we do not encourage such impulses, especially in a person's earlier years. How much more intense would be the prevailing social 'tenor.' *Anywhere else, perhaps, but not here.* And why is that? Because we are a race of compromisers. And the Chinese will likely walk over us the way the hordes of Kublai [?] or Genghis Khan overran others, and we shall repel the invaders – not by force but by sheer mediocrity – and return once again to queasy, good-hearted, mealy-mouthed democracy" – thus spoke the immortal Sturfan Abnol, one of the most cynical beasts of our age. That he had survived such acrimonious times was one of the unacknowledged miracles of that unforgettable epoch, even though, after his death and long after the Chinese occupation, during what came to be known as the "Golden Age" of Polish literature, volumes were consecrated to the man – that is, hordes of rotten parasites and literary hyenas feasted on his spiritual carcass.) Oh, to see it simultaneously broadcast on telecinema: the commander's mounted artillerymen, freshly mobilized and wild with hero worship, as they went about night exercises; the Council of Three (a triple phantom capable of outsmarting not a few apparitions at any halfway decent spiritual seance) sitting in session; shots of Jacek Boroeder cutting deals with Western business agents; and the great x of that differential equation, with all its multiple derivatives, wallowing in the most insane, the most obscene, Franco-Prussian debauchery with one of the purest women in the country, who had begun to see herself as a latter-day Jeanne d'Arc, so greatly confused had she become in her little female brain because of the attention lavished on her by the general's closest "buddies." A certain clique had convinced her that she had a patriotic duty to sacrifice her body to that sinisterly winged bull whose very approach filled her with boundless terror. But this fear entailed a thrill of its own. With her, he was not at all the bugaboo of the academies, ministries, board meetings, and of every other equally boring institution. It was he who groveled before her – ahh! When she demurred, the general became furious: eighteen adjutants were needed to detain him in his black office while terror-stricken orderlies brought in ice water by the bucketful. ("Ma'am, how would you like to see the greatest mind in the modern world rot away in the glass jar of some commie psychiatrist?" Colonel Kuźma Huśtański would say to her. "Madam, how would you like to have on your conscience not only the fate of that genius but of the whole country, maybe even the world?" Robert Monkempt-Unster would say during his exhortations while entertaining who knows what thoughts of his own. "Without *it*, my dear Perse," this from her Aunt Frumporzewska, a woman known for her unwavering discretion, "think of the subconscious pressure exerted by those dark forces? You alone can unravel that knot of bestial drives and give him a sense of Unity Within Plurality; only in your tender embrace can that fiendish mechanism find repose; only you can keep it well oiled and lessen the pain of a soul parched by the fervor of unsatisfied lust. You alone can disembowel him with those marvelous fingernails of yours.") So it happened that in a few months this girl, once pure at heart as a lily, was excelling in the worst depravity, even pleasurably so. And it was happening *right now*, that hatched-from-the-most-licentious-dream-come-true "reality" – just a few flights and corridors away, here in the very same building. And to think that THEY had been engulfed by the same demoralizing music (only in a somewhat milder way) as poor Zip and this massive incarnation of the GREAT SWINE. For they were also a part of that incarnation – perhaps the grandest part of all. Only the proportion of the "secondary products" (all those battles, military reforms, social activities, heroic exploits, political scams, etc.) (as far as women are concerned, what else are these things if not secondary?) was different. Scale can justify anything except stupidity and cowardice.

Zip was choking on insuperable contradictions: his mother, somewhat in her cups but in a sophisticated sort of way, was fondly reminiscing with Michalski about the past; Lilian, still in raptures over the success of her debut, was quite deliberately driving Sturfan Abnol insane – and this in an atmosphere of a sexual, dance-hall ragout, of panic at the prospect of meeting an officer from the school, and the memory of that body into which he was drowning, as in a swamp, all possibility of pure love . . . Oh, Zip was surely Hell-bent! "He was a wee thing that sped away my soul, / But snatch it he did, down to that fiery hole" – he recalled one of Lilian's childhood verses. "Break away, man, from all these female imbroglios!" But where was he to go? He felt like a prisoner. "Maybe this she-brute will help me to overcome HER." He actually entertained this shabby thought, this disgusting kid who for the first time in his life had fallen for someone. Today he stood at the highest point of his life's parabola, at the very pinnacle of his existence. But this peak was disappearing in a feculent fog, in life's prosaic filth at the base, while high above, at an unscalable height, there towered the true summits of the spirit: Kotzmolochowicz, Boroeder, Quilty, and those *consummate* Chinese officers atop the ruins of a Kremlin recently entered a new czarist phase. Who was he beside such giants?! Even if he lived another three hundred years on this planet? Still, he had the ambition and appetite of a true titan. And these were being kindled at that very moment – here, in this brothel. The mastications of the greedy Swine echoed obscenely in his hot and lusting guts. These celebrities were also *produits secondaires*. Revel to the teeth, feast till you puke! So this was where he had landed: first love. But how to salvage that *private* world (affirmed by art, science, and philosophy), or rather that isolated, below-summit ledge upon which to live one's life confidently and uniquely? It was hopeless. How frantically he longed for a brush with greatness, with its most extreme tip now vanishing forever. Oh, to be sitting in some military office in the capital (at the end of HIS tentacle), or to be driving somewhere by car with a document bearing his signature – how vastly different that seemed compared to his present surroundings! He could have stomached anything then, risen above it, instead of bumbling along passively, an insignificant nobody. Or so it seemed to him. The world had become such a messed up place; nothing was right due to the immediate, fluctuating, distorting social climate. The shift in rhythm and tempo had made it impossible to live one's life radically. Zip, for all his faults, was something of an exception.

By and large (or so Abnol claimed), that postwar, dance-hall-sports-crazy generation had been rapidly succeeded (that is to say, it had rapidly given way to the next generation, not just agewise but in terms of exercising authority). The age gap between the generations had diminished, ridiculously so: people only a few years younger than their peers were referring to the latter as their "seniors." A portion of this generation was already hopelessly cretinized (with competitive sports, the radio, party-throwing, jitterbugging, an increasingly vulgar cinema, when was there time to think? The daily tabloids, growing steadily thicker by the year, and literary kitsch had finished the job); another segment, reacting in panic, was seized with a spurious work ethic and had begun slaving away senselessly and unproductively. Only a minute portion tried to deepen themselves, to live more intensely, mainly mental freaks equipped for neither life nor art. The next generation (separated by a decade from the preceding one) was more intense, but impotent. Not in the muscular sense – a physical renaissance was plainly under way – but the will, my good sir, was not quite what it ought to have been, and the spirit, the spirit, my dear fellow, was not the best sort of scaffolding. The ambient social atmosphere meant that apart from a strictly banned communism there were few utopian theories left to snort. What, then, were those rachitic brains supposed to feed on? Moderation is death to youth – youth in the old-fashioned sense, not today's mindless jock types. The national campaign aimed at breeding a new type, on the pretext that the country should be represented abroad by the pole vault and discus, had backfired miserably. What would these kids be like in their thirties if they had never known radicalism in their teens? This third generation, the one to which Genezip belonged and which had been educated by the syndicate, did not differ from your average kids from before the war. At last! A new foundation for the future, time permitting! But no. It was this group that the general had hastily *militarized* – or better, *officerized:* the general dreamed of an army of officers headed by a top brass of ultrahyperfeldzeugmeisters. Ha! The results of *that* dream remain to be seen.

Dancing with the princess, Zip felt in his arms not a symbol of life but an abominable jelly of echinococci. He could see only her face, but that was enough . . . Why "enough"? He gloomily pondered the mechanics of the trap into which he had fallen. Apart from the onanistic practices of his youth, this was his first vice – not only his addiction to the physical refinements of sex, but to the habit of self-justification, of curling up in some comfy little corner of "coolness," the sort that comes from weakness and not from a spirit of adventure. Quit, man! But he who was so close to becoming an officer hesitated. Later they drove out to the suburb of Jada where Zip thrilled to the most awful pleasures. (The princess had surreptitiously slipped a little cocaine into his wine.) Worse, where he knew the thrill of desecrating the most sacred things and, worst of all, enjoyed every minute of it. From that moment on, a new man dwelt within (this was in addition to that surly, underground gent, who, pleased with events, had kept strangely quiet in recent days, though he continued to labor below). This new tenant had fashioned for himself a transformer for inverting values. Revolting? Yes, but only when done maliciously (i.e., "perversely"). Difficult? To realize, yes. Of no value whatsoever? Not when it elevates someone to the stature of life's essence. In the hands of a Kotzmolochowicz such a transformer could have led to things magnificent in their madness. But lodged in the brain of that "future madman from Ludzimierz," it might well lead to disaster.

Tor*ch*ures and the Debut of the "Gent from Below"

Without sleep; suffering, without knowing it, from a ferocious cocaine hangover (he had been left only with a sense of unfathomable marvels and revelations – why?); after a day of exercises outside the city in a landscape as lackluster as a high school graduation (it was a grey, sultry, mawkish spring day, redolent of grass); and at around six in the evening, Genezip hurried down Holy Bombast Street in the direction of Persy's place. He felt tremendously nervous, tongue-tied, sweaty in his tight-fitting uniform, and had a vile taste in his mouth.

She, that numbfish, lived with a Madame Tease (Isabella), a sort of combination cook-chaperon. The name of her chaperon capped the list of horrors in that male torturium, such as those "loving quarters" (to quote Madame Tease) of the renowned Miss Bestialskaya indeed were. Even in the hall he detected, through some obscure faculty, a morbid air of resignation. Everything was permeated with the smell of prolonged and unmitigated "tor*ch*ure" (as the princess pronounced it). And then to be exposed to such an atmosphere after yesterday's surfeit – . Ooooo! It was dangerous – ho, ho! He knew it, yet a demon kept prodding him on, with one pitiless claw clasped around his neck. He knew the sort of woman she was – and how he knew, the poor fellow. She received him in bed surrounded by a feathery affair à la Vrubel, hypertransparent lace, and by pillows whose pillowyness infinitely surpassed the most luxurious dream of idleness ever dreamed by the most Oriental prince. (The whole arrangement was rather inexpensive, but put together with remarkably sadistic taste. It was aimed at the maximal dissipation of male power, an aim soon to be realized.) Poor Zip, he was completely dazzled by her "angelic" beauty, though certain details that had been overlooked yesterday now came to his attention. He noticed, for example, that she was more beautiful "in a natural state" than onstage – a fatal discovery, by the way. Not a single flaw with which to console himself *en cas de quoi*. A wall. Her nose was "so straight it was nearly aquiline," as Rajmund Malczewski once remarked; her mouth, while not very large, was despair itself, not to mention her wonderful strawberry blush on a bed of celestial, almondlike, superchamois softness; and violet eyes whose dark lashes, curled slightly at the corners, lent her glance an undulant, elliptical quality receding into an infinity of as-yet-unsated passion. Clearly no man, even the most fiendishly sexed, was "up to" her, that is, could please her, plumb her depths, and generally perform with her. She was indestructible. Only death: his or hers. A wall not-to-be-surmounted. Ha! It was from this very futility that Kotzmolochowicz derived the most primal elements of his fury. Plainly this was not your common, even luscious little tart, many of which he had ruined like a brat who willfully breaks his toys. Here, he might lower his omnipotent battering ram, blast in there, and still fall short; he might rage like a beast, fuck up a storm with his stormtrooper of a trooper, spew his golden-black lust like a lava-spitting volcano – in a word, he might find in her a détente for his metaphysical need of devouring the All. She was a symbol of all that. Meanwhile, what about Zip? Be serious!

Her peevish chaperon had no sooner laid out the tea service and left the room (grinning all the while, as if to say: "I have a good notion what's going to happen here in a moment") than Persy threw back a puff the color of rose tea and drew her nightie up to her neck. Genezip, petrified (all sexual desire had fled to the tip of his intellect), beheld an avatar of seduction and the perfection of feminine beauty, from her ash-blonde hair (in *both* places) to the tips of her toenails. He froze. The impenetrability, the invincibility of this sight bordered on the absolute. Compared to this obstacle, what was the wall of Mount Everest when attacked from the side of the Rongbuk glacier? A farce. That which yesterday had struck him as absurd (that she could be endowed with *it*) had become real. But the absurdity of the real image was infinitely more gross than his daydreams in the theater when he had tried to imagine *it* as belonging to HER . . . Oh, horrors! And he heard, in the dark torture chamber of his soul, the words uttered from the stage by that seductive little voice ("*her* voice, no less . . .") through the medium of that woman lying before him in all the obscene splendor of her nudity (not nakedness), without abandoning for a moment her angelic pose. What a beauty she must have been at the moment of orgasm! . . . It was only a bad dream. But no: her words had crept into his ears like ants into his drawers and were already nibbling away at his aching, spiritual-corporeal knot of sexual confusion.

"For goodness's sake, sit down, Zip. By the way, I hope you don't mind if I call you by your first name. It'll make things easier." (For whom, for God's sake?!) "The truth of any emotion lies in deception and insatiability. A satisfied male doesn't lie, and I only want lies." (There was also a "truth of satiation," the kind only a Kotzmolochowicz – a brute and a bully, in other words – could give her.) "I love you, but you'll never possess me. You can only look, and then only sometimes. But soon you will start thinking deceitful thoughts, and you will tell them to me, and I will make them my life and through them create my own deceitful act. You see, I need it for the theater. And you'll come to hate me because of all the torture, and you'll want to kill me, only you won't have the stomach for it, and then I'll love you even more. Won't that be fun . . . !" She stretched, parting her lips somewhat and spreading her legs ever so slightly, while her eyes misted over. Zip began to squirm. Oh, with your crude mitts disembowel her, young man, and gobble up her guts while they still reeked of her . . . "Soon you'll be just the thought of me, a single orgasm of pain, one prolonged explosion of unrequited lust, and then maybe . . . But it's not likely I shall ever let you touch me; I prefer death to the hideous truth of boredom and contentment. I'd rather crucify myself . . . I love you, I love you . . . " And writhing as if her source of carnal delight were being jabbed with a red-hot poker, she pulled the quilt up to her neck. Her rosy pink heels flashed before his eyes, and he caught a whiff of a female not-of-this-world. (She always smelled a little after her sessions with Kotzmolochowicz.) Persy felt the same near-psychic chill, which the master of masochistic raunchiness used to call, in true "soldierly fashion" (my good sir), "baring your ass to the interplanetary void," and which was always a prelude to pleasures of a more physical kind. Starting with that wicked tongue so skilled in driving her to a frenzy. . . inside *there* . . . and to think that it was HE who – Oh, no! Zip was okay as a decoration, a childish decal on a metaphysical urinal in which the heart of that titan swam in a medium of suspicious-looking secretions. For she was certain that, for all his quirky notions of "détente," the general loved her. How marvelously full her life had become, not another pin could have been stuck in it. Aunt Frumporzewska had been right: the trick was to hold in your hand such a bomb of destiny and then play with the fuse, knowing the thing could blow sky-high at any moment: "That, my good fellow, would be positively first-rate."

For a moment Persy was convulsed by a faintly hysterical but dry sob. Fixing her gaze on Genezip, who continued to stand there in acute sexual dysfunction, she said, with the most profound sisterly affection and in the most graciously solicitous tone:

"Won't you have some tea, Zip? Madame Tease has baked some excellent petits fours today. Please help yourself – you look so undernourished." Then, in a voice full of predatory passion, she added: "Now you're mine, all mine." (On her lips was another word, the general's favorite; unable to check it, she murmured it softly, at the same time lowering her eyes, which, in the flurry of eyelashes, seemed to convey only one message: "You know what a marvelous, fragrant, tasty thing I have . . . But it's not for you, you little jack-off, only for the really big he-men of this world." [What can be more indecent that a woman's shaded eyelids lowered in affected modesty?] Genezip was sure that he had misheard, otherwise life would have been too outrageous.) "You'll never forget me. Even when you're in the grave your coffin lid will rise up whenever you think of me." She was not above such cheap, third-rate cracks! But as it came from her unassailable mouth this wisecrack resounded like a sinister, morbid, aching-with-female-insatiability truth. Mademoiselle Bestialskaya sank into his pallid face made exquisite by a transcendental despair; devoured the intolerable, adolescent sexual dolor in his feverish eyes, and with her brown-framed, innocent, violet eyes dug into his contorted mouth and quivering jaws that, in a fit of frustration, were grinding Madame Tease's truly superb petits fours to a pulp. And she was right: it was indeed a marvel. Not that it was recommended for getting the commander's officer corps into fighting shape! Ooo . . . – but what if Zip had been suddenly privy to yesterday's tryst? Now *that* would have raised his hackles! Such a "jolly" scene it would have made! But now he could ill afford it. Though it was bound to come – a time as precious as a highly polished stone, a time for dissolving in a lovely little sauce of torture . . . *Then* he would show her. There actually were such types.

It was quite obvious that her "insatiability" was only an act; actually she was more than satisfied by that demigod, that mustached brute, by that autocratic wild man rummaging in her own body, who, after prostrating himself, got his kicks by beating, slapping, kneeing – ! Aah . . . ! (It was no accident that a turbogenerator like Kotzmolochowicz had chosen such a woman. He had discerned her from among tons of female flesh and made her what she was now: sovereign of a realm of nearly metaphysical deception [the sort that denies *everything*] and truly high-grade torture. With the general behind her [psychically speaking], Persy feared no one.

She could immobilize and coolly devour anyone [even someone she loved – in her own way, of course] like a praying mantis.)

Genezip turned numb under his mountain of frustration. Various inviting little valleys offering a last-minute escape had been blocked by a scheming perversity. In a parched voice he mumbled a few nonsensical words inadvertently blossomed forth from the freshly dissipated image of her marvelously long and slender but nonetheless ample legs that, as he suddenly came to realize, *were completely covered with bruises*. And these bruises had the same effect on him as that of fulminate of mercury on pyroxylin.

"Did someone . . . I mean, why those . . . those spots?" He lacked the nerve to come right out and say "bruises." He motioned with his hand above her bedspread.

"I fell down the stairs yesterday after the third act," Persy sulked with a smile full of unspeakable sweetness. With this smile there appeared before the young martyr's intuitive navel the mute and forbidding image of some wild, inconceivable rape. And even though he was *conscious* of some monstrous foreboding, he also knew, as if by a weird hypnosis, that instead of deterring him it was making him even more fiendishly eager. He was igniting like paper in a Bessemer converter, quietly howling away in the waterless desert of his soul. There was no escaping this torture, nor could he free himself from that officero-virilo-inspirational mystique symbolized by the general, but which came down, in fact, to a crass opportunism (nationalism played no part in it at all). Even Kotzmolochowicz had stopped believing in the revival of moldy national sentiments. In the schools, lip service was paid to them at the beginning of the term, after which certain abstract notions were paraded about like the sacraments: ideas like honor and duty, which now took their place beside dependability, fortitude, punctuality, precision in drawing, clarity in elocution, and a purely physical fitness. The leveling process had spared nothing. (Apparently even the teachings of Murti Bing were in favor of this.) Meanwhile, spooked mannequins roamed the intellectual gloom. Those of a deeper cast kept it carefully hidden from the masses: such things (*which* things?) had a low exchange rate, even more so if they were connected with traditional metaphysics or religion. The same psychosis reigned everywhere: the fear of madness. Genezip was truly an exception.

Suddenly, at that fatal moment, something flung him to the ground, and he, that asymptotic officer, the commander's future aide, member of his private bodyguard, began to sink his teeth into the carpet, causing him to gag on a strand of wool and to drool on the rug's Persian designs. A black wall of dense but soft resistance separated him from ecstasy. Beyond that wall all could be conquered, whereas on this side – nothing. Rape was out of the question; at the slightest commotion her chaperon would enter. The tactics used against the princess would not work, either; against demonism there were no antidotes. Besides, there was nothing demonic about this woman: he believed in her sincerity, regardless of her confession. In fact, it was a demonism of a higher order: sweet, affectionate (affected would be more like it), and coated all over with a make-believe suffering. She was plainly unhappy. But her unhappiness only made her more appealing (like those girls dressed in mourning from his childhood) and raised the hidden, mysterious evil of this stinking situation to a frenzy. Yes, only the word "stink" (or *shtink*, to Russify it, for those who cannot abide ordinary words) could convey the awfulness of it. His first real fit of rage – *and with all the symptoms of a normal case of delirium having nothing to do with lunacy*. She leapt out of bed (wrapped in a long, nearly transparent nightie) with her naked feet and began to caress his head, calling him by the most endearing names:

"My sweetheart, my darling, my dearest kitten, my innocent little cherub, my busy little bee (whatever did she mean by that?!), my adorable affliction – calm yourself, have pity on me (this last was meant to provoke contradictory emotions), kiss me." (While he was not allowed to touch her, there was nothing to prevent her from touching him.) She pressed his head against the lower part of her belly, and Genezip could feel on his face the heat from *down there*, could smell the delicate, extraordinary trace . . . Oh, no!!! And her voice seemed to touch his body's deepest sexual sources. ("You slut – you're the sexiest woman anyone could possibly imagine, but you're a bitch just the same," the general used to say, knowing full well the good fortune of his discovery.) It was a voice that sucked the marrow from his bones, stupefied his brain, and made a hollow bladder of him. And it all happened so quickly! No more than three minutes had passed since his arrival. Somehow he got over his fit. His momentary delirium now seemed delectable. He was presently admiring her bare feet as she stood beside him (those lovely, long toes shaped – as the general knew only too well – for exotic caresses): it was the equivalent of being crowned with a club, of having a red-hot poker shoved into the testicles of his being. Again he pounded the floor with his head, howling in silence. This was love, all right – the bestial, unadulterated kind, free of any idealistic garnish.

Persy, self-suckingly content with herself (how wonderfully huge, beautiful, and suffused with herself the world had suddenly become!), continued to caress that manly little head, which struck her as "charmingly cute" in its oddity. ("The sperm rushed to his head," as her "Moloch" liked to put it. Sometimes he referred to it as a "bull spasm.") If only she could have seen the effects of her punishment *from the inside,* experienced them herself, at the very limit of the impossible where two rather contradictory concepts of the brain existed: the first, that of the brain as an organ of a nonexistent mind, as a structure of living cells reducible to a chemical system; and the other, that which each of us has in his head as something *immediately given,* the site of complexes and less empirical sequences comprising the psychological process of cognition itself. That was it: *to contemplate it as one bloody, naked brain sticking out his skull* = a third concept, but unfortunately one that necessarily involved another brain. Alarming notions had hold of that Persy, a stranger to philosophy and to the exact sciences. Even the general's metaphysics (God forbid!) was too bold for her. She believed blindly and obediently in a Catholic God and even attended confession and communion regularly – the monster! So? What about Alexander VI who prayed to the Holy Virgin for the death of certain cardinals whom he had poisoned for financial reasons; to the discrepancies between today's Catholicism and the true teachings of Christ? A trifle, a bagatelle.

"Oh, my sweet little head! What marvelous, silky hair; what naughty eyes – like those of a fidgety male who knows there's a female in the cage next door and can't get to her . . . What a thirsty, unquenched mouth; what a feverish little body!" She slipped her hand inside his uniform. "Oh, you marvel – how magnificent it all is!" And clapping her hands, she commenced to dance on the carpet, kicking her legs above his head and revealing that chasm of pleasure and original sin. Genezip knelt and stared. Like a monster from some peyote vision, the world was transformed into a hyper-grotesque monstrosity – horned, jagged, bristling, sinister, and in-con-ceiv-ably ugly. A pain both moral and physical in essence, yet somehow painless and soothing, reduced him to a hideous, evil-smelling cataplasm. He closed his eyes and felt more dead than alive. Centuries passed. Persy put on a desperate "wooden stomach" and danced herself delirious. Meanwhile, a voice that was alien both to herself and to the world (she regarded it as the voice of Satan) was saying, off to the side, unaffected by what was going on: "Suffer, you dirty male, you half-baked embryo, you wimpy little shithead – I'll crucify the hell out of you; I'll flagellate you with your own lust; I'll whip your dirty little imagination to death. You can screw me all you like in your thoughts, yell your head off, but you'll never touch me, never – that's the whole fun of it. Go ahead, scream with pain, beg me to stroke those wildly excited guts of yours with just one little hair of mine." Etcetera, etcetera. This was pure love dished up for the reverse side of the ego. She felt like a dirty sack turned inside out. This oscillation between a reality bordering on the graspable (i.e., the general and his fits) and an inner duplicity so thoroughgoing it bordered on the truth – this oscillation somehow exacerbated her will to live. For Persy suffered from acute chronic depression, and at heart was a pitiful little creature, as, weltering in self-pity, she called herself while calmly eviscerating some male, driving him *simultaneously* to a whining pity and a screaming, animal rage. For she combined, in a hideous mélange, psychic sadism with unbounded charity toward all misfits, cripples, poor in spirit, morons, and weaklings (oh, the perverse woman!). Women either worshiped her insanely (she had received several marvelous lesbian propositions but had rejected them with contempt) or despised her, often for no reason, as if she had been the mistress of their lovers, although Persy had a clear conscience in this respect – with the possible exception of the general's wife.

(Once married, the general had avoided any *official* mistresses. Persy was the first [and the last] with whom he had betrayed his wife. Tarts, of course, did not count.)

Suddenly Zip jumped to his feet and zoomed out the door, almost forgetting to grab his cap on the way out. The tea and petits fours remained untouched as a symbol of his narrow escape from those demonic pincers. The chaperon, who had been standing lookout at the door, nearly fainted at the sight of his face and the speed of his getaway. His face was indeed a sight: blackened with anguish, swollen from some mysterious thing . . . Oh, for a portrait of him at that moment, or at least a photograph! But no such luck.

Quietly, but with a hideously voluptuous grin, Persy gracefully climbed back into bed (she had a habit, even on the bidet, of always behaving as if she were being watched) and, after a brief inspection in the mirror, sensuously wrapped herself and curled up in the pillows. Now she could really fantasize: to herself, for her self's self; could screw-unscrew herself at will, withdraw into herself as easily as into a tight-fitting scabbard. Now she truly *was*, whereas the events of a moment ago had begun to fade, to become an almost abstract but necessary backdrop for the efflorescence of her pure ego, which was emerging from the mist of the quotidian and glowing in the Black Void like an alpine peak in the sunset, against a nearly nocturnal sky and above the dark valleys of vulgarity. She was the belly button of the world, Persy = the Persian shah every day of the week: she was happy. Her ego was dissolving in a voluptuous vapor (there was only this vapor, as when one is under anesthesia just before passing out); it had begun, that "merging with the cosmos": the total disappearance of the body (while a tiny spark of consciousness still flickers at the farthest perimeter of empty Space) and a glorious sleep from which to awaken fresh and healthy as a cow, serenely satisfied. It was enough to last her for one – perhaps two – weeks. And let's not begrudge her such moments, because except for them (plus those she enjoyed with that titan of mind and body) she, the renowned Persy Bestialskaya, was actually a drab and pathetic little creature (in essence, *au fond*).

Meanwhile, Zip was racing back to the school by car. (It was too late for the kind of fix used in the princess's bathroom – he knew what *that* reeked of. By now, everything had turned rank. Slowly and systematically, the world was conspiring to quicken him to the *n*th degree. Among other things, there was that unforgettable fragrance . . . Never, never! He kept banging his skull against a black wall, kept squirming in the fiercest convulsions.) In the empirical world a fine, warm, spring drizzle was coming down. Everything appeared so common, so prosaic, a veritable balm for his wounds: the street lamps, a few scattered passersby, the cafés that were beginning to revive at that hour – while in his guts he suffered the strangeness of it all, a strangeness so grotesquely obscene that he wanted to howl. His desecrated guts felt as if they were being towed through the filthy, muddy streets. A howl of abomination went up from the basement of his being, from the place where that shady character resided. The latter was not the least bit perturbed, even though a wave of discontent had managed to reach his cell. After three solid hours of horseback riding that same evening, which left his black horse lathered with foam, Genezip was able to sleep a little. But it was a tortured corpse and not he who dozed.

How to survive until he could die a glorious death? But by six the next evening he was already at the princess's and banging that mama-vampire something awful. That same evening found him back for another performance at Quintofron's theater, and at midnight at Persy's. This time, he behaved like a lamb: she had entangled him in the worst kind of torture – the addictive kind. The acute stage had passed. She had brought him to the profound conviction that she was an angel and he a sinner unworthy of a single caress. She spoke only of her sufferings, seemingly oblivious of his existence, but in fact she was studying his every move, every twitch of his eyelids weighed down by a leaden insatiability; the slightest, most fugitive aberration of his tortured body, and she feasted on him like a cuttlefish, a greedy tick, and a bedbug. Love, in her diabolical crucible, became elevated to an empyrean of sacrifice and devotion – theoretically, of course, since it was never put to the test, and even if it had been, the outcome would have been uncertain, for, apart from its external expression, that love of hers was more like a fanatic hatred toward an *inanimate object* than the state whereby one is "emotionally" affected by another human being.

The problem was this: how to exploit the affair for a proper end, and, more importantly, what *was* that "end"? If not for the proximity of Kotzmolochowicz's spirit in the capital, Zip would never have withstood it. The kettle kept boiling away in his carnal depths, spewing its black tar with an intensity nearly equal to that of his first explosion. The "gutting process" was now much more subtle, profound, real. The soul, like mucus or purulent corpuscles, was being discharged piecemeal into this solution which was nourishing her like a phosphatide so that, at the appointed time, she could give herself unconditionally to her idol – just once, but in grand style (or ten times, as long as they were "in a row") – in a kind of purple, ocherous Mass.

So it went for quite some time. A tremendous layer cake of contradictory emotions – due to the fact that he was consummating with the princess his real love for Persy – was lifting Zip's soul to increasingly higher levels of self-knowledge, to a vision of life's elusive core; and with each new height achieved, the lower tiers, so final only a short while ago, now seemed childish notions unworthy of a nineteen-year-old officer. How to explain the superiority of these new "insights"? Of *Einsichten* so different from those of Husserl, of these "intuitions" which in no way resembled the *blagues* of Henri Bergson? Call it an emotional fathoming of the unfathomable rather than a conscious perception: here reality remained something fluid, volatile, vibrant, untrappable. Genezip realized now that the only clear and precise thing in the world was suffering; that, whereas everything else was "concave," pain was convex. Let us add that he had never read Schopenhauer. (What could be more banal than a pessimistic view of the world? More to the point, of course, is how deeply this pessimism went in the metaphysical sense.) Hence his theory of the "pessimum," as opposed to a concept of the "optimum." "My optimum is precisely my pessimum," he used to say without conviction. Somehow he had to transpose his frustration into something positive; left to itself, it was taking on a bad-boring character. At times he found himself contemplating suicide, but he went on living out of sheer curiosity about what was going to happen next and about what God, so mysterious in His ability to devise temporal torments (Hell, for example, was just eternal boredom), had cooked up for him. ("*Il a de la combine, ce bougre-là*" – to quote Lebac.) Besides, he could hardly renounce life – even one as rotten as his – without having tasted at least a sip of what it meant to serve as the commander's aide. Poor Zip! He knew that even if Persy submitted to him now, nothing would have changed. Hers was a love not penetrable; she was the personification of opacity. But at the thought that with this girl who was worthy of fierce boyish idolatry he might do what he had done with that other frump, the young cadet was morally transformed into a gaseous vapor. Meanwhile, he was being kept well in hand as material for an exquisite hors d'oeuvre. Due to his having inverted the normal (relatively speaking) sequence of events, consisting of a youthful infatuation followed by an affair with an experienced woman, he had suffered a dislocation, a certain emotional detachment from his surroundings, a condition that would prove disastrous. The princess had become, well . . . a sexual pail, a trained monkey. In the strategy devised by this teenaged cad, she was now being used as a deterrent along a sector of life's front on Holy Bombast Street. The old woman suspected nothing; for her, Zip had simply become psychologically mysterious and enigmatic. Oddly, she was so sure of herself that she never entertained the slightest suspicion; she observed only that he had become terribly passionate and more sophisticated in his demands. It was not the sex that sent her into raptures now, but the knowledge that she could still gratify her young "pasha's" fantasies, one who was becoming even more steeped in the most subtle perversions.

But as to how *it* took place – the manner in which that distillery apparatus was able to transport this stud's psychophysical nourishment to Persy's grey, mothlike, murky little soul – was hard to say. He, buttoned up in his uniform like a tank, and she, disrobed, disheveled, displaying herself most lewdly, with her own, special, inimitable charm. Once he caught a glimpse (for example) of her left breast with its strawberry-colored (*fraise vomie*) little knob (otherwise known by that horrible word *nipple* – phooey!), a portion of her right thigh with its slightly blue (*bleu gendarme*) veins, and the pink (*laque de garance rose de Blocks*) little toes of her turned-up left foot (inspired by the lady in Strug's story, she was wearing a pair of sandals the color of milk and cinnamon). He was sitting on a low ottoman the color of *orange Witkacy* (getting people to sit in a low position was an essential part of Persy's method: Why? There was no telling – a diabolical intuition, perhaps), rigidly arched, transformed into one black-and-blue mass of sexual soreness. All the while, he loved her with the fervor of a madman – literally: there were times, for example, when for her sake he would have betrayed Kotzmolochowicz himself if she had willed it. But her demands were of a more modest nature: to indulge in a little fun of the "squirm-like-a-worm" variety, then "fiddle with selfie," as she put it, caressing herself like a pussy purring in the kitchen's warmth. A sample of their conversation:

"My darling, it's only when I'm with you that I don't suffer, my precious little morphine shot. I feel so good when I know you're mine, when you get all set for the pounce that you know will never take place. You're as taut as a bow whose arrow has never been shot. Would you like to know what's inside that other room? Come on – " And she took him by the hand (ah, what supreme skin it was, too, the kind that is so perfect it can only be hacked to bits with a knife dipped in vitriol) and, with a grandly seductive gesture, wrapped herself with the other hand in an *unusual* (why unusual? because *hers!*) white *robe de chambre*. He stood up, mortified. She took a key out of a Chinese jewel box and proceeded to open the door that stood to the left of the bed. The adjoining room was practically empty. With the eyes of a famished vulture, Genezip surveyed the room that was costing him so much morbid curiosity. Why today of all days? The room was furnished with an officer's cot, two armchairs on which some books were lying (a book of Mokrzycki's aeronautical designs, Love's work on theoretical mechanics, Bergson's *L'Evolution créatrice*, and the first volume of a novel by the senile Kaden Bandrowski, *Brute or Robot?*, confiscated some seventy years ago – oh yes, lying on her bed were Sigwart's logic and Gide's *Corydon:* a strange bag), and a hideous-looking metal knout lying under a shattered icon of Our Lady of Poczajów. There was no washroom – such was life. The smell of cigarette smoke hung in the air, as well as something vaguely and obscenely masculine. Zip shuddered. She was speaking now, provoking him by her drawling voice and by certain well-placed pauses in appropriately chosen places, which caused his eyebrows, lids, and mouth to twitch and a greyish, scarlet shadow to move across his contorted face. She devoured each of these symptoms like a hungry dog attacking a piece of meat. A notorious and exceedingly trite method. It would take pretty naive sucker to fall for it. Why didn't the numskull opt for a more normal life? Part company with both bitches and shack up with some floozy? Well, why not? Ha! You might as well have talked to a deaf man. That she-carcass went on:

"That's nothing; don't be afraid. Once in a while I have an overnight guest . . . an old uncle." (Only good that she didn't say "a friend of mine" [?]) "Whenever he's on a binge and hasn't the nerve to go home. And that cot there – it once belonged to my brother. He enlisted in the German army during the last damned crusade and lost his life: he was impaled the way Tuchej-Bey impaled Azja. Our mother was German – the Baroness Trendelendelendelendelenburg. An odd name, but very old. It's from her I inherited that gentle disposition that excites you so much. I won't deny I love to get you aroused – so cruelly, fiendishly excited that you don't know your own family when you go home." Her marvelously violet eyes flashed before his face made grimy by sex, plunged his eyes in a madman's fog that reeked of *it*, that *thing* . . . "When you can no longer think of anything except that poor little freak between my legs, then you'll be mine." He flinched as if about to attack, but she restrained him with one touch of her menacing finger on his chest. "Uh-uh – today I want you to rest up before your next and most serious trial. I'm through for today. I promise – ," she added with alarm, noticing a flash of real lunacy in his bloodshot pupils. He snapped out of it but nonetheless sank a few stories lower in rank misery. The world reeled, threatened to explode at any moment, but somehow held together for a while longer.

Did she know what she was doing? The extent to which she was crucifying this little upstart, this spiritual guttersnipe now rendered thoroughly defenseless? If asked such a question, she would not have known how to reply: sorry, not her department. She was capable of living only on the string of someone's lust when stretched to the breaking point. The poor thing was only trying to get through life – nothing more. Let's not judge her too harshly: it's always the man who's to blame.

"What I'd give to know her inside out! To climb inside that splendid, well-shaped little head and to rip open the cells of that weird (oh, how ordinary it was in reality!) little brain and scratch, lick, sniff, devour everything . . . " But Persy was rather frugal when it came to giving explanations. And even if she hadn't been so stingy, she was incapable of differentiating her thoughts. While she was able to *perform* her thought processes in Quintofron's disgusting brothel, she was powerless to verbalize them. She showed a talent only for uttering sadistic nonsense: she *had* to – to survive. But then that gabble came not from her mouth but was whispered in the bizarre "dialect" spoken by what are scientifically and sickeningly referred to as "lips of the pudendum." For all her prating about omnisuperhypermendacity, Zip had taken things at their face value. So, then, why try to fool him with this room and its secret? He had trusted in her. Her every word – the word itself, minus its corresponding object in reality – signified a reality infinitely more profound than the existence of any object, and yet she seemed intent on arousing his suspicion. Why? For God's sake, why?! Oh, you dope!

Suddenly, abruptly, even hastily she led him away by the hand and forced him to listen to one of Tenzer's latest theatrical scores. She played the piano jerkily, spasmodically, emotionally – lousily, in other words. It served purely as background music, as a way of enhancing the sexual ambience. Or was all this racket being used to cover up the fact that someone else was entering the other room? She had never played for Zip before. Dreadful uncertainty gnawed at his insides, but only briefly. Better to endure some obscure torture than to let anything come between them.

It was a hot, stifling, humid June night. Although it had not yet started to rain, buckets of lukewarm water hung suspended in the air, black as pitch, sultry as a steam bath. Swarms of moths and mosquitoes buzzed in the air and banged against the electric street lamps. The unremitting drone outside complemented the already hostile atmosphere inside. Everything seemed to be drooping like a pair of stockings without any garters, felt sticky and irritable; disturbed. Against such a background, Tenzer's bordellesque in Persy's erratic version was in-tol-er-able. Luckily, she had just finished. The only escape from all this was a life sentence of voluntary ennui, a colorless, crystalline edifice erected (who knew for how long) over a steaming, polluted swamp. Through the window flung open to the darkness came a June fragrance, the same fragrance which in his childhood had promised some sublime apotheosis. Was this how his life was to be fulfilled? Was this its climax? No: beyond this wretched swamp of self-immolation on behalf of a bawd's morbid fantasies there arose, in *sketch* form, a picture of the general political situation prevailing on this piddly pill of a planet. "God, if this is the sort of crap You've dished up generally, is life really worth living?" said one of his doubles to the other. "But why should I have to pay for Your screwups?" Enough – this last was a trifle insincere: the last thing he cared about was the "Almighty God" of childhood, he who had never been a believer anyway. Still, he could have gladly used some friendly assistance from the other world . . . Kotzmolochowicz was a just surrogate. Even so, there were times when not even he was enough. Then he recalled the discussions held in Prince Basil's retreat, and was panic-stricken: Had he been exposed prematurely to those three, causing him to miss out on the most crucial of revelations, that of his own destiny, a wild and solitary truth that should have been hunted down like an animal in the wilderness, caged like a prize beast, like a woman . . . ? Standing before him was the star of his destiny, no more than a step away, with that hellish between-the-legs gizmo of hers, and he, blinded by adulterous idolatry (the sense of which not even he understood), impotent and tremulous before the mystery (whose? none other than that of his own being – which meant everyone's), had not the nerve to perform that one pathetic little gesture (never mind that he had done it repeatedly in the palazzo of the Ticonderogas and in the suburb of Jada) that might have given him possession of her, the prize, and of himself. Was this what it was all about? Maybe her desperation was only skin deep; maybe violence was really what she needed. So be it. And without warning he flung himself at her: a metaphysical animal, a transcendental brute. She had finally driven him crazy. Yet – and this was the strangest thing of all – that moment *persisted:* the moment-symbol of his destiny and those of his many fellow travelers; the shady character and the defunct lad; his filthy (why filthy?) spermatozoa, each of which aspired to be his son, begotten by this very wench. If only he were in his prime! But all this was happening at an age when a person becomes what he or she is meant to be, a most dangerous time for a man. This was life's turning point – on this asinine June night, in the apartment of this ruthless bitch: either he would surmount this peak or he would be lost forever. A conqueror or a slave of cowardice. Greatness came not only from triumph, but from a defeat inwardly transformed into victory; such was a noble defeat. So get on with it: take that saintly martyr, that metaphysical prunt of a cunt by the neck, by the hair – come on! Yeah, that's it! Oh . . . but what did he see? Instead of executing his will, he suddenly found himself staring wide-eyed, from the depths of his being, at that inscrutable *other* before him. Again the mystery of another ego pressed on him from out of infinite space; instead of being bludgeoned, he was hit in the face with a soft ball of cotton. Down below, somewhere on the fifteenth story, there squirmed not a prize but an abomination. There was nothing to conquer. He had fought his way through an absolute void. *She no longer possessed a body.* Drunk on a sexual dolor and a secret exultation ("At last he's flipped; he couldn't take it anymore," she kept repeating in a whisper, and then came that special frisson which not even Kotzmolochowicz could give her; when HE snapped, it was different, it was with her, while this guy was doing it on his own – *alone!* Oh, wonders!), Persy's eyes turned up in supreme ecstasy (she was so unspeakably beautiful at that moment, it was more than he could handle, not even by an act of violence, not even a *Lustmord*), and he was struck by an inner bolt of lightning (in reality, an ordinary schizophrenic *Schub* = jolt), reduced to ashes in a spontaneous outburst of compassion bordering on self-annihilation. A moment later he was lying at her feet and tenderly, sensually kissing the rim of her sandal, not even daring to brush her exquisite toes with his lips; he kissed her the way his mother or the princess kissed him on the head in moments of filiomaternal weakness. Persy had scored another triumph.

Then came a spell of nightmarish, cloudy, muggy, rotten June days – the sort fit for petty people and their petty experiences. Greatness was nowhere to be found (oh, how much longer, how much longer? . . .). A permanent ritual had been established: he would lie beside her on the carpet, consumed by an ardor transcending sexual lust, while into his ear she would whisper words capable of turning a gelding into a stallion, a stud bull into an infinite number of impersonal studs (into the idea of studness itself), flocks of capons into cocks, and of restoring a eunuch's balls – even those of Basil the Great, minister of the Empress Theophano. Meanwhile, he was saving his sexual ammunition for that other strumpet, drinking at the very source, rather than from more distant rivers polluted by life's filth, the unbearable sting of a profaned love. He loved her quite sincerely now, and he shared with her her profane and phony suffering. Until at last he would quiver, rend the air, and sprawl out before her like a beast gutted alive in some horrible cannery of torture, like an insect flattened on a hot and dusty road in summer. (It so happened that it was one of those loathsome June-going-on-July sort of days, full of promise and heat and idle dreams about another [only, please, not this one!] life.) O life, when would you begin in earnest?! He prayed to the nameless powers in himself to grant him death, though he still had a long way to go.

That same day Persy had planned to leave for the capital – for what foul purpose we poor sinners who know everything are well aware. A very much overworked Kotzmolochowicz desperately looked forward to a moment of détente before the unleashing of certain critical events. Coded messages were coming in from Huśtański (Kuźma) – it was already the second day in a row – and were presently being decoded in the next room (the one where her intemperate uncle spent the night – ha, ha!). Persy was later briefed; the "messages" suffused her sumptuous thighs with a sweet warmth and provoked a tingling sensation in the region of the tailbone. Her winged bull was waiting, tense as a steel cable, for the usual. In the dark night she beheld his tar-pupils turned upward in the heat of a humiliating passion; saw his mouth, convulsed in the "fornicator's labor" seconds before orgasm, the awesome taking of a man by a woman. After she had left, Zip, who quite mistakenly saw himself as the chief figure in this debacle, chose to remain, bound to the school and to his carnal addiction to that other woman, in the god-forsaken hole of C. Now imagine there had been no Irina Vsevolodovna ("That, my good fellow, would have been quite a scandal"), imagine if she had not been around to serve as a safety valve or, more bluntly, a sperm bucket, what then? Possibly then he could have gotten his uncommitted crimes out of the way and, sated forever, broken with the Grand Tits of existence. But, no, he would have to persevere in his present state, a miserable, solitary, disgusting wreck. And this was *he*, Zip, "fortune's pet," bred for happiness as though he were a kind of rare plant, a *Luxustierchen*, as his aunt, Princess Waffles-Boobescu, always called him. And just as she was about to leave (packed in her luxurious trunk [from Picton's] were a golden bowl and a whip mounted with little lead balls), by means of shy allusions and discreet flickings of the tongue, she had aroused in him states terrifying in their repressed criminality. More than ever he had an urge to commit murder – but did not know *whom* to murder. Benevolence and devotion, in their inverted form, turned inside out *(Transformationsgleichungen von Gut und Böse mit dem unendlichen Genitalkoeffizienten des Fraulein v. Bestialskaya)*, were acquiring the character of a nebulous and utterly senseless crime: "quite a disinterested murder,"as the English say. A plot against himself, inside himself. The leader of it was that shady character from the basement of his soul, evil incarnate – impersonal, indifferent, and unbelievably foul.

Finally, one night (the third or fourth, though it hardly matters) after Persy's return from the capital (she was in an outrageously pious and sentimental mood), everything inside Zip's head flipped, as if his pitiful skull had been spun around at the speed of alpha particles and the cells of his brain had switched places: absolute mayhem. He held on, held on – till he could no longer stand it and blew apart in a sickening, deafening internal roar. His ego collapsed in a pile of random, disconnected, indeterminate states. The latter were "intentional acts," as posited by the phenomenologists: suspended in a void, impersonal. The anguish of a frustrated life, the failure to accomplish what, above all, *ought* to have been accomplished – this was all that kept the disparate elements of his soul together.

After a routine day at school (less than a week remained before commencement exercises and before the syndicate's revolt [against whom, though?], now rumored to be imminent), looking outwardly composed and psychologically fit (which was the greatest joke of all) but internally resembling a field of rubble littered with undetonated bombs, mines, and camouflets; given to a chronic, monumental eruption in slow motion that now went beyond a purely animal lust for life, Zip walked down Holy Bombast Street toward Persy's apartment. He moved like a live bullet; he should have had a death's-head painted on him, zigzagging red arrows and all the prescribed inscriptions. If Dr. Bekhmetev had seen him now, he would have committed an astronomical error in predicting the next sequence of events. She, that sweet and sullen miss, had no great liking for death; she merely wished to "brush against it." Those who were in a position to know disputed this: according to them, Persy was waiting for death at the hands of Kotzmolochowicz; too cowardly to commit suicide herself, she was waiting for the general to lose his self-control (he did have his dangerous moments) and, in a moment of fury, "scatter her to the void," "return her to the cosmic belly button," and "pack her off to the place of life's great nemesis" – to quote the asinine phrases being whispered in johns, public lavatories, garrets, and granaries left unattended since the Protestant Reformation. These fleeting encounters with death graced moments of sexual . . . inadequacy – yes, indeed. Fishing for such moments was one of Persy's favorite pastimes, and her principal fishing rod at the moment was Zip, whereas her net was a certain Colonel Michael Sump, who had been watching and listening from the other room (via acoustical tubes and periscopes) nearly the whole time, a bearded, rotund man, known as a bungler and a screaming homosexual but a trusted employee of the general who was used for complex errands of a private nature (usually involving some overheated countess or particularly squeamish virgin). When it came to suspected rivals, nothing – not the cruelest tortures – was spared. (The intelligence gathered by Sump drove the commander to new heights of explosive energy. Sometimes if her duties in the theater delayed her, or if she was detained for reasons of a more physiological nature [like at the moment], that energy would assume maniacal proportions: at times his subordinates feared an outright seizure. But in the end, Persy always managed to channel this fury in a harmless, socially beneficial way.) Everything was allowed – everything except touching. Here she was perfectly in her element, her sense of reality was satisfied. Zip spoke with a genital lisp, while all around him, in the form of towering black phantoms, life pressed from above, coming closer and closer until it completely shrouded him. He was vanishing like a tiny worm ingested by some weird, invisible monster. Persy listened while wickedly sprawled out in the most licentious manner (she was, *moreover,* decked out in a tailor-made black suit – you know, ma'am, tight in the hips, a trifle masculine-looking, with little hoops and stays, hemstitches along the gimps and jets, a salmon-pink blouse of crepe de chine, draped with georgettes and pleats and bordered with meticulously stitched Valenciennes lace), exposing without the slightest scruple those weary and painful places that had just been "desecrated" by her lover. He said (not exactly him, but that pug from the underground):

"You've got to today." She smiled voluptuously. "Or else, or else – I'll kill myself." In his excitement he had neglected to take off his coat and gloves. It was an unspeakably hot and sultry July day. "I've had it; I no longer know who I am . . . or who you are . . . I . . . I don't even want you anymore . . . I'm all mixed up inside; I don't know *what* I want anymore . . . But something has to happen, otherwise I'll snap . . . *I can't stand it any longer.*" His face looked menacing, full of a kind of terrifying exaltation combined with a healthy dose of repressed brutality – along with something else, something that eluded her, something she was seeing for the first time. She was seized with panic, still a relatively mild one, while her body was coated with tremendous curiosity about what was going to happen next: she could feel it pulsating in her thighs, in her calves. The time was ripe, or had she overplayed her hand? On with it, on with it . . . It was Zip's turn to speak now, and he vomited out the words in gruesome, undigested lumps. Actually, the words he chose were rather banal – words, if we exclude poetry, are powerless to express anything out of the ordinary. But the tone, the tone, and the "diction," and that choking sensation in the throat: it was as if his innards had risen to his throat like a ball of worms, as if momentarily he was going to puke his entire being all over this Persian carpet ("Persy's caviar," as she used to say) and all that would remain of him (Zip) would be a piece of skin turned inside out like a woman's nylon stocking. "You've got to, or I'll . . . No . . . Saints above, hold onto me, because in a second I'm going to . . . to do I don't know what. And that's just it – I don't know. I don't even have the nerve to rape you, that's how much I love you." He was alarmed by his state of absolute sexual inertia: an ominous calm before the arrival of a hurricane. He felt as if he were without any genitals – now as well as in the past. The worst that could have happened in these hypergenital spheres of sexuality, the one thing that was as irreversible as the third stage of syphilis, had happened. "You've got to do it, you've got to – though *what* it is you've got to do I don't know," he practically screamed, transfixing her with a sinister, murderous glower – a stare in which he was firing his last bullet of sanity, behind which there lurked some mysterious, nameless, unfettered element, and right beside it, looking silly as a loon: death in all its banality and monstrosity (the Polish word for it is *Lustmord* [from the German], which is not your village-idiot-behind-a-bush kind of murder perpetrated on some old crone on her way to or back from market [the forensic medicine of Wachholz; a summer landscape with a little white cross drawn next to a bush, and alongside it a photograph of some imbecile and a snapshot of the poor woman's horribly mutilated corpse: cheese curds mixed with brain, a liver wrapped in a tattered petticoat, legs covered all over with black-and-blue marks and dried mushrooms – the "scene of the crime," as they say – brrrr! – while over the woods night is falling and frogs are croaking in the loam pits . . .] [Some such image flashed through Persy's mind, and suddenly she became alarmed – like a human being for once, without any perverse complications]; no, this was [in Zip's eyes] a potential *Lustmord* so subtle as to defy comprehension. The wildest imagination could not have foreseen the manner and conditions in which it might have occurred; only he, that gent from below, could have known. But the latter had lost all connection with Zip's nature, leaving him alone in his struggle with the secret menace of existence).

"Sit down, Zip. Let's talk. I'll explain everything. Just relax and let me do the talking. What do you care about such stuff? Forget about it; don't you give it another moment's thought." She was sitting in an entirely respectable pose, only her teeth were chattering – faintly, briskly, nervously, like weird, ratlike little creatures with an existence all their own. "Zip – my poor little darling. Please don't look at me that way." Suddenly she lost her nerve and buried her face in her hands: the party was over. She had overplayed her hand. He was standing there, rigid and erect. Everything had returned to the depths where, in the caves of the subconscious, a real scuffle was in progress. His face remained calm, only incredibly worn and stunned. Occasionally a slight spasm rippled through the muscles of his contorted face twitching like the muscles of some animal being mechanically skinned alive in a meat cannery. Through the dark hole of the open window came the damp smell of freshly mown fields. (In that backwater town, everything was within walking distance; in any direction, you ran smack into the suburbs; and Holy Bombast Street was located on the town's "outer lip," as Persy was wont to phrase it.) A dog barked in the distance, now and then a fly was heard buzzing in the room – with one foot caught in a spider's web, no doubt. (Only Whitehead's theory, and then in an approximate, peripheral way, does justice to the mysterious simultaneity of distantly related events.) The dead silence was charged with panting expectation. Genezip was stricken with inertia (in the erotic sense); his muscles had contracted into a gnawing ache capable of mercilessly blowing the world to smithereens. But down below, in his body's pulpy scrota, not a twitch. Persy opened her eyes and tearfully gazed at her "lab specimen." A smile brightened up her beautiful little face: she was now confident of her superiority. But it grieved her to think that the wondrous moment had passed irretrievably. She lamented the danger which only now, vaguely, she had begun to sense: the enchanting, boundless realm of crimes not yet committed; life's magic, so acutely felt a moment ago that it had vanished. Boredom. Depression. Was this all there was to it? . . .

Zip tried, without success, to summon the image of the general, the heretofore efficacious symbol of human will overcoming obstacles. Something alien and scary was germinating in his psychic tubes, now seemingly independent of his body. The machine had not yet been plugged in (that nefarious electropsychotechnician was working on it around the clock) and already the arrows on the gauge were fluttering anxiously above the danger level. The machine was running by itself, like a madman: it only needed to be thrust into gear. As good as done. His solitary, sluggish muscles, with their disjointed and erratic movements, were only waiting for the command like sails ready to be hoisted, like soldiers standing at attention; while the soul was ailing, his muscles, straining for action and saturated with healthy animal blood, awaited their orders from the higher centers controlled by that brooding workman from below – that *sane madman.* He himself was basically sane. Only in combination with the Zip-Stud (the princess's lover; the future adjutant; in the excremental town of C.; on Holy Bombast Street) did this produce a *real madman.* He was a madman when he bossed the former; in himself he was simply *another* person, logical in his ideas, even somewhat intelligent. But two egos cannot occupy the same body; this happens exceptionally, and then only briefly. There is no general equation here. That's why it's called (and aptly so) insanity. Meanwhile, the poor girl, fooled by his dazed look, went on speaking to that not-to-be-recognized (in any human terms) psychological wreck. (Contrary to popular belief, the most celebrated thinkers often have, at the moment of their greatest discoveries [that is, when they skip a logical progression = a rational definition of intuition], the most asinine expressions on their faces – unless they happen to be posing before an audience.) And so she said, ruthlessly, with her customary coquetry (to put it mildly):

"I know. You can't anymore. Even so, you must, you *must.* That's the whole secret of it, the inexpressible mystery and beauty of our love. An unfulfilled dream, more beautiful than anything on earth.

What could be more sublime? . . ." Her voice broke off and was lost in a welter of tears. There was something so outrageously sensual about that voice of hers, so horribly alluring, so cruel and willfully evil that Zip began to seethe, like a laundry tub full of rags, with a sudden, thundering desire. He had nothing to lose. He was as hollow as a lobster shell – gutted, desiccated, emptied: *ausgepumpt und ausgezüzelt.* He lived only as a mathematical extraction carried to infinity: empty, ever yearning, dangerously bored. His muscles grew tense, while through his intestines a call went out to all the reserves of his sexual forces. A fire suffused his veins like a thick and oily liquid – but quickly, under extreme pressure. It had happened. Out of him came an excremental, constipated, and repulsive voice that belonged not to him but to that other person below. He was at a loss for words. It was his first appearance.

"No – I've had enough of this disgusting talk. I'm going to strangle you like a squirrel!" (Why had he chosen this particular animal when he had never strangled one as long as he had lived?) She burst out laughing. He was ridiculous: she ruled him completely. Even so, she sensed the alarming ferocity of his *bezumnykh zhelany,* as she liked to call them. She was inside him, deep in his sexual core, within his swollen glands, bossing that gang of internal brutes according to her will, assuming dominion over the whole man – well, almost. ("Oh, when will I get *complete* control?") Suddenly her body's esoteric realm, the source of orgastic thrill, now more beautiful than ever, opened up again. Never had it been like *this* before! Tenzer's music was nothing by comparison. At most, a foretaste of metaphysical reality. But here was metaphysics itself, woven into a wreath of the most exquisite tortures that could be inflicted on the male species – painlessly, caressingly . . . Oh, the things she knew now, knew about *it,* about everything! The whole world brightened and assumed astronomical proportions. The moment of the most exquisite ecstasy had arrived. What was Quinty's cocaine compared to this?! (Although Quintofron had treated her to the stuff, as he had everyone else, he had never managed to get her hooked.) Or the theories of Ganglioni, international "connoisseur of the world's wildest theaters," who, starting from Chwistek, said that only what was not, was. But Persy knew that she would *have* to refuse, otherwise that guy next door would see what he wasn't supposed to see, and that having gotten wind of it that ox would suffer a stroke in the middle of some big conference and she would die the most awful, vile death – possibly by torture . . . ugh . . . Besides, if she surrendered to this "fab" little stud (which she wanted to do at times, even after doing *it* with *him* . . .), he would have instantly dropped in value. It was already unfolding before her, that sea of boredom into which she was plunged whenever she mentally indulged her sexual desires. (She had simulated it in her w*iii*ldest, most secret fantasies, but that didn't count.) Meanwhile, death was flashing in the nut-brown eyes of that would-be, Valentinolike officer, twisting his darling, blissful, adolescent, as-yet-unkissed mouth in a brooding rage.

....

NOTE: The princess had ceased to act as an antidote.

"Wait; I'll be right back," she whispered in a tone of affected willingness, with an air so filled with promise that Zip was transformed into a stiff, buff-red, stinking flame with the temperature of blazing helium. He began to shake, fixing her with a doglike but devastating look, and those few seconds were like a death vigil. With his fists clenched in their white gloves, he stood there, an animal poised for the kill, with a nearly catatonic immobility, entirely ankylosed with his bulging desire.

She walked out of the room with a voluptuous stride, swaying the hemispheres of her derriere like an Arabian belly dancer, deliberately trailing a smile from her moist, strawberry-red mouth. And all this fuss over a slab of meat! Horrific, no?!

Somewhere close by, possibly in the adjoining room once belonging to her "deceased brother" (ha, ha!), the inevitable was looming large, swelling, towering. A paralyzing wave of some awful premonition, a foreboding of unimaginable disaster, struck him in the back. She had no intention of making love! She had deceived him! A fury reared up in him like a dog on a chain, then immediately subsided. It was still a *normal* fury, though any second now . . . (Time was being stretched like a piece of rubber.) Zip suddenly spun around, even though he had not detected the slightest sound, and stood face to face with an enormous blowup of Persy in the role of Witkacy's "Cuttlefish" (from a shot by Tadeusz Langier [the grandson]), which hung to the right of the entrance to that other room. There was no denying it: he loved that metaphysical tormentrix – in spite of it all. Such love, such diabolical passion (a great combination, by Beelzebub!) – and all of it wasted! The feeling of *Pech* (again there is no Polish equivalent here: "bad luck," "tough luck," "losing streak," "bad break," "slump," "losing battle," "losing kick," "losing jag," "flop," "flub," "jinx," "screw," "raw deal," "washout," "bind," "jam," "downhill," "comedown," "drag," "bust," "fuck-up," "fizzle," "dud," "letdown" – enough of this mugger's lexicon! What the hell – can't we have a sophisticated *Pech* in our language?) again thrust him into a clammy, sticky, gooey despair.

All of a sudden the door opened with a bang. In the doorway stood a bearded, fair-haired galoot in his mid-fifties, with shoulders like a bear, with clean and honest-looking eyes, but with a suction power that was difficult to resist. Dressed in civilian clothes, but reeking of the army from a mile away. It was the general's factotum – Sump, Michael, Colonel. He had decided to intervene. Persy's exit had been his cue. He took three steps toward Zip and, in a tone of affected ease, as though what he was about to say required a great effort on his part, said:

"Well, well, my boy, step over here. I'll simmer you down a bit. First, a bit of advice: hands off that piece of tail – if you value your life." Then he immediately switched to a tone that seemed to contain, at one and the same time, a child's supplication, checked tears, shame, and impatience. From the start the colonel had fallen terribly for "the wee lad," suffering as he watched through his periscope, mourning how that noble "soul" worthy of a Socrates was being wasted, humiliated by these useless "heterosexual" impulses. Now, in carrying out the general's orders, he could act with a clear conscience. "I'm Colonel Sump, here to teach you a more noble pleasure: the union of two pure, masculine souls. But first you must pass certain tests that will reveal – but never mind that for the moment . . . It's a minor thing, anyway . . . although without it . . . Enough . . . I'll be your friend; I'll even take the place of your father for a while – until you and the commander (with whom, as with God, we are one here on earth) are on more intimate terms. Do you believe in God?" Genezip made no reply. Inwardly convulsed, mired in a seemingly irredeemable inertia (oh, in his subterranean regions there were worlds of activity!), he remained where he was, staring vacantly into Sump's smiling, knowing, gracious, light green, tearful, seal-like, and unmistakably sexualized (how so?) eyes. Not a twitch. He stood at the edge of some awful precipice which he couldn't see; like a sleepwalker he somehow held himself erect, leaning with one finger against the weather vane of a gigantic tower. "Have you ever heard Szymanowski's *Stabat Mater* and its devastating parody *Stabat Vater*, composed by that maniac Tenzer for the sake of some miserable tail? Two irreconcilable worlds. I used to be an aviator. Even flew acrobatics – honest. But now I can't. Fouled myself up during the last crusade. But I'm no coward."

"What on earth is he getting at?" the ex-Zip wondered inside the present Zip. "He's blabbing, and to a corpse at that." Suddenly, in his innards, the gent hiding out in the bush of his manifold soul went for his own throat and that of the world. And he realized at once, with a delectable certainty, that this was how he was supposed to behave. Without knowing yet exactly how, he felt equal to a Tenzer, to Kotzmolochowicz himself. An absolute cleavage between this moment, which "lingered" (in the same way as *stoyalo kogdato divnaya osennaya pogoda* or *stoyali chudnye dni* – imagine the weather, for days on end, "standing still"!), stranded in time, and that which had been and, more importantly, which was yet to be. Unknown grottoes opened before him, unknown "parts," nebulous vistas like those in the eastern half of a cumuli-filled sky at sunset. That's where he was now; it was no longer a dream; he *was* there. It was a weird sort of giddiness, the kind you get after tossing off a few vodkas on an empty stomach or after the first snort of cocaine following fourteen shots of vodka. Genezip had never felt such exultation – or rather, not he but that fearful customer inside him, the one who had caused him such terror and loathing. It (he) was himself; they were one; the sane Zip no longer existed. And this sense, this miraculous sense (the state experienced by those who profess to *love God [!]* – about which Sturfan Abnol was so skeptical, except perhaps in the company of women) of everything, of even the wildest, most improbable of events! Oh, for an eternity of it! (Apparently it can last eternally – for those able to stare at their own navels for twenty years and subsist on a steady diet of little food and no drink – which seems unlikely.) But, alas, some kind of action, however vague, was unavoidable, for Zip was *tout de même* a man of the West. Action can also be pleasurable – even more than the sexual kind, only in different way, dammit. Maybe he was on the verge of a pure, flawless, not-a-cloud-in-the-sky sort of happiness . . . This bearded and somehow infinitely convex (as though viewed with a stereoscope) brute, who stood outlined against the black abyss of that enigmatic room, was, was, *was a dog on a chain who had to be unleashed.* From the outskirts of town he heard again a dog's sad wail – a real dog, adoring, one whose seemingly otherworldly bark derived from the empirical world of a normal, earthly night. Meanwhile, a fly had begun buzzing in his vicinity (in the vicinity of that internal fellow?). The simultaneity of unrelated events. All right, let it happen. Let what happen? He knew now (in reality he knew nothing, so why this divination?). A prescient darkness of perfection flooded his soul. The *creative* moment was approaching (such creativity would have amused Tenzer and even the Great Moloch, although the general was no stranger to such moments, he being, horns, hooves, and all, such a storehouse of emotion): the unknown, the improbable was about to spring from nowhere and be transformed into a movement of electrons, a displacement of gravitational fields; into a crossbreed, on a relatively grand scale, of exceedingly small animalcules, forever mysterious. (That they were living, thinking, sentient creatures seems indisputable, whereas the existence of inorganic matter, of the sort physics would like to posit on the basis of data derived from its own mundane vision of the world, would seem highly problematic, unless one assumes the existence of a mundane dualism, a mundane "pre-conceived order," and that people have altogether ceased to think in a mundane way – so there!)

Meanwhile, that other galoot kept on standing and waiting – bearded, gracious, and sinister – for what seemed like centuries, although no more than three minutes had passed. The "collapsing of time" was un-en-dur-able. Life teetered on an arête like a seesaw. On one side were sunny valleys of normality and great numbers of cozy little retreats; on the other loomed the murky gorges and chasms of madness, smoking with thick gases and glowing with molten lava – *valle inferno*, kingdom of eternal remorse and unbearable guilt. So there *was* an escape, after all! A vague temptation, tiny but powerful as hell, was gnawing its way deeper into his body, tunneling a passage through to his as-yet-unscathed motors. He was wholly oblivious to Persy's existence. Nothing mattered but the deed that had yet to be executed. The world was reduced to a tiny segment of its field of vision wherein, although still fairly relaxed, a tiny clump of muscular sensations was beginning to stir. Beyond that, nothing – trust me: even Mach would have been content, possibly even Chwistek. Lying on a small table was a long upholstering hammer with an iron handle sheathed in wood – oh, how such objects can tempt one at times! – an anomalous intruder in a kingdom of knickknacks and whatnots. A black Chinese Buddha smiled down at him from above. The forgotten hammer (which he had used only yesterday to help Persy move a Persian miniature some three inches to the left; Persy was a great aesthete, *very* great) seemed to be waiting. Locked inside it was all the tension of a live creature imprisoned in a cage. It, too, longed to be liberated, to make a splash, not to rot away by having to hammer in some miserable little nails – not to blow it, in other words. There you are. Zip had no wish to blow it, either, and that shady, faceless gent from below had even less. (One day he would crawl out onto Zip's face, worm his way into it, merge with it so that people would marvel at the uncanny expression in the young cadet's eyes, not realizing that *it was no longer him* but that *postpsychopatische Personalität* having nothing to do with his former self.) His musculature hummed like a flawless machine; with an unsteady hand he gripped the hammer by its long metal handle sheathed, I repeat, in wood. The weight of the object was perfect, ideally balanced . . . He looked again into the other man's startled rather than frightened eyes, now bulging out of their sockets as though no longer of this world, and with all his might struck the bearded, bushy-blonde, brute skull that had become so inexplicably hateful to him. A soft, damp, *live* crack, and the man's hulking body fell to the carpet (whose pattern Zip would never forget) with a thud. The hammer remained stuck in the skull, a little above the left frontal lobe. Zip walked out of the room like a robot, showing not the slightest hint of any thought or emotion. Simplified to the extreme. Life's conundrums, past and present? Gone. "Life is beautiful," an unfamiliar voice said inside him, and this voice was his own. His body felt light as fluff; it soared above an absurd world of officer's commissions, Kotzmolochowicz, the Chinese, the general political situation, all those funny creatures hideously referred to as "women." Neither Persy nor her chaperon were anywhere to be seen; the place was empty. Their absence did not astonish him. He was tasting true freedom now, an unprecedented levity. "Gawd! Who am I?" he thought, going down the stairs. (He slammed the door shut behind him. He had his own key to the front gate – a present from Persy.)

It was that deepest hour of the night: two A.M. An inexplicable force propelled him in the direction of the school as though a deliverance awaited him there. And yet, he was not in any need of deliverance; things had worked out splendidly – so why, why, dammit to hell? A light summer drizzle was falling. On such a night, that which might have appeared insuperably ugly and banal (the hush of a deserted town; the wet streets; the stifling air; and that muggy, musty, sweet, manure-and-onionlike, small-town smell) now seemed to him the most fantastic, necessary, perfect thing of all: *this and no other*. The sense of "thisness" as opposed to "otherness" – how wonderful to apprehend the quality of absolute necessity in this outrageous kingdom of chance and nonsense such as is *raw existence* when it is stripped of fictitious social laws concealing the most abominable contingencies. If Zip had knowingly consumed a large dose of cocaine (which the princess, in desperation, had been pestering him to do), he might have compared his present mood with the slight case of euphoria induced by that seemingly harmless but in fact devastatingly toxic stuff.

Suddenly, the horrifying flash of lucid awareness: "I'm a murderer; I've killed someone – don't know who or why. Not because of her, though. She . . . she . . . " – the word swirled among other equally dead, unattached words without meaning. "Will I never understand? Maybe after serving a twelve-year sentence. Then again, the Chinese . . . nothing will stop them . . . " It was all right for him to think so "cavalierly"; he was in no condition to grasp the horror of the moment. Actually, such thoughts were not his; they belonged to that other fellow, who, having acquired the features of the defunct kid, had somehow become disgustingly mollified.

With alarm he perceived the horror implied by the very fact of existence, even in its most benign forms: in this sense, even saints could become perfidious monsters. "Everything that exists contradicts the principle by which it exists; all stems from an irreparable metaphysical injustice. Even if I were the best man on earth, I would never be more than a pile of warring molecular beings. The world inside a man is as cruel as the one outside" – so said Sturfan Abnol while in a drunken state. Today these words had become manifestly clear to Genezip – not rationally, but through the blood, as if his artery-sewer system suddenly swam with some rank and putrescent liquid. The world contained nothing but rotten impurity, though he saw no harm in that. He dismissed it with a wave of his hand. If the whole world was flawed, why shouldn't he be, too? In the memory of what appeared to *another self* he beheld the pale and spectral face of Eliza until it was extinguished like phosphorescence in some greenish-black water. He was left with the sense of a crime somehow connected to something equally but vaguely criminal. But *wherefrom* this connection?! Let the psychologists fret over it. Still, two postulates might be mentioned: the *coloration* of a quality existing in a state of duration, and, secondly, the notion of Cornelius's "*gemischter Hintergrund*" (not consciously perceived). Whatever the reason, the fact was that Zip was strangely content with the crime he had committed. Persy, the cunning little cuttlefish (made heady by her recent success with the general), was a thing of the past. And he was not sorry in the least. Ethics? A mere fart, gentlemen. Idle phrases, at least for certain schizophrenics for whom nothing matters but themselves. A magnificent remedy for an unrequited love affair: kill some third party, some outsider, the first passerby who comes along. He then recalled the lines of a poem written by some frigging pseudofuturist from another era, from the time of Boy:

And the first fella came –
Bop went the club! And the second? The same!
But surely it's no crime.
What else, if not a crime, I mean?
Nothing, a bop on the bean
For purging old coots
Without an ax or a hangman's noose.

He forgot how the rest of the poem went. The sudden flash of hyperillumination radiating his schizophrenic doubles had already faded, but *alongside* his personality there arose thoughts of a more conventional nature. But they were no longer geared (ho, ho – not by a long shot) to his motors, which were now controlled by that gent from below. He had assumed power with the hammer blow; he had accomplished something new, something artless; he had earned himself a prize. And, of course, if you have someone's motors in your hands, then you are his master: dead was Zip – born was the postpsychotic Zipon. As for the jolt itself, the so-called *Schub*, it had lasted no more than a second. Then came the usual afterthoughts (who cares, anyway?) = good God, that man must have been involved in Persy's life, in that private life of hers, about which he, Genezip, was so abysmally ignorant. Perhaps not erotically involved; all the same, there was something weird about it, even for one as deranged as Zip was on that memorable evening. Not for nothing had the bitch lied about the room belonging to her deceased brother: clearly it had been occupied by that galoot. But his instincts (which had erred so often in the past [although in this case Genezip was sure they were telling the truth]) told him that this bearded ape had been of no sexual interest to her. No, something more profound, if oblique, was involved here, the exact nature of which he might never learn. He felt stranded in a perfect social void. He was a criminal, certain to be hounded by absolutely everyone – except perhaps by a couple of thousand other weirdos. The feeling of social isolation gradually gave way to a state of metaphysical solitude: that of a unique and solitary existence in a universe infinite both spatially and temporally. (For the mathematicians can say what they will and merrily distort the world however they wish, our real space is still Euclidean, and a straight line is fundamentally different from all others.) Intuitively – that is, without knowing the appropriate theories and terminology, relying only on his own mental images – he grasped immediately, in an animal sort of way, Being in all its infinite grandeur, its essential inscrutability relative to a particular existence. And there it ended: a wall of absolute indifference. Suddenly, almost without his realizing it, he was homeward bound. Only Lilian meant anything to him now. The problem of an alibi had risen up in all its pristine clearness, exactly as in that recent but now distant dream. Perhaps no one would see him, and Lilian would say – sure, she would – his dear sis! – that he had been with her the whole time. How convenient was a family at times! The bastard! The only person in whom he could now believe was not his mother, even less the princess, but that little outcast Lily. So come on, let's go! *Allons alors!* It was most unlikely that he would run into an acquaintance and be recognized in the dismal lighting of this perennially comatose town. Although he was convinced that life had somehow ended (the future spread itself out before him like a bowl of mush, nondescript, protoexistential, undifferentiated, containing all the old anguish but three times as intense and prolonged to infinity); while not believing in the future, while seeing before him only perpetual indifference (big deal!), he decided to play it safe and secure an alibi. And all because of that subterranean creep – the sinking Zip was making the fellow responsible for everything. He could feel him physically, his hooves and claws (the flippancy came from him, from that other character); felt the way he made himself at home, threw his weight around, tried to force the old Zip out through all his psychic pores like a soft jelly or pie dough. Just then, as bad luck would have it, there appeared before him, at the corner of Well and Filter Streets, two figures stumbling along with their flabby legs sticking to the wet flagstones, clinging with their tentaclelike arms to each other, to the walls, to the posts, and to the newsstands. Soon the air was rent by a disgusting song crooned in a hoarse baritone and a thick Marseilles accent:

Quel sale pais que la Pologne,
Cette triste patrie des gouveniages.
Pour faire voir un peu de vergogne
Ils n'ont même pas de courage.

They drew near. Civilians. One fat, short, and round, the other short and lean. The latter accompanied the heftier one with a sort of nasal hiss that seemed to issue from his body's poisonous glands. Both reeked of freshly extinguished and still warm spirit lamps. The Pole in Zip had been aroused. *(Vous autres, Polonais . . .)* It was all so simple, an open-and-shut case. Perhaps that automated joker from the underground was more Polish than he himself. His blood, gentlemen, began to seethe, so he slugged the stout one in the jaw; just as he was raising his arm he glimpsed in the shadows the insolently wry and jovial face of Lebac – familiar to him from a military review at the school. (It flashed through his mind that Persy and her chaperon might have . . . "No, they wouldn't betray me," said a voice inside him, and it was right. The thought never entered his head again: that newcomer had other tricks up his sleeve.) The man in the shadows turned out to be Lebac's aide, the Duke de Troufières. Zip rammed his fist into the pit of the adjutant's stomach and flipped him over backward into a puddle, which splashed with delight to receive the Frenchman's slender little ass. In his cadet's overcoat, Zip was scarcely distinguishable from an ordinary cavalryman. The alley was impenetrably dark: they would never recognize him. He continued on his way, as robotlike in his movements as he had been ever since the crime. Lebac tried to overtake him but soon gave up. He grabbed the post of an extinguished street lamp with his flabby arm, swung around, and fell to his knees crying, "Pol*iii*ce! Pol*iii*ce!" (The clocks had been set back two hours [part of the new labor speedup]: in another hour it would be daylight.) Zip could feel nothing, not the slightest anxiety. As a Pole he was satisfied. "A pretty alibi," he muttered to himself. "Actually, I didn't have to do that, but it was a nice way to end the day. How wonderfully light I feel! How come I didn't know about this lightness before?!" Still, it worried him that he felt nothing but this levity. "What can I do? There's no way I can make myself feel something I can't feel." He wrapped himself in this last thought as if it were a warm cloak and headed down the muddy street toward home.

He woke up Lilian, who was ter-ri-fied. She listened to his story, trembling and gripping his hand, which she even squeezed – only intermittently, of course – from excitement. Even though Sturfan Abnol did not cease to be her lover, only now was she discovering the true depths of her emotion. Suddenly her brother, so remote until now (she had often wondered whether she was in love with him; now she knew otherwise) had drawn close to her like a meteor racing from outer space, penetrating her still-dormant body with a force equal in its intensity to the violent events being described. (Poor Sturfan – thus far he had set only her delicate little head afire, though it was not for want of trying.) Something told her that she had just lost her celebrated virginity, the subject of so many legends told her by her salivating lesbian friends and even by the baroness herself. And to think it was with *him*, with this pure spirit in uniform, this truly brotherly spirit, and that she could have him like *this* anytime, *without him inside her!* Naturally, she was unaware of what this meant, but she had a rough idea. Period. For her, it was truly a happy moment: the promise of a full and unadulterated intimacy with this adorable stud-artist descended from Romanian boyars. For such moments she might serve him for a lifetime. She might perform the most abominable acts as long as he followed the course dictated by the force latent in him. She saw reflected in her (at the moment she was all mirrors) her brother's infinite possibilities, and she swallowed him whole the way a cannon devours a cannonball. But she lacked the strength to eject him from herself. He alone could launch himself into the murky, stormy expanses of life. She envisioned the "secret target of his destiny" as a bright and radiant bull's-eye on some kitschy "black hill of Death." Contained in this bull's-eye was the ultimate sense of everything. She recalled one of her father's maxims: "Fix your sights beyond life's barriers." This was also one of Sturfan's obsessions. But for Sturfan these belonged to the realm of artistic *perezhivaniya*. Let him perform such an *acte gratuit!* Then he might have reason to snap. And to think that she would be privy to everything: the true motives (or lack of same) of that bizarre crime, which no one but she would ever comprehend. For on that macabre but splendid night, perhaps the most splendid of all, she understood him so intensely and so intimately that she might have been he himself. She would have to preserve it (and remember it she would) for her wedding night, to add *this* to *that* to form her life's summit. And never, never climb down from that peak! Better to die in anguish than to descend to the flat and boring valley of banality, where everything was what it appeared to be. For all his capriccios in the realm of art (or *Kronpriccios*, as he was fond of calling his plays), Sturfan had never shown her *this*. It had taken the sacrifice of her dear brother to make *it* happen: a perception as to the mysterious charm inherent in a perverse reality. She prayed in silence to her mother's erstwhile God – her own private deities, which she had yet to arouse in herself, were still napping at the border of awareness. And she grasped so clearly that he could not have acted otherwise that she was overcome with joy, much as if she had just received some exquisite present. It was so divinely simple! She felt not the slightest pity for that innocent (as like as not) fellow with the beard (some colonel or other whose name had escaped Zip). More than likely he had deserved such a death. It was every bit as weird as one of Sturfan's plays in Quintofron's staging: absurd, but necessary. Only here it was for real! Truly a miracle. But gradually the initial ecstasy wore off, everything descended to the level of a routine conversation about everyday affairs, and soon disgust set in. Even though the aftereffects of their previous state kept them formally at a certain level, something had gone sour, rotten; things were beginning to decompose at phenomenal speed. It was reminiscent of a cocaine high, when during its final stages, *without altering their outward appearance*, things grow ten times more awesome and at the same time more banal, in inverse proportion to the preceding state of exaltation and wonder.

Lilian: Why didn't you tell me you loved her like that? I thought she was your first real passion, a reaction to your affair with Irina. She's incapable of erotic feeling; no one has ever been her lover, at least not at the theater, nor has there been any talk of her having had one. But if I had known, I would have advised you against it, tried to talk you out of it, or at least tried to stop her from leading you on unnecessarily. And possibly she might have listened to me. (She was lying gleefully and revoltingly by deliberately exaggerating [at least a little] her own self-importance.)

Zip: You talk like an old woman, but you're mistaken. No one can influence her; she's the void incarnate, a vamp. If my love didn't impress her, then she doesn't exist. I'm beginning to think – a bit late, of course – that she hides some abomination, some vile and inscrutable secret, and that this is what attracted me to her. I discovered in myself layers of evil, baseness, and weakness that I never dreamed were there. I tried to convince myself that it was love, the sort I'd never known. I wonder if I'll ever know it . . . ("Oh, my dear boy," Lilian thought with emotion. "Fresh from killing an innocent man, he complains of never having known love! It's too wonderful for words!") "I felt so paralyzed. She used some drug to overpower me and rob me of my will. I now believe it was she who killed the colonel, through me. I behaved like a robot, I tell you. It was all a nightmare. Even so, I feel different now – like I'm a different *person.* I can't explain it. Maybe I am that person's reincarnation. I crossed some line in myself, now there's no going back to what I was." (Lilian was again squirming with admiration and envy. Yes, to be continually reincarnated, to constantly change one's identity without losing the continuity of one's self! Meanwhile, he sat beside her, that everyday brother who now inhabited another world. *"Il a une autre vision du monde, ce bougre-là, à deux pas de moi – e mua kua?"* she concluded in "Polish.") "By that monstrous crime I liberated myself – both from her and from myself. If they don't lock me up, my life may yet turn out splendidly . . . " He broke off, suddenly confronted with absolute nothingness: his own and that of the circumscribing world. The devils had lowered the curtain; the show was over. And there was no telling how long the intermission might last – till the very end, perhaps. He shuddered. He was seized with a desire for action. To do something, anything, even in one's pants, as long as it constituted an action. But it was not so easy. Once again events (appalling events, to be sure) came to the rescue of this ill-starred "child of fortune." He must hold out until the morning. "I don't even know who he was." It was now so that only that troublemaker from below spoke; he had coalesced with the remains, the facade of the former Zip, to form an undifferentiated, hardened mass. And so good was his disguise that, if not for the eyes through which he peered out at the world from Zip's body, no one (not even Bekhmetev) would have suspected that it was no longer the old Zip but someone else, fearful and universally estranged. Hence the meaning of the term "madness." "The worst thing is, I don't even know who that man was," he repeated. It was by no means the *worst* thing, but so it seemed to him at the moment.

"We'll find out from the newspapers," Lilian replied with a vivacity and presence of mind typical for a girl of that generation. (O you tricky little fish, you cagey little mice, you cunning little lizards! Shall we never come to know you, we who by 1929 were already middle-aged fogies condemned to stand idly by and see the next generation gripped by a mindless, "rah-rah" sports mania! But never mind all that.) "I'll stand by you completely. Since nine o'clock you've been in my company and haven't set foot outside. Mother and Mr. Michalski were already home by nine. Trust in me. It'll be a pleasure for me. But will *she* betray you? That will depend on how much that bearded man meant to her. None of my acquaintances ever saw her with him. A guest from out of town, perhaps?"

Zip: No, he'd been living in that room for a long time. I'm positive of it now. Oddly enough, I have the impression that he knew me quite well, from before. He must have been spying on me every night, the scum, and laughing at my impotence. I'll bet he heard all those asinine things I said. Gawd, how embarrassing! But I could have sworn he wasn't her lover.

Lilian: How can you be so sure? You won't listen to me, but my advice is: try not to drown the pain. Swallow the worst right away. (She had completely forgotten her previous words. Or else she had not forgotten but was just rambling, having lost track of the conversation.)

Zip: I've gotten over it already. I'm sure of that. What worries me is what it may conceal, in me and in the situation itself. He was no ordinary house guest, and I'm not the person I once was. ("Here he goes again," thought Lilian, who was on the verge of falling asleep.)

Lilian: Okay, run along now, and be brave. I've got to get a good night's sleep before tomorrow's rehearsal.

Genezip was deeply wounded, but managed not to show it. The world again appeared extraordinary, so wonderfully suffused with the fiery essence of life's weirdness – not the sort which is grasped intellectually but which is immediately given. How so? Through the mere opposition of an individual to all that is not himself: a gloomily absurd world, ablaze in metaphysical horror like a mountainous landscape bathed in sunset, and a lonely, solitary wisp of an existence imbued with the same mystery that filled the universe. Instead of surrendering to the world, instead of ceasing to be, Genezip's uncannily specific "I" persisted, much to its own horror and that of other kindred wretches. Here was the zenith of Zip's metaphysics. Yes, that's how it *was*, but what about her? . . . The dumb cluck! Let her give you an alibi, then to hell with her . . . He stared at the vanity holding Lilian's toiletries as if it were the most wondrous thing in the world. The fact that all these quaint little articles (belonging to that other, metaphysically estranged world) were the property of another being, i.e., his sister, struck him as monstrously pathetic. Rarely does a brother who has a sister experience this extraordinary fact. But it was happening now. The differentiation of this person – independently of his will – from among millions seemed to him an insufferable burden, a weight greater, say, than the force of gravity or the equations of Maxwell or Einstein. (When it is finally understood that physics is powerless before the inscrutability of Being, then no one will care *how* approximately the world can be described. Between Planck and Heraclitus there exist only quantitative differences. Philosophy, of course, is another matter – but more on that subject later.) But this continual brush with mystery at every juncture of life, even in the most trivial situations . . . Fortunately, one is not always aware of it, otherwise nothing would ever be accomplished in this sorry world of ours.

• "Run along," Lilian repeated in a tired, childlike voice. He no longer resented that she could not speak to him in the language of his strangeness. He had been unjust toward her; he must treat her not as an element in a sinister and alien world, but as part of himself in that internal sea of nullity. Again he turned away from himself in horror.

"Forgive me, Lily," the murderer said tenderly to his little sister. "I was horribly unfair to you just now. I'm much too obsessed with life. Now that I've done something real and – because I lacked a motive – unreal, I have a much greater sense of myself as a cog in the whole machinery of our perverse society. Ugh, what a vile race we Poles are, and yet . . . " He then told her of the incident with Lebac. For a moment she perked up. Meanwhile, her brother rambled on as though by this endless stream of chatter he might keep himself among the living. He *was* because he spoke; he was dead the moment he was interrupted – some would have said he was dead already. Soon he was philosophizing again, paying not the slightest attention to Lilian's fatigue. "How hard it is to be original, even in this ungodly age of ours! Everything has been said long ago. Our minds may have become richer, more diversified, but not our language; there the possibilities are limited by practical reality. All the nuances and permutations have been exhausted. It was that beast of a poet Tuwim and his school who castrated our language out of existence. It's gotten to the point where you can't say anything; all you can do is repeat, with certain variations, things said long ago. It's called devouring your own vomit. At one time writers could plumb all the nuances of the human soul, even if two normal and respectable types, in whom those souls were found, might utter the same commonplaces." How it bored his sister to listen to such talk! But he was also uncomfortable: he was summoning up the words, trying to end this scene in which he found himself grossly out of his depth. And these were people of the final revolution, the chronic semirevolution going on ever since the French Revolution! At this rate, the next generation would speak only of concrete objects, not daring to rummage about in the "soul," a thing rendered odious by all manner of mangy literatniks. Nothing new there, comrades! Meanwhile, the external conditions, which are variable and which affect the psyche but slightly, gave only the pretense of infinite possibilities. Even Russian literature was nearing the end; the possibilities were *indeed* shrinking. People tread an ever smaller patch, like those clinging to a sinking iceberg. Fiction, following the example of the Pure Arts, was headed for the abyss. And are we not right to be scornful? While a good narcotic is still okay, a fake narcotic that fails to work the way it should but still produces all the bad side effects is worthy of contempt, and its manufacturers are a bunch of swindlers. But, alas, fiction written for the sake fiction, without a *purely* artistic justification (as in poetry, for example, where a violation of the sense is justified), fiction without substance, has proved to be an invention on the part of verbally gifted morons and graphomaniacs.

An awful, otherworldly (in the sense that there was no relief *in sight*) boredom suddenly descended on this unhappy couple. Through the dining room (a dark, rather modestly furnished room: oil tablecloth, the faint smell of chicory, the tick-tock of a clock) Michalski's loud snore could be heard reverberating in the nocturnal quiet of the town. Water dripped from a drainpipe in the yard. How he yearned to inhabit this banality, wallow in it forever, to drive this boredom to a murderous frenzy! Wishful thinking, alas. Searching for weirdness in the ordinary was out of fashion. Even the Norwegians had exhausted themselves literarily on the subject, to say nothing of the *Landsturmmänner* of our own belles lettres. The age brimmed with a social humdrum of a higher order, one that was about to inundate the world in the most extraordinary of explosions. Zip kissed Lilian passionately on the mouth and ached with regret: Why did she have to be his sister, why not that other woman? Why was everything so misplaced and displaced? Interchangeable. Roles, souls, coiffures, disguises, intellects.

He returned to the damp streets now being suffused with a pale light. About a block from the house he was approached by a shadow. At first Zip took him for a secret agent. He dropped into a crouch, instinctively, not with any criminal intent. Before him stood a house he recognized. On the ground floor a light had just been switched on. This house was somehow *different;* it was not located here in this sleepy town, in this country, or even on this planet. Its occupants were likely ordinary, average, even respectable people: creatures not of *this* (his) world. He was the outcast, the one who would never know peace. Unleashed, but still homeless. He longed for a corner in which to weep over himself and to die. But reality, in the form of that ominous figure advancing toward him, was compelling him to an action most foul. Henceforward, everything, all of his life's endeavors, would turn out negatively: a constant wriggling out of predicaments of his own making. An unidentified corpse floating down a river was more at home in this world. Still, no choice but to go on. Although nothing would have been simpler, suicide was out. The future yawned before him like a gigantic, disemboweled belly, but he was not fazed. His only hope? Squirm your way into someone's furiously aching intestines, immune to the insufferable agony of an existence stripped of all ties.

In the light of a gradually fading street lamp, he saw, under a black hat, the swarthy face and blazing (no kidding), inspired eyes of a young Hindu.

"I come from Mr. Djevani. Do you know who he is?" the stranger whispered in Polish with a strange accent. His mouth reeked of rotten meat and damp moss. Genezip recoiled with disgust, automatically reaching for the revolver in his rear pocket. "Don't be afraid, Sahib," resumed the other calmly. "We know everything and we have just the cure for all your woes. Here are some pills." He pressed into Genezip's hand a little box and a card on which, in the flickering light of the same street lamp (this struck him as odd, this indifferent sameness) (he stuck the box into his pocket like an automaton), he deciphered the following words written in round, English characters in a woman's hand:

> To sin in humility means to sin half as much. Do not admit to yourself that you are mad, even though madness is the reason for your actions. Our business is to make use of your madness, and that of our whole happy world, for the sake of higher aims. You must want to *know*.

Genezip raised his head, but the Hindu was gone. Down a little side street to the left came the sound of *soft*, hurrying footsteps retreating into the distance, although it sounded more like a reptile slithering away. A shudder that was more mystical in origin (not metaphysical – there's a big difference: one is a terror before the whole of Being and the other a terror before one of life's imperfections) coursed through Zip's body. So, someone (who, for pity's sake?!) had been dogging his every step?! Good God! He felt like an infusorian caught in a droplet of water on a glass slide, as if being examined under the glaring light of some gargantuan supermicroscope, with all his aplomb and self-assurance hopelessly blown. It was because of his "liberating act" that he was caught in this invisible net, this wolf's trap set long ago. He, who had once pasted Piętalski; he, the general's future aide, mama's pet, that *bum;* he, whose mistress was the most prominent whore in the land! He turned cold all over. It was not possible to lead a life where the most capricious accident would comprise a compelling necessity, where the most inescapable necessity would become a miracle of absolute whimsy. He felt like the mangiest cur, but how strange was this new leash! He desperately jerked his head; the invisible leash held. "You must want to know" – how ironic! No doubt some wench had written that. "Could anyone be more eager to know than I? Show me how! Don't abandon me now!" he kept shouting in a mute voice, while a cold terror mounted astronomically in him. He bristled, ruffled his feathers, got his hackles up against his invisible enemies or saviors – he didn't know which. He fumbled in his pocket for the little box containing the pills and instantly relaxed, like a raving madman sedated with morphine. Davamesque B_2: the last resort. The present now seemed a mere particle, a mere scrap of the Grand Mystery, which was grander than anything he had ever known. But this mystery was equipped with tentacles and those tentacles were brutally sucking everything into the sphere of its own activity. The foul-smelling Hindu was one of those tentacles – though obviously an inferior one.

Zip had heard of the religion of Djevani, a cult apparently persecuted by Buddhist fanatics on the other side of the yellow wall. Why "apparently"? Because there were those who claimed that Djevani was not at all an emissary of that (perhaps fictitious) Murti Bing from the island of Balampang, but was an agent of those yellow monkeys presently marching on Europe; that from Djevani to Buddhism it was but a small step backward; that it was actually a bogus religion designed for the Great White Fools of the West, an opiate facilitating the conquest of those same Great White Fools and their transformation into manure for the yellow masses of the Far East. In the past, Zip had been irritated by the sect's political naïveté, by ideas that seemed to him powerless to regenerate mankind and effect history. Yet, he would soon attest to the power of those ideas in a personal way: through the fiendish hallucinogenic drug Davamesque B_2. Previously, human history had presented itself to Zip as something grand, structurally beautiful, and necessary. A deeper examination revealed that its primary forces were: (a) the ordinary belly (either a lord's or a lout's) and (b) stupid fads masquerading in a thousand different forms and all scrupulously avoiding the – nowadays – intellectually balding Mystery of Being. One such fad was the cult of Djevani, supposedly being proselytized by such people as the Minister of Education Colonel Ludomir Swędziagolski and Chancellor of the Exchequer Jacek Boroeder, the latter being – again if rumors were correct – the third incarnation of "Extreme Consciousness" in the sect, i.e., third in rank after Murti Bing. And this was the same Boroeder, a confirmed profligate and cynic suspected of gross misconduct in the awarding of war contracts during the time of the Crusade! Ha, maybe it was they who . . .

Rat-tat-tat . . . etc. The silence was suddenly broken by machine-gun fire quite close by, which, for Zip, came as an even greater shock than the encounter with the stinking Hindu. He flinched, only not from fear but the way a circus horse starts at the sound of a cavalry charge. At last! Real gunfire that was not just part of some exercise! A revolt; the syndicate; Kotzmolochowicz; Piętalski; Mama; that corpse with the hammer stuck in its head; Persy; Lilian; the pills – such were the many associations. "I exist again; I really do exist," the former Zip proclaimed through the mouth of the gent from below. "See if I surrender! I'll show them." Quickly he made for the school, which was only a short distance away. Two and a half minutes later he could already make out, between some houses, a brooding structure towering above the limestone cliffs. Not a single light was on in the wing facing the town. Panting for breath, he bounded up the front stairs carved into the cliff. The shock had had its effects. It could not have been better timed. The recent burst of gunfire had made all the rest seem like a bad dream.

His father and the general now had him in their clutches, not knowing *whom* they held: the former schoolboy or that gent from below. Therein lay the real meaning of that clatter of machine-gun fire. Reduced to the level of an anonymous cadet, he reached the lower gate. It was open and was being guarded by six hulking giants from the Fifteenth Uhlan Regiment. Something new. They let him pass.

Yes, reality had spoken up in the irrefutable and unequivocal language of human death on a grand scale; it had penetrated, possibly for the last time, the magic circle of schizophrenic solitude. It is difficult, for example, to find an abstract, metaphysical element in a screeching barrage of eleven-inch howitzers, except perhaps in retrospect. Such an event, when it is actually experienced, can provoke (in many, but not all) a more primal religious emotion, renew one's faith in a personal deity, and has been known to cause the most devout atheists to pray.

A Battle and Its Consequences

Rounding a dark corner, Genezip noticed that all the windows at the rear of the building were ablaze, *à giorno* (as his grandmother, the countess, used to say), even though it was already daybreak. (The lights could not be seen from the front because the side wings stood at a right angle to the main building – a detail to be noted!) Filled with a feral, martial fervor (at the moment he was a mechanical brute, although there shone above his brow, as above the lady's head in Grottger's drawings, a star of *anonymous* ideals), the young cadet, now purged of any human trace, dashed up the main stairs and ran to join his squadron. The faces of the men, especially among the senior ranks, were decidedly pale, their eyes troubled and glum. Only a few of the younger faces shared Genezip's expression of idiotic fervor. Naturally, if there had been an orchestra on hand and if the Great Kotzmolochowicz had been there in person . . . Alas, he could not be everywhere at once. How much simpler – from the point of view of individual conduct – were those battles of the past!

Genezip reported to the duty officer.

"Another hour and you would have been court-martialed. As it is you'll be placed under arrest."

"I never received any order. My sister came down with an acute case of angina. I spent the whole night at her place." These words, making up his first official lie, blossomed from the muckheap of the past like white orchids. Across this heap lay a corpse with a hammer in its skull. Zip banished the image from his mind. A voice from another, quasi-real world continued:

"No excuses. Tonight's order, which you deliberately ignored by being absent before nine o'clock, clearly stated that all cadets would be confined to quarters tonight."

"Lieutenant, do you seriously think . . . "

"I don't think anything. Now return to your place," ordered the young man (Wasiukiewicz) in such a cool and malevolent tone (the tone of a working-class upstart) that Genezip, ablaze internally and even externally on his cheeks, with the "sacred" fire of youth's impetuosity, with the urge to *hunt* rather than to *kill* (he had had enough killing for a while), was turned into a block of congealed *military* iron – or rather scrap iron fit for trains, hospitals, kitchens, but under no circumstances for the front! And here they were spoiling it with their stupid formalities! Still, he was insanely glad to be a part of this "adventure." The ideological side of the contest did not interest him, only the personal implications, while death never entered his thoughts (great "military exploits" at the lower ranks of the military begin here, with just such stupidity).

The corpse of the mysterious man with the beard would vanish without a trace, osmotically absorbed by coming events – the meaning of which, for all Zip's earlier musings, completely eluded him.

Another burst of machine-gun fire sounded in the distance, followed by rifle shots somewhere in the neighborhood and by the faint roar of a crowd. It was rumored that the infantry would see action first; so far, there had been no talk of horses being used. All, with the possible exception of a few inveterate circus riders, were happy with this decision, since the average cavalryman did not relish the prospect of riding over wet cobblestones and asphalt.

"Attention!" The men fell into a double formation. "Right face! Double file, forward, march!" Genezip recognized the voice of Wołodyjowicz, now invisible behind the pillars. So *he* would be in command of the squadron, his archenemy at school. How unlucky can you get! Even so, Zip was the picture of military stiffness, having reached that stage of aggression where thoroughly mindless cattle kill for the sake of other cattle. Ideologies! God, what halcyon times those were when principles still flew like banners above such carnage – now they are utterly passé. All his doubts were lifted from him, shed like a pair of overtight suspenders; he had imploded; will had given way to absolute inertia; only his musculature, commanded by that internal gent, remained tense and alert – like a transmission waiting to be slammed into gear. His light and empty head teemed with images – detached, dematerialized, disembodied. His head felt *concave,* a chasm over which these fantasies swarmed like brilliantly hued butterflies in the sun. And what was this sunny radiance if not the Great Fundament of Being: the mystery of infinite space and the vanishing personality; that black screen on which discreet images may appear but which are finally overshadowed by the ineffable All. "I'm going to live, dammit, because I have to achieve my destiny!" his muscles said. His present estrangement had as its setting the stable's red wall and, overhead, the lead-grey sky of a hazy summer morning. "So this is how it's to be!" It seemed as if years had passed. "I'll never know what's real again." A thick pane of glass had fallen between Genezip and the world. Not even the bullets fired by the syndicate's men could pierce that glass. Would it shatter at the moment of his death, he wondered? What was once the engine of a glorious art (the mystery of the ego), what was once a heroic striving for a place in the cosmos – in the metaphysical rather than social sense – had become a rotten, half-demented rear guard made up of a degenerate race of schizoids soon to be overrun by a gang of pyknics and women.

When that happened, no one would feel the slightest pain in the splendidly organized anthill.

The voice of that detestable captain, so resonant with *real* and minatory commands, made Zip recall the princess's first visit to the school. How long ago it seemed! He barely recognized himself in the cowed lad, he who was about to march off into a real battle as a full-grown murderer and madman. Maybe this was the last . . . ? Too late now. He had a final image of himself and that gent symbiotically twinned; here and there (in the soul, principally) a few traces of the former boy were still visible through the dark and faceless figure of his double. Zip saw it vividly, objectively. The one who had been his prisoner but was now his master wore a beard just like that of the dead colonel, only darker.

They marched into the town, tramping through the sticky mud toward what appeared to be the main theater. From his soul's reserves Zip summoned a magnificent nonchalance and detachment. Cheers of "Hoorah! Hooray!" etc. (revolting enough in themselves) might have been expected. Instead, a coolheaded, sangfroid attitude prevailed – this despite the "fire of purgation licking at the edges of the social pigsty" – for which Genezip could thank that meeting with Djevani's agent. The cult of Djevani was the only point of mystery, the last repository of magic in the garish vulgarity of modern times – and not only locally. The old world, its miracles and mysteries, had been turned into a chaos, alarming, minatory, full of sweet hideouts and sordid traps, of unknown possibilities and schizophrenic hangups. Like that episode with the colonel. Zip did not care to undergo such an "experience" again, but how to control something without the proper steering mechanism? (He kept the pills on him at all times – that much he could still manage.) The present (with the possible exception of this "domestic disturbance" and the Chinese Wall in the distance – in other words, mysteries belonging to the second degree) was blatantly clear, simple, and, physically speaking, even safe, free of hideouts for hostile doubles but also of any "lotusland" in which to escape a tedious reality. And the present was, above all else, tedious – like the plague, chronic gonorrhea, classical art, materialistic philosophy, and indiscriminate kindness. If not for this morning's convenient battle, who knew where this tedium might have led – possibly even to suicide. The only spark of Mystery left was this new religion, now being seized on as a "last straw" by all who saw in it a salvation from the scientific management of labor. But for some it was not enough. Those who suffered most were people whose brains had been stuffed from infancy with pious platitudes and who later tried to stand up for those pieties like mindless little machines. Oh, how could they! Fie!

Genezip swore that if he survived this "minor disturbance" (as the revolution instigated by the syndicate was being called in circles close to the general) he would look into this new religion. Normally a person would take the pills, then proceed to the indoctrination stage. Zip decided to do the opposite: to become initiated first, then take the pills. But such decisions do not always work out in practice. Was Kotzmolochowicz "on" the pills? It was hotly debated, but no one could say for sure.

Just before they reached Dziemborowski Square (who exactly was this Dziemborowski, anyway?), they spread out in a firing line down a wide boulevard lined with chestnut trees. The shelling was growing more fierce by the second. A grey, cloying, lachrymose day was breaking. How far removed was this as-yet-unmaterialized but potentially humdrum battle from that spring day when, to the gut-wringing sounds of the school orchestra, *der geniale Kotzmolokowitsch* had "inspired" his personal robo-battalion. Why couldn't he have perished (theoretically speaking, of course) *then,* with pomp and circumstance? The discrepancy between such prewar ceremonies and the work of war itself – which, for the nonspecialist, was as boring as any other job – palled. Genezip brooded over his life's "comedown" *(Pech);* nothing had worked out, dammit, and someone surely had it in for him. But in a twinkling his anger was turned into a "martial fury": in his present mood he could have ground the syndicate to bits with his bare teeth – the leaders, of course, not these poor, deluded officers and soldiers who were "shedding their blood" so that a person like Piętalski might breakfast (!) on champagne and oysters.

Suddenly, from a seemingly deserted street, the first carbine shots rang out. A tremendous barrage between the houses – the sound of heavy artillery. Magnificent rage was again turned into a nasty discontent: it was just a minor skirmish, not a "full-scale" battle . . . ! To hell with it! More rage, etc. Not even Kotzmolochowicz, who was off in the capital, could have compensated for it; while he might have worked on the former kid, he had no clout whatever on that "gent from below," although it was rumored, under sofas and in certain privies (and then only in a whisper), that, that, well, that he may have been such a "gent from below" himself – one of his own making, of course – not he, not the true Kotzmolochowicz. Whew! A stone was lifted from his heart.

The insurgent Forty-eighth Infantry Regiment, whose ranks the nationalist platform had (inexplicably) failed to penetrate (some attributed it to their innate patriotism, but a fart on that, sir! Ridiculous. Why, then, in the Forty-eighth and not the Forty-ninth? Regionalism owing to the partitions of Poland? Pure myth. Peachy times, huh?! And now the Chinese. As Buxenhein used to say to Lebac after having had too much to drink: "In its lack of punctuality lies Poland's strength. If she were punctual, she would have disappeared long ago." Oh, let's teach that bad-mouthing bunch a lesson! But no, those "friends of the last democracy" were untouchable, unless one went about it Zip-style: hitting them while they were drunk, dressing incognito, in a dark alley, etc.) – as I was saying, this regiment kept up a sporadic fire around the plaza bordering the boulevard, using as its base two corner houses, typically modern but which at the moment loomed quite weird and amazing. Houses from another dimension, non-Euclidean houses, hyperhouses, houses straight out of a fairy tale. They were like sinister palaces inhabited by death itself, death incarnated by a bunch of crackpots armed with obsolete German rifles – who, in turn, had been "set up" by a couple of even worse crackpots who believed themselves the embodiment of the national soul but who in fact only wanted to eat well, drink well, and whore well.

A cannon exploded outside of town. An approaching thunderstorm could not have been more ominous; but whereas nature's storms happen sporadically, here everything was *humanly* concentrated in a given point in space, which may have been the belly of the listener (how else to signify a *man-made* elemental storm?).

Genezip was transformed into an enormous ear; he developed bat-like ears. It was a real battle, even if on a measly scale. He would have to remain attentive, if only to form an opinion about it and render an adequate account later. Above all, he would have to commit these sounds to memory. For all his military training, the future officer could muster no technical interest in the battle as a tactical drill. If had been given command of a division . . . ? But the confusion was so great that later, try as he might, he was never able to reconstruct his impressions in their original order. Both the previous night and this mercilessly dawning day were multidimensional vis-à-vis the passage of time; they could not be integrated in the usual chronological way. This much was certain: the previous night was being soaked up – like an unsavory secretion by a benevolent sponge – by this morning's events, turning ever paler and more diluted in the process.

Apart from these "minor perturbations" in the course of events, Genezip greeted the whine of the first shells with a truly prodigious delight. At last! (Bombardments were the dream of every young cadet. Naturally, he would have preferred a slaughter *en règle* complete with trenches, tanks, and artillery barrages. But better this than nothing.) Less appealing was the sound of those same shells slamming into the walls of the apartment houses at his back. Maybe his zeal was flagging? Now was the time to attack with fixed bayonets! But no, they were pinned down by a senseless fire (from a soldier's point of view, everything his co does is senseless). Meanwhile, a brooding, trite, washing-and-shaving sort of summer day, clad in the well-worn rags of grey and eerily mundane clouds, crept out from behind the not-so-nice apartment buildings on Dziemborowski Square. "Things are moving too fast, short-circuiting; soon there won't be any time left," Genezip lamented during a pause in the firing. Work out a plan, make a breach, then barrel in there with guns blazing! Nasty illusions. The battle, elusive as Tenzer's wild harmonics, was slipping through his fingers. A series of senseless situations and actions, lacking any composition and, worse, any elegance. Occasionally an internal light flashed, and the world was briefly set aglow, as by lightning, in the beauty of ultimate wisdom, only to dim again and be plunged into the dregs of banality, compounded by the fact that, relatively speaking (e.g., relative to sipping your morning coffee, yoga exercises, erotic experiences, etc.), this was a highly unusual scene, without ceasing to be drab and tedious as only a military drill book can be. Zip was lying behind one of the posts of the balustrade surrounding a little garden in the center of the plaza. This spot, flat and ordinary to the point of being painful, without a single redeeming aspect, grew in Zip's imagination to a terrain laced with hills and valleys, utterly mysterious vis-à-vis the immutable workings of fate, and inexplicably important: a stunning example of an infantryman's tactical drill. Theoretically speaking, that is; the command to fire had not yet been given; inactivity had prolonged time beyond eternal bounds. The day was turning brighter, increasingly pedestrian. The folly of this battle was ridding life of any charm. The present moment and Kotzmolochowicz's review at school stood worlds apart, unbridged by any connection or transformational formula. He had underestimated the absurdity: for the ordinary soldier, but also for company and squadron leaders, even for battalion chiefs and regimental commanders, especially those still awaiting orders, every battle was a folly. For officers in command of more strategic units it was different. "*Réflechir et puis exécuter – voilà la guerre,*" he recalled Lebac having said at one of his reviews. But at the moment neither of these exhortations applied. How to plan strategy in a state of "immobility," while lying on one's belly behind a post on a cheerless and asinine (necessarily so) town square? What, "execute" a battle under such conditions? There was nothing and nobody to shoot at! Meanwhile, the other side had begun pounding away again, shells whizzed overhead and landed with a thud against the walls of the houses and the tree trunks directly behind them. The absurdity of it grew more and more lethal; around the hard core of "heroism," a nimble and marionettelike thought was beginning to twirl: in a moment there might be nothing left of him (or at most a savagely aching hole somewhere in his body), since, by the theory of probability, one of these crackpots was bound to score a hit.

Suddenly, the second in command, Major Sump, emerged from behind a newsstand and roared. But before he did so, Genezip had time to note (and just in time) that he bore the same name as that corpse. The coincidence gave him pause; his instincts told him that he would not escape unpunished, that even if he went undetected as a murderer, some horrendous punishment lay in store for him: *"Ili ranyat, ili ubiyut,"* as Czar Cyril's agent, Prince Blusterosov, used to say. Then he put two and two together: this one must have been the other man's uncle, a former pilot. The major let loose a bellicose cry:

"After me, children of the Great Moloch!" And with sword in hand he charged like a lunatic the house across the way, which the hazy morning light had turned a rosy pink. The riflemen rushed after him. Genezip caught sight of four tiny flames in the windows of a corner café and again heard machine-gun fire, not an isolated burst but round after round. "Why now of all times? In another hour, even quarter of an hour, I would have been gung-ho for anything. Right – only not *here!* In some ravine, on the ramparts of some fort, on a bridgehead, dammit, but not here on this crappy Dziemborowski Square!" (May that great and unknown town worthy, D., and the surrounding hamlets be cursed until the hundredth generation!) Genezip was overwhelmed by an utterly pointless rage. He charged like a man possessed, as did the others. All – were they thinking the very same thoughts? – fell in behind Sump, who was now under a hail of bullets (or so it *seemed*). But the machine-gun fire was aimed too high, and the cadets, without suffering a single loss, landed on the café terrace, where they were immediately engaged in hand-to-hand combat. Panic-stricken, their adversaries, those poor misguided fools from the fraternal Forty-eighth, came pouring out of the café and ran straight into a double line of cadets, who meanwhile had reassembled along their flanks. A horrible melee followed. Someone (maybe one of his "own") landed a blow with his rifle butt on Genezip's shinbone. The wicked pain made what was happening all the more absurd; at the same time it raised the level of savagery to almost sexual proportions (and, frankly, can there be any greater jolt than *that?*). No one knew anymore what, where, how, or why – particularly not this last. But once unleashed, the outbreak of animal rage and terror – terror before the enemy and before the grey specter of military discipline – drove them to a hideous killing rampage. "Ideas" were irrelevant, the stuff of staffs and secret committees, though even here, given the greyness of the age, their presence was rather dubious. If you can call ideas the sort of well-chewed pap spat out by one's ancestors – whitish, without taste or smell, having roughly the same texture as sawdust. But not a few people saw in these notions a way of hanging onto life's remaining "perks." It was for their sake that these fools were butchering each other on that wretched day, there on the streets of that comatose town marinating in its own juice.

The cadets had a colossal advantage over these fresh recruits. Two minutes into the fighting, a disorderly mob was seen fleeing down the street leading from the square to some vacant fields outside the town; behind them in hot pursuit, heady with their effortless triumph, came the "children of the Great Moloch." Genezip, limping badly, bravely brought up the rear. A moment ago, he had seen a noncom ram his rifle butt into Sump's skull. Even above the din of battle he heard the moist (not unlike the time before . . .) crack on that skull once so loyal to the general. In the space of forty-eight hours, two Sumps had perished practically in the same manner, though under quite different circumstances. He mused over the coincidence with a wild satisfaction secretly linked to his body's sexual catacombs, which in turn seemed to be buried even deeper in the earth, in the very navel of the universe. "The metaphysical monstrosity of existence": Abnol, Lilian, Persy. He was also one of that cartwheeling horde of zombies (no longer fantasies!) running in bestial pursuit of those poor foot soldiers. An ecstasy of willful brutality and evil: if only he could last out the day . . . But just as his wish was coming true, Genezip began to fret over his fate. Finally they had merged into one: this ghastly daybreak and that fateful afternoon at school. Only the music and the booze were missing – but even without the trimmings it was not a bad show. For a split second Kotzmolochowicz ceased to be his "commander-idol." So this was what his work looked like from up close! Thus was the superman, the dynamo-statue, toppled: an eccentric beast on a shattered pedestal, the remains of which lay scattered on that pathetic Dziemborowski Square. The wedding of incommensurabilities had taken place behind the commander's back, at the expense of his own aura. That shady slouch, once so fearful, turned out to be not such a bad fellow; not his enemy but a cunning ally – quite a bold cuss, too. A great deal more courageous, in fact, than the former cadet; a true officer. It was he who had taken command of his fretting body, organizing and marshaling his gutstrings into a uniform system; it was he who was unleashing that mechanism in pitiless pursuit of these sheep. For these minions of the syndicate were no ordinary people; they were sorry, deluded animals. Suddenly, from out of the cracks, the old Zip (the one who used to free dogs from their captivity) crawled forth like an earwig and whispered frantically something about "murdering his own people," "love," "little flowers"; about the spring that would never return; about the weird dreams he had dreamed before his awakening. But no one would listen to him anymore, and thus did he die, trampled to death by the soulless mob, by this herd of cadets giving chase, of which he himself was a small and unwilling part. Someone (Wołodyjowicz perhaps?) from the other side suddenly hollered, like that general in the story by Zola, in a thunderous, bull-like voice *(voix tonnante):*

"Against the wall, against the wall, you sons of whores!!" The retreating infantrymen scattered as, from the far end of a long street trailing off into the buff dawn, a series of scarlet flashes and a barrage of four explosions came rumbling toward them at a horrendous clip. It was as if a gigantic sheet of linen were being rent in the air, as though a behemothian mouth several yards wide was hissing and whistling the name of the philosopher Hume: "H-e-e-y-o-o-m, H-e-e-e-y-o-o-o-m!" Then came the sound of exploding shrapnel, but of another sort: metallic, flat, short, followed by a hail of bullets (the real thing this time) against the walls and windowpanes. "Friendly" artillery was brought up from the rear and positioned in the middle of the square. A duel of light artillery followed, as infantrymen on both sides, lying face down in the gutters and along the walks, took cover along the walls. At last! Something resembling a true battle! But somewhere, in some obscure compartment of the soul, the feeling of absurdity persisted. Above the rumbling and whistling and howling and clanging and banging that split the air, men were heard crying and groaning. On both sides the batteries kept up a ceaseless barrage. Genezip, prostrate and still unaware of the two pieces of shrapnel in his right calf, also kept up a steady fire. It was now daylight, everything ached with a mediocrity that was extraordinary in its limpidity. Three more barrages of "friendly" fire, followed by silence. Soon they heard the rumbling of artillery pieces: the enemy was pulling back into the side streets. Then, directly overhead, or so it seemed, just as all were sighing that "the worst was over," a barrage of shrapnel – heavy, long-range – exploded with an excruciating racket, spewing its discharge on the last of the reserves crawling along on all fours. A blast of hot gas descended on their heads with a leaden weight. Genezip could now feel the pain in his leg along with a strange numbness that had begun to spread through his body; his head felt light and weightless, as if hollow. Anxiety suddenly piped up in this void like a stupid, irritating, darling little bird. The tension and strain were making themselves felt as he made his way back to reality. Who would reward him for his anxiety? Nobody. In fact, he was probably in for a "dressing down" over some minor breach. More anxiety. Still, something had happened, something pretty serious. He tried to stand up; the right leg felt as if it was no longer his. A gargantuan leg, proportionate to the grandeur of (1) the explosion, (2) the forces at work, and (3) the historical moment *als soche*. His wound brought home the gravity of the situation, not only here, in this pint-sized country, but universally, perhaps even cosmically. The animal part of the battle was over; now began the period of sublimation – subjectively speaking, of course, only where Zip was concerned; for others this second phase did not exist. (Kotzmolochowicz, for example, had spent the time in bed with Persy, grudgingly picking up the telephone receiver whenever it rang. While he might call out, no one was allowed to call him. This skirmish was much too minor to warrant the attention of such a titan. He was saving his ganglia for a truly great confrontation, i.e., with that mobile Chinese Wall.) "All the same, I'm alive and wounded," thought Zip, fiendishly satisfied, a Zip now relieved of the problem of a dual personality, not recognizable either to his friends or to himself due to his estrangement; possibly a little more "virile" because of recent experiences, more "morally mature" (?); and, finally, a trifle more "serious" – ha, ha – though no one suspected, nor did anyone have reason to do so, that someone else lay on the ground, a person who only outwardly was continuous with Zip's ego – the corporeal rather than spiritual one – and, well, that it was just a *certain* officer who had fallen during the attack on Tom Foolery Street. He had again stumbled into the gutter (sewer?), aglow with the thought that he had done his duty, that he had acquitted himself. His previous life was vindicated, his crimes effaced (or defaced). Henceforth, life's every moment would have to be justified. Whoever chooses such a path must, if he or she is to balance dream and reality, either (a) perfect it, (b) become unredeemably corrupt, or (c) go mad. The death of that mysterious man with the beard was totally wiped from his memory and would remain so forever. Too minor an incident when measured by his new scale of experiences. If the murder had been committed by the old Zip, it might have been catastrophic, but as the work of his alter ego it amounted to little more than the crushing of a cockroach. "The pills! Oh, the pills! Now's the time! If I don't die from these wounds, I may live to see a new and wonderful life wherein the most random things, unspoiled by life's limitation, breathe with the world's infinity." Narcotics can sometimes work such wonders.

He gradually lost all sense of his ego. The sky – a glaring, dun-yellow, cloudy-drab, backwater sky – rocked back and forth in a broad arc, so distant as to seem endless, as only a starry firmament can appear in moments of extreme astronomical wonder. The houses, by contrast, momentarily rimmed the opening of some gargantuan cavern exposing the hollow, milky, ochre-hued hole of infinity, now manifestly real in its monotony and metaphysical humdrum, far beyond earth's partisan concerns. He lay there, stuck to the asphalt by some weak glue, hovering above an interminable pit. The sidewalk acted as the floor-ceiling of a cave suspended over this vacancy. Soft black flakes whirled in glittering circles – quietly, discreetly, ominously; one would have expected something more dramatic at that penultimate moment. All was draped in dark nausea, in an insufferable but obscure pain, in which his physical pain had vanished without a trace. It engulfed the All, and not only his body, to the brim, banishing to the bleak, dark extremities of the soul all of life's previous joys. It was beyond endurance. His consciousness was dimming on the top floor of perception where, at long last, all should have become clear, certain, comprehensible, like this unendurable "sort-of-pain" *(malaise)* spreading to the farthest reaches, the deepest corners, of the cosmos: "Maybe it's death – but, then, I only got it in the fucking leg . . . " This last thought was etched in mysterious and *nearly* incomprehensible signs, in an absolute void without name, thick with sulphurous vapor, a place unwelcome to the psyche. Punctured by a pinlike flash of consciousness ("this was the end . . . "), the void burst, and Genezip, overpowered by a profound lassitude (of the psycho-metaphysical-physical variety), temporarily ceased to exist.

The Final Metamorphosis

When he awoke he was lying in the school's white-walled infirmary, at the same time he was plummeting furiously downward, and these two contradictory sensations soon manifested themselves as an irrepressible urge to vomit. He bent over while someone held his head. Just before he vomited he recognized Eliza, the girl at the princess's first soirée. It was she who was holding that enormous, aching thing he had once called his head. She wore a nurse's uniform on which a huge cross bled between her albatrosslike breasts and abdomen. A keen embarrassment suddenly stifled all desire to vomit. But her hands kept his head bent over the bucket, and, profoundly humiliated, he did what he had to do, his face a deep shade of purple and bathed with sweat. So here was where his fate had brought him (he had no sensation in his leg, which had blossomed to the size of a furnace, which did not belong to him anymore, and which hurt so badly it was as if it hurt someone else – and yet there was this awful, awful pain . . .), that he might prostrate himself so vilely before this his only possible love, this third woman whom he had entirely forgotten: the one destined to be his wife. For he had decided, instantly and irrevocably, that he would marry her, even though he was sure that after this encounter – between an unshaven, puke-stained, flushed, and sweaty cadet and an angelically beautiful, sublimely soulful creature – marriage was forever precluded. This did not stop him from tendering, along with his vomit, as a prenuptial present, his own revolting and pathetic love, including his childish and gratuitous little crime – potentially, that is, for he was still unable to speak. Clearly, this was all the work of that subterranean cad, about whom neither he nor anyone else had a clue. May this be the last mention of him who henceforth would be the only one to reside in the mildly catatonic body of this magnificent bruiser.

He fell back onto the pillows – his head had become one unbearable spinning sensation – having been rescued by the salubrious hands of this woman from that bucket located somewhere in infinity. "To do it without the body; to be joined to another body without all this fucking scramble of intestines," thought Zip. Pure love had, at last, arrived – and at such a rotten time! Actually, it was all quite simple, inscrutably so; those who talk and write about it obsessively are only filling a void, that of their own talent, are only rehashing things, because all that *can* be said *has* been said long ago. This according to Sturfan Abnol. (He had also taken part in last night's action, but as an orderly in one of the many neutral hospitals organized by Djevani in the more strategic cities [how this swarthy devil foresaw the exact day and could set up his hospitals in time remained forever a mystery].)

The pain in his thigh and shinbone made him recall the battle in all its reality. Until now it had not been *his* to experience. The fact remained: he had stood and fought – true, nervously, but without cowardice; maybe he was officer material after all. He was so comforted, so reassured by this last thought, that he blurted out:

"Please don't. Thanks, anyway. I don't want you to nurse me. Why am I having these attacks of nausea? Tell them to send an older woman. I look awful now, but I'll shape up." Eliza's innocent and sexually chaste hand (so different from the hands of the other females he had known) caressed his clammy and perspiring brow, then his unshaven cheeks (whose "growth" was barely noticeable).

"In the name of Murti Bing and the telos of unity-in-duality, be still. I know that you are on the path to wisdom. You must have gone through horror. I know all. But things will get better, everything will work out. Right now you're suffering from shell shock, but it will pass. Bekhmetev is on his way here to consult with the local doctors."

A sudden delectable calm descended, from what seemed like "otherworldly parts," onto this mangled ball of shame, loathing, despair, disenchantment, onto this fleeting, flufflike, gossamer hope (this was by far the worst; outright despair would have been better) such as his body indeed was. His spirit had fled to distant, far-off places, withdrawn to some dark and secluded spot, and there was biding its time. (His execrable destiny gave him no rest. It was thrusting him into a cyclone of events without giving him time to reflect on or digest anything – a "furious but unproductive life," as it was called, the kind so eagerly courted by so many from that offal from which such flowers bloom. How could one *not* go insane given the circumstances?) Was this second brush with the new religion, the one now incarnated in Eliza, a sign? Was this the way out of that wicked tangle into which he had stumbled? A confirmation of his initial nocturnal encounter with the mystery of Murti Bing and that "unity at the limit"? Alongside such idiotic thoughts – by which we try to invest and embellish with an inferior quality of mystery the most banal coincidences and the consequences of actions performed by beings who consider life a chess game, something planned several moves at a time – alongside these thoughts there seethed, in some tiny kettle rescued from the last disaster, a nascent and perfectly insane affection for Eliza. An explosion, but in slow motion. He began sinking mentally into her like a crab, fortified by the knowledge that he could not be torn from her except by removing a chunk of her flesh. In this atmosphere so highly charged it threatened the ambient space, the poor lass, despite all her indoctrination in Murtibingian metaphysics, reeled from an unknown and uncontrollable urge to make love. She had no idea how it should be performed. That which seemed like an infusion of infinity, but was in fact such a simple, finite thing.

Wasn't he ashamed to fall in love a third time while still so fresh from his other (!) adventures? His first, that abortive affair with the princess, posed no obstacle now, nor did the second, with its unfortunate and frustrating end – to put it delicately. The ease with which he surrendered was shocking. These affairs were no sooner behind him than he was defenseless before a new calamity, one still more hypothetical than real. It was not that he lacked the will, but no sooner was it born in him than it escaped like liquid from a leaky pot, and the leak was that loathsome and conniving emotion consecrated by a crime – or, who knew, not emotion but . . . : *gadost'*. Lying there calmly with his eyes closed, holding his still-dirty soldier's paw in Eliza's "celestial" palm, few would have guessed that this noble young man was host to such a perfidious snake nest of contradictions. All that was evil in him rushed through that hand and journeyed straight to this she-monster's heart, which circulated it through her poison-absorbing glands, building a store of antidotes, or rather antibodies, for a rainy day. The wretch had no idea what lay in store for her, for, oddly, the religion and pills of Djevani, while giving temporary relief, while providing an instantaneous suppressant against the demands of the personality (what is evil if not an unruly personality?), had nonetheless killed in its disciples and sympathizers all intuition of the future, all capacity for marshaling life's individual moments into a long-range project. The result was a pulverization of the ego into discrete moments, a submission to any, even the most mechanical, tyranny. Not for nothing had the greatest chemical brains among the Chinese worked on the formula of Davamesque B_2 in order to isolate and combine the innocuous groups of C, H, O, and N into fantastic molecular structures. Just as the religion had sprung up from the little-known

Malayan island of Balampang, so, too, the means for its realization had been furnished by the "Celestial Empire" and a "consortium of bolshevized Mongolian princes and lords."

Genezip suddenly grew curious about his family, but was loath to inquire about them. Why? Very simply, he welcomed this disengagement from reality: the necessity of an "alibi"; his chat with Lilian; the theater; Persy; and God knew what else may have arisen. Sooner or later it must end, anyway. Oh, to drift like this forever, with a head like a pumpkin, and, yes, to go on vomiting for an eternity – in a universe void of all except that bucket. To live in continual indecision; in *a continuous and endless intentionality,* in a world of promise: here was the way to fullness and plenitude. And what about the coup? The answer was obvious: the general had triumphed. She had guessed his thoughts and nodded in the affirmative. If only it were a triumph on behalf of some idea; of something worthy of belief, beyond oneself, beyond the perfunctory functions imposed by the irrevocable fact of existence – functions ranging from the purely physiological to those of a more sociomilitary kind – it might have been a joyful affair. Alas, there are lucky stiffs who can find justification for their lives in any sort of action, and then there are the eternal exiles, not of a country or social group, not even of humanity itself, but those Sturfan Abnol used to call "the world's exiled lot." We are not speaking of those who by sheer accident are dislocated, but of the *déveineurs,* the "born losers" for whom there will never be a place or a chance, not even in some vastly superior (or *inferior*) cultures hatched by weird creatures from other galaxies. Once upon a time they made up the religious founders, great artists, occasionally even thinkers; today they are all quite bonkers, or suffer terribly their whole superfluous lives long because they don't even know how to go properly insane. Luckily, they are growing fewer in number. Then he was struck by a single, solitary, third-rate little thought: there must have been at least a grain of sense in all this if (a) he had met a Hindu, (b) he was still alive, (c) he had met HER, and (d) she, too, believed in Murti Bing. He tried not to think about it: every effort brought more dizzy spells and vomiting. He started heaving again, his sweaty brow supported by her benevolent hands, soft as flower petals. But this time he did it freely, naturally, without the slightest trace of humiliation.

....

INFORMATION: The attacks were not so much the result of shell shock as of morphine poisoning, a fact later confirmed by the ingenious Bekhmetev.

He said to himself: "Come what may, I obey my destiny." He lay there without moving. It was one of those moments of genuine contentment he had never known before – the complete isolation of the naked ego, a sensation not unlike losing consciousness during anesthesia: freedom, timelessness, the "ideal world of ideas," but experienced in reality – and yet it was still him, Genezip Kapen, identical to himself, seemingly immutable, beyond all the contingencies of temporal affairs. Carried a step further, he might have reached nirvana: a "fusion with the duo-unity" à la Murti Bing.

....

INFORMATION: Murtibingism did not profess metempsychosis or posit a hierarchy or gradation of "planes"; instead, there were merely different ways (rather than degrees) of being dissolved in this unity here, in the only form of existence possible, that governed by time and space. Its superiority over other "theosauces" (as Kotzmolochowicz called them) lay in the fact that it offered no "payback" on some other "plane"; everything had to be done here, otherwise the manner of that "coalescing with the unity" could have been so nasty it made one's flesh creep to contemplate it. This was not lost on those who had taken a dose (as a rule, only one was necessary) of the wicked pills being distributed by the Supreme Chemical Council of the Celestial Empire, headed by the immortal Chang-Wei. The pills gave them a foretaste of what ultimately (time did not figure in their calculations – how, no one could say, though this by no means implied a belief in eternity) they would have to endure if they wished to be spared the tyranny of a living death, i.e., the total mechanization of life's manifold functions, which was held to be a minor irritation comparable to shortness of breath, indigestion, nausea, and heartburn when each of these four elements is raised to the infinite power.

Eliza continued to hold Zip's hand: she had become his umbilical cord to the rest of the world. Here was true love at last; a "lover" to shield him from treacherous entanglements, to forge for him a suit of armor capable of insulating him from existence, dying in him as another ego and becoming a mere symbol of absolute solitude. Of course, what he (or rather that "gent from below") took to be real love was vastly different from what is normally understood by love; in a personality as overcrowded as his, there was barely room – not only for admitting someone "internally" or for a "caring solicitude" in the broadest possible sense, but for brute recognition of the fact that a psychic entity other than his own might actually exist. Not to mention any capacity for self-sacrifice, or a willingness to reform one's personal habits to please another! He was a true vampire without knowing it; yet, if he was totally unaware of the possibility of another ego, it was through this very "otherness," through this absolute opposition (in this case, his "craving for a victim"), that he instinctively grasped his own existence – not so much consciously or with premeditation but through his body's system of cells organized with all the rigor of a specialized machine. To others he might appear "good," he might even come to see himself as such, but as Kretschmer says: "*Hinter dieser glänzenden Fassade waren schon nur Ruinen.*" In this gloomy world of a disintegrating personality, Eliza's soul was to wander till doomsday, in some otherworldly hell born of the perverse accident of just such a body and just such a lovely, boyish face: eternally unsatisfied, a woman-victim burning with unquenchable desire for the absolute fuck – a prospect Zip feared inasmuch as it would have put him face to face with reality, the very thing he loathed. He would suck her blood through a tube like a mosquito – and thus find happiness in life. Thoroughly ignorant of such psychological complications, they fell in love like a couple of "turtledoves," like one of those banal little couples at the end of a fairy tale when "all live happily ever after."

Suddenly, just when it seemed that ugly reality had been banished to the farthest outpost of this empty and perfectly senseless world, a ferocious insatiability (that absolutely nothing would appease), the bane of all those caught in the initial stages of schizophrenia, grabbed him from below. He let out a groan and tensed his muscles until he felt like a bridge suspended above a canyon, as though his navel were rubbing the very "nadir" itself buried somewhere in infinity.

"What day is today?"

"Tuesday. You've been unconscious for two days."

"I'd like to see a newspaper."

"It's too early."

"I've got to." She stood up and a moment later returned with one. As she handed it to him, she said:

"I was in love with you that night at the Ticonderogas'; I knew you'd come back to me."

"That night . . . ?"

"Yes; I was already a convert then."

He started reading, but his head swam. At times he caught a glimpse of her embodied in the print and in the events described by this print. It had happened again, and this time for real, on some drawing-board surface beyond our own stratosphere, out there in the fuzzy realm of nothingness (which he had briefly visited before losing consciousness during the street battle), which somehow commenced from a point in the Ludzimierz hills. His whole life lay rolled out like a piece of dough. Who if not he was to make ravioli out of this dough? But what to fill them with if nothing existed except this dough? And how much filling, how much?! God, what a stupendous, superhuman task! He puked again and went on. The account of the battle on Dziemborowski Square disturbed him most of all. He had a spectator's view of himself caught up in that disgusting "operation"; he relived that moment of absolute absurdity – but without the urge to justify it, without the same enthusiasm, which nothing could justify. Yes, Irina Vsevolodovna had been right: it was lunacy born of the poverty of ideas. Cavalry marches were not a substitute, nor was the savage, youthful, horse-soldierly power radiating from the general's black eyeballs and testicles. The

scientific management of labor and the regulation of production were not ideas in any real sense of the word. But no others existed, nor would they ever exist – except for the bunkum found in decadent religions like that of Murti Bing. Full stop.

On the last page of yesterday's edition of *The Watchdog* he found the following notice: "*A Bloody Reprisal.* In an apartment belonging to the well-known actress from Quintofron Crepuscolo's theater, Miss P. B., a subtenant of the above-named, Colonel Michael Sump, a former Air Force pilot and chief of staff under Quartermaster General Kotzmolochowicz, was slain by an unknown assailant by means of a blow on the head from an upholstery hammer. Mr. Sump was living incognito in C. while on special assignment for the Ministry of War. Tests have yet to turn up any fingerprints, as the wary suspect took the precaution of wearing gloves." ("Hee, hee – 'wary suspect'!" He had simply forgotten to remove his gloves. What disgusting journalism! It was his first "press." Who was it who said? . . . ah yes, Tenzer: "A man with no clippings is a zero. Show me your clippings and I'll tell you who you are." "Well, now I have one – the first and probably the last." He chuckled and went on reading.) "The victim of this tragic incident unfortunately had a great many acquaintances, recruited from the lowest elements of the local population known to congregate at the Café Euphoria, a notorious hangout for local and out-of-town homosexuals. Apart from the victim, the apartment was empty, for on that same evening Miss B. had left town with her housekeeper on a night express to the capital." "So the whole thing had been planned ahead of time! The bawd!" His humiliation and self-hatred now reached unbearable proportions. He would have to make a full confession or it would choke him to death like a clump of worms rising up in his gullet. He tore his right hand out of Eliza's and crumpled the newspaper into a ball.

"I told you it was unwise . . . "

"It was I – I who did it . . . "

He unfolded the crumpled issue of *The Watchdog* and showed her the disastrous clipping. It was like an instant replay: the battle, his show of courage, courage itself, and honor. He watched her face through his hands while she read. She did not bat an eyelash. Then she calmly folded the newspaper and said:

"Why, though?"

"I loved her, but believe me, not in the way I love you. It was ghastly. The creep came barging in after she slipped out. Don't you see, Eliza?" (He called her by her first name without realizing it.) "The whole thing was a setup. I dirtied my hands. And to think that I loved her! Not the same way, but even so . . . " (He was incapable of deceiving her.) "But it wasn't from jealousy. He wasn't her lover. Impossible. I don't love her anymore, but there's some godawful thing inside me, I don't understand it . . . "

"Relax. She was your commander's mistress. He had to have her around, but not all the time – too enervating. So she used to visit him once a month. After crushing the revolt he had to have her immediately or go berserk." Coming from her (HER!) mouth, these words and the manner in which they were spoken were the height of perversion. But he sensed at once that they were not her words, that someone was prompting her, that she was only parroting them. All the same, a dam had burst; at last the sensual image of Eliza became wedded to pure love. He desired her more ardently than he had ever desired the princess or Persy, more than all the world's women multiplied to infinity, but somehow differently . . . How to explain this difference? Possibly those other women (including the princess, whose only handicap was her age) had loomed as powers not to be conquered or annihilated. Yes, annihilated – that was the only solution; Eliza, too, he could have liquidated like a wild animal, even though he found her the most alluring of the three. Or maybe *because* he loved her – and had done so even before he had fallen for her. But by loving her did he not also wish to devour her? Actually, it was his old dream of isolating himself from the world, but pushed to the extreme: he would isolate himself by devouring and destroying – it was as simple as that. Naturally, Zip was not aware of this need, and Eliza even less so. Still, love raised his desire to an inhuman level. If only he was not nagged by a disgust (over what?) so faint and yet so profound that only death (whose?) could have drowned it.

The news came as a devastating blow.

 "Kotzmolochowicz?" he stammered, still in a state of disbelief, still reeling from the changes transpiring on the rear screen of his consciousness.

"Yes," Eliza answered calmly. "Anyhow, it's all for the better." How did she know what lay ahead for him, dammit?! How could this naive kid possibly have known that it was "for the better"? From Murti Bing, no doubt . . . The last internal light beam had faded, snuffed out by the dark paw from a childhood dream. At last the music had stopped – one of Karol Szymanowski's rousing marches played on the commander's visit to the school. So it was he – that infernal titan, that most enigmatic man of our times, that not so much apocalyptic as "apoplectic brute," as he was called by his secret enemies – who had deprived him of her. He felt somehow flattered, even though the luminous past was now irrevocably extinguished; behind Zip stretched a dark night of dead guilt, dead angst. But that is what made it so perfect, for, clearly, in this way his *whole* past was annulled by this love, absorbed like a sponge. There was only one minor hitch: he could never draw on that past again. Enough. Eliza, as the one who had brought this news from a world now defunct, gradually began to assume astronomical proportions (in the spiritual sense), to flood his battered horizon with a mild and milky sauce, to soak up the general monstrosity of life. Now was her quarry ripe, like a rabbit carefully covered with saliva by an anaconda, for devouring. Abnormal and dangerous, yes (this psychological clinging to another being), but delectable all the same. All chance for a normal life had been kicked out from under him like a stool from a hangman. With head lowered, he was sinking, without even a farewell glance at the irretrievable stars glittering on the far shore, into the quagmire of madness: *"Polzushchaya forma skhizofrenii,"* Bekhmetev would have called it.

"How do you know?"

"From my master, Lambdon Tiger, second in authority after the Supreme Master, Djevani. You'll meet him. He'll teach you how to bear life's adversity. Then you'll feel right about me and about the Mystery of Maximal Oneness."

"Your master must have better spies than our own."

"Not so loud." She clasped his mouth with her hand. Zip shut his eyes and froze. "You'll meet him, but only after our wedding night. Or maybe sooner. It has to happen, and you must believe it." The girl spoke so solemnly that Genezip almost roared with laughter, which of course would have been a gross impropriety. But even *that* would have been forgiven. Inexhaustible was the patience exercised by the disciples of Djevani. Murtibingism, all that business about "maximal unity": what crap, what lifeless drivel – *Begriffsmumien*, as Nietzsche used to say.

"Didn't your know-it-all friend tell you it was me? . . . "

"Evidently he wanted you to confess it to me yourself."

Zip then told her about his brush with the mysterious Hindu on the night of the crime. Eliza was unfazed. Her deadpan response to minor bombshells was starting to grate. But there was something sexually exciting about it. It aroused in him an animal fury that fused indissolubly (yes!) with this – quite new for him – feeling of "affection" (why are we so stuck for synonyms here?). More: he was sure that he would never tire of her, never tolerate the sight of other women. "In any event," he squeezed her hand as a sign of eternal assent. Suddenly he was reduced to a mass of chilling pain, an almost metaphysical terror: What if he should never live to see their wedding night, if he should die with a guilty conscience? Again his life seemed not his own but at the mercy of others, of some awful people who were eavesdropping on his most private thoughts, pretending to be omniscient, they who dabbled in pure rubbish, or did they only make it appear so for the benefit of the masses – as a form of enticement? Was the general also in their clutches, or was he exploiting *them* for his own inscrutable aims? Suddenly a pride overcame him that he, a would-be officer, was of such concern to such a powerful organization as the followers of Murti Bing – bigshits, really, in their own way. They at least were engaging the real world, not running away from it like Prince Basil. (His visit to the prince's retreat in the forest, along with his whole Ludzimierz past, now belonged to someone else's biography. Not a trace was left of the adolescent – he could feel the loss; for a split second he was *not*, being at the border of two personalities. That sly gent, jailed in his interior by his father, was now he, and it was that Zip who loved Eliza; the other Zip was dead to such emotions. But if the old Zip had fallen in love with her, he might have known a "fairy-tale happiness" others only dream about. If only one could control the personality shifts! But no, everything comes either too late or too soon. It was for Eliza's sake [and indirectly for the sake of Bing's followers] that he was being urged to sanctify his [that gent's] existence in another, more worthwhile dimension.) Provided, of course, that the sect was not just a blind tool in the hands of a still more powerful Mafia, which in turn was using it for its own nefarious and criminal aims. Still – it was nice to belong to something; how much nicer, then, to belong to such a secret fraternity. Genezip was sure that alone – if he had been marooned, say, on some desert island – he would have been nothing. He was a force whose control lay outside him. He thought: "I must be the plaything of mysterious powers incarnated in others. But was not everyone, despite the illusion of freedom, a toy? A tool of higher, universal forces, i.e., of economic laws that have taken the place of ideas? Historical materialism is not an eternal verity; *it began to pose as one* starting around the eighteenth century. See what sort of life was begot by that social behemoth! And we are all its puppets – including the greatest personalities of our times." Thoroughly depressed, he collapsed into a near state of delectable unconsciousness.

She waited. She had time. All the disciples of Murti Bing – not only young girls but greybeards, too, already wasted by the fever of the times and by sybaritic excesses from before their conversion – had, and still have, time. Hurrying was something foreign to them. (Hence that remarkable tranquillity that spread [literally, like grease] over converts immediately after the moment of revelation. As to what really happened during that moment of revelation, no one could say. Later, even Zip, for all his determination, missed the most crucial moment. Or was that gent [i.e, he himself] merely shamming conversion? Because, judging by what occurred later – but more on that presently.) Because of the "asymptotic convergence of oneness within twoness," there was no need to hurry. The moments passed – white, ethereal, sublime, but only for Eliza. Genezip was not yet sensitive to this sublimity; in him a struggle between two worlds was being waged: between a blackhearted scoundrel and the blissful nothingness of future centuries. A futile struggle it was, too; for, given the tenor of the times, the individual was bound to surrender (all except Kotzmolochowicz, perhaps, though even this was doubtful; history would have something to say on that score, even if he was unaware of it as yet). Individualists of a certain breed might appear from time to time, but only in the form of madmen. There are, of course, madmen who at a given phase and in a given social milieu might be treated as sane, but who in a different epoch and milieu could not help but be madmen; and then there are those unqualified madmen who would be outcasts in any milieu. Zip belonged to the former category.

Again (for the umpteenth time) she took his hand. Each time she was luring him (like an animal being tracked through the forest) more and more to the side of a gentle and soporific absurdity where her nature could reveal itself in a "magnificent bouquet of feminine virtues." But for the fanatics, life-warriors, would-be artists, madmen, for statesmen, and in general for all transformers of reality, such bunk can act as a lethal poison with multiple effects, depending on the configuration of one's soul. On some it might have a narcotic effect; others – i.e., madmen – might be transported to visionary heights having no equivalent in life. "So, she knows, and she's a disciple of his." This last pronoun referred to someone occupying a place somewhere between that mysterious Hindu and Murti Bing, someone on whom one could push all responsibility for everything. Again the glow of supreme grace brushed the crowns of his soul mired in the nocturnal gloom of crime and insanity. Or was it all delirium? Only those as steeped in their insanity as in the air they breathed could treat their feelings as normal; in reality, that air was a toxic gas which not even the Chinese masters of chemistry would have been ashamed of. If only such illnesses were contagious – but perish the thought! Waves of a nearly unconscious but powerful anguish rippled through the limp body of the former Zip – a body gutted by the fire of doubt. The time would come when cases like his would be treated as "stories for naughty children," insofar as such children would exist.

The sudden crash of a door being flung open announced a doctor's visit. But her hand (was there really nothing but this hand, dammit? That hand, that hand, nothing but her hand; for the time being the whole universe was concentrated in it) didn't twitch, not even at the frightful commotion made by the sovereigns of the ward as they burst in without knocking. The great Bekhmetev, surrounded by the head doctor and a swarm of assistants, made a tumultuous entrance. All necks craned toward this group of potentates in white uniforms (some fifty wounded lay in Zip's ward). Zip and Eliza nearly lost sight of them. A second later Eliza got up and walked away in a calm and self-assured manner, as if to say, "I'll be right back." It may have been the most delectable moment of his life: this feeling of certitude, this trust unbounded. If only he had known! So many glorious moments squandered because one could not tell which was the most glorious!

The celebrated soul expert strode up to Zip's bed with the step of a mean-tempered lion. The others stopped and snapped to "medical attention." Meanwhile, Bekhmetev affixed something to his eyes, closing one and then the other with a hand that reeked of cigars, chypre, and sweat; then he tapped here and there, outlined something on Zip's skin, scratched, tweaked, and tickled. At last, he asked:

"Do you sometimes have the feeling that it's all a cheat? That everything is right, yet not right? As if things were all wrong? Eh?" And with his all-knowing, nut-brown eyes he transfixed Zip to his psychic marrow. *"Dusha skhizotimika v tele tsiklotimika,"* he thought even before his victim had answered.

"Yes," was the quiet answer of the intimidated patient. This ruthless "mind-picker" was even better than Eliza at divorcing him from the world. Zip felt as though placed under a bell glass, surrounded by a billion-mile void. "Nearly all the time. But there's someone inside me – "

"I know – that stranger. Has he been there – "

"Since the battle," he broke in, daring to interrupt *such* an authority.

"And before that?" asked Bekhmetev, and this question flooded Zip's soul like molten lead. The Evil One rose up in arms. "Is there another subterranean level?" Zip wondered. "When will I hit bottom?" A black and empty abyss opened up in him – a real (i.e., free of literary hyperbole) abyss, pierced by the fearful, nut-brown eyes bulging from that blonde-bearded face, from that archbestial skull, like stakes in a wolf pit. One false move and he might impale himself. "Admit nothing," a voice whispered. "Even HE can be fooled."

"No," he said quietly, but firmly. "I never felt anything like it before the battle." The golden, nut-brown stars dimmed, but from their slight eclipse Zip knew that he knew everything – not the actual facts, but their essence, their abstract extract, and not from Djevani's spies but on his own, from his own spiritual power. He bowed before this true connoisseur of souls. He was willing to be dissected, firmly convinced that at his command he could have been made whole beyond the pale of time. (What? Who said so?) "The oneness of spirit and flesh. Beyond the periphery of time" – so had Eliza spoken a moment ago. Through her he was assimilating the thoughts of Murti Bing's followers.

But the great psychiatrist was showing a discretion commensurate with his greatness, that of the timeless, unconventional sort. He withdrew a step, and Zip heard him say to the school's head doctor:

"On vsegda byl nemnozhko sumasshedshy, no eta kontuziya emu zdorovo podbavila." So he was mad, then; this was as interesting as it was terrifying. But at least the shell shock was real! This news brought inexplicable relief. Only later, much later, would he discover that the pronouncement of temporary insanity had opened a credit account for the wildest acts imaginable, providing him at least with an internal alibi and, more importantly, with an aura of innocence.

They left. Eliza again (!) took his hand, and he collapsed in an aimless glow. He was through vomiting. A blissful nothing. Sleep.

He was awakened by the princess. He hardly recognized her. Her face beamed with a mysterious ardor. She traversed the hall like a bird, superterrestrial, pure, exalted. Eliza calmly rose to meet her. They pressed hands warmly. Genezip, dazzled by this unexpected good fortune, stared at the two women. It was a miracle that they should have taken so well to one another, that their first meeting should have been so cordial, that they should have exchanged glances like a couple of angelic sisters.

They ignored him (he was not the least bit offended); they were so spiritually exalted, so transported to another dimension (Eliza, in fact continually found herself in such a state, now raised to the *n*th degree) . . . Was it possible that they had sexual organs, that they urinated and defecated like others? Neither of them spoke; it was plain that this was their first meeting, that they had not met during the time Zip had lain unconscious. Having consumed Eliza with her gaze, the princess turned to her former pupil (her whole bearing, ever since entering the ward, bespoke a sense of "formerness") and gave him her hand, which he kissed with unusual respect. He was aware of it himself; the act was intensely gratifying. Incredulous, Zip saw before him that poisoner from out of the not-too-distant past, who, it appears, had infected his soul with a sick love. So, the "matronization" of Irina, which Marquis de Scampi had predicted, had come about – finally and naturally, thanks to Murtibingism. The princess had fought on what was known as the "Barricade of the Bees" immediately adjacent to Dziemborowski Square – on the side of the syndicate, of course – and they had almost met during the attack. She had escaped injury. But the battle and a tete-à-tete with Djevani (and, oh yes, the pills) had done the trick.

At the moment, Zip was numb to her poison: it had penetrated him too deeply. He would not realize how deeply until later. Neither Eliza nor Persy were what they might have been had he met them earlier, before he was introduced to love from the "darker side," in a version as demonic as that served up by this deteriorating ex-demon. Only a perverse streak inspired by the princess had allowed him to endure, until the final release, Persy's morbid insatiety; his latest shift compelled him to seek insulation from life in Eliza's troubled, bewildered little soul, in whose vapors one could dissolve without losing the illusion of life, thus permitting a momentary escape from catatonia. The poison continued to circulate slyly in his psychic arteries; this was the stuff presently nourishing and sustaining the dark tumor-gent, the author of that first senseless crime, who was looming steadily larger in Zip.

The princess began to speak as if reciting a prepared speech. But during the recitation of it something got tangled up inside her;

through repressed tears came words unfamiliar to her and which caused even her to be astonished as she listened to them being uttered.

"It's over between us, Zip." Here she injected one of her hysterical laughs. Even Zip had to laugh, but briefly, laconically. Eliza looked on with curiously rounded eyes, but without a trace of bewilderment. The princess spoke now with unaccustomed gravity: "You can love her; I'm not blind. As soon as I found out that she was a nurse in the school, I knew right away what would happen. I am wiser now. Murti Bing has enlightened me through Master Djevani." ("This Djevani is a real sickness – is this how they're going to get control of everyone?" wondered Zip.)

He asked bluntly: "Have you been taking the pills, princess?"

"Yes, but that's beside the point . . . "

"I have nine of them, and I plan on swallowing them today. I'm fed up with all this crap."

"Don't take them prematurely, not before you've arrived at the first stage of ethereal grace . . . "

"He's already arrived," Eliza whispered.

"Otherwise, it's disaster. But maybe because you knew me you'll escape harm. One day you'll appreciate what I've given you, provided you grow old, something I wish both of you. Djevani has relieved me of the burden of my body. What I saw after taking the pills and after the battle only confirmed in me the Unique Truth. I am now embarked on the arduous path to perfection, and I shall persevere." ("A consolation fit for losers and old hags," thought Genezip, but he made no reply.) "I loved you then, and I love you still" (there were tears in her voice, deep down, gurgling like an underground spring), "but I don't wish to defile our relationship, and so I relinquish all claims to you – actually I did so long ago, even before I knew she was here at your side. Forgive me for poisoning you." She fell to her knees beside the bed and burst out sobbing – only for a short while, however, a very short while, for as long as was necessary. Neither Genezip nor Eliza had the faintest idea what was going on, nor did they have the nerve to ask. The poor wretch was referring to the dose of cocaine she had slipped him at their last meeting. She sat down again and, through tears so thick they might have been resin or syrup, said: "You have no idea what a joy it is to transcend yourself, especially for one as maltreated, externally and internally, as I. You know, after one session with the master, I am a changed woman."

Eliza: How lucky you were, Auntie, to talk with him . . .

Zip: The master only has time for big fish, apparently. We'll have to content ourselves with Lambdon. Better him than nothing, I suppose. *Bone pour en sheeyen eh la moosh* (Genezip said willfully, viciously).

Something had riled him. Eliza was staring at him without reproach, and this excited him so much that, if not for the pain in his thigh, he might have raped her in front of everyone. Or maybe because of the pain, as one might demolish a chair. But lust was immediately drowned in pure love. It expired with a hiss, exploding somewhere in the dark regions of his body like a distant meteor. The princess rambled on:

"As far as I'm concerned, the syndicate is defunct. How petty and shallow is a nationalism not founded on genuine sentiment." (Zip thought: "Just as I expected. So the pills can affect one's political thinking, too. Ho, ho! Can't wait to see what effect they have on me!") "Mankind will become one, universally the same, yet the mass will not impede man's inner progress, no, he'll be sheltered from himself like a jewel in a jewel box. They say the Chinese neo-Buddhists abandoned the concept of the personality from the start; not so, the disciples of Murti Bing." She spoke inelegantly, naively, but not that anyone cared in those days. "Matronization" was enveloping her in the solemn robe of atonement; it almost lent her a touch of the sacred. The purely formal, aesthetic satisfaction of seeing the old whore come to such an end was so great that there was not a single verbal or conceptual "howler" she might not have been forgiven. But Zip was not in the mood for conversation, any more than a serious intellectual will join in frivolous conversation at some tedious reception. Still, he had to say something.

"Unfortunately, I find that very hard to believe. The individual is expiring so gradually, so imperceptibly, as to not feel the painful effects of that process. A few people may still suffer the material effects of social dislocation, but in a few decades such problems will vanish." That all his miseries sprang *indirectly* from a profound social dislocation was totally lost on him. No one need be conscious of such dependencies for them to exist. It's enough if *someone* correlates certain effects with social transformations. This will suffice the future historian.

The princess: Zip, you probably think that I'm doing this from cowardice, that I was searching for a compensation and that I grabbed the first palliative to come along. But that's where you're mistaken . . .

Zip: I never thought any such thing . . . (Those had been exactly his thoughts.)

The princess: That's good, because it's simply not so. Not until Djevani did I grasp what I could never admit to myself: that it had to end between us, for your sake. Before that, you know, I would have fought with him against you.

Suddenly she broke into tears, this time in earnest. But her tears bespoke no regret or self-pity concerning the irretrievable past; only exultation at having risen *above* the past, that mire of humiliation, doubt, and an artificially sustained faith in her own physical indestructibility. "I even thought, 'How nice if he killed me in battle, so nice . . . ' How sorry I am that it didn't turn out that way." Genezip was writhing. The poor girl was still fighting. If she had been killed, he would never, but never, have forgiven himself. Now that he was relieved of the physical burden of this woman's love, he could assess how much he had loved this perverse – but sensuously fine – old tramp (and still loved, perhaps more so than at the beginning). In his present tangle of emotions he vaguely sensed what he would be grateful to her for. Time permitting, he would know its true value, so long as antibodies could be found to take the place of her poison. This intuition was prompted by the following shabby thought: "What if I hadn't found in this one an antidote against Persy? Would I have come away with so few losses – one colonel, a bout of lunacy, and only 'love's labor lost'?" Genezip suffered delectably to see Irina Vsevolodovna's tear-stained face. The prevailing mood had become wonderfully exalted, and the princess had been one of the factors in the general equation. Eliza feebly tried to console her, yet the effect was quite noticeable. A moment later the princess smiled through her tears. She looked so beautiful with her mixed expression of joy and suffering that Genezip's whole body quivered with the strangest emotions that, any moment now, might have turned decidedly and uniformly sexual. To make matters worse, he was visited by his family – his mother, Michalski, Lilian, and Sturfan Abnol – and was immediately subjected to the usual domestic doting. Lilian stared at Zip with her all-knowing eyes. He felt sure about her, which was fiendishly satisfying. He knew that she adored him, even more than those other two did, and he was insanely glad that Lilian had in her possession that secret of his, which no one, not even Abnol, would ever learn. And then there was his mother . . . At last he was in the zenith of his happiness. The crime he had committed became suffused with this cluster of feminine feelings; it figured into his relationship with Lilian and Eliza, compounding his joy. There was simply no room for a guilty conscience. (Perhaps if he had been on more intimate terms with the victim . . . But as it was? Well, you can hardly expect any remorse from someone who kills a man a moment after being introduced to him. Nonsense. Such experiences are rare, and the masses ought to be the last to judge such cases.) The order had been given, making it official: he was now an officer, promoted in the field, not while in command of a fighting regiment but in a lousy shootout. Promotion was still a week away (tactical exercises had been scheduled for this week), but the recent battle was deemed to have been a sufficient test and the cadets were to be awarded the rank of second lieutenant, or *kornet,* to use the Russian term favored by the general. Even the debacle with Persy disappeared in the sherbet of contentment, which Zip lapped up with the ample proboscis of his newly acquired roguish personality. When everyone had gone home, Eliza gave him ten pills of Davamesque B_2 – the same pills he had been given that time on the street – from her rather ample supply. He fell into a deep sleep, thinking to himself: "I wonder whether I'll turn pussy-headed like all the others."

He awoke at two in the morning with a weird sensation. He no longer lay in the school hospital, and, although he was without pain, his legs felt as though they were paralyzed. A dark, thick curtain seemed to flutter before his eyes. He was mortified that he had lost his vision. He gazed over at the windows, which even on the darkest night shone red. Nothing – darkness, absolute and restless. Something writhed, much as if the ponderous bodies of terrifying reptiles had locked in battle in the impenetrable penumbra. At the same time he was visited by an absolute calm – the calm was normal, apparently. He lay scarcely conscious of who he was; he had transcended himself, was peering down into himself as though into mysterious caverns where something unknown was being fashioned. Till suddenly the billowing curtain exploded and he was showered with brilliant sparks. From the sparks strange and recondite objects began to form and to compete with one another: weird combinations of machines and insects, avatars of objective nonsense in greyish brown, yellow, and violet, embodied in a queer matter and constructed with a hellish precision. Suddenly the shower stopped, and Zip realized that this was *a three-dimensional curtain* of a higher order, concealing another world in another space. A distinct and three-dimensional image, but *where,* in what continuum? And later, though able to summon the images, he could never fully reconstruct this remarkable impression in all its immediacy and freshness, being left with only comparisons: its essence eluded man's normal senses and spatial sense generally. It began with relatively common things, whose sense was confided to Zip by a secret internal voice. He listened to this voice not with his ears but with his belly. Hence: a tiny island in a spherical ocean – like a miniature planet viewed from an enormous distance, through eyes that were thousands of miles wide. But such measures were out of place. Here distance was not distance but rather the sensation of a spiraling point, which his head, elongating itself, had become in order to reach the *ceiling of the world* beyond infinity.

These were the words he later used when trying to describe his impressions to Eliza. But they failed to convey even a fraction of the elusive wonder inspired by the scrambling of all planes bordering on space-less-ness. (Eliza merely nodded indulgently her small blonde head: Zip's visions paled beside her own. "Each of us has the visions he deserves – but for you, for your gloomy little soul, these will do." His inferiority only enhanced the insane desire he felt for her; nothing, not the most savage rape, could have destroyed the distance separating him from her: she was, in a way, untouchable. And it was precisely this invulnerability that was conveyed by the irritating calm with which she responded to the most startling events.) Suddenly Zip beheld an endless path, which turned out to be a large-toothed snake crawling into the boundless distance. He was standing on its back and being transported as on an escalator. All this was happening on the tiny island. Someone inside him said: "This is Balampang; in a moment you shall behold the Light of Lights, the only person to merge with the Maximal Oneness during his lifetime." The serpent came to an end (it had lasted an eternity; in general, time seemed willfully distorted, depending on the type of experience consuming it), and at last Zip saw *the thing* itself – that which those lucky enough to have tried Davamesque B_2 have seen: a tiny hut in the middle of a low and arid jungle (purple flowers swayed before his nose, and he could hear the song of a little bird that kept repeating, by way of a warning, the same melody in sequences of three, as if to say: "Don't go near there, don't go near there . . . "). Squatting before the hut was an old man with a café au lait complexion. His enormous, black, and shiny eyes shot furtively around, while a young priest (shaved head, yellow robe) fed him from a bowl of rice with a wooden spoon. Instead of arms (and this Zip noticed only *later*), the old man had sticking out of his shoulders a pair of gigantic amaranthine wings, which he would flap from time to time like a bored vulture in a cage. "So he does exist, he does exist," Genezip whispered ecstatically. "I see him and believe in him; I believe in him forever. This is the truth." What was the truth? He couldn't say. *Anything shown to him in the name of Murti Bing had necessarily to be the truth.* All this in the same enigmatic space which, while not ceasing to be our own normal, three-dimensional, and even *concave* space, was not contained in our universe. Where *was* it taking place, then? Just as he was about to find out, the old man transfixed him with his eyes. Zip felt an inner refulgence; he was a beam speeding through the infinite void toward a crystalline creature (not really a creature; hell only knew what) iridescent with unknown colors, which turned out to be the eternally untrappable Maximal Duo-Unity. The vision vanished;

again confusion, the same diabolical curtain of *invisible,* writhing reptiles. And he saw his entire life, but as though engulfed in flame: deficient, riddled with gaps of appalling darkness in which some mysterious fellow (the same as before, only wearing Murti Bing's expression) was performing amazing feats, now expanding to nearly unlimited proportions, now shrinking to something imperceptible and microscopically small, that something being *the world's very intestines* – which was, in fact, a pile of improbable guts heaving in an erotic trance: the agitation of impersonal sex organs. This was his life, but now viewed with a critical eye from the vantage point of a higher – that is, not-of-the-human – purpose: its aims lay beyond this world (in that mysterious spatial realm?), but *this* life still had to be measured by them, otherwise the world's potential would be diminished, even reduced to zero, in which case (O, horrors!) not only would a Non-Spatial Nothingness exist – something inconceivable – but also *everything that had already been would be canceled out,* and this would imply that *nothing had ever existed or ever could exist.* The prospect of this vacancy inspired incalculable horror. Hence that zealous obedience shown by the followers of Murti Bing. Self-annulment, cancellation of the past? How was that possible? Yet under the influence of Davamesque B_2 such things were grasped as readily as the theory of functions.

Zip had revisited his entire life and vowed to reform it. His crime appeared in this retrospective version as the coupling of two crystalline powers in the land of Eternal Fire. The colonel's existence had become his own, Zip's, and was far from having expired. Zip had become a duo-person, simply. But he, like everyone, had missed the moment of revelation. The crux of the vision had seemed that weird and penetrating gaze, but exactly *when and how* all this was assimilated by his former psyche was impossible to say. And another thing: those already exposed to such visions said nothing to those who had yet to be exposed. Discretion came naturally, without any exhortations on the part of the sect's higher powers. Who would have believed them, anyway? Still, the fact that so many had experienced these visions produced a solidarity among the followers of Murti Bing: they clung to one another like burrs to a dog's tail.

Zip awoke around eleven the next morning and immediately felt like a new person. He beamed with delight as he slowly – but *slowly* – recalled his vision. Eliza was *already* holding his hand, and it was not the least bit tiresome. He was delving deeper into himself, entering those now-empty caverns where he had been nurturing that gent. (It was the latter, not the former adolescent, who had been converted.) There he ferreted out a new ego, a new presence. Who the hell could it be? Madness, along with the toxic effect of the pills, a morbidity impossible to reproduce synthetically, was yielding results completely unforeseen by those Chinese psychiatrists. In a moment, the results of this revelation would receive an "intellectual" (!) interpretation. This was Eliza's task, that notoriously unintelligent mademoiselle from the spheres of the demiaristocracy.

The Wedding Night

It was one of those semisummerlike, quasi-autumnal Augusts when the drab and dreary verdure of July gives way to a whole spectrum of hues, ranging from emerald green to a dark olive grey. Genezip had gradually begun to recover. He was troubled not so much by his shrapnel-riddled thigh as by the aftereffects of his shell shock, which manifested themselves not only physically (dizzy spells, blackouts, minor convulsions) but in various psychic states, more subtle variations of those he had been experiencing since the crime. He was nagged by the feeling – sometimes reaching an exceedingly nasty intensity – that *it was not he who was experiencing all this.* He observed himself as one would a stranger, but *literally so*, not like one of Chwistek's "endlessly proliferating observers." This was not cant: such is how *it was*. Those who have not experienced it can never know the feeling. Such things defy explanation. Pyknic types can approximate how schizoids deviate from the norm by downing a large dose of Merck's mescaline (a hallucinatory alkaloid of peyote). A real "schizo" will immediately grasp what is happening, whereas a pyknic cannot even get off the ground without the aid of more powerful narcotics. Between Zip's two identities there arose awkward pauses fraught with terror. What transpired in those pauses? What filled this persistent void, the void not filled by either of his two selves? Lurking in it were deeds so horrifying as to breach the armor shielding us from the laws of existence; to permit one to experience, in a split second, the infinity immanent in the Omnibeing. Oh, those voids! We do not wish them on our worst enemy. A moment which appears unattached, but which is nonetheless the cement joining two distinct natures that, without it, would *indeed* be separate egos. At such times there existed that other *indestructible* in life – until the final phases of acute catatonia.

Despite his nocturnal vision, Zip was not a "confirmed" Murtibingist. His conversion had not gone as smoothly as it should have, and the poor aspirant was deemed unworthy of a personal interview with Lambdon Tiger. On the other hand, he had gazed into his fiancée's soul, or rather into its emanation, which he himself had conjured up: Eliza could exist only as a negative in relation to someone else, a *positive* negative (a benign specter); in herself she was a null. She came alive the moment she had insinuated herself into Genezip's spiritual guts. Yes, he had come to know Eliza's soul, insofar as she possessed one (in the masculine sense) and was not merely a mannequin neatly assembled by Lambdon Tiger, which, because of her physical perfection, might have been assumed. A certain boredom, the price of every perfection, was inescapable. Perfection breeds suspicion; at times it can conceal an absolute negativity: empty form. Zip was insulated from such matters by a serene contentment. He grew delightfully bored, not knowing that his delight came precisely from that boredom. For Eliza was one of those women who throve on elevating some fallen angel or ordinary devil to her own "height" – provided that the person in question was of purely sexual value. But a sane and healthy brute divested of all problems was as useless as the other extreme: no, he would have to be both. In Zip she had found such a person, and she was determined never to let him out of her hands till her dying day.

....

INFORMATION: The political situation remained as before. After his "litmus victory," as the rout of the syndicalists was being called, Kotzmolochowicz assumed at least partial command of the syndicate's forces and became even more enigmatic than before. The syndicate had turned out to be a hoax, an inflated bladder, lacking credibility as a social force and being obsessed with one thing only: the defense of the White Race. Was this fixation what lay behind the general's celebrated and inscrutable "scheme"? Was he himself possibly a projection of the racial instinct of the Whites? Hmm. Apart from some incorrigible communists, political parties had ceased to exist: the country was obsessed, subconsciously at least, with the "bulwark," though not so much for national as for racial reasons: people saw themselves as Whites, simply – whereas the "Yellows" belonged to some other species. They might as easily have been waging war against a pack of rats or cockroaches; not even the most nationalistic among the sociologists could detect any strictly national elements in their movement. As to the state of things in China or in yellow-occupied Moscow, no one had even the remotest idea. Not because the noble-minded Poles were incapable of running something as ugly as an efficient secret service – no – for, in point of fact, the West was not much wiser, either. Those blasted yellow-skinned monkeys had built about them such an impenetrable wall of secrecy and were known for inflicting such hideous tortures – not only on spies caught red-handed, but even on those who looked suspicious – that there was not an agent alive who, given enough time, could not be compromised. Spy missions, in fact, had ceased. Decent spies can be recruited only when national sentiment runs high, or through social propaganda: for money – never. Neither factor applied in our case, while sinophobia in the rest of Europe was hardly a breeding ground for heroes. Self-defense arises when there is no escape; for mounting an attack more positive motives are needed.

The waiting grew more and more frantic. Not so for the adepts of Djevani, for whom individual time extended beyond their lives – in either direction (thus contradicting that punitive cancellation of the past – a mystery incarnate they appeared to grasp without the slightest effort). Even while meditating on the benign metaphysical state of the world, their time did not appear linear but ultraspatial, globlike – so stretched had the range of their empathy become. Minor telepathic occurrences became, in certain circles, commonplace; everyone "intercoursed" with everyone else, forming one huge, amorphous mass in which each could do as he or she pleased, as long as it was done according to the rules. People were drowning in mutual exultation, thus adding to their own self-exultation. Petty grievances were dissolved in a sauce of universal charity, and even the more passionate hatreds were being reconciled. The ebullience of the Djevanists, so manifest to all, aroused such jealousy among their contemporaries that people – people whose beliefs were in many cases incompatible with, or even antithetical to, the teachings of Murti Bing – began, for purely pragmatic reasons, to gravitate in their direction, only to be swallowed up in the mass hypnosis. The rest was accomplished by those fiendish DB_2 pills. It was around this time that Prince Basil arrived in C. on matters pertaining to the forest. The master's emissaries had even managed to penetrate the prince's retreat in the Ludzimierz wilds and to lure this prized beast from his sanctuary. After a dose of nine pills, the prince had decided that this was indeed the religion of his quest, as it seemed to contain a little bit of "intellect" (God have mercy!) and a modicum of faith – a lovely compromise requiring no more self-denial and, above all, no more intellectual labor. But the new faith affected people differently. Even Afanasol Benz, who, through the efforts of Djevani himself, was appointed a junior lecturer somewhere, managed to reconcile this system of Asymptotic Oneness with his own kingdom of symbols, in effect logicizing certain aspects of Murti Bing's doctrines – only certain aspects, however. Meanwhile, events were acquiring a momentum of their own. Until one day the walls of the Chinese-Muscovite cauldron cracked, and the yellow magma advanced a few kilometers farther – till it stood, surrounded by an ominous silence, at our own humble Polish border. But more on that later.

The newly commissioned officer and his exalted fiancée grew used to sitting together in the school garden where the belated (?) roses, coral lilacs, plum and apple trees, and the cherry and barberry blossoms interlaced with umbellets, sorrel, and gentian formed a positively idyllic backdrop for their budding romance. And they were like a pair of bluish-gold beetles – as these insects are called in the vernacular – copulating on a russet blackberry leaf in the golden August sun. Nature breathed a serene languor, and the azure days, borne by the airy sails of eastward-bound clouds, drifted by like flower petals spirited by a blustery wind – or something like that. (Enough of these idylls that have so polluted our literature. There is simply no substituting setting for substance; no escaping psychological complexities through sentimental postcards.) How bothered they were by their swelling love! It was not they who devoured one another spiritually (physical *prikosnoveniya* were, for the time being, unthinkable), but their love – bipersonal, bound beyond the personality, objectivized, hypostatic, peripheral, and not internal – that was sucking them dry like a cuttlefish and satisfying its own inscrutable laws. This fundamentally depraved specter stood behind them as they sat cuddled on the little garden bench beneath a rowan tree, its clusters of red berries aflame against the clear blue sky; or on a small sofa in the cool shade of a green lamp shade on long, early winter evenings. During their strolls on the outskirts of town (Zip now sported his new officer's uniform, that of the Adjutant's Academy), the phantom bellied behind them (or so it seemed) through the parched and yellowing grass, peered into their skulls from above in the form of billowing August clouds, made cautious but subtle advances in the gentle autumnal breezes, and, in the rustle of heat-rumpled leaves, whispered false, deceitful, seemingly happy words that were actually full of sadness and the promise of future disenthrallment.

But Zip did not have long to savor this blessed convalescence, to revel blithely in his own heroism, his premature promotion, or in this pure emotion "unclouded by reason." The Sons of Duo-Unity had begun to increase the ambient pressure on behalf of what they considered to be more crucial tasks. Eliza had been holding secret conferences with low-ranking members of the Murtibingist hierarchy. Soon he was attending formal classes. During one of these classes (they were scheduled from six to seven in the evening, a fact that disturbed Zip inasmuch as it reminded him of a required school course) they were introduced to Lambdon Tiger, a short old man with a grey beard and bright yellow eyes that shone like topaz in his smooth and tawny face. (He was reputed to have been a former coffee planter.) But Zip said nothing. He only listened and chewed some mysterious little nuts. Eliza, on the other hand, inspired by her master's presence, launched into a fury of lecturing. From her mouth streamed whole rivers of blatantly sweet nonsense about infinite contiguities in the *x*th dimension, about a duality verging on unity, the sublimation of demonstrable feelings, about some tiny ethereal orifices through which unity can engulf the most divided creatures. She was in absolute command of her subject; she could explain all; there was nothing she could not elucidate, nothing that held any mystery for her. Lambdon listened and nodded. In a way, the world of Murti Bing was as banal as our own, with which it was of course identical, only the philosophical problems common to both were barely grazed – something its zealous commentators chose to ignore. They ignored the fact that their rambling pieties were killing the mystery in a higher, never-never land as surely as the most ordinary profligates, *jouisseurs*, and devotees of "life for life's sake" were doing. Why, then, this whole comedy? So thought, subconsciously at least, this convert to the new religion. But before such thoughts could solidify, he would be reminded of his vision; maybe there really *was* something to it after all. To this doubt his philosophically untrained mind could find no reply.

Initially, even Genezip rebelled against all this claptrap – shyly and ineptly, but even so. Gradually, however, he began to associate some of Eliza's words with emotions experienced during his "afternoon awakening." His affair with the princess, followed by his era of torture with Persy, had blurred into an unreal nightmare, which he managed to shake off one August day like a snake shedding its skin. And lo, he stood naked (spiritually) before himself, young and inviolable, on the threshold of a new miracle: a love so elemental and perfect that it was as if this lecherous little stud had never known any other woman, as if he had stumbled on some wholly unknown creature. His past did *indeed* belong to someone else. A swarm of hitherto repressed feelings – not anticipated even in his wildest dreams – suddenly gushed forth: Genezip was genuinely in love. He carried his aching, bleeding heart around like a huge, gaping wound; but inwardly he howled. What else to do in the circumstances but to sit and chat? The most harmless little peck would have equaled a horribly sacrilegious act of ruthless depravity. He was moved by her, stressfully so; pitied her as he would have pitied a kennel of dogs; ripped and tore himself apart – but in vain; nothing else to do but sit, go for a stroll, chat. Oh, abomination! This outrageous sublimation had him so frustrated that he could not imagine performing the most modest sexual act with her. Strangest of all, he now loved her consciously – loved her as that dark and shady character from below (only slightly illuminated on the night of the vision): metaphysical experiences were now all that recalled the defunct kid. The murder had faded entirely. "Now that you are reborn, there's no need to worry about it, is there?" Eliza had once remarked, and with that the matter was closed.

But the sexual urge, halted in its development by the aftereffects of the shell shock and by this recent surge of sanctimonious feeling, gradually reasserted itself. Not desire as such but rather a mild case of "concupiscence," infinitely more subtle than the first impressions of sexual excitement produced by Eliza's calm and poised exterior, now all but extinguished by his consumption of the pills. For all her beauty, Eliza appeared at first glance to be almost totally sexless. (This sort are known to be extremely dangerous the moment they fall for someone.) Her large, grey, innocent, and ecstatic eyes, inspiring otherworldly respect rather than slimy, unchaste thoughts (to see such eyes squinting in the heat of unslaked lust . . . ah!); her mouth arched in an expression of prayer, neither too narrow nor too wide, but denoting a slight benevolence in the corners ("why not make him suffer a little for his own good") (to pulverize that mouth with a kiss until it meekly surrendered . . . ah!); and her seemingly fragile body that was as supple as an acrobat's (in orgasm she could touch her head with her heels) and like a steel spring when nervously excited (such an indifferent little body – to see it coiled, like a reptile, in carnal convulsion . . . ahhh!) – such "sensual data" of seemingly mild erotic intensity portended fiendish, unexplored possibilities about which Genezip, being hoisted to ever higher plateaus of spiritual perfection, did not dare to think consciously. Her frailty was an illusion, of course, something that completely escaped this inexperienced whelp, who had considered self-evisceration to be the true expression of one's passion; sometimes he was so overcome by his fiancée's spiritual exaltation that he dared not rouse her from it. By an unspoken pact they abstained from even the most modest physical contact before their wedding night. His desire, already concentrated in him thanks to Persy, grew rather impersonal; it was a depersonalized desire, objectified, made abstract through his soul's sublime surrender. Antidotes, of the sort used against Irina's erotic *trucs*, were not the thing, either, although at times . . . but more about that later. (What won't a man entertain in the fraction of a second? If every shade of feeling were recorded and analyzed, what would remain of history's greatest celebrities? It's the proportions that count. Yes – while all are host to various germs, not everyone catches the diseases caused by them.)

Subconsciously, with his grubby male instinct, Genezip detected awesome and mysterious tensions in her who was so close and yet so enigmatic to him. She was infinitely more enigmatic, in fact, than either the princess or Persy had been. He would have been blind to such enigmas a few months ago, but now, as that *other*, he sank into her the impotent claws of his demented thoughts (absolute insatiability) and fell back as if he had collided with some slippery wall. She was nearly as transparent as a hydra or a jellyfish; he could almost see the process of her psychic digestion when she tutored him on Murti Bing's sublime gospel. And yet . . . For Zip, her greatest mystery was the coolly burning sexuality sequestered deep inside her body, for what can be more mysterious in a woman (qua female, not as a metaphysical ego) than *that*, apart from her moodiness, which may be ignored à la Napoleon I. So thought Genezip, who had inherited the idea from Sturfan. Eliza had a wry and mischievous look in her eye, which petrified Zip's insides. There, in those depths, were feelings unknown to him, unimaginable feelings: he would never understand them, never, never . . . A split second of demoniacal fury and humiliation, followed by an even more exalted and resplendent love illuminating both his own world and the world around him . . . Subsequently a spray of orange-red rowan berries against the cobalt blue of an August horizon; a leaf shading into yellow; a luminous dragonfly, fluttering, whirring, while its body remained perfectly immobile in the warm breeze from the hot stubble fields – all became symbols of sublime and inscrutable things and, momentarily, the common property of both Genezip and Eliza, like their own private, but mutually unexplored, bodies. For what could be more private than one's own body – unless it was one's own soul? Disguised self-infatuation and the usual banalities associated with the first stirrings of emotions. But there was no arresting it, no converting it into something more enduring, no fixing it forever. The moments went by, and the incremental past became more and more tinged with sadness. Yet Zip's freakish past, distorted by its twisted beginning, could not become Eliza's property. And is that not love's crowning moment, when lovers' pasts converge? But here the differences were too overwhelming: Eliza lacked the proper organs (what a disgusting word) for digesting the former Zip and his dual personality. Whenever he brooded over the past, distant and yet so recent, he seemed remote and had to be left alone, however rational their relationship. This distance lent a tragic quality to even their brightest moments together. A mysterious fear was encircling them, and quite often, prescient of some obscure and impending atrocity (that "yellow wall," perhaps?), they would flinch simultaneously. At times, the angelic face of reality would be transformed, imperceptibly, for an infinitesimally brief period, into an unbelievably hideous mug. But it lasted such a short while as to seem an illusion.

Because of these emotional permutations, the pieties of Murti Bing slowly but surely began to infiltrate Genezip's stunted and metaphysics-hungry brain. The bulk of these inchoate feelings, moods, thoughts – allied with a sense of the world's infinite mystery and the personality that was as self-contained as a locked trunk – failed to blossom into the structure, however rudimentary, of any *genuinely* religious feeling having God as its object; would not crystallize, solidify into a system of primitive but precise thoughts. Gradually they disintegrated into a boneless, undifferentiated pulp. The vague and blurry outlines of a conceptual framework, randomly composed of such banal notions as "maximal oneness within twoness," could hardly serve as an agent of mental crystallization – a facile narcotic anesthetizing all intellectual endeavor in the embryonic stage. Oh, yes, to plug (with any cork) that little hole leading to the bottomless abyss, as long as it palliated the monstrosity of existence, everywhere in evidence. To relax in some halfway perfect world as in an easy chair – not forever, but for a while, for an instant of that sublime love imperiled by powers mounting on all sides. But the new religion could not fortify Zip or give him the power to stomach reality in all its forms. And how to entertain great ambitions when the future remained opaque, unresolved? What would life be like if the Chinese prevailed? And what if, which was highly improbable and which no one *seriously* believed, Poland, that eternal bulwark, were to repel the Mongolian avalanche? An even more uncertain future. Poland, the shell of an artificial fascism, subsidized by Western communism, was threatened, if not by the Chinese then by its own communists. Genezip soon quit delving into life's cruel show, satisfied that ultimate wisdom had been conferred on Murti Bing by the Maximal Oneness – as was apparent from his vision. Suffice it to say that only those who have had such visions can know their terrifying power. Here is not the place to elucidate them; not even a dog would sit through such an ordeal. It was a cross between religion and philosophy, by itself an obscenity; deliberately vague, improperly thought out, everything wrapped in idea-masks so as to fudge and to conceal the really serious issues. The result? A simpleminded benevolence and stupefaction tolerating every violation. To it submitted all those infected with *Murtibingitis acuta*, as Kotzmolochowicz called it (still?). The trend was greatly accelerated by the events of July: some diversion before the final catastrophe was the only thing approaching a common goal – no one thought in long-range terms anymore. Thus did those "yellow devils" prepare the way for their unstoppable conquest: first lull all to sleep and then strangle them. One who did not submit to the New Faith was Tenzer. He had no mind to, as he put it, decipher the "signs of the end in the sky of reason"; he turned out even wilder things, drank, dabbled in depravity, and had his fill of girls – what better way to go? Artists – ugh – the most revolting concept of the age: worms in a carcass. Such, then, was the general narcosis (on the eve of universal stupefaction) (science, in the popular sense, was defunct, and philosophy had reached a dead end) toward which the world was heading, and it was spreading before our very eyes. But how many "simplifiers," noble-minded (really?) optimists, and traders in psychic goods could see it, or even *wanted* to?

And so, even before Eliza had exhausted herself in conversation, Zip was all but indoctrinated. Pure love was about to consume, prematurely, a love not as yet divided into the spiritual and the sensual. Meanwhile, sensual outrages were waiting in the future, planted along the high road of life like sphinxes on the way to the Egyptian temple. Toward the end, their chats went more or less like this:

Genezip (without conviction): I feel as if, in the radius of your soul, I grow more perfect the closer I get to where the two lines of the personality intersect – the spatial and the temporal, which you talked about yesterday . . .

Eliza (staring aimlessly into the distance, as if through two different windows, with one gaze wandering about the island of Balampang and the other, the darker one, combing the recesses of Zip's body, touching and probing his internal organs; rousing herself): You know, at times I'm visited by a horrible doubt: if the source of ultimate wisdom – that which we must accept – is not a benign but an indifferent power, why should the world be a progression and not an aimless, oscillating motion? And if that is so, which phase are we in? Or are we already in the stage of steady decline? (She delighted in getting at the truth through a succession of doubts.) Our human limitation gives no certainty as to the sign before Existence: whether a plus or a minus.

Genezip (disagreeably roused): I've always said that ethics was relative. The relation of the individual to the species is specific to a given species – this dependency we call ethics. The Maximal Oneness of Existence is indifferent to status. We always run up against the same thing: infinity.

Eliza: Since infinity is really finite, it might as well not exist . . .

A few leaves of yellowing maple broke loose and, wobbling, fell to the ground, which heaved with a dry heat. They contemplated the leaves floating through the motionless air, and (for a brief moment) the concepts they invoked seemed so trivial that they were embarrassed by their own pseudophilosophical cant. But Eliza obstinately plodded on (how much misery they would have spared themselves if they had simply made love): "In finite segments of time the hierarchy is absolute. The goal of our Master is to maintain the fiction of the individual so that he becomes socially harmless."

Genezip: Impossible. Observe what's happening in the theater: the death throes of pure nonsense. You haven't been to Quintofron's theater. Music, too, has reached a dead end with Tenzer. Art will never march in the front ranks again, a fact irreversible.

Eliza: Until now, no one, much less a state, has consciously tried to isolate artists and scientists from the rest of a hopelessly mechanized society –

Genezip: Bunk! But even that's possible. Who knows what might be hidden in a future freighted with such a present?

Eliza: Thanks to our religion, we can pickle in aspic *any* political system of government. But philosophy must be ruthlessly exterminated as a squandering of the brain's supply of phosphorus.

Genezip: It makes me nervous to sit and think such thoughts with you. I want to live, but this – this is suffocating me! Help!

He was momentarily speechless, gasping in real terror – a black, sweaty, bug-eyed terror fixing on him from out of infinity; he cried out but failed to recognize his own voice. An abyss opened inside him. *Nothing was right.* Something pounced on him from his own interior; not a stranger (his ex-prisoner – oh! – what joyous times those had been!) but *something*, unnamed, as final as death itself – not only his own but the death of everything: Nothingness. Eliza was motionless, her pristine profile was turned toward him, but across her lips there strayed an enigmatic, provocative grin. Genezip beat the air where, with furious speed, the *blazing* beard of the man he had killed consumed the entire universe, stretching, as in his Davamesque vision when all had transpired extraterrestrially, beyond the finite. Simultaneously, he saw before him the whole of reality with stunning clarity, as never before, but as something alien, uncanny, as though viewed through someone else's eyes. It was ghastly. His eyes bulged from their sockets, he was breathing heavily. Not able to bear it, Eliza grabbed his head and pulled him, even as he thrashed about, toward her. Oh, yes, to have him like this forever, in her power, hers to remake, to recast into someone *unrecognizable.* Eliza loved his madness, *loved him as a madman;* in this and only this was her contentment; now it was at hand; she felt as if she had a body, that she had him, as well as *it,* inside her. Naturally, she could not account for such a sensation – oh, joy! Now that he had purged himself, now that he had deceased the person he once was, he belonged to her. The first kiss of his life – light as the brush of a moth's wings grazing the cup of a night flower but as perverse in its lightness as the sexual evil lurking in all of existence – descended on Genezip's half-open, contorted mouth, ripping the veil of madness from his awe-struck, wide-open eyes. It was over. He longed for Kotzmolochowicz. He was ready to die, with or without any cavalry music. Oh, why do such valorous moments always occur at the wrong time! He woke up. How passionately he adored Eliza at the moment! (Her passion, meanwhile, had cooled somewhat.) She who had freed him from the wolf's trap into which he had been thrust by the pitiless paw of his father, who had been running his life from the beginning. Not the one who had died, but that eternal, almost Godlike Father whose boundless fury – the fury of a titan – was now developing in him who was as spiritually weak as an infusorian. Horribly unjust, you say? Was it a lesser folly to demand justice from existence as a whole? But such was the pleasure of the most celebrated thinkers: sanctifying, persistently and to no effect, a chaos of moral contingencies and elevating them to the stature of metaphysical laws.

Now and then, Eliza would say with fervor: " . . . and there, in the endless distance, the most sublime concepts will converge in an absolute union of everything with everything, and beyond the intercourse of panexistence we shall become one. Imagine it! The gap between the real and ideal, between a concept and the thing it designates – annulled at last! Existence will be identical with its most profound essence. Everything will coalesce with itself" – and so on. Genezip felt slightly embarrassed by her but, swept up by the ardor of her words, his discomfort soon turned to lust. He knew of a way to coalesce right here on earth – through the sexual act – however reluctant he was to talk about it. ("Duo-unity" – ha, ha! – such words had the Chinese staff officers in stitches as they washed down with rice brandy a dish of rats' tails fried in linseed oil. Even Wang laughed, the commander in chief of Asia's bolshevized Mongols, the only man to cause Kotzmolochowicz the slightest tremor.)

Summer languished in its own beauty. The sapphire face of night was shrouded by the mourning veil of a hopeless, star-infested void. The world now seemed truly finite, in conformity with Einstein's theory: one huge prison. (Even though physics no longer insisted on this theory [what a hoax was perpetrated by that infinitely great gravitational potential!], some individuals grew so used to the idea of an elliptical universe that they came to accept subconsciously the notion of its finiteness and did so without reservation. A dangerous symptom.) "Out there" was silence; between the unattainable truth and existence as such there hung the curtain of Murtibingism, although it sooner resembled a torn curtain of rain obscuring a sunny horizon that had once radiated an enlightened optimism. The word *knowledge* had long ago been dumped, leaving only ordinary cretinism and its cousin: the certitude that all must be according to the gospel of Murti Bing. Otherwise, nothing – except, perhaps, for Benz's symbols. Like the rattle of yellow leaves falling from sorry tree skeletons to the frozen ground, the words of Murti Bing's soporific gospel seemed to murmur as they lighted on the brittle ganglia of the poor adjutant's brain. The final military drills, the most subtle in an adjutant's career, had begun; post assignments were due any day now. Then a trip to the capital, the start of a new life . . . Genezip found it hard to think about the future as he sank into a painful, soggy boredom. Only the thought of his approaching marriage galvanized his musty ganglia. But here, too, a sea of complications. How was this, his last (he was sure it was to be his last, despite his youth) affair, to end? At times he was seized by the prongs of a wild panic, transforming the skin on his loins into crocodile scales. How to satisfy this terrific, previously untasted lust that was as swollen as the bud of a monstrous flower and which was branching out in his body like a fibrous tumor, devouring him with smacking lips, paralyzing his ability to perform the most primary act: he was as impotent with her as he had been with that other woman . . . And then such boundless and unfathomable boredom . . . Ha! Suppose he managed it, what then? Only one woman had he ever really known, the princess, and he was nauseatingly afraid of the sexual state of war, so depressing in its mendacity, that would come of consummating their erotic relations. Thus did their spiritual love persist, so much so that it seemed impossible to imagine a life without it.

The fateful, longed-for day was approaching. It was almost at hand – tomorrow or the next day. Genezip planned to have one last conversation with her. From whom could he expect sympathy if not from her, his mistress in the realm of the occult? He cornered her, embraced her, implored her help, not realizing that she was to be the cause of his derangement, which, without her, he might have overcome. He had intended to speak, but all he could do was to whisper incoherently while burying his head in her left armpit and to inhale, with dilated nostrils, the "bloodied" (he could think of no other word for it) but subtle fragrance of her unexplored body. "Oh, that body – you'll find the mystery *there*, not in a system suspended in some ideal realm where the world's greatest minds have been screwing around with nothing to show for it." (The late Bergson would have been pleased to "hear" such a "notion.") (We may think such thoughts beforehand – but afterward?) He began whispering things, and every word she uttered in reply to his dirty whispering was both sacred and diabolically boring – a powerful stimulant for his insatiable and feckless lust. The trite but seductive gospel of the Polish Djevanists was – in Eliza's mouth – like drops of water landing on the red-hot walls of a steaming cauldron. Too embarrassing for words. And all this in a manner best described as *dry:* a desert simoom. More scary than the Chinese! Here, in this tiny microcosm of personal tragedies, the tragedy of generations was reflected – semaphorically, symbolically. Its name? "The failure to experience great emotions." No doubt some shoemaker was passionately in love with some cook or other, but this did not make for a public life, at least not in Poland with its elite made up of schizoids and schizophrenics. The pyknics were not yet in power; thanks to the Chinese, however, they were becoming a true contender. Zip finally broke off Eliza's lecture.

"Listen, Eliza," he said (this was not what he had intended to say, as often happens with young people). "I hesitate even to call you Liz – how that hurts me! If you can't rouse me to greatness, what then? . . . " he asked with a helpless little grin of abject despair, staring into a September sky tinged with the willow green of evening. A cool breeze blew from the distant fields, where a knoll bearing the name of some nearly forgotten national hero was casting an emerald shadow. The earth around them radiated the heat of day. A horrible longing weighed on them. How they envied a swarm of mosquitoes (mosquitoes in September?) that whirled and hopped before a yellowing willow. Envied the swarm, not the individual mosquitoes; envied being segregated into groups, losing oneself in a multitude . . . they were that far gone. The long-needled pines soughed in the evening breeze. To capture eternity in just such a moment and then cease to exist.

"I would gladly sacrifice myself for the sake of that greatness. I desire no glory for myself, only that you have the chance to become great in your own eyes."

"No, no – that's not it," Genezip moaned.

"I know – you'd like it to be with military music and pennants in the background, you'd like Kotzmolochowicz (she permitted herself this license) to tap you on the shoulder with the sword of the brave." (Oh, how he despised her at that moment, in reality loving her to distraction. What a drag!) "No, for you this will be a mere stepping stone. Once you've outgrown it, you'll become disenchanted. You'll have to suffer through the war whether you like it or not."

"So, you'd like to see me a great robot?!" cried Zip, and he stood before her in all his grandeur, in his quaint adjutant's uniform, legs astride in tight-fitting, brick-red trousers and riding boots with spurs. (This splendor bore traces of the Napoleonic *Guides*. The general reveled in decorations.) Oh, how handsome her Zip looked! Now was the moment, there on that scorching ground, with him pouncing like a hawk on a bird, and her howling like a cat, voluptuously, painfully: she had witnessed such a scene not long ago. And then with that thing of his . . . Both wanted it, but hesitated. Oh, why hadn't they done it when the time was right? The conversation resumed as Eliza continued to hound Genezip with that *sacrifice* of hers — another of those cursed specters of the past that was undergoing a revival: the voluntary sacrificing of the individual to society, sublimation in the stinking entrails of the masses so that, bloated with pride, it might perfume the whole thing all over again, now in a sanitized version (arrived at through psychic brutalization: this stage was indispensable), producing an externally well-fed, well-washed, clean-looking, well-housed tribe of contented people — or rather the wheels, cogs, screws, and brackets needed to construct the flawless machines of future centuries, whose first draft could be seen in various countries. It made one's bones freeze to contemplate the future.

In his office at the War Ministry on Holy Cross Square, the general stood before the fireplace, rocking gently to warm his hemorrhoids, which today itched especially. An operation was unlikely at the moment; yesterday, after getting drunk with Persy, he had indulged in things perverse even by his standards. Presently he was dictating to Oleśnicki what appeared to be a minor order. Since this was history in the very making, we render it word for word: " . . . and for that reason harmful. We hereby declare the barrack off limits to the disciples of Murti Bing. A soldier's mechanization must proceed in the manner prescribed by paragraph 3. We view the aforementioned religion as harmless only for the elite, from the rank of ensign on up. At the lower levels, the third stage of initiation can arouse old-fashioned, anachronistic beliefs involving a materialistic approach to history. I therefore urge all officers, from the rank of captain up, to get in there and clean up this whole fucking mess. (Such was the general's style, even in official orders.) To be read aloud at all officers' meetings convened expressly for this purpose." Just then an orderly came in to announce the arrival of Djevani. (Why here of all places?) Kotzmolochowicz felt as if he were covered with leeches in a Ceylon jungle. Into the room strode a young and noble-looking Hindu in a dinner jacket. On his head he wore a turban fastened with a sapphire the size of a pigeon's egg. The two powers stood there and sized each other up: the one the secret envoy of eastern communism whose motto was "destroy everything first, then create a new man and rid the world of the poison of the white race"; the other the unwitting slave of furious communist machinations in the West who was a force in his own right, tempestuous, a man without direction, one of the last of the vanishing tribe of individualists. Their conversation was brief.

Djevani: Why does Your Excellency bar soldiers of this excellent bulwark (the arrogant Hindu pronounced these words with a barely perceptible irony) from the grand truth, which embraces not only the infinity of pure being but also the future of rational creatures throughout the cosmos, on all planets, both real and hypothetical?

Kotzmolochowicz replied calmly, almost sweetly, but it was a terrifying sweetness:

"How so, worthless spy of the yellow avalanche . . . ?"

Djevani: We have nothing to do with the Mongol invasion. No one has proved that we . . .

General: Don't interrupt. Only ideas that are stored here (he tapped his protruding and sagacious forehead) can go undetected.

Djevani was endowed with a phenomenal sense of hearing, further enhanced by the use of special acoustical antennae – a Chinese invention unknown in the West. He had overheard the general dictating the order of the day and had done so from a waiting room three rooms away, each having an upholstered door. He had been listening through the furnace and chimney ducts. And what is fakirism if not trained senses combined with an aptitude for hypnosis. Still, the valiant "Kotz" was not to be taken in by such subterfuges. Djevani did not flinch.

"Only thoughts unborn can go undetected," he said in a decidedly knowing manner, fixing his passionate gaze on the black, brilliant, vivacious eyes of his host. It was an unmistakable allusion to the commander's esoteric plan. Until now no one had even implied such a thing. The Hindu's gaze was so pregnant with meaning that the gaiety momentarily vanished from those black eyeballs like a coat of powder suddenly blown away. "What if he's wise to my mechanism?" wondered the general, and his body turned cold. A sudden jerk and his hemorrhoids stopped itching: an intestine had snapped back into place. This visit was not without its benefits. Moreover, effective immediately he tightened security in the rooms adjoining his office – not to mention his own internal-external security. To act on a hunch inspired by the most subtle observations – yes, that was the whole secret of his success. The conversation proceeded as if nothing had ever happened, as if nothing vital had been said or decided. The two scrutinized each other continuously. The general wondered what else this tawny-colored monkey knew. The Hindu, on the other hand, was testing his own power of intuition, for rarely had he, a yoga of the second class, met a white man of such enigmatic appearance. *Der geniale Kotzmolokowitsch* had taught him, as he had others, the lesson of secrecy. Never put anything in writing; keep all in your head. On his way out, Djevani handed the general twenty-five pills of Davamesque in an exquisitely carved box. "For an eagle like you, twenty-five is hardly enough. But I know that Your Excellency is in pain." These were his last words.

When Genezip awoke on the day after his final exam, it was again with that mysterious expanse of freedom he had felt after his graduation. He knew the challenge that awaited him "at his commander's side." But it was not only that. He was a free man. His apprenticeship was now over (including his apprenticeship with Eliza). Yes, free to make something of himself – a terrifying moment for schizoids who relish being suspended between a decision and its execution. What could be worse than being free and not knowing what to do with that freedom? He would rather not have awakened that morning. But the day stood before him, huge, implacable, and hollow, waiting to be filled: time was flying. And it was his wedding day, a fact that had not dawned on him until now, some ten minutes after waking, and it made him doubly horrified. He drew the curtain aside and peered out the window. The autumn trees ablaze in the sun seemed to be growing on another planet. Why another planet? *This* world was a bottomless pit filled with a strangeness incarnated in external objects. But where was that world worth inhabiting? Where? It did not exist; it *could not exist*. This was the unkindest truth. "What am I living for?" he whispered, his throat filling with tears. Oh, what an insufferable drag! Why had he not understood?! In the past he might have killed himself without hesitation; now he *had* to live. Why had he passed up the chance? Because of some trifles; because of some women; his family. Aha, *à propos*, where were they: his mother, his sister, that all-knowing Abnol, all those who might have meant something to him but had now become impersonal ghosts, powerless to help him in this dead and impersonal world of his? Was Eliza one of the phantoms? Distinguishable from the others only because of her seductive face and her desirable, as-yet-unprobed body? Genezip was so pathetic, so eager for sympathy, for the soft caress of a loving hand (the person wasn't important, just the hand). A hand? Ridiculous. Why a hand? What did all this mean? He was alone and suffering wretchedly. There was no discussing it, either, not even with her. He knew what he would have gotten from her: a short lecture on ethereal orifices. Even though he had contemplated marriage (in the abstract, without reference to anyone in particular), only now was he conscious of her as his fiancée, as someone real. She really did exist, his Liz – ha, ha! And he wrapped himself in her (in his love for her) as in death. She who would fill his empty and alienated world. To think that he had forgotten that!! Yes, he had forgotten; the world was so filled with her presence that the recognition of it had passed unnoticed. Was it all true? Who could say? And to think that such tragedies, which once might have altered the history of the world had they occurred in certain social circles, were now reduced to expectorated fruit pits, cigarette butts, scraps. No one cared a damn about such things now; they were being exterminated like bedbugs. Comical dreamers were a dying breed. Only here on this patch of planet miraculously spared the general upheaval, here in our mighty paralysis, could one still find vestiges of the past. But hollowed out, gutted; a void reverberating like a dried-out gourd. The pernicious gospel of Murti Bing was devouring people's brains, or rather the leftovers, like a hideous, brooding vulture hiding its ugliness beneath brilliant feathers. On the surface it looked like a nice, small, harmless little panacea. Eliza: the name was enough to flood the brain with a poisonous syrup. And yet, her omniscient eyes bespoke an unknown fury, an unknown passion, promising fulfillment of the most outrageous, most improbable desires; intense devotion verging on hatred. Only some utter monstrosity could give him satisfaction. But what sort of satisfaction? However he racked his brains, no solution offered itself. By God, routine hysterics would have been better!

And just as suddenly as it had appeared, his confusion was shed like some gruesome mask. Eliza again became his sweetheart and not some specter or succubus infecting him with the occult; his family became his beloved family; Sturfan, his true friend; and he himself, a splendid candidate for the post of the general's aide, one whose equally splendid career was assured. And a good thing it was, too.

NOTE: A soul that can heal one person can be deadly for another, can make a great man out of a third, can reduce a fourth to the level of a psychic sewer. It is worrisome to think that kindness, self-sacrifice, unstinting devotion, and self-effacement can provoke, in the object of these feelings and deeds, the complete opposite of those virtues. Souls should be as opaque as Leibniz's monads; better for things to proceed according to some objective law. Alas, people were crawling all over one another in the most revolting manner.

Zip washed up in the bathroom like the sanest and healthiest of young men. Then an orderly (that relic of an almost prehistoric martial age) supplied him with his freshly laundered clothes, a pair of gleaming boots with spurs, his epaulets, and other trimmings of a bygone era. The early morning sun purged his bedroom of any melancholic strangeness. He was a young officer recovered from a long and serious but invigorating illness. He had never felt stronger or healthier; he was totally oblivious of the sinister ghost looking over his shoulder, winding threads onto spools, installing springs, inserting hardly noticeable pins between the convoluted layers of his brain. Even his orderly Ciompała detected something eerie in the air. But not Zip, who had the sensitivity of a rock.

The wedding preparations proceeded "as in a dream," commencing with the usual *kanitel* of formalities, rituals, and ceremonies. There were three weddings: a civilo-military one, a Catholic one (for mama), and a Murtibingist one, otherwise known as a "duo-unitary wedding." Marriage was a symbol of the duo-maximal union = absolute imbecility, the temporary surrender of the individual to society. The ceremony was performed by Lambdon Tiger with the customary incantations. Eliza, reserved, concentrated, wore in the corners of her mouth a martyr's slightly contorted grimace, which only aroused the most evil, craven desires in the body of the young adjutant. This was not only normal but, under the circumstances, desirable.

The next day the young couple planned to leave for the capital, where a real job awaited Genezip. "Fabulous, utterly fabulous," he kept saying to himself, his teeth chattering, his eyes restless with an anxiety issuing from the marrow of his being. He looked feverish – from ordinary excitement, and it was regarded as such by others. Meanwhile, the evening newspapers brought some disturbing news. The yellow wall was beginning to stir. The first detachments had already reached Minsk: within three hours the entire Byelorussian Republic had been "sinocized." That afternoon a general mobilization was declared; by five, a communist-inspired revolt had swept three regiments stationed in the capital, all under the command of Monkempt-Unster, whose sweaty hands and hygienic neglect had justly earned him the nickname of Unkempt Monster. After meeting privately with Kotzmolochowicz (during which a little face-bashing had been indulged in, a rare occurrence), the unsightly man, without enlightening his subordinates, had quelled the regimental riots abruptly. It remained one of the miracles of the age, never to be elucidated by history. Among the other miracles of that age was the general's involvement with Monkempt (Napoleon in his dealings with Talleyrand and Fouché). Some claimed the general needed the treacherous beast as an internal backup and for "keeping his finger on the pulse of certain events," which was highly probable. Others attributed this association to the prevailing idiocy of the times.

The wedding was attended by the former ambassador to China, Prince Adam Ticonderoga, whose stay in prison had left him severely emaciated. He remained bitterly taciturn before his mother and the others. Only the princess observed that he was not the same person and proceeded to inject him with a colossal dose of Murtibingism. The young prince simply nodded despairingly: he had heard enough platitudes. The topic was "the arresting of culture": Was this the final phase of the Chinese ideology, or only the penultimate one beyond which lay something not yet foreseen in either Europe or America? Prince Adam had refused to divulge any information except to the Syndicate for National Salvation. Hence his ambush and detainment in prison. After a session with the general, who (according to dubious sources) had personally supervised his torture (the less said about it the better), it was rumored that a tiny gland had been removed from his brain, causing instant amnesia. This left the general as the only person in the know.

The details of this forced debriefing were too grisly for words. Ticonderoga had been turned over to the highest mandarin, Wu (and had almost died in the process), though he had Wu to thank for his having been released at all. Or was it all disinformation, deliberately leaked? – the general agonized over such thoughts. Now, at last, he could do battle on the level of "ideas," and maybe this was a blessing – who knew? The question was: should this "idea" be allowed to spread? No, better not. The whole *Ideengang* had been set in motion by the prince's confession. As he writhed in horrendous pain, he had (so it was rumored) spilled his guts as follows: "When everything clicks into place, all will form a solid mass, free of internal tensions and dynamic forces. Only by its aberrations and deviations shall we follow that fantastic spiral (not forward trend) of an expanding culture, that runaway process threatening mankind with absolute extermination through the sheer complexity of life. This complexity has not only outstripped the individual – now spent, thanks to organization – *but even the very forces needed to organize the masses.* The catastrophe was foreseen by only a handful of Chinese. The prophecy has already been vindicated in China, on a modest scale at least, to say nothing of the West, which still affects ignorance. But not even the Chinese – despite their intellectual potential, which the introduction of a Western-style alphabet has helped to liberate – could cope with this complexity. When their experiments projected a new race of Aryan-

Mongolian crossbreeds, off they marched, westward, to join the two races, to revitalize mankind! All right, but then what? Ah – unforeseen possibilities! The suppression of culture may prove only temporary. A new destiny may await mankind, one presently beyond our imagination. Meanwhile, we must strive to control and channel the forces of 'rampant capital,' the engine of this accelerated pace, and to set up a provisional communist system to act as a *peredyshka*. Western communism, now so fascist as to be indistinguishable from the latter, has not fulfilled the Chinese expectations."

Kotzmolochowicz reflected while pacing about in his spacious new office housed in the former palace of the Radziwiłłs – or "post-Radziwiłłian," as it was now called. (A week ago he had ordered the eviction of the Radziwiłł family for refusing to submit to him. He tolerated the aristocracy only when it licked his boots. Ever since his victory over the syndicate he could not suffer the pompous little squires, and by God if he wasn't right.) Like an eagle he hovered in midair above his own ego, which lay before him spread with the rotten mediocrity of the present like a steel plate smeared with jam. But panic – the source of his most brilliant maneuvers – did not grip him. He would take the twenty-five pills given him by Djevani – then come what may! The mobilization, the war – all was under way; the plans were set; it was time to relax and to "sound the depths." But were those depths still there, whence to conjure up some new stratagem? He knew how to duck burning problems when it suited him: therein lay his strength. He rang up Oleśnicki and ordered that Persy be brought to the former Radziwiłł residence. Persy had been staying in a hotel for the past two days: the deadly pills would be popped in her presence. (The next day, the official transcript of their visions, drafted that same night by Oleśnicki, was sent to Bekhmetev. The latter arranged for the dangerous document to be interred with him in his coffin. Its contents thus remained a secret. However, judging from Zip's vision, one can imagine what it was like.) Just then Monkempt-Unster (bearded, with bulging, hazel-brown eyes; altogether a repulsive type) came into the office to report the quelling of the very revolt he had helped to instigate. The left side of his face was bandaged, but otherwise he seemed to be in good shape. Their conversation was lively and cordial. The general had calmly (not in one of his fits) decided to reveal a smidgeon of his thoughts to his "counterweight," as he called Monkempt in his most intimate moments of self-evisceration. Monkempt felt extremely honored. For the first time they parted on excellent terms.

While such events were taking place in the background, there in the district capital of C., the modest wedding of the officer destined to serve as the principal hero of those same events was being celebrated. Linking these two series of events was a cable conveying the general's congratulations: "'Zip, carry on. Kotzmolochowicz." It was immediately framed in a hastily improvised passe-partout and strung to a lamp above the table. Genezip drank little, yet an inner illumination was engulfing the upper regions of his not yet perfectly shaped mind. In a word, he was beginning to feel more intelligent than himself, and that made him uneasy. He confided this to Eliza.

"It's because of my prayer to the Double Nothingness. I felt a wave dispatched by Murti Bing himself. May eternal light be shed upon his head," whispered this omniscient lass. Genezip had indeed noticed a wave, but a wave of boredom transmitted by some metaphysical power station housed inside this creature: her power was indeed awesome. The entire wedding scene, including the guests (the list included nearly everyone who appeared in Part One, even Prince Basil), impressed him as petty and frivolous, as something as accidental as, say, the entrails of that cockroach ambling across the kitchen – only just vacated by the cooks – of the officers' club of the Fifteenth Uhlan Regiment, where supper was being prepared for the guests. (He had just gone in there to hand out the tips.) Eliza's words aroused in him a sudden and unmotivated anger he had never known before. He would have gleefully outraged everyone: yanked the tablecloth off the table, for example; hurled a few dishes at the guests; screamed a madman/martyr's laugh before his terrified mother, before Lilian, the princess, and Eliza; smeared the mustached mug of the school director, General Mildew, with mayonnaise, and then ran, ran, ran – but where to? The world was too small to escape. Only one sanctuary: the metaphysical abyss, which unfortunately was sealed off forever, guarded by a number of excellent corks – a purely military stupidity, a bad education, intellectual laziness, and, of course, Murti Bing, that great demystifier of everything. The safety valve was stuck (the same valve that once constituted every world religion): follies intended for the masses, shielding humanity from an explosion in the void of the universe, from sudden and panicky flight into interstellar space. Another second and he would make his move. But with a final effort of consciousness he subdued his rage, checked it at the periphery of his muscles quivering beneath his silky smooth skin. "No, I shall marry for Liz's sake." He would sacrifice everything for her. How he adored her (both spiritually and sensually, to the *n*th power). She had saved him from a dumb "metaphysical" (ha, ha!) act.

After sitting through some abominable speeches by Sturfan, Mildew, and Michalski, they got up from the table. Things were in a bad way. In some small recess of his heart – a heart so swollen with love it bordered on hatred – there arose a slight satisfaction, a wee joy, a tiny, pint-sized premonition that, at this rate, he would drown Eliza and the world in some sticky ooze, in some idiotic bliss. Dangerous. Suddenly a flash of sanity, a vivid image having all the clarity of a cocaine vision. But Zip felt as if cast down into his chair from some *other*, more fantastic world where the reflection of this image signified *something else entirely*, where it possessed its own elusive, terrifying, wholly mysterious sense. He took a deep breath. There he sat; beside him were his mother, Michalski's mustache, the darling face of some wayward uncle, the khan Murľa-Mamzelowicz; coffee, assorted liqueurs. Oh, how nice to be a part of the normal world! Why did they have to postpone their departure until tomorrow?! District headquarters had failed to process his papers in time; so all had been decided by some silly little stamp. If only they had left for the station immediately after supper. Reality: a big word, perhaps the biggest of all. Unfortunately, Zip no longer saw it; his eyes were rolling around in the presence of the guests, of the mothers, sisters, and wives (yes, it was true; she was his wife, his very own – un-be-liev-able!), gazing into the forbidden treasures of inner perversity where true freedom reigned and where some supersublimated brute was committing imaginary crimes, thus adding to the world's store of iniquity. But woe if his overwrought nodes and ganglia should allow a nervous reflex to reach the periphery and paralyze his inert muscles. What then? A cry, a crime, a straitjacket: the muffled, metaphysical shriek of the ego, rending the guts with the infernal heartache of a wasted life. His howling entrails, torn by infernal, painful defection from implacable worldly phenomena, could be heard, it seemed, for miles. But here, nothing: the guests drank their coffee and liqueurs in the normal world – his wife included. She had to be made a partner to his madness, to be made his own property. But how? His eyes searched his brain, which was engaged in the formidable task of catapulting the ego into infinity – unaided by art, science, religion, philosophy, or any other tricks – here in this life; in the drawing room of the officers' club of the Fifteenth Uhlan Regiment on Vista Street, at house number 6. Never would she know those normal eyes of his again. The hand of fate ticking loudly in his head had finally passed the little red arrow: Keep clear – danger, hands off, high voltage, *Vorsicht!* Full steam ahead! Oof – at long last! The worst was having to wait for madness; in itself, it was not so awful, just knowing that it was madness was a relief. The abyss had opened; he had already caught a glimpse of it as it sprawled before him, a wicked and promiscuous female, seductive beyond all hell.

Suddenly Putricides, drunk as could be and high on cocaine, started playing. Genezip felt something snap inside him, but it was only a little membrane covered with the loathsome mucus of childhood sentiments. If it had ruptured altogether, collapsing all his brattices and sluice gates, he might have been saved. But it was just a little membrane. He took refuge in the men's room and broke down, sobbing tearlessly (which made it all the more pathetic) as he listened to the distant sounds of Tenzer's music suffusing the entrails of the universe. A sudden calm; and everything subsided – but not entirely. Inside him, crouched for the kill, lurked the ogre of metaphysical self-indulgence. When he returned to the drawing room, the music no longer affected him. The ultimate narcotic – a performance by that brilliant glutton and conjurer of otherworldly abysses – had no effect on him whatever. It was gruesome. The avalanche had started on its downward path – quietly, as before a storm.

The telephone rang. There was a vacancy in the Hotel Splendid. The coveted "Splendid" (coveted by whom?) was theirs. It was there, at the Hotel Splendid, they would find the place ordained, *for all eternity*, for their wedding night and where, in the name of Murti Bing, the sacrificial act would take place. "One day the Chinese will understand," thought Genezip as he slipped into his military coat and buckled on his saber. He later returned to this thought in astonishment, never able to trace its origin.

The world had emptied: only Eliza remained, his medium for exploring the mystery which those three had obfuscated with their pious drivel that night in Basil's retreat. They strolled through the nearly empty streets of that pathetic provincial capital. The "ancestral voice" beckoned to them from the "cloisters, towers, and ramparts." A bugle call from the tower sounded the hour of midnight, flatly and without echo. The Hotel Splendid blazed in a dark desert of houses seemingly seized by an epidemic. Yes, it was indeed an epidemic; the perfidious gospel of Murti Bing was mandating a sexless revolution by force (yes, by force; by yourselves – *vous autres, Polonais* – you would never have acquiesced in such a thing). "I'll never fuck Eliza unless she makes the 'first move,'" he thought. At the moment, she seemed alien and remote, estranged by the invincible wall of his own indecision. He confided this to her in the most casual terms, as if he had been the most normal of officers, and the husband of a normal young lady, for some two hundred years.

"You know, you seem oddly distant at the moment – as if I were seeing only your shell, some automaton pretending to be you. You seem utterly unapproachable. Will I ever possess you?" He laughed over the discrepancy between what he was saying and what was going on inside him.

Eliza replied in a perfectly calm voice: "Don't be nervous; relax. Act with me the way you would with some paid street girl. I'm yours from the tips of my toes to the hair on my head. You have no idea what sort of legs I have; they're so beautiful that even I'm in love with them. I want to drown in love. That's the wish of our master. To tell you the truth, there's nothing in me except my religion and my love for you. Sometimes I feel guilty that I made you so attached to me; I'm emptiness incarnate. But through me you'll excel in this hateful little graveyard of worlds in which the only shining light is our religion. You have to be freed from yourself . . ." She pressed against him her whole body, which mounting passion had softened and relaxed. Her distant air vanished; she had unleashed the beast in him, for which he was extremely grateful to her. He hustled her limp body off to the hotel.

A powerful longing seized him as he removed Eliza's little coat, oddly redolent of Australian wild thyme. He would have moved mountains for her, but he would never have forsaken her body. He was nagged by a fierce curiosity; after all, this was only his second woman. After some foreplay, his wife – his lawfully wedded wife, how handy! – made love to him in the most normal way possible, and everything seemed (only "seemed," alas) headed for a routine conjugal bliss. There was even a formal little rape that assisted Eliza, who affected a slight embarrassment, in her passage from a state of virginity to that of a married woman with no great psychological complications. But suddenly, during their next round of permissible pleasures (how simple, how utterly simple!), something extraordinary happened: "*Quelque chose de vraiment insamovite à la manière polonaise*," to quote Lebac. Zip's silklike skin; his impeccable muscles; his adolescent, Valentinolike, lust-contorted face brought on by the recollection of the pleasure just had but not consummated (due to the speed of events), all became transformed into something totally transcending Eliza's understanding of love. In her wildest dreams she had never imagined it to be like *this*. The world assumed unknown, astronomical proportions – became metaphysicized, as it were. As she lay beside him, she felt a sublime thrill just gazing into his face. She wanted it again, with him, with him inside her, at once, otherwise something awful would happen. She could not live without it. The naked Zip, lying motionless in her lovely arms, elusive in his beauty, invulnerable and thus infuriating, was suddenly become in her eyes a demigod, became something inexpressible, beyond the possible, something – oh, may it go on and on; never a moment without it; it was the only way to go; without it there was death; to hell with the country, Kotzmolochowicz, Murti Bing, the Duo-Unity (as it were), China, social revolution, war – as long as he was here and that inconceivable thing he did could last forever. Here was twoness in oneness, free of fatuous symbols; this, and not the sentimental claptrap preached by Lambdon Tiger, was the only true reality. And her darling Zip was driving her so insane! She moaned with a calamitous joy. The poor creature knew next to nothing about the limits of masculine potency; she was too well educated, had scrupulously guarded against premature initiation. She had been living in a bubble. Now the bubble had exploded, revealing to her the heretofore ungrasped mission of her life, namely, having her body's panting interior ripped apart by the weirdest pleasure; being violated by him, that dearest, most gorgeous, most exquisite stud-boy. Nothing else mattered. Some unsatisfied beast inside her howled for it to go on indefinitely. There was nothing, *nor could there ever be anything else*, but this: it was the culmination of everything. So it was that on the first assault on the mysterious rampart of pleasure, preceded by delicate grazings, poor Eliza had been stricken with acute nymphomania. Such cases are known to occur, and it was Zip's fate that it should have happened to him – to him, who was already teetering on the edge of a rotting ego (what vile words!), of a personality turned thoroughly savage, and of ordinary dementia.

And then suddenly it started up again, but with such hellish ferocity that Zip registered something he had never known with the princess – etcetera. It seemed to him, as it had to her, that nothing else mattered but this. The world had receded, leaving only this room in the Hotel Splendid, an isolated system, inexplicably sucked into the orbit of infernal forces sprung from their own bodies – which, like their souls, were locked in a living frenzy, bipersonal, Murtibingist, and bordering on a death wish, itself a contradiction. In diabolical fashion (as was later revealed) Eliza had intuited every sort of perversion, blossoming that night like the flower of the agave; internally she had exploded like a grenade loaded with lust. At that moment they lived for the millions unable to grasp the metaphysical profundity of things; they were consumed by the flame of a bestial-celestial desire to coalesce, ineffably, into one being. It ran completely contrary to the division of cells. But it was not to be realized; hence the asymptotic anguish raised to an infinity, a violation of the most fundamental law by which individuals are differentiated like Cantor's transfinite numbers, like those pernicious Hebraic alephs raised to C, the *continuum*, and even higher perhaps, into an infinitely infinite infinity, etc., etc. (Transfinite functions do not and cannot exist: the late Sir Tumor Brainard tried to prove their existence and broke his neck – or rather his brain – in the process.)

How marvelous Eliza was in her depravity! Everything in her that had appeared sacred, aloof, and distant in its expression (her eyes, her mouth, her gestures) now acquired a bestial aspect, without losing in sanctity: such was how an angel-become-pervert might have looked. Everything that Zip had found serenely, sublimely, *inviolably* beautiful in her was suddenly set ablaze by the powerful fire of the body – not that statuelike body, but the real one, palpable in its indecencies, odors, and even (ah!) its blemishes. Therein lay the terrific erotic allure: namely, that such an angel *(tout court)*, with a face as beautiful as a sunset-tinged cloud in a violet evening sky, could boast such legs, such magnificent, well-shaped calves of living flesh, and such hideousness that, without ceasing to be such, constituted, *at the very same time*, an unfathomable miracle. Hence the diabolical power of such things; the mysterious, forever incomprehensible pleasure they can bestow: the sinister, despondent – like all things too profound – pleasure. All the same, what could be more humiliating for a man than the sexual act? As a bestial relaxation enjoyed by warriors after battle, as an expression of male conquest over his female captive, it was tolerable. But in our day – what an abomination! Children and domestic life were something else again, though even these had been drastically transformed; the stultified and beleaguered male of today could hardly be compared to the paterfamilias of the past. Leaving aside some primitive forms of matriarchy, true "bagiarchy" is a modern phenomenon. No one has triumphed more fully over the world and the mystery of the personality than women. Oh, if that moron Ovsusenko, chief Taylorizor in the erotic realm, could have beheld Zip and the innocent Liz right now! All the seemingly wasted motions invented by this couple! At one point Zip's body was convulsed as though he had been bitten by a scorpion. He would have to make up for lost time and lost opportunities; if infinity was not to be his, here was something to take its place. This room, Eliza, her insurmountable allure. His mind may have stopped working, but a great perversity was taking shape within him. All his inscrutable, bygone dreams lay before him on this hotel bed. Life stopped here; the future was a dead and hollow word. His family, friends, the general, Poland, and the war hanging over it – all were as nothing compared to swallowing the world and oneself in a single dose of some outrageous act. Just start, and the rest would take care of itself. Blue coils spun at the center of his being, an endless spiral which became the entire universe when he peered into his wife's innocent but now unfamiliar, upturned, animal-angelic eyes, this woman who was neither his wife nor his mistress now but some preposterous animal-idol, the incarnation of life's perishability, of priceless duration, the most precious thing of all. And to think that it was real! Oh! How to assent to it; how to capture a flicker of the most sublime wonder; how, out of the volatile mist, the one that pained by reason of the elusive and irrevocable character of the moment – to effect at least *a fragment of eternity* congealed in the hard and bony claws of the will? A lost cause. His perverse fantasies at the wedding reception? Mere clowning. Only now did his human ego, that work of millions of generations, only now did it begin to stir, snort, bolt, split, splinter – to shatter finally in a slow and laborious explosion in a bottomless pit teeming with pure death. He saw before him a twitching neck, a white, supple, tempting neck, felt under his frantic hands the exquisite *eternally* perfect forms of the hemispheres gracing the reverse side of her arched body. He spread them apart and rammed his whole being into that sex incarnate, nonspatial, embracing all the circles of an earthly Hell and the true, unattainable Sky of Nothingness. But death eluded him. He stopped loving her at that moment – began hating her with unfathomable ferocity. And why? For his having been liquidated alive; because he could never be himself and her at the same time; for the horrendous, unendurable pleasure made all the more diabolically mysterious because of Eliza's complicity in it; and for the reason that he could never destroy her, never overcome her insufferable allure. His arteries and tendons snapped, his bones and muscles convulsed, his brain was a hideous, flaming, maniacal howl of delight at the Poverty of Existence. He let go of her buttocks and dug his hands into that detestable neck. Eliza's eyes bulged from their sockets and became even more beautiful than before. She offered no resistance, evidently preferring to drown in ecstasy. Pain became fused with pleasure, death with eternal life in praise of the unfolding Mystery of Panexistence, which was on the verge of being illuminated. She took a deep breath, but it was no longer a living breath that came out of her. Her body shook in the final convulsions of death, the brutal victor was supremely satisfied in knowing he had destroyed her. This certainty was the last flicker of dimming consciousness; Genezip was now definitively, irrevocably mad. He fall asleep with the corpse in his arms, totally oblivious to anything temporal. A crime? Not likely, for at that terrifying moment Zip was unaware that by his violent act he was depriving someone of life. At last he could love Eliza in his own way; at last they were one.

He awoke, like Marchal Ney on the day of his execution, *avec une exactitude militaire* at seven the next morning. He freed himself from his lover's death grip, got up, washed in the adjoining bathroom, left without as much as a backward glance (not that he would have known what to make of the body had he turned around), and, after slipping on his uniform and overcoat, took his hand valise and went downstairs. He behaved mechanically, obeying the same mechanism that impels bees to gather honey, ants to transport pine needles, gallflies to deposit their eggs in caterpillars, and myriads of other creatures to perform similar acts. Not a single trace of his former self remained. Though he could remember everything down to the last detail, his memory was dead; his living memory belonged to someone else.

It was an ordinary fall day, one of those days suitable for ordinary people. Genezip, too, fit this category, so burnt out was he. These were the first symptoms of his catatonia.

"Did the documents arrive?" he asked the hotel attendant.

"Yes, Lieutenant. The orderly delivered them at 6:30 this morning. I was just about to have you awakened."

"The lady won't be leaving until tomorrow," a voice from another world said through him. He paid his hotel bill and left for the train depot. Someone performed these actions on his behalf. Zip was dead forever, but his outward person remained unchanged. He ate lunch in the restaurant car, staring out at the frost-covered Mazovian plain as it receded and then was lost in the bright haze of an autumnal sun, and listened no less absently to the utterly profound imbecilities being spouted by Lambdon Tiger, who sat opposite him. Naturally, that strange old man already knew everything and could even justify the atrocity. Intrigued, Zip listened to him lecture, even pleasurably so, although his theoretical pronouncements fell on deaf ears; such things no longer stuck to Zip's automated brain. Perhaps this was standard procedure. It seemed that all Murtibingists had to suffer a severe crisis and then be lulled to sleep, as on a cushy bed, by the Murtibingist system. (Only the severely traumatized were used as propagandists.) Lambdon foresaw that Eliza would have abandoned her faith the moment she achieved her erotic ambitions. He also knew, inexplicably, that she was unable to have children: she was barren. What did he care about the rest? She had died at the peak of her life; only a slow breakdown and suicide awaited her. So wasn't she better off dead? . . .

In the capital, Zip reported to the local headquarters and then made straight for the commander's place. The general was just then supping with his wife and daughter. He looked oddly pale, and by contrast the black of his mustache created a funereal impression. The night before had been one of Davamesque visions. Something had clearly transpired there, in that titanic brain of his. But what? No one knew; nor would anyone ever find out. His dark, jet-black, *smorodinovye* eyes flashed their customary wild gaiety. Tomorrow, at long last, the army was leaving for the front. It marked the end of these stupid, petty little games, for the grandest game of all was about to commence – that of life and death. But tucked away in his soul was a secret; curled up on the floor of his soul was a great surprise, the only true and loyal mistress worthy of him. Zip, who was invited to join them for supper, ate with appetite, even though he had polished off a full-course meal a couple of hours ago on the train. Still, the poor guy was suffering from mild exhaustion. Kotzmolochowicz, oddly, failed to make any special impression on him. Of course, he was tickled to have as his commander a giant among men – but there it ended. They were no longer rivals where Persy was concerned. At the moment the general was relaxing before tomorrow's expedition – *détente*ing, *entspannung*ing, "loosening up." He had a knack for squeezing in these calculated, carefree moments even when he was swamped with work. He did nothing: chatted with his wife, even clapping her on occasion; horsed around with his daughter and their red-haired cat, Puma; lounged about the house. He reveled in this family atmosphere – for what may have been the last time, which in no way dampened his mood. On the contrary, he enjoyed the occasion all the more because of it. The enjoyment of life is a supreme art. It cannot be acquired; one has to have a gift for it. At 5:30 he and Zip sat in the general's study drinking coffee. In reply to a harmless inquiry, Zip told him his life's story, talked about his father, his military service and the recent battle, and even alluded vaguely to his affair with the princess. When in his recitation he came to his meeting with Persy, the general looked queerly at his adjutant. But his catatonic aide withstood it: "*Un aide de camp catatonisé, quel luxe!*" as the general told Troufières.

A telephone message. From the general's words Genezip guessed that it was about Eliza's death. He rose, snapped to attention, and as soon as Kotzmolochowicz had hung up and again fixed on him those marvelous, vacant eyes full of mild bewilderment, he immediately began in the manner of a report:

"I strangled her because I loved her too much. Maybe I was mad to do it, but that's how it happened. I want to serve nobody but the army. My marriage would have stood in the way. I ask for mercy. I'll make up for everything at the front. Please grant me this one favor, general; you can punish me later." He remained stiffly at attention, his doglike eyes fixed on the general's magnificent face. The latter studied him for what seemed like an eternity – studied and envied. Zip moved not a muscle. "A madman if ever there was one – a first-class madman," the commander mused. "And in a way, it's partly my fault," he added, recalling one of Sump's last reports. Had this imbecile kid gotten a taste something he himself could not even begin to comprehend? Time dragged on interminably. The after-dinner mood of a second-rate city apartment. The tick-tock of a clock; various household odors trickling into the study, mingling with the aroma of cigars: *melkoburzhuazynaya skuka.* Such a bourgeois background!

If he were now being sentenced to prison, even to death, his reaction would not have been less indifferent. "But when I snap out of this and the day of enlightenment comes – what then?" he thought lethargically, vapidly. "Then it's death – but the nasty, painful kind! Ugh . . . " This last was spoken by a newcomer, someone risen from the cellar of his being to take control of his catatonic body. Between these two psychoidentities – the one currently in progress and the one which as a child (oh, shed a little tear!) used to unleash dogs – there was a gulf not to be filled, "a gap in the soul," as Bekhmetev not very astutely described this state. It takes a madman to grasp it, which of course precludes a true and objective grasp of this or any other phenomenon: a vicious circle. Meanwhile, the general kept staring at the son of his former friend (and his own "would-be" son), and it was as if, with his clairvoyant eyes, he could decipher not only this erratic killer's brain but even its albuminous links, its electrons, and those smaller (infinitesimally small), almost fictional (or were they as real as galactic systems? Good God, if that were actually so . . . And yet who knows? But that would be too ghastly for words . . .) elements of matter-energy mentally stimulated by (a) arbitrary objects, (b) motion, and (c) our muscular activity, which is immediately given. The ingenious general saw not only the present and the past (he had been partially briefed on Zip's past, just as he was briefed on the lives of all his adjutants), but also the fate of this truly remarkable young officer: he would lead a long and happy life even as the walking corpse he had lately become. And his own fate? Ha – better not to think about that! There the struggle was with something infinitely more powerful, with no prospect of victory: like trying to stop an express train with one finger. Still, it must end beautifully. If all else failed, he would lead his general staff in a final charge and go down fighting. Now, didn't *that* bottomless (?) thought brighten the present! All one could say was "Wow!" "Though the little turd might stick it to her . . . later . . . " (in the back of his mind was that criminal do at

Persy's). He never pursued this thought – not now or later. He walled it up the way Mazepa was immured (?). Half an hour, perhaps three-quarters of an hour, went by. Suddenly that young man said (but not before the general had time to reflect: "What fun it must have been for that hysterical little piece [he had been introduced to Eliza at some ball or other] to die at the hands of such a stud. Too bad I'm not a fag – I'd fuck him like a greyhound."):

"I wish to report that . . . etc. Before that I killed a colonel – his name escapes me – when I was desperately in love with Miss Bestialskaya." The general flinched even though he had just been dwelling on the very same theme. But her name never failed to impress him. He was perversely in love with everything that belonged to her: her slippers, stockings, makeup, her ribbons, even the sound of her first and last names. "It's hers, all hers," he told himself in his scarier moments. Right now he craved those habitual marvels as a conclusion to what was likely his last moment of escape. He rose to his feet, clanged his spurs, and, stretching his creaking bones, said:

"I know everything and won't pry. As for what lies ahead, those are *melochy – a melochy k chortu*. Persy told me; she's my secretary now. Tomorrow we're leaving for the front. To the front – do you understand, you clown? Such a front the world has never seen, and such a confrontation as the one Wang and I are going to have has never been seen, either. I'm not exaggerating, you little dope. You'll see for yourself, so be happy. By the time they figure out that it was you, we'll be far from here. You'll pay a price, and most likely we shall all die. Now you're mine. I need people like you – that's right, even madmen. And you're one helluva madman, Zip, but I like people like you; I need them and look after them. You're a vanishing breed. Who knows, maybe I'm just as bonkers as you. Ha, ha!" A laugh full of fiendish, devastating levity broke from him. He kissed Zip on the brow and then rang. His aide calmly sat down in an armchair, leaning forward in silence. If only it had been like this before! Now it no longer mattered. Then the orderly, or "The Blob," as he was called, came in. (He knew his master inside and out and diligently performed the most outrageous errands entrusted to him. He sensed moods of which his master was not even dimly aware. He could decipher them from a twitch of the general's cheek, from the imperceptible flash of his omnipotent pitch-black eyes. But on the whole he was a "blob" – that was true – but he had that – oh, what's it called? – intuition – yes – the female, short-range sort.) "Tell my wife, that *gavno sobachee*, that I've gone to the office for a while. I'll be back before nine. We'll move out at eight tomorrow morning. Make sure everything's ready. Now show the lieutenant to his room. The guest room, number three. To bed, Zip – at once. You'll have much to do tonight." He gave him his hand, his sovereign but gentle hand, and strode out of his study briskly, with a youthful step. Then he got into his car (which was always parked in front, day and night) and drove over to Persy's place, later to become the scene of events too ghastly to contemplate. Kotzmolochowicz confided everything to his mistress, and she repaid him with unknown details concerning Zip and his trials, a titillation that grew to a passion when Persy persuaded the general that it was actually she who had killed Eliza through Zip out of jealousy. It was not true, of course, as is clear from the above – unless subconsciously? But who was to say? Psychoanalysts were no longer practicing in those jolly times. But from that moment on, Persy saw the future differently – oh, a lot differently. There loomed up, in that marvelous little head of hers, the barest premonition of some bizarre prospect. She asked to be taken along to the front and bribed him into consenting. For, even though she was terribly afraid (not to worry: a woman will always find a way out), she had to act as she did.

The Last Convulsion

Eight A.M. In half an hour the staff train would depart for the front, hastily thrown together by the general at the last minute. His ingenious plan, conceived almost subconsciously in the awesome turbogenerator that was this invincible strategist's brain, had materialized, with a magical exactitude, in the distant plains, swamps, and woods of Polish Byelorussia. The Chinese would have given anything to know the details of this plan, so marvelous in its simplicity. No such luck: *der geniale Kotzmolokowitsch* kept it all in his head. The corps leaders were to be notified by telephone as to where to position the various companies, squadrons, and batteries. Not a single scrap of paper was used.

An immaculately clean map, without a single marking, before the eyes; a telephone, in a *quadruply* upholstered office called the Operations Room (where even a wiretap would have produced nothing); a special underground cable, whose approximate position was known only to a handful of people, and, oh, yes, to the officers – always different ones – in charge of installing the various sections of the cable. A sample of the field commands two days before the defensive offensive: "Hello. Headquarters of III Corps. General Niekrzejko? Listen and make a note of this. Thirteenth Division: a sector four kilometers long stretching from Gizzard Gulch to Comatosia. Twenty-first Infantry Regiment: Gizzard Gulch – Slopville. First Battalion: Gizzard Gulch. General Staff: elevation point 261, the coal miner's shack next to the birch forest. Front O.S.O.: three hundred steps to the right of the large oak tree with the red cross on it. Second Battery, First Division, Fifth Regiment: 150-mm mortars. Two howitzers in an easterly direction, thirty meters to the left of the blue cottage along the road to Comatosia," etc., etc. Enough to confuse anyone. But not him. His voice was already hoarse, yet he kept at it tirelessly. Alone in the room for hours, never cracking, never losing an ounce of his composure. Did the group commanders lack initiative? Well, so what, no great loss; the imbeciles would only have spoiled everything. Excitable dogs. He alone *knew*, this master of masters.

For the first time since leaving Peking, the mandarin Wang and his Japanese adviser Fudsujito Johikomo were stumped. They had not a scrap of intelligence on the enemy's defenses. Not a single spy had met with success. In fact, almost all had perished, while those who had returned reported a state of general ignorance. Not even torture had worked. The plan of operations was to go out to the group commanders, and from there to the division commanders, on the evening before the offensive. It was as clearly outlined in the general's truly august head as the troop disposition itself. ("What a shame to waste such a man on such a crummy epoch," even his critics were saying.) And it was this plan that would force the enemy's hand. Of course, minor modifications might occur, but then what was the telephone for? The general reacted to the unexpected with the same ease as to the familiar. Obviously, the Chinese had an enormous numerical advantage; they were a fearsome and inscrutable people, indifferent to pain and death, able to get along for days without food or drink, and capable of fighting like the dickens. In recent years their technology had far outstripped that of the White Devils from Beyond the Seas. In a word, defeat was imminent. Although, a miracle was still possible. Hadn't the Great Moloch already performed several such miracles in his lifetime? He was determined to "show his stuff," as the saying about him went. The first battle had to be won. Life wasn't worth a tinker's damn, anyway. If he came through it alive, the Chinese would have to make him a field commander, a cushy rank at which to retire: first he would whip the Germans, next the French, then the English, and even the devil himself. Either way, he was ready: whichever side won was almost irrelevant. Almost – for despite everything, that night of Davamesque had made a slight, almost imperceptible breach. But he knew how to conceal it, both from himself and from others.

Eight in the morning. A fall day was breaking, which, despite the sunrise, augured a bleak day. It was the second day of frost. Digging trenches was hard, but there were enough men on hand and the ground was only hard on the surface. Soon the cavalry would be staging a spectacle such as never has been recorded – neither then nor since. Future military historians had their work cut out for them, not a single document would survive – not the tiniest scrap, hee-hee! Steam poured from the cylinder cocks of an enormous American locomotive. The greatest figures of the Polish military swarmed like phantoms in the damp mist. A festive day before the grand performance. Everyone was aboard the train: Monkempt-Unster, Kuźma Huśtański, Rammer, and members of the cabinet who had come to give their final blessing – all those Boroeders, Zifferblatowiczes, and Quiltys, who positively reeked of treason. Gaze on, fellas! *Nech sa paczy* – as the Czechs say. Oh yes – there were even a few gullible counts, "dressed for the kill," among them. The more the merrier! The smart-asses hadn't a clue. It's what made it so enjoyable. He stood alone – His Onlyness – against that yellow crap bearing light from the East. If only they didn't reek so much! You can't breathe within a three-mile radius of them. The train was being conducted by the general's brother, Isidore, the director of public transportation. Wasn't it time to leave? Not yet. At last, walking with a light step, Persy appeared on the platform. With an elegant gesture, the general kissed the hand of the woman who had now become his official mistress. There was no stopping him now; he was headed for certain death. His wife greeted her warmly, like a sister. Everyone was whispering. The members of the cabinet looked on with astonished, sleepy eyes. The general lifted up his little daughter Ileanka and pressed her face against his black mustache. Persy, light as a wagtail, flitted from the platform to the club car. Would she or wouldn't she indulge his perverse whims? Then Zip reported to the general (he had been sent to check on someone's trunk in the baggage car). The eyes of this bizarre, would-be couple met. At the moment, Miss Bestialskaya's recent victim had more the look of a corpse: there was not a trace of emotion in him. Pouting, she withdrew into the wagon's interior, which glittered with the very essence of club-car elegance, and drew the curtain. She was a sore loser, and besides, ever since the killing, Genezip had grown fonder in her eyes. It was, after all, she who had provoked him to vent his rage in such a quaint manner. This last thought thrilled her as only the commander had been able to do until now. Was the general amusing himself with these two before his death? Most unlikely, since Zip already was a living corpse in uniform, sensitive to nothing save his own fatal state of insensitivity.

Isidore's whistle rent the frosty air. There was another kiss on the forehead of his martyred wife (Saint Ann the Martyr), yet another immersion of his mustache in his daughter's lovely pink puss (at this point a tear, black as a black pearl, rolled [inwardly] from the eye of that glorious specimen of a vanishing race: What would become of the poor woman after the yellow vermin had conquered the earth?), and they entered the well-heated car. (Kotzmolochowicz was not very attached to the earth, only to the landscape – or so he claimed when he was drunk.) The train, panting under the glass vault of the station, slowly pulled out, floated phantomlike past the station's squalid outbuildings, and disappeared into the city fog, now turned reddish brown by the morning sun. The historical destiny of a country now rolled along in this luxurious car headed for the east, toward that unfathomable abyss of the future waiting in the form of a sullen, brooding, autumnal, Byelorussian landscape. It was all so petty and drab and humdrum – compared, say, to the mystery of intergalactic space. It felt lovely to be traveling in a well-heated Pullman car. The circumstances were by no means the worst. Clad in his field uniform, Zip sat erect, giving notice that he was the general's aide. Betraying a growing unease, Persy thought only of how she might escape a certain disaster. She was counting on her diabolical sexiness – that plus the Chinese chief of staff's furious passion for white women of quality. But what if that maniac Erasmus, her "Erico," whom she adored in her own special way, should put her on parade??? The very thought annoyed her. And yet her passivity before his omnipotence excited her, aroused her in the presence of all men – something she had never known. She was suddenly, for example, overcome by lust for that gorgeous young murderer in the adjutant's uniform. The imminent danger, the *prospect of ineluctable death* (how so?) rendered everything – at the same time and nearly to the same degree – both terrifying and marvelous, desirable and detestable, and wildly enchanting. Damn – how to escape this, by what genital stunt – now, there was a challenge. Poor Persy did not feel it within her power, and therein lay the horrific, unsurpassed magic of the moment. She had not the knack of transposing good into evil as did that all-powerful bull of hers, enviably so. The devils! Still, she had never felt better. She had the whole world in her hand, like some poisonous dagger: on whom should the first and decisive blow fall? It was maddening, this being stranded between abject despair and life's apotheosis . . . Suppose she cheated fate and escaped her stubborn destiny, life would not be *this*, supreme but . . . but . . . And so it would go, up and down, down and up, a sort of psychic seasickness, vertigo above the abyss of life's ultimate weirdness. It was there that they had really met, had come within an infinitesimally small fraction of absolute coition; it was there she and Zip had met asymptotically.

The train whizzed along like a bullet, impossible to stop or deflect, toward the unknown "verdict of history," toward that bristling, two-horned Chinese something that not even Murti Bing (assuming he really existed) understood. The commander of this terrible expedition was in excellent spirits. He, too, was in his life's zenith. He had become that "mortal blow incarnate," as his staff officers used to call him and as he imagined himself to be, longingly, during peacetime. At last the umbilical cord connecting him with coarse, everyday reality had snapped. It would be brief, but for all time. The wretch was mistaken (who said that? To the wall!!!) in believing this to be the climax. The latter lay hidden in a point-moment of space-time and was designated on our relative, earthly calendar as follows: 9 A.M., October 5; Sublimity; here at the front mapped out in the general's ingenious brain. Not even an apparatus as splendid as the commander's brain could foresee the exact ending. More on that subject later. So, for the time being, this was to serve as his life's climax. Let there be others, even more splendid; the general was intimate with the world's most awesome powers: with life at the summit, or with death – wherever it might occur, as long as it was a noble, that is, heroic, death, occurring as his spirit was fulfilling its historical mission on this planet; and beautiful, dammit, a knight's glorious death as dreamed by a virgin descended from a race of warriors. All things pointed toward such an end. The commander surveyed, without regret, the receding emerald fields, the yellow stubble, the pine forest, possibly for the last time . . . unless? Perish the thought. Celebrate the miracle, if and when it should happen. Because what awaited him was a catastrophe of cosmic proportions, as inevitable as the ending of a Greek tragedy. This much was certain: there was not, nor could there be, any other resolution. He always thought ahead – never backward – such was his method. His mind was always one step ahead of life; it never trailed behind. Meanwhile, things would be done his way, dammit – then we'd see. He buried his mouth in Persy's fluffy curls and through the strands of her blonde hair devoured the surrounding countryside framed by the car's generous window. The majority of the commander's overworked companions dozed on the red plush couches. A few, spent from last night's intense farewells to life, had actually gone to bed. The operational plan was ready: it had only to be dictated to the company commanders in such a way so as to be unintelligible in its entirety. In the meantime: "*entspannen.*" Grabbing Persy as though she were an object, he carried her out of the club car toward their sleeping compartment. Zip was unfazed. Had he lost all erotic sensation, or what? Certain natures can achieve maximal happiness only through madness; not since birth had he felt this buoyant. He remained motionless, completely obedient to someone else's will: close to the main turbine of historical events, the very nexus of forces embodied in the general (what more could he have wanted?); curled up in a tranquil little corner on a roaring projectile, a tiny flea on a fifteen-inch artillery shell splitting the breathless air. Only occasionally, with some spare motor of his brain, did he fear being jarred from his complacency. In his imagination he distinctly recalled the last scene with Eliza, but he could not, emotionally, admit to having committed a crime. Everything that had thus far transpired formed a quaint, necessary little picture in which the living appeared as actors in disguise. And all in a normal light, without a trace of lunacy – only for him, of course.

It was a springlike day in autumn, one of those days when aging summer lounges above the somnolent earth in a second adolescence, like a reformed alcoholic or drug addict who suddenly says to himself: no, just one more drink, one more fix. It was quiet as a morgue at the front – compared to an artillery barrage, of course. As for poor Persy, it was war at its most horrifying: the Chinese artillery was merely "target practicing," sounding out the enemy while adjusting its sights. Time and again, multicaliber guns could be heard firing from the Chinese side, and isolated shells came flying in our direction, screeching in the peaceful air until they landed in the trenches and occasionally inflicted heavy losses. We had engaged in the same exercise the day before, unable to put it off any longer, though it greatly facilitated the task of the Chinese. They had time; we, that is, the general, did not. It was a windless autumnal day, and most of the trees still had their leaves, now browned by the hoarfrosts. The stubble fields and meadows glistened with gossamer and reflected the lusterless, gentle, comatose sun like ponds covered with duckweed. The infinite calm of space aroused a superstitious fear. Everyone, from the simplest camp followers to the company and corps commanders, was strangely and solemnly disturbed by "something" – not to be confused with ordinary fear. From time to time Kotzmolochowicz, accompanied by Zip and Oleśnicki, would tour the front in a small and elegant "fartolette," as the torpedolike tank was called. The ban instituted by the Antiwar League against aerial bombardments and gases was a great relief. High above circled reconnaissance planes that now and then were garlanded with the white puffs of exploding antiaircraft shells, but no one feared being hit by shells hundreds of kilometers behind the lines – unless by our own side, in the form of shrapnel, although to be hit in this fashion was the mark of a born loser. And yet this is precisely what happened to the general. While he was conferring with the commander of III Corps, Niekrzejko, a fragment of one of our own shells struck the general's boot on the toe, completely demolishing the sole and ruining the tip. Niekrzejko turned pale as the commander swayed but kept his balance. In the mayhem that followed, Zip had an opportunity to admire the perfection of his mask: not for a moment did those pitch-black eyes lose their insolent gaiety. Unfortunately, although Zip had the *opportunity* to admire, he failed to do so: nothing could impress him anymore. The earthworks were near completion – only the attack zones were left – and the defense line had been drawn up long ago, some twenty kilometers to the rear. The Chinese occupied a position approximately ten to twelve kilometers from our lines. Our most advanced cavalry patrols had made contact with the enemy in an area located some seven kilometers away.

The general was in an excellent mood. He had already crossed the line of doubt and hesitation and was now like a bullet in flight. Miracles sometimes happened, dammit. Having a fair knowledge of himself, he could always expect the unexpected of himself. What brainstorm would issue from that indomitable, next-to-last individualist on earth, preserved until that day (October 5) in the devilish marinade of Poland's social hierarchy? He could be proud of his army-machine: one press of the button and – ka-bloom!! But he could take equal pride in his own mind, where, almost without a single scrap of paper, that whole impending battle was kept stored in the abstract. Fleetingly, the general felt visited by Poland's ancient warriors, by those who had fought against similar Mongolian "avalanches." But suddenly a strange sorrow effaced this glorious moment, as dust is wiped from a tabletop. Why had such a "domestic" comparison come to mind? A dazzling and immaculate boredom, born of the absolute folly of great deeds, overpowered him. He desired, *quite simply*, to live. And here was death staring boldly at him from underneath the wide visor of his cap of the First Light Cavalry Regiment, whose uniform, festooned with general's stripes and braids, he wore especially for the occasion. It was not a lack of courage, but a pure instinct for life, uncomplicated by the fear of death. A soft voice whispered internally of another existence, of a bungalow in a military cooperative outside the city; of geraniums in the windows; his daughter playing in the garden; his lovely wife Ann busily pursuing her own philosophy (soon his to explore, as well). To hell with that "tart," with the sort of wild "entshpanoongs" and "daytaunts" demanded by work's fury! They were not essential, merely a substitute for satisfying an unconscious metaphysical urge to be everything, but literally *everything*. Yet here it was: the Void. How close he was to that Void on the giant hierarchy of infinite possibilities! No sooner had he broken with the world of base mediocrity (he, a former stable boy, and later broncobuster, employed by Count Chraposkrzecki, the lord of Bathos and Bunkum, whose youngest son, a major and commander of a squadron of his guards, was presently a blind instrument in his hands) than it enticed with the temptation of a peaceful sleep, a vulgar, vegetablelike existence. "Is this my peasant blood, or what?" the commander chided himself. Then he had to laugh. "It's even better this way; if I were a count, it wouldn't be half as great." If only he could retire after executing this desperate mission, this blasted battle that was to have been his life's magnum opus. Then what? Then travels with his daughter, showing her marvels hidden from ordinary eyes, bringing her up to be a monster like Persy or himself – a secret voice whispered. Ugh! . . . His successes on the Romanian front, the crusades in Bolshevia, the brilliant street battles in which he had shown himself such a master – all not enough for him, a cavalry man of blood and spirit down to his most inscrutable guts, this Moloch-centaur, as he was called during regimental orgies, when, in an alcoholic frenzy, as wobbly on his feet as an infantryman, he showed off his diabolical, dragon-centaurian cavalryman's skills, thus setting an impossible example for the wilder junior officers. But had he been, at the outset, in his most profound essence, that which he was at the moment? What might he have become in "more favorable circumstances"? The owner of a racing stable or stud farm, a professor of horse breeding at the University of Vilno? His career had been anything but normal, being mainly indebted to chance and, well, perhaps a little to his own doing. But what might he have accomplished had it not been for this crusade? He could always become a professor. But he had deserved better, a noble birth, that of a count at the very least; but it was all come to naught, there was no undoing the past. He was a slave of some higher force; there was no turning back. His schedule: an inspection, followed by an orgy with light cavalry, then a nap and a little morning *Entspannung* with Persy (she was waiting for him at the manor of the Cockleburs of Lumbagonia, behind a sleepy [?] cluster of copper-colored trees, most likely sipping her morning coffee in her strawberry nightie . . . Oh!!). And then would come the greatest battle history had ever known, from which he would emerge as an awesome myth of vanishing individuality, the bugaboo of automated mothers wishing to frighten their future descendants. Boo! He shook off this last attack of weakness in which he had made himself snug – as snug as in a soft dressing gown fit for a lazy, holiday morning. His aides stared at him, not daring to breathe. At the thought of what might be stirring inside that diabolical skull, they were struck with superstitious (necessarily superstitious) fear. Among them sat seemingly ordinary flesh in a general's finest dress, harboring a supremely unique moment in the history of an expiring world. Before them stood mankind's passage into its second fundamental phase, incarnated now in that diabolical doll whose head teemed with incomprehensible thoughts – here, before their very eyes, on an October morning, in a "fartolette" racing across the cobweb-covered stubble.

Zip was beginning to rouse himself, but he had already passed into another world. The horror of the past, coated with the mysterious varnish of madness and the expectation of approaching events, shimmered like the tarnished but once-vibrant colors in a painting by some ancient master. This state was due as much to the "trauma" experienced that awful night of initiation into the infinite and the bizarre as to the impending disaster that precluded profound changes. How delectable was the ephemeral quality of these irreversible moments! On the day of their departure the commander's orderly had confided to both aides in a whisper that no one would return from this campaign. Not even the general had ever shown such clairvoyance. That Blob had let drop this observation while dressing the general one morning. (Later the general's mask betrayed only grim determination, concentrated like sun rays in a lens: "He dug into his brain the spur of his will" – indeed he had.) Besides, was there anything that psychopath had not already experienced? Both the commander and his aide were borderline cases. Zip may have gone farther in realizing his fantasies, may have reached a more advanced stage of insanity, but the general was teetering on the edge. Only he was unaware of it: his terrific workload had such a grip on him that the symptoms escaped him. He literally had not had time to go insane. Not infrequently (but not too often, either) Bekhmetev, half-pityingly and half-admiringly, would shake his head. "There won't be time for any treatment in the grave, Erasmus Wojciechowicz," he would say. "Too early for the booby hatch," the general would reply. "When it's time for me to go, I prefer to be taken out behind a fence and shot in the ear. As for the fence, I have one back at the officer's co-op in Żoliborz, and a revolver is bound to turn up – some sport will always do me the favor." He was referring to his bitterest enemies in the capital, who, even as he risked his life, were probably getting out the welcome mat and polishing up the keys to the city. Genezip felt content in his emotional void. He would never socialize with sane people again; suicidal death, whether or not he went to prison, awaited him. Life had resolved his fate. He recognized neither himself nor the surrounding world. But in his estrangement he felt as comfortable as in a jewel box. Was this not a symptom of incipient madness? The prospect of madness terrified him. A clinical madman who could go on functioning only because of the excess force exerted by an external situation and, well, because he was catatonic – was it not already too late? But there was no time for such piddling questions. Just as they were driving past a camouflaged battery installation, the general began delivering one of his celebrated speeches rousing one's most secret, most militant insides. (These speeches were never transcribed or published; without his presence, his voice, his bearing, and the ambience he created, they appeared clumsy and mediocre. He was of the same opinion himself.) He had no sooner finished speaking than a high-caliber eleven-inch shell came flying, as if on command, from the remote positions of the enemy and exploded directly before their artillery line, showering everyone with dirt and splinters from the demolished wooden barriers. Miraculously, no one was killed, but the commander was struck on the head by a large piece of wood. A second omen. Zip regretted not being able to muster the same enthusiasm he had felt in school; then a few trumpet blasts and the sound of his commander's voice had sufficed to light up the world in a furious explosion of life's concentrated magic. With head bowed, embarrassed by Kotzmolochowicz's tasteless jokes, he listened to these *balivernes* like a condemned man for whom life has lost all meaning.

The next sequence of events took place with alarming speed. On the following morning, the Great Moloch stood surrounded by his staff on elevation point 261, the spot from which he was to observe the battle (the ban on gases and airplanes [whew!] had made for relative safety: they were still ten kilometers behind their own front line), or rather, the point from which it was to be launched. The front was three hundred kilometers long; the battle itself was expected to last a minimum of five days. Camped approximately one thousand feet behind the general staff were three regiments of mounted guardsmen under the command of Czar Cyril's adjutant, Karpeka, one of the best cavalrymen in all of Russia. Oh, yes! We forgot to mention the execution: yesterday, at midnight, they had summarily executed Monkempt-Unster, who, at a sham war council (immediately following an orgy), had ranted like a bolshevik. He was gagged and taken outside. A quarter of an hour later he was no longer among the living. Even Zip had helped to drag him outside while he had desperately tried to free himself from the irate staff officers, and had done so without the slightest emotion. The drunken Huśtański (Kuźma) had wanted personally to castrate Monkempt before he died but was refused permission: the commander had strenuously forbidden it. By now Zip was infused with the general's spirit; the execution made not the slightest impression on him; he was now a complete automaton.

The battle was organized in the Napoleonic style, since the last performance for the benefit of history could not be staged without a certain decor: the general staff, the cavalry, the general's Grey, gala uniforms, and parades. At last they proceeded to the dirty work scheduled for that festive day. The tactical command was relayed by telephone – by the general himself, of course – from a closed booth that trailed him everywhere. The artillery was set to begin firing shortly; the attack was scheduled for three P.M.

It was a pale, autumnal dawn, overcast from the start. Gradually the clouds stacked in the east turned red underneath as a magnificent day began to unfold, slowly but systematically. Kotzmolochowicz was mounted on horseback before his staff (on his famous Grey, whose rump had been turned into a veritable storage room by the general's exhortative style). In his hand he held a telephone receiver. His face looked calm, his black eyes remained fixed on the cottages of Sublimity blocking the distant horizon. His eyes brimmed with individualism. A hush. Suddenly the customary (but brilliant) darkness of his brain was rent by a black thunderbolt. Back, everyone back! There would be no battle! He was prepared to sacrifice his personal glory for the sake of those poor soldiers, our poor country, and the rest of poor Europe. One way or another the Chinese were bound to conquer. Why should thousands go to their deaths? What for? To suit his ambition and that of his general staff? For the sake of a noble death? Horrifying doubts flashed through the precise but opaque skull of this weary titan. He spoke on the telephone in a sure and decisive voice, while the grey clouds overhead turned ever more jagged and red-streaked. The staff officers sensed that the general was pronouncing the words with an unusual but painful emphasis:

"Hello – signal exchange? Yes. Listen carefully, General Knuckle: there is not going to be any battle. Canceled. Raise the signal of surrender in every sector. The front is being opened." (A sudden thought in the midst of these irreversible commands: "Could it be that I just want to go on living?" The geraniums in the window of the little bungalow in Żoliborz flashed through his mind.) "Once the enemy has received the signal, all divisions are to abandon their positions, lay down arms, and head in an easterly direction to begin fraternizing with the troops of the yellow coalition. Long live" – he hesitated, then whispered feebly to himself – "mankind!" He let go of the receiver, which fell to the frozen ground with a hollow, weak thud. The telephone operator stood riveted to the spot, not daring to move. The general staff was awestruck. But these troops were so disciplined that not a murmur was heard. Besides, there was not one who did not yearn to go on living: all realized the situation was hopeless. Then a cry went up: "Long live the general!" – a disorderly, spasmodic, tumultuous cry. The crimson clouds were shading into orange-red. Kotzmolochowicz turned toward his loyal comrades and saluted. At the moment he was as much an automaton as his aide-de-camp, Zip Kapen; something had snapped. They were then approached by Chraposkrzecki, the orderly of the commanding officer of the "Legion of Molochs" and the second son of the general's former employer.

"General, may I ask what's going on around here? I've just been talking to Ciunzik, and he claims that . . . "

"Lieutenant" – on duty, Kotzmolochowicz was a strict observer of ranks and never tolerated any familiarity – "we are surrendering for humanitarian reasons. There will be no unnecessary bloodshed. Go and inform my guards." There followed a moment of silence. The clouds were now a bright yellow. Huge patches of willow-green sky appeared in the east. The hills behind the general staff were ablaze with morning sunlight. With a single motion, Chraposkrzecki yanked an enormous six-cylinder revolver from his holster and fired it at the general. Then, without waiting to see the outcome of his shot, he mounted his horse and galloped off to where the guards were stationed some eight hundred feet to the west. There the sun already shone brightly. Kotzmolochowicz touched his left shoulder. The bullet had ripped off an epaulet in the place where his general's aiguillettes were attached; now they dangled despondently at his side, tickling the flank of his Grey.

"He humiliated me in front of my general staff. The moron!" The commander laughed. "Not for a moment!" he shouted to his loyal officers, who all turned to the west. Chraposkrzecki was galloping toward the solid line of cavalry mustered on the plain. He yelled something. A crowd of officers gathered around him. Someone delivered a speech – a brief one. A command was given . . . What sort of command? Only the last words could be heard distinctly – it was the voice of General Sergei Karpeka: "Tighten the reins, ready arms for the attack, maaarch!" This was followed by an abrupt, "March! March!" The troops moved out slowly, their swords gleaming in the warm, rose light.

"Well, gentlemen, now it's our turn," the commander said calmly, lighting a cigarette. "Full tilt to Thirteenth. Direction – Sublimity, E, General Staff Map No. 167." He broke out in a loud guffaw and dug his spurs into his horse. They charged *ventre à terre* toward the first cottages of Sublimity, to the place on the map corresponding to the letter E, the first letter of the locale hitherto unknown but now become world famous. There the "Legion of Molochs" fought its last battle with the Thirteenth Division, which remained loyal to the commander, as did the rest of the army. Meanwhile, its staff fled in scattered array, but it was no easy task chasing down twenty riders with three regiments. The officers reached the village two hundred feet ahead of their pursuers.

"They've revolted! Fire!! Return their machine-gun fire!!" the general shouted wildly, never losing any of his customary sangfroid. He studied himself from a distance, this reputed hysteric and bunkoturbogenerator. How splendidly that heroic fighter comported himself, as did the automated companies of the Thirteenth Division. A barrage roared through the limpid air of that autumnal morning. Forty machine guns began rattling in the direction of the sun-drenched zone. The sun stood high now. The magnificent light cavalry charged but fell short of that beastly sector of E. Kotzmolochowicz calmly surveyed the fighting. When all three regiments had regrouped in the fields in the blazing sun (the weather was now perfect; the clouds had parted like curtains drawn by invisible cords), he had the mobile hospitals brought up while he himself drove out to what were once his front lines. He believed more than ever that he was making a personal sacrifice of absolutely monumental proportions for the good of mankind – even greater than Napoleon's sacrifice at Waterloo. On "his" front all was quiet, as the first detachments of "fraternizers" were already setting out. The commander was greeted courteously but without enthusiasm, as befitted an army of robots in a time of crisis. Kotzmolochowicz had shown his stuff – and this time he wasn't kidding.

They were sitting in front of a cottage next to what were once the earthworks. With a strangely glassy look, the general gazed into the black hole of the trench that had been dug in the magnificent black earth of Old Konstantinov. For the first time he began contemplating the grave, and his heart constricted with a secret, unaccustomed grief. The eternity of the universe produced a fleeting *Minderwertigkeitsgefühl.* His wife and daughter (was this about-face for their sake and that of the geraniums in the window?) now loomed in his eyes as the only things of value in the whole universe. He was sickened by the presence of Persy, who, delighted by the turn of events, gaily twittered with his staff officers, who behind affectedly despondent masks leapt for joy at their having been spared. The ghost of the senselessly murdered Monkempt momentarily cast a shadow over that bright, serene, October morning. "He'll soon be taking me with him," thought the general. "After all, I did today what he wanted to do yesterday. But to want and to do are two different things. He could never have brought it off by himself – at the most he might have caused a minor ruckus. That's how it's always been in Poland: they'll kill for something they themselves will do tomorrow." Any moment they were expecting the Chinese liaison, who was to arrange for a formal meeting of the two commanders in chief. The general was now curious about the "other side," which he never believed (until this morning) he would ever visit under peaceful conditions. The Chinese general staff was stationed in Old Konstantinov, twenty miles from the front trenches. The tumult produced by the fraternizing troops spread along the entire front, disturbing the morning calm that cringed before the oncoming winter and slyly stole from the warmth of a lingering summer. Summer and winter seemed to have coalesced on this glorious day, combining as it did elements of both seasons.

The general's doubts did not last long. With his indomitable will he quickly resumed his previous stance born of momentary hysteria over the sheer whimsicality of his about-face, topped with a bit of theoretical "icing" *("eine zugedachte Theorie"?)*, namely, the good of the country and of the human race, whereby military genius was sacrificed on behalf of an even greater (who knew?) fame and glory, for: "Better a live sheep than a dead lion." The turnabout was later ascribed to the inductive effect of the "psycho-magnetic fields" created by the presence of the millions of Chinese obsessed with a single idea. (Such scientific trends actually existed in the West.) Others alluded mysteriously to "the night of twenty-five pills"; still others chalked it up to madness pure and simple. However, it happened exactly as we have described, and that's the truth. Suddenly all pricked up their ears in silence. An automobile was heard rumbling down the road. Soon a luxurious red Bridgewater pulled up in front of the cottage on the opposite side of the line of demarcation. Out of it stepped a retiring Chinese homunculus in an ochre-yellow uniform decorated with a red and yellow sash. With a sprightly jump, he crossed the black hole of the trench, lifting up his long, curved sword with astonishing grace, and approached the group of Polish officers. He saluted, as did the general's staff, and then turned to their commander (all this time Zip remained expressionless; he was the only one who was neither gladdened nor saddened by what had occurred. But in view of the circumstances, why bother with the psychology of some pissant? A madman or not a madman: who cares?):

"Have I the honor of speaking with His Excellency Kotzmolochowicz?" he asked in the most impeccable English.

The general's reply was a curt "Yes." "Okay, now let's keep up this game of masks," he coached himself through clenched teeth.

The other went on, but instead of holding out his hand he kept bowing in the Chinese fashion. "I am General Ping-Fang-Lo, chief of the general staff and a knight of the order of the Yellow and Red Cornflower." (Here he bowed.) "Our Commander, Wang-Tang-Tsang, a mandarin of the first order" (this tsetselike name had a genuinely sinister ring to it) "has the honor of inviting Your Excellency, your entire staff, and, of course, your – hmm – spouse to lunch with him at one o'clock in the Old Konstantinov palace." Fear was evident in the Mongol's beady black eyes.

"What's the mummy so afraid of?" wondered the general. "They're normally not afraid of anything. Something's going on here." And for some reason he answered in French, in an "effusive" manner:

"My dear general *(mon général)*, I am highly honored to receive you . . . *(je suis énormément flatté de pouvoir saluer en votre personne . . .)*."

"Thank you," the other interrupted in English. He saluted, then jumped across the trench and climbed back into the car, which had already been turned around in the meantime. This car, thanks to its giant supercharger, immediately accelerated to sixty miles an hour. A second later it was out of sight. There was an awkward silence, then a great tumult arose among the members of the general staff. Kotzmolochowicz was noticeably (for Blob, of course, had he been there) shaken; the giveaway was a slight wrinkle between his eyes. Something had gone wrong.

"Who does that bastard think he is, anyway?" he said to Persy. "What a nerve . . . No matter. I'll have to eat the fruit of my deeds in true communist fashion. But I'll show them!"

"You won't show them anything," chirped his beaming mistress. "You've just pulled off the greatest feat since Alexander the Great. Just think how glorious our life will be! If a coward had done what you did, it would have been awful. But such a boar, such a winged bull, such a Leviathan as you! . . . It was miraculous, absolutely miraculous! Only I understand you." She took his hand and fixed him with one of those gazes that could cloud the most crystalline thoughts. It was reflected in his eyes as in two metallic discs: the commander was gazing into himself. Again, the image of his wife (a born countess, by the way) and daughter passed through his exhausted brain. But with renewed effort the general quickly reverted to his previous automatism, now tinged with resignation. He sent for his car. Nearby, the men wounded in this morning's conflict were being transported to the Chinese hospitals. That was the order. But who had given it? The Chinese. So now he was forced to submit to Chinese orders! A vicious, almost physical pain jabbed his spiritual intestines, then faded away in the black desert that had suddenly, and insidiously, unfolded. Hearing the men's groans the general buried his face in his hands – but only for a second. "How many more casualties if I hadn't done what I did? Still, something has snapped inside my skull, dammit! I don't feel a thing anymore." A boundless lassitude and boredom assailed him from all sides – even from the west where THEY were, his wife and daughter. The world around him had expired, emptied. He was all by himself, alone in some anonymous pit of automatons – perhaps the last real man on earth. Curiously, since the Chinaman's departure, none of his friends had paid him any attention, something unheard of. The counts gloomily spoke in a whisper with Oleśnicki. Kuźma Huśtański, who had been drunk since morning, strutted about and clanged his enormous saber threateningly. Rammer, whistling the tango "Jealousie" through his teeth, looked anxiously out at the Chinese lines. But so complete was their faith in the perfection of their commander's actions that no one dared to utter a peep. No one, that is, except that imbecile Chraposkrzecki – the hero! Zip reported that Chraposkrzecki had been fenestrated but had died in excellent spirits: his fame was assured. But what about the others? It was all Karpeka's fault. What in hell's name could have possessed me to put a Russian in command of my guards? Did he hypnotize them, or what? Or had they simply miscalculated? An exaggerated discipline was to blame: no one dared to oppose an order, no matter whose it was. Ha, we shall see what really happened.

Traveling in the car with him were Persy, Zip, and Oleśnicki. The men were silent; only Persy would, from time to time, rhapsodize over the beauty of the landscape. The young prince never took his magnificent eyes, which brimmed with a desperate and melancholic lust, from her. As for Zip, nothing: he was barely among the living. He was a small tumor on the brains of the others. Even so, he sensed perfectly what was going on inside them – one of the benefits bestowed on him by Davamesque B_2 – but what good would it do him now? Poor Liz was not around, nor would she ever be. Still, as much as he grieved over her death, he could not squeeze out the slightest internal tear. A stone.

They drove up to the gate of the Old Konstantinov estate. The Chinese soldiers saluted in grand style and let the car pass through. The bizarre guests drove past clumps of yellow and copper-red trees scattered among emerald-green lawns. The typical Byelorussian landscape (the same as the one they had just left behind) made an eerie impression on them; it was as if they were already in China, as if the shapes of the trees had already been sinocized, as if everything had been colored differently, as on a map.

Suddenly they witnessed a curious spectacle. At the point where the lane turned, a lawn ran up to a manor house whose walls and columns shone with a dazzling whiteness in a clump of purple rowan trees. Men could be seen kneeling on the gentle slope. Only two were standing – an officer and a man who turned out to be an executioner. "We're just in time," said Kotzmolochowicz as he jumped from the moving car. The car skidded to a halt, and the others scrambled out after the general. Oh. Now he understood. "*Unser liebenswürdiger Gastgeber hat uns eine kleine Überraschung vorbereitet – nach Tisch werden ein paar Mandarinen geköpft,*" he thought, suddenly recalling a *Witz* from the celebrated *Simplicissimus*. Only here it was *vor Tisch*. The general and the others stopped before the first of the condemned men.

"Why are those men being punished?" the general asked the officer on duty. (There was no armed escort in sight.) "What the blazes have they done?"

"*Ne me parlez pas, Excellence – je suis des gardes,*" replied the baby-faced lieutenant coldly but courteously, with only the barest trace of reproach in his voice.

The condemned man stared blankly at the park trees glowing in the sun and seemed to be either totally enlightened (in the metaphysical sense) or ignorant – one of the two. The other prisoners (their hands were untied – how amazing!) looked on attentively, like athletes awaiting the announcement of a record-breaking score. The executioner walked up to the first prisoner and stood over him with a straight-edged sword in his hand. The officer in charge of the execution had ceased to pay the general and the others any attention. Although the general stood only three feet away from him in full uniform, the other deliberately ignored him. Incomprehensible! Suddenly, as though now anxious to "have done" with the exercise, the baby-faced lieutenant gave a shout. The executioner swung the arm holding the sword and the head of the first "bloke" bounced, baring its yellow teeth, several feet down the slope. But at the very moment it was being lopped off (that is, when it was already airborne), Kotzmolochowicz's attention was drawn to something like a section of headcheese, grey in the center, then a ring of white, then red, some specks, and, finally, a thin line of skin going completely around the circumference of the severed trunk. A second, maybe a quarter of a second, later, a bubbling stream gushed forth, while the head went on baring its teeth on the lawn. (What artistry! What artistry!) It may have been only his imagination, but the general could have sworn the eyes in the amputated head had winked knowingly at him. A few of the other prisoners commented on what appeared to be the purely technical aspects of the execution. It must have been complimentary, because afterward the executioner bowed in their direction, before drawing up to the next man kneeling on the grass. The prisoners were as like as peas. Again a barked command, the same motion by the executioner, and another head rolled down the ancient, manorial lawn, now flooded by the light of a perfect autumnal afternoon. They had all seen it with their own eyes — it was not a hallucination. A few seconds later Persy fainted, and Zip and Oleśnicki had to take her under the arms and drag her behind the silent general, who was already making for the house. As he went he chewed the left corner of his mustache, muttering to himself, "What finesse! What finesse!" The execution had obviously had an uplifting effect on the general, who now braced himself for a talk with the invincible Wang. At last the moment had arrived. He had feared that it might escape him, but no, there it was, standing before his very nose. It was indeed his lucky day! They passed beneath the columns of the "old gentlemen's nest" — for centuries the site of so much servant-bashing, here and elsewhere. "Revenge is at hand," suddenly crossed through the general's mind as he mounted the steps of the manor house. He had already caught sight of the shriveled, yellow face with small, black, cunning eyes that stuck out like raisins in a saffron cake.

There to meet them was the commander in chief himself —

Wang-Tang-Tsang. He was dressed as modestly as the other officers in his company. They entered the dining room. Just then the rest of the general's staff pulled up in front of the house. Persy and Kotzmolochowicz were seated in the first two places of honor. On Persy's left was none other than Wang-Tang-Tsang; seated to the general's right was the chief of staff, Ping-Fang-Lo, the same who had visited him earlier in the morning. An enormous pyramid of food piled in the center of the table blocked his view of the other guests. After swallows' nests dipped in a sauce of pressed cockroaches (here and there the leg of one of these smart little creatures swam in the stuff), Wang stood up and, raising an enormous glass of authentic Dubois, delivered the following speech in an impeccable English:

"Your Excellency, I am honored to welcome you, as first among men, to our headquarters after the capital deed you performed this morning on humanitarian grounds. As much as I respect your personal merits, I must acknowledge you as a dangerous individualist belonging to a bygone era. And so, for the good of that same mankind in whose name, Mr. Kotzmolochowicz, you willingly sacrificed the ambition of the commanding officer of your country, I must sentence you to death by beheading – a very noble death, I might add – since your continued existence, in light of what this morning's heroic deed revealed to us, would surely threaten the very goals for whose sake that deed was performed. But nothing compels us to expedite this irreversible sentence, so let us indulge the gifts of the gods and by all means drink, drink, drink to the happiness and well-being of that same mankind for whose sake, in one way or another, we all sacrifice our paltry personal lives."

Zip never took his eyes from his former idol. Only when the subject of his death arose, and then only for a fraction of a second, did the general knit his magnificent eyebrows, as if struck by some purely rhetorical phrase. Zip tried to probe the general's thoughts with his vacuous eyes. Nothing: the mask remained unruffled. It was a spectacle too beautiful to behold. What marvelous balls to weather a blow like that! So will a seasick passenger feel when he sees someone strolling peacefully on deck in a storm and knows how much it costs him not to be able to vomit.

"What gall!" Zip thought admiringly. He still looked on Kotzmolochowicz as his commanding officer, still trusted him in the hour of his hideous death. For what could be worse than a death sentence? The Chinese were notorious for not joking around. This show of greatness on the general's part, however, stirred Zip's torpid gut. He awaited that proud demon's reply. But after tossing off a brandy, Wang went on. "Gentlemen, you are entitled to a few words of explanation as to our aims and methods. The whole thing is as simple as the structure of our prayer mill: you cannot govern yourselves and you are racially exhausted. We, on the other hand, know how to govern. Once our intellectuals seized hold of your ingenious alphabet, they instantly shook off their centuries-old slumber. Almost overnight our science overtook yours. It was then we discovered that you could not govern, whereas we could. Every country has its own system for achieving the greatest prosperity. That our system is superior to yours is seen in our system of organization and that of our racial brethren. We shall teach you. Politics does not exist for us as such – by politics we understand productivity that is scientifically organized and regulated. We will organize you and you will be happy. We do not wish to repress human culture per se, but to create something that will serve as a springboard. As for what lies ahead for a humanity organized on sound economic principles, I must admit not even we can predict. Perhaps it can only be made happy, perhaps the higher forms of creativity are bound to vanish. Who knows. Of course, that in itself would be a great achievement, very great indeed. But there is another problem. We, too, are a spent race, not in the same way you are, but nonetheless. We must invigorate our race; we must swallow and digest you and build a new yellow-white race that, as our sociobiological institutes have shown, faces untold possibilities. That is why we are introducing compulsory mixed marriages – hereafter, only artists will be free to choose the women of their desire – white or yellow, it's all the same. And so I have the honor to ask His Excellency in advance for the hand of his widow-to-be and for the hand of his daughter for my son. One of our guiding precepts is that future captains should be selectively bred and deindividualized in the better sense of the word." After toasting this last pronouncement, Wang wiped his bald pate with a white silk handkerchief and sat down. "Silence is said to be a sign of affirmation," Wang spoke up finally, suddenly addressing the general in a less official tone.

Kotzmolochowicz wore an expression more suited to one of Huśtański's speeches given, say, at some regimental ceremony. While listening to Wang's speech, he had passed through the following mental states: on hearing the sentence, so quaintly formulated, the general felt blazing-hot needles being driven through all his nerve tips – or rather, he felt as if his nerve tips were squirting tiny jets – the fires of Saint Elmo, perhaps. It was painful. Next, he distinctly saw purple flames on his hands. He looked up and through the bay window saw a park bathed in the colors of a sunny autumnal afternoon. Was this real or merely the distilled magic left by memories from the irretrievable past and conjured up in a mirror by an evil spirit? This scenic nostalgia wrung his insides like a painful cramp. Ho! Ho! Never . . . This was worse than any battle! All his forces to the front – only here the front was his mask. Nothing could make him flinch, though he might allow himself an occasional twitch of the eyebrows. "Too much sangfroid might give me away." The image of the park was succeeded by another image – that of his wife and daughter – which memory now invoked. Suddenly he saw little Ileanka sitting in her highchair over a bowl of porridge with the dining room's dark interior at her back, and leaning over her shoulder "Saint Ann the Martyr," who appeared to be whispering something in her ear. (It was as he imagined it.) No – no turning to them for deliverance. A momentary weakness. Żoliborz and geraniums. Only Persy, now masquerading as his wife, offered him any real support. Meanwhile, Persy had just fainted, and two officers belonging to Wang's staff, as like as peas in a pod and obviously trained to deal with such emergencies, were in the other room trying to revive her. The general again "put reason into the saddle" and caught up with his body on the brink of its foul plunge into fear and dishonor. "Maybe death by fire would have been better." What terrible doubts! And what was all this talk about "humanitarian grounds"? He had never lacked for courage, but this was something different. Even Long John Silver was appalled by the thought of the hangman's noose. Hmm . . . Decapitation . . .

Really *ganz Pomade* . . . All of a sudden, in the place where Persy had sat only a few short moments ago, Kotzmolochowicz saw the diaphanous, slovenly, bearded figure of Monkempt-Unster. It was an hallucination – his first (not counting his Davamesque B_2 visions). But somehow his spur-impaled brain survived even this shock. The general stared at the vacant chair as if it were a ghost in broad daylight. There was bewilderment on all sides. It was diabolical. Suddenly he was reminded of how, as a small boy, he had seen an edition of Shakespeare's *Macbeth* illustrated by Seluze. The book was shown to him – he was still a stableboy then – by Chraposkrzecki, who was younger than Kotzmolochowicz and a brother of the same Chraposkrzecki cut down by machine-gun fire earlier that morning in the senseless attack on the Thirteenth Division. Banquo's dark, opaque spirit had spooked him so much that he had lain awake for hours. Then the ghost of Monkempt-Unster vanished. When Wang had concluded his speech, the general unexpectedly broke the silence with a thunderous peal of laughter. There was nothing hysterical about his laugh – it was just the beginning phase. (He had been holding back this laugh ever since the old "Chink" had asked for his wife's hand. Ha! Ha! *C'est le comble!* No sense in disillusioning the beggar! *Pust razbirut potom!!*) All eyes were on him. Persy revived and, assisted by two members of Wang's staff, returned to the dining room, grinning from ear to ear. Such a hush had descended that they could hear Persy's wicked teeth rattling against the glass which the chief of staff, Ping-Fang-Lo, had offered her. At last the general stood up and in a relaxed, easygoing voice – the voice of a "trooper" – said (in French):

"Marshal Wang, the honor is too great to be refused. '*Slishkom mnogo chesti, chtob otkazatsya,*' as one of our officers told his seconds in 1831 after being challenged to a duel by the Russian governor, the grand duke. Besides, what good would it do. And so, deeply respectful of the laws of history, I accept the compliment paid to me by Your Excellency *(Votre Eminence)*. You may have been right, marshal, in calling me a dangerous breed given to mysterious impulses – mysterious even for me. Witness the events of this morning. If not for that about-face of mine, you would have lost three-fourths of your army. Ultimately, your numerical advantage would have proven decisive. But you can forget about the plan, it's all up here." (The general tapped his skull and imitated an echo with a piglike grunt in the hollow between his nose and throat. The Chinese were dumbfounded.) "Not a single scrap in writing. In me you might have had a swell chief of staff in your fight against the Germans – no offense meant, General Ping," he added, bowing in the direction of this young, repulsive, yellow mummy. "Because the German communists won't go down without a fight. We fell for lack of an original idea – oh, we had one all right, but one imposed upon us from outside. Then again, it would not do to breed any more of my type. But even if you spared my life, marshal, I would decline such a favor and would rather pump a jelly bean into my noggin with this Browning which I received from Czar Cyril and which I now surrender." Kotzmolochowicz laid the cute black gadget before the marshal's plate and sat down. All conversation ceased, even though the topic was fairly interesting. ("The crowd, from shame, stowed all feeling in its breast" a poet would have added.) Eventually they took up the problem of automation and the preservation of culture; the process of automation itself; methods for automating the processes of automation; and, finally, life in the perfectly automated society. The condemned man astonished the gathering by the "acerbity" of his wit. After a serving of rats' tails in a sauce of bedbugs stewed in tomatoes, and after all this vile stuff had been washed down with a superb rice brandy and rose water, Wang stood up and said:

"Gentlemen, the time has come." Kotzmolochowicz asked Wang if he could have a few words with him in confidence.

"My only request, marshal, is to be given half an hour in which to speak in private with my wife. Moreover, permit me to write two letters – one to my first wife and another to my daughter."

"But of course, general," Wang said affably. "Oh – your first wife is still alive?" he asked. "That's splendid, really splendid. I had no idea your daughter was from your first – But no matter . . . It doesn't alter our plans, does it?"

"Not in the least. Where?"

"In that small parlor over there," said Wang, patting Kotzmolochowicz gently on the back. This friendly gesture, unprecedented among the Chinese, brought tears to the eyes of all. Even so, the general's men were loath to approach him, thus creating an insurmountable distance, an invisible wall between them and their commander. Nor did the general feel like company. What could one possibly say at such a moment? A stiff upper lip! Not so, Persy, who in the meantime had begun sharing her culinary impressions with Genezip and the Chinese chief of staff. "You're a strong fellow, general," the marshal continued. "It's a pity you weren't born Chinese. With a different education, you might have become truly great. But as it is – I have no other choice. What a shame."

"Where?"

"I'll show you the way."

"Come on, Persy. You'll have plenty of time to flirt this evening." They passed into a small parlor furnished in the rococo style.

"You have half an hour," Wang said with compassion, and he departed the room quietly. A lieutenant, formerly a Mongolian prince, a plundered saber at his side, was told to stand watch in front of the door. Beneath the windows a pair of bayonets strolled back and forth, now and then crossing paths. "Lieutenant, you will remain here," Wang said to Zip, pointing to a divan beside the door. "In half an hour you will please knock." Time dragged. Somewhere a clock struck three. It was dark in the hallway. Zip dozed off; a few minutes later he roused himself and looked down at his watch. "My God, it's time!" He knocked on the door. Silence. He knocked again, louder, then a third time – nothing. He entered and was met by a curious odor. Suddenly he saw something awful. A saucer, red welts, and, beside the plate, a horsewhip with a diamond stud that Zip recognized at once as Persy's, it having been in her possession ever since her arrival at the front. Persy stood by the window, crying. The world performed a furious tarantella inside Zip's skull. With a desperate effort he pulled himself together. Something inexplicable coursed through him, but then passed. Whew! And good that it did . . .

The general sprang to his feet and hurriedly tidied himself. Persy began striding over to Zip from the windows, her hands outstretched. In one hand (the left) lay a crumpled handkerchief. Zip quickly withdrew and went into the dining room. It was deserted.

He poured himself a large glass of rice whiskey and gulped it down, then ate a sandwich of God-only-knew-what. The sun was orange-red.

A moment later they stepped out onto the manor's magnificent lawn. The heads and bodies of those beheaded that afternoon still lay on the grass.

"Officers who committed some tactical errors in preparing the battle against Your Excellency, which, as you know, failed to take place," Wang graciously explained. Kotzmolochowicz looked pale, but still wore his impenetrable mask. He was no longer among the living. (This, incidentally, is really what is meant by courage — the body pretends; the soul drifts.) The general handed Zip the letters.

"Good-bye, Zip." With a final wave to everyone, the general added: "This is not farewell, because we shall see each other again soon. 'When choosing my destiny / I chose insanity,'" he said, quoting Miciński. From that moment on, the general was all protocol and military stiffness. He saluted. All snapped to attention. Then he threw his cap — the cap of the First Regiment, Light Cavalry — on the ground, knelt down on the grass, and began staring fixedly at the long, aquamarine shadows thrown by a clump of copper-red trees glowing in the sunset. The executioner stepped forward — the same as before. An ineffable spell suddenly descended on the world. Never had a sunset affected him with such diabolical allure — his last session with Persy had something do to with it (how much murderous delight from that finality!). So why should he now feel sorry? Wasn't this October afternoon a climax?

"I'm ready," the general said firmly. His friends had tears in their eyes. The wall separating them from their commander had cracked. For them, too, the world had loomed strangely beautiful at that moment. At a signal from Wang ("*Il était impassible comme une statue de Bouddha*" were the words always used by Persy to describe this scene), the executioner raised his straight-edged sword and . . . Wiuuu! Then Zip saw what they and the general had seen some four hours ago: a section of some sinister headcheese, overrun in a second or two with a torrent of blood — blood that spurted from the arteries of this inveterate individualist. The head rolled across the lawn. At the actual moment of decapitation, however, Kotzmolochowicz had felt only a slight chill about the base of the neck; as his head began spiraling downward, the world suddenly made a somersault in his eyes, similar to the way the earth behaves when viewed from an airplane in the process of banking. Afterward a heavy darkness enveloped the head on the grass. Once and for all the general's ego had terminated its existence in this head, independently of the trunk, which still knelt in an upright position and had on it the uniform of a general. (The severed trunk maintained this posture for some fifteen seconds.) Persy could not decide whether to throw her arms around the head or the trunk. She chose the former, inspired by Salome in the New Testament, Queen Margaret, and by Stendhal's Mathilde de la Mole. (The next woman in her predicament can now draw on the example of Persy Bestialskaya, who by then will surely be as famous as the forementioned.) She picked up the general's mad and obstinate head, which was still spitting blood and bits of marrow through the opening at the neck, leaned over cautiously, and kissed him in the middle of the mouth, which still smelled of her own. Oh God, it was obscene! With blood running from her mouth, Persy turned to Zip and pressed her crimson lips (known later on as *rouge Kotzmoloukowitsch*) against his. Then she threw herself on the universally astonished Chinese and friends of the general. She worked herself into such a frenzy that she began foaming about the mouth and had to be tied up. With disgust, Zip wiped off his uniform, but however furiously he rubbed he could not get it clean enough. That night (after confessing that she had never been Kotzmolochowicz's wife) Persy became Zip's lover, who, for all intents a robot, "possessed her sans pleasure" as Cymisches did Basilissa Teophanu. Afterward, Persy went to bed with the Chinese chief of staff, even though he reeked like a corpse, and with still other "Chinks," even though they, too, reeked like corpses – perhaps even because of that, who knew. Zip, now grown completely indifferent, let her do as she pleased.

* * * *

A sudden snowstorm from the west prevented the Chinese from occupying the country at once. So, for the present, they reorganized the enemy's "fraternal forces." Zip was kept so busy that he hardly had any time for love.

When the storm had abated they started for the west. During the first days of November the Chinese troops entered the capital, lately become a house of horrors. The Syndicate for National Salvation had given the communists quite a battle. They were crushed. Two ghosts, those of Monkempt-Unster and his murderer, Kotzmolochowicz, who by this last "feat," redeemed himself in the eyes of the former, mercilessly played one side against the other. It was their revenge for not being around to enjoy life. "Saint Ann the Martyr" became devoted to her daughter, the fiancée of the younger Wang. She herself refused the hand of the elder Wang – period. Zip became completely "functional." In his absence they had begun investigating the Eliza affair, but with the invasion of the Chinese the case was dropped. Many criminals, in fact, were able to begin a new life.

Artists were subsidized. Both Sturfan and Tenzer made out well. After turning over the upbringing of his children to his wife, by now completely "city-slickered," Putricides was allowed to compose freely and to wallow, like Sardanapalus, among bales of multicolored women supplied by the Section for the Preservation of Art in the Ministry of Cultural Automation. Sturfan wrote abominable things – novels with "group heroes" – in collaboration with Lilian, who also went on performing in a theater for high-ranking mandarins. He operated exclusively with the collective psyche, dispensing with dialogue. Art and literary criticism were at last banned. Prince Basil and Benz, as men of science (the former with his Murtibingism, the latter with his symbols), lived in the lap of luxury. But the masses of dukes, counts, farmers, peasants, workers, craftsmen, the army, women, etc., suffered penitentially at having to be crossbred for the sake of the Mongolian race. (Ultimately sex is a trivial thing, not worth the fuss made over it!) Still, the good souls got accustomed to it in relatively short time (two months, to be exact), because the Universe knows no beast worse than man. The Chinese made feverish preparations for their fight against the Germans, who, to the Chinese way of thinking, were not considered orthodox communists. The invasion was scheduled for the beginning of spring.

Zip, by now a consummate lunatic, a mild catatonic, was forced to marry a Chinese girl of exquisite beauty who traced her ancestry back to some Mongolian khans. He was increasingly in demand as a model officer and more and more neglected Persy, who, after marrying one of these yellow bureaucrats, sided completely with the Chinese. Oh, yes. The Princess di Ticonderoga perished on the barricades during the anti-Chinese riots that broke out later on, whereas the Michalskis made out fairly well. By a special dispensation, marriages previously contracted were allowed to remain intact.

The situation degenerated into something that the Polish language is ill-equipped to describe. One day, perhaps, some very learned Chinese with the incorrigible soul of a "Chink" might be able to record all of this in English, provided he could look at it with un-Chinese eyes. But this is highly unlikely.

DECEMBER 16, 1927

Notes

PART ONE: THE AWAKENING

The Awakening

intraductible . . . et par excellence irrationel (Fr.): Untranslatable, irreducible, untransmittable, and preeminently irrational.
au fond des fonds (Fr.): At the bottommost bottom – based on the idiom *au fond*, "at bottom, in essence."
précieuse (Fr.): A sophisticate.
déclenchement (Fr.): A launching, release.
Valentino obraznoe sushchestvo (Russ.): A Valentinolike creature.

A Soirée at the Princess di Ticonderoga's

zakhlyobyvalsya (Russ.): He choked.
gomon (Russ.): A hubbub.
interesselose Anschauung (Ger.): A disinterested observation.
svetleyshy (Russ.): A princely title in czarist Russia, roughly equivalent to "Your Excellence."
Etot Tenzer pishet kak khochet (Russ.): That Tenzer writes as he pleases.

A Visit with Tenzer

gebrauchsfähig (Ger.): Permissible.
svoeobraznym fashizmom na psevdosindikalistichnom fone (Russ.): With its own special [brand of] fascism based on pseudosyndicalism.
Überkerle (Ger.): Superguys.
Zufall von Büchern und Menschen (Ger.): A coincidence of books and men.
Musik ist höhere Offenbarung als jede Religion und Philosophie (Ger.): Music is a higher [form of] revelation than any religion or philosophy.
Vy zhivyote na bolshoy schyot, gospodin Tenzer (Russ.): You do things in grand style, Mr. Tenzer.

A Visit to Prince Basil's Retreat

Ce ne sont que les gens . . . des classes (Fr.): It's only those who have been rejected by their class *[déclassés]* who talk of nothing save of classes and the classes of classes.
en règle (Fr.): Official, regular.

aristos (Fr.): *Aristo* is a common abbreviation of the French *aristocrat.*
ganz gleich (Ger.), *égal* (Fr.), *vsyo ravno* (Russ.): It's all the same.
denknotwendig (Ger.): Conceptually necessary.
unerlaubte Gedankenexperimente (Ger.): Forbidden thought experiments.
Evo Velichestvo (Russ.): His Majesty.

Sexphyxiation

Wovon man nicht sprechen kann . . . schweigen (Ger.): What cannot be expressed should be left unsaid.
sukhostoy (Russ.): Literally "dry rot"; a vulgarism for the male condition known as priapism.
bas-bleu (Fr.): A bluestocking.
vykinut takuyu shtuku . . . Evrope (Russ.): To pull off such a stunt as to confound all of Europe.
mégère (Fr.): A shrew, a vixen.
Ah non, pas si bête que ça! (Fr.): Oh no, not [something] as silly as that!
y compris (Fr.): Including.
chut-chut (Russ.): Ever so slightly.
je ne 'zipe' qu'à peine (Fr.-Pol.): Literally, "I can hardly breathe"; from a Polish verb *zipać* ("to breathe") the author contrives a nonexistent French *ziper* and then transposes it to an analogous French phrase corresponding to the Polish *ledwie zipać*, "to be on one's last legs."
sur ce paquet de muscles (Fr.): On top of this bundle of muscles.
trucs (Fr.): Tricks.
après nous vsyo propadaet (Fr.-Russ.): After us let everything collapse.
un simple 'gouveniage' polonais (Fr.-Ger.): A simple Polish shitass. The word *gouveniage* is nearly a French transcription of the Polish *gowniarz* (shitass).
Oh, vous autres . . . et elle vaincra (Fr.): Oh, you Poles – all the same, democracy, true democracy, is one and indivisible and it will prevail.
kruzhok samoopredeleniya (Russ.): A circle for self-definition.

The Return, or Life and Death

Gli piccoli sadismi (It.): The little sadisms.
tout court (Fr.): Simply.
mesquinerie (Fr.): Baseness, shabbiness.

tryn-trava (Russ.): Idiomatic for "it's all the same."
qu'est-ce qu'on ne fait pas pour une dupe polonaise! (Fr.): What one wouldn't do for a Polish dupe!
bafonites: *Bafon* in the original; from the French *bas-fond* (lower class, dregs) and then transcribed into Polish.
vo chtoby ni stalo (Russ.): By all means, at all costs.

Demonism

mal de je ne sais quoi (Fr.): An ailment [affliction] of some kind or other.
vsekh ne pro . . . (Russ.): The complete phrase would read *vsekh ne proebyosh,* "you can't fuck them all."
fond de feminité . . . permanente (Fr.): [That] element of impersonal and lasting femininity.
mais ou là-bas! (Fr.): Nothing of the sort. The more usual expression is *mais non!*
le principe de la contingence (Fr.): The princple of contingency, as used in modern logic.
shkurny vopros (Russ.): A question of self-interest, of personal convenience.
Des hommes d'État . . . j'en fasse? (Fr.): Statesmen, statesmen – now whatever am I to do with them?
Das balivernes, ma chérie (Fr.): Nonsense, my dear.
Tiens, tiens (Fr.): Well, well.
printsipialny razgovor (Russ.): A fundamental discussion; a discussion involving basic principles.
blanc-bec (Fr.): A greenhorn.
blagueur (Fr.): A fake, a joker.
V kazhdom russkom samom blagorodnom cheloveke . . . i svinstva (Russ.): Deep down in every Russian, even in the most noble of them, one can find a little dirt and filth.
Vous avez exagéré votre importance, princesse (Fr.): You exaggerate your importance, princess.
lovkost ruk (Russ.): Sleight of hand.
cochonnerie féminine pure (Fr.): A purely feminine swinishness.
einer lockeren Masse . . . ohne "Gestaltsqualität" (Ger.): A loosely connected mass of disconnected emotions without any formal quality.
Inhalt (Ger.): Content.
ganz Pomade (Ger.): Idiomatic for "it's all the same."

demonicheskaya shtuchka (Russ.): A diabolical stunt.
a molodets (Russ.): Nice going!
Katzenjammer (Ger.): Hangover.

Domestic Affairs and Destiny

Oberkontroler (Ger.): Head controller.
au commencement BYTHOS était (Fr.-Gk.): In the beginning there was the abyss [Gk.: *bythos*].
vseobshchee babyo (Russ.): A universal hag.
Ah, nom d'un chien! (Fr.): Drat it!
zavedenie (Russ.): Establishment.

PART TWO: INSANITY

School

When such a *psychopatisch angehauchtes Individuum tombera dans un pareil engrenage,* then *vsyo propalo* (Ger.-Fr.-Russ.): The sense of this multilingual salmagundi is roughly the following: "When such a psychopathically prone individual gets into a comparable fix, then all is lost."
Wesenszusammenhang (Ger.): Intrinsic connection.
die Erwartung an und für sich (Ger.): Waiting in and for itself.
Erwartungspolitik (Ger.): A policy of anticipation.
perihelium (Gk.): Perihelion, in the astronomical sense.
ostervenenie (Russ.): Frenzy.
bezalabernost (Russ.): Disorder, chaos.
Il faut prendre . . . se brûler la cervelle (Fr.): One should take life cheerfully, or else blow out one's brains.
espirit d'escalier (Fr.): Idiomatic for a delayed mental reaction.
onyswakeemalipawnse: From the French expression *Honni soit qui mal y pense,* "Shame on him who thinks evil."
Hochexplosivum (Ger.-Lat.): From the German *Hochexplosiv* (high-explosive) plus the Latin ending *-um.*
Sovnarkom (Russ.): An abbreviation for *Sovet Narodnych Komissarov,* Soviet of People's Commissars.

A Meeting and Its Consequences

reine Fingermusikanten (Ger.): Pure-fingered musicians.

A Repeat Performance

Das ist nur in Polen möglich (Ger.): Only in Poland is that possible.

semimesyanchniki (Russ.): Literally, a seven-month-old [child].

Minderwertigkeitsgefühl (Ger.): A feeling of inferiority.

podkhodyashchy fon (Russ.): The appropriate background.

tout de même (Fr.): Still, nonetheless.

portupeyny (Russ.): From the Russian *portupeya* (Fr.: *porte-épée*), denoting the sort of sword worn by Russian cadets before the revolution; *portupeyny-junker* was a military rank in prerevolutionary Russia.

escrime (Fr.): Fencing.

tretevo razryada (Russ.): Third class.

Glupie poetniki (Russ.): Stupid [little] poets.

obolochka (Russ.): Casing, shell.

Selbstbefriedigungsmaschine (Ger.): A self-gratification machine.

servelka (Fr.-Russ.): From the French *cervelle* (brain) plus the Russian diminutive suffix *-ka*.

Der Mann ist selbst (Ger.): Man is [stands] alone.

en compôte (Fr.): To a pulp. *Compôte* is a desert of mixed stewed fruit.

als soche (Ger.): As such.

Die Freude zu stinken (Ger.): The joy of stinking.

der Wille zum Wahnsinn (Ger.): The desire for madness. A parodistic allusion to Friedrich Nietzsche's famous *der Wille zur Macht* (the desire for power).

Die leute sind dieselben, aber der Geruch ist anders (Ger.): People are the same, only their odor is different.

Bonne la nôtre (Fr.): Just our luck. The more conventional idiom would be *À nous la chance.*

Die Kerle haben keine Ahnung . . . kein Zeitgefühl (Ger.): The guys have no idea what work means, and, what's more, they have no sense of time.

podozritelnaya parochka (Russ.): A suspicious [little] couple.

geroj nashego vremeni (Russ.): A hero of our time.

A Commander's Thoughts and the Little Theater of Quintofron Crepuscolo

himmelblau (Ger.): Sky-blue.

raspolozheniya (Russ.): Dispositions.

A beau se raider le cadavre (Fr.): Roughly, what's dead is dead.

Wille zur Ohnmacht (Ger.): The desire for impotence. See above, *der Wille zum Wahnsinn.*

qu'est-ce que j'avais dans le cul o dans le ventre même (Fr.): That which I have up my rump or in my very belly.

Meine Wahrheiten sind nicht für die Anderen (Ger.): My truths are not for the others.

Trebiono nat (Russ.): A distortion of *ebiono mat,* "fuck your mother."

parbleu (Fr.): Damn!

rugatelstva (Russ.): Obscenities.

otpravlyayut v zholty dom (Russ.): [The ones] they ship off to the mental asylum.

Il a de la poigne, ce bougre-là (Fr.): That fellow has a firm grip [on things].

dévergondified: Zdewergondowana in the original; from the French *dévergonder,* to debauch, pervert, lead astray.

cherezvychayka (Russ.): Colloquial for Cherezvychaynaya Komissiya, or the Cheka, the Soviet security police set up by Lenin in 1918.

Erasm Wojciechowicz ne imeet . . . kamimnibud vzrywom (Russ.): Erasmus Wojciechowicz [Russian patronymic] doesn't even have time to go insane. But it's bound to end in some kind of bang.

peregrupirovka (Russ.): Regrouping, in the military sense.

le problème de la détente (Fr.), *das Entspannungsproblem* (Ger.): The relaxation problem.

pust plachut (Russ.): Let them weep.

bezobrazie (Russ.): A scandal, an outrage.

ofitserov i bladey (Russ.): Officers and whores.

couches d'émergence (Fr.): Levels [stages, degrees] of awakening.

osoby obrazets (Russ.): A prize specimen.

coup de foudre (Fr.): A thunderclap.

kudrefudrennoe raspolozhenie dukha (Fr.-Russ.): A polyglotal invention involving a Russified *coup de foudre* and the Russian phrase for "affinity of the soul."

polnejshy bardak i Untergang (Russ.-Ger.): Sheer chaos [lit. *bardak* = brothel] and collapse.

Kein Posten für mich hier (Ger.): There's no place for me here.

à la fourchette (Fr.): On the spur [of the moment].

bonbonnières (Fr.): Boxes of candy.

Kokettenduft (Ger.): Coquette's Scent.

more po kolena (Russ.): Idiomatic for "it's all the same."

Quelque chose vraiment ineffable (Fr.): Something truly enigmatic.

Von (Russ.): Away! Off!

malum purum elementarium (Lat.): Element of pure evil.

Griff (Ger.): Hold.

idée fixe . . . Fide X (Fr.-Lat.): Fixed idea . . . Faith X.

bezzabotnost (Russ.): Lightheartedness, levity.

Gefärlich ist's zu trennen . . . und auch zu Taxis (Ger.): It is dangerous to separate theory from practice, but it is equally difficult to find princesses *von Thurn auch zu Taxis*. Thurn und Taxis was once a principality of northern Italy and an Austrian princely house.

der geniale Kotzmolokowitsch (Ger.): The brilliant Kotzmolochowicz.

lettres de cachet (Fr.): Sealed letters.

les moeurs, vous savez (Fr.): [It's a case of] morals, you know.

Prosikhodil protses psevdomorfozy (Russ.): A process of pseudomorphosis was taking place.

kanitel (Russ.): Rigmarole.

Ein Künstler, der Wahnsinnig wird . . . mit seiner eigenen Natur (Ger.): An artist who's going mad is always in conflict with his own nature.

rançon de genie (Fr.): The price of genius.

exkrementale Inhalte mit Edelsteinen zu neuen Elementen verbunden (Ger.): Excremental contents mixed with precious stones [to form] new elements.

Knyaginya (Russ.): Princess (wife of a prince).

ultrahyperfeldzeugmeisters: From the German *Feldzeugmeister* (quartermaster).

Torchures and the Debut of the "Gent from Below"

en cas de quoi (Fr.): Just in case.

Einsichten (Ger.): Insights, views.

blagues (Fr.): Hoaxes.

Il a de la combine, ce bougre-là (Fr.): He has some sort of plan, that fellow has.

fraise vomie (Fr.): Strawberry puke.

bleu gendarme (Fr.): Policeman's blue.

laque de garance rose de Blocks (Fr.): Laquer of Block's madder.

orange Witkacy (Fr.): "Witkacy" was the name the author assumed to distinguish himself from his father, Stanisław Witkiewicz, a well-known artist and critic.

Luxustierchen (Ger.): Prize pet.

Transformationsgleichungen . . . des Fraulein v. Bestialskaya (Ger.):

Transformation equations of good and evil by means of the infinite genital coefficient of Miss von Bestialskaya.

augepumpt und ausgezüzelt (Ger.): Pumped out and fizzled out.

bezumnych zhelany (Russ.): Insane desires.

stoyalo kogdato . . . or *stoyali chudnye dni* (Russ.): "A marvelous fall weather lingered" and "there followed [a string of] marvelous days," respectively. In both Russian expressions, the verb *stoyat* (to stand) is used in the sense of "to be."

postpsychopatische Personalität (Ger.): A postpsychotic personality.

Cornelius's *"gemischter Hintergrund"* (Ger.): Cornelius's "complex background."

Allons alors! (Fr.): Let's be off, then!

Quel sale pays que la Pologne . . . (Fr.): The following is a literal translation of this Witkiewicz-concocted song.

What a dirty country this Poland is,
This depressing land of shitasses [*gouveniage* = Pol. *gówniarz*]
To show even a little shame
They haven't the slightest courage.

Vous autres, Polonais (Fr.): You Poles.

perezhivaniya (Russ.): Experiences.

Kronpriccios (Ger.-It.): A coalescence of the German *Kronprinz* and the the Italian *capriccio.*

Il a une autre vision . . . à deux pas de moi (Fr.): He has another vision of the world, this fellow [sitting] only two steps away from me.

Landsturmmänner (Ger.): Local militiamen.

A Battle and Its Consequences

à giorno (It.): Openworked, as used in architecture.

Réflechir et puis exécuter – voilà la guerre (Fr.): First think and then execute – that's war for you.

Ili ranyat, ili ubiyat (Russ.): Either they wound [you] or they kill [you].

voix tonnante (Fr.): [In] a thunderous voice.

The Final Metamorphosis

gadost' (Russ.): Vile stuff.

déveineurs (Fr.): Losers.

 Hinter dieser glänzenden Fassade waren schon nur Ruinen (Ger.):

Behind that facade only ruins were left.

Polzushchaya forma skhizofrenii (Russ.): An incipient form of schizophrenia.

Begriffsmumien (Ger.): Idea mummies.

Dusha skhizotimika v tele tsiklotimika (Russ.): The soul of a schizothymic in the body of a cyclothymic.

On vsegda byl . . . emu zdorovo podbavila (Russ.): He was always a little crazy, but this shellshock has him fixed up good and proper.

Bone pour en sheeyen eh la moosh (Fr.): In the original, Witkiewicz transcribed into Polish a French expression meaning, literally, "What's good for a dog is good for a fly"; in other words, "it's better than nothing."

kornet (Russ.): First officer rank, equal to an infantry lieutenant, in the army of prerevolutionary Russia.

The Wedding Night

prikosnoveniya (Russ.): Contacts.

jouisseurs (Fr.): Pleasure-seekers.

Ideengang (Ger.): Train of thought.

peredyshka (Russ.): Breathing spell.

Vorsicht! (Ger.): Caution!

Quelque chose de vraiment insamovite à la manière polonaise (Fr.): Something truly remarkable [*insamovite* = Pol. *niesamowity*] in the Polish style.

avec une exactitude militaire (Fr.): With a military precision.

smorodinovye (Russ.): Currant-colored.

Un aide de camp catatonisé, quel luxe! (Fr.): A catatonic aide-de-camp – what a luxury!

melkoburzhuazynaya skuka (Russ.): A petty-bourgeois tedium.

melochy – a melochy k chortu (Russ.): The sense here is "what's coming are trifles – and to hell with trifles."

gavno sobachee (Russ.): Dog shit.

The Last Convulsion

ventre à terre (Fr.): At full speed.

minderwertigheitsgefühl (Ger.): A feeling of inferiority.

eine zugedachte Theorie (Ger.): A theoretical afterthought.

Unser liebenswürdiger Gastgeber . . . ein paar Mandarinen geköpft (Ger.):

Our gracious host has prepared a small surprise for us – after supper a few mandarins are going to be beheaded.

vor Tisch (Ger.): Before supper.

C'est le comble! (Fr.): That's the limit!

Pust razbirut potom! (Russ.): Let them figure it out afterward!

Il était impassible comme une statue de Bouddha (Fr.): He was as expressionless as a statue of Buddha.

rouge Kotzmoloukowitsch (Fr.): Kotzmolochowicz red.